PENGUIN ACADEMICS

CANADIAN SHORT STORIES

PENGUIN ACADEMICS

CANADIAN SHORT STORIES

Edited by **RUSSELL BROWN** *University of Toronto*

DONNA BENNETT *University of Toronto*

PEARSON
Longman

Toronto

Library and Archives Canada Cataloguing in Publication

Canadian short stories / edited by Russell Brown and Donna Bennett.

ISBN 0-321-24850-3

1. Short stories, Canadian (English)   2. College readers.
I. Brown, Russell, 1942–   II. Bennett, Donna, 1945–

PS8319.C355 2005   C813'.0108   C2004-904599-7

ISBN 0-321-24850-3

Vice President, Editorial Director: Michael J. Young
Acquisitions Editor: Patty Riediger
Marketing Manager: Toivo Pajo
Developmental Editor: Jennifer Murray
Production Editor: Söğüt Y. Güleç
Copy Editor: Nancy Carroll
Proofreader: Maryan Gibson
Production Coordinator: Janis Raisen
Page Layout: Jansom
Permissions Research: Beth McAuley
Art Director: Julia Hall
Interior Design: Dave McKay
Cover Design: Michelle Bellemare
Cover Image: Katherine Knight, *Dock*, 2000

2 3 4 5   09 08 07 06 05

Printed and bound in Canada.

PEARSON
Longman

For Kathryn and Michael

Contents

Introduction   1

Canadian Short Stories   9

Alphabetical List by Author

Preface

The thirty-nine short stories in this volume appeared in books and journals published between 1838 and 2004. They show writers responding to all of the regions of Canada, to both rural and urban settings, and to a wide variety of cultures—as well as to their thirty-nine different internal landscapes.

Long before we undertook this anthology, we discussed Canadian short stories with so many friends, colleagues, and students that our debts go beyond repaying or recounting. Among those who made suggestions or patiently answered questions for us about stories in this volume, we would like to thank Petal Almeida, Chelva Kanaganayakam, Margaret Reeves, Joanne Rochester, Glenn Willmott, Michael Trussler, and, especially, Jack David. We would also like to thank the following instructors for their thoughtful reviews of and comments on this volume: Alison Calder, University of Manitoba; Carrie Dawson, Dalhousie University; Paul Denham, University of Saskatchewan; Robyn Fowler, University of Alberta; Susan Gingell, University of Saskatchewan; Gwendolyn Guth, University of Ottawa; Dean Irvine, Dalhousie University; Ed Jewinski, Wilfrid Laurier University; Manina Jones, University of Western Ontario; Peggy Kelly, University of Ottawa; Sophie McCall, Simon Fraser University; Kevin McNeilly, University of British Columbia; Laura Moss, University of British Columbia; and Tracey Ware, Queen's University.

Russell Brown
Donna Bennett

About the Editors

Russell Brown has taught Canadian and contemporary literature at the University of Toronto at Scarborough and in University of Toronto Department of English graduate program for the last 27 years (before that he taught at Lakehead University for 8 years). He is the co-editor of *A New Anthology of Canadian Literature in English*, of *Tasks of Passion: Dennis Lee at Mid-Career*, and of the *University of Toronto Quarterly*. While editorial director for poetry at McClelland & Stewart from 1983 to 1988, he edited *The Collected Poems of Al Purdy* and other books. In addition to the short monograph, *Borderlines and Borderlands in English Canada: The Written Line*, his critical essays have been published in *Modern Fiction Studies*, *Essays on Canadian Writing*, *Open Letter*, *Journal of Commonwealth Literature*, *Mosaic*, and elsewhere. They treat a variety of writers including Robert Kroetsch, Margaret Laurence, Al Purdy, Margaret Atwood, Alice Munro, Leon Rooke, Northrop Frye, Robertson Davies, and Marshall McLuhan, and of topics such as Canadian thematic criticism, Canadian postmodernism, and the differences between American and Canadian literary traditions.

Donna Bennett teaches courses in Canadian literature, literature and myth, and literature and media at the University of Toronto at Scarborough and as a member of the University of Toronto Department of English graduate faculty. Currently a co-editor of the *University of Toronto Quarterly*, she is also the co-editor of *An Anthology of Canadian Literature in English* and *Tasks of Passion: Dennis Lee at Mid-Career*, and served for many years as an editor of *Descant*. Her essays on Margaret Laurence, Margaret Atwood, Alice Munro, Bronwen Wallace, Robert Kroetsch, Fred Wah, Adele Wiseman, and others, and on broad topics such as the Canadian critical tradition, the Canadian canon, and Canadian feminist theory can be found in *Modern Fiction Studies*, *Essays on Canadian Writing*, *Journal of Commonwealth Literature*, *Room of One's Own*, *Atlantis*, *Queen's Quarterly*, *The Canadian Forum*, *A Mazing Space*, *The Oxford Companion to Canadian Literature*, and elsewhere.

PENGUIN ACADEMICS

CANADIAN SHORT STORIES

Introduction

I   Origins

The short story has been described as the newest literary form, one that was born early in the nineteenth century. In Europe, Nikolai Gogol, whose tales of the Ukraine were collected in *Evenings on a Farm near Dikanka* (1831–32), is hailed as its originator; while in the United States, Edgar Allan Poe, who began to publish his stories in 1832, is thought of as the progenitor of the short story written in English. In this way of looking at its history, the short story came into existence a century after the emergence of the novel and is closely related to that longer form.

In the nineteenth century, these two prose forms coexisted with the long narrative poem. Although poetry had been thought of as more artful than prose, the novel and the short story matured and began to be understood as also having a capacity for artfulness in style and structure.

A different way of understanding the origins and nature of the short story is to trace its roots back to oral narratives. Every culture has its fireside and its bedtime stories, its mythic tales and its accounts of the day's activities. Seeing these as the source of the short story makes it the oldest, not the newest, of forms. Such a view emphasizes not so much the literary art of the story as its enduring appeal and may lead us to focus on aspects of structure, style, and content that still show traces of the spoken story.

These two accounts of the short story's beginnings may be somewhat contradictory but they are not entirely exclusive. The history of the short story is different in every national literature, but always includes both literary and non-literary antecedents. Because national cultures sometimes define their literatures in strictly literary terms, they may resist acknowledging those sources that lie outside the literary sphere.

The Origins of the Canadian Short Story

Because literary writing in Canadian literature is still so young, oral and non-literary written sources *have* often been recognized as components of our literature. Indeed, one traditional oral storyteller can be found in this book—Harry Robinson, whose Okanagan tales were recorded, just as he told them, in *Write It on Your Heart* (1989). Most of Robinson's stories were handed down from previous tellers; some, including the one anthologized here, look back to the distant past. An awareness of such oral storytelling has had an effect on our writers. Thomas King has remarked on how reading transcriptions of Robinson's speech rhythms influenced his understanding of how the story could be told.

Several other stories in this collection, while they do not have the long ancestry of Robinson's tales, also respond to the oral roots of short fiction. A second oral tradition—that of the early settlers' use of folktale and anecdote to communicate their values and to convey information about the place to which they had come—had an impact on writers like Thomas Chandler Haliburton, who draws on the tradition of the tall tale. Contemporary stories, such as Michael Crummey's "Bread," recall the oral folktale and show how it continues to exert power. Stephen Leacock's *Sunshine Sketches of a Little Town* attests to the anecdote as a part of the Canadian short story tradition (Leacock rehearsed versions of his stories of small-town life over many a dinner table before he put them into print). Anecdotes remain a powerful element today in the work of contemporary writers such as Lisa Moore.

Thomas Raddall's "The Wedding Guest" marries anecdote and folktale in its blending of an old story of his region with folkloric motifs. Alistair MacLeod's narrator in "The Closing Down of Summer" draws on a spoken art passed down from Celtic bards. Alice Munro's "Open Secrets" shows a current event passing from anecdote into folklore.

The Canadian short story also has sources in non-literary written forms such as the letters of settlers and early journalism. The letters written home by newcomers manifested their authors' desires to provide old friends and family with a sense of life in a new land by including sketches—written portraits of individuals and events. (These early letters were sometimes turned into books, such as Catharine Parr Traill's *The Backwoods of Canada*, 1836.) The forms of the letter and its sketch were adapted for newspaper publication by Thomas McCulloch, whose short satirical accounts of early farm life, later published as *The Mephibosheth Stepsure Letters*, began to appear in a Nova Scotian newspaper in 1821.

Haliburton's Sam Slick tales similarly began in a newspaper. (They were published in *The Nova Scotian* from 1835.) And Traill and her sister, Susanna Moodie, wrote sketches independent of the letter for the Montreal-based *Literary Garland* (1838–51), an important venue for early English–Canadian writing. For much of its history, writers of the Canadian short story, from Haliburton to Leacock and beyond, have looked to periodicals for their standards as much as to literary aesthetics.

In Canada, a conception of literariness that valued poetry over prose forms lingered until the second half of the twentieth century. Because prose was seen as less important than poetry and because there was uncertainty as to whether a Canadian literary tradition for fiction even existed, short story writers felt free to explore their form in a way that might not have been possible had they been working in a more established tradition.

II   The Form of the Short Story

In the nineteenth century Poe argued that the short story was, like the short poem, superior to both the novel and the long poem because "unity of effect or impression" was what gave a literary work its power, and "this unity cannot be thoroughly preserved in productions whose perusal cannot be completed at one sitting."

Since Poe, many have tried to define the story or to isolate its special qualities. But the short story is a Protean form, constantly evolving beyond its definitions. Other than being a narrative of a certain length, the short story has had only a few characteristics that seem stable, all of them responding to a sense that the essence of the short story is its condensation. They include

- compression or curtailment of narrative events
- elision of detail and of background information—which may make special demands on the reader

- closure that does not necessarily depend on narrative resolution, but instead may emphasize the gaining of insight (an epiphany) or evoke an emotion in the reader or present a resolving image—as a poem would.

The Form of the Canadian Short Story

But how short can a short story be? Although Poe (following Aristotle) thought it possible for a literary work to be too short (Poe wrote that "a certain degree of duration is absolutely requisite for the production of any effect at all"), contemporary story writers, especially in Canada, have experimented with very brief narratives—called "short short stories" or, at their briefest, "postcard stories." Readers of this volume will find that "Bread" is less than a page—yet it seems fully satisfactory as a story.

Given that its name announces a limit to its length, how long can the *short* story be? Alice Munro's stories move outward, in length often approaching the borderline of the novella, and they are so richly textured that they contravene traditional ideas about singleness of effect. (Her short stories have been called novels in miniature.) Such complex stories, as well as the splintered forms used by Lisa Moore or the internal monologue employed by Dionne Brand, suggest that limiting notions of unity or structure will not serve to define the short story in Canada.

As well, Canadian short story writers have been particularly attracted to a special use of the story—as a building block in constructing something larger. These longer works are not novels but are made up of separate stories capable of standing on their own, though these can be quite interconnected with other stories in the volume. Such works are called short story sequences or "short story suites," or referred to as "thematically unified" collections. Several such collections have been a source for stories in this anthology: Duncan Campbell Scott's *In the Village of Viger*, Leacock's *Sunshine Sketches of a Little Town*, Margaret Laurence's *A Bird in the House*, Mordecai Richler's *The Street*, Sandra Birdsell's *Agassiz Stories*, Rohinton Mistry's *Tales from Firozsha Baag*, Antanas Sileika's *Buying on Time*, and David Bezmozgis's *Natasha and Other Stories*.

Because journalism, the letter, and the journalistic sketch were more important than the novel in furnishing a context for the emergence of the short story in Canada, an indirect impact of these non-literary forms can still be felt. Canadian short story writers such as Scott, Morley Callaghan, and Thomas Raddall continued to work in a simple and direct style, to emphasize direct experience, to make detail and essential facts important, and to seek to capture a specific setting and particular character. As it developed, the Canadian story drew on a wide range of influences and aesthetics, yet these traits inherited from its early history have remained within our literary tradition and can still be seen shaping the stories of writers such as Margaret Laurence, Sandra Birdsell, Isabel Huggan, Bronwen Wallace, and Antanas Sileika.

At the same time, as we suggested above, Canadian short story writers have not felt restricted. Their freedom to experiment can be seen, in this volume, in the way writers such as P.K. Page, Dionne Brand, and André Alexis test the boundaries of the short story form.

III   The Importance of the Short Story

The story was an important literary form from its emergence in the nineteenth century to the middle of the twentieth century. In that time stories usually appeared first in periodicals and then might later be collected in bound volumes. During the first half of the twentieth century, modernist writers like Ernest Hemingway and F. Scott Fitzgerald achieved both prominence and financial success by first publishing their short stories in *The Atlantic Monthly, Cosmopolitan, Esquire*, the *Saturday Evening Post*, and *Scribner's* before issuing them as collections. In the 1950s, these magazines began to disappear or to change. Once the commercial markets for short fiction declined precipitously, many writers turned away from the form. Often they were further encouraged to avoid the short story by agents and publishers who thought novels were more commercial than short story collections. For about three decades, until the 1980s, the story became a minor form—and publishers became leery of short story collections—in the United States and elsewhere. But this was not the case in Canada.

The Importance of the Canadian Short Story

The short story has been important to the development of English Canadian literature and to the way it is now perceived. Until the explosion of Canadian novelists that began in the late 1960s and

1970s, short fiction and sketches were more often cited as an example of Canadian literary excellence in prose than were novels. F.P. Grove's sketches, for example, were preferred by most Canadian critics over his novels; and Callaghan's stories were frequently said to be superior to his long works.

The short story has also been the form that, before the present era, most often crossed borders to bring international success to Canadian authors. Thomas Chandler Haliburton, revered by the American storyteller Mark Twain among others, was Canada's first writer to be widely recognized abroad. So immense was his popularity that more than a hundred editions of his Clockmaker sketches were printed in Canada, the United States, England, and, in translation, in France and Germany. A century later, Leacock, whom Timothy Findley once called "the grandfather of us all," became one of the best-known and most sought-after writers in the English language. And during the period when the literary modernists were placing their short stories in top American magazines, Callaghan took his place alongside writers like Hemingway and Fitzgerald in these venues.

Although the larger market for the short story may have crashed after World War II, in Canada—where the commercial stakes had never been as high and at a time when the publishing of Canadian novels was not yet a common occurrence—short fiction became an increasingly important outlet for Canadian writers. Some of Canada's most important writers—including Mavis Gallant, Alice Munro, Alistair MacLeod, and Margaret Atwood—began their careers with the short story and influenced how short stories were being written both in Canada and beyond. As a result, in the last twenty years, at a time when the short story has begun to enjoy a new international popularity, Canadian writers have become recognized as world leaders and innovators in the creation of short fiction.

Excellence breeds excellence: the short story is flourishing in Canada today as never before. While it is not uncommon for aspiring novelists to use the story as a way of beginning their career or for the purpose of honing their craft, a number of Canadian writers have not viewed the short story as a means to an end but have made it their principal form, resisting the allure of the novel; and other writers, like Atwood, have made collections of short stories a regular part of their larger output.

IV   Reading for Content in Canadian Short Stories

An old critical question in Canada, now often held up to sceptical examination, is whether or not there are themes that typify Canadian literature (and that therefore tell us something about the culture that has produced this literature). The stories in this volume were selected for quality and range, not for thematic content. Yet, some themes emerge. The significance of landscape, often described as an important topos in Canadian writing, is evident, even when the landscape becomes, in the more modern era, an urban one. The sense of the past impinging on, even inhabiting, the present is noticeable in a way that suggests much about how Canadians understand their relationship to history.

While the importance and the difficulties of human relationships have been central to all literature, it is worth remarking how many of these stories take as their primary focus the tensions inherent in these relationships and examine the small nuances of human interactions in a way that makes the Canadian short story seem different from the Canadian novel, which often pursues larger social or mythic themes. In these short stories, feelings of displacement and loss—and the questions of identity they provoke—figure largely. These topics may be prominent because, throughout its history, the Canadian story has so often responded to the experience of coming to a new land. When the feeling of displacement that results from exchanging a familiar world for an unfamiliar one combines with a crisis in human relationships, then emotional desolation—*heartbreak*—becomes a reiterated topic. The title of Mavis Gallant's story "My Heart Is Broken" could serve for many of the stories. In spite of this recurrence, Canadian short stories are rarely grim. The edgy humour that is frequently a quality of Canadian writing leavens most of the stories found in this collection.

To read for themes is one way to organize an understanding of a large body of work. It should never be allowed to reduce the nuances and uniqueness of a story, or the individuality of a writer. To read this way need not be limiting; every reader will find a different set of themes or construct a different hierarchy of concerns. One function of short stories is that they allow us to identify what is important to us as readers and let us view our own concerns at a distance. They offer us opportunities for reflection.

Thomas Chandler Haliburton
1796–1865

*In Judge Thomas Chandler Haliburton's time, newspapers and periodicals were the
main source for readers of sketches and other narratives—books being expensive
and sometimes unattainable commodities in the colonies. Haliburton's Sam Slick
stories appeared in* The Nova Scotian, *a Halifax newspaper run by reformer
Joseph Howe, before being collected in book form.*

*These satirical sketches of his native Nova Scotia brought Haliburton an inter-
national reputation. They are among the earliest examples we have of North
American humour, a humour that is playful, colourful, and witty, and that records
emerging North American speech patterns. Through his many portrayals of this
persuasive Yankee peddler, who travels through Nova Scotia selling the clocks he
manufactures to the "blue-noses," Haliburton sought to stir up his colony's citizens,
characterizing them as a lethargic and complacent populace in contrast to Slick,
whose actions might initially suggest those of a dishonest trickster but whose post-
revolutionary "go a-head" turns out to be exemplary, based on common sense and
a keen understanding of human behaviour.*

*Most of the Slick stories are told by a man known only as the Squire—a
Nova Scotian of the leisure class who learns from Slick's observations. "A Cure for
Smuggling," however, is a departure: a dramatic monologue addressed by Slick to
the Squire. The tale shows the reader something about the stereotypes of Americans
and Nova Scotians in Haliburton's time.*

A Cure for Smuggling

Wherever natur' does least, man does most, said the Clockmaker. Gist
see the difference atween these folks here to Liverpool and them up the
bay of Fundy. There natur' has given them the finest country in the
world,—she has taken away all the soil from this place, and chucked it
out there, and left nothin' but rocks and stones here. There they gist
vegetate, and here they go a-head like anything. I was credibly
informed, when Liverpool was first settled, folks had to carry little light
ladders on their shoulders to climb over the rocks, and now they've got
better streets, better houses, better gardens, and a better town than any
of the baymen. They carry on a considerable of a fishery here, and do a
great stroke in the timber-business.

I shall never forget a talk I had with Ichabod Gates here, and a frolic him and me had with a tide-waiter.[1] Ichabod had a large store o' goods, and I was in there one evenin' adrinkin' tea along with him, and we got atalkin' about smugglin'. Says he, Mr. Slick, your people ruin the trade here, they *do* smuggle so; I don't know as I ever shall be able to get rid of my stock of goods, and it cost me a considerable of a sum too. What a pity it is them navy people, instead of carryin' freights of money from the West Indgies warn't employed more a protectin' of our fisheries and our trade. Why don't you smuggle then too, says I, and meet 'em in their own way?—tit for tat—diamond cut diamond—smuggle yourselves and seize *them*;—free trade and sailors' rights is our maxim. Why, says he, I ain't gist altogether certified that it's right; it goes ag'in my conscience to do the like o' that are,[2] and I must say I like a fair deal. In a gineral way a'most, I've observed what's got over the devil's back is commonly lost under his belly. It don't seem to wear well. Well, that's onconvenient, too, to be so thin skinned, said I; for conscience most commonly has a hide as thick as the sole of one's foot; you may cover it with leather to make it look decent-like, but it will bear a considerable hard scrubbin' without anything over it. Now, says I, I will put you on a track that will sarve you without bringin' corns on your conscience either. Do you gist pretend to smuggle and make believe as if you were agoin' the whole hog in it. It's safer and full out as profitable as the rael thing; and besides there's no sort o' risk in it in the world. When folks hear a thing is smuggled they always think it's cheap, and never look into the price; they bite directly— it's a grand bait that. Now always onload your vessels at night, and let folks hear a cart agoin' into your place atween two and three o'clock in the mornin'; fix one o' the axles so it will squeak like a pig, and do you look suspicious, mysterious, and oneasy. Says you, (when a chap says, I guess you were up late last night,) ax me no questions and I'll tell you no lies. There are so many pimpin'[3] eyes about now, a body has to be cautious if he don't want to get into the centre of a hobble.[4] If I'm up late I guess it's nobody's business but my own I'm about any how; but I hope you won't make no remarks about what you seed or heerd.

Well, when a feller axes arter a thing, do you gist stand and look at him for a space without sayin' a word, enquirin' like with a dubersum'[5]

---

[1] A customs officer who boarded ships upon their arrival in port.
[2] *Are* is dialect for *there*.
[3] Prying.
[4] A hobble is an awkward situation.
[5] Doubtful.

look, as if you didn't know as you could trust him or no; then gist wink, put your finger on your nose, and say mum is the word. Take a candle and light it, and say, foller me now, and take him into the cellar. Now, says you, friend, don't betray me, I beseech you, for your life; don't let on to any one about this place;—people will never think o' suspectin' me if you only keep dark about it. I'll let you see some things, says you, that will please you, I know; but don't blow me—that's a good soul. This article, says you, atakin' up one that cost three pounds, I can afford to let you have as low as five pounds, and that one as cheap as six pounds, on one condition,—but mind you it's on them terms only,— and that is that you don't tell any one, not even your wife, where you got it; but you must promise me on the word and honour of a man. The critter will fall right into the trap, and swear by all that's good he'll never breathe it to a livin' soul, and then go right off and tell his wife, and you might as well pour a thing into a filterin' stone[6] as into a woman's ear; it will run right thro', and she'll go a braggin' to her neighbours of the bargain they got, and swear them to secrecy, and they'll tell the whole country in the same way, as a secret of the cheap things Ichabod Gates has. Well, the excise folks will soon hear o' this, and come and sarch your house from top to bottom, and the sarch will make your fortin', for, as they can't find nothin', you will get the credit of doin' the officers in great style.

Well, well, said Ichabod, if you Yankees don't beat all natur'. I don't believe in my soul there's a critter in all Nova Scotia would a' thought o' such a scheme as that, but it's a grand joke, and comports with conscience, for it parallels pretty close with the truth: I'll try it. Try it, says I, to be sure; let's go right off this blessed night, and hide away a parcel of your goods in the cellar,—put some in the garret and some in the gig-house.[7] Begin and sell to-morrow, and all the time I'm to Liverpool I'll keep a runnin' in and out o' your house; sometimes I'll gist come to the corner of the fence, put my head over and draw it back ag'in as if I didn't want folks to see me, and sometimes I'll make as if I was agoin' out, and if I see any one acomin' I'll spring back and hide behind the door; it will set the whole town on the lookout,—and they'll say it's me that's asmugglin' either on my own hook or yourn. In three days he had a great run o' custom, particlarly arter night-fall. It was fun alive to see how the critters were bammed by that hoax.

---

[6] A porous stone, such as sandstone, that permits the flow of water.
[7] Carriage house.

On the fifth day the tide-waiter came. Mr. Slick, says he, I've got
information th——Glad to hear it, says I: an officer without information
would be a poor tool—that's a fact. Well, it brought him up all standin'.
Says he, Do you know who you are atalkin' to? Yes, says I, I guess I do;
I'm talkin' to a man of information, and that bein' the case I'll be so
bold as to ax you one question,—have you any thing to say to me, for
I'm in a considerable of a hurry? Yes, said he, I have. I'm informed you
have smuggled goods in the house. Well, then, says I, you can say what
many galls can't boast on at any rate. What's that? says he. Why, says
I, that you are *miss*informed.

Mr. Gates, said he, give me a candle—I must go to the cellar.
Sartainly, sir, said Ichabod, you may sarch where you please: I've never
smuggled yet, and I am not agoin' now to commence at my time of life.
As soon as he got the candle, and was agoin' down to the cellar with
Gates, I called out to Ichabod. Here, says I, Ich, run quick, for your
life—now's your time; and off we ran up stairs as fast as we could leg it,
and locked the door; the sarcher heerin' that, up too and arter us hot
foot, and bust open the door. As soon as we heerd him adoin' of that we
out o' the other door and locked that also, and down the back stairs to
where we started from. It was some time afore he broke in the second
door, and then he follered us down, lookin' like a proper fool. I'll pay
you up for this, said he to me. I hope so, said I, and Ichabod too. A
pretty time o' day this when folks can tare and race over a decent man's
house, and smash all afore him this way for nothin', ain't it? Them
doors you broke all to pieces will come to somethin', you may depend;—
a joke is a joke, but that's no joke. Arter that he took his time, sarched
the cellar, upper rooms, lower rooms, and garret, and found nothin' to
seize; he was all cut up, and amazin' vexed, and put out. Says I, Friend,
if you want to catch a weasel you must catch him asleep; now if you
want to catch me asmugglin', rise considerable airly in the mornin', will
you? This story made Ichabod's fortin' a'most: he had smuggled goods
to sell for three years, and yet no one could find him in the act, or tell
where onder the sun he hid 'em away to. At last the secret leaked out,
and it fairly broke up smugglin' on the whole shore. That story has done
more nor twenty officers[8]—that's a fact.

There's nothin' a'most, said the Clockmaker, I like so much as to see
folks cheat themselves. I don't know as I ever cheated a man myself in

---

[8] Been more effective than twenty customs officials at impeding the trade in smuggled goods.

my life: I like to do things above board handsum', and go strait ahead; but if a chap seems bent on cheatin' himself, I like to be neighbourly and help him to do it. I mind once, when I was to the eastward of Halifax atradin', I bought a young horse to use while I gave old Clay a run to grass. I do that most every fall, and it does the poor old critter a deal of good. He kinder seems to take a new lease every time, it sets him up so. Well, he was a most aspecial horse, but he had an infarnal temper, and it required all my knowledge of horse flesh to manage him. He'd kick, sulk, back, bite, refuse to draw, or run away, gist as he took the notion. I mastered him, but it was gist as much as a bargain too; and I don't believe, tho' I say it myself, there is any other gentleman in the province could have managed him but me. Well, there was a parson livin' down there that took a great fancy to that horse. Whenever he seed me adrivin' by he always stopt to look at his action and gait, and admired him amazin'ly. Thinks I to myself; that man is inokilated[9]—it'll break out soon—he is detarmined to cheat himself, and if he is, there is no help for it as I see, but to let him. One day I was adrivin' out at a most a duce of a size,[10] and he stopped me. Hallo! says he, Mr. Slick, where are you agoin' in such a desperate hurry? I want to speak a word to you. So I pulls up short. Mornin', says I, parson, how do you do to-day? That's a very clever horse of your'n, says he. Middlin', says I; he does my work, but he's nothin' to brag on; he ain't gist equal to old Clay, and I doubt if there's are a blue-nose horse that is either. Fine action that horse, said he. Well, says I, people do say he has considerable fine action, but that's better for himself than me, for it makes him travel easier.

How many miles will he trot in the hour? said he. Well, says I, if he has a mind to and is well managed, he can do fifteen handsum'. Will you sell him? said he. Well, said I, parson, I would sell him, but not to you; the truth is, said I, smilin', I have a regard for ministers; the best friend I ever had was one, the Reverend Joshua Hopewell, of Slickville, and I wouldn't sell a horse to one I didn't think would suit him. Oh! said he, the horse would suit me exactly; I like him amazin'ly: what's your price? Fifty pounds to anybody else, said I, but fifty-five to you, parson, for I don't want you to have him at no price. If he didn't suit you, people would say I cheated you, and cheatin' a parson is, in my mind, pretty much of a piece with robbin' of a church. Folks would think considerable

[9] Inoculated; here, in the sense of having been infected with a disease.
[10] At a high speed.

hard of me sellin' you a horse that warn't quite the thing, and I shouldn't blame them one morsel if they did. Why, what's the matter of him? said he. Well, says I, minister, says I, alarfin' right out, everything is the matter of him. Oh! said he, that's all nonsense; I've seen the horse in your hands often, and desire no better. Well, says I, he will run away with you if he gets a chance to a sartainty. I will drive him with a curb,[11] said he. He will kick, says I. I'll put a back strap[12] on him, said he. He will go backwards faster than forward, said I. I will give him the whip and teach him better, says he. Well, says I, larfin' like anything, he won't go at all sometimes. I'll take my chance of that, said he; but you must take off that five pounds. Well, says I, parson, I don't want to sell you the horse—that's a fact; but if you must have him I suppose you must, and I will substract the five pounds on one condition, and that is, if you don't like the beast, you tell folks that you would have him, tho' I tried to set him out as bad as I could, and said everything of him I could lay my tongue to. Well, says he, the horse is mine, and if he don't suit me, I acquit you of all blame.

Well, he took the horse, and cracked and boasted most prodigiously of him; he said he wouldn't like to take a hundred pounds for him; that he liked to buy a horse of a Yankee, for they were such capital judges of horse flesh they hardly ever a'most had a bad one, and that he knew he was agoin' to get a first-chop one, the moment he found I didn't want to sell him, and that he never saw a man so loath to part with a beast. Oh dear! how I larfed in my sleeve when I heerd tell of the goney talkin' such nonsense: thinks I, he'll live to larn yet some things that ain't writ down in Latin afore he dies, or I'm mistakened—that's all. In the course of a few days the horse began to find he'd changed hands, and he thought he'd try what sort o' stuff his new master was made on; so he gist took the bit in his mouth one fine mornin' and ran off with him, and kicked his gig all to flinders, and nearly broke the parson's neck; and findin' that answer, he took to all his old tricks ag'in, and got worse than ever. He couldn't do nothin' with him,—even the helps were frightened out of their lives to go into the stable to him.

So he come to me one day lookin' quite streaked,[13] and says he, Mr. Slick, that horse I bought of you is a perfect divil; I never saw such a

---

[11] A curb bit is a part of a bridle placed in a horse's mouth to restrain it from running.
[12] A back strap (or hock strap) is attached to the upper hind legs of the horse to limit its movement.
[13] Confused or agitated.

critter in my life; I can neither ride him nor drive him. He gist does what he pleases with us, and we can't help ourselves nohow. He actilly beats all the onruly animals I ever seed in my life. Well, says I, I told you so, minister—I didn't want to sell him to you at all, but you would have him. I know you did, said he; but you larfed so all the time I thought you was in jeest. I thought you didn't care to sell him, and gist said so to put me off, jokin' like: I had no idee you were in airnest: I wouldn't give ten pounds for him. Nor I neither, said I; I wouldn't take him as a gift, and be bound to keep him. How could you then, said he, have the conscience to ax me fifty pounds for him, and pocket it so cooly? To prevent you from buyin' him, parson, said I, that was my reason. I did all I could for you, I axed you five times as much as he was worth, and said all I could think on to run him down too; but *you took yourself in.* There's two ways of tellin' a thing, said he, Mr. Slick,—in airnest and in jeest. You told it as if you were in jeest, and I took it so; you may call it what you like, but I call it a deception still. Parson, says I, how many ways you may have of tellin' a thing I don't know; but I have only one, and that's the true way: I told you the truth, but you didn't choose to believe it. Now, says I, I feel kinder sorry for you too; but I'll tell you how to get out o' the scrape. I can't take him back, or folks would say it was me and not you that cheated yourself. Do you ship him. You can't sell him here without doin' the fair thing, as I did, tellin' all his faults; and if you do no soul would take him as a present, for people will believe you, tho' it seems they won't always believe a Clockmaker. Gist send him off to the West Indgies, and sell him at auction there for what he will fetch. He'll bring a good price, and if he gets into a rael right down genu*wine* horseman's hands, there's no better horse. He said nothin', but shook his head, as if that cat wouldn't jump.[14]

Now, says I, there's another bit of advice I'll give you free gratis for nothin',—*never buy a horse on the dealer's judgment, or he will cheat you if he can; never buy him on your own, or you will cheat yourself as sure as you are born.* In that case, said he, larfin', a man will be sure to be cheated either way: how is he to guard ag'in bein' taken in, then? Well, says I, he stands a fair chance any way of havin' the leake put into him—that's sartain, for next to woman kind there is nothin' so deceitful as horse-flesh that ever I seed yet. Both on 'em are apt to be spoiled in

---

[14] As if the event couldn't happen.

the breakin'; both on 'em puzzle the best judges sometimes to tell their age when well vamped up, and it takes some time afore you find out all their tricks. Pedigree must be attended to in both cases, particularly on the mother's side, and both require good trainin', a steady hand, and careful usage. Yes; both branches require great experience, and the most knowin' ones do get bit sometimes most beautifully. Well, says he, as touchin' horses, how is a man to avoid bein' deceived? Well, says I, I'll tell you—never buy a horse of a total stranger on no account,—never buy a horse of a gentleman, for—— Why, said he, he's the very man I should like to buy of, above all others. Well, then, says I, he's not the man for my money anyhow; you think you are safe with him, and don't inquire enough, and take too much for granted: you are apt to cheat yourself in that case. Never buy a crack horse; he's done too much. Never buy a colt; he's done too little; you can't tell how he'll turn out. In short, says I, it's a considerable of a long story to go all through with it; it would take me less time to teach you how to make a clock, I calculate. If you buy from a man who ain't a dealer, he actilly don't know whether his horse is a good one or not; you must get advice from a friend who does know. If you buy from a dealer, he is too much for you or your friend either. If he has no honour, don't trade with him. If he has, put yourself wholly and entirely on it, and he'll not deceive you, there's no mistake—he'll do the thing genteel. If you'd a' axed me candidly now about that are horse, says I.—At that he looked up at me quite hard for a space, without sayin' a word, but pressed his lips together quite miffy like, as if he was a strivin' for to keep old Adam down,[15] and turned short off and walked away. I felt kinder pity for him too; but if a man will cheat himself in spite of all you can do, why, there is no help for it as I see, but to let him. Do you, squire?

—1838

---

[15] To keep his unregenerate nature in check; to hold his temper.

Catharine Parr Traill 1802–1899

As the success of her Backwoods of Canada *(1836), a book addressed to prospective female settlers, suggests, Catharine Parr Traill adapted to life in rural Canada more readily than most nineteenth-century British immigrants—including her sister, Susanna Moodie, whose* Roughing It in the Bush *recorded the difficulties of establishing a home in a new land. Inspired by the recent emergence of women of science such as Jane Marcet (whose 1806* Conversations on Chemistry, *a popular and influential science book in its day, is mentioned in "The Old Doctor"), Traill became an excellent naturalist, documenting her early observations of the local flora. As in her instructional books, Traill's more literary writing depends on close observation. Working within the conventions of the sketch and drawing from experience, her stories record the manners and conditions of her time and place.*

In "The Old Doctor" Traill, seeking to capture the nature of an individual, unifies her sketch around character rather than plot. She presents two aspects of the central figure: first, as a scientific Englishman trying to adapt his knowledge to frontier conditions; second, as a social commentator, arguing in dialogue with a "lady" that, because of the demands settlement places on immigrants to a new country, the customs of genteel English society must be modified in Canada if the new settlers are to prosper.

The Old Doctor: A Backwoods Sketch

"This is comfort Sir—old Canadian comfort such as I rarely meet with now, even in the backwoods," said the old doctor as he extended his half frozen hands to the cheerful blaze of the log fire that roared and crackled in the ample stone chimney at "Braehead."

"This fire, my dear Sir, is worth all the fine gim-crack stoves that ever came out of a foundry—lung-destroying, life-destroying, house-destroying, stoves."

"You are eloquent Doctor. What has moved your wrath against iron today?"

"The misery of my fellow creatures and their stupidity moreover," said the old man, rapidly divesting himself of sundry woollen mufflers that were wrapped around his throat and chin, of a thick homespun greatcoat and spencer of super-fine cloth, that old-fashioned sort of overjacket that used to be worn fifty years ago by elderly gentlemen, especially medical men.

The doctor was a model of strength, both mental and physical, of middle height and half as much above it but not fat; his hair silvered, but not white, still curled in thick masses above a high broad brow. The form of the head indicated mental power, firmness and decision; the height from ear to the crown showed a little too much destructiveness but the fine arch over the upper region of the forehead displayed benevolence in a still greater degree. The keen blue fiery eye, mouth slightly sarcastic, indicated to those who were skilled in reading the human mind from the human face the decisive character of the man.

The old doctor was a Radical in his way, but it was against abuses and follies, all, as he said, for the good of his species. He ran atilt at idleness and vice, knocking down all opponents with the power of his keen sarcasm and downright bluster. However, when real sympathy was required to the sick and unfortunate he was tender and generous and loving as a father. But while he shewed benevolence to such as were suffering from the visitation of God or incidental causes, he gave no comfort to the idler who was content to fold his arms and sit down in hopeless apathy lamenting over a hard fate that might have been averted by energy of body or prudent forethought. "Up and be doing," "Set your shoulder to the wheel," "God helps those who help themselves," and many other such pithy maxims were among his household words. Such was the old doctor who now stood on the wide grey hearthstone of the log house at "Braehead."

One of his great antipathies was a parlour stove. "Let the women use a cooking stove in the kitchen, though I do not even like that, but give me the soul-cheering, heartwarming ruddy blaze of a good large log fire with a backlog that needs a stout arm to bring in. Hurl into the chimney back split maple, birch or oak, a few chips judiciously placed to keep up the draft and a kindling of cedar or pine below. There, Sir, is a fire such as our ancestors used to sit beside of a Christmas eve or a cool fall night."

"The stoves give more warmth," timidly interposed a delicate young girl who sat in the chimney corner.

The old man turned and eyed her for a minute, "How is your cough Miss Ellen? Did the burgundy pitch plaister ease your chest?"

"Not much, Doctor."

"No Madam, and it never will while you continue to breathe that stifling over-heated atmosphere of your father's house—thermometer rising daily from 85 to 100 degrees; no ventilation by means of a good wide chimney like this; air rushes in at an open door in a current and you may yourself be sitting in the direct line between it and the hot stove. No wonder you are a sick child."

"I am never too hot Doctor when you come to see us and make such a fuss . . ."

"You were going to say—about the heated room," the old man interrupted.

"Well, I am often quite chilly."

"No wonder Madam. Flesh and blood cannot stand it. Why, man is not a salamander to live in the fire. You would have been a good subject for that tyrannical old King of Babylon to have exercised his authority over. I think you would have stood the fiery furnace as well as Shadrach, Meshach and Abednego."[1]

The invalid laughed, though she felt a pang of conscience in doing so.

"Then at night you have a fire lighted in your bedroom and sleep under a weight of blankets and coverlets and the room is again heated to a degree that is quite inimical to health. Fever, restless nights and languor is the consequence."

"I am perished when I awake if the stove is out Sir."

"There it is. You are roasted or stewed half the night and literally frozen the other half. You feel the cold twice as much as you would do if you went to bed in a moderately cold room and covered yourself up warmly. I do not object to an open fireplace, or a hall stove if there must be a stove at all to take off the keen edge of the frosty air, but no bedroom stove at all. I never sleep in a hot room—neither allow one for my children and look at them—cheeks like roses, eyes bright and lively as kittens—do you think those English cheeks would bloom so brightly in a hot house? Half the sickness that prevails in this naturally fine climate arises from the folly of those who make iron ovens of their houses and then think to breathe like the hardy children of the soil. Why they might as well expect fish to live out of their own element. What makes all our women fade and their cheeks lose their colour and turn yellow? The hot stove. It puts one in a rage to think of it!"

"You think the stove heat hurts the lungs Doctor?" asked his nervous patient.

"Yes I do. The air is completely changed by the heated iron. I could explain it from chemical causes, only you would be none the wiser if I did."

"I have read 'Conversations on Chemistry.'"

---

[1] In the biblical Book of Daniel, Nebuchadnezzar, the King of ancient Babylon, condemns three Israelites—Shadrach, Meshach, and Abednego—to death in a "burning fiery furnace" for their refusal to obey his command to worship a golden image. They are saved from the flames by a miracle. This idea of being able to withstand fire extends the doctor's earlier reference to the folk belief that salamanders were born from flames.

"Pooh, poor child. Stuff. Girls never do understand these things from reading books. Learn the practical chemistry of the kitchen. That is the thing for them. The rapid change that the delicate respiratory organs undergo passing from a heated room into the open air when the mercury is below zero must be very trying to them. You girls will coddle yourselves up in one of these hot rooms and then think nothing of going out for a sleigh drive by moonlight, into the air perhaps ten or fifteen degrees below zero, or dance away till morning at your picnics and enjoy a good mouthful of cold in the coldest part of the twenty-four hours just before sunrise and yet are surprised that you are delicate and are subject to influenza and coughs and chest disease."

"It is singular, the prevalence of colds and coughs, influenza and consumption, that we hear of in late years,"[2] said Mr. Gradewell, who had been listening attentively to the pronouncements of his guest.

"It is not at all singular, Sir. It is just what was to be expected from the insane folly of the settlers."

"The dearness of wood in the towns is one of the reasons for the adoption of stove heat," said Mr. Gradewell.

"The government ought to have restricted settlers from cutting down too much wood. A forest reserve might have been made and the right of cutting it paid for at a moderate price. The people would have grumbled a little at first but would have found the blessing of it after a time. They should be prevented in their deeds from clearing up all the timber land on their lots. People are fools and should be curbed in their folly and ruled for their own good."

This was a pet refrain of the old doctor's, who also believed in preserving a portion of pleasantly wooded land in the vicinity of large towns for public walks and parks. It roused his furious indignation when he beheld the natural beauties of a place disfigured, and spots that seemed by nature fitted for man's recreation despoiled of trees and turf and crowded with buildings. He considered it a great oversight that a portion of such land was not reserved by the government for the use of the people.

Ellen Eastwood was the daughter of a gentleman residing in the neighbouring town whose delicate consumptive habit had alarmed her friends. Yielding to the doctor's advice she was on a visit to her uncle, Mr. Gradewell, who lived on a cleared farm five or six miles out of the town.

---

[2] There were worldwide influenza pandemics in 1831 and 1833; epidemics of consumption (i.e., tuberculosis) became a matter of general concern in the nineteenth century.

In summer, in spite of the distance, the hale active old man used to walk to visit his patients with no other help than the twisted thorn staff that he had cut on one of his botanizing rambles through the woods. In winter he drove himself in a stout dark-painted cutter, the woodwork made by his own hands, for the doctor was no mean mechanic. So active was he that he considered it one of the seven deadly sins to be idle. If he was not working with his hands, he was with his head. The first question that he put when he heard of a fresh arrival in the township was: "Are they sober? Can they use their hands?" He believed "Mere bookworms will starve in Canada. Idle hands make no head. If the young men can only drink and shoot let them get back from whence they came. They are not the right sort for a colony." The first thing in his estimation was to know how to use tools and with this idea he constantly advised any young men who came from the old country to learn a little of the craft of the carpenter, the blacksmith, and even the mason, before they settled on a farm. It was one of his maxims that no man should emigrate as a farmer to a Colony till he could help to build his own house. He had been settled many years in the Province and had seen a great deal of the ups and downs of life in Canada.

The hardships and toils of a Backwoodsman's life he knew from his constant acquaintance with settlers of all sorts and conditions. He would predict from his experience who would drive and thrive and who would sink utterly or drag on in a more shifting sort of life, ever in need, and who would go down and perish. The doctor was a great utilitarian. He valued most those who did most, but it must be for others as well as themselves. He was not selfish and did not love those who were.

The doctor was always a favoured visitor at "Braehead" and its cheerful log fire always put him in good humour—that is as soon as he had had his grumble out, for he was sure to have seen in the exercise of his vocation some thing that had roused his anger at deeds done or deeds undone that ought to have been done.

He was always pleased to see the girls usefully occupied in a household and took pleasure in praising the bread or puddings, pies or preserves if he knew they had been prepared by the hands of any of the ladies of the family. He loved to see a girl spinning at the large wheel. The hum of it, he said, was more pleasing to his ear than the sound of a piano, though he loved music too. He viewed with satisfaction the busy fingers plying the knitting needles and always commended any of the young folks whose hands were thus employed.

One of his lady friends reproached the doctor for his leveling system.

"Nay Madam," he replied curtly, "it is that you would level your family by managing idleness among them. The diligent hand maketh rich and the sluggard shall starve in harvest."

His friend Gradewell's family he regarded as patterns to the country. "They will be happy and respected," he used to say, "when others have gone down in the world, merely because they have wisely conformed to the lot in life to which Providence has called them. There is Bessy, now. See how bright and neat and cheerful she looks. I hear her voice singing by sunrise as she trips to her dairy. She is not ashamed to help milk the cows and make the butter and cheese. She never seems idle, for the knitting needles are going if she sits down by the fire. She loses no time lolling on a couch reading a novel. No, she is up and doing. And there is Anna. See how steadily she attends to all her employments. She is a pattern for girls of her age."

"These girls are complete household drudges," observed the lady to whom the remark was made, with a shrug. "The poor girls are worked like slaves. What time can they have for enjoyment? I wonder what their mother and father think is to become of them."

The doctor almost glared at the speaker. "I will tell you Madam. They will become good wives and sensible mothers and will be blessings to their husbands and children. They will flourish when others fail. If there were thousands more brought up like the girls and boys in that house the Province would in time be the wonder and glory of all lands."

"They can have no time for recreation of any sort. It is always the same—work, work, work."

"You are quite mistaken there. I know of no family that enjoys more pleasure than the Gradewells. Not a day in the winter, if the horses can be spared, that my friend or one of the boys does not take out a load of them, young and old, and merry enough they are—singing and enjoying themselves with all their hearts. Then at night they dance to Edward's fiddle and make a great circle round the fire and chat and sing and talk till bedtime."

"How do they get time for all this enjoyment?"

"By order Madam, which, like economy, makes a little go a long way. They have time for everything, for work and also for play."

The lady sighed wearily and went away, but did not profit by the Doctor's exhortations. He complained that very few did.

—1985 [3]

[3] This sketch, based on a doctor who attended Traill from around 1836 to 1844, was not published in her lifetime.

Duncan Campbell Scott 1862–1947

Although Duncan Campbell Scott was better known as a poet, his short stories are landmarks in the development of short fiction in Canada. In the Village of Viger *(1896) is innovative because, like Stephen Leacock's* Sunshine Sketches of a Little Town *(1912) and James Joyce's* Dubliners *(1914), it unifies its stories around a single setting. "Paul Farlotte," the conclusion to this collection, is, like Haliburton's sketches, a response to a culture that seems deeply conservative. But, in contrast to the Sam Slick stories, "Paul Farlotte" suggests that "progress" is at best ambiguous and may be futile; it can disrupt society and destroy individuals by tempting them to sacrifice the present for a longed-for future. Fable-like in its increasingly nightmarish vision of the machine, this story is an early expression of concern about the potential dangers of technology.*

Paul Farlotte

Near the outskirts of Viger, to the west, far away from the Blanche, but having a country outlook of their own, and a glimpse of a shadowy range of huts, stood two houses which would have attracted attention by their contrast, if for no other reason. One was a low cottage, surrounded by a garden, and covered with roses, which formed jalousies for the encircling veranda. The garden was laid out with the care and completeness that told of a master hand. The cottage itself had the air of having been secured from the inroads of time as thoroughly as paint and a nail in the right place at the right time could effect that end. The other was a large gaunt-looking house, narrow and high, with many windows, some of which were boarded up, as if there was no further use for the chambers into which they had once admitted light. Standing on a rough piece of ground it seemed given over to the rudeness of decay. It appeared to have been the intention of its builder to veneer it with brick; but it stood there a wooden shell, discoloured by the weather, disjointed by the frost, and with the wind fluttering the rags of tar-paper which had been intended as a protection against the cold, but which now hung in patches and ribbons. But despite this dilapidation it had a sort of martial air about it, and seemed to watch over its embowered companion, warding off tempests and gradually falling to pieces on guard, like a faithful soldier who suffers at his post. In the road, just between the two, stood a beautiful Lombardy poplar. Its shadow fell upon the little cottage in the morning, and travelled across the garden, and in the evening touched the corner of the tall house, and faded out with the sun, only to float there again in the moonlight, or to commence the journey next morning with the dawn. This shadow seemed, with its constant movement, to figure the connection that existed between the two houses.

The garden of the cottage was a marvel; there the finest roses in the parish grew, roses which people came miles to see, and parterres of old-fashioned flowers, the seed of which came from France, and which in consequence seemed to blow with a rarer colour and more delicate perfume. This garden was a striking contrast to the stony ground about the neighbouring house, where only the commonest weeds grew un-regarded; but its master had been born a gardener, just as another man is born a musician or a poet. There was a superstition in the village that all he had to do was to put anything, even a dry stick, into the ground, and it would grow. He was the village school-master, and Madame Laroque would remark spitefully enough that if Monsieur Paul Farlotte had been as successful in planting knowledge in the heads of his schol-ars as he was in planting roses in his garden Viger would have been cele-brated the world over. But he was born a gardener, not a teacher; and he made the best of the fate which compelled him to depend for his living on something he disliked. He looked almost as dry as one of his own hyacinth bulbs; but like it he had life at his heart. He was a very small man, and frail, and looked older than he was. It was strange, but you rarely seemed to see his face; for he was bent with weeding and digging, and it seemed an effort for him to raise his head and look at you with the full glance of his eye. But when he did, you saw the eye was honest and full of light. He was not careful of his personal appearance, clinging to his old garments with a fondness which often laid him open to ridicule, which he was willing to bear for the sake of the comfort of an old pair of shoes, or a hat which had accommodated itself to the irregularities of his head. On the street he wore a curious skirt-coat that seemed to be made of some indestructible material, for he had worn it for years, and might be buried in it. It received an extra brush for Sundays and holidays, and always looked as good as new. He made a quaint picture, as he came down the road from the school. He had a hesitating walk, and constantly stopped and looked behind him; for he always fancied he heard a voice calling him by his name. He would be working in his flower-beds when he would hear it over his shoulder, "Paul"; or when he went to draw water from his well, "Paul"; or when he was reading by his fire, someone calling him softly, "Paul, Paul"; or in the dead of night, when nothing moved in his cottage he would hear it out of the dark, "Paul." So it came to be a sort of companionship for him, this haunting voice; and sometimes one could have seen him in his garden stretch out his hand and smile, as if he were welcoming an invisible guest. Sometimes the guest was not invisible, but took body and shape, and was a real presence; and often Paul was greeted with visions of things that had been, or that would be, and saw figures where, for other eyes, hung only the impalpable air.

He had one other passion besides his garden, and that was Montaigne.[1] He delved in one in the summer, in the other in the winter. With his feet on his stove he would become so absorbed with his author that he would burn his slippers and come to himself disturbed by the smell of the singed leather. He had only one great ambition, that was to return to France to see his mother before she died; and he had for years been trying to save enough money to take the journey. People who did not know him called him stingy, and said the saving for his journey was only a pretext to cover his miserly habits. It was strange, he had been saving for years, and yet he had not saved enough. Whenever anyone would ask him, "Well, Monsieur Farlotte, when do you go to France?" he would answer, "Next year—next year." So when he announced one spring that he was actually going, and when people saw that he was not making his garden with his accustomed care, it became the talk of the village: "Monsieur Farlotte is going to France"; "Monsieur Farlotte has saved enough money, true, true, he is going to France."

His proposed visit gave no one so much pleasure as it gave his neighbours in the gaunt, unkempt house which seemed to watch over his own; and no one would have imagined what a joy it was to Marie St. Denis, the tall girl who was mother to her orphan brothers and sisters, to hear Monsieur Farlotte say, "When I am in France"; for she knew what none of the villagers knew, that, if it had not been for her and her troubles, Monsieur Farlotte would have seen France many years before. How often she would recall the time when her father, who was in the employ of the great match factory near Viger, used to drive about collecting the little paper match-boxes which were made by hundreds of women in the village and the country round; how he had conceived the idea of making a machine in which a strip of paper would go in at one end, and the completed match-boxes would fall out at the other; how he had given up

[1] Michel de Montaigne, sixteenth-century French thinker. In his essays, Montaigne was sceptical about our human ability to know truth yet he advocated the search for self-knowledge.

his situation and devoted his whole time and energy to the invention of this machine; how he had failed time and again, but continued with a perseverance which at last became a frantic passion; and how, to keep the family together, her mother, herself, and the children joined that army of workers which was making the match-boxes by hand. She would think of what would have happened to them then if Monsieur Farlotte had not been there with his help, or what would have happened when her mother died, worn out, and her father, overcome with disappointment, gave up his life and his task together, in despair. But whenever she would try to speak of these things Monsieur Farlotte would prevent her with a gesture, "Well, but what would you have me do—besides, I will go some day—now who knows, next year, perhaps." So here was the "next year," which she had so longed to see, and Monsieur Farlotte was giving her a daily lecture on how to treat the tulips after they had done flowering, preluding everything he had to say with, "When I am in France," for his heart was already there.

He had two places to visit, one was his old home, the other was the birthplace of his beloved Montaigne. He had often described to Marie the little cottage where he was born, with the vine arbours and the long garden walks, the lilac-bushes, with their cool dark-green leaves, the white eaves where the swallows nested, and the poplar, sentinel over all. "You see," he would say, "I have tried to make this little place like it; and my memory may have played me a trick, but I often fancy myself at home. That poplar and this long walk and the vines on the arbour— sometimes when I see the tulips by the border I fancy it is all in France."

Marie was going over his scant wardrobe, mending with her skilful fingers, putting a stitch in the trusty old coat, and securing its buttons. She was anxious that Monsieur Farlotte should get a new suit before he went on his journey; but he would not hear to it. "Not a bit of it," he would say, "if I made my appearance in a new suit, they would think I had been making money; and when they would find out that I had not enough to buy cabbage for the soup there would be a disappointment." She could not get him to write that he was coming. "No, no," he would say, "if I do that they will expect me." "Well, and why not—why not?" "Well, they would think about it—in ten days Paul comes home, then in five days, Paul comes home, and then when I came they would set the dogs on me. No, I will just walk in—so—and when they are staring at my old cat I will just sit down in a corner, and my old mother will commence to cry. Oh, I have it all arranged."

So Marie let him have his own way; but she was fixed on having her way in some things. To save Monsieur Farlotte the heavier work, and allow him to keep his strength for the journey, she would make her brother Guy do the spading in the garden, much to his disgust, and that of Monsieur Farlotte, who would stand by and interfere, taking the spade into his own hands with infinite satisfaction. "See," he would say, "go deeper and turn it over so." And when Guy would dig in his own clumsy way, he would go off in despair, with the words, "God help us, nothing will grow there."

When Monsieur Farlotte insisted on taking his clothes in an old box covered with raw-hide, with his initials in brass tacks on the cover, Marie would not consent to it, and made Guy carry off the box without his knowledge and hide it. She had a good tin trunk which had belonged to her mother, which she knew where to find in the attic, and which would contain everything Monsieur Farlotte had to carry. Poor Marie never went into this attic without a shudder, for occupying most of the space was her father's work bench, and that complicated wheel, the model of his invention, which he had tried so hard to perfect, and which stood there like a monument of his failure. She had made Guy promise never to move it, fearing lest he might be tempted to finish what his father had begun—a fear that was almost an apprehension, so like him was he growing. He was tall and large-boned, with a dark restless eye, set under an overhanging forehead. He had long arms, out of proportion to his height, and he hung his head when he walked. His likeness to his father made him seem a man before his time. He felt himself a man; for he had a good position in the match factory, and was like a father to his little brothers and sisters.

Although the model had always had a strange fascination for him, the lad had kept his promise to his sister, and had never touched the mechanism which had literally taken his father's life. Often when he went into the attic he would stand and gaze at the model and wonder why it had not succeeded, and recall his father bending over his work, with his compass and pencil. But he had a dread of it, too, and sometimes would hurry away, afraid lest its fascination would conquer him.

Monsieur Farlotte was to leave as soon as his school closed, but weeks before that he had everything ready, and could enjoy his roses in peace. After school hours he would walk in his garden, to and fro, to and fro, with his hands behind his back, and his eyes upon the ground, meditating; and once in a while he would pause and smile, or look over his shoulder when the haunting voice would call his name. His scholars had commenced to view him with additional interest, now that he was going to take such a prodigious journey; and two or three of them could always be seen peering through the palings, watching him as he walked up and down the path; and Marie would watch him, too, and wonder what he would say when he found that his trunk had disappeared. He missed it fully a month before he could expect to start; but he had resolved to pack that very evening.

"But there is plenty of time," remonstrated Marie.

"That's always the way," he answered. "Would you expect me to leave everything until the last moment?"

"But, Monsieur Farlotte, in ten minutes everything goes into the trunk."

"So, and in the same ten minutes something is left out of the trunk, and I am in France, and my shoes are in Viger, that will be the end of it."

So, to pacify him, she had to ask Guy to bring down the trunk from the attic. It was not yet dark there; the sunset threw a great colour into the room, touching all the familiar objects with transfiguring light, and giving the shadows a rich depth. Guy saw the model glowing like some magic golden wheel, the metal points upon it gleaming like jewels in the light. As he passed he touched it, and with a musical click something dropped from it. He picked it up: it was one of the little paper match-boxes, but the defect that he remembered to have heard talked of was there. He held it in his hand and examined it; then he pulled it apart and spread it out. "Ah," he said to himself, "the fault was in the cutting." Then he turned the wheel, and one by one the imperfect boxes dropped out, until the strip of paper was exhausted. "But why,"—the question rose in his mind—"why could not that little difficulty be overcome?"

He took the trunk down to Marie, who at last persuaded Monsieur Farlotte to let her pack his clothes in it. He did so with a protestation, "Well, I know how it will be with a fine box like that, some fellow will whip it off when I am looking the other way, and that will be the end of it."

As soon as he could do so without attracting Marie's attention Guy returned to the attic with a lamp. When Marie had finished packing Monsieur Farlotte's wardrobe, she went home to put her children to bed; but when she saw that light in the attic window she nearly fainted from apprehension. When she pushed open the door of that room which she had entered so often with the scant meals she used to bring her father, she saw Guy bending over the model, examining every part of it. "Guy," she said, trying to command her voice, "you have broken your promise." He looked up quickly. "Marie, I am going to find it out—I can understand it—there is just one thing, if I can get that we will make a fortune out of it."

"Guy, don't delude yourself; those were father's words, and day after day I brought him his meals here, when he was too busy even to come downstairs; but nothing came of it, and while he was trying to make a machine for the boxes, we were making them with our fingers. O Guy," she cried, with her voice rising into a sob, "remember those days, remember what Monsieur Farlotte did for us, and what he would have to do again if you lost your place!"

"That's all nonsense, Marie. Two weeks will do it, and after that I could send Monsieur Farlotte home with a pocket full of gold."

"Guy, you are making a terrible mistake. That wheel was our curse, and it will follow us if you don't leave it alone. And think of Monsieur Farlotte; if he finds out what you are working at he will not go to France—I know him; he will believe it his duty to stay here and help us, as he did when father was alive. Guy, Guy, listen to me!"

But Guy was bending over the model, absorbed in its labyrinths. In vain did Marie argue with him, try to persuade him, and threaten him; she attempted to lock the attic door and keep him out, but he twisted the lock off, and after that the door was always open. Then she resolved to break the wheel into a thousand pieces; but when she went upstairs, when Guy was away, she could not strike it with the axe she held. It seemed like a human thing that cried out with a hundred tongues against the murder she would do; and she could only sink down sobbing, and pray. Then failing everything else she simulated an interest in the thing, and tried to lead Guy to work at it moderately, and not to give up his whole time to it.

But he seemed to take up his father's passion where he had laid it down. Marie could do nothing with him; and the younger children, at first hanging around the attic door, as if he were their father come back again, gradually ventured into the room, and whispered together as they watched their rapt and unobservant brother working at his task. Marie's one thought was to devise a means of keeping the fact from Monsieur Farlotte; and she told him blankly that Guy had been sent away on business, and would not be back for six weeks. She hoped that by that time Monsieur Farlotte would be safely started on his journey. But night after night he saw a light in the attic window. In the past years it had been constant there, and he could only connect it with one cause. But he could get no answer from Marie when he asked her the reason; and the next night the distracted girl draped the window so that no ray of light could find its way out into the night. But Monsieur Farlotte was not satisfied; and a few evenings afterwards, as it was growing dusk, he went quietly into the house, and upstairs into the attic. There he saw Guy stretched along the work bench, his head in his hands, using the last light to ponder over a sketch he was making, and beside him, figured very clearly in the thick gold air of the sunset, the form of his father, bending over him, with the old eager, haggard look in his eyes. Monsieur Farlotte watched the two figures for a moment as they glowed in their rich atmosphere; then the apparition turned his head slowly, and warned him away with a motion of his hand.

All night long Monsieur Farlotte walked in his garden, patient and undisturbed, fixing his duty so that nothing could root it out. He found the comfort that comes to those who give up some exceeding deep desire of the heart, and when next morning the market-gardener from St. Valérie, driving by as the matin bell was clanging from St. Joseph's, and seeing the old teacher as if he were taking an early look at his growing roses, asked him, "Well, Monsieur Farlotte, when do you go to France?" he was able to answer cheerfully, "Next year—next year."

Marie could not unfix his determination. "No," he said, "they do not expect me. No one will be disappointed. I am too old to travel. I might be lost in the sea. Until Guy makes his invention we must not be apart."

At first the villagers thought that he was only joking, and that they would some morning wake up and find him gone; but when the holidays came, and when enough time had elapsed for him to make his journey twice over they began to think he was in earnest. When they knew that Guy St. Denis was chained to his father's invention, and when they saw that Marie and the children had commenced to make match-boxes again, they shook their heads. Some of them at least seemed to understand why Monsieur Farlotte had not gone to France.

But he never repined. He took up his garden again, was as contented as ever, and comforted himself with the wisdom of Montaigne. The people dropped the old question, "When are you going to France?" Only his companion voice called him more loudly, and more often he saw figures in the air that no one else could see.

Early one morning, as he was working in his garden around a growing pear-tree, he fell into a sort of stupor, and sinking down quietly on his knees he leaned against the slender stem for support. He saw a garden much like his own, flooded with the clear sunlight, in the shade of an arbour an old woman in a white cap was leaning back in a wheeled chair, her eyes were closed, she seemed asleep. A young woman was seated beside her holding her hand. Suddenly the old woman smiled, a childish smile, as if she were well pleased. "Paul," she murmured, "Paul, Paul." A moment later her companion started up with a cry; but she did not move, she was silent and tranquil. Then the young woman fell on her knees and wept, hiding her face. But the aged face was inexpressibly calm in the shadow, with the smile lingering upon it, fixed by the deeper sleep into which she had fallen.

Gradually the vision faded away, and Paul Farlotte found himself leaning against his pear-tree, which was almost too young as yet to support his weight. The bell was ringing from St. Joseph's, and had shaken the swallows from their nests in the steeple into the clear air. He heard their cries as they flew into his garden, and he heard the voices of his neighbour children as they played around the house.

Later in the day he told Marie that his mother had died that morning, and she wondered how he knew.

—1896

Stephen Leacock 1869–1944

Already well established as a popular humorist, Stephen Leacock created his masterwork, Sunshine Sketches of a Little Town —*a series of stories about life in the Canadian community of Mariposa—in 1912. A satiric comic idyll, the collection shows the emergence of an urban perspective that invites the reader to look at small-town Canada with a mixture of irony and nostalgia.*

"The Hostelry of Mr. Smith," the opening story in the collection, uses the comedic techniques of malapropism and of inflation and deflation (often through renaming or inept comparison) to establish the characters' misperceptions and their aggrandizing estimates of their own self-worth and their small town's importance. Behind the foolishness displayed by Mariposans lies a goodness that allows Leacock to forgive all their self-delusions.

The Hostelry of Mr. Smith

I don't know whether you know Mariposa. If not, it is of no consequence, for if you know Canada at all, you are probably well acquainted with a dozen towns just like it.

There it lies in the sunlight, sloping up from the little lake that spreads out at the foot of the hillside on which the town is built. There is a wharf beside the lake, and lying alongside of it a steamer that is tied to the wharf with two ropes of about the same size as they use on the Lusitania.[1] The steamer goes nowhere in particular, for the lake is landlocked and there is no navigation for the Mariposa Belle except to "run trips" on the first of July and the Queen's Birthday, and to take excursions of the Knights of Pythias and the Sons of Temperance to and from the Local Option Townships.[2]

In point of geography the lake is called Lake Wissanotti and the river running out of it the Ossawippi, just as the main street of Mariposa is called Missinaba Street and the county Missinaba County. But these names do not really matter. Nobody uses them. People simply speak of the "lake" and the "river" and the "main street," much in the same way as they always call the Continental Hotel, "Pete Robinson's" and the Pharmaceutical Hall, "Eliot's Drug Store." But I suppose this is just the same in every one else's town as in mine, so I need lay no stress on it.

The town, I say, has one broad street that runs up from the lake, commonly called the Main Street. There is no doubt about its width. When Mariposa was laid out there was none of that shortsightedness which is seen in the cramped dimensions of Wall Street and Piccadilly. Missinaba street is so wide that if you were to roll Jeff. Thorpe's barber shop over on its face it wouldn't reach half-way across. Up and down the Main Street are telegraph poles of cedar of colossal thickness, standing at a variety of angles and carrying rather more wires than are commonly seen at a transatlantic cable station.

On the Main Street itself are a number of buildings of extraordinary importance,—Smith's Hotel and the Continental and the Mariposa House, and the two banks (the Commercial and the Exchange), to say nothing of McCarthy's Block (erected in 1878), and Glover's Hardware Store with the Oddfellows' Hall above it. Then on the "cross" street that intersects Missinaba Street at the main corner there is the Post Office and the Fire Hall and the Young Men's Christian Association and the office of the Mariposa Newspacket,—in fact to the eye of discernment a perfect

---

[1] When the *Lusitania* was launched in 1906, it was the largest ship in the world.
[2] The Knights of Pythias and the other fraternal organizations mentioned throughout this story were or are real men's social clubs, modelled on ancient fraternal groups whose exclusiveness and initial practices are meant to insure that their members are worthy to carry out charitable and civic functions. Local Option Townships: townships that have voted individually on whether or not to prohibit or permit the sale of liquor.

jostle of public institutions comparable only to Threadneedle Street or Lower Broadway. On all the side streets there are maple trees and broad sidewalks, trim gardens with upright calla lilies, houses with verandahs, which are here and there being replaced by residences with piazzas.

To the careless eye the scene on the Main Street of a summer afternoon is one of deep and unbroken peace. The empty street sleeps in the sunshine. There is a horse and buggy tied to the hitching post in front of Glover's Hardware Store. There is, usually and commonly, the burly figure of Mr. Smith, proprietor of Smith's Hotel, standing in his chequered waistcoat on the steps of his hostelry, and perhaps, further up the street, Lawyer Macartney going for his afternoon mail, or the Rev. Mr. Drone, the rural dean of the Church of England Church, going home to get his fishing rod after a mothers' auxiliary meeting.

But this quiet is mere appearance. In reality, and to those who know it, the place is a perfect hive of activity. Why, at Netley's butcher shop (established in 1882) there are no less than four men working on the sausage machines in the basement; at the Newspacket office there are as many more job printing; there is a long distance telephone with four distracting girls on high stools wearing steel caps and talking incessantly; in the offices in McCarthy's block are dentists and lawyers, with their coats off, ready to work at any moment; and from the big planing factory down beside the lake where the railroad siding is, you may hear all through the hours of the summer afternoon the long-drawn music of the running saw.

Busy—well, I should think so! Ask any of its inhabitants if Mariposa isn't a busy, hustling, thriving town. Ask Mullins, the manager of the Exchange Bank, who comes hustling over to his office from the Mariposa House every day at 10:30 and has scarcely time all morning to go out and take a drink with the manager of the Commercial; or ask—well, for the matter of that, ask any of them if they ever knew a more rushing go-a-head town than Mariposa.

Of course if you come to the place fresh from New York, you are deceived. Your standard of vision is all astray. You do think the place is quiet. You do imagine that Mr. Smith is asleep merely because he closes his eyes as he stands. But live in Mariposa for six months or a year and then you will begin to understand it better; the buildings get higher and higher; the Mariposa House grows more and more luxurious; McCarthy's block towers to the sky; the 'buses roar and hum to the station; the trains shriek; the traffic multiplies; the people move faster and faster; a dense crowd swirls to and fro in the post-office and the five and ten cent store—and amusements! well, now! lacrosse, baseball, excursions, dances, the Firemen's Ball every winter and the Catholic picnic every summer; and music—the town band in the park every Wednesday evening, and the Oddfellows' brass band on the street every other Friday; the Mariposa Quartette, the Salvation Army—why, after a few months' residence you begin to realize that the place is a mere mad round of gaiety.

In point of population, if one must come down to figures, the Canadian census puts the numbers every time at something round five thousand. But it is very generally understood in Mariposa that the census is largely the outcome of malicious jealousy. It is usual that after the census the editor of the Mariposa Newspacket makes a careful re-estimate (based on the data of relative non-payment of subscriptions), and brings the population up to 6,000. After that the Mariposa Times-Herald makes an estimate that runs the figures up to 6,500. Then Mr. Gingham, the undertaker, who collects the vital statistics for the provincial government, makes an estimate from the number of what he calls the "demised" as compared with the less interesting persons who are still alive, and brings the population to 7,000. After that somebody else works it out that it's 7,500; then the man behind the bar of the Mariposa House offers to bet the whole room that there are 9,000 people in Mariposa. That settles it, and the population is well on the way to 10,000, when down swoops the federal census taker on his next round and the town has to begin all over again.

Still, it is a thriving town and there is no doubt of it. Even the transcontinental railways, as any townsman will tell you, run through Mariposa. It is true that the trains mostly go through at night and don't stop. But in the wakeful silence of the summer night you may hear the long whistle of the through train for the west as it tears through Mariposa, rattling over the switches and past the semaphores and ending in a long sullen roar as it takes the trestle bridge over the Ossawippi. Or, better still, on a winter evening about eight o'clock you will see the long row of the Pullmans and diners of the night express going north to the mining country, the windows flashing with brilliant light, and within them a vista of cut glass and snow-white table linen, smiling negroes and millionaires with napkins at their chins whirling past in the driving snowstorm.

I can tell you the people of Mariposa are proud of the trains, even if they don't stop! The joy of being on the main line lifts the Mariposa people above the level of their neighbours in such places as Tecumseh and Nichols Corners into the cosmopolitan atmosphere of through traffic and the larger life. Of course, they have their own train, too—the Mariposa Local, made up right there in the station yard, and running south to the city a hundred miles away. That, of course, is a real train, with a box stove on end in the passenger car, fed with cordwood upside down, and with seventeen flat cars of pine lumber set between the passenger car and the locomotive so as to give the train its full impact when shunting.[3]

Outside of Mariposa there are farms that begin well but get thinner and meaner as you go on, and end sooner or later in bush and swamp and the rock of the north country. And beyond that again, as the background of it all, though it's far away, you are somehow aware of the great pine woods of the lumber country reaching endlessly into the north.

Not that the little town is always gay or always bright in the sunshine. There never was such a place for changing its character with the season. Dark enough and dull it seems of a winter night, the wooden sidewalks creaking with the frost, and the lights burning dim behind the shop windows. In olden times the lights were coal oil lamps; now, of course, they are, or are supposed to be, electricity,—brought from the power house on the lower Ossawippi nineteen miles away. But, somehow, though it starts off as electricity from the Ossawippi rapids, by the time it gets to Mariposa and filters into the little bulbs behind the frosty windows of the shops, it has turned into coal oil again, as yellow and bleared as ever.

After the winter, the snow melts and the ice goes out of the lake, the sun shines high and the shanty-men[4] come down from the lumber woods and lie round drunk on the sidewalk outside of Smith's Hotel—and that's spring time. Mariposa is then a fierce, dangerous lumber town, calculated to terrorize the soul of a newcomer who does not understand that this also is only an appearance and that presently the rough-looking shanty-men will change their clothes and turn back again into farmers.

Then the sun shines warmer and the maple trees come out and Lawyer Macartney puts on his tennis trousers, and that's summer time.

[3] Changing cars from one track to another in making up the string of cars in a train.
[4] Men who go into the woods during the winter for seasonal labour and, while living in shanties, cut and prepare logs for spring shipping.

The little town changes to a sort of summer resort. There are visitors up from the city. Every one of the seven cottages along the lake is full. The Mariposa Belle churns the waters of the Wissanotti into foam as she sails out from the wharf, in a cloud of flags, the band playing and the daughters and sisters of the Knights of Pythias dancing gaily on the deck.

That changes too. The days shorten. The visitors disappear. The golden rod beside the meadow droops and withers on its stem. The maples blaze in glory and die. The evening closes dark and chill, and in the gloom of the main corner of Mariposa the Salvation Army around a naphtha lamp lift up the confession of their sins—and that is autumn. Thus the year runs its round, moving and changing in Mariposa, much as it does in other places.

If, then, you feel that you know the town well enough to be admitted into the inner life and movement of it, walk down this June afternoon half way down the Main Street—or, if you like, half way up from the wharf—to where Mr. Smith is standing at the door of his hostelry. You will feel as you draw near that it is no ordinary man that you approach. It is not alone the huge bulk of Mr. Smith (two hundred and eighty pounds as tested on Netley's scales). It is not merely his costume, though the chequered waistcoat of dark blue with a flowered pattern forms, with his shepherd's plaid trousers, his grey spats and patent leather boots, a colour scheme of no mean order. Nor is it merely Mr. Smith's finely mottled face. The face, no doubt, is a notable one,—solemn, inexpressible, unreadable, the face of the heaven-born hotel keeper. It is more than that. It is the strange dominating personality of the man that somehow holds you captive. I know nothing in history to compare with the position of Mr. Smith among those who drink over his bar, except, though in a lesser degree, the relation of the Emperor Napoleon to the Imperial Guard.

When you meet Mr. Smith first you think he looks like an over-dressed pirate. Then you begin to think him a character. You wonder at his enormous bulk. Then the utter hopelessness of knowing what Smith is thinking by merely looking at his features gets on your mind and makes the Mona Lisa seem an open book and the ordinary human countenance as superficial as a puddle in the sunlight. After you have had a drink in Mr. Smith's bar, and he has called you by your Christian name, you realize that you are dealing with one of the greatest minds in the hotel business.

Take, for instance, the big sign that sticks out into the street above Mr. Smith's head as he stands. What is on it? Simply: "Jos. Smith, Prop." Nothing more, and yet the thing was a flash of genius. Other men who had had the hotel before Mr. Smith had called it by such feeble names as the Royal Hotel and the Queen's and the Alexandria. Every one of them failed. When Mr. Smith took over the hotel he simply put up the sign with "Jos. Smith, Prop.," and then stood underneath in the sunshine as a living proof that a man who weighs nearly three hundred pounds is the natural king of the hotel business.

But on this particular afternoon, in spite of the sunshine and deep peace, there was something as near to profound concern and anxiety as the features of Mr. Smith were ever known to express.

The moment was indeed an anxious one. Mr. Smith was awaiting a telegram from his legal adviser who had that day journeyed to the county town to represent the proprietor's interest before the assembled License Commissioners. If you know anything of the hotel business at all, you will understand that as beside the decisions of the License Commissioners of Missinaba County, the opinions of the Lords of the Privy Council are mere trifles.

The matter in question was very grave. The Mariposa Court had just fined Mr. Smith for the second time for selling liquors after hours. The Commissioners, therefore, were entitled to cancel the license.

Mr. Smith knew his fault and acknowledged it. He had broken the law. How he had come to do so, it passed his imagination to recall. Crime always seems impossible in retrospect. By what sheer madness of the moment could he have shut up the bar on the night in question, and shut Judge Pepperleigh, the district judge of Missinaba County, outside of it? The more so inasmuch as the closing up of the bar under the rigid license law of the province was a matter that the proprietor never trusted to any hands but his own. Punctually every night at 11 o'clock Mr. Smith strolled from the desk of the "rotunda" to the door of the bar. If it seemed properly full of people and all was bright and cheerful, then he closed it. If not, he kept it open a few minutes longer till he had enough people inside to warrant closing. But never, never unless he was assured that Pepperleigh, the judge of the court, and Macartney, the prosecuting attorney, were both safely in the bar, or the bar parlour, did the proprietor venture to close up. Yet on this fatal night Pepperleigh and Macartney had been shut out—actually left on the street without a drink, and compelled to hammer and beat at the street door of the bar to gain admittance.

This was the kind of thing not to be tolerated. Either a hotel must be run decently or quit. An information[5] was laid next day and Mr. Smith convicted in four minutes, his lawyers practically refusing to plead. The Mariposa court, when the presiding judge was cold sober, and it had the force of public opinion behind it, was a terrible engine of retributive justice.

So no wonder that Mr. Smith awaited with anxiety the message of his legal adviser.

He looked alternately up the street and down it again, hauled out his watch from the depths of his embroidered pocket, and examined the hour hand and the minute hand and the second hand with frowning scrutiny.

Then wearily, and as one mindful that a hotel man is ever the servant of the public, he turned back into the hotel.

"Billy," he said to the desk clerk, "if a wire comes bring it into the bar parlour."

The voice of Mr. Smith is of a deep guttural such as Plancon or Edouard de Reske[6] might have obtained had they had the advantages of the hotel business. And with that, Mr. Smith, as was his custom in off moments, joined his guests in the back room. His appearance, to the untrained eye, was merely that of an extremely stout hotel-keeper walking from the rotunda to the back bar. In reality, Mr. Smith was on the eve of one of the most brilliant and daring strokes ever effected in the history of licensed liquor. When I say that it was out of the agitation of this situation that Smith's Ladies' and Gent's Café originated, anybody who knows Mariposa will understand the magnitude of the moment.

Mr. Smith, then, moved slowly from the doorway of the hotel through the "rotunda," or more simply the front room with the desk and the cigar case in it, and so to the bar and thence to the little room or back bar behind it. In this room, as I have said, the brightest minds of Mariposa might commonly be found in the quieter part of a summer afternoon.

To-day there was a group of four who looked up as Mr. Smith entered, somewhat sympathetically, and evidently aware of the perplexities of the moment.

Henry Mullins and George Duff, the two bank managers, were both present. Mullins is a rather short, rather round, smooth-shaven man of

---

[5] A complaint lodged with a magistrate in order to initiate criminal charges.
[6] Paul Plançon and Edouard de Reszke, operatic bassos of the period.

less than forty, wearing one of those round banking suits of pepper and salt, with a round banking hat of hard straw, and with the kind of gold tie-pin and heavy watch-chain and seals necessary to inspire confidence in matters of foreign exchange. Duff is just as round and just as short, and equally smoothly shaven, while his seals and straw hat are calcu-lated to prove that the Commercial is just as sound a bank as the Exchange. From the technical point of view of the banking business, neither of them had any objection to being in Smith's Hotel or to taking a drink as long as the other was present. This, of course, was one of the cardinal principles of Mariposa banking.

Then there was Mr. Diston, the high school teacher, commonly known as the "one who drank." None of the other teachers ever entered a hotel unless accompanied by a lady or protected by a child. But as Mr. Diston was known to drink beer on occasions and to go in and out of the Mariposa House and Smith's Hotel, he was looked upon as a man whose life was a mere wreck. Whenever the School Board raised the salaries of the other teachers, fifty or sixty dollars per annum at one lift, it was well understood that public morality wouldn't permit of an increase for Mr. Diston.

Still more noticeable, perhaps, was the quiet, sallow looking man dressed in black, with black gloves and with black silk hat heavily craped and placed hollow-side-up on a chair. This was Mr. Golgotha Gingham, the undertaker of Mariposa, and his dress was due to the fact that he had just come from what he called an "interment." Mr. Gingham had the true spirit of his profession, and such words as "funeral" or "coffin" or "hearse" never passed his lips. He spoke always of "interments," of "caskets," and "coaches," using terms that were calculated rather to bring out the majesty and sublimity of death than to parade its horrors.

To be present at the hotel was in accord with Mr. Gingham's general conception of his business. No man had ever grasped the true principles of undertaking more thoroughly than Mr. Gingham. I have often heard him explain that to associate with the living, uninteresting though they appear, is the only way to secure the custom of the dead.

"Get to know people really well while they are alive," said Mr. Gingham; "be friends with them, close friends, and then when they die you don't need to worry. You'll get the order every time."

So, naturally, as the moment was one of sympathy, it was Mr. Gingham who spoke first.

"What'll you do, Josh," he said, "if the Commissioners go against you?"

"Boys," said Mr. Smith, "I don't rightly know. If I have to quit, the next move is to the city. But I don't reckon that I will have to quit. I've got an idee that I think's good every time."

"Could you run a hotel in the city?" asked Mullins.

"I could," said Mr. Smith. "I'll tell you. There's big things doin' in the hotel business right now, big chances if you go into it right. Hotels in the city is branching out. Why, you take the dining-room side of it," continued Mr. Smith, looking round at the group, "there's thousands in it. The old plan's all gone. Folks won't eat now in an ordinary dining-room with a high ceiling and windows. You have to get 'em down underground in a room with no windows and lots of sawdust round and waiters that can't speak English. I seen them places last time I was in the city. They call 'em Rats' Coolers.[7] And for light meals they want a Caff, a real French Caff, and for folks that come in late another place that they call a Girl Room that don't shut up at all. If I go to the city that's the kind of place I mean to run. What's yours, Gol? It's on the house."

And it was just at the moment when Mr. Smith said this that Billy, the desk clerk, entered the room with the telegram in his hand.

But stop—it is impossible for you to understand the anxiety with which Mr. Smith and his associates awaited the news from the Commissioners, without first realizing the astounding progress of Mr. Smith in the three past years, and the pinnacle of public eminence to which he had attained.

Mr. Smith had come down from the lumber country of the Spanish River, where the divide[8] is toward the Hudson Bay, "back north" as they called it in Mariposa.

He had been, it was said, a cook in the lumber shanties. To this day Mr. Smith can fry an egg on both sides with a lightness of touch that is the despair of his own "help."

After that, he had run a river driver's[9] boardinghouse.

After that, he had taken a food contract for a gang of railroad navvies[10] on the transcontinental.

---

[7] Malapropism for "rathskeller" (a basement saloon or restaurant)—as "caff" is for café and "Girl Room" is for Grill Room.

[8] A watershed; here referring to the point at which all rivers to the north drain into the Hudson Bay and the Arctic Ocean.

[9] A river-driver follows the logs as they float downriver in the spring to keep them from getting jammed.

[10] Manual labourers.

After that, of course, the whole world was open to him.

He came down to Mariposa and bought out the "inside" of what had been the Royal Hotel.

Those who are educated understand that by the "inside" of a hotel is meant everything except the four outer walls of it—the fittings, the furniture, the bar, Billy the desk-clerk, the three dining-room girls, and above all the license granted by King Edward VII and ratified further by King George, for the sale of intoxicating liquors.

Till then the Royal had been a mere nothing. As "Smith's Hotel" it broke into a blaze of effulgence.

From the first, Mr. Smith, as a proprietor, was a wild, rapturous success.

He had all the qualifications.

He weighed two hundred and eighty pounds.

He could haul two drunken men out of the bar each by the scruff of the neck without the faintest anger or excitement.

He carried money enough in his trousers pockets to start a bank, and spent it on anything, bet it on anything, and gave it away in handfuls.

He was never drunk, and, as a point of chivalry to his customers, never quite sober. Anybody was free of[11] the hotel who cared to come in. Anybody who didn't like it could go out. Drinks of all kinds cost five cents, or six for a quarter. Meals and beds were practically free. Any persons foolish enough to go to the desk and pay for them, Mr. Smith charged according to the expression of their faces.

At first the loafers and the shanty men settled down on the place in a shower. But that was not the "trade" that Mr. Smith wanted. He knew how to get rid of them. An army of charwomen, turned into the hotel, scrubbed it from top to bottom. A vacuum cleaner, the first seen in Mariposa, hissed and screamed in the corridors. Forty brass beds were imported from the city, not, of course, for the guests to sleep in, but to keep them out. A bar-tender with a starched coat and wicker sleeves[12] was put behind the bar.

The loafers were put out of business. The place had become too "high toned" for them.

To get the high class trade, Mr. Smith set himself to dress the part. He wore wide cut coats of filmy serge, light as gossamer; chequered

---

[11] Welcome to.
[12] Protectors slipped over the lower part of the sleeves to keep them clean.

waistcoats with a pattern for every day in the week; fedora hats light as autumn leaves; four-in-hand ties of saffron and myrtle green with a diamond pin the size of a hazel nut. On his fingers there were as many gems as would grace a native prince of India; across his waistcoat lay a gold watch-chain in huge square links and in his pocket a gold watch that weighed a pound and a half and marked minutes, seconds and quarter seconds. Just to look at Josh Smith's watch brought at least ten men to the bar every evening.

Every morning Mr. Smith was shaved by Jefferson Thorpe, across the way. All that art could do, all that Florida water[13] could effect, was lavished on his person.

Mr. Smith became a local character. Mariposa was at his feet. All the reputable business men drank at Mr. Smith's bar, and in the little parlour behind it you might find at any time a group of the brightest intellects in the town.

Not but what there was opposition at first. The clergy, for example, who accepted the Mariposa House and the Continental as a necessary and useful evil, looked askance at the blazing lights and the surging crowd of Mr. Smith's saloon. They preached against him. When the Rev. Dean Drone led off with a sermon on the text "Lord be merciful even unto this publican Matthew Six," it was generally understood as an invitation to strike Mr. Smith dead. In the same way the sermon at the Presbyterian church the week after was on the text "Lo what now doeth Abiram in the land of Melchisideck Kings Eight and Nine?"[14] and it was perfectly plain that what was meant was, "Lo, what is Josh Smith doing in Mariposa?"

But this opposition had been countered by a wide and sagacious philanthropy. I think Mr. Smith first got the idea of that on the night when the steam merry-go-round came to Mariposa. Just below the hostelry, on an empty lot, it whirled and whistled, steaming forth its tones on the summer evening while the children crowded round it in hundreds. Down the street strolled Mr. Smith, wearing a soft fedora to indicate that it was evening.

"What d'you charge for a ride, boss?" said Mr. Smith.

"Two for a nickel," said the man.

---

[13] A men's cologne.
[14] In his citations of the Bible, Rev. Drone is inaccurate—recasting events and garbling names ("Abiram" for Abraham; "Melchisideck" for Melchizedek).

"Take that," said Mr. Smith, handing out a ten-dollar bill from a roll of money, "and ride the little folks free all evening."

That night the merry-go-round whirled madly till after midnight, freighted to capacity with Mariposa children, while up in Smith's Hotel, parents, friends and admirers, as the news spread, were standing four deep along the bar. They sold forty dollars' worth of lager alone that night, and Mr. Smith learned, if he had not already suspected it, the blessedness of giving.

The uses of philanthropy went further. Mr. Smith subscribed to everything, joined everything, gave to everything. He became an Oddfellow, a Forester, a Knight of Pythias and a Workman. He gave a hundred dollars to the Mariposa Hospital and a hundred dollars to the Young Men's Christian Association.

He subscribed to the Ball Club, the Lacrosse Club, the Curling Club, to anything, in fact, and especially to all those things which needed premises to meet in and grew thirsty in their discussions.

As a consequence the Oddfellows held their annual banquet at Smith's Hotel and the Oyster Supper of the Knights of Pythias was celebrated in Mr. Smith's dining-room.

Even more effective, perhaps, were Mr. Smith's secret benefactions, the kind of giving done by stealth of which not a soul in town knew anything, often, for a week after it was done. It was in this way that Mr. Smith put the new font in Dean Drone's church, and handed over a hundred dollars to Judge Pepperleigh for the unrestrained use of the Conservative party.

So it came about that, little by little, the antagonism had died down. Smith's Hotel became an accepted institution in Mariposa. Even the temperance people were proud of Mr. Smith as a sort of character who added distinction to the town. There were moments, in the earlier quiet of the morning, when Dean Drone would go so far as to step in to the "rotunda" and collect a subscription. As for the Salvation Army, they ran in and out all the time unreproved.

On only one point difficulty still remained. That was the closing of the bar. Mr. Smith could never bring his mind to it,—not as a matter of profit, but as a point of honour. It was too much for him to feel that Judge Pepperleigh might be out on the sidewalk thirsty at midnight, that the night hands of the Times Herald on Wednesday might be compelled to go home dry. On this point Mr. Smith's moral code was simplicity itself,— do what is right and take the consequences. So the bar stayed open.

Every town, I suppose, has its meaner spirits. In every genial bosom some snake is warmed,—or, as Mr. Smith put it to Golgotha Gingham— "there are some fellers even in this town skunks enough to inform."

At first the Mariposa court quashed all indictments. The presiding judge, with his spectacles on and a pile of books in front of him, threatened the informer with the penitentiary. The whole bar of Mariposa was with Mr. Smith. But by sheer iteration the informations had proved successful. Judge Pepperleigh learned that Mr. Smith had subscribed a hundred dollars for the Liberal party and at once fined him for keeping open after hours. That made one conviction. On the top of this had come the untoward incident just mentioned and that made two. Beyond that was the deluge. This then was the exact situation when Billy, the desk clerk, entered the back bar with the telegram in his hand.

"Here's your wire, sir," he said.

"What does it say?" said Mr. Smith.

He always dealt with written documents with a fine air of detachment. I don't suppose there were ten people in Mariposa who knew that Mr. Smith couldn't read.

Billy opened the message and read, "Commissioners give you three months to close down."

"Let me read it," said Mr. Smith, "that's right, three months to close down."

There was dead silence when the message was read. Everybody waited for Mr. Smith to speak. Mr. Gingham instinctively assumed the professional air of hopeless melancholy.

As it was afterwards recorded, Mr. Smith stood and "studied" with the tray in his hand for at least four minutes. Then he spoke.

"Boys," he said, "I'll be darned if I close down till I'm ready to close down. I've got an idee. You wait and I'll show you."

And beyond that, not another word did Mr. Smith say on the subject.

But within forty-eight hours the whole town knew that something was doing. The hotel swarmed with carpenters, bricklayers and painters. There was an architect up from the city with a bundle of blue prints in his hand, There was an engineer taking the street level with a theodolite,[15] and a gang of navvies with shovels digging like fury as if to dig out the back foundations of the hotel.

"That'll fool 'em," said Mr. Smith.

---

[15] An instrument for surveying.

Half the town was gathered round the hotel crazy with excitement. But not a word would the proprietor say.

Great dray loads of square timber, and two-by-eight pine joists kept arriving from the planing mill. There was a pile of matched spruce sixteen feet high lying by the sidewalk.

Then the excavation deepened and the dirt flew, and the beams went up and the joists across, and all the day dawn till dusk the hammers of the carpenters clattered away, working overtime at time and a half.

"It don't matter what it costs," said Mr. Smith; "get it done."

Rapidly the structure took form. It extended down the side street, joining the hotel at a right angle. Spacious and graceful it looked as it reared its uprights into the air.

Already you could see the place where the row of windows was to come, a veritable palace of glass, it must be, so wide and commodious were they. Below it, you could see the basement shaping itself, with a low ceiling like a vault and big beams running across, dressed, smoothed, and ready for staining. Already in the street there were seven crates of red and white awning.

And even then nobody knew what it was, and it was not till the seventeenth day that Mr. Smith, in the privacy of the back bar, broke the silence and explained.

"I tell you, boys," he says, "it's a caff—like what they have in the city—a ladies' and gent's caff, and that underneath (what's yours, Mr. Mullins?) is a Rats' Cooler. And when I get her started, I'll hire a French Chief to do the cooking, and for the winter I will put in a 'girl room,' like what they have in the city hotels. And I'd like to see who's going to close her up then."

Within two more weeks the plan was in operation. Not only was the caff built but the very hotel was transformed. Awnings had broken out in a red and white cloud upon its face, its every window carried a box of hanging plants, and above in glory floated the Union Jack. The very stationery was changed. The place was now Smith's Summer Pavilion. It was advertised in the city as Smith's Tourists' Emporium, and Smith's Northern Health Resort. Mr. Smith got the editor of the Times-Herald to write up a circular all about ozone and the Mariposa pine woods, with illustrations of the maskinonge[16] (piscis mariposis) of Lake Wissanotti.

The Saturday after that circular hit the city in July, there were men with fishing rods and landing nets pouring in on every train, almost too

---

[16] The northern pike.

fast to register. And if, in the face of that, a few little drops of whiskey were sold over the bar, who thought of it?

But the caff! that, of course, was the crowning glory of the thing, that and the Rats' Cooler below.

Light and cool, with swinging windows open to the air, tables with marble tops, palms, waiters in white coats—it was the standing marvel of Mariposa. Not a soul in the town except Mr. Smith, who knew it by instinct, ever guessed that waiters and palms and marble tables can be rented over the long distance telephone.

Mr. Smith was as good as his word. He got a French Chief with an aristocratic saturnine countenance, and a moustache and imperial[17] that recalled the late Napoleon III. No one knew where Mr. Smith got him. Some people in the town said he was a French marquis. Others said he was a count and explained the difference.

No one in Mariposa had ever seen anything like the caff. All down the side of it were the grill fires, with great pewter dish covers that went up and down on a chain, and you could walk along the row and actually pick out your own cutlet and then see the French marquis throw it onto the broiling iron; you could watch a buckwheat pancake whirled into existence under your eyes and see fowls' legs devilled, peppered, grilled, and tormented till they lost all semblance of the original Mariposa chicken.

Mr. Smith, of course, was in his glory.

"What have you got to-day, Alf?" he would say, as he strolled over to the marquis. The name of the Chief was, I believe, Alphonse, but "Alf" was near enough for Mr. Smith.

The marquis would extend to the proprietor the menu, "Voilà, m'sieu, la carte du jour."

Mr. Smith, by the way, encouraged the use of the French language in the caff. He viewed it, of course, solely in its relation to the hotel business, and, I think, regarded it as a recent invention.

"It's comin' in all the time in the city," he said, "and y'aint expected to understand it."

Mr. Smith would take the carte between his finger and thumb and stare at it. It was all covered with such devices as Potage à la Mariposa— Filet Mignon à la proprietaire—Côtelette à la Smith, and so on.

But the greatest thing about the caff were the prices. Therein lay, as everybody saw at once, the hopeless simplicity of Mr. Smith.

---

[17] Small beard grown just below the lower lip (what is now known as a "soul patch").

The prices stood fast at 25 cents a meal. You could come in and eat all they had in the caff for a quarter.

"No, sir," Mr. Smith said stoutly, "I ain't going to try to raise no prices on the public. The hotel's always been a quarter and the caff's a quarter."

Full? Full of people?

Well, I should think so! From the time the caff opened at 11 till it closed at 8.30, you could hardly find a table. Tourists, visitors, travellers, and half the people of Mariposa crowded at the little tables; crockery rattling, glasses tinkling on trays, corks popping, the waiters in their white coats flying to and fro, Alphonse whirling the cutlets and pancakes into the air, and in and through it all, Mr. Smith, in a white flannel suit and a broad crimson sash about his waist. Crowded and gay from morning to night, and even noisy in its hilarity.

Noisy, yes; but if you wanted deep quiet and cool, if you wanted to step from the glare of a Canadian August to the deep shadow of an enchanted glade,—walk down below into the Rats' Cooler. There you had it; dark old beams (who could believe they were put there a month ago?), great casks set on end with legends such as Amontillado Fino done in gilt on a black ground, tall steins filled with German beer soft as moss, and a German waiter noiseless as moving foam. He who entered the Rats' Cooler at three of a summer afternoon was buried there for the day. Mr. Golgotha Gingham spent anything from four to seven hours there of every day. In his mind the place had all the quiet charm of an interment, with none of its sorrows.

But at night, when Mr. Smith and Billy, the desk clerk, opened up the cash register and figured out the combined losses of the caff and the Rats' Cooler, Mr. Smith would say:

"Billy, just wait till I get the license renood, and I'll close up this damn caff so tight they'll never know what hit her. What did that lamb cost? Fifty cents a pound, was it? I figure it, Billy, that every one of them hogs eats about a dollar's worth a grub for every twenty-five cents they pay on it. As for Alf—by gosh, I'm through with him."

But that, of course, was only a confidential matter as between Mr. Smith and Billy.

I don't know at what precise period it was that the idea of a petition to the License Commissioners first got about the town. No one seemed to know just who suggested it. But certain it was that public opinion began to swing strongly towards the support of Mr. Smith. I think it was perhaps on the day after the big fish dinner that Alphonse cooked for the Mariposa

Canoe Club (at twenty cents a head) that the feeling began to find open expression. People said it was a shame that a man like Josh Smith should be run out of Mariposa by three license commissioners. Who were the license commissioners, anyway? Why, look at the license system they had in Sweden; yes, and in Finland and in South America. Or, for the matter of that, look at the French and Italians, who drink all day and all night. Aren't they all right? Aren't they a musical people? Take Napoleon, and Victor Hugo; drunk half the time, and yet look what they did.

I quote these arguments not for their own sake, but merely to indicate the changing temper of public opinion in Mariposa. Men would sit in the caff at lunch perhaps for an hour and a half and talk about the license question in general, and then go down into the Rats' Cooler and talk about it for two hours more.

It was amazing the way the light broke in in the case of particular individuals, often the most unlikely, and quelled their opposition.

Take, for example, the editor of the Newspacket. I suppose there wasn't a greater temperance advocate in town. Yet Alphonse quelled him with an Omelette à la License in one meal.

Or take Pepperleigh himself, the judge of the Mariposa court. He was put to the bad with a game pie,—pâté normand aux fines herbes—the real thing, as good as a trip to Paris in itself. After eating it, Pepperleigh had the common sense to realize that it was sheer madness to destroy a hotel that could cook a thing like that.

In the same way, the secretary of the School Board was silenced with a stuffed duck à la Ossawippi.

Three members of the town council were converted with a Dindon farci à la Josh Smith.

And then, finally, Mr. Diston persuaded Dean Drone to come, and as soon as Mr. Smith and Alphonse saw him they landed him with a fried flounder that even the apostles would have appreciated.

After that, every one knew that the license question was practically settled. The petition was all over the town. It was printed in duplicate at the Newspacket and you could see it lying on the counter of every shop in Mariposa. Some of the people signed it twenty or thirty times.

It was the right kind of document too. It began—"Whereas in the bounty of providence the earth putteth forth her luscious fruits and her vineyards for the delight and enjoyment of mankind—" It made you thirsty just to read it. Any man who read that petition over was wild to get to the Rats' Cooler.

When it was all signed up they had nearly three thousand names on it.

Then Nivens, the lawyer, and Mr. Gingham (as a provincial official) took it down to the county town, and by three o'clock that afternoon the news had gone out from the long distance telephone office that Smith's license was renewed for three years.

Rejoicings! Well, I should think so! Everybody was down wanting to shake hands with Mr. Smith. They told him that he had done more to boom Mariposa than any ten men in town. Some of them said he ought to run for the town council, and others wanted to make him the Conservative candidate for the next Dominion election. The caff was a mere babel of voices, and even the Rats' Cooler was almost floated away from its moorings.

And in the middle of it all, Mr. Smith found time to say to Billy, the desk clerk:

"Take the cash registers out of the caff and the Rats' Cooler and start counting up the books."

And Billy said: "Will I write the letters for the palms and the tables and the stuff to go back?"

And Mr. Smith said: "Get 'em written right away."

So all evening the laughter and the chatter and the congratulations went on, and it wasn't till long after midnight that Mr. Smith was able to join Billy in the private room behind the "rotunda." Even when he did, there was a quiet and a dignity about his manner that had never been there before. I think it must have been the new halo of the Conservative candidacy that already radiated from his brow. It was, I imagine, at this very moment that Mr. Smith first realised that the hotel business formed the natural and proper threshold of the national legislature.

"Here's the account of the cash registers," said Billy.

"Let me see it," said Mr. Smith. And he studied the figures without a word.

"And here's the letters about the palms, and here's Alphonse up to yesterday———"

And then an amazing thing happened.

"Billy," said Mr. Smith, "tear 'em up. I ain't going to do it. It ain't right and I won't do it. They got me the license for to keep the caff and I'm going to keep the caff. I don't need to close her. The bar's good for anything from forty to a hundred a day now, with the Rats' Cooler going good, and that caff will stay right here."

And stay it did.

There it stands, mind you, to this day. You've only to step round the corner of Smith's Hotel on the side street and read the sign: LADIES' AND GENT'S CAFÉ, just as large and as imposing as ever.

Mr. Smith said that he'd keep the caff, and when he said a thing he meant it!

Of course there were changes, small changes.

I don't say, mind you, that the fillet de beef that you get there now is perhaps quite up to the level of the filet de boeufs aux champignons of the days of glory.

No doubt the lamb chops in Smith's Caff are often very much the same, nowadays, as the lamb chops of the Mariposa House or the Continental.

Of course, things like Omelette aux Trufles practically died out when Alphonse went. And, naturally, the leaving of Alphonse was inevitable. No one knew just when he went, or why. But one morning he was gone. Mr. Smith said that "Alf had to go back to his folks in the old country."

So, too, when Alf left, the use of the French language, as such, fell off tremendously in the caff. Even now they use it to some extent. You can still get fillet de beef, and saucisson au juice, but Billy the desk clerk has considerable trouble with the spelling.

The Rats' Cooler, of course, closed down, or rather Mr. Smith closed it for repairs, and there is every likelihood that it will hardly open for three years. But the caff is there. They don't use the grills, because there's no need to, with the hotel kitchen so handy.

The "girl room," I may say, was never opened. Mr. Smith promised it, it is true, for the winter, and still talks of it. But somehow there's been a sort of feeling against it. Every one in town admits that every big hotel in the city has a "girl room" and that it must be all right. Still, there's a certain—well, you know how sensitive opinion is in a place like Mariposa.

—1912

Frederick Philip Grove 1879–1948

In his fiction, Frederick Philip Grove recorded the life of Canadian prairie farmers and the challenges they faced in a landscape that could nurture them or subject them to ecological disaster. In a 1968 essay called "The Prairie: A State of Mind," Henry Kreisel describes how in Grove's fiction, "Man, the giant-conqueror, and man, the insignificant dwarf always threatened by defeat, form the two polarities of the state of mind produced by the sheer physical fact of the prairie." In "Lazybones," however, it is woman who becomes the conqueror. This story and Sinclair Ross's "A Field of Wheat" make an interesting pair in that they show the reader not only the narrow margin on which family farms operated but also the pressures that farm life exerted on male and female roles.

Lazybones

The bare hills, in the first level rays of the rising sun, were suggestive of a sea with enormous billows gone rigid. There was not a tree on this rolling prairie; there was nothing to arrest the eye as it swept around from the summit on which stood the grey-painted house.

Elizabeth Hurst, who at this moment issued from its door, was a strong, bony young woman, clad in a short, washed-out gingham dress. She was not a beauty, but energy and capability betrayed themselves in her least movement. So far, the hush of the night lay over the landscape: within half-an-hour the diurnal wind of the prairie would be blowing, which explained the tight, grey-checked cloth she wore tightly knotted over her short-cut hair. On each arm she carried a milking-pail.

Before issuing in the chill, she had called her still sleeping husband. But as the door closed behind her, she stopped to listen. At her feet cringed three dogs that had come from under the house, a black-and-tan terrier in his middle age and two collie pups, still woolly. Since she heard nothing stirring, she took a few steps and knocked at the bedroom window. "Sun's up, Walt," she called. A grunt answered her.

Going to the corner of the house, she turned west. Below her lay a "draw," a hollow between the hills. One of these rose to the northwest, and against its flank the barn was built, a large, decrepit unpainted building, grey with exposure, looking as if any wind would blow it this way or that; the third hill, to the southwest, had a dugout let into its steep acclivity. Below the barn a dozen cows were tethered by long ropes, since the fields were unfenced. Every morning Elizabeth noted their pale gold: they were choked with tumbling mustard in bloom.

Descending, she passed a rickety buggy, an old wagon, a seeder and a binder, all standing under the open sky. This drew no comment from her; she was used to it; you do not complain when there is no implement shed on a rented farm. You are glad if the dwelling provides the family with reasonable accommodation; and the house on the hill was the best they had had in the ten years of their wandering tenants' life.

Elizabeth reached the bottom of the draw and picked up a box to serve as a stool. She sat down by the flank of the nearest cow and began to milk. At this time of day she felt joyful and equal to any task.

She was alone and engaged in work of which she had dreamt as a young girl. She was not old yet, thirty-five, and strong and active. Throughout the milking she felt at one with some mysterious thing pervading the world. She did not think about it; she did not care what it was; but it made her happy. By her labour she was supporting the family and working for what little progress was possible. She had looked on without envy when her sisters had married into towns and cities, while for her it was work, work, work on the farm. She had borne five children—four boys (two pairs of twins), and a girl: that, too, was something to hold on to. She had borne her children and worked: she had worked in the fields, in the house, and at milking. She thought of the time, during the first years of her married life, when, before she could light a fire in the morning, she had had to go out to gather "prairie-coal," the dried manure of horses and cows.

Yet occasionally there was a twitching in her upper lip, uncovering her large, strong, white teeth, which told of disappointment, of nervous strain, of repressed angers. Occasionally she would face her disappointment critically. It had to do with Walter Hunt, the man she had married in the face of much opposition at home, where brothers and sisters had spoken contemptuously of her suitor, son of the blacksmith in town. "How's the cowboy today?" Or, "Seen anything of the horse-wrangler?" When she thought of it, there was a quick rush of blood to her heart. She must defend Walt. He had done this one thing for her: he had stayed on the farm. He was lazy, yes; he was unsuccessful; but he had enabled her to remain within her own tradition. She could not have put it that way; she did not have the words; but had anyone said it for her, she would have assented.

She felt softened; suddenly she thought of certain moments in Walt's courtship, which had been largely conducted on horseback. Walt came over, before or after dark, to the parental homestead in the sun-baked, rain-washed hills of the prairie; and she threw a saddle on the old race-horse which one of her brothers had given her. They sped over the hills together, racing, to the warming of their blood, or talking while the horses walked. Walt was handsome, big, tall, with a striking face and large, dreamy black eyes, a figure to attract a girl; and he wanted to farm, or, rather, to live on a farm. His occasional coarseness of speech had rather won than repelled her. But he would have to rent before he could homestead; he had no equipment; his parents were poor.

Elizabeth recalled the final moments when he had put the decisive question. She realized that, in spite of her disappointment, in spite of his laziness, in spite of everything, she loved him. Yet his words during those final moments had been trivial and commonplace. What made them great was her own emotional response, not to him, but to the destiny she was fulfilling.

They had dismounted, letting the horses graze on the roadside; they were sitting on the usual seats of strollers on the prairie: the boulders of a stone pile in the edge of a field.

"You know, Liz," he had said, "I'm doggone poor. I'll have to rent. But I've two cows and a calf. If we milked and shipped cream, we might make it a go."

"Beginners are poor," she had replied. "Life is long, Walt; we're young."

"It's agreed, then? We hook up next fall?"

"I suppose so," Elizabeth had whispered, lowering her eyes. . . .

Under her swift strokes the milk purled into the pail. If only Walt were up, feeding the horses, so that he could start on the summer-fallow[1] right after breakfast! The one thing needed to complete her happiness fate had denied her. Yet they had these cows. There had been a year when, with four children born, and a fifth child coming, the sheriff had taken their stock. It was so no longer.

When she had finished milking, she briskly picked up the two pails and carried them to the seeder, lifting them to its box. Unencumbered, she went up to the barn, reaching for a fork in the open door, and on to the haystack where hay still trailed from the last wagon that had been drawn. Gathering huge trusses, big enough for any man to carry, she returned to the barn and fed the horses. Then she fetched her pails and took them to the house.

---

[1] In semi-arid areas such as the Canadian prairies, some wheat fields are kept out of production (i.e., kept fallow) each year to preserve the moisture and nutrients in the soil. These fallow fields still need to be plowed to break up the soil and to prevent weeds from taking hold.

When she entered the kitchen, a glance showed her that Walt was not up; a second glance, that the kettle on the stove was simmering. She took the milk to the rear and emptied one pail into the bowl of the separator. At last she went into the bedroom.

Walt, his covers in disorder, was lying on his back, one arm bent over his face. She shook him. "Walt, Lazybones, wake up!"

He gasped, yawned, stretched, and opened his eyes. "Oah!" he said, "I'm never so tired as when I'm to get up."

"High time! I'm done milking; and I've fed the horses."

"Have you?" And, curling up, ingratiatingly, "Doggone it, Liz! Five minutes more!"

"All right. Five minutes. I'll call the children." And she left the room to go to the narrow stairway which led from the corner by the separator to the attic of the house. "Hello, kids! Time to get up!"

Yawns and the creaking of bedsteads answered her.

She made the coffee, knowing that all but one of the children had gone to sleep again. The one, a little girl of five, big for her age, fat, fair-haired, and all smiles, came crawling down.

"Well, Vi," said Elizabeth, going over to pick her up from the steps, "as usual, you are the only one, aren't you?"

The child was in her nightgown; and Elizabeth reached for her clothes, which were hanging over a baby-chair. The child said nothing, but smiled at her mother as the garments were slipped on.

That done, Elizabeth, with a look at the battered alarm-clock on the warming-closet of the range—it refused to go if placed anywhere else—wiped the oilcloth on the large table by the outside door. The five minutes were gone; but she set the table. She opened the cellar-trap, jumped into the shallow hole, and fetched a butter-dish of green glass and a crockery pitcher of milk. Then she returned to the range and stirred the porridge. With another look at the clock she entered the bedroom again.

Again she had to shake the handsome man with his smooth, white skin and black, glossy hair. He stretched, yawned and gasped. "Walt, wake up! I've given you ten minutes instead of five!"

"Doggone it, why can't it always be night?" His smile was sad as forgiveness in spite of knowledge.

"Walt, you've got to work on the summer-fallow today. It must be finished tomorrow. If Mr. Bock comes out. . . ." Mr. Bock was the landlord.

Walt groaned. "The ground ain't hardly fit to plow."

"I know. But you've got to try. Without last year's fallow we'd have no crop this year."

"There ain't any crop. It's all choked with weeds. That shows that fallowing's no use. The horses can't hardly pull in the weeds."

"That's our fault. We should have plowed before they grew up."

"There won't be any wheat unless we get rain; but the weeds grow, rain or shine."

"That's what makes them weeds. But we can't do our share with empty promises."

"All right," said Walt. "You know me, Liz. I ain't one who won't do what he says he'll do. Be there in a minute."

Elizabeth knocked a broom handle against the ceiling, a signal answered by a wild scampering upstairs; for it meant, "No breakfast unless you're ready within five minutes!"

Soon there was pushing and pulling by the two washbasins on the bench by the door. Walt, who appeared from the bedroom in trousers and undershirt, his feet bare, looked complacently down on the children. He stood six feet tall and shook his long, glossy hair back with a lazy swing of his head. Elizabeth was cutting bread.

Walt went to the door. "Another hot, dry day," he said with his dreamy smile. "Hard on the horses. With no oats to feed!"

"Whose horses get oats hereabouts?" Elizabeth asked. "Hey, children! Hurry up! You have to fill the barrel from the slough before school."

A yell answered her; but the children obeyed to the extent of wetting faces and hands and rushing for the roller-towel on the wall. Walt, too, washed while Elizabeth put the porridge in bowls. A few minutes later he was sitting over his breakfast, eating slowly.

Long before he finished, Elizabeth had sent the boys down to the slough, armed with two lard pails each, to dip water and bring it up to the barrel. She herself turned the cream separator with vigorous bendings and straightenings of her back. When Walt had eaten, he turned sideways on his chair, folding knee over knee.

"Doggone it," he said, picking his teeth, "everlastingly working for others!"

"We knew when we married that we'd be renting."

"We knew it all right. But that don't change the fact."

Elizabeth made no reply. She was pouring the skim-milk into two huge pails half full of dishwater, potato-peelings and scraps for the pigs; the cream she took to the cellar.

Walt was looking out on the hills where the grass was bending before the wind of the day. Elizabeth reached for the grey-checked cloth.

"What you going to do, Liz?"

"Help the children drive the cows to pasture."

Under the implied reproach of her tone he rose and went into the bedroom to put on shoes. Since these were somewhat short, he removed them more than once to nurse his toes between his hands.

The pasture being half-a-mile north, Elizabeth led the procession, pulling Bess, the bell-cow. The five children followed, swinging their arms and running gingerly, with bare feet, over the baked ground. When they returned, it was time for Elizabeth to start the boys on their way to school, the roof of which just showed above the hills.

At half-past eight Elizabeth, having told the little girl to stay around the house, went down to the stable. In passing the pig-pen, she made sure that the pigs had been fed. Walt was not at the barn.

She went through the draw to the dug-out which served as a black-smith shop. Apart from the cows and the scant furniture of the house, its equipment was all they owned; it had been inherited from Walt's father. Unfortunately, instead of adding much to their income, it helped to supply Walt with a pretext to stay at home instead of working in the field. He was tinkering with a piece of harness. This was the time of day when she felt critical and burdened with a load hard to bear.

"Come on," she said briefly. "I'll help you hitch up."

He followed her to the barn. It took half-an-hour to put the gear on the five horses that Mr. Bock furnished. When Walt emerged from the driveway, Elizabeth was pumping water into the trough. The well was alkaline and unfit for the use of the house; but the horses drank. When they had had enough and stood for a moment, raising their heads while the water dripped from their nether lips, Elizabeth turned away.

"Have you seen the potatoes?" she asked.

"Say, I was going to tell you. We better not figure on our own potatoes this year. They're choked with bindweed."

"Not figure on our own potatoes? What are we to figure on?"

"I know, Liz, but what is a fellow to do?"

She stood, thinking. "You must plow," she decided. "I'll go over when I've washed the dishes. We'll have a late lunch."

To keep the chickens from scratching them up, the potatoes had been planted in the eastern margin of the wheat, half-a-mile away.

Elizabeth hurried through her housework, doing the dishes, sweeping, making up the beds. Full of vitality, she burst into snatches of song. It was half-past-nine when she finished; and she went out at once, reached for a hoe which was leaning against the house, took Vi by the hand, and set out. Two furry pups whined after her; they did not yet dare to leave the house, though Paddy, the terrier, had followed his master.

When she passed the prospective fallow, now a waste of pale yellow mustard, she saw that a single furrow had been turned; but when she looked from the draw up the hill to her left, she saw the plow standing on the crest, without the horses.

"Well!" she said, told Vi to wait, and ran up the hill till she could see Walt, holding the lines of his five horses and walking alongside a buggy driven by a man leaning on the arm-rest of the seat. Walt did not look lazy now. *"Well!"* she repeated.

She went on to the potato patch, where she put the child to play. The potatoes were invisible under the bindweed; the hoe was useless. She gathered the twining stems in armfuls and pulled them up by main force.

Now and then she straightened and looked at the sun. And she seemed to see the farm she had dreamt of in the days of her girlhood: the yard surrounded by tall, rustling trees, with garden patches in it, and with vistas of wide, waving grain fields, her house the centre of it all.

Half the patch had been cleared when she thought it time to go home. Since Walt was not in the field, they must have an early lunch. Leaving the hoe, she retraced her steps through the winding draw, carrying Vi.

At the house, she put her to play again, stirred the fire, added coal, put water on to boil, and fetched eggs from the cellar. This was the time of day when she felt angry and rebellious.

Leaving the house, she went down to the shop where she knew Walt would be with his visitor. She also knew that if this caller stayed for lunch Walt would not plow in the afternoon. In the presence of a stranger she would be unable to shame him into it.

The buggy stood in front of the dug-out. She stepped into the opening, said briefly, "Walt, I need you," and stepped back.

The two men were squatting on a pile of shavings. Walt was speaking humorously of a woman called Irene. He rose, but did not answer his wife. "Yeh," he said, "she's a looker, all right; and a high-stepper, too."

The other man rose likewise. "Well, that's the way we like 'em, eh?"

"Sure," Walt said, coming forward. "Though Liz ain't a looker exactly; and as for stepping high. . . ." He pinched her cheek as he passed her.

Angrily she climbed halfway up the hill. If she went out of sight, the stranger would never leave. He was a sponger, or he would not have brought his shares[2] for Walt to sharpen. Walt would not take pay from a neighbour. In revolt against him and the world, she listened to the leave-taking.

"Well," said Walt, "be good, fellah! Don't take any wooden money!"

Even this cheap vulgarity irritated her now; but she made sure that the caller was leaving. Then she went quickly to the house.

When Walt entered, he asked, raising the child to his arm, "What is it?"

"What is what?"

"You said you needed me."

"I didn't need you. I had to send young Armstrong about his business." And, facing Walt, she added fiercely, "You've got to plow, Walt."

"Shucks! It's too doggone dry and windy."

"Walt," she said, "you plow this afternoon, or I'll take the team out myself."

"Oh, all right. It ain't no use. I've got to get off every few yards and pull the bloody weeds away from the coulter."[3]

She was still looking at him. "Take the coulter off. I'll come along for a couple of hours and attend to the weeds. When the boys come home, they'll help you. Bock's the best landlord we've had."

"As far as that goes, let him tell me to get off! Blast his dirty land!"

"He wants to get it clean."

"And I'm to do his work?"

"Exactly. Don't forget he gives the pasture free."

"I can rent pasture cheap enough."

Elizabeth, knowing that it was useless to argue and that she would only weaken whatever impression she had made, turned back to her work.

After lunch, taken in silence, she left everything, put the child to bed, returned to the kitchen, said briefly, "Come on," and went out.

In the field, she called to the horses whenever she had pulled away the weeds, "Get up there! Step lively!" It was hard work, but her anger subsided because something was being done. This was the time of day when she felt resigned.

---

[2] Ploughshares; a ploughshare is the large cutting blade of the plow.
[3] A small secondary blade that runs ahead of the ploughshare.

Thus, two weeks ago, she had pitched the hay to the rack; thus, a few weeks hence, she would stook the wheat. Work, work! But it kept the place going. In the fall, after threshing, there would be two or three hundred dollars to buy clothes with and fuel. It kept the place going; it kept life going, advancing if ever so slowly.

The hours fled. It was four o'clock. She saw the flag being lowered at the school. She went on for another half hour; and then she spoke quietly, without the anger of noonday: "I'll go to get a bite ready for the kids. Then I'll send Jack and Bill." She did not even object when she saw that Walt was going to sit down till the children came. She counted the furrows: eight. It would take many days to plow this field of sixty acres; but a beginning was made.

At the house, she took the little girl up and then hurried to get the dishes washed and supper prepared. But she did not mind any longer. . . .

It was half-past eight, and the sun was touching the horizon, when she had cleared the supper things away and put the children to bed. She no longer hurried. There still remained much to do; but she could do it less anxiously.

Dusk was rising in the hollows of the hills when, attired as in the morning, milk-pails on her arms, she stepped into the open.

Walt was lying on the grass, barefooted, for his shoes hurt him. . . .

And as, through the gathering dusk, leaving her pails behind, she went to the pasture where the cows were waiting, anxious to get to the yard with its smudge[4] of smoke, she felt at peace with herself and the world. With swinging strides she stepped along behind the herd, feeling tired, with a lassitude honestly come by, yet pervaded with an inner gladness: the night was coming and, with the night, rest.

Between dug-out and barn, Walt had actually started the smudge; and, the day having waned, she sat there, leaning against the flank of a cow, and listening to the purring of the milk in the pail. The draw was shut off from the rest of the world by the roof of smoke from the smouldering smudge. She did not dream; her mind was a blank; but life itself seemed a dream in which she was merely one of the shadowy actors. This was the time of day when she knew contentment.

—1971[5]

---

[4] A low fire that produces dense smoke to keep insects away.
[5] Collected in *Tales from the Margin* (ed. Desmond Pacey). This story first appeared in *Queen's Quarterly* in 1944; an earlier version was published in the *Winnipeg Tribune* in 1927.

Ethel Wilson 1888–1980

Although born in the nineteenth century, Ethel Wilson did not begin her career as a writer until the middle of the twentieth century. In her four novels and three books of short fiction, she deals with women seeking self-definition and struggling against society's constraints. Her short story "We Have to Sit Opposite" treats a topic often explored in Canadian writing—travel abroad—to suggest something about propriety and the balance of power in male–female relationships; about the strains that such power-struggles place on social conventions; about the use of humour as a buffer; and even about the dangerous conflicts associated with territorial claims. (The story, though set in 1931, was written around the end of World War II and responds to Hitler's assertions, when he came to power in 1933, that German expansion was justified by its need for more "living space.") Sharing a train compartment with an imperious man who makes unreasonable demands, even traditional women like the two Canadian "clinging vines" (as the narrator calls them) find ways to refuse to be bullied.

We Have to Sit Opposite

Even in the confusion of entering the carriage at Salzburg, Mrs. Montrose and her cousin Mrs. Forrester noticed the man with the blue tooth. He occupied a corner beside the window. His wife sat next to him. Next to her sat their daughter of perhaps seventeen. People poured into the train. A look passed between Mrs. Montrose and Mrs. Forrester. The look said, "These people seem to have filled up the carriage pretty well, but we'd better take these seats while we can as the train is so full. At least we can have seats together." The porter, in his porter's tyrannical way, piled their suitcases onto the empty rack above the heads of the man with the blue tooth, and his wife, and his daughter, and departed. The opposite rack was full of baskets, bags and miscellaneous parcels. The train started. Here they were. Mrs. Montrose and Mrs. Forrester smiled at each other as they settled down below the rack which was filled with miscellaneous articles. Clinging vines that they were, they felt adventurous and successful. They had travelled alone from Vienna to Salzburg, leaving in Vienna their doctor husbands to continue attending the clinics of Dr. Bauer and Dr. Hirsch. And now, after a week in Salzburg, they were happily on their way to rejoin their husbands, who had flown to Munich.

Both Mrs. Montrose and Mrs. Forrester were tall, slight and fair. They were dressed with dark elegance. They knew that their small hats were smart, suitable and becoming, and they rejoiced in the simplicity and distinction of their new costumes. The selection of these and other costumes, and of these and other hats in Vienna had, they regretted, taken from the study of art, music and history a great deal of valuable time. Mrs. Montrose and Mrs. Forrester were sincerely fond of art, music and history and longed almost passionately to spend their days in the Albertina Gallery and the Kunsthistorische Museum. But the modest shops and shop windows of the craftsmen of Vienna had rather diverted the two young women from the study of art and history, and it was easy to lay the blame for this on the museums and art galleries which, in truth, closed their doors at very odd times. After each day's enchanting pursuits and disappointments, Mrs. Montrose and Mrs. Forrester hastened in a fatigued state to the café where they had arranged to meet their husbands who by this time had finished their daily sessions with Dr. Bauer and Dr. Hirsch.

This was perhaps the best part of the day, to sit together happily in the sunshine, toying with the good Viennese coffee or a glass of wine, gazing and being gazed upon, and giving up their senses to the music that flowed under the chestnut trees. (Ah Vienna, they thought, Vienna, Vienna.)

No, perhaps the evenings had been the best time when after their frugal pension dinner they hastened out to hear opera or symphony or wild atavistic gypsy music. All was past now. They had been very happy. They were fortunate. Were they too fortunate?

Mrs. Montrose and Mrs. Forrester were in benevolent good spirits as they looked round the railway carriage and prepared to take their seats and settle down for the journey to Munich to meet their husbands. In their window corner, opposite the man with the blue tooth, was a large hamper. "*Do* you mind?" asked Mrs. Montrose, smiling sweetly at the man, his wife, and his daughter. She prepared to lift the hamper on which the charming view from the carriage window was of course wasted, intending to move it along the seat, and take its place. The man, his wife, and his daughter had never taken their eyes off Mrs. Montrose and Mrs. Forrester since they had entered the carriage.

"*If* you please," said the man loudly and slowly in German English, "*if* you please, that place belongs to my wife or to my daughter. For the moment they sit beside me, but I keep that place for my wife or my daughter. That seat is therefore reserved. It is our seat. You may of course use the two remaining seats."

"I'm sorry," said Mrs. Montrose, feeling snubbed, and she and Mrs. Forrester sat down side by side on the two remaining seats opposite the German family. Beside them the hamper looked out of the window at the charming view. Their gaiety and self-esteem evaporated. The train rocked along.

The three continued to stare at the two young women. Suddenly the mother leaned toward her daughter. She put up her hand to her mouth and whispered behind her hand, her eyes remaining fixed on Mrs. Montrose. The daughter nodded. She also stared at Mrs. Montrose. Mrs. Montrose flushed. The mother sat upright again, still looking at Mrs. Montrose, who felt very uncomfortable, and very much annoyed at blushing.

The man ceased staring at the two young women. He looked up at the rack above him, which contained their suitcases.

"Those are your suitcases," he asked, or rather announced.

"Yes," said Mrs. Montrose and Mrs. Forrester without smiles.

"They are large," said the man in a didactic manner, "they are too large. They are too large to be put on racks. A little motion, a very little motion, and they might fall. If they fall they will injure myself, my wife, or my daughter. It is better," he continued instructively, "that if they fall, they should fall upon your heads, not upon our heads. That is logical. They are not my suitcases. They are your suitcases. You admit it. Please to move your suitcases to the opposite rack, where, if they fall, they will fall upon your own heads." And he continued to sit there motionless. So did his wife. So did his daughter.

Mrs. Montrose and Mrs. Forrester looked at the suitcases in dismay. "Oh," said Mrs. Forrester, "they are so heavy to move. If you feel like that, please won't you sit on this side of the carriage, and we will move across, under our own suitcases, though I can assure you they will not fall. Or perhaps you would help us?"

"We prefer this side of the carriage," said the man with the blue tooth. "We have sat here because we prefer this side of the carriage. It is logical that you should move your suitcases. It is not logical that my wife, my daughter and I should give up our seats in this carriage, or remove your suitcases."

Mrs. Montrose and Mrs. Forrester looked at each other with rage in their hearts. All their self-satisfaction was gone. They got up and tugged and tugged as the train rocked along. They leaned resentfully across the erectly sitting man, and his wife and his daughter. They experienced with exasperation the realization that they had better make the best of it. The train, they knew, was crowded. They had to remain in this carriage with this disagreeable family. With much pulling and straining they hauled down the heavy suitcases. Violently they removed the parcels of the German family and lifted their own suitcases onto the rack above their heads, disposing them clumsily on the rack. Panting a little (they disliked panting), they settled down again side by side with high colour and loosened wisps of hair. They controlled their features so as to appear serene and unaware of the existence of anyone else in the railway carriage, but their hearts were full of black hate.

The family exchanged whispered remarks, and then resumed their scrutiny of the two young women, whose elegance had by this time a sort of tipsy quality. The girl leaned toward her mother. She whispered behind her hand to her mother, who nodded. Both of them stared at Mrs. Forrester. Then they laughed.

"Heavens!" thought the affronted Mrs. Forrester, "this is outrageous! Why can't Alice and I whisper behind our hands to each other about these people and make them feel simply awful! But they wouldn't feel awful. Well, we can't, just because we've been properly brought up, and it would be too childish. And perhaps they don't even know they're rude. They're just being natural." She breathed hard in frustration, and composed herself again.

Suddenly the man with the blue tooth spoke. "Are you English?" he said loudly.

"Yes—well—no," said Mrs. Forrester.

"No—well—yes," said Mrs. Montrose, simultaneously.

A derisive look came over the man's face. "You must know what you are," he said, "either you are English or you are not English. Are you, or are you not?"

"No," said Mrs. Montrose and Mrs. Forrester, speaking primly. Their chins were high, their eyes flashed, and they were ready for discreet battle.

"Then are you Americans?" said the man in the same bullying manner.

"No," said Mrs. Montrose and Mrs. Forrester.

"You can't deceive *me*, you know," said the man with the blue tooth, "I know well the English language. You *say* you are not English. You *say* you are not American. What, then, may I ask, are you? You must be something."

"We are Canadians," said Mrs. Forrester, furious at this catechism.

"*Canadians,*" said the man.

"Yes, Canadians," said Mrs. Montrose.

"This," murmured Mrs. Forrester to Mrs. Montrose, "is more than I can bear!"

"What did you say?" said the man, leaning forward quickly, his hands on his knees.

"I spoke to my friend," said Mrs. Forrester coldly, "I spoke about my bear."

"Yes," said Mrs. Montrose, "she spoke about her bear."

"Your bear? Have you a bear? But you cannot have a bear!" said the man with some surprise.

"In Canada I have a bear. I have two bears," said Mrs. Forrester conceitedly.

"That is true," said Mrs. Montrose nodding, "she has two bears. I myself have five bears. My father has seven bears. That is nothing. It is the custom."

"What do you do with your bears?" asked the man.

"We eat them," said Mrs. Forrester.

"Yes," said Mrs. Montrose, "we eat them. It is the custom."

The man turned and spoke briefly to his wife and daughter, whose eyes opened wider than ever.

Mrs. Montrose and Mrs. Forrester felt pleased. This was better.

The man with the blue tooth became really interested. "Are you married?" he asked Mrs. Forrester.

"Yes," she replied. (We'll see what he'll say next, then we'll see what we can do.)

"And you?" he enquired of Mrs. Montrose. Mrs. Montrose seemed uncertain. "Well, yes, in a way, I suppose," she said.

The man with the blue tooth scrutinized Mrs. Montrose for a moment. "*Then,*" he said, as though he had at last found her out, "if you are married, where is your husband?"

Mrs. Montrose took out her pocket handkerchief. She buried her face in her hands, covering her eyes with her handkerchief. She shook. Evidently she sobbed.

"Now you see what you've done!" said Mrs. Forrester. "You shouldn't ask questions like that. Just look at what you've done."

The three gazed fascinated on Mrs. Montrose. "Is he dead or what is he?" asked the man of Mrs. Forrester, making the words almost quietly with his mouth.

"Sh ! !" said Mrs. Forrester very loudly indeed. The three jumped a little. So did Mrs. Montrose.

There was silence while Mrs. Montrose wiped her eyes. She looked over the heads opposite. The wife leaned toward her husband and addressed him timidly behind her hand. He nodded, and spoke to Mrs. Forrester.

"Well," he said, "at least you admit that *you* have a husband. If you have a husband then, where is he?"

"Oh, I don't know," said Mrs. Forrester lightly.

"No, she doesn't know," said Mrs. Montrose.

The three on the opposite seat went into a conference. Mrs. Montrose and Mrs. Forrester did not dare to look at each other. They were enjoying themselves. Their self-esteem had returned. They had impressed. Unfavourably, it is true. But still they had impressed.

The man with the blue tooth pulled himself together. He reasserted himself. Across his waistcoat hung a watch chain. He took his watch out of his pocket and looked at the time. Then to the surprise of Mrs. Montrose and Mrs. Forrester he took another watch out of the pocket at the other end of the chain. "You see," he said proudly, "I have two watches."

Mrs. Montrose and Mrs. Forrester were surprised, but they had themselves well in hand.

Mrs. Montrose looked at the watches disparagingly. "My husband has six watches," she said.

"Yes, that is true," nodded Mrs. Forrester, "her husband *has* got six watches, but my husband, like you, unfortunately has only two watches."

The man put his watches back. Decidedly the battle was going in favour of the two young women. How horrid of us, he was so pleased with his watches, thought Mrs. Montrose. Isn't it true that horridness just breeds horridness. We're getting horrider every minute. She regarded the man, his wife and his daughter with distaste but with pity.

"You *say*," said the man, who always spoke as though their statements were open to doubt, which of course they were, "that you come from Canada. Do you come from Winnipeg? I know about Winnipeg."

"No," said Mrs. Montrose, and she spoke this time quite truthfully, "I come from Vancouver." Mrs. Forrester remained silent.

"And you, where do you come from?" persisted the man in a hectoring tone, addressing Mrs. Forrester. Mrs. Forrester remained silent, she had almost decided to answer no more questions.

"Oh, do not tell, please do not tell," begged Mrs. Montrose in an anguished way.

"No," said Mrs. Forrester importantly, "I shall not tell. Rest assured. I shall not tell."

"Why will she not tell?" demanded the man. He was tortured by curiosity. So was his wife. So was his daughter.

"Sh ! !" said Mrs. Montrose very loudly.

The man seemed ill at ease. By this time nothing existed in the world for him, or for his wife, or for his daughter but these two Canadian women who ate bears.

"How is it," asked the man, "that you no longer buy my trousers?"

"I beg your pardon?" faltered Mrs. Montrose. For a moment she lost ground.

"I said," replied the man, "why is it that you no longer buy my trousers?"

The ladies did not answer. They could not think of a good answer to that one.

"I," said the man, "am a manufacturer of trousers. I make the most beautiful trousers in Germany. Indeed in the world." (You do not so, thought Mrs. Forrester, picturing her husband's good London legs.) "For three years I receive orders from Winnipeg for my trousers. And now, since two years, yes, since 1929, I receive no more orders for my trousers. Why is that?" he asked, like a belligerent.

"Shall we tell him?" asked Mrs. Forrester, looking at Mrs. Montrose. Neither of them knew why he had received no more orders for his trousers, but they did not wish to say so. "Shall we tell him?" asked Mrs. Forrester.

"You tell him," said Mrs. Montrose.

"No, *you* tell him," said Mrs. Forrester.

"I do not like to tell him," said Mrs. Montrose, "I'd rather you told him."

The man with the blue tooth looked from one to the other.

"Very well, I shall tell him," said Mrs. Forrester. "The fact is," she said, looking downward, "that in Canada men no longer wear trousers."

"What are you saying? That is not true, never can that be true!" said the man in some confusion.

"Yes," said Mrs. Montrose, corroborating sombrely. "Yes, indeed it is true. When they go abroad they wear trousers, but in Canada, no. It is a new custom."

"It is the climate," said Mrs. Forrester.

"Yes, that is the reason, it is the climate," agreed Mrs. Montrose.

"But in Canada," argued the man with the blue tooth, "your climate is cold. Everyone knows your climate is cold."

"In the Arctic regions, yes, it is really intensely cold, we all find it so. But not in Winnipeg. Winnipeg is very salubrious." (That's a good one, thought Mrs. Montrose.)

The man turned and spoke rapidly to his wife. She also turned, and looked askance at her daughter. The expressions of the man, his wife, and his daughter were a blend of pleasure and shock. The two liars were delighted.

At last the man could not help asking, "But they *must* wear something! It is not logical."

"Oh, it's logical, all right!" said Mrs. Forrester.

"But what *do* they wear?" persisted the man.

"I never looked to see," said Mrs. Montrose. "*I* did, I looked," said Mrs. Forrester.

"Well?" asked the man.

"Oh, they just wear kilts," said Mrs. Forrester.

"Kilts? What are kilts? I do not know kilts," said the man.

"I would rather not tell you," said Mrs. Forrester primly.

"Oh," said the man.

Mrs. Montrose took out her vanity case, and inspected herself, powder puff in hand.

"I do not allow my wife and daughter to paint their faces so," said the man with the blue tooth.

"No?" said Mrs. Montrose.

"It is not good that women should paint their faces so. Good women do not do that. It is a pity."

(Oh, Alice, thought Mrs. Forrester in a fury, he shall not dare!) "It is a pity," she hissed, "that in your country there are no good dentists!"

"Be careful, be careful," whispered Mrs. Montrose.

"What do you mean?" demanded the man with the blue tooth.

(She will go too far, I know she will, thought Mrs. Montrose, alarmed, putting out her hand.)

"In our country," said the rash Mrs. Forrester, "anyone needing attention is taken straight to the State Dentist by the Police. This is done for aesthetic reasons. It is logical."

"I am going to sleep," said Mrs. Montrose very loudly, and she shut her eyes tight.

"So am I," said Mrs. Forrester, in a great hurry, and she shut her eyes too. This had been hard work but good fun for Mrs. Montrose and Mrs. Forrester. They felt, though, that they had gone a little bit too far. It might be as well if they slept, or pretended to sleep, until they reached Munich. They felt that outside their closed eyes was something frightening. The voice of the man with the blue tooth was saying, "I wish to tell you, I wish to tell you . . . " but Mrs. Montrose was in a deep sleep, and so was Mrs. Forrester. They sat with their eyes tightly closed, beside the hamper which still occupied the seat with the view by the darkening window. Mrs. Montrose had the inside corner, and so by reason of nestling down in the corner, and by reason of having an even and sensible temperament, she really and truly fell asleep at last.

Not so Mrs. Forrester. Her eyes were tightly closed, but her mind was greatly disturbed. Why had they permitted themselves to be baited? She pondered on the collective mentality that occupied the seat near to them (knees almost touching), and its results which now filled the atmosphere of the carriage so unpleasantly. She had met this mentality before, but had not been closely confined with it, as now. What of a world in which this mentality might ever become dominant? Then one would be confined with it without appeal or relief. The thought was shocking. She felt unreasonably agitated. She felt rather a fool, too, with her eyes shut tightly. But, if she opened them, she would have to look somewhere, presumably at the family, so it seemed safer to keep them closed. The train sped on. After what seemed to her a very long time, she peeped. The wife and daughter were busy. The husband sat back, hands on knees, chin raised, expectant, eyes closed. His wife respectfully undid his tie, his collar, and his top shirt button. By this time the daughter had opened the hamper, and had taken from it a bottle and a clean napkin. These she handed to her mother. The wife moistened the napkin from the bottle and proceeded to wash her husband, his face, his ears, round the back of his neck, and inside his shirt collar, with great care. "Like a cat," thought Mrs. Forrester, who had forgotten to shut her eyes.

The man with the blue tooth lowered his raised chin and caught her. "You see," he said loudly, "you see, wives should look properly after their husbands, instead of travelling alone and . . ." But Mrs. Forrester was fast asleep again. The whole absurd encounter had begun to hold an element of terror.

They had been tempted into folly. She knew—as she screwed up her closed eyes—that they were implicated in fear and folly.

The two young women took care to sleep until the train reached Munich. Then they both woke up.

Many people slept until they reached Munich. Then they all began to wake up.

—1961[1]

---

[1] Originally published in *Chatelaine* in 1945.

Harry Robinson 1900–1990

Although Harry Robinson's stories only became known to the general public in the 1990s, they are among the oldest we have in Canada. Robinson was a traditional Okanagan oral storyteller, who learned many of his stories from his grandmother, who first heard them in the middle of the nineteenth century. Some are anecdotes about real people, while others are legends with long Native traditions. Such oral stories are both stable and unstable: storytellers keep the germ of the tale intact but may alter material to suit specific performances.

"Coyote Tricks Owl" has at its centre one of the major trickster–transformer figures in traditional Native lore. Already in existence in a legendary past before humans came into the world, but still having an effect on the present, Coyote is often mischievous but sometimes helpful. Like other Native mythic figures, Coyote is a shape-shifter, taking both animal and human forms. By limiting Owl's ability to change his form from animal to human, he restricts Owl's power, thereby making the world a safer place.

We owe the preservation of Robinson's stories to Wendy Wickwire, an ethnographer who gained Robinson's permission to record him in his act of telling. Wanting to capture in print the oral nature of these stories and to indicate the rhythmic patterns of Robinson's delivery, Wickwire and Robinson decided to set his speeches in lines, almost like lines of verse.

Coyote Tricks Owl

Owl is bad. He preys on people. So Coyote devises a crafty plan to end Owl's killings.

The Owl is bad.
He kills people.
Owl, he's supposed to be big man.
Big tall man.
And he kills people, that Owl.
He's tall and he got the power,
    that Owl, he got the power
Was a big man.
Tall and long arms.
Big arms.
Big man.
Big person, the Owl was.
Big woman or big man.
And he can kill people.
Kill 'em and eat 'em.
He bad.

And he can turn himself into a bird.
Into an Owl.
But in another way, it's a person.
Big man or big woman.
But he can change himself into Owl.
And that's a bird.
Then sometimes he could change himself or herself
    into a big person
        so he can kill people.

So Coyote find that out.

All right.
He look for Owl.
They call that *sa-NEE-na*.
That's an Indian word, *sa-NEE-na*.

And he look around.
And he going along,
    and he see some people.
And he ask and they tell them,
  "You go that way.
    He was over there.
    And you can find 'em if you go over that way."

So he keep going and get closer.
Finally he find 'em.
And this time
    when he found 'em,
        and he change into Owl.
He was Owl.
He was Owl Woman when he found 'em.

And Coyote, he know.
He's a big man.
Strong man or big woman.
He couldn't kill 'em.
Too strong.
He use his power whenever he met 'em,
    whenever he find 'em.
It can be an Owl.
That way it can kill easy.
So he's smart because he's got the power to use.
So that's why that Owl, she changed herself.
Was a woman.

Changed herself into Owl.
And it was Owl already
   when Coyote met 'em.

And he was going along.
And he see a woman walking along.
And they met together.
And he see this woman.
And Coyote say to that woman,
   "You going along here.
   Where are you going?"
So this woman, she said,
   "I'm going along to look for some people.
   I kill 'em and I eat 'em.
   I eat people."
And Coyote says,
   "So do I.
   I do the same.
   That's what I'm looking for."

See?
He tell 'em a lie.
He's got to tell 'em lie,
He's got to tell 'em something.
He got to fool 'em, you know, to kill 'em.
He says,
   "I'm the same.
   I'm looking for some people.
   I eat people too.
   So we both the same.
   We can go together."

So all right.
The Owl Woman, she went along with Coyote.
They both people-eater.
They look for people
   so they could kill 'em and eat 'em.

All right.
They kept a'going,
   and Coyote told 'em,
      "You stop here.
      We stop here.
      Then you build a fire.
      Then we can cook something."

They got something to cook.
"Then I'm going to look around here.
I might find some berries.
If I find something to eat,
    maybe I'll let you know
    and then we can both get 'em."
So that's just to fool, you know.

So Owl Woman build a fire.
And Coyote went out.
Get on the other side so she couldn't see him.
And he use his power.
And finally he came back with a person.
Coyote, he use his power,
    then he make a person out of his power.
And while he were out there
    he bring the two girls and two boys,
        just young people.
And he bring 'em
    and he come to Owl Woman
        and he says to Owl Woman,
            "I found these young people over there
                and I see them and tell them to come.
            Come along with me and then we going to be here."
And he says
    "Build a bigger fire,"
    he says to these young people.
    "Gather some wood from long ways,
        and get 'em,
            and make a big fire,
                so we'll have a good light."
It's getting to be dark, you know, at night.
And, he said,
    "We'll cook something.
    Roast 'em on the stick
        and eat that."
I don't know what they cook,
    but anyway they had a meal.
They eat something.
I think it was,
    they used to tell that, but I forget.
Mushroom, I think they get that.
And then they roast 'em on the stick, you know.
They eat that.

Then after supper, they say,
   "We are glad to get together.
   Now we're six of us.
   We gonna dance.
   We gonna dance and we sing our song.
   And we gonna dance right around the fire."

So they did after supper and they sing their song.
Coyote sing his song and he dance.
The whole bunch of 'em, you know,
   they dance around the fire.
And keep going.
And Coyote, he change the song.
And he sing another song, a better song.
Then he dance and dance.

And Owl Woman, she was pretty happy.
She like that.
She hear that good song, Coyote's song.
And she stop and Coyote told 'em,
   "You got a song.
     You sing your song, and we dance on your song."

All right.
Owl Woman, she sing her own song.
Dance around.
And again.
And Coyote sing his song.
Owl Woman, she was happy.
Then they dance around
   and again Coyote sing his song.
Then he says to the young people,
   "You go out and find me a stick,
     not too big.
   Kinda long, and kinda fork.
   Fork stick.
   Cut it with a knife."
Coyote, he got a knife.

And Owl Woman tell 'em,
   "What did you want that stick for?"
   "Well," he says,
   "When I sing one song I sing
   I gotta have that in my hand.
   That's the way I was.

It's more like Indian doctor.
So I gotta have that stick.
So I got one more song to sing,
    when I get that stick,
        sing that song,
            I have that stick in my hand."

So the young people went out
    and get 'em a stick
        and bring 'em.
They cut 'em and they got a long stick.
Got kinda fork, you know.
Then he had that and he dance around the fire.
And she dance, Owl.
And he kinda pushed her, you know.
Pushed her towards the fire.

And then,
    "Ah," she says,
    "I was so happy, and I danced that way and that way."

She keep doing it for a while.
And one time he know that he just push her.
Push her to the fire.

And then, she fall about halfways.
And then, he get that stick.
And then, he stick her at the back of the head towards the fire
    and he leave her there.

Then he get her burned, you know.
She breathe the fire.
And she burned her face.
He burn her.
They kill her.

See?
He fool 'em around.
And these people they had there,
    that's his power only.
That's not real people.
He just had that so they could help him
    so he could fool that Owl
        to kill her.

So after that these other people,
    they disappeared.
They disappeared on the air.
That's not a real people.
Just himself, you know.
Then he killed the Owl.

In the morning when the fire was all off,
    he gather the bone.
And he get them and pick them up.
Then he get the water,
    and he put water and he wrap 'em on something.
Then he take 'em up to a tree.
He climb on a tree,
    and this is just a bone.
And some of the meat, you know,
    it's been burned.
But it's not all burned.
He get them together
    and he wrap 'em up with something.
And he climb up to a tree.
Then he put 'em up there on the limbs,
    on the forks of the limbs.
He put them there.
Stick 'em there.
Then he come back and he look.
And then he says,
    "Now you're there.
    You not going to kill the people no more.
    When the human people come *shtil-SHKAYL* come,
        You going to be Owl only.
    At night you can be sitting on the limb like that,
        on the tree.
    And you could speak like, at night.
    Then, if the children,
        the people have the children
            if the children, they were cry,
                maybe one year old, two years old,
                    you could tell 'em,
                        'Shut up.
                        Don't cry.
                        You hear that Owl?
                        He going to come and get you.'

Then you could speak and the child could hear.
And that's Owl.
Because you're sitting up there
   and you speak,
      'Mmmm Mmmm Mmmm.'
That's the way the Owl speaks at night,
   sitting on the tree.
And the child hear that.
Told 'em.
   'Hear that?
    If you cry all the time,
      he'll come and pick you up,
        kill you.'
And the kid'll be scared,
   quit crying.
You can be used only that way.
You can only scare the kids.
And you can do that at night.
Not only for the kids,
   but once in awhile
     if anybody could hear you,
       you could fly and you sitting on the tree,
         and you could say that at night.
Even in daytime you could say that sometimes.
But most of the time,
   you could do that at night.
And you could scare the kids.
That you're going to do.
No more killing people.
No more eat people."

See?
He judge 'em.
He tell 'em what to do.
And not only that.
There's a lot of these people-killer,
   and people-eater, when he kill 'em,
     he always judge 'em,
       and tell 'em what they should do.

And that's Coyote did that.

—1989

Morley Callaghan 1903–1990

*Beginning in the last years of the 1920s and for more than a decade, Morley
Callaghan was Canada's most highly regarded and successful short story writer—
keeping company with Ernest Hemingway and F. Scott Fitzgerald in prestigious
American magazines such as* Scribner's, The New Yorker, *and* Esquire.
*"Rigmarole" is a good example of North American modernist fiction of this period,
which used straightforward descriptions of sensory experience—from which the
reader may be able to extrapolate the characters' submerged feelings. Callaghan's
interest in new ideas about the human unconscious as riven by psychological conflict
can be seen in the way both characters are uncertain of what they really want or
need and by how hard it is for them to express their feelings of love or even kindness.
Because Callaghan employs the modernist technique of restricted point of view, this
conflict is shown chiefly through the consciousness and perceptions of only one of the
characters, but the story reveals the confusions of both. Its conclusion is typical of
Callaghan's short fiction in that we leave its characters before they or we can know
for certain what the future holds.*

Rigmarole

After they had come in from the party, Jeff Hilton, the advertising man,
looked up and saw his young wife, Mathilde, standing there beaming at
him. She seemed to him to be glowing from the memory of many whispered conversations with young men who had been anxious to touch her
hand or her arm; she smiled and went on dreaming and her wide dark
eyes grew soft with tenderness. She began to hum as she walked over to
the window and stood there looking down at the street in the early winter
night; and as Jeff went on watching her he kept resenting that she should
have had such a good time at a party that he had found so dull. She had
left him alone a lot, but he had always remained aware of the admiration
she aroused in the young men around her. And now she turned, all warm
and glowing, and burst out, "Didn't you like the party, Jeff?"

"It was a lousy party," he said vindictively. "I'm fed up with that
crowd. No one ever has anything new or bright to say. They've all gone
a little stale."

Mathilde tried to stop smiling, but her dark, ardent face still glowed
with warmth as she stood there with her hands clasped in front of her.
Though Jeff went on talking with a kind of good-humored disgust his

earnest face began to show such a desolate loneliness that she suddenly felt guilty; she longed to offer up to him all the tenderness, all the delight it had been so enchanting to have in her since the party. "I had an awfully good time," she said. "But I kept my eye on you. I know who you were with. Were you watching me, Jeff?" and she rushed over to him and threw herself on his lap and began to kiss him and rub her hand through his hair, laughing all the time like a little girl. "Did you think I was flirting? Did you think I laughed and whispered too much? Don't you love people to think I'm pretty?"

But Jeff who had had such a dull time felt only that she was trying to console him and make him feel good so he said irritably, "You don't need to feel you neglected me. Don't feel guilty. Nobody ever has to worry about me trailing you around. You can feel free."

"Jeff," she said very softly, "I don't want to feel free. I don't feel free now."

"Sure you do. You would be the first to complain if you didn't."

"Didn't you worry a little about me once tonight, Jeff?"

"Listen here, Mathilde," he said shortly, "jealous men are the greatest bores in the world."

"Jeff, put your arms around me."

"What's the matter with you? You don't need to mollify me or feel guilty because you had a good time. Surely we've got beyond that."

"I wasn't trying to mollify you," she said, looking quite lost, and she began to show in her face much of that curious discontent he had felt growing in her the last three months. She was pouting like a child and she had the shame of one whose innocent gift has been rejected curtly, and then she went away from him awkwardly and curled herself upon the couch, almost crouching, her eyes hardening as she stared at him.

After a while he said, "You're childish, Mathilde. Why are you sitting there as if you hate me?" But he began to feel helpless against her silent, unreasonable and secret anger. "These last few months you've become about as unreasonable as a sick woman. What on earth is the matter with you?" he said. And he got up and paced up and down and his voice rose as he went on questioning her, but every time he passed the couch where she was crouching he became more disturbed by the passionate restlessness he felt in her.

So he tried to laugh and he said, "This is a lot of nonsense, Mathilde," and he sat down beside her. In a rough, good-natured way he tried to pull her against him. When she pushed him away he stared at her for a long time till at last he began to desire her, and again he put his arm around her, and again she pushed him away. Then he lost his temper; he threw his arms around her and held her down while he tried to caress her. "Stop it, stop it Jeff," she cried. "Haven't you got any sense at all? Doesn't it mean anything to you that you didn't want me near you a few minutes ago? What do you think I am?" As she pulled away roughly from him she was really pleading for him to see that she was struggling to hold on to something he had been destroying carelessly month after month. "Doesn't it mean anything?" she asked.

"There you go," he said. "Why can't you be direct about things instead of sentimental?"

"Because I don't want things that way," she said. And then she cried passionately, "You can't touch me whenever you like. You can't do that to me just when you feel like it," and her eyes were full of tears as if at last she had touched the true source of all her disappointment.

But he grabbed hold of her, held her a moment to show he could possess her, then pushed her away. "I'm not a little boy playing that old game," he shouted. "We've been married three years. Why all the rigmarole?" and he expressed the rage that was growing in him by banging her on the knee with his fist.

"Oh, you've hurt me," she said, holding the spot. "Why did you do that?" and she began to cry a little. "That ends it. You'll never hit me again," she said.

"Damn it all, I didn't hit you."

"You did. Oh, dear, you did. That settles it. I'll not stay around here. I'll not stay another night. I'm going now."

"Go ahead. Do what you want to."

"Don't worry. I'll soon be gone," she said, and with tears streaming from her eyes she ran into the bedroom. He stood gloomily at the door with his arms folded across his chest. He watched her pull out drawers, toss dresses into a suitcase, sweep silver at random from the top of the dresser. Sometimes she stopped to press her fists against her eyes. He began to feel so distressed, watching, that he shouted at last, "I won't stand for this stupid exhibition," and he jumped at her and flung his arms around her and squeezed her as though he would crush forever the unreasonable revolt in her soul. Then he grew ashamed and he said, "I won't stop you, and I won't stay and watch this stupid performance either. I'm going out." And when he left her she was still pulling out dresser drawers.

As soon as Jeff walked along the street from the apartment house on that early winter night he began to feel that he really had not left that room at all, that wherever he walked, wherever he went, he would still be pulled back there to the room to watch her, and when he went into the corner tavern to have a glass of beer he sat there mopping his forehead and thinking, "Not just when I want, not just when I feel like it! I can't go on with that stuff when we're so used to each other. I'd feel stupid."

In the crowded tavern men and women leaned close together and whispered and while he listened Jeff kept hearing her voice beneath the murmuring voices and the clink of glasses and seeing her face in the smoke of the tavern. As he looked around, a dreadful fear kept growing in him that whatever was warm and vital among people was being pushed out of his reach; and then he couldn't stop himself from getting up and hurrying back to the apartment house.

He saw her coming out wearing her brown coat, and her felt hat was pulled over her eyes. She was carrying her bag. A taxi was waiting. In a foolish way, to hide his eagerness, he smiled and said, "May I take the bag for you, madam?" He even made a little bow.

"No, thanks," she said, and she swayed the bag away from his outstretched hand, looking at him in that shy pleading way.

"Are you sure you wouldn't like me to take it?"

"Quite sure," she said.

"All right," he said politely, trying to smile while she got into the cab, and when the cab actually moved off along the street, he stood there, worried and unbelieving, feeling there was no place to go.

But he went into the apartment and as he wandered aimlessly into the bedroom and looked at the empty dresser drawers his loneliness deepened, and he thought, "I tried to use some common sense anyway. She'll come back. If I went on struggling with her like that all the time I'd never be able to hold my job. I'll bet a million dollars she'll be back."

And he waited and was desolate remembering the shy pleading look in her eyes as she swayed the bag away from him on the sidewalk, and he listened for every small sound from the street, the stairs and the door; and when at last he heard the key turning in the lock he jumped up triumphantly and rushed to meet her.

She came in quietly with a timid, apologetic smile, and as she pulled off her hat she said in a bantering tone, "What were you doing, Jeff? What was keeping you up till this hour?"

"Waiting for you, of course."

"You mean you missed me?"

"Sure I missed you. You know I did, too," he said. He helped her off with her coat, begged her to sit down, rushed to the ice box to get a snack for them and his face kept showing all of his childish triumph. She was delighted to be waited on in this different way. Every time the broad smile came on his face she asked, "What are you laughing at, Jeff?"

"How does it feel to be free?" was all he said.

But when they were going to bed and she had buried her dark head in the pillow she began to cry brokenly, and no matter how he coaxed her, or how gently he spoke she would not be quiet. "Aren't we happy now, Mathilde? Isn't it all over now?" he kept saying.

"No, I'm not happy. I can't bear it," she said.

"You can't bear what?"

"The way you let me go. No matter what happened I didn't think you'd ever let me go. You wouldn't have done it two years ago."

"But you wanted to go, Mathilde, and if I thought you wanted to . . ."

"Two years ago you would have made me come back. You would have been afraid of losing me."

"I knew you'd come back like a homing pigeon."

"Yes, you were so sure of it. You were so very sure," she said, and then she put her hands over her face and turned her head away, mumbling, "I'm silly. I guess I sound silly. I guess I don't know what I want," and he could only see the back of her neck and her hand moving over her cheek.

As he walked around the bed, looking at her, he thought, "Why didn't I stop her? Why can't she see that knowing we love each other is better than worrying that we don't," but he began to feel terribly afraid. "Nobody loves insecurity," he said, knowing his words sounded weak and apologetic. For a while he watched her, then went to speak, but he found himself shyly fumbling what seemed to be old words, so he stood there, silent, with his love becoming an ache, for it seemed a terrible thing that such words should sound strange just because they had grown used to each other. Then he knew that his fear had been that he would never be able to express all the feeling he had for her. And all he said was, "I had a glass of beer at the corner and I began to feel terrible."

"Did you?" she said without looking up.

"I think I know what you've been missing," he said.

"Yes?" she said.

"I couldn't stay away from here," he said. "I felt you'd be pulled back too."

She looked up at him timidly for though the words he used were neither new, nor warm, nor strange, she began to feel his awkward shyness, she began almost to hear him thinking, "What happens that you can't keep showing your love when it's so strong in you?" She just waited there and grew shy too, and the feeling between them at that moment seemed so much deeper than any earlier time of impulse and sudden joy.

—1959; 2003[1]

Thomas Raddall 1903–1994

The author of over eighty short stories and eleven novels, Thomas Raddall was able to support himself solely by his writing, even though all his fiction was focused on the history and environment of Nova Scotia:

> *In all of my stories I* made clear *that it was Nova Scotia I was talking about, that these were Nova Scotian people. I was determined to do this. When the* [Saturday Evening] *Post . . . wanted me to change the stories so that they occurred in the United States, I could have gone on selling to them, doing what Callaghan did in his early stories, carefully setting them nowhere distinct so that readers could perceive them as American, but I didn't. I preferred to sell my stories elsewhere, even if for less money.*

> *While many of his narratives followed the conventions of twentieth-century historical romance, as "The Wedding Gift" shows, Raddall—an avid collector of the old stories he encountered throughout the province—also drew on local folk traditions to tell anecdotal tales of love's attractions and complexities, and of cunning and escape from apparently predestined fate. Like many folktales, this narrative depends on a trick that allows its surprising young woman, Kezia Barnes, to exercise choice in a world of constraint. Indeed, Kezia seems to embody what Raddall describes, in his memoir,* In My Time *(1976), as his own philosophy: "to face things on your own feet and with eyes wide open, watchful for trouble and maybe a bit of luck here and there along the way."*

[1] Originally published in *Story Magazine* in 1935.

The Wedding Gift

Nova Scotia, in 1794. Winter. Snow on the ground. Two feet of it in the woods, less by the shore, except in drifts against Port Marriott's barns and fences; but enough to set sleigh bells ringing through the town, enough to require a multitude of paths and burrows from doors to streets, to carpet the wharves and the decks of the shipping, and to trim the ships' yards with tippets of ermine. Enough to require fires roaring in the town's chimneys, and blue wood smoke hanging low over the roof tops in the still December air. Enough to squeal under foot in the trodden places and to muffle the step everywhere else. Enough for the hunters, whose snowshoes now could overtake the floundering moose and caribou. Even enough for the always-complaining loggers, whose ox sleds now could haul their cut from every part of the woods. But not enough, not nearly enough snow for Miss Kezia Barnes, who was going to Bristol Creek to marry Mr. Hathaway.

Kezia did not want to marry Mr. Hathaway. Indeed she had told Mr. and Mrs. Barclay in a tearful voice that she didn't want to marry anybody. But Mr. Barclay had taken snuff and said "Ha! Humph!" in the severe tone he used when he was displeased; and Mrs. Barclay had sniffed and said it was a very good match for her, and revolved the cold blue eyes in her fat moon face, and said Kezia must not be a little fool.

There were two ways of going to Bristol Creek. One was by sea, in one of the fishing sloops. But the preacher objected to that. He was a pallid young man lately sent out from England by Lady Huntingdon's Connexion,[1] and seasick five weeks on the way. He held Mr. Barclay in some awe, for Mr. Barclay had the best pew in the meetinghouse and was the chief pillar of godliness in Port Marriott. But young Mr. Mears was firm on this point. He would go by road, he said, or not at all. Mr. Barclay had retorted "Ha! Humph!" The road was twenty miles of horse path through the woods, now deep in snow. Also the path began at Harper's Farm on the far side of the harbour, and Harper had but one horse.

"I shall walk," declared the preacher calmly, "and the young woman can ride."

Kezia had prayed for snow, storms of snow, to bury the trail and keep anyone from crossing the cape to Bristol Creek. But now they were setting out from Harper's Farm, with Harper's big brown horse, and all

---

[1] A religious group of like-minded worshippers.

Kezia's prayers had gone for naught. Like any anxious lover, busy Mr. Hathaway had sent Black Sam overland on foot to find out what delayed his wedding, and now Sam's day-old tracks marked for Kezia the road to marriage.

She was a meek little thing, as became an orphan brought up as house-help in the Barclay home; but now she looked at the preacher and saw how young and helpless he looked so far from his native Yorkshire, and how ill-clad for this bitter trans-Atlantic weather, and she spoke up.

"You'd better take my shawl, sir. I don't need it. I've got Miss Julia's old riding cloak. And we'll go ride-and-tie."

"Ride and what?" murmured Mr. Mears.

"I'll ride a mile or so, then I'll get down and tie the horse to a tree and walk on. When you come up to the horse, you mount and ride a mile or so, passing me on the way, and you tie him and walk on. Like that. Ride-and-tie, ride-and-tie. The horse gets a rest between."

Young Mr. Mears nodded and took the proffered shawl absently. It was a black thing that matched his sober broadcloth coat and small-clothes,[2] his black woollen stockings and his round black hat. At Mr. Barclay's suggestion he had borrowed a pair of moose-hide moccasins for the journey. As he walked a prayer-book in his coat-skirts bumped the back of his legs.

At the top of the ridge above Harper's pasture, where the narrow path led off through gloomy hemlock woods, Kezia paused for a last look back across the harbour. In the morning sunlight the white roofs of the little lonely town resembled a tidal wave flung up by the sea and frozen as it broke against the dark pine forest to the west. Kezia sighed, and young Mr. Mears was surprised to see tears in her eyes.

She rode off ahead. The saddle was a man's, of course, awkward to ride modestly, woman-fashion. As soon as she was out of the preacher's sight she rucked her skirts and slid a leg over to the other stirrup. That was better. There was a pleasant sensation of freedom about it, too. For a moment she forgot that she was going to Bristol Creek, in finery second-hand from the Barclay girls, in a new linen shift and drawers that she had sewn herself in the light of the kitchen candles, in white cotton stockings and a bonnet and shoes from Mr. Barclay's store, to marry Mr. Hathaway.

The Barclays had done well for her from the time when, a skinny weeping creature of fourteen, she was taken into the Barclay household

---

[2] Knee-breeches.

and, as Mrs. Barclay so often said, "treated more like one of my own than a bond-girl from the poorhouse." She had first choice of the clothing cast off by Miss Julia and Miss Clara. She was permitted to sit in the same room, and learn what she could, when the schoolmaster came to give private lessons to the Barclay girls. She waited on table, of course, and helped in the kitchen, and made beds, and dusted and scrubbed. But then she had been taught to spin and to sew and to knit. And she was permitted, indeed encouraged, to sit with the Barclays in the meetinghouse, at the convenient end of the pew, where she could worship the Barclays' God and assist with the Barclay wraps at the beginning and end of the service. And now, to complete her rewards, she had been granted the hand of a rejected Barclay suitor.

Mr. Hathaway was Barclay's agent at Bristol Creek, where he sold rum and gunpowder and corn meal and such things to the fishermen and hunters, and bought split cod—fresh, pickled or dry—and ran a small sawmill, and cut and shipped firewood by schooner to Port Marriott, and managed a farm, all for a salary of fifty pounds, Halifax currency, per year. Hathaway was a most capable fellow, Mr. Barclay often acknowledged. But when after fifteen capable years he came seeking a wife, and cast a sheep's eye first at Miss Julia, and then at Miss Clara, Mrs. Barclay observed with a sniff that Hathaway was looking a bit high.

So he was. The older daughter of Port Marriott's most prosperous merchant was even then receiving polite attentions from Mr. Gamage, the new collector of customs, and a connection of the Halifax Gamages, as Mrs. Barclay was fond of pointing out. And Miss Clara was going to Halifax in the spring to learn the gentle art of playing the pianoforte, and incidentally to display her charms to the naval and military young gentlemen who thronged the Halifax drawingrooms. The dear girls laughed behind their hands whenever long solemn Mr. Hathaway came to town aboard one of the Barclay vessels and called at the big house under the elms. Mrs. Barclay bridled at Hathaway's presumption, but shrewd Mr. Barclay narrowed his little black eyes and took snuff and said "Ha! Humph!"

It was plain to Mr. Barclay that an emergency had arisen. Hathaway was a good man—in his place; and Hathaway must be kept content there, to go on making profit for Mr. Barclay at a cost of only £50 a year. 'Twas a pity Hathaway couldn't satisfy himself with one of the fishermen's girls at the Creek, but there 'twas. If Hathaway had set his mind on a town miss, then a town miss he must have; but she must be the right kind, the sort who would content herself and Hathaway at Bristol Creek and not go nagging the man to remove and try his capabilities elsewhere. At once Mr. Barclay thought of Kezia—dear little Kezzie. A colourless little creature but quiet and well-mannered and pious, and only twenty-two.

Mr. Hathaway was nearly forty and far from handsome, and he had a rather cold, seeking way about him—useful in business of course— that rubbed women the wrong way. Privately Mr. Barclay thought Hathaway lucky to get Kezia. But it was a nice match for the girl, better than anything she could have expected. He impressed that upon her and introduced the suitor from Bristol Creek. Mr. Hathaway spent two or three evenings courting Kezia in the kitchen—Kezia in a quite good gown of Miss Clara's, gazing out at the November moon on the snow, murmuring now and again in the tones of someone in a rather dismal trance, while the kitchen help listened behind one door and the Barclay girls giggled behind another.

The decision, reached mainly by the Barclays, was that Mr. Hathaway should come to Port Marriott aboard the packet schooner on December twenty-third, to be married in the Barclay parlour and then take his bride home for Christmas. But an unforeseen circumstance had changed all this. The circumstance was a ship, "from Mogador in Barbary" as Mr. Barclay wrote afterwards in the salvage claim, driven off her course by gales and wrecked at the very entrance to Bristol Creek. She was a valuable wreck, laden with such queer things as goatskins in pickle, almonds, wormseed, pomegranate skins and gum arabic, and capable Mr. Hathaway had lost no time in salvage for the benefit of his employer.

As a result he could not come to Port Marriott for a wedding or anything else. A storm might blow up at any time and demolish this fat prize. He dispatched a note by Black Sam, urging Mr. Barclay to send Kezia and the preacher by return. It was not the orthodox note of an impatient sweetheart, but it said that he had moved into his new house by the Creek and found it "extream empty lacking a woman," and it suggested delicately that while his days were full, the nights were dull.

Kezia was no judge of distance. She rode for what she considered a reasonable time and then slid off and tied the brown horse to a maple tree beside the path. She had brought a couple of lamp wicks to tie about her shoes, to keep them from coming off in the snow, and she set out afoot in the big splayed tracks of Black Sam. The soft snow came almost to her knees in places and she lifted her skirts high. The path was no wider than the span of a man's arms, cut out with axes years before. She stumbled over a concealed stump from time to time, and the huckleberry bushes dragged at her cloak, but the effort warmed her. It had been cold, sitting on the horse with the wind blowing up her legs.

After a time the preacher overtook her, riding awkwardly and holding the reins in a nervous grip. The stirrups were too short for his long black-stockinged legs. He called out cheerfully as he passed, "Are you all right, Miss?" She nodded, standing aside with her back to a tree. When he disappeared ahead, with a last flutter of black shawl tassels in the wind, she picked up her skirts and went on. The path climbed and dropped monotonously over a succession of wooded ridges. Here and there in a hollow she heard water running, and the creak of frosty poles underfoot, and knew she was crossing a small stream, and once the trail ran across a wide swamp on half-rotten corduroy, wind-swept and bare of snow.

She found the horse tethered clumsily not far ahead, and the tracks of the preacher going on. She had to lead the horse to a stump so she could mount, and when she passed Mr. Mears again she called out, "Please, sir, next time leave the horse by a stump or a rock so I can get on." In his quaint old-country accent he murmured, "I'm very sorry," and gazed down at the snow. She forgot she was riding astride until she had passed him, and then she flushed, and gave the indignant horse a cut of the switch. Next time she remembered and swung her right leg back where it should be, and tucked the skirts modestly about her ankles; but young Mr. Mears looked down at the snow anyway, and after that she did not trouble to shift when she overtook him.

The ridges became steeper, and the streams roared under the ice and snow in the swales. They emerged upon the high tableland between Port Marriott and Bristol Creek, a gusty wilderness of young hardwood scrub struggling up amongst the grey snags of an old forest fire, and now that they were out of the gloomy softwoods they could see a stretch of sky. It was blue-grey and forbidding, and the wind whistling up from the invisible sea felt raw on the cheek. At their next meeting Kezia said, "It's going to snow."

She had no knowledge of the trail but she guessed that they were not much more than half way across the cape. On this high barren the track was no longer straight and clear, it meandered amongst the meagre hardwood clumps where the path-makers had not bothered to cut, and only

Black Sam's footprints really marked it for her unaccustomed eyes. The preacher nodded vaguely at her remark. The woods, like everything else about his chosen mission field, were new and very interesting, and he could not understand the alarm in her voice. He looked confidently at Black Sam's tracks.

Kezia tied the horse farther on and began her spell of walking. Her shoes were solid things, the kind of shoes Mr. Barclay invoiced as "a Common Strong sort, for women, Five Shillings"; but the snow worked into them and melted and saturated the leather. Her feet were numb every time she slid down from the horse and it took several minutes of stumbling through the snow to bring back an aching warmth. Beneath her arm she clutched the small bundle which contained all she had in the world—two flannel nightgowns, a shift of linen, three pairs of stout wool stockings—and of course Mr. Barclay's wedding gift for Mr. Hathaway.

Now as she plunged along she felt the first sting of snow on her face and, looking up, saw the stuff borne on the wind in small hard pellets that fell amongst the bare hardwoods and set up a whisper everywhere. When Mr. Mears rode up to her the snow was thick in their faces, like flung salt.

"It's a nor-easter!" she cried up to him. She knew the meaning of snow from the sea. She had been born in a fishing village down the coast.

"Yes," mumbled the preacher, and drew a fold of the shawl about his face. He disappeared. She struggled on, gasping, and after what seemed a tremendous journey came upon him standing alone and bewildered, looking off somewhere to the right.

"The horse!" he shouted. "I got off him, and before I could fasten the reins some snow fell off a branch—startled him, you know—and he ran off, over that way." He gestured with a mittened hand. "I must fetch him back," he added confusedly.

"No!" Kezia cried. "Don't you try. You'd only get lost. So would I. Oh, dear! This is awful. We'll have to go on, the best we can."

He was doubtful. The horse tracks looked very plain. But Kezia was looking at Black Sam's tracks, and tugging his arm. He gave in, and they struggled along for half an hour or so. Then the last trace of the old footprints vanished.

"What shall we do now?" the preacher asked, astonished.

"I don't know," whispered Kezia, and leaned against a dead pine stub in an attitude of weariness and indifference that dismayed him.

"We must keep moving, my dear, mustn't we? I mean, we can't stay here."

"Can't stay here," she echoed.

"Down there—a hollow, I think. I see some hemlock trees, or are they pines?—I'm never quite sure. Shelter, anyway."

"Shelter," muttered Kezia.

He took her by the hand and like a pair of lost children they dragged their steps into the deep snow of the hollow. The trees were tall spruces, a thick bunch in a ravine, where they had escaped the old fire. A stream thundered amongst them somewhere. There was no wind in this place, only the fine snow whirling thickly down between the trees like a sediment from the storm overhead.

"Look!" cried Mr. Mears. A hut loomed out of the whiteness before them, a small structure of moss-chinked logs with a roof of poles and birch-bark. It had an abandoned look. Long streamers of moss hung out between the logs. On the roof shreds of birch-bark wavered gently in the drifting snow. The door stood half open and a thin drift of snow lay along the split-pole floor. Instinctively Kezia went to the stone hearth. There were old ashes sodden with rain down the chimney and now frozen to a cake.

"Have you got flint and steel?" she asked. She saw in his eyes something dazed and forlorn. He shook his head, and she was filled with a sudden anger, not so much at him as at Mr. Barclay and that—that Hathaway, and all the rest of menkind. They ruled the world and made such a sorry mess of it. In a small fury she began to rummage about the hut.

There was a crude bed of poles and brushwood by the fireplace—brushwood so old that only a few brown needles clung to the twigs. A rough bench whittled from a pine log, with round birch sticks for legs. A broken earthenware pot in a corner. In another some ash-wood frames such as trappers used for stretching skins. Nothing else. The single window was covered with a stretched moose-bladder, cracked and dry-rotten, but it still let in some daylight while keeping out the snow.

She scooped up the snow from the floor with her mittened hands, throwing it outside, and closed the door carefully, dropping the bar into place, as if she could shut out and bar the cold in such a fashion. The air inside was frigid. Their breath hung visible in the dim light from the window. Young Mr. Mears dropped on his wet knees and began to pray in a loud voice. His face was pinched with cold and his teeth rattled as he prayed. He was a pitiable object.

"Prayers won't keep you warm," said Kezia crossly.

He looked up, amazed at the change in her. She had seemed such a meek little thing. Kezia was surprised at herself, and surprisingly she went on, "You'd far better take off those wet moccasins and stockings and shake the snow out of your clothes." She set the example, vigorously shaking out her skirts and Miss Julia's cloak, and she turned her small back on him and took off her own shoes and stockings, and pulled on dry stockings from her bundle. She threw him a pair.

"Put those on."

He looked at them and at his large feet, hopelessly.

"I'm afraid they wouldn't go on."

She tossed him one of her flannel nightgowns. "Then take off your stockings and wrap your feet and legs in that."

He obeyed, in an embarrassed silence. She rolled her eyes upward, for his modesty's sake, and saw a bundle on one of the low rafters—the late owner's bedding, stowed away from mice. She stood on the bench and pulled down three bearskins, marred with bullet holes. A rank and musty smell arose in the cold. She considered the find gravely.

"You take them," Mr. Mears said gallantly. "I shall be quite all right."

"You'll be dead by morning, and so shall I," she answered vigorously, "if you don't do what I say. We've got to roll up in these."

"Together?" he cried in horror.

"Of course! To keep each other warm. It's the only way."

She spread the skins on the floor, hair uppermost, one overlapping another, and dragged the flustered young man down beside her, clutched him in her arms, and rolled with him, over, and over again, so that they became a single shapeless heap in the corner farthest from the draft between door and chimney.

"Put your arms around me," commanded the new Kezia, and he obeyed.

"Now," she said, "you can pray. God helps those that help themselves."

He prayed aloud for a long time, and privately called upon heaven to witness the purity of his thoughts in this strange and shocking situation. He said "Amen" at last; and "Amen," echoed Kezia, piously.

They lay silent a long time, breathing on each other's necks and hearing their own hearts—poor Mr. Mears' fluttering in an agitated way, Kezia's as steady as a clock. A delicious warmth crept over them. They relaxed in each other's arms. Outside, the storm hissed in the spruce tops and set up an occasional cold moan in the cracked clay chimney. The down-swirling snow brushed softly against the bladder pane.

"I'm warm now," murmured Kezia. "Are you?"

"Yes. How long must we stay here like this?"

"Till the storm's over, of course. Tomorrow, probably. Nor'easters usually blow themselves out in a day and a night, 'specially when they come up sharp, like this one. Are you hungry?"

"No."

"Abigail—that's the black cook at Barclay's—gave me bread and cheese in a handkerchief. I've got it in my bundle. Mr. Barclay thought we ought to reach Bristol Creek by supper time, but Nabby said I must have a bite to eat on the road. She's a good kind thing, old Nabby. Sure you're not hungry?"

"Quite, I feel somewhat fatigued but not hungry."

"Then we'll eat the bread and cheese for breakfast. Have you got a watch?"

"No, I'm sorry. They cost such a lot of money. In Lady Huntingdon's Connexion we—"

"Oh well, it doesn't matter. It must be about four o'clock—the light's getting dim. Of course, the dark comes very quick in a snowstorm."

"Dark," echoed young Mr. Mears drowsily. Kezia's hair, washed last night for the wedding journey, smelled pleasant so close to his face. It reminded him of something. He went to sleep dreaming of his mother, with his face snug in the curve of Kezia's neck and shoulder, and smiling, and muttering words that Kezia could not catch. After a time she kissed his cheek. It seemed a very natural thing to do.

Soon she was dozing herself, and dreaming, too; but her dreams were full of forbidding faces—Mr. Barclay's, Mrs. Barclay's, Mr. Hathaway's; especially Mr. Hathaway's. Out of a confused darkness Mr. Hathaway's hard acquisitive gaze searched her shrinking flesh like a cold wind. Then she was shuddering by the kitchen fire at Barclay's, accepting Mr. Hathaway's courtship and wishing she was dead. In the midst of that sickening wooing she wakened sharply.

It was quite dark in the hut. Mr. Mears was breathing quietly against her throat. But there was a sound of heavy steps outside, muffled in the snow and somehow felt rather than heard. She shook the young man and he wakened with a start, clutching her convulsively.

"Sh-h-h!" she warned. "Something's moving outside." She felt him stiffen.

"Bears?" he whispered.

Silly! thought Kezia. People from the old country could think of nothing but bears in the woods. Besides, bears holed up in winter. A caribou, perhaps. More likely a moose. Caribou moved inland before this, to the wide mossy bogs up the river, away from the coastal storms. Again the sound.

"There!" hissed the preacher. Their hearts beat rapidly together.

"The door—you fastened it, didn't you?"

"Yes," she said. Suddenly she knew.

"Unroll, quick!" she cried . . . "No, not this way—your way."

They unrolled, ludicrously, and the girl scrambled up and ran across the floor in her stockinged feet, and fumbled with the rotten door-bar. Mr. Mears attempted to follow but he tripped over the night-gown still wound about his feet, and fell with a crash. He was up again in a moment, catching up the clumsy wooden bench for a weapon, his bare feet slapping on the icy floor. He tried to shoulder her aside, crying "Stand back! Leave it to me!" and waving the bench uncertainly in the darkness.

She laughed excitedly. "Silly!" she said. "It's the horse." She flung the door open. In the queer ghostly murk of a night filled with snow they beheld a large dark shape. The shape whinnied softly and thrust a long face into the doorway. Mr. Mears dropped the bench, astonished.

"He got over his fright and followed us here somehow," Kezia said, and laughed again. She put her arms about the snowy head and laid her face against it.

"Good horse! Oh, good, good horse!"

"What are you going to do?" the preacher murmured over her shoulder. After the warmth of their nest in the furs they were shivering in this icy atmosphere.

"Bring him in, of course. We can't leave him out in the storm." She caught the bridle and urged the horse inside with expert clucking sounds. The animal hesitated, but fear of the storm and a desire for shelter and company decided him. In he came, tramping ponderously on the split-pole floor. The preacher closed and barred the door.

"And now?" he asked.

"Back to the furs. Quick! It's awful cold."

Rolled in the furs once more, their arms went about each other instinctively, and the young man's face found the comfortable nook against Kezia's soft throat. But sleep was difficult after that. The horse whinnied gently from time to time, and stamped about the floor. The decayed poles crackled dangerously under his hoofs whenever he moved, and Kezia trembled, thinking he might break through and frighten himself, and flounder about till he tumbled the crazy hut about their heads. She called out to him "Steady, boy! Steady!"

It was a long night. The pole floor made its irregularities felt through the thickness of fur; and because there seemed nowhere to put their arms but about each other the flesh became cramped, and spread its protest along the bones. They were stiff and sore when the first light of morning stained the window. They unrolled and stood up thankfully, and tramped up and down the floor, threshing their arms in an effort to fight off the gripping cold. Kezia undid her bundle in a corner and brought forth Nabby's bread and cheese, and they ate it sitting together on the edge of the brushwood bed with the skins about their shoulders. Outside the snow had ceased.

"We must set off at once," the preacher said. "Mr. Hathaway will be anxious."

Kezia was silent. She did not move, and he looked at her curiously. She appeared very fresh, considering the hardships of the previous day and the night. He passed a hand over his cheeks and thought how unclean he must appear in her eyes, with this stubble on his pale face.

"Mr. Hathaway—" he began again.

"I'm not going to Mr. Hathaway," Kezia said quietly.

"But—the wedding!"

"There'll be no wedding. I don't want to marry Mr. Hathaway. 'Twas Mr. Hathaway's idea, and Mr. and Mrs. Barclay's. They wanted me to marry him."

"What will the Barclays say, my dear?"

She shrugged. "I've been their bond-girl ever since I was fourteen, but I'm not a slave like poor black Nabby, to be handed over, body and soul, whenever it suits."

"Your soul belongs to God," said Mr. Mears devoutly.

"And my body belongs to me."

He was a little shocked at this outspokenness but he said gently, "Of course. To give oneself in marriage without true affection would be an offense in the sight of heaven. But what will Mr. Hathaway say?"

"Well, to begin with, he'll ask where I spent the night, and I'll have to tell the truth. I'll have to say I bundled with you in a hut in the woods."

"Bundled?"

"A custom the people brought with them from Connecticut when they came to settle in Nova Scotia. Poor folk still do it. Sweethearts, I mean. It saves fire and candles when you're courting on a winter evening. It's harmless—they keep their clothes on, you see, like you and me—but Mr. Barclay and the other Methody[3] people are terrible set against it. Mr. Barclay got old Mr. Mings—he's the Methody preacher that died last year—to make a sermon against it. Mr. Mings said bundling was an invention of the devil."

"Then if you go back to Mr. Barclay—"

"He'll ask me the same question and I'll have to give him the same answer. I couldn't tell a lie, could I?" She turned a pair of round blue eyes and met his embarrassed gaze.

"No! No, you mustn't lie. Whatever shall we do?" he murmured in a dazed voice. Again she was silent, looking modestly down her small nose.

"It's so very strange," he floundered. "This country—there are so many things I don't know, so many things to learn. You—I—we shall have to tell the truth, of course. Doubtless I can find a place in the Lord's service somewhere else, but what about you, poor girl?"

"I heard say the people at Scrod Harbour want a preacher."

"But—the tale would follow me, wouldn't it, my dear? This—er— bundling with a young woman?"

"'Twouldn't matter if the young woman was your wife."

"Eh?" His mouth fell open. He was like an astonished child, for all his preacher's clothes and the new beard on his jaws.

"I'm a good girl," Kezia said, inspecting her foot. "I can read and write, and know all the tunes in the psalter. And—and you need someone to look after you."

He considered the truth of that. Then he murmured uncertainly, "We'd be very poor, my dear. The Connexion gives some support, but of course—"

---

[3] Methodist.

"I've always been poor," Kezia said. She sat very still but her cold fingers writhed in her lap.

He did something then that made her want to cry. He took hold of her hands and bowed his head and kissed them.

"It's strange—I don't even know your name, my dear."

"It's Kezia—Kezia Barnes."

He said quietly "You're a brave girl, Kezia Barnes, and I shall try to be a good husband to you. Shall we go?"

"Hadn't you better kiss me, first?" Kezia said faintly.

He put his lips awkwardly to hers; and then, as if the taste of her clean mouth itself provided strength and purpose, he kissed her again, and firmly. She threw her arms about his neck.

"Oh, Mr. Mears!"

How little he knew about everything! He hadn't even known enough to wear two or three pairs of stockings inside those roomy moccasins, nor to carry a pair of dry ones. Yesterday's wet stockings were lying like sticks on the frosty floor. She showed him how to knead the hard-frozen moccasins into softness, and while he worked at the stiff leather she tore up one of her wedding bed-shirts and wound the flannel strips about his legs and feet. It looked very queer when she had finished, and they both laughed.

They were chilled to the bone when they set off, Kezia on the horse and the preacher walking ahead, holding the reins. When they regained the slope where they had lost the path, Kezia said, "The sun rises somewhere between east and southeast, this time of year. Keep it on your left shoulder a while. That will take us back towards Port Marriott."

When they came to the green timber she told him to shift the sun to his left eye.

"Have you changed your mind?" he asked cheerfully. The exercise had warmed him.

"No, but the sun moves across the sky."

"Ah! What a wise little head it is!"

They came over a ridge of mixed hemlock and hardwood and looked upon a long swale full of bare hackmatacks.[4]

"Look!" the girl cried. The white slot of the axe path showed clearly in the trees at the foot of the swale, and again where it entered the dark mass of the pines beyond.

[4] A long marshy hollow with tamaracks (larches).

"Praise the Lord!" said Mr. Mears.

When at last they stood in the trail, Kezia slid down from the horse.

"No!" Mr. Mears protested.

"Ride-and-tie," she said firmly. "That's the way we came, and that's the way we'll go. Besides, I want to get warm."

He climbed up clumsily and smiled down at her.

"What shall we do when we get to Port Marriott, my dear?"

"Get the New Light preacher[5] to marry us, and catch the packet for Scrod Harbour."

He nodded and gave a pull at his broad hat brim. She thought of everything. A splendid helpmeet for the world's wilderness. He saw it all very humbly now as a dispensation of Providence.

Kezia watched him out of sight. Then, swiftly, she undid her bundle and took out the thing that had lain there (and on her conscience) through the night—the tinderbox[6]—Mr. Barclay's wedding gift to Mr. Hathaway. She flung it into the woods and walked on, skirts lifted, in the track of the horse, humming a psalm tune to the silent trees and the snow.

—1947

---

[5] A preacher associated with the Protestant New Light doctrines, which were more liberal than the Puritanism out of which the New Light movement developed. In Nova Scotia, this sect tended to emphasize individual pentecostal experience.

[6] A box containing flint, steel, and bits of dried wood, for kindling fires.

Sinclair Ross 1908–1996

Perhaps more than any other fiction we have, the work of Sinclair Ross has shaped Canadian perceptions of prairie farm and small-town life and of the grave conditions experienced by westerners in the thirties as a result of the prolonged drought and economic collapse during the Great Depression. In his slim novel As for Me and My House *(1941) and in the stories written in the 1930s and early 1940s (collected in* The Lamp at Noon and Other Stories, *1968), Ross chronicles the human consequences of the continuing struggle to bring fertility to a difficult land. In brief but evocative narratives, such as "A Field of Wheat," he displays a keen eye for the repression demanded by the intensity of farm work and for the way emotional attachments to the land disrupt human relationships.*

A Field of Wheat

It was the best crop of wheat that John had ever grown; sturdy, higher than the knee, the heads long and filling well; a still, heat-hushed mile of it, undulating into a shimmer of summer-colts and crushed horizon blue. Martha finished pulling the little patch of mustard that John had told her about at noon, stood a minute with her shoulders strained back to ease the muscles that were sore from bending, then bunched up her apron filled with the yellow-blossomed weeds and started towards the road. She walked carefully, placing her feet edgeways between the rows of wheat to avoid trampling and crushing the stalks. The road was only a few rods distant, but several times she stopped before reaching it, holding her apron with one hand and with the other stroking the blades of grain that pressed close against her skirts, luxuriant and tall. Once she looked back, her eyes shaded, across the wheat to the dark fallow land beside it. John was there; she could see the long, slow-settling plume of dust thrown up by the horses and the harrow-cart. He was a fool for work, John. This year he was farming the whole section of land without help, managing with two outfits of horses, one for the morning and one for the afternoon; six, and sometimes even seven hours a shift.

It was John who gave such allure to the wheat. She thought of him hunched black and sweaty on the harrow-cart, twelve hours a day, smothering in dust, shoulders sagged wearily beneath the glare of sun. Her fingers touched the stalks of grain again and tightened on a supple blade until they made it squeak like a mouse. A crop like this was coming to him. He had had his share of failures and set-backs, if ever a man had, twenty times over.

Martha was thirty-seven. She had clinched with the body and substance of life; had loved, borne children—a boy had died—and yet the quickest aches of life, travail, heartbrokenness, they had never wrung as the wheat wrung. For the wheat allowed no respite. Wasting and unending it was struggle, struggle against wind and insects, drought and weeds. Not an heroic struggle to give a man courage and resolve, but a frantic, unavailing one. They were only poor, taunted, driven things; it was the wheat that was invincible. They only dreaded, built bright futures; waited for the first glint of green, watched timorous and eager while it thickened, merged, and at last leaned bravely to a ripple in the wind; then followed every slip of cloud into the horizon, turned to the wheat and away again. And it died tantalizingly sometimes, slowly; there would be a cool day, a pittance of rain.

Or perhaps it lived, perhaps the rain came, June, July, even into August, hope climbing, wish-patterns painted on the future. And then one day a clench and tremble to John's hand; his voice faltering, dull. Grasshoppers perhaps, sawflies or rust; no matter, they would grovel for a while, stand back helpless, then go on again. Go on in bitterness and cowardice, because there was nothing else but going-on.

She had loved John, for these sixteen years had stood close watching while he died—slowly, tantalizingly, as the parched wheat died. He had grown unkempt, ugly, morose. His voice was gruff, contentious, never broke into the deep, strong laughter that used to make her feel she was living at the heart of things. John was gone, love was gone; there was only wheat.

She plucked a blade; her eyes travelled hungrily up and down the field. Serene now, all its sting and torment sheathed. Beautiful, more beautiful than Annabelle's poppies, than her sunsets. Theirs—all of it. Three hundred acres ready to give perhaps a little of what it had taken from her—John, his love, his lips unclenched.

Three hundred acres. Bushels, thousands of bushels, she wouldn't even try to think how many. And prices up this year. It would make him young again, lift his head, give him spirit. Maybe he would shave twice a week as he used to when they were first married, buy new clothes, believe in himself again.

She walked down the road towards the house, her steps quickening to the pace of her thoughts until the sweat clung to her face like little beads of oil. It was the children now, Joe and Annabelle: this winter perhaps they could send them to school in town and let them take music lessons, Annabelle, anyway. At a pinch Joe could wait a while; he was only eight. It wouldn't take Annabelle long to pick up her notes; already she played hymn tunes by ear on the organ. She was bright, a real little lady for manners; among town people she would learn a lot. The farm was no place to bring her up. Running wild and barefoot, what would she be like in a few years? Who would ever want to marry her but some stupid country lout?

John had never been to school himself; he knew what it meant to go through life with nothing but his muscles to depend upon; and that was it, dread that Annabelle and Joe would be handicapped as he was, that was what had darkened him, made him harsh and dour. That was why he breasted the sun and dust a frantic, dogged fool, to spare them, to help them to a life that offered more than sweat and debts. Martha knew. He was a slow, inarticulate man, but she knew. Sometimes it even vexed her, brought a wrinkle of jealousy, his anxiety about the children, his sense of responsibility where they were concerned. He never seemed to feel that he owed her anything, never worried about her future. She could sweat, grow flat-footed and shapeless, but that never bothered him.

Her thoughts were on their old, trudging way, the way they always went; but then she halted suddenly, and with her eyes across the wheat again found freshening promise in its quiet expanse. The children must come first, but she and John—mightn't there be a little of life left for them too? A man was young at thirty-nine. And if she didn't have to work so hard, if she could get some new clothes, maybe some of the creams and things that other women had. . . .

As she passed through the gate, Annabelle raced across the yard to meet her. "Do you know what Joe's done? He's taken off all his clothes and he's in the trough with Nipper!" She was a lanky girl, sunburned, barefoot, her face oval and regular, but spoiled by an expression that strained her mouth and brows into a reproachful primness. It was Martha who had taught her the expression, dinning manners and politeness into her, trying to make her better than the other girls who went to the country school. She went on, her eyes wide and aghast, "And when I told him to come out he stood right up, all bare, and I had to come away."

"Well, you tell him he'd better be out before I get there."

"But how can I tell him? He's all bare."

Then Joe ran up, nothing on but little cotton knee-pants, strings of green scum from the water-trough still sticking to his face and arms. "She's been peekin'." He pointed at Annabelle. "Nipper and me just got into the trough to get cooled off, and she wouldn't mind her own business."

"Don't you tell lies about me." Annabelle pounced on him and slapped his bare back. "You're just a dirty little pig anyway, and the horses don't want to drink after you've been in the trough."

Joe squealed, and excited by the scuffle Nipper yelped and spattered Martha with a spray of water from his coat and tail. She reached out to cuff him, missed, and then to satisfy the itch in her fingers seized Joe and boxed his ears. "You put your shirt on and then go and pick peas for supper. Hurry now both of you, and only the fat ones, mind. No, not you, Annabelle." There was something about Annabelle's face burned and countrified that changed Martha's mind "You shell the peas when he gets them. You're in the sun too much as it is."

"But I've got a poppy out and if he goes to the garden by himself he'll pick it—just for spite." Annabelle spun round, and leaving the perplexity in her voice behind her bolted for the garden. The next minute, before Martha had even reached the house, she was back again triumphant, a big fringed pink and purple poppy in her hand. Sitting down on the doorstep to admire the gaudy petals, she complained to herself, "They go so fast—the first little wind blows them all away." On her face, lengthening it, was bitten deeply the enigma of the flowers and the naked seed pods. Why did the beauty flash and the bony stalks remain?

Martha had clothes to iron and biscuits to bake for supper; Annabelle and Joe quarrelled about the peas until she shelled them herself. It was hot—heat so intense and breathless that it weighed like a solid. An ominous darkness came with it, gradual and unnoticed. All at once she turned away from the stove and stood strained, inert. The silence seemed to gather itself, hold its breath. She tried to speak to Nipper and the children, all three sprawled in a heap alongside the house, but the hush over everything was like a raised finger forbidding her.

A long immobile minute; suddenly a bewildering awareness that the light was choked; and then, muffled, still distant, but charged with resolution, climaxing the stillness, a slow, long brooding heave of thunder.

Martha darted to the door, stumbled down the step and around the corner of the house. To the west there was no sky, only a gulf of blackness, so black that the landscape seemed slipping down the neck of a funnel. Above, almost overhead, a heavy, hard-lined bank of cloud swept its way across the sun-white blue in august, impassive fury.

"Annabelle!" She wanted to scream a warning, but it was a bare whisper. In front of her the blackness split—an abrupt, unforked gash of light as if angry hands had snatched to seal the rent.

"Annabelle! Quick—inside—!" Deep in the funnel shaggy thunder rolled, emerged and shook itself, then with hurtling strides leaped up to drum and burst itself on the advancing peak of cloud.

"Joe, come back here!" He was off in pursuit of Nipper, who had broken away from Annabelle when she tried to pull him into the house. "Before I warm you!"

Her voice broke. She stared into the blackness. There it was—the hail again—the same white twisting little cloud against the black one— just as she had seen it four years ago.

She craned her neck, looking to see whether John was coming. The wheat, the acres and acres of it, green and tall, if only he had put some insurance on it. Damned mule—just work and work. No head himself and too stubborn to listen to anyone else.

There was a swift gust of wind, thunder in a splintering avalanche, the ragged hail-cloud low and close. She wheeled, with a push sent Annabelle toppling into the house, and then ran to the stable to throw open the big doors. John would turn the horses loose—surely he would. She put a brace against one of the doors, and bashed the end into the ground with her foot. Surely—but he was a fool—such a fool at times. It would be just like him to risk a runaway for the sake of getting to the end of the field.

The first big drops of rain were spitting at her before she reached the house. Quietly, breathing hard, she closed the door, numb for a minute, afraid to think or move. At the other side of the kitchen Annabelle was tussling with Joe, trying to make him go down cellar with her. Frightened a little by her mother's excitement, but not really able to grasp the imminence of danger, she was set on exploiting the event; and to be compelled to seize her little brother and carry him down cellar struck her imagination as a superb way of crystallizing for all time the dreadfulness of the storm and her own dramatic part in it. But Martha shouted at her hoarsely, "Go and get pillows. Here, Joe, quick, up on the table." She snatched him off his feet and set him on the table beside the window. "Be ready now when the hail starts, to hold the pillow tight against the glass. You, Annabelle, stay upstairs at the west window in my room."

The horses were coming, all six at a break-neck gallop, terrified by the thunder and the whip stripes John had given them when he turned them loose. They swept past the house, shaking the earth, their harness jangling tinny against the brattle[1] of thunder, and collided headlong at the stable door.

John, too; through Joe's legs Martha caught sight of his long, scarecrow shape stooped low before the rain. Distractedly, without purpose, she ran upstairs two steps at a time to Annabelle. "Don't be scared, here comes your father!" Her own voice shook, craven. "Why don't you rest your arms? It hasn't started yet."

As she spoke there was a sharp, crunching blow on the roof, its sound abruptly dead, sickening, like a weapon that has sunk deep into flesh. Wildly she shook her hands, motioning Annabelle back to the window, and started for the stairs. Again the blow came; then swiftly a stuttered dozen of them.

She reached the kitchen just as John burst in. With their eyes screwed up against the pommelling roar of the hail they stared at each other. They were deafened, pinioned, crushed. His face was a livid blank, one cheek smeared with blood where a jagged stone had struck him. Taut with fear, her throat aching, she turned away and looked through Joe's legs again. It was like a furious fountain, the stones bouncing high and clashing with those behind them. They had buried the earth, blotted out the horizon; there was nothing but their crazy spew of whiteness. She cowered away, put her hands to her ears.

Then the window broke, and Joe and the pillow tumbled off the table before the howling inrush of the storm. The stones clattered on the floor and bounded up to the ceiling, lit on the stove and threw out sizzling steam. The wind whisked pots and kettles off their hooks, tugged at and whirled the sodden curtains, crashed down a shelf of lamps and crockery. John pushed Martha and Joe into the next room and shut the door. There they found Annabelle huddled at the foot of the stairs, round-eyed, biting her nails in terror. The window she had been holding was broken too; and she had run away without closing the bedroom door, leaving a wild tide of wind upstairs to rage unchecked. It was rocking the whole house, straining at the walls. Martha ran up to close the door, and came down whimpering.

There was hail heaped on the bed, the pictures were blown off the walls and broken, the floor was swimming; the water would soak through and spoil all the ceilings.

[1] Loud clatter.

John's face quietened her. They all crowded together, silent, averting their eyes from one another. Martha wanted to cry again, but dared not. Joe, awed to calmness, kept looking furtively at the trickle of blood on his father's face. Annabelle's eyes went wide and glassy as suddenly she began to wonder about Nipper. In the excitement and terror of the storm they had all forgotten him.

When at last they could go outside they stumbled over his body on the step. He had run away from Joe before the storm started, crawled back to the house when he saw John go in, and crouching down against the door had been beaten lifeless. Martha held back the children, while John picked up the mangled heap and hurried away with it to the stable.

Neither Joe nor Annabelle cried. It was too annihilating, too much like a blow. They clung tightly to Martha's skirts, staring across the flayed yard and garden. The sun came out, sharp and brilliant on the drifts of hail. There was an icy wind that made them shiver in their thin cotton clothes. "No, it's too cold on your feet." Martha motioned them back to the step as she started towards the gate to join John. "I want to go with your father to look at the wheat. There's nothing anyway to see."

Nothing but the glitter of sun on hailstones. Nothing but their wheat crushed into little rags of muddy slime. Here and there an isolated straw standing bolt upright in headless defiance. Martha and John walked to the far end of the field. There was no sound but their shoes slipping and rattling on the pebbles of ice. Both of them wanted to speak, to break the atmosphere of calamity that hung over them, but the words they could find were too small for the sparkling serenity of wasted field. Even as waste it was indomitable. It tethered them to itself, so that they could not feel or comprehend. It had come and gone, that was all; before its tremendousness and havoc they were prostrate. They had not yet risen to cry out or protest.

It was when they were nearly back to the house that Martha started to whimper. "I can't go on any longer; I can't, John. There's no use, we've tried." With one hand she clutched him and with the other held her apron to her mouth. "It's driving me out of my mind. I'm so tired—heart-sick of it all. Can't you see?"

He laid his big hands on her shoulders. They looked at each other for a few seconds, then she dropped her head weakly against his greasy smock. Presently he roused her. "Here come Joe and Annabelle!" The pressure of his hands tightened. His bristly cheek touched her hair and forehead. "Straighten up, quick, before they see you!"

It was more of him than she had had for years. "Yes, John, I know—I'm all right now." There was a wistful little pull in her voice as if she would have had him hold her there, but hurriedly instead she began to dry her eyes with her apron. "And tell Joe you'll get him another dog."

Then he left her and she went back to the house. Mounting within her was a resolve, a bravery. It was the warming sunlight, the strength and nearness of John, a feeling of mattering, belonging. Swung far upwards by the rush and swell of recaptured life, she was suddenly as far above the desolation of the storm as a little while ago she had been abject before it. But in the house she was alone; there was no sunlight, only a cold wind through the broken window; and she crumpled again.

She tried to face the kitchen to get the floor dried and the broken lamps swept up. But it was not the kitchen; it was tomorrow, next week, next year. The going on, the waste of life, the hopelessness.

Her hands fought the broom a moment, twisting the handle as if trying to unscrew the rusted cap of a jar; then abruptly she let it fall and strode outside. All very fine for John: he'd talk about education for Joe and Annabelle, and she could worry where the clothes were to come from so that they could go clean and decent even to the country school. It made no difference that she had wanted to take out hail insurance. He was the one that looked after things. She was just his wife; it wasn't for her to open her mouth. He'd pat her shoulder and let her come back to this. They'd be brave, go on again, forget about the crop. Go on, go on—next year and the next—go on till they were both ready for the scrap-heap. But she'd had enough. This time he'd go on alone.

Not that she meant it. Not that she failed to understand what John was going through. It was just rebellion. Rebellion because their wheat was beaten to the ground, because there was this brutal, callous finish to everything she had planned, because she had will and needs and flesh, because she was alive. Rebellion, not John at all—but how rebel against a summer storm, how find the throat of a cloud?

So at a jerky little run she set off for the stable, for John. Just that she might release and spend herself, no matter against whom or what, unloose the fury that clawed within her, strike back a blow for the one that had flattened her.

The stable was quiet, only the push of hay as the horses nosed through the mangers, the lazy rub of their flanks and hips against the stall partitions; and before its quietness her anger subsided, took time for breath. She advanced slowly, almost on tiptoe, peering past the horses' rumps for a glimpse of John. To the last stall, back again. And then there was a sound different from the stable sounds. She paused.

She had not seen him the first time she passed because he was pressed against one of the horses, his head pushed into the big deep hollow of its neck and shoulder, one hand hooked by the fingers in the mane, his own shoulders drawn up and shaking. She stared, thrust out her head incredulously, moved her lips, but stood silent. John sobbing there, against the horse. It was the strangest, most frightening moment of her life. He had always been so strong and grim; had just kept on as if he couldn't feel, as if there were a bull's hide over him, and now he was beaten.

She crept away. It would be unbearable to watch his humiliation if he looked up and saw her. Joe was wandering about the yard, thinking about Nipper and disconsolately sucking hailstones, but she fled past him, head down, stricken with guilty shame as if it were she who had been caught broken and afraid. He had always been so strong, a brute at times in his strength, and now—

Now—why now that it had come to this, he might never be able to get a grip of himself again. He might not want to keep on working, not if he were really beaten. If he lost heart, if he didn't care about Joe and Annabelle any more. Weeds and pests, drought and hail—it took so much fight for a man to hold his own against them all, just to hold his own, let alone make headway.

"Look at the sky!" It was Annabelle again, breathless and ecstatic. "The far one—look how it's opened like a fan!"

Withdrawn now in the eastern sky the storm clouds towered, gold-capped and flushed in the late sunlight, high still pyramids of snowiness and shadow. And one that Annabelle pointed to, apart, the farthest away of them all, this one in bronzed slow splendour spread up mountains high to a vast, plateau-like summit.

Martha hurried inside. She started the fire again, then nailed a blanket over the broken window and lit the big brass parlour lamp—the only one the storm had spared. Her hands were quick and tense. John would need a good supper tonight. The biscuits were water-soaked, but she still had the peas. He liked peas. Lucky that they had picked them when they did. This winter they wouldn't have so much as an onion or potato.

—1968[2]

[2] Originally published in 1935 in *Queen's Quarterly*.

Sheila Watson 1909–1998

*Challenging the conservative literary milieu of the 1950s, Sheila Watson's experi-
mental and almost abstract fiction signalled a new direction in Canadian writing.
Unlike the many mid-twentieth century literary narratives that remained within
the confines of mimetic realism and that made only limited allusions to other texts,
Watson's three short stories of this period ("Brother Oedipus," "The Black Farm,"
and "Antigone") and her influential short novel* The Double Hook *(1959)
stripped away much of the action, description, and individuality of characters
that make fiction seem representative of lived experience. Her works are instead
constructed around multiple intertexts that are unified thematically. For example,
in addition to the story of Oedipus alluded to in its title, "Antigone" contains references to several other Greek myths, to the Bible, and to T.S. Eliot's* The Waste
Land; *the way Watson interweaves these with plant names recalls the fertility
themes of these intertexts.*

*At the same time, "Antigone" is located in the everyday world of the twentieth
century. Indeed, Watson, who generally avoided the personal, draws here on her own
family history. Knowing that her father, a physician, was the superintendent of the
Provincial Mental Hospital; that it was located next to the penitentiary in the
Vancouver suburb of New Westminster, B.C. (on the Fraser River); that the whole
family lived in a wing of that hospital; and that Watson was home-schooled on the
hospital grounds until she was ten allows the reader of "Antigone" to glimpse a
unifying design.*

Antigone[1]

My father ruled a kingdom on the right bank of the river. He ruled it
with a firm hand and a stout heart though he was often more troubled
than Moses, who was simply trying to bring a stubborn and moody
people under God's yoke.[2] My father ruled men who thought they were
gods or the instruments of gods or, at very least, god-afflicted and god-

---

[1] In Greek mythology, the ill-fated Oedipus unwittingly married his mother, Jocasta, Queen of
Thebes, and fathered four children—two sons (Etiocles and Polynices) and two daughters (Antigone
and Ismene)—who were also his half-siblings. After Oedipus stepped down as king, his sons killed
one another in a dispute over who should rule the kingdom. When their uncle Creon succeeded to the
throne and forbade burial rites for Polynices, Antigone defied him. Creon punished her, though she
was betrothed to his son Haemon, by interring her alive in a cave. When the prophet Tiresias subsequently convinced Creon that Antigone was following the will of the gods, he went to the cave to
release her but found she had already taken her life. Grief-stricken, Haemon attacked his father and
then killed himself; learning of this news, Creon's wife also committed suicide, leaving Creon devas-
tated and alone.
[2] The biblical books of Exodus, Leviticus, Numbers, and Deuteronomy tell the story of how Moses,
following God's instructions, led the Israelites out of Egyptian bondage and to the Promised Land—
and of how in the desert they frequently struggled against his authority.

pursued. He ruled Atlas who held up the sky, and Hermes who went on endless messages, and Helen who'd been hatched from an egg, and Pan the gardener, and Kallisto the bear, and too many others to mention by name. Yet my father had no thunderbolt, no trident, no helmet of darkness. His subjects were delivered bound into his hands. He merely watched over them as the hundred-handed ones watched over the dethroned Titans so that they wouldn't bother Hellas again.[3]

Despite the care which my father took to maintain an atmosphere of sober common sense in his whole establishment, there were occasional outbursts of self-indulgence which he could not control. For instance, I have seen Helen walking naked down the narrow cement path under the chestnut trees for no better reason, I suppose, than that the day was hot and the white flowers themselves lay naked and expectant in the sunlight. And I have seen Atlas forget the sky while he sat eating the dirt which held him up. These were things which I was not supposed to see.

If my father had been as sensible through and through as he was thought to be, he would have packed me off to boarding school when I was old enough to be disciplined by men. Instead he kept me at home with my two cousins who, except for the accident of birth, might as well have been my sisters. Today I imagine people concerned with our welfare would take such an environment into account. At the time I speak of most people thought us fortunate—especially the girls whose fathers' affairs had come to an unhappy issue. I don't like to revive old scandal and I wouldn't except to deny it; but it takes only a few impertinent newcomers in any community to force open cupboards which had been decently sealed by time. However, my father was so busy setting his kingdom to rights that he let weeds grow up in his own garden.

As I said, if my father had had all his wits about him he would have sent me to boarding school—and Antigone and Ismene too. I might have fallen in love with the headmaster's daughter and Antigone might have learned that no human being can be right always. She might have found out besides that from the seeds of eternal justice grow madder flowers than any which Pan grew in the gardens of my father's kingdom.

---

[3] That is, even though they came to his domain bound, those whom the narrator's father ruled over thought they belonged among the Greek gods on Olympus. The narrator suggests that since his father was not endowed with Zeus's power, a better parallel would be to see them analogous to the Titans, whom Zeus had banished to Tartarus (the lowest level of the Greek underworld) and his father as analogous to "the hundred-handed ones," who served to keep the Titans from getting free and interfering with Zeus's rule of Hellas (ancient Greece) and its human population.

Between the kingdom which my father ruled and the wilderness flows a river. It is this river which I am crossing now. Antigone is with me. How often can we cross the same river, Antigone asks.

Her persistence annoys me. Besides, Heraklitos made nonsense of her question years ago.[4] He saw a river too—the Inachos, the Kephissos, the Lethaios. The name doesn't matter. He said: See how quickly the water flows. However agile a man is, however nimbly he swims, or runs, or flies, the water slips away before him. See, even as he sets down his foot the water is displaced by the stream which crowds along in the shadow of its flight.

But after all, Antigone says, one must admit that it is the same kind of water. The oolichan run in it as they ran last year and the year before. The gulls cry above the same banks. Boats drift towards the Delta and circle back against the current to gather up the catch.

At any rate, I tell her, we're standing on a new bridge. We are standing so high that the smell of mud and river weeds passes under us out to the straits. The unbroken curve of the bridge protects the eye from details of river life. The bridge is foolproof as a clinic's passport to happiness.

The old bridge still spans the river, but the cat-walk with its cracks and knot-holes, with its gap between planking and hand-rail has been torn down. The centre arch still grinds open to let boats up and down the river, but a child can no longer be walked on it or swung out on it beyond the water-gauge at the very centre of the flood.

I've known men who scorned any kind of bridge, Antigone says. Men have walked into the water, she says, or, impatient, have jumped from the bridge into the river below.

But these, I say, didn't really want to cross the river. They went Persephone's way,[5] cradled in the current's arms, down the long halls under the pink feet of the gulls, under the booms and tow-lines, under the soft bellies of the fish.

Antigone looks at me.

There's no coming back, she says, if one goes far enough.

I know she's going to speak of her own misery and I won't listen. Only a god has the right to say: Look what I suffer. Only a god should say: What more ought I to have done for you that I have not done?

---

[4] Heraklitos was an ancient Greek philosopher who emphasized the way flux was the chief characteristic of the world; an aphorism attributed to him embodies that idea: "We can not step into the same river twice."

[5] To the underworld.

Once in winter, she says, a man walked over the river.

Taking advantage of nature, I remind her, since the river had never frozen before.

Yet he escaped from the penitentiary, she says. He escaped from the guards walking round the walls or standing with their guns in the sentry-boxes at the four corners of the enclosure. He escaped.

Not without risk, I say. He had to test the strength of the ice himself. Yet safer perhaps than if he had crossed by the old bridge where he might have slipped through a knot-hole or tumbled out through the railing.

He did escape, she persists, and lived forever on the far side of the river in the Alaska tea[6] and bulrushes. For where, she asks, can a man go farther than to the outermost edge of the world?

The habitable world, as I've said, is on the right bank of the river. Here is the market with its market stalls—the coops of hens, the long-tongued geese, the haltered calf, the bearded goat, the shoving pigs, and the empty bodies of cows and sheep and rabbits hanging on iron hooks. My father's kingdom provides asylum in the suburbs. Near it are the convent, the churches, and the penitentiary. Above these on the hill the cemetery looks down and on the river itself.

It is a world spread flat, tipped up into the sky so that men and women bend forward, walking as men walk when they board a ship at high tide. This is the world I feel with my feet. It is the world I see with my eyes.

I remember standing once with Antigone and Ismene in the square just outside the gates of my father's kingdom. Here from a bust set high on a cairn the stone eyes of Simon Fraser look from his stone face over the river that he found.

It is the head that counts, Ismene said.

It's no better than an urn, Antigone said, one of the urns we see when we climb to the cemetery above.

And all I could think was that I didn't want an urn, only a flat green grave with a chain about it.

A chain won't keep out the dogs, Antigone said.

But his soul could swing on it, Ismene said, like a bird blown on a branch in the wind.

And I remember Antigone's saying: The cat drags its belly on the ground and the rat sharpens its tooth in the ivy.

---

[6] A shrub, also known as Labrador tea.

I should have loved Ismene, but I didn't. It was Antigone I loved. I should have loved Ismene because, although she walked the flat world with us, she managed somehow to see it round.

The earth is an oblate spheroid, she'd say. And I knew that she saw it there before her comprehensible and whole like a tangerine spiked through and held in place while it rotated on the axis of one of Nurse's steel sock needles. The earth was a tangerine and she saw the skin peeled off and the world parcelled out into neat segments, each segment sweet and fragrant in its own skin.

It's the head that counts, she said.

In her own head she made diagrams to live by, cut and fashioned after the eternal patterns spied out by Plato as he rummaged about in the sewing basket of the gods.

I should have loved Ismene. She would live now in some prefabricated and perfect chrysolite by some paradigm which made love round and whole. She would simply live and leave destruction in the purgatorial ditches outside her own walled paradise.

Antigone is different. She sees the world flat as I do and feels it tip beneath her feet. She has walked in the market and seen the living animals penned and the dead hanging stiff on their hooks. Yet she defies what she sees with a defiance which is almost denial. Like Atlas she tries to keep the vaulted sky from crushing the flat earth. Like Hermes she brings a message that there is life if one can escape to it in the brush and bulrushes in some dim Hades beyond the river. It is defiance not belief and I tell her that this time we walk the bridge to a walled cave where we can deny death no longer.

Yet she asks her questions still. And standing there I tell her that Heraklitos has made nonsense of her question. I should have loved Ismene for she would have taught me what Plato meant when he said in all earnest that the union of the soul with the body is in no way better than dissolution.[7] I expect that she understood things which Antigone is too proud to see.

I turn away from her and flatten my elbows on the high wall of the bridge. I look back at my father's kingdom. I see the terraces rolling down from the red-brick buildings with their barred windows. I remember

---

[7] Plato taught in *The Phaedo* that, because the soul was incorruptible and would pass on to the divine world, the soul's condition was better once it left the body after death.

hands shaking the bars and hear fingers tearing up paper and stuffing it through the meshes. Diktynna, mother of nets and high leaping fear. O Artemis, mistress of wild beasts and wild men.

The inmates are beginning to come out on the screened verandahs. They pace up and down in straight lines or stand silent like figures which appear at the same time each day from some depths inside a clock.

On the upper terrace Pan the gardener is shifting sprinklers with a hooked stick. His face is shadowed by the brim of his hat. He moves as economically as an animal between the beds of lobelia and geranium. It is high noon.

Antigone has cut out a piece of sod and has scooped out a grave. The body lies in a coffin in the shade of the magnolia tree. Antigone and I are standing. Ismene is sitting between two low angled branches of the monkey puzzle tree. Her lap is filled with daisies. She slits the stem of one daisy and pulls the stem of another through it. She is making a chain for her neck and a crown for her hair.

Antigone reaches for a branch of the magnolia. It is almost beyond her grip. The buds flame above her. She stands on a small fire of daisies which smoulder in the roots of grass.

I see the magnolia buds. They brood above me, whiteness feathered on whiteness. I see Antigone's face turned to the light. I hear the living birds call to the sun. I speak private poetry to myself: Between four trumpeting angels at the four corners of the earth a bride stands before the altar in a gown as white as snow.

Yet I must have been speaking aloud because Antigone challenges me: You're mistaken. It's the winds the angels hold, the four winds of the earth.[8] After the just are taken to paradise the winds will destroy the earth. It's a funeral, she says, not a wedding.

She looks towards the building.

Someone is coming down the path from the matron's house, she says.

I notice that she has pulled one of the magnolia blossoms from the branch. I take it from her. It is streaked with brown where her hands have bruised it. The sparrow which she has decided to bury lies on its back. Its feet are clenched tight against the feathers of its breast. I put the flower in the box with it.

---

[8] The narrator's "private poetry" draws on imagery from the Book of Revelation; Antigone responds by alluding to Revelation 7:1.

Someone is coming down the path. She is wearing a blue cotton dress. Her cropped head is bent. She walks slowing carrying something in a napkin.

It's Kallisto the bear, I say. Let's hurry. What will my father say if he sees us talking to one of his patients?

If we live here with him, Antigone says, what can he expect? If he spends his life trying to tame people he can't complain if you behave as if they were tame. What would your father think, she says, if he saw us digging in the Institution lawn?

Pan comes closer. I glower at him. There's no use speaking to him. He's deaf and dumb.

Listen, I say to Antigone, my father's not unreasonable. Kallisto thinks she's a bear and he thinks he's a bear tamer, that's all. As for the lawn, I say quoting my father without conviction, a man must have order among his own if he is to keep order in the state.

Kallisto has come up to us. She is smiling and laughing to herself. She gives me her bundle.

Fish, she says.

I open the napkin.

Pink fish sandwiches, I say.

For the party, she says.

But it isn't a party, Antigone says. It's a funeral.

For the funeral breakfast, I say.

Ismene is twisting two chains of daisies into a rope. Pan has stopped pulling the sprinkler about. He is standing beside Ismene resting himself on his hooked stick. Kallisto squats down beside her. Ismene turns away, preoccupied, but she can't turn far because of Pan's legs.

Father said we never should
Play with madmen in the wood.

I look at Antigone.

It's my funeral, she says.

I go over to Ismene and gather up a handful of loose daisies from her lap. The sun reaches through the shadow of the magnolia tree.

It's my funeral, Antigone says. She moves possessively towards the body.

An ant is crawling into the bundle of sandwiches which I've put on the ground. A file of ants is marching on the sparrow's box.

I go over and drop daisies on the bird's stiff body. My voice speaks ritual words: Deliver me, O Lord, from everlasting death on this dreadful day. I tremble and am afraid.[9]

The voice of a people comforts me. I look at Antigone. I look her in the eye.

It had better be a proper funeral then, I say.

Kallisto is crouched forward on her hands. Tears are running down her cheeks and she is licking them away with her tongue.

My voice rises again: I said in the midst of my days, I shall not see—

Antigone just stands there. She looks frightened, but her eyes defy me with their assertion.

It's my funeral, she says. It's my bird. I was the one who wanted to bury it.

She is looking for a reason. She will say something which sounds eternally right.

Things have to be buried, she says. They can't be left lying around anyhow for people to see.

Birds shouldn't die, I tell her. They have wings. Cats and rats haven't wings.

Stop crying, she says to Kallisto. It's only a bird.

It has a bride's flower in its hand, Kallisto says.

We shall rise again, I mutter, but we shall not all be changed.[10]

Antigone does not seem to hear me.

Behold, I say in a voice she must hear, in a moment, in the twinkling of an eye, the trumpet shall sound.

Ismene turns to Kallisto and throws the daisy chain about her neck.

Shall a virgin forget her adorning or a bride the ornament of her breast?

Kallisto is lifting her arms towards the tree.

The bridegroom has come, she says, white as a fall of snow. He stands above me in a great ring of fire.[11]

Antigone looks at me now.

Let's cover the bird up, she says. Your father will punish us all for making a disturbance.

[9] A version of a passage from the Requiem mass: "Deliver me, O Lord, from everlasting death on that dreadful day when heaven and earth shall be shaken, when thou shalt come to judge the world by fire. I am seized with trembling and fear."
[10] See 1 Corinthians, 15:51 (Douay translation). The narrator's next speech paraphrases 1 Corinthians 15:52, which also promises the resurrection of the dead.
[11] A paraphrase of Jeremiah 2:32.

He has on his garment, Kallisto says, and on his thigh is written King of Kings.

I look at the tree. If I could see with Kallisto's eyes I wouldn't be afraid of death, or punishment, or the penitentiary guards. I wouldn't be afraid of my father's belt or his honing strap or his bedroom slipper. I wouldn't be afraid of falling into the river through a knot-hole in the bridge.

But, as I look, I see the buds falling like burning lamps and I hear the sparrow twittering in its box: Woe, woe, woe because of the three trumpets which are yet to sound.[12]

Kallisto is on her knees. She is growling like a bear. She lumbers over to the sandwiches and mauls them with her paw.

Ismene stands alone for Pan the gardener has gone.

Antigone is fitting a turf in place above the coffin. I go over and press the edge of the turf with my feet. Ismene has caught me by the hand.

Go away, Antigone says.

I see my father coming down the path. He has an attendant with him. In front of them walks Pan holding the sprinkler hook like a spear.

What are you doing here? my father asks.

Burying a bird, Antigone says.

Here? my father asks again.

Where else could I bury it? Antigone says.

My father looks at her.

This ground is public property, he says. No single person has any right to an inch of it.

I've taken six inches, Antigone says. Will you dig the bird up again?

Some of his subjects my father restrained since they were moved to throw themselves from high places or to tear one another to bits from jealousy or rage. Others who disturbed the public peace he taught to walk in the airing courts or to work in the kitchen or in the garden.

If men live at all, my father said, it is because discipline saves their life for them.

From Antigone he simply turned away.

—1979[13]

---

[12] An allusion to Revelation 8:13, a prediction of coming catalysm.
[13] Originally published in 1959 in *The Tamarack Review*.

P.K. Page b. 1916

Better known for her long career as a poet and (under her married name, P.K. Irwin) as a visual artist, P.K. Page is also the author of a number of innovative short stories. A selection of these, spanning fifty years, was published as A Kind of Fiction *in 2001. In her eighties, Page continues to produce new work, including "Ex Libris." (This Latin phrase, which literally means* from—*or out of*—books, *has long been used as a heading on bookplates followed by a name that identifies the personal library from which a book comes.)*

A highly intertextual postmodern fantasy that emerges from the world of books, "Ex Libris"—with its I-narrator who tells us that he likes doubt—challenges the boundaries of the text and questions our assumptions about identity, whether determined by the self or another, by one's family or associates, by one's environment or profession, or even by one's membership in the human species. As well, we find ourselves wondering: who is speaking to us in the opening and closing italicized frame of this story and what is the relationship between this authorial voice and the I-narrator who speaks in the rest of this tale? Indeed, what is the relationship of the voracious reader within this fiction and us, the readers who stand outside of it?

Ex Libris

PUBLICATION DATE

The book, worked on for years, was finally published the day he was born. It was waiting for him, so to speak, on 3 December. Of course he was too young to read, so his mother read it aloud to him—between feedings. The first snow was falling outside and the household was turned upside down—broken nights and nappies and—a baby! With Christmas looming. Reading it exhausted his poor dear mother and it is unlikely that he understood a word. But it was a major influence in his life, none the less. In fact, it was his life.

His mother read the four-volume edition. It has since been edited, hopefully improved, with certain episodes deleted entirely.

THE EDITED VERSION

I was born into a literate family, literate but far from wealthy—or so I thought. Why have I used "but" where I might have used "and"? As if wealth and literacy are opposed—as indeed they are, today. But surely not then. Many of my parents' friends were layabouts—bookish and broke—so that may be where the idea came from. Today a so-called education prepares you for commerce, not scholarship.

My parents were such avid readers it surprises me that I was conceived at all. I don't quite understand that "at all." Except that it must have been nip and tuck—between the end of *War and Peace* and the start of *The Brothers Karamazov*, perhaps. I think I belonged to the Russian period. It would account for my name.

I WAS AN ONLY, LONELY CHILD.

Oh, they loved me, I feel sure. But it was a literary love—nursery rhymes and Beatrix Potter, faitytales and King Arthur. I liked *Mrs. Tiggy Winkle* and *The Tale of Two Bad Mice*. I also liked Merlin a lot. Dreamed I was the young Arthur. Looked for an excalibur in every stone, thought there might be miniature excaliburs no bigger than darning needles waiting for the bright-eyed. How I polished my eyes! And I longed to be the youngest son in those fairytales where three brothers set out to win the treasure. I suppose I *was* the youngest, but as I was also the oldest and the middle one as well it seemed to cancel me out.

They didn't converse much, my parents—even with each other. "Brilliant!" my mother would say, handing a hardcover to my father who would give her a metallic glance through his reading glasses. That was about all that passed between them. And the books kept piling up. Everywhere. In my tiny bedroom a narrow path between stacks of books—read and unread—led to my cot. My nightmares—I was a fire child, and the least fever induced hallucinations—usually consisted of two people building a wall of books higher and higher. No room for windows or doors. No room for the light. Just little me in my sleepers tossing on my cot in a paper canyon.

BUT IT WAS NOT A NARROW LIFE.

I defy anyone to contradict me. What most people didn't know was that I was given to out-of-body experiences. Or, out of *my* body and into that of a dog. Always a dog. Sometimes rough-haired, sometimes smooth-haired. I can still feel the collar of rough hair, the taste of a leather leash. The sleekness of hair as smooth as skin. Even today I cannot see a dog—any dog—without feeling my being enter into its being, rejoice in its being. Feel the difference in the blood—the astonishing difference in the blood. Don't think dogs don't think—you, who have never been one. Take my word for it. They do.

Serious long thoughts about bones. A flutter of thoughts about running and jumping and the most extraordinary thoughts about smells—near-epiphanies.

You might have expected me to react against this life of books and parents and dogs' bodies and seek out other kids, tough ones maybe, or at least, jocks. But I suppose genes play a large part, especially before experience has entered the picture. I was pretty much the cat that walked by itself. But there were kids, occasionally. One little girl on our street took down her underpants in her dad's garage and I stared in a kind of bewilderment at her malformation. Thought about it a lot, actually. A sort of pink wall. It stays in my mind mixed with the smell of engine oil. Other than that my world was mainly books, just as my parents' was. I believe I was precocious. Used words like "fenestration" and "lazareto" and "recanalization." I liked to see the look on people's faces.

I don't remember being unhappy, beyond having spots. All the other manifestations of puberty and adolescence were dealt with adequately by my father. He was intelligent. And scientific in a way for all his love of literature.

AT COLLEGE I LIVED IN THE STACKS.

Where else? They were just like my bedroom, but organized. Besides, I was bred for stacks. Long legs, long arms. Good eyes that I had polished. I began by reading the As. It took me a long time to get to Auden. You can imagine. Even with *my* eyes. But when I did, I fell in love. At home I had been immersed in the classics. I knew my Shakespeare and I loved him, even tolerated wordy old Wordsworth. My parents were into modern translations of all kinds—Rilke, Lorca, Seferis. Although translations intrigued me, I wanted the real thing. Auden was it. He was like jazz. I devoured him. Funny, really, because he was dead, for pete's sake. Long dead.

There are people on earth who are dead and don't know it. Walking about. I read it in a book. Are the dead—Auden, for instance—those who have returned, believing themselves still alive? Slow learners, you might say. Or are they the living—my Mum and Dad? Me? It makes me uneasy. How can I prove to myself I am living?

> Dead: having the appearance of death; lacking power to move, feel, or respond; very tired; incapable of being stirred emotionally or intellectually; grown cold; no longer producing or functioning; no longer having interest, relevance or significance.

What if I answer "yes" to those definitions—am I dead, then? Dead before achieving anything. Unlike Auden. Alack, alas. Alas, alack.

BUT BLESS MY LONG ARMS AND LEGS.

I was made for basketball. My game drove spectators wild. In a team I moved slow motion, or so it appeared. People who watched said they were caught in two time streams. It affected the circuits in their brains.

> *Ivor moves like slow honey. All the other guys are like bees.*

I didn't know what they meant. I was just playing the game. But as they liked it, I was happy for them. At first I had played unselfconsciously. Then the shouts of the crowd reached me and I began to love those shouts. Soon I played for the shouts alone. Became aware of every move I made. It wasn't that I was actually slow but my long arms and legs made me look slow. I took one step where others took two or three. Then I developed a taste for slowness and began to test just how slowly I could pass and run without actually stopping. A slow dribble drove the crowd mad. It was as if all the clocks had run down, they told me. Dreamy. For me *and* the spectators. Our team was a sensation. We won every game.

We were national champions when a scout got to me and I found myself on an all-black team. The Tall Boys. We matched, The Tall Boys and I. Arms and legs long. Polished eyes. There was no difference in our timing. We were all slow honey. But I was the only white. It was the first time such a thing had happened in the annals of the sport. I was called "nigger-lover." I was called "piss-ass." But the crowd loved me and we took all the games. Slow and dreamy. Even my parents raised their eyes from their books and looked at me with surprise. Between *War and Peace* and *The Brothers* . . . they had conceived a star.

The year we took the world I married Esmeralda.

My black orchid, I called her.

A cliché, I know. Long arms and long legs. Eyes polished. Like me. Black and white, white and black, our languorous, violent love. Nothing had prepared me for Esmeralda. To love her was my career. I embraced it. My body, her body—I no longer knew which was which. I loved her as I loved myself.

I am not proud of this blatant declaration of self-love. It makes me uneasy. *We love ourselves first, our friends second, God last. It should be the reverse.* Where had I read *that*? Interesting that friends remain in the middle, either way. If I were to say, I loved myself as I loved Esmeralda, would anything change? The idea is provocative. And let me provoke myself further, blaspheme, perhaps: I loved her as I love God.

An observant reader will notice the tenses: I loved her as I love God. Do I not love her still? I do.

But I cannot go into that yet.

I was wealthy, of course, I had amassed a fortune. Basketball became a thing of the past. I didn't even watch the games. I might have coached, I suppose, and without Esmeralda, I probably would have. But with Esmeralda there, in my arms as I wakened—long arms, long legs—what choice did I have? We made love. It was my vocation; my avocation.

On Sundays we went to her church and sang. Holy Saints. She was another Kathleen Battle.[1] And the whole congregation sang too. Lordy! Lordy! There had been nothing like that in my literary childhood. Nothing like that at all. No room for music among all the words. And now I was swamped by it, overwhelmed, in fact. What was this art that demanded your entire lung power—took your breath and gave it back, took your breath and gave it back. It was more like a kind of sport. Writing, painting, sculpture required no special breathing. Only dance. And music. My voice came out of some hidden vault. "They crucified my Lord."

---

[1] Black American soprano. Regarded as one of the greatest opera singers of the twentieth century, Battle expanded her repertoire beyond classical music to take in jazz, spirituals (including "Were You There When They Crucified My Lord?"), and other musical forms.

I WENT TO SEE MY PARENTS FROM TIME TO TIME.

Their world didn't change. They had neither computer nor TV. The house was solid with books—a book meatloaf. They couldn't bring themselves to get rid of any of them. Easier they said, to get rid of furniture. They sold the chesterfield, all but two armchairs, and the spare bed. As a concession to me, they read Tony Morrison. Living through books, as they did, with no time for life, nothing had readied them for *Beloved*. Surely, I thought, in all that reading, they would have learned something about racism. But, "White people don't behave like that," they said, a questioning tone in their voices, as if asking me to agree. I replied that white people do. All people do. We are half animal and half angel. A very difficult mix. They could only shake their heads—my father's, now, a shock of grey, my mother's turning white at the temples. They were old.

AS FOR ME....

I was putting on weight—thickening through the waist. Even my once so muscular thighs were becoming flabby.

One morning Esmeralda wakened, and instead of turning to me lazy and drowsy as usual, she sprang out of bed and turned on the shower. The scent of her gel, heavy as gardenias, filled the air. Oh, Proust, do I not know what you mean?[2] That smell would come to conjure up my whole life with Esmeralda.

"What's up?" I asked, unbelieving.

"I've got a job," she said. "Modelling."

"Modelling! A job! What the heck? We don't need the money, honey."

"Somebody in this family's got to work. It's only right."

The logic of it was absurd. I saw, in a flash, that I didn't know Esmeralda—how her mind worked, what her thoughts were. It was terrifying. I went into the bathroom and pulled her beautiful black naked body to me. "Honey," I said. "Don't leave me. We've got to get to know each other."

---

[2] A reference to the famous scene in the opening section of Marcel Proust's *Remembrance of Things Past* (also translated as *In Search of Lost Time*), in which a world of forgotten experience is brought back to the narrator by the tastes of a small cake called a *petit madeleine*.

"No talk of leaving," Esmeralda said. "I just need to find myself. I don't want to be a sex object all my life."

A sex object! Esmeralda? "You are my love, my life," I said. There were tears in my eyes.

"*Yours,*" she said. "That's the whole point."

IF I WERE TO TELL YOU MY WORLD FELL APART. . . .

It did. Morning to night, my life was a vacuum. Her hatbox, her cosmetic case, her beautiful long arms and legs, her polished eyes. She had no place left in her heady, hectic life for her lover. With those looks, with that voice, she was destined for stardom and she knew it. Something any fool could see.

And now I was any fool. Every fool. Why had I not seen it before?

I took to pacing back and forth like an Alzheimer's patient. As if the very action of my feet could heal my heart. I saw Esmeralda less and less. Photo shoots, fashion shows, beauty parlours. New York, Paris, Rome, Singapore. She bought a pale Afghan hound—her perfect match, even as I had been—who walked at the end of a golden leash. They modelled together. Sometimes she phoned, sometimes she was too busy. Lonely, I sought her on TV. She was on shampoo ads—her long shiny black hair lifted by a fan. Tampons, pantyhose, face cream. Sometimes because of the lighting, the camera angle, the hairdo, I barely knew her. Recognized her just as the image faded, and my heart broke.

I spent more and more time in front of TV. Took to drinking beer. Alone.

When she came home with the dog after months abroad, I was waiting for her, avid for her. And the dog. I had begun to see the dog as me—or me as the dog. Which? Those long legs, that pale fur. I wondered if that was why she bought it.

She was astonishing. I could hardly believe her. Always dazzling, she was now perfect, with the dog on a long golden leash. I wanted to fling my arms around her but as soon as my eyes fell on the dog I had an out-of-body experience.

I was that dog. And hostile. I strained at the leash. "Heel, Holly, heel," she said firmly, and yanked my collar. It was a choke-leash and she almost strangled me. "This is Ivor. Nice Ivor," she said, and patted me. But Holly hated "nice Ivor" and lunged again. *And I was Holly. Holly was me.*

It lasted no longer than a minute or so. I don't think Esmeralda even noticed but it unnerved me. Of all the dogs I had ever been, I had never been a dog that disliked me.

"He usually loves people," Esmeralda said and I felt accusation in her tone. Then her eyes looked me over. My thick waistline had become a paunch. It was not disguised by the new Armani jacket I had bought especially for her. With my unmanicured hands I reached out to her. "Don't touch me!" she said in a sharp voice I had not heard her use before. And Holly lunged again.

IN SHORT, HER HOMECOMING WAS A DISASTER.

We never made love. That dog wouldn't let us. And the telephone, the fax machine, the e-mails all interfered. A steady stream of beauticians came to the house. She worked out.

"I have to tell you," she said, between appointments, "I'm leaving for Hollywood."

"Hollywood!"

"Yep. I'm going to play Josephine Baker. They tell me I'm made for it."

"Josephine Baker!" I could only repeat what she said. I had no words of my own, apparently. "Josephine Baker," I said again.

"The great jazz singer!" She was impatient.

"Can you sing jazz?"

"I can sing anything, honey. Just you watch."

I didn't know this Esmeralda. I had never seen this confident metallic woman in my life before. Where had she come from? "Esmeralda . . ." I pleaded. But she was on the phone again and that goddam dog was between us, always between us. A canine wall.

BEFORE I KNEW IT SHE HAD GONE.

I looked at the desolation of the house. Garment bags, tissue paper, cardboard boxes. Our bathroom full of lotions and creams and gels. There was barely room for my razor.

WHEN THE TELEPHONE RANG I DIDN'T ANSWER.

I was not going to be her appointments secretary. Let it ring. She isn't here. Let it go on ringing. But the persistent bell in the empty house was intolerable. Just to shut it up, I lifted the receiver. It was my father's voice.

"Ivor, I've been trying to reach you. Your mother is dying."

My head was so full of Esmeralda I couldn't take it in.

"Ivor, did you hear me?"

"Mum?" I said. Mum couldn't die. He must be wrong.

"She had a stroke and they say. . . . Oh, son, can you not come home?"

AND SO I WENT.

Threw my razor into a bag along with my pyjamas and a change of shirt and shorts and caught the first plane out.

I hardly knew my father. He was a stick of skin. Small, grey, broken. He led me through walls of books, up the dusty stairs and into their bedroom. There was barely room for both of us beside the bed. My mother lay, her right side paralyzed. Her face twisted. Unrecognizable. But on the floor beside her bed, open and face down, as if she had put it there before turning off the light, lay Emily Dickinson's poems.

"She wouldn't have been able to read," I said, looking at the book and then at her.

"What? What's that you said?" Perhaps my father was deaf.

"Left hemisphere," I continued, not believing my words, my mother, the crypt of books we stood in.

"Speak to her, son," my father said,

I didn't know what to say. Then, "It's Ivor, Mum. Ivor." My voice sounded like a kid's.

"Mum. Mum!" Her left eyelid flickered. "Oh, Mum!" But her face closed again into that contorted mask.

I thought my chest would break. I had to get out of there. I pushed past my father, past all those piles of books, looking for a place to sit down. The house smelled like an antiquarian bookstore. At last, in the kitchen, I found a chair. My chest broke. I began to sob. I sobbed for my mother, for my father, for Esmeralda. And I sobbed for myself.

OH, I LOOKED AFTER WHAT HAD TO BE DONE.

Hired a nurse. Cleared a wider passageway to the bedroom between the books. Got some order in the kitchen. Bought some eggs. And settled in to wait. There is a lot of waiting in a house of death. A lot of standing, hands hanging helpless. Useless rearranging of sheets and pillows. "A little jelly, Mum?" "Some mango ice cream?"

I had picked up the Emily Dickinson beside her bed and now I opened it. It had been read and re-read, marked in pencil with stars, asterisks, underlinings. Poems about Death.

> Because I could not stop for Death
> He kindly stopped for me.

Did she suspect, in her pell-mell race through literature, that He was about to stop? Probably not. More likely it was the poetry she loved. The turn of phrase. Dickinson's unique turn of phrase.

When I began basketball I forgot books. Really didn't miss them. And then Esmeralda wiped my tapes completely. Now, suddenly, I longed for literature. A spring of fresh water gushed as I read. Plants bloomed. I read hungrily.

> The manner of the Children—
> Who weary of the Day—
> Themself—the weary Plaything
> They cannot put away—

How did she know all that—that spinster Emily in her white house behind white curtains? How could she possibly know what I felt? A weary Plaything. Weary to death.

I was astonished by my grief. This old lady who had conceived me between books, given birth to me between books and read to me, sometimes at great cost to herself, would read to me no more. But as her farewell present she gave me Emily Dickinson.

MY FATHER AND I WERE THE ONLY MOURNERS.

My father a little stick figure clutching a bunch of summer flowers. Delphiniums, daisies, roses—yellow and pink.

We returned, drained, from the crematorium to that comfortless warehouse he called home. With the nurse gone, my mother gone, the place was dust and debris. We hardly spoke, my father and I. I poured us a whisky. Later, I scrambled us some eggs. Then we crashed.

What to do now? I thought, as I wakened. The books towered above and around me, stacked helter-skelter. I heard my father moving about downstairs. I thought of Esmeralda, beautiful Esmeralda in Hollywood with that goddam dog. And I wondered where I—the star, the guy with the beautiful wife—had vanished to? The whole tone of my life had altered. No longer a figure to be envied, I was a deserted husband with a father bereft, in a house of despair. Psychologists have a name for it: mid-life crisis, they call it. Damn them.

THEN MY FATHER DIED.

I found myself the sole inheritor of a surprising amount of money, an old house in a run-down neighbourhood, and thousands of books. My first thought was to call in a second-hand bookseller and get rid of them all. But I moved slowly, hobbled by inertia. Esmeralda's absence, the death of both parents—the enormity of my inheritance. . . .

But little by little, book by book, I got sucked into that dust-filled vortex. A most eclectic library—if a jumble could be graced by such a name. I was interested to see that the largest single category was poetry.

Art books were perhaps second—the surrealists from Bosch to Ernst and Carrington—and the whole history of art. Folktales, science fiction: Verne and H.G. Wells and Abbott's *Flatland* as well as Clarke and Sturgeon and the inner space fiction of Lessing, plus people I had never heard of. Their astonishing thoughts about time and space turned me upside down. The literature of ideas. I had read nothing like it in contemporary fiction—a genre noticeably absent in my parents' collection, as far as I could see. "If you don't read the bestsellers when they first come out," my father had said, "you don't need to read them at all." Perhaps he was right.

Had my parents absorbed this wealth of ideas, I wondered? And if so, what did it profit them? Why had I not spent more time at home, asking them questions, instead of goofing off with Esmeralda? But that was what I thought with Esmeralda *gone*. What would I have thought if she had suddenly appeared?

DID I SAY I LOVED HER?

I do.

BOOKS, BOOKS, BOOKS.

They became my life, even as they had been my parents' life. Lethargy and inertia were things of the past. I was on fire.

I found an unemployed librarian and together we began the interminable work of sorting and cataloguing. I installed a computer and the software required for itemizing what, at times, felt like the contents of the city dump. We wore masks against the dust of decades. We found treasures and learned skills I could not have dreamed of. And although, originally, I thought we should construct a special building for the books, I soon discovered that the house was well enough built for us to renovate. So I hired carpenters and designers. Shelves rose in all the rooms. Floors were reinforced. Temperature and humidity controls installed.

When not working on the project, I was reading. I became a vessel for all that print to pour into. And the hallucination of my childhood—of book building upon book and blocking the light—was now reversed, and book building upon book was letting the light *in*. I had had no idea how many combinations and computations of words there were, no idea of the extent of human thought—psychological, philosophical, spiritual. I began to sense space/time, stretching back to the beginnings of language and beyond, and forward beyond my imagination's reach. The world that had seemed large enough to me when I had Esmeralda—a bed-sized world—was now, without her, immense. A vast glass-house, light-filled. A night sky by day, if one can conceive of such a thing.

I had calls from her occasionally. The filming was going well. She was "a natural," they told her. Everyone loved Holly. And what did I think about a divorce?

And then it came to me. A vast glass-house was exactly what I wanted—an atrium with a glass ceiling—UV glass, of course—around which the books. . . . How my thoughts raced. The property next door was for sale. I snapped it up. And hired an architect, the best I could find. To hell with the cost. I wanted the space to reflect the contents. A glass bomb.

THE WORK WAS A WONDER.

Even before it was finished—half-finished—librarians and architects beat a path, as they say. The architects were stunned by the cantilevered extension which took in the property next door. And the light pouring in. The librarians didn't quite know why I featured Auden so prominently. Not only did I include his complete works, but all books with references to him—*Evening Light at Sandover*, for example, in which he comes back as a shade, conjured by Merrill. And the David Hockney drawing, blown up, life size, of his raddled face—the only face I know with actual runnels in it. I told them I planned to do the same with certain other authors—chosen in a somewhat idiosyncratic manner, or seemingly so. Persian miniatures for Hakim Sanai, perhaps, or elegantly handset, a quotation from him: "The human's progress is that of one who has been given a sealed book written before he was born." The Modigliani drawing of Akmatova for her section, of course. What would I use for Immanuel Velikovsky and his *Worlds in Collision*?[3] Something from an observatory—the heavens blazing. Or I could hire an artist, for

---

[3] This 1950 book argued—not on the basis of scientific inference or observation but from Velikovsky's interpretative synthesis of ancient sacred texts and myths—that in early human history the planet Jupiter had expelled a large comet, which, before becoming the contemporary planet Venus, had grazed earth. Although scientists unanimously rejected this theory, these imaginative arguments were initially received with enthusiasm by some of the American literati.

pete's sake. Why not? And why Velikovsky, come to that? Was he one of my faves? Actually no. He may have been a nut. But that Immanuel shook things up—questioned all those scientists locked in their certainties. I like doubt cast on conventional wisdom. I guess I like doubt a lot.

The librarians shook their serious heads—this was not according to the book, ha, ha—but they took notes.

MEANWHILE

The neighbourhood altered. Old houses became boutiques and delis. Were remodelled for the wealthy young. What a change-about. And at its centre, at its very heart—the library. It shone.

A PHENOMENON, NOT A FOLLY.

My parents' obsession, now an idiosyncratic collection of paintings and books, was written up in the press, in architectural journals, in librarians' bulletins. It created world-wide attention.

And that attention generated work—more than our small staff could handle. We appointed a Board, a Chairman of the Board—me. We hired experts. And we had an official opening where speeches were made and ribbons cut. There had never been such an event. Artists and writers, bureaucrats of culture—celebrities of all kinds—fought to attend.

Esmeralda swanned in—a creature from another planet. All jewels and line. "Where is Holly?" I asked. Her beautiful eyes swam with tears. "Dead," she said. "Run over." I put my arm around her. "Ivor," she said, "you are like a brother," and for the briefest moment her glittering body relaxed against me. But then she was on stage again, camera men crowding, flashbulbs popping. And before I knew it she was gone.

DO I STILL LOVE HER?

I do.

I HAD BUILT MY SHINING PALACE.

Out of tears, perhaps. It was dedicated to the memory of my parents, to Emily Dickinson, and W.H. Auden. Their names were engraved on a tablet in the foyer. The foyer that had once been our small book-jammed hall.

The days after the opening were crammed with appointments—the Ministry of Culture, the International Commission on the Arts. No time to read. Once again, no time to read. Exhausted, I dashed from interviews to meetings, from hotels to boardrooms.

BECAUSE I COULD NOT STOP FOR DEATH

I was late for my last appointment of the day—a TV appearance. It was rush hour. I stood on the curb waiting for the light. And then I saw a dog, a terrified dog, running in and out between the cars. In a flash I was out of my body and into that dog.

HE STOOD ON THE CURB WAITING FOR THE LIGHT.

He had no idea he was approaching death. But as he entered the body of the dog, he suddenly remembered what his mother had read him when he lay in her arms—a babe, newborn—tiny, squalling, wanting to be fed.

—2002[4]

---

[4] Published in the magazine *Border Crossings* and subsequently reprinted in *Best Canadian Stories 02* (ed. Douglas Glover).

Mavis Gallant b. 1922

Although she grew up in Montreal, Mavis Gallant has spent most of her adult life in Paris, where she established herself as one of the leading writers of the short story. The setting of "My Heart Is Broken," the northern Canadian bush, is not typical of Gallant's fiction: her narratives, often international in locale, more often take place in urban settings. This story does, however, develop many of her recurring themes: the difficulty of communication, disappointments brought on by misguided expectations, and the heartbreaks that result from the inability to bridge differences—those between cultures, those that separate the generations, and those that divide men and women. As well, the almost gothic setting in "My Heart Is Broken," with its isolating and claustrophobic qualities, intensifies the sense of displacement that is often at the centre of Gallant's fiction.

My Heart Is Broken

"When that Jean Harlow died,"[1] Mrs. Thompson said to Jeannie, "I was on the 83 streetcar with a big, heavy paper parcel in my arms. I hadn't been married for very long, and when I used to visit my mother she'd give me a lot of canned stuff and preserves. I was standing up in the streetcar because nobody'd given me a seat. All the men were unemployed in those days, and they just sat down wherever they happened to be. You wouldn't remember what Montreal was like then. *You* weren't even on earth. To resume what I was saying to you, one of these men sitting down had an American paper—the *Daily News*, I guess it was—and I was sort of leaning over him, and I saw in big print 'JEAN HARLOW DEAD.' You can believe me or not, just as you want to, but that was the most terrible shock I ever had in my life. I never got over it."

Jeannie had nothing to say to that. She lay flat on her back across the bed, with her head toward Mrs. Thompson and her heels just touching the crate that did as a bedside table. Balanced on her flat stomach was an open bottle of coral-pink Cutex nail polish. She held her hands up over her head and with some difficulty applied the brush to the nails of her right hand. Her legs were brown and thin. She wore nothing but shorts and one of her husband's shirts. Her feet were bare.

---

[1] Jean Harlow, an early and widely popular Hollywood sex symbol known as "the Blonde Bombshell," died in 1937 when she was only twenty-six years old.

Mrs. Thompson was the wife of the paymaster in a road-construction camp in northern Quebec. Jeannie's husband was an engineer working on the same project. The road was being pushed through country where nothing had existed until now except rocks and lakes and muskeg. The camp was established between a wild lake and the line of raw dirt that was the road. There were no towns between the camp and the railway spur, sixty miles distant.

Mrs. Thompson, a good deal older than Jeannie, had become her best friend. She was a nice, plain, fat, consoling sort of person, with varicosed legs, shoes unlaced and slit for comfort, blue flannel dressing gown worn at all hours, pudding-bowl haircut, and coarse gray hair. She might have been Jeannie's own mother, or her Auntie Pearl. She rocked her fat self in the rocking chair and went on with what she had to say: "What I was starting off to tell you is you remind me of her, of Jean Harlow. You've got the same teeny mouth, Jeannie, and I think your hair was a whole lot prettier before you started fooling around with it. That peroxide's no good. It splits the ends. I know you're going to tell me it isn't peroxide but something more modern, but the result is the same."

Vern's shirt was spotted with coral-pink that had dropped off the brush. Vern wouldn't mind; at least, he wouldn't say that he minded. If he hadn't objected to anything Jeannie did until now, he wouldn't start off by complaining about a shirt. The campsite outside the uncurtained window was silent and dark. The waning moon would not appear until dawn. A passage of thought made Mrs. Thompson say, "Winter soon."

Jeannie moved sharply and caught the bottle of polish before it spilled. Mrs. Thompson was crazy; it wasn't even September.

"Pretty soon," Mrs. Thompson admitted. "Pretty soon. That's a long season up here, but I'm one person doesn't complain. I've been up here or around here every winter of my married life, except for that one winter Pops was occupying Germany."

"I've been up here seventy-two days," said Jeannie, in her soft voice. "Tomorrow makes seventy-three."

"Is that right?" said Mrs. Thompson, jerking the rocker forward, suddenly snappish. "Is that a fact? Well who asked you to come up here? Who asked you to come and start counting days like you was in some kind of jail? When you got married to Vern, you must of known where he'd be taking you. He told you, didn't he, that he liked road jobs, construction jobs, and that? Did he tell you, or didn't he?"

"Oh, he told me," said Jeannie.

"You know what, Jeannie?" said Mrs. Thompson. "If you'd of just listened to me, none of this would have happened. I told you that first day, the day you arrived here in your high-heeled shoes, I said, 'I know this cabin doesn't look much, but all the married men have the same sort of place.' You remember I said that? I said, 'You just get some curtains up and some carpets down and it'll be home! I took you over and showed you my place and you said you'd never seen anything so lovely."

"I meant it," said Jeannie. "Your cabin is just lovely. I don't know why, but I never managed to make this place look like yours."

Mrs. Thompson said, "That's plain enough." She looked at the cold grease spattered behind the stove, and the rag of towel over by the sink. "It's partly the experience," she said kindly. She and her husband knew exactly what to take with them when they went on a job, they had been doing it for so many years. They brought boxes for artificial flowers, a brass door knocker, a portable bar decorated with sea shells, a cardboard fireplace that looked real, and an electric fire that sent waves of light rippling over the ceiling and walls. A concealed gramophone played the records they loved and cherished—the good old tunes. They had comic records that dated back to the year 1, and sad soprano records about shipwrecks and broken promises and babies' graves. The first time Jeannie heard one of the funny records, she was scared to death. She was paying a formal call, sitting straight in her chair, with her skirt pulled around her knees. Vern and Pops Thompson were talking about the Army.

"I wish to God I was back," said old Pops.

"Don't I?" said Vern. He was fifteen years older than Jeannie and had been through a lot.

At first there were only scratching and whispering noises, and then a mosquito orchestra started to play, and a dwarf's voice came into the room. "Little Johnnie Green, little Sallie Brown," squealed the dwarf, higher and faster than any human ever could. "Spooning in the park with the grass all around."

"Where is he?" Jeannie cried, while the Thompsons screamed with laughter and Vern smiled. The dwarf sang on: "And each little bird in the treetop high/Sang 'Oh you kid!' and winked his eye."

It was a record that had belonged to Pops Thompson's mother. He had been laughing at it all his life. The Thompsons loved living up north and didn't miss cities or company. Their cabin smelled of cocoa and toast. Over their beds were oval photographs of each other as children, and they had some Teddy bears and about a dozen dolls.

Jeannie capped the bottle of polish, taking care not to press it against her wet nails. She sat up with a single movement and set the bottle down on the bedside crate. Then she turned to face Mrs. Thompson. She sat cross-legged, with her hands outspread before her. Her face was serene.

"Not an ounce of fat on you," said Mrs. Thompson. "You know something? I'm sorry you're going. I really am. Tomorrow you'll be gone. You know that, don't you? You've been counting days, but you won't have to any more. I guess Vern'll take you back to Montreal. What do you think?"

Jeannie dropped her gaze, and began smoothing wrinkles on the bedspread. She muttered something Mrs. Thompson could not understand.

"Tomorrow you'll be gone," Mrs. Thompson continued. "I know it for a fact. Vern is at this moment getting his pay, and borrowing a jeep from Mr. Sherman, and a Polack driver to take you to the train. He sure is loyal to you. You know what I heard Mr. Sherman say? He said to Vern, 'If you want to send her off, Vern, you can always stay,' and Vern said, 'I can't very well do that, Mr. Sherman.' And Mr. Sherman said, 'This is the second time you've had to leave a job on account of her, isn't it?,' and then Mr. Sherman said, 'In my opinion, no man by his own self can rape a girl, so there were either two men or else she's invented the whole story.' Then he said, 'Vern, you're either a saint or a damn fool.' That was all I heard. I came straight over here, Jeannie, because I thought you might be needing me." Mrs. Thompson waited to hear she was needed. She stopped rocking and sat with her feet flat and wide apart. She struck her knees with her open palms and cried, "I *told* you to keep away from the men. I told you it would make trouble, all that being cute and dancing around, I said to you, I remember saying it, I said nothing makes trouble faster in a place like this than a grown woman behaving like a little girl. Don't you remember?"

"I only went out for a walk," said Jeannie. "Nobody'll believe me, but that's all. I went down the road for a walk."

"In high heels?" said Mrs. Thompson. "With a purse in your arm, and a hat on your head? You don't go taking a walk in the bush that way. There's no place to walk to. Where'd you think you were going? I could smell Evening in Paris a quarter mile away."

"There's no place to go," said Jeannie, "but what else is there to do? I just felt like dressing up and going out."

"You could have cleaned up your home a bit," said Mrs. Thompson. "There was always that to do. Just look at that sink. That basket of ironing's been under the bed since July. I know it gets boring around here, but you had the best of it. You had the summer. In winter it gets dark around three o'clock. Then the wives have a right to go crazy. I knew one used to sleep the clock around. When her Nembutal ran out, she took about a hundred aspirin. I knew another learned to distill her own liquor, just to kill time. Sometimes the men get so's they don't like the life, and that's death for the wives. But here you had a nice summer, and Vern liked the life."

"He likes it better than anything," said Jeannie. "He liked the Army, but this was his favorite life after that."

"There," said Mrs. Thompson. "You had every reason to be happy. What'd you do if he sent you off alone, now, like Mr. Sherman advised? You'd be alone and you'd have to work. Women don't know when they're well off. Here you've got a good, sensible husband working for you and you don't appreciate it. You have to go and do a terrible thing."

"I only went for a walk," said Jeannie. "That's all I did."

"It's possible," said Mrs. Thompson, "but it's a terrible thing. It's about the worst thing that's ever happened around here. I don't know why you let it happen. A woman can always defend what's precious, even if she's attacked. I hope you remembered to think about bacteria."

"What d'you mean?"

"I mean Javel,[2] or something."

Jeannie looked uncomprehending and then shook her head.

"I wonder what it must be like," said Mrs. Thompson after a time, looking at the dark window. "I mean, think of Berlin and them Russians and all. Think of some disgusting fellow you don't know. Never said hello to, even. Some girls ask for it, though. You can't always blame the man. The man loses his job, his wife if he's got one, everything, all because of a silly girl."

Jeannie frowned, absently. She pressed her nails together, testing the polish. She licked her lips and said, "I was more beaten up, Mrs. Thompson. It wasn't exactly what you think. It was only afterwards I thought to myself, Why, I was raped and everything."

Mrs. Thompson gasped, hearing the word from Jeannie. She said, "Have you got any marks?"

"On my arms. That's why I'm wearing this shirt. The first thing I did was change my clothes."

[2] Also marketed as Javex: a liquid bleach.

Mrs. Thompson thought this over, and went on to another thing: "Do you ever think about your mother?"

"Sure."

"Do you pray? If this goes on at nineteen—"

"I'm twenty."

"—what'll you be by the time you're thirty? You've already got a terrible, terrible memory to haunt you all your life."

"I already can't remember it," said Jeannie. "Afterwards I started walking back to camp, but I was walking the wrong way. I met Mr. Sherman. The back of his car was full of coffee, flour, all that. I guess he'd been picking up supplies. He said, 'Well, get in.' He didn't ask any questions at first. I couldn't talk anyway."

"Shock," said Mrs. Thompson wisely.

"You know, I'd have to see it happening to know what happened. All I remember is that first we were only talking . . ."

"You and Mr. Sherman?"

"No, no, before. When I was taking my walk."

"Don't say who it was," said Mrs. Thompson. "We don't any of us need to know."

"We were just talking, and he got sore all of a sudden and grabbed my arm."

"Don't say the name!" Mrs. Thompson cried.

"Like when I was little, there was this Lana Turner movie. She had two twins. She was just there and then a nurse brought her in the two twins. I hadn't been married or anything, and I didn't know anything, and I used to think if I just kept on seeing the movie I'd know how she got the two twins, you know, and I went, oh, I must have seen it six times, the movie, but in the end I never knew any more. They just brought her the two twins."

Mrs. Thompson sat quite still, trying to make sense of this. "Taking advantage of a woman is a criminal offense," she observed. "I heard Mr. Sherman say another thing, Jeannie. He said, 'If your wife wants to press a charge and talk to some lawyer, let me tell you,' he said, 'you'll never work again anywhere,' he said. Vern said, 'I know that, Mr. Sherman.' And Mr. Sherman said, 'Let me tell you, if any reporters or any investigators start coming around here, they'll get their . . . they'll never . . .' Oh, he was mad. And Vern said, 'I came over to tell you I was quitting, Mr. Sherman.'" Mrs. Thompson had been acting this with spirit, using a quiet voice when she spoke for Vern and a blustering tone for Mr. Sherman. In her own voice, she said, "If you're wondering how I came to hear all this, I was strolling by Mr. Sherman's office window— his bungalow, that is. I had Maureen out in her pram." Maureen was the Thompsons' youngest doll.

Jeannie might not have been listening. She started to tell something else: "You know, where we were before, on Vern's last job, we weren't in a camp. He was away a lot, and he left me in Amos, in a hotel. I liked it. Amos isn't all that big, but it's better than here. There was this German in the hotel. He was selling cars. He'd drive me around if I wanted to go to a movie or anything. Vern didn't like him, so we left. It wasn't anybody's fault."

"So he's given up two jobs," said Mrs. Thompson. "One because he couldn't leave you alone, and now this one. Two jobs, and you haven't been married five months. Why should another man be thrown out of work? We don't need to know a thing. I'll be sorry if it was Jimmy Quinn," she went on slowly. "I like that boy. Don't say the name, dear. There's Evans. Susini. Palmer. But it might have been anybody, because you had them all on the boil. So it might have been Jimmy Quinn—let's say—and it could have been anyone else, too. Well, now let's hope they can get their minds back on the job."

"I thought they all liked me," said Jeannie sadly. "I get along with people. Vern never fights with me."

"Vern never fights with anyone. But he ought to have thrashed *you*."

"If he . . . you know. I won't say the name. If he'd liked me, I wouldn't have minded. If he'd been friendly. I really mean that. I wouldn't have gone wandering up the road, making all this fuss."

"Jeannie," said Mrs. Thompson, "you don't even know what you're saying."

"He could at least have liked me," said Jeannie. "He wasn't even friendly. It's the first time in my life somebody hasn't liked me. My heart is broken, Mrs. Thompson. My heart is just broken."

She has to cry, Mrs. Thompson thought. She has to have it out. She rocked slowly, tapping her foot, trying to remember how she'd felt about things when she was twenty, wondering if her heart had ever been broken, too.

—1965

Margaret Laurence 1926–1987

One of Canada's most beloved authors, Margaret Laurence is best known for her five books set in or associated with Manawaka, a prairie town (based on Neepawa, Manitoba) that she populated with interrelated characters spanning several generations. Characters such as Morag Gunn in The Diviners *(1975) and Vanessa MacLeod, the unifying figure in the stories in* A Bird in the House *(1970), live under the shadows of the morally rigid founders of the community, such as Hagar Shipley of* The Stone Angel *(1964) and Vanessa's Grandmother MacLeod. Their Scots Calvinist code of sobriety and restraint and its doctrine of predestination so pervade the Manawaka world that while family, church, and community may be nourishing, they are also dangerously entrapping. As the image of the bird in the house suggests, these institutions can confine a vital force that would seek a less limited space. But escape is never easy and may bring unlooked-for consequences.*

A Bird in the House

The parade would be almost over by now, and I had not gone. My mother had said in a resigned voice, "All right, Vanessa, if that's the way you feel," making me suffer twice as many jabs of guilt as I would have done if she had lost her temper. She and Grandmother MacLeod had gone off, my mother pulling the low box-sleigh with Roddie all dolled up in his new red snowsuit, just the sort of little kid anyone would want people to see. I sat on the lowest branch of the birch tree in our yard, not minding the snowy wind, even welcoming its punishment. I went over my reasons for not going, trying to believe they were good and sufficient, but in my heart I felt I was betraying my father. This was the first time I had stayed away from the Remembrance Day parade. I wondered if he would notice that I was not there, standing on the sidewalk at the corner of River and Main while the parade passed, and then following to the Court House grounds where the service was held.

I could see the whole thing in my mind. It was the same every year. The Manawaka Civic Band always led the way. They had never been able to afford full uniforms, but they had peaked navy-blue caps and sky-blue chest ribbons. They were joined on Remembrance Day by the Salvation Army band, whose uniforms seemed too ordinary for a parade, for they were the same ones the bandsmen wore every Saturday night when they played "Nearer My God to Thee" at the foot of River Street. The two bands never managed to practise quite enough together, so they did not keep in time too well. The Salvation Army band invariably played faster, and afterwards my father would say irritably, "They play those marches just like they do hymns, blast them, as though they wouldn't get to heaven if they didn't hustle up." And my mother, who had great respect for the Salvation Army because of the good work they did, would respond chidingly, "Now, now, Ewen—" I vowed I would never say "Now, now" to my husband or children, not that I ever intended having the latter, for I had been put off by my brother Roderick, who was now two years old with wavy hair, and everyone said what a beautiful child. I was twelve, and no one in their right mind would have said what a beautiful child, for I was big-boned like my Grandfather Connor and had straight lanky black hair like a Blackfoot or Cree.

After the bands would come the veterans. Even thinking of them at this distance, in the white and withdrawn quiet of the birch tree, gave me a sense of painful embarrassment. I might not have minded so much if my father had not been among them. How could he go? How could he not see how they all looked? It must have been a long time since they were soldiers, for they had forgotten how to march in step. They were old—that was the thing. My father was bad enough, being almost forty, but he wasn't a patch on Howard Tully from the drugstore, who was completely grey-haired and also fat, or Stewart MacMurchie, who was bald at the back of his head. They looked to me like imposters, plump or spindly caricatures of past warriors. I almost hated them for walking in that limping column down Main. At the Court House, everyone would sing *Lord God of Hosts, be with us yet, lest we forget, lest we forget.* Will Masterson would pick up his old Army bugle and blow the Last Post. Then it would be over and everyone could start gabbling once more and go home.

I jumped down from the birch bough and ran to the house, yelling, making as much noise as I could.

I'm a poor lonesome cowboy
An' a long way from home—

I stepped inside the front hall and kicked off my snow boots. I slammed the door behind me, making the dark ruby and emerald glass shake in the small leaded panes. I slid purposely on the hall rug, causing it to bunch and crinkle on the slippery polished oak of the floor. I seized the newel post, round as a head, and spun myself to and fro on the bottom stair.

I ain't got no father
To buy the clothes I wear,
 I'm a poor lonesome—

At this moment my shoulders were firmly seized and shaken by a pair of hands, white and delicate and old, but strong as talons.

"Just what do you think you're doing, young lady?" Grandmother MacLeod enquired, in a voice like frost on a windowpane, infinitely cold and clearly etched.

I went limp and in a moment she took her hands away. If you struggled, she would always hold on longer.

"Gee, I never knew you were home yet."

"I would have thought that on a day like this you might have shown a little respect and consideration," Grandmother MacLeod said, "even if you couldn't make the effort to get cleaned up enough to go to the parade."

I realised with surprise that she imagined this to be my reason for not going. I did not try to correct her impression. My real reason would have been even less acceptable.

"I'm sorry," I said quickly.

In some families, *please* is described as the magic word. In our house, however, it was *sorry*.

"This isn't an easy day for any of us," she said.

Her younger son, my Uncle Roderick, had been killed in the Great War. When my father marched, and when the hymn was sung, and when that unbearably lonely tune was sounded by the one bugle and everyone forced themselves to keep absolutely still, it would be that boy of whom she was thinking. I felt the enormity of my own offence.

"Grandmother—I'm sorry."

"So you said."

I could not tell her I had not really said it before at all. I went into the den and found my father there. He was sitting in the leather-cushioned armchair beside the fireplace. He was not doing anything, just sitting and smoking. I stood beside him, wanting to touch the light-brown hairs on his forearm, but thinking he might laugh at me or pull his arm away if I did.

"I'm sorry," I said, meaning it.

"What for, honey?"

"For not going."

"Oh—that. What was the matter?"

I did not want him to know, and yet I had to tell him, make him see.

"They look silly," I blurted. "Marching like that."

For a minute I thought he was going to be angry. It would have been a relief to me if he had been. Instead, he drew his eyes away from mine and fixed them above the mantelpiece where the sword hung, the handsome and evil-looking crescent in its carved bronze sheath that some ancestor had once brought from the Northern Frontier of India.

"Is that the way it looks to you?" he said.

I felt in his voice some hurt, something that was my fault. I wanted to make everything all right between us, to convince him that I understood, even if I did not. I prayed that Grandmother MacLeod would stay put in her room, and that my mother would take a long time in the kitchen, giving Roddie his lunch. I wanted my father to myself, so I could prove to him that I cared more about him than any of the others did. I wanted to speak in some way that would be more poignant and comprehending than anything of which my mother could possibly be capable. But I did not know how.

"You were right there when Uncle Roderick got killed, weren't you?" I began uncertainly.

"Yes."

"How old was he, Dad?"

"Eighteen," my father said.

Unexpectedly, that day came into intense being for me. He had had to watch his own brother die, not in the antiseptic calm of some hospital, but out in the open, the stretches of mud I had seen in his snapshots. He would not have known what to do. He would just have had to stand there and look at it, whatever that might mean. I looked at my father with a kind of horrified awe, and then I began to cry. I had forgotten about impressing him with my perception. Now I needed him to console me for this unwanted glimpse of the pain he had once known.

"Hey, cut it out, honey," he said, embarrassed. "It was bad, but it wasn't all as bad as that part. There were a few other things."

"Like what?" I said, not believing him.

"Oh—I don't know," he replied evasively. "Most of us were pretty young, you know, I and the boys I joined up with. None of us had ever been away from Manawaka before. Those of us who came back mostly came back here, or else went no further away from town than Winnipeg. So when we were overseas — that was the only time most of us were ever a long way from home."

"Did you want to be?" I asked, shocked.

"Oh well—" my father said uncomfortably. "It was kind of interesting to see a few other places for a change, that's all."

Grandmother MacLeod was standing in the doorway.

"Beth's called you twice for lunch, Ewen. Are you deaf, you and Vanessa?"

"Sorry," my father and I said simultaneously.

Then we went upstairs to wash our hands.

That winter my mother returned to her old job as nurse in my father's medical practice. She was able to do this only because of Noreen.

"Grandmother MacLeod says we're getting a maid," I said to my father, accusingly, one morning. "We're not, are we?"

"Believe you me, on what I'm going to be paying her," my father growled, "she couldn't be called anything as classy as a maid. Hired girl would be more like it."

"Now, now, Ewen," my mother put in, "it's not as if we were cheating her or anything. You know she wants to live in town, and I can certainly see why, stuck out there on the farm, and her father hardly ever letting her come in. What kind of life is that for a girl?"

"I don't like the idea of your going back to work, Beth," my father said. "I know you're fine now, but you're not exactly the robust type."

"You can't afford to hire a nurse any longer. It's all very well to say the Depression won't last forever—probably it won't, but what else can we do for now?"

"I'm damned if I know," my father admitted. "Beth—"

"Yes?"

They both seemed to have forgotten about me. It was at breakfast, which we always ate in the kitchen, and I sat rigidly on my chair, pretending to ignore and thus snub their withdrawal from me. I glared at the window, but it was so thickly plumed and scrolled with frost that I could not see out. I glanced back to my parents. My father had not replied, and my mother was looking at him in that anxious and half-frowning way she had recently developed.

"What is it, Ewen?" Her voice had the same nervous sharpness it bore sometimes when she would say to me, "For mercy's sake, Vanessa, what is it *now?*" as though whatever was the matter, it was bound to be the last straw.

My father spun his sterling silver serviette ring, engraved with his initials, slowly around on the table.

"I never thought things would turn out like this, did you?"

"Please—" my mother said in a low strained voice, "please, Ewen, let's not start all this again. I can't take it."

"All right," my father said. "Only—"

"The MacLeods used to have money and now they don't," my mother cried. "Well, they're not alone. Do you think all that matters to me, Ewen? What I can't bear is to see you forever reproaching yourself. As if it were your fault."

"I don't think it's the comedown," my father said. "If I were somewhere else, I don't suppose it would matter to me, either, except where you're concerned. But I suppose you'd work too hard wherever you were—it's bred into you. If you haven't got anything to slave away at, you'll sure as hell invent something."

"What do you think I should do, let the house go to wrack and ruin? That would go over well with your mother, wouldn't it?"

"That's just it," my father said. "It's the damned house all the time. I haven't only taken on my father's house, I've taken on everything that goes with it, apparently. Sometimes I really wonder—"

"Well, it's a good thing I've inherited some practicality even if you haven't," my mother said. "I'll say that for the Connors—they aren't given to brooding, thank the Lord. Do you want your egg poached or scrambled?"

"Scrambled," my father said. "All I hope is that this Noreen doesn't get married straightaway, that's all."

"She won't," my mother said. "Who's she going to meet who could afford to marry?"

"I marvel at you, Beth," my father said. "You look as though a puff of wind would blow you away. But underneath, by God, you're all hardwood."

"Don't talk stupidly," my mother said. "All I hope is that she doesn't object to taking your mother's breakfast up on a tray."

"That's right," my father said angrily. "Rub it in."

"Oh Ewen, I'm sorry!" my mother cried, her face suddenly stricken. "I don't know why I say these things. I didn't mean to."

"I know," my father said. "Here, cut it out, honey. Just for God's sake please don't cry."

"I'm sorry," my mother repeated, blowing her nose.

"We're both sorry," my father said. "Not that that changes anything."

After my father had gone, I got down from my chair and went to my mother.

"I don't want you to go back to the office. I don't want a hired girl here. I'll hate her."

My mother sighed, making me feel that I was placing an intolerable burden on her, and yet making me resent having to feel this weight. She looked tired, as she often did these days. Her tiredness bored me, made me want to attack her for it.

"Catch me getting along with a dumb old hired girl," I threatened.

"Do what you like," my mother said abruptly. "What can I do about it?"

And then, of course, I felt bereft, not knowing which way to turn.

My father need not have worried about Noreen getting married. She was, as it turned out, interested not in boys but in God. My mother was relieved about the boys but alarmed about God.

"It isn't natural," she said, "for a girl of seventeen. Do you think she's all right mentally, Ewen?"

When my parents, along with Grandmother MacLeod, went to the United Church every Sunday, I was made to go to Sunday school in the church basement, where there were small red chairs which humiliatingly resembled kindergarten furniture, and pictures of Jesus wearing a white sheet and surrounded by a whole lot of well-dressed kids whose mothers obviously had not suffered them to come unto Him until every face and ear was properly scrubbed. Our religious observances also included grace at meals, when my father would mumble "For what we are about to receive the Lord make us truly thankful Amen," running the words together as though they were one long word. My mother approved of these rituals, which seemed decent and moderate to her. Noreen's religion, however, was a different matter. Noreen belonged to the Tabernacle of the Risen and Reborn, and she had got up to testify no less than seven times in the past two years, she told us. My mother, who could not imagine anyone's voluntarily making a public spectacle of themselves, was profoundly shocked by this revelation.

"Don't worry," my father soothed her. "She's all right. She's just had kind of a dull life, that's all."

My mother shrugged and went on worrying and trying to help Noreen without hurting her feelings, by tactful remarks about the advisability of modulating one's voice when singing hymns, and the fact that there was plenty of hot water so Noreen really didn't need to hesitate about taking a bath. She even bought a razor and a packet of blades and whispered to Noreen that any girl who wore transparent blouses so much would probably like to shave under her arms. None of these suggestions had the slightest effect on Noreen. She did not cease belting out hymns at the top of her voice, she bathed once a fortnight, and the sorrel-coloured hair continued to bloom like a thicket of Indian paintbrush in her armpits.

Grandmother MacLeod refused to speak to Noreen. This caused Noreen a certain amount of bewilderment until she finally hit on an answer.

"Your poor grandma," she said. "She is deaf as a post. These things are sent to try us here on earth, Vanessa. But if she makes it into Heaven, I'll bet you anything she will hear clear as a bell."

Noreen and I talked about Heaven quite a lot, and also Hell. Noreen had an intimate and detailed knowledge of both places. She not only knew what they looked like — she even knew how big they were. Heaven was seventy-seven thousand miles square and it had four gates, each one made out of a different kind of precious jewel. The Pearl Gate, the Topaz Gate, the Amethyst Gate, the Ruby Gate—Noreen would reel them off, all the gates of Heaven. I told Noreen they sounded like poetry, but she was puzzled by my reaction and said I shouldn't talk that way. If you said poetry, it sounded like it was just made up and not really so, Noreen said.

Hell was larger than Heaven, and when I asked why, thinking of it as something of a comedown for God, Noreen said naturally it had to be bigger because there were a darn sight more people there than in Heaven. Hell was one hundred and ninety million miles deep and was in perpetual darkness, like a cave or under the sea. Even the flames (this was the awful thing) *did not give off any light.*

I did not actually believe in Noreen's doctrines, but the images which they conjured up began to inhabit my imagination. Noreen's fund of exotic knowledge was not limited to religion, although in a way it all seemed related. She could do many things which had a spooky tinge to them. Once when she was making a cake, she found we had run out of eggs. She went outside and gathered a bowl of fresh snow and used it instead. The cake rose like a charm, and I stared at Noreen as though she were a sorceress. In fact, I began to think of her as a sorceress, someone not quite of this earth. There was nothing unearthly about her broad shoulders and hips and her forest of dark red hair, but even these features took on a slightly sinister significance to me. I no longer saw her through the eyes of the expressed opinions of my mother and father, as a girl who had quit school at grade eight and whose life on the farm had been endlessly drab. I knew the truth—Noreen's life had not been drab at all, for she dwelt in a world of violent splendours, a world filled with angels whose wings of delicate light bore real feathers, and saints shining like the dawn, and prophets who spoke in ancient tongues, and the ecstatic souls of the saved, as well as denizens of the lower regions—mean-eyed imps and crooked cloven-hoofed monsters and beasts with the bodies of swine and the human heads of murderers, and lovely depraved jezebels torn by dogs through all eternity. The middle layer of Creation, our earth, was equally full of grotesque presences, for Noreen believed strongly in the visitation of ghosts and the communication with spirits. She could prove this with her Ouija board. We would both place our fingers lightly on the indicator, and it would skim across the board and spell out answers to our questions. I did not believe whole-heartedly in the Ouija board, either, but I was cautious about the kind of question I asked, in case the answer would turn out unfavourable and I would be unable to forget it.

One day Noreen told me she could also make a table talk. We used the small table in my bedroom, and sure enough, it lifted very slightly under our fingertips and tapped once for *Yes*, twice for *No*. Noreen asked if her Aunt Ruthie would get better from the kidney operation, and the table replied *No*. I withdrew my hands.

"I don't want to do it any more."

"Gee, what's the matter, Vanessa?" Noreen's plain placid face creased in a frown. "We only just begun."

"I have to do my homework."

My heart lurched as I said this. I was certain Noreen would know I was lying, and that she would know not by any ordinary perception, either. But her attention had been caught by something else, and I was thankful, at least until I saw what it was.

My bedroom window was not opened in the coldest weather. The storm window, which was fitted outside as an extra wall against the winter, had three small circular holes in its frame so that some fresh air could seep into the house. The sparrow must have been floundering in the new snow on the roof, for it had crawled in through one of these holes and was now caught between the two layers of glass. I could not bear the panic of the trapped bird, and before I realised what I was doing, I had thrown open the bedroom window. I was not releasing the sparrow into any better a situation, I soon saw, for instead of remaining quiet and allowing us to catch it in order to free it, it began flying blindly around the room, hitting the lampshade, brushing against the walls, its wings seeming to spin faster and faster.

I was petrified. I thought I would pass out if those palpitating wings touched me. There was something in the bird's senseless movements that revolted me. I also thought it was going to damage itself, break one of those thin wing-bones, perhaps, and then it would be lying on the floor, dying, like the pimpled and horribly featherless baby birds we saw sometimes on the sidewalks in the spring when they had fallen out of their nests. I was not any longer worried about the sparrow. I wanted only to avoid the sight of it lying broken on the floor. Viciously, I thought that if Noreen said, *God sees the little sparrow fall*, I would kick her in the shins. She did not, however, say this.

"A bird in the house means a death in the house," Noreen remarked.

Shaken, I pulled my glance away from the whirling wings and looked at Noreen.

"What?"

"That's what I've heard said, anyhow."

The sparrow had exhausted itself. It lay on the floor, spent and trembling. I could not bring myself to touch it. Noreen bent and picked it up. She cradled it with great gentleness between her cupped hands. Then we took it downstairs, and when I had opened the back door, Noreen set the bird free.

"Poor little scrap," she said, and I felt struck to the heart, knowing she had been concerned all along about the sparrow, while I, perfidiously, in the chaos of the moment, had been concerned only about myself.

"Wanna do some with the Ouija board, Vanessa?" Noreen asked.

I shivered a little, perhaps only because of the blast of cold air which had come into the kitchen when the door was opened.

"No thanks, Noreen. Like I said, I got my homework to do. But thanks all the same."

"That's okay," Noreen said in her guileless voice. "Any time."

But whenever she mentioned the Ouija board or the talking table, after that, I always found some excuse not to consult these oracles.

"Do you want to come to church with me this evening, Vanessa?" my father asked.

"How come you're going to the evening service?" I enquired.

"Well, we didn't go this morning. We went snowshoeing instead, remember? I think your grandmother was a little bit put out about it. She went alone this morning. I guess it wouldn't hurt you and me, to go now."

We walked through the dark, along the white streets, the snow squeaking dryly under our feet. The streetlights were placed at long intervals along the sidewalks, and around each pole the circle of flimsy light created glistening points of blue and crystal on the crusted snow. I would have liked to take my father's hand, as I used to do, but I was too old for that now. I walked beside him, taking long steps so he would not have to walk more slowly on my account.

The sermon bored me, and I began leafing through the Hymnary for entertainment. I must have drowsed, for the next thing I knew, my father was prodding me and we were on our feet for the closing hymn.

Near the Cross, near the Cross,
    Be my glory ever,
Till my ransomed soul shall find
    Rest beyond the river.

I knew the tune well, so I sang loudly for the first verse. But the music to that hymn is sombre, and all at once the words themselves seemed too dreadful to be sung. I stopped singing, my throat knotted. I thought I was going to cry, but I did not know why, except that the song recalled to me my Grandmother Connor, who had been dead only a year now. I wondered why her soul needed to be ransomed. If God did not think she was good enough just as she was, then I did not have much use for His opinion. *Rest beyond the river*—was that what had happened to her? She had believed in Heaven, but I did not think that rest beyond the river was quite what she had in mind. To think of her in Noreen's flashy Heaven, though—that was even worse. Someplace where nobody ever got annoyed or had to be smoothed down and placated, someplace where there were never any family scenes—that would have suited my Grandmother Connor. Maybe she wouldn't have minded a certain amount of rest beyond the river, at that.

When we had the silent prayer, I looked at my father. He sat with his head bowed and his eyes closed. He was frowning deeply, and I could see the pulse in his temple. I wondered then what he believed. I did not have any real idea what it might be. When he raised his head, he did not look uplifted or anything like that. He merely looked tired. Then Reverend McKee pronounced the benediction, and we could go home.

"What do you think about all that stuff, Dad?" I asked hesitantly, as we walked.

"What stuff, honey?"

"Oh, Heaven and Hell, and like that."

My father laughed. "Have you been listening to Noreen too much? Well, I don't know. I don't think they're actual places. Maybe they stand for something that happens all the time here, or else doesn't happen. It's kind of hard to explain. I guess I'm not so good at explanations."

Nothing seemed to have been made any clearer to me. I reached out and took his hand, not caring that he might think this a babyish gesture.

"I hate that hymn!"

"Good Lord," my father said in astonishment. "Why, Vanessa?"

But I did not know and so could not tell him.

Many people in Manawaka had flu that winter, so my father and Dr. Cates were kept extremely busy. I had flu myself, and spent a week in bed, vomiting only the first day and after that enjoying poor health, as my mother put it, with Noreen bringing me ginger ale and orange juice, and each evening my father putting a wooden tongue-depressor into my mouth and peering down my throat, then smiling and saying he thought I might live after all.

Then my father got sick himself, and had to stay at home and go to bed. This was such an unusual occurrence that it amused me.

"Doctors shouldn't get sick," I told him.

"You're right," he said. "That was pretty bad management."

"Run along now, dear," my mother said.

That night I woke and heard voices in the upstairs hall. When I went out, I found my mother and Grandmother MacLeod, both in their dressing-gowns. With them was Dr. Cates. I did not go immediately to my mother, as I would have done only a year before. I stood in the doorway of my room, squinting against the sudden light.

"Mother—what is it?"

She turned, and momentarily I saw the look on her face before she erased it and put on a contrived calm.

"It's all right," she said. "Dr. Cates has just come to have a look at Daddy. You go on back to sleep."

The wind was high that night, and I lay and listened to it rattling the storm windows and making the dry and winter-stiffened vines of the Virginia creeper scratch like small persistent claws against the red brick. In the morning, my mother told me that my father had developed pneumonia.

Dr. Cates did not think it would be safe to move my father to the hospital. My mother began sleeping in the spare bedroom, and after she had been there for a few nights, I asked if I could sleep in there too. I thought she would be bound to ask me why, and I did not know what I would say, but she did not ask. She nodded, and in some way her easy agreement upset me.

That night Dr. Cates came again, bringing with him one of the nurses from the hospital. My mother stayed upstairs with them. I sat with Grandmother MacLeod in the living room. That was the last place in the world I wanted to be, but I thought she would be offended if I went off. She sat as straight and rigid as a totem pole, and embroidered away at the needlepoint cushion cover she was doing. I perched on the edge of the chesterfield and kept my eyes fixed on *The White Company* by Conan Doyle, and from time to time I turned a page. I had already read it three times before, but luckily Grandmother MacLeod did not know that. At nine o'clock she looked at her gold brooch watch, which she always wore pinned to her dress, and told me to go to bed, so I did that.

I wakened in darkness. At first, it seemed to me that I was in my own bed, and everything was as usual, with my parents in their room, and Roddie curled up in the crib in his room, and Grandmother MacLeod sleeping with her mouth open in her enormous spool bed, surrounded by half a dozen framed photos of Uncle Roderick and only one of my father, and Noreen snoring fitfully in the room next to mine, with the dark flames of her hair spreading out across the pillow, and the pink and silver motto cards from the Tabernacle stuck with adhesive tape onto the wall beside her bed—*Lean on Him, Emmanuel Is My Refuge, Rock of Ages Cleft for Me.*

Then in the total night around me, I heard a sound. It was my mother, and she was crying, not loudly at all, but from somewhere very deep inside her. I sat up in bed. Everything seemed to have stopped, not only time but my own heart and blood as well. Then my mother noticed that I was awake.

I did not ask her, and she did not tell me anything. There was no need. She held me in her arms, or I held her, I am not certain which. And after a while the first mourning stopped, too, as everything does sooner or later, for when the limits of endurance have been reached, then people must sleep.

In the days following my father's death, I stayed close beside my mother, and this was only partly for my own consoling. I also had the feeling that she needed my protection. I did not know from what, nor what I could possibly do, but something held me there. Reverend McKee called, and I sat with my grandmother and my mother in the living room. My mother told me I did not need to stay unless I wanted to, but I refused to go. What I thought chiefly was that he would speak of the healing power of prayer, and all that, and it would be bound to make my mother cry again. And in fact, it happened in just that way, but when it actually came, I could not protect her from this assault. I could only sit there and pray my own prayer, which was that he would go away quickly.

My mother tried not to cry unless she was alone or with me. I also tried, but neither of us was entirely successful. Grandmother MacLeod, on the other hand, was never seen crying, not even the day of my father's funeral. But that day, when we had returned to the house and she had taken off her black velvet overshoes and her heavy sealskin coat with its black fur that was the softest thing I had ever touched, she stood in the hallway and for the first time she looked unsteady. When I reached out instinctively towards her, she sighed.

"That's right," she said. "You might just take my arm while I go upstairs, Vanessa."

That was the most my Grandmother MacLeod ever gave in, to anyone's sight. I left her in her bedroom, sitting on the straight chair beside her bed and looking at the picture of my father that had been taken when he graduated from medical college. Maybe she was sorry now that she had only the one photograph of him, but whatever she felt, she did not say.

I went down into the kitchen. I had scarcely spoken to Noreen since my father's death. This had not been done on purpose. I simply had not seen her. I had not really seen anyone except my mother. Looking at Noreen now, I suddenly recalled the sparrow. I felt physically sick, remembering the fearful darting and plunging of those wings, and the fact that it was I who had opened the window and let it in. Then an inexplicable fury took hold of me, some terrifying need to hurt, burn, destroy. Absolutely without warning, either to her or to myself, I hit Noreen as hard as I could. When she swung around, appalled, I hit out at her once more, my arms and legs flailing. Her hands snatched at my wrists, and she held me, but still I continued to struggle, fighting blindly, my eyes tightly closed, as though she were a prison all around me and I was battling to get out. Finally, too shocked at myself to go on, I went limp in her grasp and she let me drop to the floor.

"Vanessa! I never done one single solitary thing to you, and here you go hitting and scratching me like that! What in the world has got into you?"

I began to say I was sorry, which was certainly true, but I did not say it. I could not say anything.

"You're not yourself, what with your dad and everything," she excused me. "I been praying every night that your dad is with God, Vanessa. I know he wasn't actually saved in the regular way, but still and all—"

"Shut up," I said.

Something in my voice made her stop talking. I rose from the floor and stood in the kitchen doorway.

"He didn't need to be saved," I went on coldly, distinctly. "And he is not in Heaven, because there is no Heaven. And it doesn't matter, see? *It doesn't matter!*"

Noreen's face looked peculiarly vulnerable now, her high wide cheekbones and puzzled childish eyes, and the thick russet tangle of her hair. I had not hurt her much before, when I hit her. But I had hurt her now, hurt her in some inexcusable way. Yet I sensed, too, that already she was gaining some satisfaction out of feeling sorrowful about my disbelief.

I went upstairs to my room. Momentarily I felt a sense of calm, almost of acceptance. *Rest beyond the river.* I knew now what that meant. It meant Nothing. It meant only silence, forever.

Then I lay down on my bed and spent the last of my tears, or what seemed then to be the last. Because, despite what I had said to Noreen, it did matter. It mattered, but there was no help for it.

Everything changed after my father's death. The MacLeod house could not be kept up any longer. My mother sold it to a local merchant who subsequently covered the deep red of the brick over with yellow stucco. Something about the house had always made me uneasy—that tower room where Grandmother MacLeod's potted plants drooped in a lethargic and lime-green confusion, those long stairways and hidden places, the attic which I had always imagined to be dwelt in by the spirits of the family dead, that gigantic portrait of the Duke of Wellington at the top of the stairs. It was never an endearing house. And yet when it was no longer ours, and when the Virginia creeper had been torn down and the dark walls turned to a light marigold, I went out of my way to avoid walking past, for it seemed to me that the house had lost the stern dignity that was its very heart.

Noreen went back to the farm. My mother and brother and myself moved into Grandmother Connor's house. Grandmother MacLeod went to live with Aunt Morag in Winnipeg. It was harder for her than for anyone, because so much of her life was bound up with the MacLeod house. She was fond of Aunt Morag, but that hardly counted. Her men were gone, her husband and her sons, and a family whose men are gone is no family at all. The day she left, my mother and I did not know what to say. Grandmother MacLeod looked even smaller than usual in her fur coat and her black velvet toque. She became extremely agitated about trivialities, and fussed about the possibility of the taxi not arriving on time. She had forbidden us to accompany her to the station. About my father, or the house, or anything important, she did not say a word. Then, when the taxi had finally arrived, she turned to my mother.

"Roddie will have Ewen's seal ring, of course, with the MacLeod crest on it," she said. "But there is another seal as well, don't forget, the larger one with the crest and motto. It's meant to be worn on a watch chain. I keep it in my jewel-box. It was Roderick's. Roddie's to have that, too, when I die. Don't let Morag talk you out of it."

During the Second World War, when I was seventeen and in love with an airman who did not love me, and desperately anxious to get away from Manawaka and from my grandfather's house, I happened one day to be going through the old mahogany desk that had belonged to my father. It had a number of small drawers inside, and I accidentally pulled one of these all the way out. Behind it there was another drawer, one I had not known about. Curiously, I opened it. Inside there was a letter written on almost transparent paper in a cramped angular handwriting. It began—*Cher Monsieur Ewen*— That was all I could make out, for the writing was nearly impossible to read and my French was not good. It was dated 1919. With it, there was a picture of a girl, looking absurdly old-fashioned to my eyes, like the faces on long-discarded calendars or chocolate boxes. But beneath the dated quality of the photograph, she seemed neither expensive nor cheap. She looked like what she probably had been—an ordinary middle-class girl, but in another country. She wore her hair in long ringlets, and her mouth was shaped into a sweetly sad posed smile like Mary Pickford's. That was all. There was nothing else in the drawer.

I looked for a long time at the girl, and hoped she had meant some momentary and unexpected freedom. I remembered what he had said to me, after I hadn't gone to the Remembrance Day parade.

"What are you doing, Vanessa?" my mother called from the kitchen.

"Nothing," I replied.

I took the letter and picture outside and burned them. That was all I could do for him. Now that we might have talked together, it was many years too late. Perhaps it would not have been possible anyway. I did not know.

As I watched the smile of the girl turn into scorched paper, I grieved for my father as though he had just died now.

—1970

Timothy Findley 1930–2002

A writer of short fiction, novels, memoirs, and plays, Timothy Findley is best remembered as the author of The Wars *(1977), a compelling short novel about the disastrous experiences of soldiers during World War I. The shattering effect of war—not only on the soldiers but also on the families to which they eventually return—is similarly central to "Stones," which has for its background one of the most traumatic battles of World War II and which shows the way national, personal, and family traumas all merge.*

Several other themes important to Findley's work are also visible in this story: struggles between father and son, the disintegration of families, the conflicts of class, the treatment of outsiders by society, and alcoholism, breakdown, and madness. Mixed in among such disturbing topics is an image of a more loving time, one that may now be irrevocably lost amid the violence of the twenty-first century.

Stones

We lived on the outskirts of Rosedale, over on the wrong side of Yonge Street. This was the impression we had, at any rate. Crossing the street-car tracks put you in another world.

One September, my sister, Rita, asked a girl from Rosedale over to our house after school. Her name was Allison Pritchard and she lived on Cluny

Drive. When my mother telephoned to see if Allison Pritchard could stay for supper, Mrs. Pritchard said she didn't think it would be appropriate. That was the way they talked in Rosedale: very polite; oblique and cruel.

Over on our side—the west side—of Yonge Street, there were merchants—and this, apparently, made the difference to those whose houses were in Rosedale. People of class were not meant to live in the midst of commerce.

Our house was on Gibson Avenue, a cul-de-sac with a park across the road. My bedroom window faced a hockey rink in winter and a football field in summer. Cy, my brother, was a star in either venue. I was not. My forte, then, was the tricycle.

Up at the corner, there was an antique store on one side and a variety shop on the other. In the variety shop, you could spend your allowance on penny candy, Eskimo pies and an orange drink I favoured then called *Stubby*. *Stubby* came in short, fat bottles and aside from everything else—the thick orange flavour and the ginger in the bubbles—there was something wonderfully satisfying in the fact that it took both hands to hold it up to your lips and tip it down your throat.

Turning up Yonge Street, beyond the antique store, you came to The Women's Bakery, Adam's Grocery, Oskar Schickel, the butcher, and Max's flowers. We were Max's flowers. My mother and my father wore green aprons when they stood behind the counter or went back into the cold room where they made up wreaths for funerals, bouquets for weddings and corsages for dances at the King Edward Hotel. Colonel Matheson, retired, would come in every morning on his way downtown and pick out a boutonnière from the jar of carnations my mother kept on the counter near the register. Once, when I was four, I caused my parents untold embarrassment by pointing out that Colonel Matheson had a large red growth on the end of his nose. The "growth" was nothing of the sort, of course, but merely the result of Colonel Matheson's predilection for gin.

Of the pre-war years, my overall memory is one of perfect winters, heavy with snow and the smell of coal- and wood-smoke mingling with the smell of bread and cookies rising from The Women's Bakery. The coal-smoke came from our furnaces and the wood-smoke—mostly birch and maple—came to us from the chimneys of Rosedale, where it seemed that every house must have a fireplace in every room.

Summers all smelled of grass being cut in the park and burning tar from the road crews endlessly patching the potholes in Yonge Street. The heat of these summers was heroic and the cause of many legends. Mister

Schickel, the butcher, I recall once cooked an egg on the sidewalk outside his store. My father, who was fond of Mister Schickel, made him a bet of roses it could not be done. I think Mister Schickel's part of the bet was pork chops trimmed of excess fat. When the egg began to sizzle, my father slapped his thigh and whistled and he sent my sister, Rita, in to get the flowers. Mister Schickel, however, was a graceful man and when he placed his winnings in the window of his butcher shop, he also placed a card that read: *Thanks to Max's Flowers one dozen roses.*

The Great Depression held us all in thrall, but its effects on those of us who were used to relative poverty—living on the west side on Yonge Street—were not so debilitating as they were on the far side in Rosedale. The people living there regarded money as something you had—as opposed to something you went out and got—and they were slower to adjust to what, for them, was the unique experience of deprivation.

I remember, too, that there always seemed to be a tramp at the door: itinerants asking if—for the price of a meal, or the meal itself—they could carry out the ashes, sweep the walks or pile the baskets and pails in which my father brought his flowers from the market and the greenhouse.

Our lives continued in this way until about the time I was five—in August of 1939. Everyone's life, I suppose, has its demarcation lines—its latitudes and longitudes passing through time. Some of these lines define events that everyone shares—others are confined to personal—even to secret lives. But the end of summer 1939 is a line drawn through the memory of everyone who was then alive. We were all about to be pitched together into a melting pot of violence from which a few of us would emerge intact and the rest of us would perish.

My father joined the army even before the war had started. He went downtown one day and didn't come back till after suppertime. I noticed that he hadn't taken the truck but had ridden off on the streetcar. I asked my mother why he had worn his suit on a weekday and she replied *because today is special.* But that was all she said.

At the table, eating soufflé and salad, my brother, Cy—who was nine years old that summer—talked about the World's Fair in New York City and pictures he'd seen of the future in magazines. The Great World's Fair was a subject that had caught all our imaginations with its demonstrations of new appliances, aeroplanes and motor cars. Everything was "streamlined" in 1939; everything designed with swept-back lines as if we were all preparing to shoot off into space.

Earlier that summer, the King and Queen of England had come to Canada, riding on a streamlined train whose blue-painted engine was sleek and slim as something in a silver glove. In fact, the King and Queen had arrived in Toronto just up Yonge Street from where we lived. We got permission from the Darrow family, who lived over Max's Flowers, to stand on the roof and watch the parade with its Mounties in scarlet and its Black Watch Band and the King and Queen, all blue and white and smiling, sitting in an open Buick called a *McLaughlin—built*, according to Cy, *right here in Canada!* For one brief moment while all these symbols of who we were went marching past, the two communities—one on either side of Yonge Street—were united in a surge of cheering and applause. But after the King and Queen were gone, the ribbon of Yonge Street divided us again. It rained.

Now, Cy and Rita were arguing over the remnants in the soufflé dish. Cy held the classic belief that what was in the dish was his by virtue of his being the eldest child. He also held the classic belief that girls were meant to be second in everything. Rita, who was always hungry but never seemed to gain an ounce, held none of these beliefs and was capable of fighting Cy for hours on end when our parents weren't present. With Mother at the table, however, the argument was silenced by her announcement that the soufflé dish and all the delicious bits of cheese and egg that clung to its sides would be set aside for our father.

Then—or shortly thereafter—our father did indeed arrive, but he said he wasn't hungry and he wanted to be left alone with Mother.

In half an hour the children were called from the kitchen where we had been doing the dishes and scooping up the remains of the meal. I—the child my mother called *The Rabbit*—had been emptying the salad bowl, stuffing my mouth with lettuce, tomatoes and onion shards and nearly choking in the process. We all went into the sitting-room with food on our lips and tea towels in our hands: Father's three little Maxes—Cy and Rita and Ben. He looked at us then, as he always did, with a measure of pride he could never hide and a false composure that kept his lips from smiling, but not his eyes. I look back now on that moment with some alarm when I realize my father was only twenty-seven years old—an age I have long survived and doubled.

"Children, I have joined the army," he said—in his formal way, as if we were his customers. "I am going to be a soldier."

Our mother had been weeping before we entered the room, but she had dried her eyes because she never allowed us to witness her tears.

Now, she was smiling and silent. After a moment, she left the room and went out through the kitchen into the garden where, in the twilight, she found her favourite place and sat in a deck-chair amidst the flowers.

Cy, for his part, crowed with delight and yelled with excitement. He wanted to know if the war would last until he was a man and could join our father at the front. Father, I remember, told him the war had not yet begun and the reason for his enlistment was precisely so that Cy and I could not be soldiers. "There will be no need for that," he said.

Cy was immensely disappointed. He begged our father to make the war go on till 1948, when he would be eighteen.

Our father only laughed at that.

"The war," he said, "will be over in 1940."

I went out then and found our mother in the garden.

"What will happen to us while he's away?" I asked.

"Nothing," she said. And then she said: "come here."

I went and leaned against her thigh and she put her arm around my shoulder and I could smell the roses somewhere behind us. It was getting dark.

"Look up there," she said. "The stars are coming out. Why don't you count them?" This was her way of distracting me whenever my questions got out of hand. Either she told me to count the stars or go outside and dig for China. *There's a shovel in the shed,* she would tell me. *You get started and I will join you.* Just as if we would be in China and back by suppertime.

But that night in August, 1939, I wasn't prepared to bite. I didn't want to dig for China and I didn't want to count the stars. I'd dug for China so many times and had so many holes in the yard that I knew I would never arrive; it was much too far and, somehow, she was making a fool of me. As for the stars: "I counted them last night," I told her. "And the night before."

"Oh?" she said—and I felt her body tense, though she went on trying to inject a sense of ease when she spoke. "So tell me," she said. "How many are there?"

"Twelve," I said.

"Ah," she said. And sighed. "Just twelve. I thought there might be more than twelve."

"I mean twelve zillion," I said with great authority.

"Oh," she said. "I see. And you counted them all?"

"Unh-hunh."

For a moment she was quiet. And then she said: "what about that one there?"

One week later, the war began. But my father had already gone.

On the 14th of February, 1943, my father was returned. He came back home from the war. He did this on a Sunday and I recall the hush that fell upon our house, as indeed it seemed to have fallen over all the city. Only the sparrows out in the trees made sound.

We had gone downtown to the Exhibition Grounds to meet him. The journey on the streetcar took us over an hour, but Mother had splurged and hired a car and driver to take us all home. The car, I remember, embarrassed me. I was afraid some friend would see me being driven— sitting up behind a chauffeur.

A notice had come that told us the families of all returning soldiers would be permitted to witness their arrival. I suspect the building they used for this was the one used to house the Royal Winter Fair and other equestrian events. I don't remember what it was called and I'm not inclined to inquire. It was enough that I was there that once—and once remains enough.

We sat in the bleachers, Cy and Rita and Mother and me, and there was a railing holding us back. There must have been over a thousand people waiting to catch a glimpse of someone they loved—all of them parents, children or wives of the men returning. I was eight years old that February—almost nine and feeling I would never get there. Time was like a field of clay and all the other children I knew appeared to have cleared it in a single bound while I was stuck in the mud and barely able to lift my feet. I hated being eight and dreaded being nine. I wanted to be ten—the only dignified age a child could be, it seemed to me. Cy, at ten, had found a kind of silence I admired to the point of worship. Rita, who in fact was ten that year and soon to be eleven, had also found a world of silence in which she kept herself secreted—often behind closed doors. Silence was a sign of valour.

The occasion was barely one for public rejoicing. The men who were coming home were mostly casualties whose wounds, we had been warned, could be distressing and whose spirit, we had equally been warned, had been damaged in long months of painful recuperation. Plainly, it was our job to lift their spirits and to deny the severity of their wounds. Above all else, they must not be allowed to feel they could not rejoin society at large. A man with no face must not be stared at.

Our father's wounds were greater by far than we had been told. There was not a mark on his body, but—far inside—he had been destroyed. His mind had been severely damaged and his spirit had been broken. No one had told me what this might have made of him. No one had said *he may never be kind again.* No one had said *he will never sleep again without the aid of alcohol.* No one had said *he will try to kill your mother.* No one had said *you will not be sure it's him when you see him.* Yet all these things were true.

I had never seen a military parade without a band. The effect was eerie and upsetting. Two or three officers came forward into the centre of the oval. Somebody started shouting commands and a sergeant-major, who could not yet be seen, was heard outside the building counting off the steps.

I wanted drums. I wanted bugles. Surely this ghostly, implacable sound of marching feet in the deadening sand was just a prelude to everyone's standing up and cheering and the music blaring forth. But, no. We all stood up, it is true, the minute the first of the columns rounded the wooden corner of the bleachers and came into sight. But no one uttered a sound. One or two people threw their hands up over their mouths—as if to stifle cries—but most of us simply stood there—staring in disbelief.

Nurses came with some of the men, supporting them. Everyone was pale in the awful light—and the colours of their wounds and bruises were garish and quite unreal. There was a predominance of yellow flesh and dark maroon scars and of purple welts and blackened scabs. Some men wore bandages—some wore casts and slings. Others used canes and crutches to support themselves. A few had been the victims of fire, and these wore tight, blue skull-caps and collarless shirts and their faces and other areas of uncovered skin were bright with shining ointments and dressings.

It took a very great while for all these men and women—perhaps as many as two hundred of them—to arrive inside the building and make their way into the oval. They were being lined up in order of columns—several long lines, and each line punctuated here and there with attendant nurses. The voices of the sergeant-major and of the adjutant who was taking the parade were swallowed up in the dead acoustics, and—far above us—pigeons and sparrows moved among the girders and beams that supported the roof. I still had not seen Father.

At last, because my panic was spreading out of control, I tugged my mother's elbow and whispered that I couldn't see him. Had there been a mistake and he wasn't coming at all?

"No," she told me—looking down at me sideways and turning my head with her ungloved fingers. "There he is, there," she said. "But don't say anything, yet. He may not know we're here."

My father's figure could only be told because of his remarkable height. He was six feet four and had always been, to me, a giant. But now his height seemed barely greater than the height of half a dozen other men who were gathered out in the sand. His head was bowed, though once or twice he lifted his chin when he heard the commands. His shoulders, no longer squared, were rounded forward and dipping towards his centre. His neck was so thin I thought that someone or something must have cut over half of it away. I studied him solemnly and then looked up at my mother.

She had closed her eyes against him because she could not bear to look.

Later on that night, when everyone had gone to bed but none of us had gone to sleep, I said to Cy: "what is it?"

"What?"

"That's happened to Dad. . . ."

Cy didn't answer for a moment and then he said: "Dieppe."

I didn't understand. I thought it was a new disease.

We were told the next day not to mention at school that our father had come back home. Nothing was said about why it must be kept a secret. That was a bitter disappointment. Other children whose fathers had returned from overseas were always the centre of attention. Teachers, beaming smiles and patting heads, would congratulate them just as if they had won a prize. Classmates pestered them with questions: *what does he look like? Have you seen his wounds? How many Germans did he kill?* But we had none of this. All we got was: *what did you do on the weekend?*

Nothing.

All day Monday, Father remained upstairs. Our parents' bedroom was on the second floor directly over the sitting-room. Also, directly underneath the bedroom occupied by Cy and me. We had heard our mother's voice long into the night, apparently soothing him, telling him over and over again that everything was going to be all right.

We could not make out her words, but the tone of her voice was familiar. Over time, she had sat with each of us, deploying her comforts in all the same cadences and phrases, assuring us that pains and aches and sicknesses would pass.

Because we could not afford to lose the sale of even one flower, neither the single rose bought once a week by Edna Holmes to cheer her ailing sister, nor the daily boutonnière of Colonel Matheson—our mother had persuaded Mrs. Adams, the grocer's wife, to tend the store while she "nipped home" once every hour to see to Father's needs. It was only later that we children realized what those needs entailed. He was drinking more or less constantly in every waking hour, and our mother's purpose was first to tempt him with food—which he refused—and then to make certain that his matches and cigarettes did not set fire to the house.

On the Wednesday, Father emerged from his shell around two o'clock in the afternoon. We were all at school, of course, and I have only the account of what follows from my mother. When she returned at two, Mother found that Father had come down into the hallway, fully dressed in civilian clothes. He had already donned his greatcoat when she arrived. She told me that, at first, he had seemed to be remarkably sober. He told her he wanted to go outside and walk in the street. He wanted to go and see the store, he said.

"But you can't wear your greatcoat, David," she told him.

"Why?"

"Because you're in civilian dress. You know that's not allowed. A man was arrested just last week."

"I wasn't here last week," said my father.

"Nevertheless," my mother told him, "this man was arrested because it is not allowed."

"But I'm a soldier!" my father yelled.

My mother had to play this scene with all the care and cunning she could muster. The man who had been arrested had been a deserter. All that winter, desertions had been increasing and there had been demonstrations of overt disloyalty. People had shouted *down with the King!* and had booed the Union Jack. There were street gangs of youths who called themselves *Zombies* and they hung around the Masonic Temple on Yonge Street and the Palais Royale at Sunnyside. Some of these young men were in uniform, members of the Home Guard: reserves who had been promised, on joining up, they would not be sent overseas. They may have disapproved of the war, but they did not disapprove of fighting. They waited outside the dancehalls, excessively defensive of their manhood, challenging the servicemen who were dancing inside to *come out fighting and show us your guts!* Men had been killed in such encounters and the encounters had been increasing. The government was absolutely determined to stamp these incidents out before they spread across the country. These were the darkest hours of the war and morale, both in and out of the Forces, was at its lowest ebb. If my father had appeared on the street with his military greatcoat worn over his civilian clothes, it would have been assumed he was a *Zombie* or a deserter and he would have been arrested instantly. Our neighbours would have turned him in, no matter who he was. Our patriotism had come to that.

"I don't have a civilian overcoat," my father said. "And don't suggest that I put on my uniform, because I won't. My uniform stinks of sweat and I hate it."

"Well, you aren't going out like that," my mother said. "That's all there is to it. Why not come to the kitchen and I'll fix you a sandwich. . . ."

"I don't want a goddamned sandwich," my father yelled at her. "I want to see the store!"

At this point, he tore off his greatcoat and flung it onto the stairs. And then, before my mother could prevent him, he was out the door and running down the steps.

My mother—dressed in her green shop apron and nothing but a scarf to warm her—raced out after him.

What would the neighbours think? What would the neighbours say? How could she possibly explain?

By the time she had reached the sidewalk, my father had almost reached the corner. But, when she got to Yonge Street, her fears were somewhat allayed. My father had not gone into Max's Flowers but was standing one door shy of it, staring into the butcher's window.

"What's going on here?" he said, as my mother came abreast of him. Mother did not know what he meant.

"Where is Mister Schickel, Lily?" he asked her.

She had forgotten that, as well.

"Mister Schickel has left," she told him—trying to be calm—trying to steer my father wide of the butcher's window and in towards their own front stoop.

"Left?" my father shouted. "He's only just managed to pay off his mortgage! And who the hell is this impostor, Reilly?"

"Reilly?"

"Arthur Reilly the bloody butcher!" My father pointed at and read the sign that had replaced *Oskar Schickel, Butcher* in the window.

"Mister Reilly has been there most of the winter, David. Didn't I write and tell you that?" She knew very well she hadn't.

My father blinked at the meagre cuts of rationed meat displayed beyond the glass and said: "what happened to Oskar, Lily? Tell me."

And so, she had to tell him, like it or not.

Mister Schickel's name was disagreeable—stuck up there on Yonge Street across from Rosedale—and someone from Park Road had thrown a stone through the window.

There. It was said.

"But Oskar wasn't a German," my father whispered. "He was a Canadian."

"But his name was German, David."

My father put his fingers against the glass and did not appear to respond to what my mother had said.

At last, my mother pulled at his arm. "Why not come back home," she said. "You can come and see the shop tomorrow."

My father, while my mother watched him, concentrated very hard and moved his finger over the dusty glass of Oskar Schickel's store.

"What are you doing, David?"

"Nothing," said my father. "Setting things right, that's all."

Then he stepped back and said to her: "now—we'll go home."

What he had written was:

Oskar Schickel: Proprietor in absentia.

Mother said that Mrs. Reilly rushed outside as soon as they had reached the corner and she washed the window clean.

This was the only remaining decent thing my father did until the day he died.

The rest was all a nightmare.

I had never seen Dieppe. I had seen its face in photographs. I had read all the books and heard all the stories. The battle, of which my father had been a victim, had taken place in August of 1942—roughly six months before he was returned to us. Long since then, in my adult years, I have seen that battle, or seen its parts, through the medium of documentary film. It was only after Cy and Rita had vetted these films that I was able to watch. Till then, I had been afraid I would catch my father's image unawares—fearful that somehow our eyes would meet in that worst of moments. I couldn't bear the thought of seeing him destroyed. So, I had seen all this—the photographs, the books, the films—but I had never seen the town of Dieppe itself until that day in May of 1987 when I took my father's ashes there to scatter them.

Before I can begin this ending, I have to make it clear that the last thing I want to provoke is the sentimental image of a wind-blown stretch of rocky beach with a rainbow of ashes arching over the stones and blowing out to sea. If you want that image, let me tell you that had been the way it was when Cy, my brother, and Rita, my sister, and I went walking, wading into the ocean south of Lunenburg, Nova Scotia— where our mother had been born—to cast her ashes into the air above the Atlantic. Then there was almost music and we rejoiced because our mother had finally gained her freedom from a life that had become intolerable. But in Dieppe, when I shook my father's ashes out of their envelope, there was no rejoicing. None.

I felt, in fact, as if had brought the body of an infidel into a holy place and laid it down amongst the true believers. Still, this was what my father had wanted—and how could I refuse him? Neither Cy nor Rita would do it for him. *Gone*, they had said. *Good riddance.*

And so it fell to me.

I was always the least informed. I was always the most inquisitive. During my childhood, nobody told me—aside from the single word *Dieppe*—what it was that had happened to my father. And yet, perhaps because I knew the least and because I was the youngest and seemed the most naïve and willing, it was more than often me he focused on.

His tirades would begin in silence—the silence we had been warned of when he first returned. He would sit at the head of the table, eating a piece of fish and drinking from a glass of beer. The beer was always dark in colour. Gold.

Our dining-room had a window facing west. Consequently, winter sunsets in particular got in his eyes.

Curtain, he would say at his plate—and jab his fork at me.

If I didn't understand because his mouth was full, my mother would reach my sleeve and pull it with her fingers. *The curtain, Ben*, she would say. *Your father's eyes.*

Yes, ma'am. Down I'd get and pull the curtain.

Then, no sooner would I be reseated than my father—still addressing his plate—would mumble *lights*. And I would rise and turn on the lights. Then, when I was back at last in my chair, he would look at me and say, without apparent rancour, *why don't you tell me to shove the goddamn curtain up my ass?*

You will understand my silence in response to this if you understand that—before he went away—the worst my father had ever said in our presence had been *damn* and *hell*. The ultimate worst had been *Christ!* when he'd nearly sliced his finger off with a knife. Then, however, he hadn't known that anyone was listening. And so, when he started to talk this way—and perhaps especially at table—it paralyzed me.

Cy or Mother would sometimes attempt to intervene, but he always cut them off with something worse than he'd said to me. Then he would turn his attention back in my direction and continue. He urged me to refuse his order, then to upbraid him, finally to openly defy him—call him the worst of the words he could put in my mouth and hit him. Of course, I never did any of these things, but the urging, the cajoling and ultimately the begging never ceased.

One night, he came into the bedroom where I slept in the bunk-bed over Cy and he shouted at me *why don't you fight back?* Then he dragged my covers off and threw me onto the floor against the bureau. All this was done in the dark, and after my mother had driven me down in the truck to the Emergency Ward of Wellesley Hospital, the doctors told her that my collar-bone was broken. I heard my mother saying *yes, he fell out of bed.*

Everyone—even I—conspired to protect him. The trouble was, my father had no wish to protect himself. At least, it seemed that way until a fellow veteran of Dieppe turned up one day in the shop and my father turned on him with a pair of garden shears and tried to drive him back onto Yonge Street. Far from being afraid of my father, the other man took off his jacket and threw it in my father's face and all the while he stood there, the man was yelling at my father: *Coward! Coward! Yellow Bastard!*

Then, he turned around and walked away. The victor.

Thinking for sure the police would come, my mother drew the blind and closed the shop for the rest of the day.

But that was not the end of it. She gathered us together out on the porch and Cy was told to open a can of pork and beans and to make what our mother called a *passel of toast.* He and Rita and I were to eat this meal in the kitchen, after which Cy, who'd been handed a dollar bill my mother had lifted from the till, was to take us down to the Uptown Theatre where an Abbott and Costello film was playing. All these ordinary things we did. Nonetheless, we knew that our father had gone mad.

It was summer then and when the movie was over, I remember Cy and Rita and I stood on the street and the sidewalks gave off heat and the air around us smelled of peanuts and popcorn and Cy said: "I don't think it's safe to go home just yet." For almost an hour, we wandered on Yonge Street, debating what we should do and, at last, we decided we would test the waters by going and looking at the house and listening to see if there was any yelling.

Gibson Avenue only has about twenty houses, most of them semi-detached—and all of them facing south and the park. The porches and the stoops that night were filled with our neighbours drinking beer from coffee cups and fanning themselves with paper plates and folded bits of the *Daily Star*. They were drinking out of cups—you could smell the beer—because the law back then forbade the public consumption, under any circumstance, of alcohol. Whatever you can hide does not exist.

Passing, we watched our neighbours watching us—the Matlocks and the Wheelers and the Conrads and the Bolts—and we knew they were thinking *there go the Max kids and David Max, their father, tried to kill a man today in his store with gardening shears. . . .*

"Hello, Cy."

"Hello."

"Ben. Rita."

"Hi."

"Good-night . . ."

We went and stood together on the sidewalk out in front of our house.

Inside, everything seemed to be calm and normal. The lights were turned on in their usual distribution—most of them downstairs. The radio was playing. Someone was singing *Praise the Lord and Pass the Ammunition.*

Cy went up the steps and turned the handle. He was brave—but I'd always known that. Rita and I were told to wait on the porch.

Two minutes passed—or five—or ten—and finally Cy returned. He was very white and his voice was dry, but he wasn't shaking and all he said was: "you'd better come in. I'm calling the police."

Our father had tried to kill our mother with a hammer. She was lying on the sofa and her hands were broken because she had used them trying to fend off the blows.

Father had disappeared. The next day, he turned himself in because, as he told the doctors, he had come to his senses. He was kept for a year and a half—almost until the war was over—at the Asylum for the Insane on Queen Street. None of us children was allowed to visit him there—but our mother went to see him six months after he had been committed. She told me they sat in a long, grey room with bars on all the windows. My father wore a dressing gown and hadn't shaved. Mother said he couldn't look her in the eyes. She told him that she forgave him for what he had done. But my father never forgave himself. My mother said she never saw his eyes again.

Two weeks after our father had tried to kill our mother, a brick was thrown through the window of Max's Flowers. On the brick, a single word was printed in yellow chalk.

Murderer.

Mother said: "there's no way around this, now. I'm going to have to explain."

That was how we discovered what had gone wrong with our father at Dieppe.

Our mother had known this all along, and I still have strong suspicions Cy had found it out and maybe Rita before our mother went through the formal procedure of sitting us down and telling us all together. Maybe they had thought I was just too young to understand. Maybe Cy and maybe Rita hadn't known. Maybe they had only guessed. At any rate, I had a very strong sense that I was the only one who received our mother's news in a state of shock.

Father had risen, since his enlistment in 1939, all the way up from an NCO to the rank of captain. Everyone had adored him in the army. He was what they called a natural leader. His men were particularly fond of him and they would, as the saying goes, have followed him anywhere. Then came Dieppe. All but a handful of those who went into battle there were Canadians. This was our Waterloo. Our Gettysburg.

There isn't a single history book you can read—there isn't a single man who was there who won't tell you—there isn't a single scrap of evidence in any archive to suggest that the battle of Dieppe was anything but a total and appalling disaster. Most have called it a slaughter.

Dieppe is a port and market town on the coast of Normandy in northern France. In 1942, the British High Command had chosen it to be the object of a practice raid in preparation for the invasion of Europe. The Allies on every front were faltering, then. A gesture was needed, and even the smallest of victories would do.

And so, on the 19th of August, 1942, the raid on Dieppe had taken place—and the consequent carnage had cost the lives of over a thousand Canadians. Over two thousand were wounded or taken prisoner. Five thousand set out; just over one thousand came back.

My father never left his landing craft.

He was to have led his men ashore in the second wave of troops to follow the tanks—but, seeing the tanks immobilized, unable to move because the beaches were made of stone and the stones had jammed the tank tracks—and seeing the evident massacre of the first wave of troops whose attempt at storming the shore had been repulsed by machine-gun fire from the cliffs above the town—my father froze in his place and could not move. His men—it is all too apparent—did not know what to do. They had received no order to advance and yet, if they stayed, they were sitting ducks.

In the end, though a handful escaped by rushing forward into the water, the rest were blown to pieces when their landing craft was shelled. In the meantime, my father had recovered enough of his wits to crawl back over the end of the landing craft, strip off his uniform and swim out to sea where he was taken on board a British destroyer sitting offshore.

The destroyer, H.M.S. *Berkley*, was ultimately hit and everyone on board, including my father—no one knowing who he was—was transferred to another ship before the *Berkley* was scuttled where she sat. My father made it all the way back to England, where his burns and wounds were dressed and where he debated taking advantage of the chaos to disappear, hoping that, in the long run, he would be counted among the dead.

His problem was, his conscience had survived. He stayed and, as a consequence, he was confronted by survivors who knew his story. He was dishonourably discharged and sent home to us. Children don't understand such things. The only cowards they recognize are figures cut from comic books or seen on movie screens.

Fathers cannot be cowards.

It is impossible.

*

His torment and his grief were to lead my father all the way to the grave. He left our mother, in the long run, though she would not have wished him to do so and he lived out his days in little bars and back-street beer parlours, seeking whatever solace he could find with whores and derelicts whose stories might have matched his own. The phone would ring and we would dread it. Either it was him or news of him—either his drunken harangue or the name of his most recent jail.

He died in the Wellesley Hospital, the place where I was born—and when he was dying he asked to see his children. Cy and Rita "could not be reached," but I was found—where he'd always found me— sitting within yelling distance. Perhaps this sounds familiar to other children—of whatever age—whose parents, whether one of them or both of them, have made the mistake of losing faith too soon in their children's need to love.

I would have loved a stone.

If only he had known.

He sensed it, maybe, in the end. He told me he was sorry for everything—and meant it. He told me the names of all his men and he said he had walked with them all through hell, long since their deaths, to do them honour. He hoped they would understand him, now.

I said they might.

He asked if his ashes could be put with theirs.

Why not, I thought. *A stone amongst stones.*

The beaches at Dieppe can throw you off balance. The angle at which they slope into the water is both steep and dangerous. At high tide you can slide into the waves and lose your footing before you've remembered how to swim. The stones are treacherous. But they are also beautiful.

My father's ashes were contraband. You can't just walk about with someone's remains, in whatever form, in your suitcase. Stepping off the *Sealink* ferry, I carried my father in an envelope addressed to myself in Canada. This was only in case I was challenged. There was hardly more than a handful of him there. I had thrown the rest of him into the English Channel as the coast of Normandy was coming into view. It had been somewhat more than disconcerting to see the interest his ashes caused amongst the gulls and other sea birds. I had hoped to dispose of him in a private way, unnoticed. But a woman with two small children came and stood beside me at the railing and I heard her explain that *this nice gentleman is taking care of our feathered friends.* I hoped that, if my father was watching, he could laugh. I had to look away.

The ferry arrived in the early afternoon and—once I had booked myself into La Présidence Hotel—I went for a walk along the promenade above the sea-wall. It being May, the offshore breeze was warm and filled with the faintest scent of apple trees in bloom.

I didn't want to relive the battle. I hadn't come to conjure ghosts. But the ghosts and the battle are palpable around you there, no matter what your wishes are. The sound of the tide rolling back across the stones is all the cue you need to be reminded of that summer day in 1942. I stood that evening, resting my arms along the wall and thinking *at last, my father has come ashore.*

In the morning, before the town awoke, I got up in the dark and was on the beach when the sun rose inland beyond the cliffs. I wore a thick woollen sweater, walking shorts and a pair of running shoes. The envelope was in my pocket.

The concierge must have thought I was just another crazy North American off on my morning run. He grunted as I passed and I pretended not to know that he was there. Out on the beach, I clambered over retaining walls and petrified driftwood until I felt I was safely beyond the range of prying eyes.

The stones at Dieppe are mostly flint—and their colours range from white through yellow to red. The red stones look as if they have been washed in blood and the sight of them takes your breath away. I hunkered down above them, holding all that remained of my father in my fist. He felt like a powdered stone—pummelled and broken.

I let him down between my fingers, feeling him turn to paste— watching him divide and disappear.

He is dead and he is gone.

Weekends, our parents used to take us walking under the trees on Crescent Road. This was on the Rosedale side of Yonge Street. My brother Cy and I were always dressed in dark blue suits whose rough wool shorts would chafe against our thighs. Our knee socks—also blue—were turned down over thick elastic garters. Everything itched and smelled of Sunday. Cy had cleats on his shoes because he walked in such a way as to wear his heels *to the bone,* as my mother said—and causing much expense. The cleats made a wondrous clicking noise and you could always hear him coming. I wanted cleats, but I was refused because, no matter how I tried, I couldn't walk like that.

The houses sat up neat as pins beyond their lawns—blank-eyed windows, steaming chimneys—havens of wealth and all the mysteries of wealth.

Father often walked behind us. I don't know why. Mother walked in front with Rita. Rita always wore a dress that was either red or blue beneath her princess coat and in the wintertime she wore a sort of woollen cloche that was tied with a knitted string beneath her chin. Her Mary Jane shoes were just like Shirley Temple's shoes—which, for a while, was pleasing to Rita; then it was not. Rita always had an overpowering sense of image.

After the advent of our father's return, she said from the corner of her mouth one Sunday as we walked on Crescent Road that she and Cy and I had been named as if we were manufactured products: *Cy Max Office Equipment; Rita Max Household Appliances* and *Ben Max Watches.* This, she concluded, was why our father had always walked behind us. Proudly, he was measuring our performance. Now, he had ceased to walk behind us and our mother led us forward dressed in black.

Tick. Tick. Tick. That's me. The Ben Max Watch.

I have told our story. But I think it best—and I like it best—to end with all of us moving there beneath the trees in the years before the war. Mister and Mrs. David Max out walking with their children any Sunday afternoon in any kind of weather but the rain.

Colonel Matheson, striding down his walk, is caught and forced to grunt acknowledgement that we are there. He cannot ignore us, after all. We have seen him every weekday morning, choosing his boutonnière and buying it from us.

—1988

Mordecai Richler 1931–2001

In the short story sequence The Street *(1969), from which "Some Grist for Mervyn's Mill" is taken, Mordecai Richler provides a fictionalized account of his experiences growing up in the Montreal Jewish enclave of St. Urbain Street. Looking back at the milieu of his childhood both fondly and unsparingly, Richler captures the cadences of the voices that shaped his own.*

Canada's foremost satirist, Richler directed his barbs at many subjects in his long career as a journalist and a prolific writer of fiction, screenplays, and essays. He attacked injustice and discrimination in whatever form he saw it, and questioned the narrow view that seemed to him the danger of every group, even his own community. As "Some Grist for Mervyn's Mill" shows, his sharpest critiques were aimed at pretension, self-delusion, and the mistaken measure of an individual's worth in terms of material success.

Some Grist
for Mervyn's Mill

Mervyn Kaplansky stepped out of the rain on a dreary Saturday afternoon in August to inquire about our back bedroom.

"It's twelve dollars a week," my father said, "payable in advance."

Mervyn set down forty-eight dollars on the table. Astonished, my father retreated a step. "What's the rush-rush? Look around first. Maybe you won't like it here."

"You believe in electricity?"

There were no lights on in the house. "We're not the kind to skimp," my father said. "But we're orthodox here. Today is *shabus*."[1]

"No, no, no. Between people."

"What are you? A wise-guy."

"I do. And as soon as I came in here I felt the right vibrations. Hi, kid." Mervyn grinned breezily at me, but the hand he mussed my hair with was shaking. "I'm going to love it here."

My father watched, disconcerted but too intimidated to protest, as Mervyn sat down on the bed, bouncing a little to try the mattress. "Go get your mother right away," he said to me.

Fortunately, she had just entered the room. I didn't want to miss anything.

"Meet your new roomer," Mervyn said, jumping up.

"Hold your horses." My father hooked his thumbs in his suspenders. "What do you do for a living?" he asked.

"I'm a writer."

"With what firm?"

"No, no, no. For myself. I'm a creative artist."

My father could see at once that my mother was enraptured and so, reconciled to yet another defeat, he said, "Haven't you any . . . things?"

"When Oscar Wilde entered the United States and they asked him if he had anything to declare, he said, 'Only my genius.'"

My father made a sour face.

"My things are at the station," Mervyn said, swallowing hard. "May I bring them over?"

---

[1] Orthodox Jews are forbidden any kind of work on the Sabbath, which includes turning on light switches.

"Bring."

Mervyn returned an hour or so later with his trunk, several suit-cases, and an assortment of oddities that included a piece of driftwood, a wine bottle that had been made into a lamp base, a collection of pebbles, a twelve-inch-high replica of Rodin's *The Thinker*, a bull-fight poster, a Karsh portrait of G.B.S., innumerable notebooks, a ball-point pen with a built-in flashlight, and a framed cheque for fourteen dollars and eighty-five cents from the *Family Herald & Weekly Star.*

"Feel free to borrow any of our books," my mother said.

"Well, thanks. But I try not to read too much now that I'm a wordsmith myself. I'm afraid of being influenced, you see."

Mervyn was a short, fat boy with curly black hair, warm wet eyes, and an engaging smile. I could see his underwear through the triangles of tension that ran from button to button down his shirt. The last button had probably burst off. It was gone. Mervyn, I figured, must have been at least twenty-three years old, but he looked much younger.

"Where did you say you were from?" my father asked.

"I didn't."

Thumbs hooked in his suspenders, rocking on his heels, my father waited.

"Toronto," Mervyn said bitterly. "Toronto the Good. My father's a bigtime insurance agent and my brothers are in ladies' wear. They're in the rat-race. All of them."

"You'll find that in this house," my mother said, "we are not materialists."

Mervyn slept in—or, as he put it, stocked the unconscious—until noon every day. He typed through the afternoon and then, depleted, slept some more, and usually typed again deep into the night. He was the first writer I had ever met and I worshipped him. So did my mother.

"Have you ever noticed his hands," she said, and I thought she was going to lecture me about his chewed-up fingernails, but what she said was, "They're artist's hands. Your grandfather had hands like that." If a neighbour dropped in for tea, my mother would whisper, "We'll have to speak quietly," and, indicating the tap-tap of the typewriter from the back bedroom, she'd add, "in there, Mervyn is creating." My mother prepared special dishes for Mervyn. Soup, she felt, was especially nourishing. Fish was the best brain food. She discouraged chocolates and nuts because of Mervyn's complexion, but she brought him coffee at all hours, and if a day passed with no sound coming from the back room my mother would be extremely upset. Eventually, she'd knock softly on Mervyn's door. "Anything I can get you?" she'd ask.

"It's no use. It just isn't coming today. I go through periods like that, you know."

Mervyn was writing a novel, his first, and it was about the struggles of our people in a hostile society. The novel's title was, to begin with, a secret between Mervyn and my mother. Occasionally, he read excerpts to her. She made only one correction. "I wouldn't say 'whore,'" she said. "It isn't nice, is it? Say 'lady of easy virtue.'" The two of them began to go in for literary discussions. "Shakespeare," my mother would say, "Shakespeare knew everything." And Mervyn, nodding, would reply, "But he stole all his plots. He was a plagiarist." My mother told Mervyn about her father, the rabbi, and the books he had written in Yiddish. "At his funeral," she told him, "they had to have six motorcycle policemen to control the crowds." More than once my father came home from work to find the two of them still seated at the kitchen table, and his supper wasn't ready or he had to eat a cold plate. Flushing, stammering apologies, Mervyn would flee to his room. He was, I think, the only man who was ever afraid of my father, and this my father found very heady stuff. He spoke gruffly, even profanely in Mervyn's presence, and called him Moitle[2] behind his back. But, when you come down to it, all my father had against Mervyn was the fact that my mother no longer baked potato kugel. (Starch was bad for Mervyn.) My father began to spend more of his time playing cards at Tansky's Cigar & Soda, and when Mervyn fell behind with the rent, he threatened to take action.

"But you can't trouble him now," my mother said, "when he's in the middle of his novel. He works so hard. He's a genius maybe."

"He's peanuts, or what's he doing here?"

I used to fetch Mervyn cigarettes and headache tablets from the drugstore round the corner. On some days when it wasn't coming, the two of us would play casino and Mervyn, at his breezy best, used to wisecrack a lot. "What would you say," he said, "if I told you I aim to out-Emile Zola?" Once he let me read one of his stories, *Was The Champ A Chump?*, that had been printed in magazines in Australia and South Africa. I told him that I wanted to be a writer too. "Kid," he said, "a word from the wise. Never become a wordsmith. Digging ditches would be easier."

---

[2] "Myrtle" (pronounced with a mocking Yiddish accent); meant to suggest that Mervyn is effeminate.

From the day of his arrival Mervyn had always worked hard, but what with his money running low he was now so determined to get his novel done, that he seldom went out any more. Not even for a stroll. My mother felt this was bad for his digestion. So she arranged a date with Molly Rosen. Molly, who lived only three doors down the street, was the best looker on St. Urbain, and my mother noticed that for weeks now Mervyn always happened to be standing by the window when it was time for Molly to pass on the way home from work. "Now you go out," my mother said, "and enjoy. You're still a youngster. The novel can wait for a day."

"But what does Molly want with me?"

"She's crazy to meet you. For weeks now she's been asking questions."

Mervyn complained that he lacked a clean shirt, he pleaded a headache, but my mother said, "Don't be afraid she won't eat you." All at once Mervyn's tone changed. He tilted his head cockily. "Don't wait up for me," he said.

Mervyn came home early. "What happened?" I asked.

"I got bored."

"*With* Molly?"

"Molly's an insect. Sex is highly over-estimated, you know. It also saps an artist's creative energies."

But when my mother came home from her Talmud Torah meeting[3] and discovered that Mervyn had come home so early she felt that she had been personally affronted. Mrs. Rosen was summoned to tea.

"It's a Saturday night," she said, "she puts on her best dress, and that cheapskate where does he take her? To sit on the mountain. Do you know that she turned down three other boys, including Ready-To-Wear's *only* son, because you made such a *gedille?*"

"With dumb-bells like Ready-to-Wear she can have dates any night of the week. Mervyn's a creative artist."

"On a Saturday night to take a beautiful young thing to sit on the mountain. From those benches you can get piles."

"Don't be disgusting."

"She's got on her dancing shoes and you know what's for him a date? To watch the people go by. He likes to make up stories about them he says. You mean it breaks his heart to part with a dollar."

"To bring up your daughter to be a gold-digger. For shame."

[3] A meeting for the parents of students at the local Jewish parochial school.

"All right. I wasn't going to blab, but if that's how you feel—modern men and women, he told her, experiment *before* marriage. And right there on the bench he tried dirty filthy things with her. He . . ."

"Don't draw me no pictures. If I know your Molly he didn't have to try so hard."

"How dare you! She went out with him it was a favour for the marble cake recipe. The dirty piker he asked her to marry him he hasn't even got a job. She laughed in his face."

Mervyn denied that he had tried any funny stuff with Molly—he had too much respect for womankind, he said—but after my father heard that he had come home so early he no longer teased Mervyn when he stood by the window to watch Molly pass. He even resisted making wise-cracks when Molly's kid brother returned Mervyn's thick letters unopened. Once, he tried to console Mervyn. "With a towel over the face," he said gruffly, "one's the same as another."

Mervyn's cheeks reddened. He coughed. And my father turned away, disgusted.

"Make no mistake," Mervyn said with a sudden jaunty smile. "You're talking to a boy who's been around. We pen-pushers are notorious lechers."

Mervyn soon fell behind with the rent again and my father began to complain.

"You can't trouble him now," my mother said. "He's in agony. It isn't coming today."

"Yeah, sure. The trouble is there's something coming to me."

"Yesterday he read me a chapter from his book. It's so beautiful you could die." My mother told him that F. J. Kugelman, the Montreal corre-spondent of *The Jewish Daily Forward*, had looked at the book. "He says Mervyn is a very deep writer."

"Kugelman's for the birds. If Mervyn's such a big writer, let him make me out a cheque for the rent. That's my kind of reading, you know."

"Give him one week more. Something will come through for him, I'm sure."

My father waited another week, counting off the days. "E-Day minus three today," he'd say. "Anything come through for the genius?" Nothing, not one lousy dime, came through for Mervyn. In fact he had secretly borrowed from my mother for the postage to send his novel to a publisher in New York. "E-Day minus one today," my father said. And then, irritated because he had yet to be asked what the E stood for, he added. "E for Eviction."

On Friday my mother prepared an enormous potato kugel. But when my father came home, elated, the first thing he said was, "Where's Mervyn?"

"Can't you wait until after supper, even?"

Mervyn stepped softly into the kitchen. "You want me?" he asked.

My father slapped a magazine down on the table. *Liberty.* He opened it at a short story titled *A Doll For The Deacon.* "Mel Kane, Jr.," he said, "isn't that your literary handle?"

"His *nom-de-plume*," my mother said.

"Then the story is yours." My father clapped Mervyn on the back. "Why didn't you tell me you were a writer? I thought you were a . . . well, a fruitcup. You know what I mean. A long-hair."

"Let me see that," my mother said.

Absently, my father handed her the magazine. "You mean to say," he said, "you made all that up out of your own head?"

Mervyn nodded. He grinned. But he could see that my mother was displeased.

"It's a top-notch story," my father said. Smiling, he turned to my mother. "All the time I thought he was a sponger. A poet. He's a writer. Can you beat that?" He laughed, delighted. "Excuse me," he said, and he went to wash his hands.

"Here's your story, Mervyn," my mother said. "I'd rather not read it."

Mervyn lowered his head.

"But you don't understand, Maw. Mervyn has to do that sort of stuff. For the money. He's got to eat too, you know."

My mother reflected briefly. "A little tip, then," she said to Mervyn. "Better he doesn't know why . . . well, you understand."

"Sure I do."

At supper my father said, "Hey, what's your novel called, Mr. Kane?"

"The DIRTY JEWS."

"*Are you crazy?*"

"It's an ironic title," my mother said.

"Wow! It sure is."

"I want to throw the lie back in their ugly faces," Mervyn said.

"Yeah. Yeah, sure." My father invited Mervyn to Tansky's to meet the boys. "In one night there," he said, "you can pick up enough material for a book."

"I don't think Mervyn is interested."

Mervyn, I could see, looked dejected. But he didn't dare antagonize my mother. Remembering something he had once told me, I said, "To a creative writer every experience is welcome."

"Yes, that's true," my mother said. "I hadn't thought of it like that."

So my father, Mervyn and I set off together. My father showed *Liberty* to all of Tansky's regulars. While Mervyn lit one cigarette off another, coughed, smiled foolishly and coughed again, my father introduced him as the up-and-coming writer.

"If he's such a big writer what's he doing on St. Urbain Street?"

My father explained that Mervyn had just finished his first novel. "When that comes out," he said, "this boy will be batting in the major leagues."

The regulars looked Mervyn up and down. His suit was shiny.

"You must understand," Mervyn said, "that, at the best of times, it's difficult for an artist to earn a living. Society is naturally hostile to us."

"So what's so special? I'm a plumber. Society isn't hostile to me, but I've got the same problem. Listen here, it's hard for anybody to earn a living."

"You don't get it," Mervyn said, retreating a step. "*I'm* in rebellion against society."

Tansky moved away, disgusted. "Gorki, there was a writer. This boy. . . ."

Molly's father thrust himself into the group surrounding Mervyn. "You wrote a novel," he asked, "it's true?"

"It's with a big publisher in New York right now," my father said.

"You should remember," Takifman said menacingly, "only to write good things about the Jews."

Shapiro winked at Mervyn. The regulars smiled, some shyly, others hopeful, believing. Mervyn looked back at them solemnly. "It is my profound hope," he said, "that in the years to come our people will have every reason to be proud of me."

Segal stood Mervyn for a Pepsi and a sandwich. "Six months from now," he said, "I'll be saying I knew you when. . . ."

Mervyn whirled around on his counter stool. "I'm going to out-Emile Zola," he said. He shook with laughter.

"Do you think there's going to be another war?" Perlman asked.

"Oh, lay off," my father said. "Give the man air. No wisdom outside of office hours, eh, Mervyn?"

Mervyn slapped his knees and laughed some more. Molly's father pulled him aside. "You wrote this story," he said, holding up *Liberty*, "and don't lie because I'll find you out."

"Yeah," Mervyn said, "I'm the grub-streeter who knocked that one off. But it's my novel that I really care about."

"You know who I am? I'm Molly's father. Rosen. Put it there, Mervyn. There's nothing to worry. You leave everything to me."

My mother was still awake when we got home. Alone at the kitchen table. "You were certainly gone a long time," she said to Mervyn.

"Nobody forced him to stay."

"He's too polite," my mother said, slipping her tooled leather bookmark between the pages of *Wuthering Heights*. "He wouldn't tell you when he was bored by such common types."

"Hey," my father said, remembering. "Hey, Mervyn. Can you beat that Takifman for a character?"

Mervyn started to smile, but my mother sighed and he looked away. "It's time I hit the hay," he said.

"Well," my father pulled down his suspenders. "If anyone wants to use the library let him speak now or forever hold his peace."

"*Please, Sam.* You only say things like that to disgust me. I know that."

My father went into Mervyn's room. He smiled a little. Mervyn waited, puzzled. My father rubbed his forehead. He pulled his ear. "Well, I'm not a fool. You should know that. Life does things to you, but . . ."

"It certainly does, Mr. Hersh."

"You won't end up a zero like me. So I'm glad for you. Well, good night."

But my father did not go to bed immediately. Instead, he got out his collection of pipes, neglected all these years, and sat down at the kitchen table to clean and restore them. And, starting the next morning, he began to search out and clip items in the newspapers, human interest stories with a twist, that might be exploited by Mervyn. When he came home from work—early, he had not stopped off at Tansky's—my father did not demand his supper right off but, instead, went directly to Mervyn's room. I could hear the two men talking in low voices. Finally, my mother had to disturb them. Molly was on the phone.

"Mr. Kaplansky. Mervyn. Would you like to take me out on Friday night? I'm free."

Mervyn didn't answer.

"We could watch the people go by. Anything, you say, Mervyn."

"Did your father put you up to this?"

"What's the diff? You wanted to go out with me. Well, on Friday, I'm free."

"I'm sorry. I can't do it."

"Don't you like me any more?"

"I sure do. And the attraction is more than merely sexual. But if we go out together it will have to be because you so desire it."

"Mervyn, if you don't take me out on Friday he won't let me out to the dance Saturday night with Solly. Please, Mervyn."

"Sorry. But I must answer in the negative."

Mervyn told my mother about the telephone conversation and immediately she said, "You did right." But a few days later, she became tremendously concerned about Mervyn. He no longer slept in each morning. Instead, he was the first one up in the house, to wait by the window for the postman. After he had passed, however, Mervyn did not settle down to work. He'd wander sluggishly about the house or go out for a walk. Usually, Mervyn ended up at Tansky's. My father would be waiting there.

"You know," Sugarman said, "many amusing things have happened to me in my life. It would make *some* book."

The men wanted to know Mervyn's opinion of Sholem Asch, the red menace, and ungrateful children.[4] They teased him about my father. "To hear him tell it you're a guaranteed genius."

"Well," Mervyn said, winking, blowing on his fingernails and rubbing them against his jacket lapel. "Who knows?"

But Molly's father said, "I read in the *Gazette* this morning where Hemingway was paid a hundred thousand dollars to make a movie from *one* story. A complete book must be worth at least five short stories. Wouldn't you say?"

And Mervyn, coughing, clearing his throat, didn't answer, but walked off quickly. His shirt collar, too highly starched, cut into the back of his hairless, reddening neck. When I caught up with him, he told me, "No wonder so many artists have been driven to suicide. Nobody understands us. We're not in the rat-race."

---

[4] Sholem Asch: an early twentieth-century Polish-Jewish author who wrote in Yiddish. "The red menace" was the phrase used in post–World War II North America as shorthand for the perceived threat of international Communism.

Molly came by at seven-thirty on Friday night.

"Is there something I can do for you?" my mother asked.

"I'm here to see Mr. Kaplansky. I believe he rents a room here."

"Better to rent out a room than give fourteen ounces to the pound."

"If you are referring to my father's establishment then I'm sorry he can't give credit to everybody."

"We pay cash everywhere. Knock wood."

"I'm sure. Now, may I see Mr. Kaplansky, *if you don't mind?*"

"He's still dining. But I'll inquire."

Molly didn't wait. She pushed past my mother into the kitchen. Her eyes were a little puffy. It looked to me like she had been crying. "Hi," she said. Molly wore her soft black hair in an upsweep. Her mouth was painted very red.

"Siddown," my father said. "Make yourself homely." Nobody laughed. "It's a joke," he said.

"Are you ready, Mervyn?"

Mervyn fiddled with his fork. "I've got work to do tonight," he said.

"I'll put up a pot of coffee for you right away."

Smiling thinly, Molly pulled back her coat, took a deep breath, and sat down. She had to perch on the edge of the chair either because of her skirt or that it hurt her to sit. "About the novel," she said, smiling at Mervyn, "congrats."

"But it hasn't even been accepted by a publisher yet."

"It's good, isn't it?"

"Of course it's good," my mother said.

"Then what's there to worry? Come on," Molly said, rising. "Let's skedaddle."

We all went to the window to watch them go down the street together.

"Look at her how she's grabbing his arm," my mother said. "Isn't it disgusting?"

"You lost by a T.K.O.," my father said.

"*Thanks,*" my mother said, and she left the room.

My father blew on his fingers. "Whew," he said. We continued to watch by the window. "I'll bet you she sharpens them on a grindstone every morning to get them so pointy, and he's such a shortie he wouldn't even have to bend over to . . ." My father sat down, lit his pipe, and opened *Liberty* at Mervyn's story. "You know, Mervyn's not that special a guy. Maybe it's not as hard as it seems to write a story."

"Digging ditches would be easier," I said.

My father took me to Tansky's for a coke. Drumming his fingers on the counter, he answered questions about Mervyn. "Well, it has to do with this thing . . . The Muse. On some days, with the Muse, he works better. But on other days . . ." My father addressed the regulars with a daring touch of condescension; I had never seen him so assured before. "Well, that depends. But he says Hollywood is very corrupt."

Mervyn came home shortly after midnight.

"I want to give you a word of advice," my mother said. "That girl comes from very common people. You can do better, you know."

My father cracked his knuckles. He didn't look at Mervyn.

"You've got your future career to think of. You must choose a mate who won't be an embarrassment in the better circles."

"Or still better stay a bachelor," my father said.

"Nothing more dreadful can happen to a person," my mother said, "than to marry somebody who doesn't share his interests."

"Play the field a little," my father said, drawing on his pipe.

My mother looked into my father's face and laughed. My father's voice fell to a whisper. "You get married too young," he said, "and you live to regret it."

My mother laughed again. Her eyes were wet.

"I'm not the kind to stand by idly," Mervyn said, "while you insult Miss Rosen's good name."

My father, my mother, looked at Mervyn as if surprised by his presence. Mervyn retreated, startled. *"I mean that,"* he said.

"Just who do you think you're talking to?" my mother said. She looked sharply at my father.

"Hey, there," my father said.

"I hope," my mother said, "success isn't giving you a swelled head."

"Success won't change me. I'm steadfast. But you are intruding into my personal affairs. Good night."

My father seemed both dismayed and a little pleased that someone had spoken up to my mother.

"And just what's ailing you?" my mother asked.

"Me? Nothing."

"If you could only see yourself. At your age. A pipe."

"According to the *Digest* it's safer than cigarettes."

"You know absolutely nothing about people. Mervyn would never be rude to me. It's only his artistic temperament coming out."

My father waited until my mother had gone to bed and then he slipped into Mervyn's room. "Hi." He sat down on the edge of Mervyn's bed. "Tell me to mind my own business if you want me to, but . . . well, have you had bad news from New York? The publisher?"

"I'm still waiting to hear from New York."

"Sure," my father said, jumping up. "Sorry. Good night. But he paused briefly at the door. "I've gone out on a limb for you. Please don't let me down."

Molly's father phoned the next morning. "You had a good time Mervyn?"

"Yeah. Yeah, sure."

"Atta boy. That girl she's crazy about you. Like they say she's walking on air."

Molly, they said, had told the other girls in the office at Susy's Smart-Wear that she would probably soon be leaving for, as she put it, tropical climes. Gitel Shalinsky saw her shopping for beach wear on Park Avenue—in November, this—and the rumour was that Mervyn had already accepted a Hollywood offer for his book, a guaranteed best-seller. A couple of days later a package came for Mervyn. It was his novel. There was a printed form enclosed with it. The publishers felt the book was not for them.

"Tough luck," my father said.

"It's nothing," Mervyn said breezily. "Some of the best wordsmiths going have had their novels turned down six-seven times before a publisher takes it. Besides, this outfit wasn't for me in the first place. It's a homosexual company. They only print the pretty-pretty prose boys." Mervyn laughed, he slapped his knees. "I'll send the book off to another publisher today."

My mother made Mervyn his favourite dishes for dinner. "You have real talent," she said to him, "and everything will come to you." Afterwards, Molly came by. Mervyn came home very late this time, but my mother waited up for him all the same.

"I'm invited to eat at the Rosens on Saturday night. Isn't that nice?"

"But I ordered something special from the butcher for us here."

"I'm sorry. I didn't know."

"So now you know. Please yourself, Mervyn. Oh, it's alright. I changed your bed. But you could have told me, you know."

Mervyn locked his hands together to quiet them. "Tell you what, for Christ's sake? There's nothing to tell."

"It's alright, *boyele*," my mother said. "Accidents happen."

Once more my father slipped into Mervyn's room. "It's O.K.," he said, "don't worry about Saturday night. Play around. Work the kinks out. But don't put anything in writing. You might live to regret it."

"I happen to think Molly is a remarkable girl."

"Me too. I'm not as old as you think."

"No, no, no. You don't understand."

My father showed Mervyn some clippings he had saved for him. One news story told of two brothers who had discovered each other by accident after twenty-five years, another was all about a funny day at court. He also gave Mervyn an announcement for the annual Y.H.M.A.[5] *Beacon* short story contest. "I've got an idea for you," he said. "Listen, Mervyn, in the movies . . . well, when Humphrey Bogart, for instance, lights up a Chesterfield or asks for a coke you think he doesn't get a nice little envelope from the companies concerned? Sure he does. Well, your problem seems to be money. So why couldn't you do the same thing in books? Like if your hero has to fly somewhere, for instance, why use an unnamed airline? Couldn't he go TWA because it's the safest, the best, and maybe he picks up a cutie-pie on board? Or if your central character is . . . well, a lush, couldn't he always insist on Seagram's because it's the greatest? Get the idea? I could write, say, TWA, Pepsi, Seagram's and Adam's Hats and find out just how much a book plug is worth to them, and you . . . well, what do you think?"

"I could never do that in a book of mine, that's what I think. It would reflect on my integrity. People would begin to talk, see."

But people had already begun to talk. Molly's kid brother told me Mervyn had made a hit at dinner. His father, he said, had told Mervyn he felt, along with the moderns, that in-laws should not live with young couples, not always, but the climate in Montreal was a real killer for his wife, and if it so happened that he ever had a son-in-law in, let's say, California . . . well, it would be nice to visit . . . and Mervyn agreed that families should be close-knit. Not all the talk was favourable, however. The boys on the street were hostile to Mervyn. An outsider, a Torontonian, they felt, was threatening to carry off our Molly.

"There they go," the boys would say as Molly and Mervyn walked hand-in-hand past the pool room, "Beauty and the Beast."

---

[5] Young Hebrew Men's Association; also known as the Y.M.H.A.

"All these years they've been looking, and looking, and looking, and there he is, the missing link."

Mervyn was openly taunted on the street.

"Hey, big writer. Lard-ass. How many periods in a bottle of ink?"

"Shakespeare, come here. How did you get to look like that, or were you paid for the accident?"

But Mervyn assured me that he wasn't troubled by the boys. "The masses," he said, "have always been hostile to the artist. They've driven plenty of our number to self-slaughter, you know. But I can see through them."

His novel was turned down again.

"It doesn't matter," Mervyn said. "There are better publishers."

"But wouldn't they be experts there," my father asked. "I mean maybe . . ."

"Look at this, will you? This time they sent me a personal letter! You know who this is from? It's from one of the greatest editors in all of America."

"Maybe so," my father said uneasily, "but he doesn't want your book."

"He admires my energy and enthusiasm, doesn't he?"

Once more Mervyn mailed off his novel, but this time he did not resume his watch by the window. Mervyn was no longer the same. I don't mean that his face had broken out worse than ever—it had, it's true, only that was probably because he was eating too many starchy foods again—but suddenly he seemed indifferent to his novel's fate. I gave birth, he said, sent my baby out into the world, and now he's on his own. Another factor was that Mervyn had become, as he put it, pregnant once more (he looks it too, one of Tansky's regulars told me): that is to say, he was at work on a new book. My mother interpreted this as a very good sign and she did her utmost to encourage Mervyn. Though she continued to change his sheets just about every other night, she never complained about it. Why, she even pretended this was normal procedure in our house. But Mervyn seemed perpetually irritated and he avoided the type of literary discussion that had formerly given my mother such deep pleasure. Every night now he went out with Molly and there were times when he did not return until four or five in the morning.

And now, curiously enough, it was my father who waited up for Mervyn, or stole out of bed to join him in the kitchen. He would make coffee and take down his prized bottle of apricot brandy. More than once I was wakened by his laughter. My father told Mervyn stories of his

father's house, his boyhood, and the hard times that came after. He told
Mervyn how his mother-in-law had been bedridden in our house for
seven years, and with pride implicit in his every word—a pride that
would have amazed and maybe even flattered my mother—he told
Mervyn how my mother had tended to the old lady better than any
nurse with umpteen diplomas. "To see her now," I heard my father say,
"is like night and day. Before the time of the old lady's stroke she was
no sour-puss. Well, that's life." He told Mervyn about the first time he
had seen my mother, and how she had written him letters with poems
by Shelley, Keats and Byron in them, when all the time he had lived only
two streets away. But another time I heard my father say, "When I was
a young man, you know, there were days on end when I never went to
bed. I was so excited. I used to go out and walk the streets better than
snooze. I thought if I slept maybe I'd miss something. Now isn't that
crazy?" Mervyn muttered a reply. Usually, he seemed weary and self-
absorbed. But my father was irrepressible. Listening to him, his tender
tone with Mervyn and the surprise of his laughter, I felt that I had reason
to be envious. My father had never talked like that to me or my sister.
But I was so astonished to discover this side of my father, it was all so
unexpected, that I soon forgot my jealousy.

One night I heard Mervyn tell my father, "Maybe the novel I sent out
is no good. Maybe it's just something I had to work out of my system."

"Are you crazy it's no good? I told everyone you were a big writer."

"It's the apricot brandy talking," Mervyn said breezily. "I was only
kidding you."

But Mervyn had his problems. I heard from Molly's kid brother that
Mr. Rosen had told him he was ready to retire. "Not that I want to be
a burden to anybody," he had said. Molly had begun to take all the
movie magazines available at Tansky's. "So that when I meet the stars
face to face," she had told Gitel, "I shouldn't put my foot in it, and
embarrass Merv."

Mervyn began to pick at his food, and it was not uncommon for him
to leap up from the table and rush to the bathroom, holding his hand to
his mouth. I discovered for the first time that my mother had bought a
rubber sheet for Mervyn's bed. If Mervyn had to pass Tansky's, he no
longer stopped to shoot the breeze. Instead, he would hurry past, his
head lowered. Once, Segal stopped him. "What's a matter," he said,
"you too good for us now?"

Tansky's regulars began to work on my father. "All of a sudden, your genius there, he's such a B.T.O.,"[6] Sugerman said, "that he has no time for us here."

"Let's face it," my father said. "You're zeros. We all are. But my friend Mervyn . . ."

"Don't tell me, Sam. He's full of beans. Baked beans."

My father stopped going to Tansky's altogether. He took to playing solitaire at home.

"What are you doing here?" my mother asked.

"Can't I stay home one night? It's my house too, you know."

"I want the truth, Sam."

"Aw, those guys. You think those cockroaches know what an artist's struggle is?" He hesitated, watching my mother closely. "By them it must be that Mervyn isn't good enough. He's no writer."

"You know," my mother said, "he owes us seven weeks' rent now."

"The first day Mervyn came here," my father said, his eyes half-shut as he held a match to his pipe, "he said there was a kind of electricity between us. Well, I'm not going to let him down over a few bucks."

But something was bothering Mervyn. For that night and the next he did not go out with Molly. He went to the window to watch her pass again and then retreated to his room to do the crossword puzzles.

"Feel like a casino?" I asked.

"I love that girl," Mervyn said. "I adore her."

"I thought everything was O.K., but I thought you were making time."

"No, no, no. I want to marry her. I told Molly that I'd settle down and get a job if she'd have me."

"Are you crazy? A job? With your talent?"

"That's what she said."

"Aw, let's play casino. It'll take your mind off things."

"She doesn't understand. Nobody does. For me to take a job is not like some ordinary guy taking a job. I'm always studying my own reactions. I want to know how a shipper feels from the inside."[7]

"You mean you'd take a job *as a shipper?*"

"But it's not like I'd really be a shipper. It would look like that from the outside, but I'd really be studying my co-workers all the time. I'm an artist, you know."

---

[6] Big-time operator.
[7] A shipper claimed incoming merchandise for local merchants and delivered it to them for a small fee.

"Stop worrying, Mervyn. Tomorrow there'll be a letter begging you for your book."

But the next day nothing came. A week passed. Ten days.

"That's a very good sign," Mervyn said. "It means they are considering my book very carefully."

It got so we all waited around for the postman. Mervyn was aware that my father did not go to Tansky's any more and that my mother's friends had begun to tease her. Except for his endless phone calls to Molly he hardly ever came out of his room. The phone calls were futile. Molly wouldn't speak to him.

One evening my father returned from work, his face flushed. "Son-of-a-bitch," he said, "that Rosen he's a cockroach. You know what he's saying? He wouldn't have in his family a faker or a swindler. He said you were not a writer, Mervyn, but garbage." My father started to laugh. "But I trapped him for a liar. You know what he said? That you were going to take a job as a shipper. Boy, did I ever tell him."

"What did you say?" my mother asked.

"I told him good. Don't you worry. When I lose my temper, you know. . . ."

"Maybe it wouldn't be such a bad idea for Mervyn to take a job. Better than go into debt he could—"

"You shouldn't have bragged about me to your friends so much," Mervyn said to my mother. "I didn't ask it."

"*I'm* a braggart? You take that back. You owe me an apology, I think. After all, *you're* the one who said you were such a big writer."

"My talent is unquestioned. I have stacks of letters from important people and—"

"I'm waiting for an apology, Sam?"

"I have to be fair. I've seen some of the letters, so that's true. But that's not to say Emily Post would approve of Mervyn calling you a—"

"My husband was right the first time. When he said you were a sponger, Mervyn."

"Don't worry," Mervyn said, turning to my father. "You'll get your rent back no matter what. Good night."

I can't swear to it. I may have imagined it. But when I got up to go to the toilet late that night it seemed to me that I heard Mervyn sobbing in his room. Anyway, the next morning the postman rang the bell and Mervyn came back with a package and a letter.

"Not again," my father said.

"No. This happens to be a letter from the most important publisher in the United States. They are going to pay me two thousand five hundred dollars for my book in advance against royalties."

"Hey. Lemme see that."

"Don't you trust me?"

"Of course we do." My mother hugged Mervyn. "All the time I knew you had it in you."

"This calls for a celebration," my father said, going to get the apricot brandy.

My mother went to phone Mrs. Fisher. "Oh, Ida, I just called to say I'll be able to bake for the bazaar after all. No, nothing new here. Oh, I almost forgot. Remember Mervyn you were saying he was nothing but a little twerp? Well, he just got a fantastic offer for his book from a publisher in New York. No, I'm only allowed to say it runs into four figures. Excited? That one. I'm not even sure he'll accept."

My father grabbed the phone to call Tansky's.

"One minute. Hold it. Couldn't we keep quiet about this, and have a private sort of celebration?"

My father got through to the store. "Hello, Sugarman? Everybody come over here. Drinks on the house. Why, of Korsakov. No, wise-guy. She certainly isn't. At her age? It's Mervyn. He's considering a five thousand dollar offer just to sign a contract for his book."

The phone rang an instant after my father had hung up.

"Well, hello Mrs. Rosen," my mother said. "Well, thank you. I'll give him the message. No, no, why should I have anything against you we've been neighbours for years. No. Certainly not. It wasn't *me* you called a piker. Your Molly didn't laugh in my face."

Unnoticed, Mervyn sat down on the sofa. He held his head in his hands.

"There's the doorbell," my father said.

"I think I'll lie down for a minute. Excuse me."

By the time Mervyn came out of his room again many of Tansky's regulars had arrived. "If it had been up to me," my father said, "none of you would be here. But Mervyn's not the type to hold grudges."

Molly's father elbowed his way through the group surrounding Mervyn. "I want you to know," he said, "that I'm proud of you today. There's nobody I'd rather have for a son-in-law."

"You're sort of hurrying things. Aren't you?"

"What? Didn't you propose to her a hundred times she wouldn't have you? And now I'm standing here to tell you alright and you're beginning with the shaking in the pants. This I don't like."

Everybody turned to stare. There was some good natured laughter.

"You wrote her such letters they still bring a blush to my face—"

"But they came back unopened."

Molly's father shrugged and Mervyn's face turned grey as a pencil eraser.

"But you listen here," Rosen said. "For Molly, if you don't mind, it isn't necessary for me to go begging."

"Here she is," somebody said.

The regulars moved in closer.

"Hi," Molly smelled richly of Lily of the Valley. You could see the outlines of her bra through her sweater (both were in Midnight Black, from Susy's Smart-Wear). Her tartan skirt was held together by an enormous gold-plated safety pin. "Hi, doll." She rushed up to Mervyn and kissed him. "Maw just told me." Molly turned to the others, her smile radiant. "Mr. Kaplansky has asked for my hand in matrimony. We are engaged."

"Congratulations!" Rosen clapped Mervyn on the back. "The very best to you both."

There were whoops of approval all around.

"When it comes to choosing a bedroom set you can't go wrong with my son-in-law Lou."

"I hope," Takifman said sternly, "yours will be a kosher home."

"Some of the biggest crooks in town only eat kosher and I don't mind saying that straight to your face, Takifman."

"He's right, you know. And these days the most important thing with young couples is that they should be sexually compatible."

Mervyn, surrounded by the men, looked over their heads for Molly. He spotted her trapped in another circle in the far corner of the room. Molly was eating a banana. She smiled at Mervyn, she winked.

"Don't they make a lovely couple?"

"Twenty years ago they said the same thing about us. Does that answer your question?"

Mervyn was drinking heavily. He looked sick.

"Hey," my father said, his glass spilling over, "tell me, Segal, what goes in hard and stiff and comes out soft and wet?"

"Oh, for Christ's sake," I said. "Chewing gum. It's as old as the hills."

"You watch out," my father said. "You're asking for it."

"You know," Miller said. "I could do with something to eat."

My mother moved silently and tight-lipped among the guests collecting glasses just as soon as they were put down.

"I'll tell you what," Rosen said in a booming voice, "let's all go over to my place for a decent feed and some schnapps."

Our living room emptied more quickly than it had filled.

"Where's your mother?" my father asked, puzzled.

I told him she was in the kitchen and we went to get her. "Come on," my father said, "let's go to the Rosens."

"And who, may I ask, will clean up the mess you and your friends made here?"

"It won't run away."

"You have no pride."

"Oh, please. Don't start. Not today."

"Drunkard."

"Ray Milland,[8] that's me. Hey, what's that coming out of the wall? A bat."

"That poor innocent boy is being railroaded into a marriage he doesn't want and you just stand there."

"Couldn't you enjoy yourself *just once?*"

"You didn't see his face how scared he was? I thought he'd faint."

"Who ever got married he didn't need a little push? Why, I remember when I was a young man—"

"You go, Sam. Do me a favour. Go to the Rosens.'"

My father sent me out of the room.

"I'm not," he began, "well, I'm not always happy with you. Not day in and day out, I'm telling you straight."

"When I needed you to speak up for me you couldn't. Today courage comes in bottles. Do me a favour, Sam. Go."

"I wasn't going to go and leave you alone. I was going to stay. But if that's how you feel. . . ."

My father returned to the living room to get his jacket. I jumped up.

"Where are *you* going?" he asked.

"To the party."

"You stay here with your mother you have no consideration."

"God damn it."

"You heard me." But my father paused for a moment at the door. Thumbs hooked in his suspenders, rocking to and fro on his heels, he

[8] Hollywood film star best known for his portrayal of an alcoholic in *The Lost Weekend* (1945).

raised his head so high his chin jutted out incongruously. "I wasn't always your father. I was a young man once."

"So?"

"Did you know," he said, one eye half-shut, "that LIVE spelled backwards is EVIL?"

I woke at three in the morning when I heard a chair crash in the living room; somebody fell, and this was followed by the sound of sobbing. It was Mervyn. Dizzy, wretched and bewildered. He sat on the floor with a glass in his hand. When he saw me coming he raised his glass. "The wordsmith's bottled enemy," he said, grinning.

"When you getting married?"

He laughed. I laughed too.

"I'm not getting married."

"Wha'?"

"Sh."

"But I thought you were crazy about Molly?"

"I was. I am no longer." Mervyn rose, he tottered over to the window, "Have you ever looked up at the stars," he said, "and felt how small and unimportant we are?"

It hadn't occurred to me before.

"Nothing really matters. In terms of eternity our lives are shorter than a cigarette puff. Hey," he said. "Hey!" He took out his pen with the built-in flashlight and wrote something in his notebook. "For a writer," he said, "everything is grist to the mill. Nothing is humiliating."

"But what about Molly?"

"She's an insect. I told you the first time. All she wanted was my kudos. My fame... If you're really going to become a wordsmith remember one thing. The world is full of ridicule while you struggle. But once you've made it the glamour girls will come crawling."

He had begun to cry again. "Want me to sit with you for a while," I said.

"No. Go to bed. Leave me alone."

The next morning at breakfast my parents weren't talking. My mother's eyes were red and swollen and my father was in a forbidding mood. A telegram came for Mervyn.

"It's from New York," he said. "They want me right away. There's an offer for my book from Hollywood and they need me."

"You don't say?"

Mervyn thrust the telegram at my father. "Here," he said. "You read it."

"Take it easy. All I said was . . ." But my father read the telegram all the same. "Son-of-a-bitch," he said. "Hollywood."

We helped Mervyn pack.

"Shall I get Molly?" my father asked.

"No. I'll only be gone for a few days. I want to surprise her."

We all went to the window to wave. Just before he got into the taxi Mervyn looked up at us, he looked for a long while, but he didn't wave, and of course we never saw him again. A few days later a bill came for the telegram. It had been sent from our house. "I'm not surprised," my mother said.

My mother blamed the Rosens for Mervyn's flight, while they held us responsible for what they called their daughter's disgrace. My father put his pipes aside again and naturally he took a terrible ribbing at Tansky's. About a month later five dollar bills began to arrive from Toronto. They came sporadically until Mervyn had paid up all his back rent. But he never answered any of my father's letters.

—1969

Alice Munro   *b. 1931*

Having perfected her craft for more than half a century, Alice Munro has created a substantial body of stories and has come to be regarded as one of the world's most important short story writers, an author whose work is both extremely influential and hard to emulate. Her short fiction is dense with character and event and unfettered by the constraints of time and by traditional ideas about narrative unity, prompting the American writer Mona Simpson to observe:

> *Her genius, like Chekhov's, is quiet and particularly hard to describe, because it has the simplicity of the best naturalism, in that it seems not translated from life but, rather, like life itself . . . Like the highest practitioners of any craft, Alice Munro seems . . . to have left old forms behind, or to have broken them open, so that she is now writing not short stories or novellas but something altogether new . . . symphonic, large, architecturally gorgeous.*

"Open Secrets" is a good example of Munro's way of telling a story. It is both about Maureen, a woman going through a difficult period in her marriage, and an account of a young girl's having vanished from the community. Moving us back and

forth between Maureen's reflections and the effects of a recent and disastrous camping trip, Munro not only leaves her readers uncertain as to where the focus of the story lies but also suggests that narrative events can be hard to interpret and that the motives of characters are often ambiguous.

One of the sources of uncertainty in Munro's short stories is the difficulty individuals sometimes have in speaking—or their surprising tendency, when their speech is unblocked, to say that which is unexpected or inappropriate. A tension between public communication and private meaning is implicit in the paradoxical expression that provides the title for "Open Secrets" (it is also the title of the collection from which the story comes) —with its suggestion that knowledge can be regarded as confidential yet generally known.

While making the short story look unfamiliar, Munro can provide deceptively familiar-looking structures. In "Open Secrets" she moves the narrative close to the whodunit, with its hidden guilt and its conventional false leads and red herrings. Its mystery—the disappearance of a young girl in the woods—resembles the central event in Margaret Atwood's "Death by Landscape," which was published just a few years before Munro's story, and it is possible to see Munro as writing in response to Atwood. "Open Secrets" offers its readers more of a solution than does "Death by Landscape," yet, as in so many Munro stories, its answers seem only provisional. What is more important than who is guilty is what Maureen experiences near the end of Munro's story: the possibility of understanding two lives at once, her own and someone else's—an experience that great fiction has always offered us.

Open Secrets

It was on a Saturday morning
Just as lovely as it could be
Seven girls and their Leader Miss Johnstone
Went camping from the C.G.I.T.

"And they almost didn't even go," Frances said. "Because of the downpour Saturday morning. They were waiting half an hour in the United Church basement and she says, Oh, it'll stop—my hikes are never rained out! And now I bet she wishes it had've been. Then it would've been a whole other story."

It did stop raining, they did go, and it got so hot partway out that Miss Johnstone let them stop at a farmhouse, and the woman brought out Coca-Colas and the man let them take the garden hose and spray themselves cool. They were grabbing the hose from each other and doing tricks, and Frances said that Mary Kaye said Heather Bell had been the worst one; the boldest, getting hold of the hose and shooting water on the rest of them in all the bad places.

"They will try to make out she was some poor innocent, but the facts are dead different," Frances said. "It could have been all an arrangement, that she arranged to meet somebody. I mean some man."

Maureen said, "I think that's pretty farfetched."

"Well, I don't believe she drowned," Frances said. "That I don't believe."

The Falls on the Peregrine River were nothing like the waterfalls you see pictures of. They were just water falling over limestone shelves, none of them more than six or seven feet high. There was a breathing spot where you could stand behind the hard-falling curtain of water, and all around in the limestone there were pools, smooth-rimmed and not much bigger than bathtubs, where the water lay trapped and warm. You would have to be very determined to drown in there. But they had looked there—the other girls had run around calling Heather's name and peering into all the pools, and they had even stuck their heads into the dry space behind the curtain of noisy water. They had skipped around on the bare rock and yelled and got themselves soaked, finally, plunging in and out through the curtain. Till Miss Johnstone shouted and made them come back.

> *There was Betsy and Eva Trowell*
> *And Lucille Chambers as well*
> *There was Ginny Bos and Mary Kaye Trevelyan*
> *And Robin Sands and poor Heather Bell.*

"Seven was all she could get," Frances said. "And every one of them, there was a reason. Robin Sands, doctor's daughter. Lucille Chambers, minister's daughter. They can't get out of it. The Trowells—country. Glad to get in on anything. Ginny Bos, the double-jointed monkey—she's along for the swimming and the horsing around. Mary Kaye living next door to Miss Johnstone. Enough said. And Heather Bell new in town. *And* her mother away on the weekend herself—yes, she was taking the opportunity. Getting off on an expedition of her own."

It was about twenty-four hours since Heather Bell had disappeared, on the annual hike of the C.G.I.T.—which stood for Canadian Girls in Training—out to the Falls on the Peregrine River. Mary Johnstone, who

was now in her early sixties, had been leading this hike for years, since
before the war. There used to be at least a couple of dozen girls heading
out the County Road on a Saturday morning in June. They would all be
wearing navy-blue shorts and white blouses and red kerchiefs round
their necks. Maureen had been one of them, twenty or so years ago.

Miss Johnstone always started them off singing the same thing.

> *For the Beauty of the Earth,*
> *For the Beauty of the Skies,*
> *For the Love that from our Birth*
> *Over and around us lies—*

And you could hear a hum of different words going along, cautiously
but determinedly, under the hymn words.

> *For the sight of Miss Johnstone's bum,*
> *Waddling down the County Road.*
> *We are the morons singing this song—*
> *Doesn't she look just like a toad?*

Did anybody else Maureen's age remember these words now? The ones
who had stayed in town were mothers—they had girls old enough to go
on the hike, and older. They would get into the proper motherly kind of
fit about rude language. Having children changed you. It gave you the
necessary stake in being grown-up, so that certain parts of you—old
parts—could be altogether eliminated and abandoned. Jobs, marriage
didn't quite do it—just made you *act* as if you'd forgotten things.

Maureen had no children.

Maureen was sitting with Frances Wall, having coffee and cigarettes
at the breakfast table that had been wedged into the old pantry, under
the high, glass-fronted cupboards. This was Maureen's house in
Carstairs, in 1965. She had been living in the house for eight years, but
she still felt as if she got around it on fairly narrow tracks, from one spot
where she felt at home to another. She had fixed up this corner so there
was a place to eat other than the dining-room table, and she had put
new chintz in the sunroom. It took a long time to work her husband
around to changes. The front rooms were full of valuable, heavy furniture, made of oak and walnut, and the curtains were of green-and-
mulberry brocade, as in a rich-looking hotel—you could not begin to
alter anything there.

Frances worked for Maureen in the house, but she was not like a
servant. They were cousins, though Frances was nearly a generation

older. She had worked in this house long before Maureen came into it—
she had worked for the first wife. Sometimes she called Maureen
"Missus." It was a joke, half friendly and half not. How much did you
give for those chops, Missus? Oh, they must have seen you coming! And
she would tell Maureen she was getting broad in the beam and her hair
did not suit her piled and sprayed like an upside-down mixing bowl. This
though Frances herself was a dumpling sort of woman with gray hair like
brambles all over her head, and a plain, impudent face. Maureen did not
think of herself as timid—she had a stately look—and she was certainly
not incompetent, having run her husband's law office before she "graduated" (as both she and he would say) to running his house. She sometimes thought she should try for more respect from Frances—but she
needed somebody around the house to have spats and jokes with. She
could not be a gossip, because of her husband's position, and she didn't
think it was her nature, anyway, but she let Frances get away with plenty
of mean remarks, and wild, uncharitable, confident speculations.

(For example, what Frances was saying about Heather Bell's mother,
and what she said about Mary Johnstone and the hike in general.
Frances thought she was an authority on that, because Mary Kaye
Trevelyan was her granddaughter.)

Mary Johnstone was a woman you were hardly supposed to mention
in Carstairs without attaching the word "wonderful." She had had polio
and nearly died of it, at the age of thirteen or fourteen. She was left with
short legs, a short, thick body, crooked shoulders, and a slightly twisted
neck, which kept her big head a little tilted to one side. She had studied
bookkeeping, she had got herself a job in the office at Douds Factory,
and she had devoted her spare time to girls, often saying that she had
never met a bad one, just some who were confused. Whenever Maureen
met Mary Johnstone on the street or in a store, her heart sank. First
came that searching smile, the eyes raking yours, the declared delight in
any weather—wind or hail or sun or rain, each had something to recommend it—then the laughing question. *So what have you been up to, Mrs.
Stephens?* Mary Johnstone always made a point of saying "Mrs.
Stephens," but she said it as if it was a play title and she was thinking
all the time, It's only Maureen Coulter. (Coulters were just like the
Trowells that Frances had remarked on—country. No more, no less.)
What interesting things have you been doing lately, Mrs. Stephens?

Maureen felt then as if she was being put on the spot and could do
nothing about it, as if a challenge was being issued, and it had something

to do with her lucky marriage and her tall healthy body, whose only misfortune was a hidden one—her tubes had been tied to make her infertile—and her rosy skin and auburn hair, and the clothes she spent a lot of money and time on. As if she must owe Mary Johnstone something, a never specified compensation. Or as if Mary Johnstone could see more lacking than Maureen herself would face.

Frances didn't care for Mary Johnstone, either, in the pure and simple way she didn't care for anybody who made too much of themselves.

Miss Johnstone had taken them on a half-mile hike before breakfast, as she always did, to climb the Rock—the chunk of limestone that jutted out over the Peregrine River, and was so rare a thing in that part of the country that it was not named anything but the Rock. On Sunday morning you always had to do that hike, dopey as you were from trying to stay awake all night and half sick from smoking smuggled cigarettes. Shivering, too, because the sun wouldn't have reached deep into the woods yet. The path hardly deserved to be called one— you had to climb over rotted tree trunks and wade through ferns and what Miss Johnstone pointed out as Mayapples and wild geraniums, and wild ginger. She would pull it up and nibble it, hardly brushing off the dirt. Look what nature provides us.

I forgot my sweater, Heather said when they were halfway up. Can I go back and get it?

In the old days Miss Johnstone would probably have said no. Get a move on and you'll warm up without it, she would have said. She must have felt uneasy this time, because of the waning popularity of her hikes, which she blamed on television, working mothers, laxity in the home. She said yes.

Yes, but hurry. Hurry and catch up.

Which Heather Bell never did do. At the Rock they looked at the view (Maureen recalled looking around for French safes—did they still call them that?—among the beer bottles and candy wrappers), and Heather had not caught up. On the way back they didn't meet her. She wasn't in the big tent, or in the little tent, where Miss Johnstone had slept, or between the tents. She wasn't in any of the shelters or love nests among the cedars surrounding the campground. Miss Johnstone cut that searching short.

"Pancakes," she called. "Pancakes and coffee! See if the smell of pancakes and coffee won't smoke Miss Mischief out of hiding."

They had to sit and eat—after Miss Johnstone had said grace, thank-
ing God for everything in the woods and at home—and as they ate, Miss
Johnstone called out, "Yum-*my*!

"Doesn't the fresh air give us an appetite?" she said at the top of
her voice. "Aren't these the best pancakes you ever did eat? Heather
better hurry up or there won't be one left. Heather? Are you listening?
Not one left!"

As soon as they were finished, Robin Sands asked if they could go
now, could they go and look for Heather?

"Dishes first, my lady," Miss Johnstone said. "Even if you never do
pick up a dishrag around home."

Robin nearly burst out crying. Nobody ever spoke to her like that.

After they had cleaned up, Miss Johnstone let them go, and that was
when they went back to the Falls. But she brought them back soon
enough and made them sit in a semicircle, wet as they were, and she
herself sat cross-legged in front of them and called out that anybody
listening was welcome to come and join them. "Anybody hiding round
here and trying to play tricks is welcome! Come out now and no questions asked! Otherwise we will just have to get along without you!"

Then she launched into her talk, her Sunday-morning-of-the-hike
sermon, without any qualms or worries. She kept going and going,
asking a question every now and then, to make sure they were listening. The sun dried their shorts and Heather Bell did not come back. She
did not appear out of the trees and still Miss Johnstone did not stop
talking. She didn't let go of them until Mr. Trowell drove into the camp
in his truck, bringing the ice cream for lunch.

She didn't give them permission then, but they broke loose
anyway. They jumped up and ran for the truck. They all started telling
him at once. Jupiter, the Trowells' dog, jumped over the tailgate, and
Eva Trowell threw her arms about him and started to wail as if he had
been the one lost.

Miss Johnstone got to her feet and came over and called out to Mr.
Trowell above the girls' clamoring.

"One's taken it into her head to go missing!"

Now the search parties were out. Douds was closed, so that every
man who wanted to go could go. Dogs had been added. There was talk
of dragging the river downstream from the Falls.

When the constable went to tell Heather Bell's mother, he found her just back from her own weekend, wearing a backless sundress and high heels.

"Well, you better find her," she said. "That's your job."

She worked at the hospital—she was a nurse. "Either divorced or never was married in the first place," Frances said. "One for all and all for one, that's her."

Maureen's husband was calling her, and she hurried away to the sunroom. After his stroke two years ago, at the age of sixty-nine, he had given up his law practice, but he still had letters to write and a bit of business to do for old clients who could never get used to anybody else. Maureen typed out all his correspondence and helped him every day with what he called his chores.

"Whaur doing out there?" he said. His speech was sometimes slurred, so she had to stay around and interpret for people who did not know him well. Alone with her he made less effort, and his tone could be testy and complaining.

"Talking to Frances," said Maureen.

"Wha' bout?"

"This and that," she said.

"Yeah."

He stretched out the word gloomily, as if to say he well knew what their talk had been about and he did not care for it. Gossip, rumor, the coldhearted thrill of catastrophe. He never went in for much talk, now or in the days when he could talk readily—even his reproofs were brief, a matter of tone and implication. He seemed to call upon a body of belief, on rules known to all decent people and maybe to all people, even those who spent their lives falling short. He seemed to be a little pained, a little embarrassed for all concerned, when he had to do this, and at the same time formidable. His reproofs were extraordinarily effective.

People in Carstairs were just growing out of the habit of calling lawyers Lawyer So-and-So, just as you would always call a doctor by his title. They no longer referred to any of the younger lawyers as Lawyer, but they always called Maureen's husband Lawyer Stephens. Maureen herself often thought of him that way, though she called him Alvin. He dressed every day just as he used to dress to go to his office—in a three-piece gray or brown suit—and his clothes, though they cost enough money, never seemed to fit well or to smooth out his long, lumpy body. Nor did they ever seem to be free of a faint sifting of cigarette ashes, crumbs, maybe even flecks of shed skin. His head wagged downward, his face sagged with preoccupation, his expression was shrewd and absentminded—you could never be sure which. People liked that—they liked that he looked a little unkempt and at a loss and then could flash out with some fearsome detail. He knows the Law, they said. He doesn't have to look it up. He's got it all in his head. His stroke hadn't shaken their faith, and it really hadn't altered his appearance or his manner much, just accentuated what was already there.

Everyone believed he could have been a judge if he had played his cards right. He could have been a senator. But he was too honorable. He wouldn't kowtow. He was a man in a million.

Maureen sat down on the hassock near him to write shorthand. His name for her, in the office, had been the Jewel, because she was intelligent and dependable, in fact quite able to draw up documents and write letters on her own. Even in the household, his wife and the two children, Helena and Gordon, had used that name for her. The children still used it sometimes, though they were grown up and lived away. Helena used it affectionately and provocatively, Gordon with a solemn, self-congratulatory kindness. Helena was an unsettled single woman who came home seldom and got into arguments when she did. Gordon was a teacher at a military college, who liked to bring his wife and children back to Carstairs, making rather a display of the place, and of his father and Maureen, their backwater virtues.

Maureen could still enjoy being the Jewel. Or at least she found it comfortable. Part of her thoughts could slip off on their own. She was thinking now of the way the night's long adventure began, at camp, with Miss Johnstone's abdicating snores, and its objective—staying awake till dawn, and all the strategies and entertainments that were relied on to achieve that, though she had never heard that they were successful. The girls played cards, they told jokes, they smoked cigarettes, and around midnight began the great games of Truth or Dare. Some Dares were: take off your pajama top and show your boobs; eat a cigarette butt; swallow dirt; stick your head in the water pail and try to count to a hundred; go and pee in front of Miss Johnstone's tent. Questions requiring Truth were: Do you hate your mother? Father? Sister? Brother? How many peckers have you seen and whose were they? Have you ever lied? Stolen? Touched anything dead? The sick and dizzy feeling of having smoked too many cigarettes too quickly came back to Maureen, also the smell of the smoke under the heavy canvas that had been soaking up the day's sun, the smell of girls who had swum for hours in the river and run and hidden in the reeds along the banks and had to burn leeches off their legs.

She remembered how noisy she had been then. A shrieker, a dare-taker. Just before she hit high school, a giddiness either genuine or faked or half-and-half became available to her. Soon it vanished, her bold body vanished inside this ample one, and she became a studious, shy girl, a blusher. She developed the qualities her husband would see and value when hiring and proposing.

I dare you to run away. Was it possible? There are times when girls are inspired, when they want the risks to go on and on. They want to be heroines, regardless. They want to take a joke beyond where anybody has ever taken it before. To be careless, dauntless, to create havoc—that was the lost hope of girls.

From the chintz-covered hassock at her husband's side she looked out at the old copper-beech trees, seeing behind them not the sunny lawn but the unruly trees along the river—the dense cedars and shiny-leaved oaks and glittery poplars. A ragged sort of wall with hidden door-ways, and hidden paths behind it where animals went, and lone humans sometimes, becoming different from what they were outside, charged with different responsibilities, certainties, intentions. She could imagine vanishing. But of course you didn't vanish, and there was always the other person on a path to intersect yours and his head was full of plans for you even before you met.

When she went to the Post Office that afternoon to send off her husband's letters, Maureen heard two new reports. A light-haired young girl had been seen getting into a black car on the Bluewater Highway north of Walley at about one o'clock on Sunday afternoon. She might have been hitchhiking. Or waiting for just one car. That was twenty miles away from the Falls, and it would take about five hours to walk it, across the country. It could be done. Or she could have got a ride in another car.

But some people tidying up family graves in a forsaken country churchyard in the swampy northeastern corner of the country had heard a cry, a scream, in the middle of the afternoon. Who was that? they remembered saying to each other. Not *what* but *who. Who was that?* But later on they thought that it might have been a fox.

Also, the grass was beaten down in a spot close to the camp, and there were fresh cigarette butts lying around. But what did that prove—people were always out there. Lovers. Young boys planning mischief.

And maybe some man did meet her there
That was carrying a gun or a knife
He met her there and he didn't care
He took that young girl's life.

But some will say it wasn't that way
That she met a stranger or a friend
In a big black car she was carried far
And nobody knows the end.

On Tuesday morning, while Frances was getting breakfast and Maureen was helping her husband to finish dressing, there was a knock at the front door, by someone who did not notice or trust the bell. It was not unheard-of for people to drop by this early, but it made difficulties, because Lawyer Stephens was apt to have more trouble with his speech early in the morning, and his mind, too, took a little time to get warmed up.

Through the pebbled glass in the front door Maureen saw the blurry outlines of a man and a woman. Dressed up, at least the woman was—wearing a hat. That meant serious business. But serious business, to the people involved, might still seem humdrum to others. Death threats had been issued over the ownership of a chest of drawers, and a property owner could pop a blood vessel over a six-inch overlap of a driveway. Missing firewood, barking dogs, a nasty letter—all that could fire people up and bring them knocking. *Go and ask Lawyer Stephens. Go and ask about the Law.*

Of course there was a slim chance this pair might be peddling religion. Not so.

"We've come to see the Lawyer," the woman said.

"Well," said Maureen. "It's early." She did not know who they were right away.

"Sorry, but we got something to tell him," the woman said, and somehow she had stepped into the front hall and Maureen had stepped backward. The man shook his head as if in discomfort or apology, indicating that he had no choice but to follow his wife.

The hall filled up with the smell of shaving soap, paste deodorant, and a cheap drugstore cologne. Lily of the Valley. And now Maureen recognized them.

It was Marian Hubbert. Only, she looked different in a blue suit—which was too heavy for this weather—and her brown cloth gloves, and a brown hat made of feathers. Usually you saw her in town wearing slacks or even what looked like men's work pants. She was a husky woman of about Maureen's age—they had been in high school together, though a year or two apart. Marian's body was clumsy but quick, and her graying hair was cut short, so that bristles showed on her neck. She had a loud voice, most of the time a rather rambunctious manner. She was toned down now.

The man with her was the man she had married not so long ago. Maybe a couple of years ago. He was tall and boyish-looking, in a cheap, cream-colored jacket with too much padding in the shoulders. Wavy brown hair, fixed with a wet comb. "Excuse us," he said in a soft voice— perhaps one that his wife was not intended to hear—as Maureen took them into the dining room. Close up, his eyes were not so young—there was a look of strain and dryness, or bewilderment. Perhaps he was not very bright. Maureen remembered now some story about Marian's getting him from an advertisement. *Woman with farm, clear title. Businesswoman with farm,* it could have been, for Marian Hubbert's other name was the Corset Lady. For years and years she had sold made-to-measure corsets and perhaps she still did, to the dwindling number of ladies who wore them. Maureen imagined her taking measurements, prodding like a nurse, bossy and professionally insulting. But she had been kind to her old parents, who lived out on the farm until they were a great age and had any number of things wrong with them. And now another story surfaced, a less malicious one, about her husband. He had driven the bus that took old folks to their therapeutic swimming session, at Walley, in the indoor pool—that was how they had met. Maureen had another picture of him, too—carrying the old father in his arms, into Dr. Sands' office. Marian charging ahead, swinging her purse by its strap, ready to open the door.

She went to tell Frances about breakfast in the dining room, and to ask her to bring extra coffee cups. Then she went to warn her husband.

"It's Marian Hubbert, or she used to be," she said. "And whatever that man's name is that she's married to."

"Slater," her husband said, the way he would dryly bring forth the particulars of a sale or lease that you wouldn't have thought he could know so readily. "Theo."

"You're more up-to-date than I am," Maureen said.

He asked if his porridge was ready. "Eat and listen," he said.

Frances brought in the porridge, and he fell to at once. Slathered with cream and brown sugar, porridge was his favorite food, winter and summer.

When she brought the coffee, Frances tried to hang about, but Marian gave her a steady look that turned her back to the kitchen.

There, thought Maureen. She can manage better than I can.

Marian Hubbert was a woman without one visible advantage. She had a heavy face, a droop to the cheeks—she reminded Maureen of some sort of dog. Not necessarily an ugly dog. Not an ugly face, really. Just a heavy and determined one. But everywhere Marian went, as now in Maureen's dining room, she would present herself as if she had absolute rights. She had to be taken account of.

She had put on a quantity of makeup, and perhaps that was another reason Maureen hadn't immediately recognized her. It was pale and pink-ish and unsuited to her olive skin, her black, heavy eyebrows. It made her look odd but not pathetic. It seemed she might have put it on, like the suit and hat, to demonstrate that she could get herself up the way other women did, she knew what was expected. But perhaps she intended to look pretty. Perhaps she saw herself transformed by the pale powder that was hanging on her cheeks, the thick pink lipstick—perhaps she turned when she finished and coyly showed herself to her husband.

Answering for his wife in regard to sugar for her coffee, he almost giggled when he said *lumps*. He said please and thank you as often as possible. He said, "Thank you very much, please. Thank you. The same for me. Thank you."

"Now, we didn't know anything about this girl until after it seems like everybody else knew," Marian was saying. "I mean, we didn't even know anybody was missing or anything. Not until yesterday when we came into town. Yesterday? Monday? Yesterday was Monday. I have got my days all mixed up, because I've been taking painkiller pills."

Marian was not the sort to tell you she had been taking pills and let it go at that. She would tell you what for.

"So I had a terrible big boil on my neck, right there?" she said. She scrunched her head around, trying to show them the dressing on it. "It was giving me pain and I started getting a headache, too, and I think it was something connected. So I was feeling so bad on Sunday I just took a hot cloth and put it to my neck and I swallowed a couple of painkillers and I went and laid down. He was off work that day, but now he's working he's always got lots to do when he's home. He's work-ing at the Atomic Energy."

"Douglas Point?" said Lawyer Stephens, with a brief look up from his porridge. There was a certain interest or respect all men showed—

even Lawyer Stephens had to show it—at the mention of the new Atomic Energy Station at Douglas Point.

"That's where he works now," Marian said. Like many country women and Carstairs women, too, she referred to her husband as *he*— it was spoken with a special emphasis—rather than calling him by his name. Maureen had caught herself doing it a few times, but had corrected the habit without anybody's having to point it out to her.

"He had to take the salt out for the cows," Marian said, "and then he went back and worked on the fence. He had to go quarter of a mile, maybe, so he took the truck. But he left Bounder. He went off in the truck without him. Bounder our dog. Bounder won't go any distance unless that he can ride. He left him on guard sort of because he knew I had went and laid down. I had taken a couple of 222s, and I went into a kind of doze more than a regular sleep, and then I heard Bounder barking. It woke me right up. Bounder barking."

She got up then, and she put on her wrapper and went downstairs. She had been lying down just in her underclothing. She looked out the front door, out the lane, and there was nobody. She didn't see Bounder, either, and by that time he had quit his barking. He quit when it was somebody he recognized. Or somebody just going by on the road. But still she wasn't satisfied. She looked out the kitchen windows, which gave on the side yard but not the back. Still nobody. She couldn't see the backyard from the kitchen—to do that, you had to go right out through what they called the back kitchen. It was just a sort of catchall room, like a shed tacked onto the house, all jumbled up with everything. It had a window looking out back, but you couldn't get near that or see out of it because of cardboard boxes piled up and the old couch springs standing on end. You had to go right and open the back door to see out. And now she thought she could hear something at that door like a kind of clawing. Maybe Bounder. Maybe not.

It was so hot in that shut-up back kitchen packed with junk that she could barely breathe. Under her wrapper she was all sticky with sweat. She said to herself, Well, at least you haven't got a fever, you are sweating like a pig.

She was more interested in getting air to breathe than she was scared of what might be out there, so she thrust the door open. It opened outward, pushing the fellow back that was up against it. He staggered back but didn't fall. And she saw who it was. Mr. Siddicup, from town.

Bounder knew him, of course, because he often went by and sometimes cut across the property on his walks and they never stopped him.
He came right through the yard, sometimes—it was just because he
didn't know any better anymore. She never yelled at him, the way some
people did. She had even invited him to sit on the steps and rest if he
was tired, she had offered him a cigarette. He would take the cigarette,
too. But he would never sit down.

Bounder was just nosing around and fawning on him. Bounder was
not particular.

Maureen knew Mr. Siddicup, as everybody did. He used to be the
piano tuner at Douds. He used to be a dignified, sarcastic little
Englishman, with a pleasant wife. They read books from the library and
were noted for their garden, especially strawberries and roses. Then, a
few years ago, misfortunes started arriving. Mr. Siddicup had an operation on his throat—it must have been for cancer—and after that he
could not talk, just make wheezing and growling noises. He had already
retired from Douds—they had some electronic way of tuning pianos
now, better than the human ear. His wife died suddenly. Then the
changes came in a hurry—he deteriorated from a decent old man into a
morose and rather disgusting old urchin, in a matter of months. Dirty
whiskers, dribbles on his clothes, a sour smoky smell, and a look in his
eyes of constant suspicion, sometimes of loathing. In the grocery store if
he could not find what he wanted, or if they had changed the places of
things, he would knock canned goods and boxes of cereal over on
purpose. He was not welcome anymore in the café, and never went near
the library. Women from his wife's church group kept going to see him
for a while, bringing a meat dish or some baking. But the smell of the
house was dreadful and the disorder perverse—even for a man living
alone it was inexcusable—and he was the opposite of grateful. He would
toss the remainders of pies and casseroles out on his front walk, breaking the dishes. No woman wanted the joke going round that even Mr.
Siddicup wouldn't eat her cooking. So they left him alone. Mostly he just
walked the roads. When you were driving along, you might spot him
standing still, standing in the ditch, mostly hidden in tall weeds and
grass, while cars whizzed by him. You could also run into him in a town
miles away from home, and there a strange thing would happen. His
face would take on something of its old expression, ready for the genial
obligatory surprise, the greeting of people who lived in one place meeting in another. It did look as if he had a hope then that the moment

would open out, that words would break through, in fact that perhaps the changes would be wiped out, here in a different place—his voice and his wife and his old stability in life might all be returned to him.

People were not unkind, usually. They were patient up to a point. Marian said she would never have chased him off.

She said he looked pretty wild, this time. Not just as he looked when he was trying to get his meaning out and it would not come, or when he was mad at some kids who were teasing him. His head was bobbing back and forth and his face looked swollen up, like a bawling baby's.

Now then, she said. Now, Mr. Siddicup, what's the matter? What are you trying to tell me? Do you want a cigarette? Are you telling me it's Sunday and you're all out of cigarettes?

Shook his head back and forth, then bobbed it up and down, then shook it back and forth again.

Come on, now. Make up your mind, said Marian.

Ah, ahh was all he said. He put both hands to his head, knocking off his cap. Then he backed farther off and started zigzagging around the yard in between the pump and the clothesline, still making these noises—*ah, ahh*—that would never turn into words.

Here Marian pushed back her chair so abruptly that it almost fell over. She got up and began to show them just what Mr. Siddicup had done. She lurched and crouched and banged her hands to her head, though she did not dislodge her hat. In front of the sideboard, in front of the silver tea service presented to Lawyer Stephens in appreciation of his many years' work for the Law Society, she put on this display. Her husband held his coffee cup in both hands and kept his deferential eyes on her by an effort of will. Something flashed in his face—a tic, a nerve jumping in one cheek. She was watching him in spite of her antics, and her look said, Hold on. Be still.

Lawyer Stephens, as far as Maureen could see, had not glanced up at all.

He did like that, Marian said, reseating herself. He did like that, and because she had not been feeling well herself, she got the idea that perhaps he was in pain.

Mr. Siddicup. Mr. Siddicup. Are you trying to tell me your head hurts? Do you want me to get you a pill? Do you want me to take you to the doctor?

No answer. He wouldn't stop for her. *Ah, ahh.*

In his stumbling around he found himself at the pump. They had running water in the house now, but still used the pump outside and filled Bounder's dish at it. When Mr. Siddicup took note of what it was, he got busy. He went to work on the handle and pumped it up and down like crazy. There wasn't any cup to drink from, like there used to be. But as soon as water came he stuck his head under. It splashed and stopped, because he had quit pumping. Back he went and pumped again, and stuck himself under again, and on like that, pumping and dousing, letting it pour over his head and face and shoulders and chest, soaking himself and still, when he could, making some noise. Bounder was excited and ran around bumping into him and letting out barks and whines in sympathy.

That's enough, you two! Marian yelled at them. Let go that pump! Let go and settle down!

Only Bounder listened to her. Mr. Siddicup had to keep on till he got himself so drenched and blinded he couldn't find the pump handle. Then he stopped. And he lifted one arm up, he lifted and pointed, back in the general direction of the bush and the river. He was pointing and making his noises. At the time, that didn't make any sense to her. She didn't think about it till later. Then he quit that and just sat down on the well cover, soaked and shivering, with his head in his hands.

Maybe it's something simple after all, she thought. Complaining because there isn't a cup.

If it's a cup you want, I'll go and get you one. No need to carry on like a baby. You stay there, I'll go and get you a cup.

She headed back to the kitchen and got a cup. And she had another idea. She fixed him up some graham crackers, with butter and jam. That was a kid's treat, graham crackers, but it was a thing old people liked, too, she remembered from her mother and daddy.

Back to the door she went and pushed it open with her hands full. But there was no sign of him. Nobody in the yard but Bounder, looking the way he did when he knew he'd made a fool of himself.

Where did he go, Bounder? Which way did he go?

Bounder was ashamed and fed up and wouldn't give any sign. He slunk off to his place in the house shade, in the dirt, by the foundations.

Mr. Siddicup! Mr. Siddicup! Come see what I got for you!

All silent as the dead. And her head was pounding. She started eating the crackers herself but she shouldn't have—a couple of bites and she wanted to puke.

She took two more pills and went back upstairs. The windows up and blinds down. She wished now they'd bought a fan when the sale was on at Canadian Tire. But she slept without one, and when she woke it was nearly dark. She could hear the mower—*he*, her husband, was out finishing the grass at the side of the house. She went down to the kitchen and saw that he had cut up some cold potatoes and boiled an egg and pulled green onions to make a salad. He was not like some men—a hopeless case in the kitchen waiting for the woman to get out of a sickbed and make him a meal. She picked at the salad but couldn't eat. One more pill and up the stairs and dead to the world till morning.

We better get you to the doctor, he said then. He phoned them up at work. I got to take my wife to the doctor.

Marian said, What if she just boiled a needle and he could lance it? But he could not stand to hurt her, and anyway he was afraid he might do something wrong. So they got in the truck and drove in to see Dr. Sands. Dr. Sands was out, they had to wait. Other people waiting told them the news. Everybody was amazed they didn't know. But they hadn't had the radio on. She was the one who always turned it on and she couldn't stand the noise, the way she felt. And they hadn't noticed any groups of men, anything peculiar, on the road.

Dr. Sands fixed the boil but he didn't lance it. His way of dealing with a boil was to strike it a sharp blow, knock it on the head, when you thought he was just looking at it. There! he said, that's less fuss than the needle and not so painful overall because you didn't have time to get in a sweat. He cleaned it out and put the dressing on and said she'd soon be feeling better.

And so she was, but sleepy. She was so useless and foggy in the head that she went back to bed and slept till her husband came up around four o'clock with a cup of tea. It was then she thought of those girls, coming in with Miss Johnstone on Saturday morning, wanting a drink. She had lots of Coca-Cola and she gave it to them in flowered glasses, with ice cubes. Miss Johnstone would only take water. *He* let them play with the hose, they jumped around and squirted each other and had a great time. They were trying to skip the streams of water, and they were a bit on the wild side when Miss Johnstone wasn't looking. He had to practically wrestle the hose away from them, and give them a few squirts of water to make them behave.

She was trying to picture which girl it was. She knew the minister's daughter and Dr. Sands' daughter and the Trowells'—with their little sheep eyes you would know a Trowell anywhere. But which of the others? She recalled one who was very noisy and jumping up trying to get the hose even when he took it away, and one was doing cartwheels and one was a skinny pretty little thing with blond hair. But maybe she was thinking of Robin Sands—Robin had blond hair. She asked her husband that night did he know which one, but he was worse than she was—he didn't know people here and couldn't separate out any of them.

Also she told him about Mr. Siddicup. It all came back to her now. The way he was upset, the pumping, the way he pointed. It bothered her what that could mean. They talked about it and wondered about it and got themselves into a state of wondering so they hardly got any sleep. Until she finally said to him, Well, I know what we have to do. We have to go and talk to Lawyer Stephens.

So they got up and came as soon as they could.

"Police," said Lawyer Stephens now. "Police. Who should gone to see."

The husband spoke. He said, "We didn't know if we should ought to do that or not." He had both hands on the table, fingers spread, pressed down, pulling at the cloth.

"Not accusation." Lawyer Stephens said. "Information."

He had talked in that abbreviated way even before his stroke. And Maureen had noticed, long ago, how just a few words of his, spoken in no very friendly tone—spoken, in fact, in a tone of brusque chastisement—could cheer people up and lift a weight off them.

She had been thinking of the other reason why the women stopped going to visit Mr. Siddicup. They didn't like the clothes. Women's clothes, underwear—old frayed slips and brassières and worn-out underpants and nubbly stockings, hanging from the backs of chairs or from a line above the heater, or just in a heap on the table. All these things must have belonged to his wife, of course, and at first it looked as if he might be washing and drying them and sorting them out, prior to getting rid of them. But they were there week after week, and the women started to wonder: Did he leave them lying around to suggest things? Did he put them on himself next to his skin? Was he a pervert?

Now all that would come out, they'd chalk that up against him.

Pervert. Maybe they were right. Maybe he would lead them to where he'd strangled or beat Heather to death in a sexual fit, or they would find something of hers in his house. And people would say in horrid, hushed voices that no, they weren't surprised. *I wasn't surprised, were you?*

Lawyer Stephens had asked some question about the job at Douglas Point, and Marian said, "He works in Maintenance. Every day when he comes out he's got to go through the check for X-rays, and even the rags he cleans off his boots with, they have to be buried underground."

When Maureen shut the door on the pair of them and saw their shapes wobble away through the pebbled glass, she was not quite satisfied. She climbed three steps to the landing on the stairs, where there was a little arched window. She watched them.

No car was in sight, or truck or whatever they had. They must have left it parked on the main street or in the lot behind the Town Hall. Possibly they did not want it to be seen in front of Lawyer Stephens' house.

The Town Hall was where the Police Office was. They did turn in that direction, but then they crossed the street diagonally and, still within Maureen's sight, they sat down on the low stone wall that ran around the old cemetery and flower plot called Pioneer Park.

Why should they feel a need to sit down after sitting in the dining room for what must have been at least an hour? They didn't talk, or look at each other, but seemed united, as if taking a rest in the midst of hard shared labors.

Lawyer Stephens, when in a reminiscing mood, would talk about how people used to rest on that wall. Farm women who had to walk into town to sell chickens or butter. Country girls on their way to high school, before there was any such thing as a school bus. They would stop and hide their galoshes and retrieve them on the way home.

At other times he had no patience with reminiscing.

"Olden times. Who wants 'em back?"

Now Marian took out some pins and carefully lifted off her hat. So that was it—her hat was hurting her. She set it in her lap, and her husband reached over. He took it away, as if anxious to take away anything that might be a burden to her. He settled it in his lap. He bent over and started to stroke it, in a comforting way. He stroked that hat made of horrible brown feathers as if he were pacifying a little scared hen.

But Marian stopped him. She said something to him, she clamped a hand down on his. The way a mother might interrupt the carrying-on of a simple-minded child—with a burst of abhorrence, a moment's break in her tired-out love.

Maureen felt a shock. She felt a shrinking in her bones.

Her husband came out of the dining room. She didn't want him to catch her looking at them. She turned around the vase of dried grasses that was on the window ledge. She said, "I thought she'd never get done talking."

He hadn't noticed. His mind was on something else.

"Come on down here," he said.

Early in their marriage Maureen's husband had mentioned to her that he and the first Mrs. Stephens gave up sleeping together after Helena, the younger child, was born. "We'd got our boy and our girl," he said, meaning there was no need to try for more. Maureen did not understand then that he might intend some similar cutoff for her. She was in love when she married him. It was true that when he first put his arm around her waist, in the office, she thought he must believe that she was headed for the wrong door and was redirecting her—but that was a conclusion she came to because of his propriety, not because she hadn't longed to feel his arm there. People who thought she was making an advantageous, though kindly, marriage, would have been amazed at how happy she was on her honeymoon—and that was in spite of having to learn to play bridge. She knew his power—the way he used it and the way he held it back. He was attractive to her—never mind his age, ungainliness, nicotine stains on his teeth and fingers. His skin was warm. A couple of years into the marriage she miscarried and bled so heavily that her tubes had been tied, to prevent such a thing from ever happening again. After that the intimate part of her life with her husband came to an end. It seemed that he had been mostly obliging her, because he felt that it was wrong to deny a woman the chance to have a child.

Sometimes she would pester him a little and he would say, "Now, Maureen. What's all this about?" Or else he would tell her to grow up. "Grow up" was an injunction that he had picked up from his own children, and had continued to use long after they had dropped it, in fact long after they had moved away from home.

His saying that humiliated her, and her eyes would fill with tears. He was a man who detested tears above all things.

And now, she thought, wouldn't it be a relief to have that state of affairs back again! For her husband's appetite had returned—or an entirely new appetite had developed. There was nothing now of the rather clumsy ceremony, the formal fondness, of their early times together. Now his eyes would cloud over and his face would seem weighed down. He would speak to her in a curt and menacing way and sometimes push and prod her, even trying to jam his fingers into her from behind. She did not need any of that to make her hurry—she was anxious to get him into the bedroom as soon as possible, afraid that he might misbehave elsewhere. His old office had been made into a downstairs bedroom with a bathroom adjoining it, so that he would not have to climb the stairs. At least that room had a lock, so Frances could not burst in. But the phone might ring, Frances might have to come looking for them. She might stand outside the door and then she would have to hear the noises—Lawyer Stephens' panting and grunting and bullying, the hiss of disgust with which he would order Maureen to do this or that, his pounding of her right at the end and the command he let out then, a command that perhaps would be incoherent to anybody but Maureen but that would still speak eloquently, like lavatory noises, of his extremity.

"Ta' dirty! Ta' dirty!"

This came from a man who had once shut Helena in her room for calling her brother a shitty bastard.

Maureen knew enough words, but it was difficult for her in her shaken state to call up just which ones might suit, and to utter them in a tone that would be convincing. She did try. She wanted above all else to help him along.

Afterward he fell into the brief sleep that seemed to erase the episode from his memory. Maureen escaped to the bathroom. She did the first cleanup there and then hurried upstairs to replace some clothing. Often at these times she had to hang onto the bannisters, she felt so hollow and feeble. And she had to keep her mouth closed not on any howls of protest but on a long sickening whimper of complaint that would have made her sound like a beaten dog.

Today she managed better than usual. She was able to look into the bathroom mirror, and move her eyebrows, her lips and jaws, around to bring her expression back to normal. So much for that, she seemed to be saying. Even while it was going on she had been able to think of other things. She had thought about making a custard, she thought about whether they had enough milk and eggs. And right through her husband's rampage she thought of the fingers moving in the feathers, the wife's hand laid on top of the husband's, pressing down.

So of Heather Bell we will sing our song,
As we will till our day is done.
In the forest green she was taken from the scene
Though her life had barely begun.

"There is a poem already made up and written down," Frances said.
"I've got it here typed out."

"I thought I'd make a custard," said Maureen.

How much had Frances heard of what Marian Hubbert had said?
Everything, probably. She sounded breathless with the effort of keeping all that in. She held up the typed lines in front of Maureen's face
and Maureen said, "It's too long, I don't have time." She started to
separate the eggs.

"It's good," Frances said. "It's good enough to be put to music."

She read it through aloud. Maureen said, "I have to concentrate."

"So I guess I got my marching orders," said Frances, and went to do
the sunroom.

Then Maureen had the peace of the kitchen—the old white tiles and
high yellowed walls, the bowls and pots and implements familiar and
comforting to her, as probably to her predecessor.

What Mary Johnstone told the girls in her talk was always more or less the
same thing and most of them knew what to expect. They could even make
prepared faces at each other. She told them how Jesus had come and
talked to her when she was in the iron lung. She did not mean in a dream,
she said, or in a vision, or when she was delirious. She meant that He
came and she recognized Him but didn't think anything was strange
about it. She recognized Him at once, though he was dressed like a doctor
in a white coat. She thought, Well, that's reasonable—otherwise they
wouldn't let Him in here. That was how she took it. Lying there in the iron
lung, she was sensible and stupid at once, as you are when something like
that hits you. (She meant Jesus, not the polio.) Jesus said, "You've got to
get back up to bat, Mary." That was all. She was a good softball player,
and He used language that He knew she would understand. Then He went
away. And she hugged onto Life, the way He had told her to.

There was more to follow, about the uniqueness and specialness of
each of their lives and their bodies, which led of course into what Mary
Johnstone called "plain talk" about boys and urges. (This was where

they did the faces—they were too abashed when she was going on about Jesus.) And about liquor and cigarettes and how one thing can lead to another. They thought she was crazy—and she couldn't even tell that they had smoked themselves half sick last night. They reeked and she never mentioned it.

So she was—crazy. But everybody let her talk about Jesus in the hospital because they thought she was entitled to believe that.

But suppose you did see something? Not along the line of Jesus, but something? Maureen has had that happen. Sometimes when she is just going to sleep but not quite asleep, not dreaming yet, she has caught something. Or even in the daytime during what she thinks of as her normal life. She might catch herself sitting on stone steps eating cherries and watching a man coming up the steps carrying a parcel. She has never seen those steps or that man, but for an instant they seem to be part of another life that she is leading, a life just as long and complicated and strange and dull as this one. And she isn't surprised. It's just a fluke, a speedily corrected error, that she knows about both lives at the same time. It seemed so ordinary, she thinks afterward. The cherries. The parcel.

What she sees now isn't in any life of her own. She sees one of those thick-fingered hands that pressed into her tablecloth and that had worked among the feathers, and it is pressed down, unresistingly, but by somebody else's will—it is pressed down on the open burner of the stove where she is stirring the custard in the double boiler, and held there just for a second or two, just long enough to scorch the flesh on the red coil, to scorch but not to maim. In silence this is done, and by agreement—a brief and barbaric and necessary act. So it seems. The punished hand dark as a glove or a hand's shadow, the fingers spread. Still in the same clothes. The cream-colored sleeve, the dull blue.

Maureen hears her husband moving around in the front hall, so she turns off the heat and lays down the spoon and goes in to him. He has tidied himself up. He is ready to go out. She knows without asking where he is going. Down to the Police Office, to find out what has been reported, what is being done.

"Maybe I should drive you," she says. "It's hot out."

He shakes his head, he mutters.

"Or I could walk along with you."

No. He is going on a serious errand and it would diminish him to be accompanied or transported by a wife.

She opens the front door for him and he says, "Thank you," in his stiff, quaintly repentant way. As he goes past, he bends and purses his lips at the air close to her cheek.

They've gone, there's nobody sitting on the wall now.

Heather Bell will not be found. No body, no trace. She has blown away like ashes. Her displayed photograph will fade in public places. Its tight-lipped smile, bitten in at one corner as if suppressing a disrespectful laugh, will seem to be connected with her disappearance rather than her mockery of the school photographer. There will always be a tiny suggestion, in that, of her own free will.

Mr. Siddicup will not be any help. He will alternate between bewilderment and tantrums. They will not find anything when they search his house, unless you count those old underclothes of his wife's, and when they dig up his garden the only bones they will find will be old bones that dogs have buried. Many people will continue to believe that he did something or saw something. *He had something to do with it.* When he is committed to the Provincial Asylum, renamed the Mental Health Centre, there will be letters in the local paper about Preventive Custody, and locking the stable door after the horse is stolen.

There will also be letters in the newspaper from Mary Johnstone, explaining why she behaved as she did, why in all good sense and good faith she behaved as she did that Sunday. Finally the editor will have to let her know that Heather Bell is old news, and not the only thing the town wants to be known for, and if the hikes are to come to an end it won't be the worst thing in the world, and the story can't be rehashed forever.

Maureen is a young woman yet, though she doesn't think so, and she has life ahead of her. First a death—that will come soon—then another marriage, new places and houses. In kitchens hundreds and thousands of miles away, she'll watch the soft skin form on the back of a wooden spoon and her memory will twitch, but it will not quite reveal to her this moment when she seems to be looking into an open secret, something not startling until you think of trying to tell it.

—1994

Rudy Wiebe b. 1934

Rudy Wiebe's experience of growing up in a Mennonite community—a Protestant sect that holds itself apart from the world—has had an impact on his writing. Wiebe focuses on figures who live outside the dominant culture or who have lost their place. Viewing official history as itself a form of cultural displacement, he is sceptical about the ability of a historian to reconstruct the past, especially the pasts of individuals not members of the historian's own culture.

These concerns are apparent in "The Naming of Albert Johnson," in which Wiebe reconsiders the legend of the Mad Trapper of Rat River, a man whose actions in the winter of 1931–32 received extensive news coverage and subsequently passed into northern mythology. By recounting the main events in reverse chronological order, Wiebe's narrative reflects the way we reconstruct history: backwards. This technique—in a story that also shows us how few facts we actually know about a man who was the subject of so much early media coverage—emphasizes the uncertainties and limits of historical knowledge.

The Naming
of Albert Johnson[1]

1. *The Eagle River, Yukon:* Wednesday, February 17, 1932
Tuesday, February 16

There is arctic silence at last, after the long snarl of rifles. As if all the stubby trees within earshot had finished splitting in the cold. Then the sound of the airplane almost around the river's bend begins to return, turning as tight a spiral as it may up over bank and trees and back down, over the man crumpled on the bedroll, over the frantic staked dogteams, spluttering, down, glancing down off the wind-ridged river. Tail leaping, almost cart-wheeling over its desperate roar for skis,

---

[1] Dubbed the "Mad Trapper of Rat River," a man identified as Albert Johnson (his actual identity is uncertain) emerged into history in the winter of 1931–32 in the Peel River area of the Northwest Territories, when the Mounties set siege to his cabin after he shot and wounded Constable Alfred King. Johnson managed to slip away and flee westward, killing Constable Edward "Spike" Millen when he caught up to him and eluding pursuit for more than a month in the first manhunt ever to make use of either aircraft or radio. His flight came to be regarded an epic feat of endurance: he is the only man ever known to have travelled by foot across the mountains into the Yukon during the winter. His survival in the harshest of northern Canadian conditions (on some days during his pursuit the temperature reached a high of only -47°C), combined with his extraordinary skill in throwing off his pursuers (he several times circled around behind them and sometimes, to confuse them more, walked backwards in his own tracks), brought him fame.

immense sound rocketing from that bouncing black dot on the level glare but stopped finally, its prop whirl staggering out motionless just behind the man moving inevitably forward on snowshoes, not looking back, step by step up the river with his rifle ready. Hesitates, lifts one foot, then the other, stops, and moves forward again to the splotch in the vast whiteness before him.

The pack is too huge, and apparently worried by rats with very long, fine teeth. Behind it a twisted body. Unbelievably small. One outflung hand still clutching a rifle, but no motion, nothing, the airplane dead and only the distant sounds of dogs somewhere, of men moving at the banks of the river. The police rifle points down, steadily extending the police arm until it can lever the body, already stiffening, up. A red crater for hip. As if one small part of that incredible toughness had rebelled at last, exploded red out of itself, splattering itself with itself when everything but itself was at last unreachable. But the face is turning up. Rime, and clots of snow ground into whiskers, the fur hat hurled somewhere by bullets perhaps and the whipped cowlick already a mat frozen above half-open eyes show-ing only white, nostrils flared, the concrete face wiped clean of everything but snarl. Freezing snarl and teeth. As if the long clenched jaws had tight-ened down beyond some ultimate cog and openly locked their teeth into their own torn lips in one final wordlessly silent scream.

The pilot blunders up, gasping. "By god, we got the son of a bitch!" stumbles across the back of the snowshoes and recovers beside the policeman. Gagging a little, "My g—" All that sudden colour propped up by the rifle barrel on the otherwise white snow. And the terrible face.

The one necessary bullet, in the spine where its small entry cannot be seen at this moment, and was never felt as six others were, knocked the man face down in the snow. Though that would never loosen his grip on his rifle. The man had been working himself over on his side, not concerned as it seemed for the bullets singing to him from the level drifts in front of him or the trees on either bank. With his left hand he was reaching into his coat pocket to reload his Savage .30-.30, almost warm on the inside of his other bare hand, and he knew as every good hunter must that he had exactly thirty-nine bullets left besides the one hidden under the rifle's butt plate. If they moved in any closer he also had the Winchester .22 with sixty-four bullets, and closer still there will be the sawed-off shotgun, though he had only a few shells left, he could not now be certain exactly how many. He had stuffed snow tight into the hole where one or perhaps even two shells had exploded in his opposite hip pocket. A man could lose his blood in a minute from a hole that size but the snow was still white and icy the instant he had to glance at it, packing it in. If they had hit him there before forcing him down behind his pack in the middle of the river, he could not have moved enough to pull out of the pack straps, leave alone get behind it for protection. Bullets twitch it, whine about his tea tin like his axe handle snapping once at his legs as he ran from the eastern river bank too steep to clamber up, a very bad mistake to have to discover after spending several minutes and a hundred yards of strength running his snowshoes towards it. Not a single rock, steep and bare like polished planks. But he had gained a little on them, he saw that as he curved without stopping towards the centre of the river and the line of trees beyond it. That bank is easily climbed, he knows because he climbed it that morning, but all the dogs and men so suddenly around the hairpin turn surprised him towards the nearest bank, and he sees the teams spreading to outflank him, three towards the low west bank. And two of them bending over the one army radioman he got.

Instantly the man knew it was the river that had betrayed him. He had outlegged their dogs and lost the plane time and again on glare-ice and in fog and brush and between the endless trails of caribou herds, but the sluggish loops of this river doubling back on itself have betrayed him. It is his own best move, forward and then back, circle forward and further back, backwards, so the ones following his separate tracks will suddenly confront each other in cursing bewilderment. But this river, it cannot be named the Porcupine, has out-doubled him. For the dogs leaping towards him around the bend, the roaring radioman heaving at his sled, scrabbling for his rifle, this is clearly what he saw when he climbed the tree on the far bank, one of the teams he saw then across a wide tongue of land already ahead of him, as it seemed, and he started back to get further behind them before he followed and picked them off singly in whatever tracks of his they thought they were following. These dogs and this driver rounding to face him as he walks so carefully backwards in his snowshoes on the curve of his own tracks.

Whatever this river is spiralling back into the Yukon hills, his rifle will not betray him. Words are bellowing out of the racket of teams hurtling around the bend. His rifle speaks easily, wordlessly to the army radioman kneeling, sharpshooter position, left elbow propped on left knee. The sights glided together certain and deadly, and long before the sound had returned that one kneeling was already flung back clean as frozen wood bursting at his axe.

He has not eaten, he believes it must be two days, and the rabbit tracks are so old they give no hope for his snares. The squirrel burrow may be better. He is scraping curls from tiny spruce twigs, watching them tighten against the lard pail, watching the flames as it seems they're licking the tin blacker with their gold tongues. The fire lives with him, and he will soon examine the tinfoil of matches in his pocket, and the tinfoil bundle in his pack and also the other two paper-wrapped packages. That must be done daily, if possible. The pack, unopened, with the .22 laced to its side is between his left shoulder and the snow hollow; the moose hides spread under and behind him; the snowshoes stuck erect into the snow on the right, the long axe lying there and the rifle also, in its cloth cover but on the moosehide pouch. He has already worked carefully on his feet, kneading as much of the frost out of one and then the other as he can before the fire though two toes on the left are black and the heel of the right is rubbed raw. Bad lacing when he walked backwards, and too numb for him to notice. The one toe can only be kept another day, perhaps, but he has only a gun-oily rag for his heel. Gunoil? Spruce gum? Wait. His feet are wrapped and ready to move instantly and he sits watching warmth curl around the pail. Leans his face down into it. Then he puts the knife away in his clothes and pulls out a tiny paper. His hard fingers unfold it carefully, he studies the crystals a moment, and then as the flames tighten the blackened spirals of spruce he pours that into the steaming pail. He studies the paper, the brownness of it; the suggestion of a word beginning, or perhaps ending, that shines through its substance. He lowers it steadily then until it darkens, smiling as a spot of deep brown breaks through the possible name and curls back a black empty circle towards his fingers. He lets it go, feeling warmth like a massage in its final flare and dying. There is nothing left but a smaller fold of pepper and a bag of salt so when he drinks it is very slowly, letting each mouthful move for every part of his tongue to hold a moment this last faint sweetness.

He sits in the small yellow globe created by fire. Drinking. The wind breathes through the small spruce, his body rests motionlessly; knowing that dug into the snow with drifts and spruce tips above him they could see his smokeless fire only if they flew directly over him. And the plane cannot fly at night. They are somewhere very close now, and their plane less than a few minutes behind. It has flown straight in an hour, again and again, all he had overlaid with tangled tracks in five weeks, but the silent land is what it is. He is now resting motionlessly. And waiting.

And the whisky-jacks are suddenly there. He had not known them before to come after dark, but grey and white tipped with black they fluffed themselves at the grey edge of his light, watching, and then one hopped two hops. Sideways. The first living thing he had seen since the caribou. But he reaches for the bits of babiche[2] he had cut and rubbed in salt, laid ready on the cloth of the riflebutt. He throws, the draggle-tail is gone but the other watches, head cocked, then jumps so easily the long space his stiff throw had managed, and the bit is gone. He does not move his body, tosses another bit, and another, closer, closer, and then draggle-tail is there scrabbling for the bit, and he twitches the white string lying beside the bits of babiche left by the rifle, sees the bigger piece tug from the snow and draggle-tail leap to it. Gulp. He tugs, feels the slight weight as the thread lifts from the snow in the firelight, and now the other is gone while draggle-tail comes towards him inevitably, string pulling the beak soundlessly agape, wings desperate in snow, dragged between rifle and fire into the waiting claw of his hand. He felt the bird's blood beat against his palm, the legs and tail and wings thud an instant, shuddering and then limp between his relentless fingers.

Wings. Noiselessly he felt the beautiful muscles shift, slip over bones delicate as twigs. He could lope circles around any dogs they set on his trail but that beast labelled in letters combing the clouds, staring everywhere until its roar suddenly blundered up out of a canyon or over a ridge, laying its relentless shadow like words on the world: he would have dragged every tree in the Yukon together to build a fire and boil that. Steel pipes and canvas and wires and name, that stinking noise. In the silence under the spruce he skims the tiny fat bubbles from the darkening soup; watches them coagulate yellow on the shavings. Better than gunoil, or gum. He began to unwrap his feet again but listening, always listening. The delicate furrow of the bird pointed towards him in the snow.

2. *The Richardson Mountains*, N.W.T: Tuesday, February 9, 1932
                                          Saturday, January 30

Though it means moving two and three miles to their one, the best trail to confuse them in the foothill ravines was a spiral zig-zag. West of the mountains he has not seen them; he has outrun them so far in crossing

---

[2] Leather strips.

the Richardson Mountains during the blizzard that when he reaches a river he thought it must be the Porcupine because he seems at last to be inside something that is completely alone. But the creeks draining east lay in seemingly parallel but eventually converging canyons with tundra plateaus glazed under wind between them, and when he paused on one leg of his zag he sometimes saw them, across one plateau or in a canyon, labouring with their dogs and sleds as it seems ahead of him. In the white scream of the mountain pass where no human being has ever ventured in winter he does not dare pause to sleep for two days and the long night between them, one toe and perhaps another frozen beyond saving and parts of his face dead, but in the east he had seen the track-ers up close, once been above them and watched them coming along his trails towards each other unawares out of two converging canyons with their sleds and drivers trailing, and suddenly round the cliff to face each other in cursing amazement. He was far enough not to hear their words as they heated water for tea, wasting daylight minutes, beating their hands to keep warm.

The police drive the dog teams now, and the Indians sometimes; the ones who best track him on the glazed snow, through zags and bends, always wary of ambush, are the two army radiomen. One of the sleds is loaded with batteries when it should be food, but they sniff silently along his tracks, loping giant circles ahead of the heaving dogs and winging arms like semaphores when they find a trail leading as it seems directly back towards the sleds they have just left. He would not have thought them so relentless at unravelling his trails, these two who every morning tried to raise the police on their frozen radio, and when he was convinced they would follow him as certainly as Millen and the plane roared up, dropping supplies, it was time to accept the rising blizzard over the mountains and find at last, for certain, the Porcupine River.

It is certainly Millen who brought the plane north just before the blizzard, and it was Millen who saw his smoke and heard him cough-ing, whistling in that canyon camp hidden in trees under a cliff so steep he has to chop handholds in the frozen rock to get out of there. Without dynamite again, or bombs, they could not dig him out; even in his unending alert his heart jerks at the sound of what was a foot slipping against a frozen tree up the ridge facing him. His rifle is out of its sheath, the shell racking home in the cold like precise steel biting. There is nothing more; an animal? A tree bursting? He crouches motionless, for if they are there they should be all around him, perhaps above on the cliff, and he will not move until he knows. Only the wind worrying spruce and snow, whining wordlessly. There, twenty yards away a shadow moves, Millen certainly, and his shot snaps as his rifle swings up, as he drops. Bullets snick from everywhere, their sound booming back and forth along the canyon. He has only fired once and is down, completely aware, on the wrong side of his fire and he shoots carefully again to draw their shots and they come, four harmlessly high and nicely spaced out: there are two—Millen and another—below him in the canyon and two a bit higher on the right ridge, one of them that slipped. Nothing up the canyon or above on the cliff. With that knowledge he gathered himself and leaped over the fire against the cliff and one on the ridge made a good shot that cut his jacket and he could fall as if gut-shot in the hollow of deadfall. Until the fire died, he was almost comfortable.

In the growing dusk he watches the big Swede, who drove dogs very well, crawl towards Millen stretched out, face down. He watches him tie Millen's legs together with the laces of his mukluks and drag him backwards, plowing a long furrow and leaving the rifle sunk in the snow. He wastes no shot at their steady firing, and when they stop there are Millen's words still

You're surrounded. King isn't dead. Will you give

waiting, frozen in the canyon. He lay absolutely motionless behind the deadfall against the cliff, as if he were dead, knowing they would have to move finally. He flexed his feet continuously, and his fingers as he shifted the rifle no more quickly than a clock hand, moving into the position it would have to be when they charged him. They almost outwait him; it is really a question between the coming darkness and his freezing despite his invisible motions, but before darkness Millen had to move. Two of them were coming and he shifted his rifle slightly on the log to cover the left one—it must have been the long cold that made him mistake that for Millen—who dived out of sight, his shot thundering along the canyon, but Millen did not drop behind anything. Simply down on one knee, firing. Once, twice bullets tore the log and then he had his head up with those eyes staring straight down his sights and he fired two shots so fast the roar in the canyon sounded as one and Millen stood up, the whole length over him, whirled in that silent unmistakable way and crashed face down in the snow. He hears them dragging and chopping trees for a stage cache[3] to keep the body, and in the darkness he chops handholds up the face of the cliff, step by step as he hoists himself and his pack out of another good shelter. As he has had to leave others.

3. *The Rat River,* N.W.T.: Saturday, January 10, 1932
Thursday, December 31, 1931
Tuesday, July 28

In his regular round of each loophole he peers down the promontory towards their fires glaring up from behind the riverbank. They surround him on three sides, nine of them with no more than forty dogs, which in this cold means they already need more supplies than they can have brought with them. They will be making plans for something, suddenly, beyond bullets against his logs and guns and it will have to come soon. In the long darkness, and he can wait far easier than they. Dynamite. If they have any more to thaw out very carefully after blowing open the roof and stovepipe as darkness settled, a hole hardly big enough for one of them—a Norwegian, they were everywhere with their long noses—to fill it an instant, staring down at him gathering himself from the corner out of roof-sod and pipes and snow: the cabin barely stuck above the drifts but that one was gigantic to lean in like that, staring until he lifted his rifle and the long face vanished an instant before his bullet passed through that space. But the hole was large enough for the cold to slide down along the wall and work itself into his trench, which would be all that saved him when they used the last of their dynamite. He began to feel what they had stalked him with all day: cold tightening steadily as steel around toes, face, around fingers.

In the clearing still nothing stirs. There is only the penumbra of light along the circle of the bank as if they had laid a trench-fire to thaw the entire promontory and were soundlessly burrowing in under him. Their flares were long dead, the sky across the river flickering with orange lights to vanish down into spruce and willows again, like the shadow blotting a notch in the eastern bank and he thrust his rifle through the chink and had almost got a shot away when a projectile arced against the sky and he jerked the gun out, diving, into the trench deep under the wall among the moose hides that could not protect him from the roof

---

[3] A platform.

and walls tearing apart so loud it seemed most of himself had been blasted to the farthest granules of sweet, silent, earth. The sods and foot-thick logs he had built together where the river curled were gone and he would climb out and walk away as he always had, but first he pulled himself up and out between the splinters, still holding the rifle, just in time to see yellow light humpling through the snow towards him and he fired three times so fast it sounded in his ears as though his cabin was continuing to explode. The shadows around the light dance in one spot an instant but come on in a straight black line, lengthening down, faster, and the light cuts straight across his eyes and he gets away the fourth shot and the light tears itself into bits. He might have been lying on his back staring up into night and had the stars explode into existence above him. And whatever darkness is left before him then blunders away, desperately plowing away from him through the snow like the first one who came twice with a voice repeating at his door.

I am Constable Alfred King, are you in there?

fist thudding the door the second time with a paper creaking louder than his voice so thin in the cold silence

I have a search warrant now, we have had complaints and if you don't open

and then plowing away in a long desperate scrabble through the sun-shot snow while the three others at the riverbank thumped their bullets hopelessly high into the logs but shattering the window again and again until they dragged King and each other head first over the edge while he placed lead carefully over them, snapping willow bits on top of them and still seeing, strangely, the tiny hole that had materialized up into his door when he flexed the trigger, still hearing the grunt that had wormed in through the slivers of the board he had whipsawn himself. Legs and feet wrapped in moose hide lay a moment across his window, level in the snow, jerking as if barely attached to a body knocked over helpless, a face somewhere twisted in gradually developing pain that had first leaned against his door, fist banging while that other one held the dogs at the edge of the clearing, waiting.

Hallo? Hallo? This is Constable Alfred King of the Royal Canadian Mounted Police. I want to talk to you. Constable Millen and they looked into each other's eyes, once, through his tiny window. The eyes peering down into his—could he be seen from out of the blinding sun?—squinted blue from a boy's round face with a bulging nose bridged over pale with cold. King, of the Royal Mounted. Like a silly book title, or the funny papers. He didn't look it as much as Spike Millen, main snooper and tracker at Arctic Red River who baked pies and danced, everybody said, better than any man in the north. Let them dance hipped in snow, get themselves dragged away under spruce and dangling traps, asking, laying words on him, naming things

> You come across from the Yukon? You got a trapper's licence? The Loucheaux[4] trap the Rat, up towards the Richardson Mountains. You'll need a licence, why not

Words. Dropping out of nothing into advice. Maybe he wanted a kicker[5] to move that new canoe against the Rat River? Loaded down as it is. The Rat drops fast, you have to hand-line the portage anyway to get past Destruction City[6] where those would-be Klondikers wintered in '98. He looked up at the trader above him on the wedge of gravel. He had expected at least silence. From a trader standing with the bulge of seven hundred dollars in his pocket; in the south a man could feed himself with that for two years. Mouths always full of words, pushing, every mouth falling open and dropping words from nothing into meaning. The trader's eyes shifted finally, perhaps to the junction of the rivers behind them, south and west, the united river clicking under the canoe. As he raised his paddle. The new rifle oiled and ready with its butt almost touching his knees as he kneels, ready to pull the canoe around.

4. *Above Fort McPherson*, N.W.T.: Tuesday, July 7, 1931

The Porcupine River, as he thought it was then, chuckled between the three logs of his raft. He could hear that below him, under the mosquitoes probing the mesh about his head, and see the gold lengthen up the river like the canoe that would come towards him from the north where the sun just refused to open the spiky horizon. Gilded, hammered out

---

[4] The Natives of the Peel River region who had the right to trap the Rat River. Johnson was accused of stealing from a Loucheaux trapline.
[5] An outboard motor.
[6] A debris-covered area in the Richardson Mountains where gold-seekers, travelling to the Klondike, had wintered over. Some died and many of the survivors suffered severe frostbite.

slowly, soundlessly towards him the thick gold. He sat almost without breathing, watching it come like silence. And then imperceptibly the black spired riverbend grew pointed, stretched itself in a thin straight line double-bumped, gradually spreading a straight wedge below the sun through the golden river. When he had gathered that slowly into anger it was already too late to choke his fire; the vee had abruptly bent towards him, the bow man already raised his paddle; hailed. Almost it seemed as if a name had been blundered into the silence, but he did not move in his fury. The river chuckled again.

"... o-o-o-o ..." the point of the wedge almost under him now. And the sound of a name, that was so clear he could almost distinguish it. Perhaps he already knew what it was, had long since lived this in that endlessly enraged chamber of himself, even to the strange Indian accent mounded below him in the canoe bow where the black hump of the stem partner moved them straight towards him out of the fanned ripples, crumpling gold. To the humps of his raft below on the gravel waiting to anchor them.

"What d'ya want."

"You Albert Johnson?"

It could have been the sternman who named him. The sun like hatchet-strokes across slanted eyes, the gaunt noses below him there holding the canoe against the current, their paddles hooked in the logs of his raft. Two Loucheaux half-faces, black and red kneeling in the roiled gold of the river, the words thudding softly in his ears.

You Albert Johnson?

One midnight above the Arctic Circle to hear again the inevitability of name. He has not heard it in four years, it could be to the very day since that Vancouver garden, staring into the evening sun and hearing this quiet sound from these motionless—perhaps they are men kneeling there, perhaps waiting for him to accept again what has now been laid inevitably upon him, the name come to meet him in his journey north, come out of north around the bend and against the current of the Peel River, as they name that too, to confront him on a river he thought another and aloud where he would have found after all his years, at long last, only nameless silence.

You Albert Johnson?

"Yes," he said finally.

And out of his rage he begins to gather words together. Slowly, every word he can locate, as heavily as he would gather stones on a Saskatchewan field, to hold them for one violent moment against himself between his two hands before he heaves them up and hurls them—but they are gone. The ripples of their passing may have been smoothing out as he stares at where they should have been had they been there. Only the briefly golden river lies before him, whatever its name may be since it must have one, bending back somewhere beyond that land, curling back upon itself in its giant, relentless spirals down to the implacable, and ice-choked, arctic sea.

—1974

Carol Shields 1935–2003

Carol Shields was a writer of short stories and novels, as well as of poetry, plays, and essays. Her three volumes of short fiction, brought together posthumously in 2004 as The Collected Stories, *show a fine eye for the small details of everyday life and the ironies we tend to overlook. Often morality tales, they tell of everymen and women who encounter situations that try their spirit and sense of worth. In "The Orange Fish," the narrator and his wife, seeking to fill a void, find their life transformed by art and themselves drawn into a new community. The surprising progress of the story turns it into a parable about how we make meaning and value, and teasingly recasts old questions about the function of art and its relationship to society.*

The Orange Fish

Like others of my generation I am devoted to food, money, and sex; but I have an ulcer and have been unhappily married to Lois-Ann, a lawyer, for twelve years. As you might guess, we are both fearful of aging. Recently Lois-Ann showed me an article she had clipped from the newspaper, a profile of a well-known television actress who was described as being "deep in her thirties."

"That's what we are," Lois-Ann said sadly, "deep in our thirties." She looked at me from behind a lens of tears.

Despite our incompatibility, the two of us understand each other, and I knew more or less what it was she was thinking: that some years ago, when she was twenty-five, she made up her mind to go to Vancouver Island and raise dahlias, but on the very day she bought her air ticket, she got a letter in the mail saying she'd been accepted at law school. "None of us writes our own script," she said to me once, and of course she's right. I still toy—I confess this to you freely—with my old fantasy of running a dude ranch, with the thought of well-rubbed saddles and harnesses and the whole sweet leathery tip of possibility, even though I know the dude market's been depressed for a decade, dead in fact.

Not long ago, on a Saturday morning, Lois-Ann and I had one of our long talks about values, about goals. The mood as we sat over breakfast was sternly analytical.

"Maybe we've become trapped in the cult of consumerism and youth worship," I suggested.

"Trapped by our *zeitgeist*," said Lois-Ann, who has a way of capping a point, especially my point.

A long silence followed, twenty seconds, thirty seconds. I glanced up from an emptied coffee cup, remembered that my fortieth birthday was only weeks away, and felt a flare of panic in my upper colon. The pain was hideous and familiar. I took a deep breath as I'd been told to do. Breathe in, then out. Repeat. The trick is to visualize the pain, its substance and color, and then transfer it to a point outside the body. I concentrated on a small spot above our breakfast table, a random patch on the white wall. Often this does the trick, but this morning the blank space, the smooth drywall expanse of it, seemed distinctly accusing.

At one time Lois-Ann and I had talked about wall-papering the kitchen or at least putting up an electric clock shaped like a sunflower. We also considered a ceramic bas-relief of cauliflowers and carrots, and after that a little heart-shaped mirror bordered with rattan, and, more recently, a primitive map of the world with a practical acrylic surface. We have never been able to agree, never been able to arrive at a decision.

I felt Lois-Ann watching me, her eyes as neat and neutral as birds' eggs. "What we need," I said, gesturing at the void, "is a picture."

"Or possibly a print," said Lois-Ann, and immediately went to get her coat.

Three hours later we were the owners of a cheerful lithograph titled *The Orange Fish*. It was unframed, but enclosed in a sandwich of twinkling glass, its corners secured by a set of neat metal clips. The mat surrounding the picture was a generous three inches in width—we liked that—and the background was a shimmer of green; within this space the orange fish was suspended.

I wish somehow you might see this fish. He is boldly drawn, and just as boldly colored. He occupies approximately eighty per cent of the surface and has about him a wet, dense look of health. To me, at least, he appears to have stopped moving, to be resting against the wall of green water. A stream of bubbles, each one separate and tear-shaped, floats above him, binding him to his element. Of course he is seen in side profile, as fish always are, and this classic posture underlines the tranquillity of the whole. He possesses, too, a Buddha-like sense of being in the *right* place, the only place. His center, that is, where you might imagine his heart to be, is sweetly orange in color, and this color diminishes slightly as it flows toward the semi-transparency of fins and the round, ridged, non-appraising mouth. But it was his eye I most appreciated, the kind of wide, ungreedy eye I would like to be able to turn onto the world.

We made up our minds quickly; he would fit nicely over the breakfast table. Lois-Ann mentioned that the orange tones would pick up the colors of the seat covers. We were in a state of rare agreement. And the price was right.

Forgive me if I seem condescending, but you should know that, strictly speaking, a lithograph is not an original work of art, but rather a print from an original plate; the number of prints is limited to ten or twenty or fifty or more, and this number is always indicated on the piece itself. A tiny inked set of numbers in the corner, just beneath the artist's signature, will tell you, for example, that our particular fish is number eight out of an existing ten copies, and I think it pleased me from the start to think of those other copies, the nine brother fish scattered elsewhere, suspended in identical seas of green water, each pointed soberly in the same leftward direction. I found myself in a fanciful mood, humming, installing a hook on the kitchen wall, and hanging our new acquisition. We stepped backward to admire it, and later Lois-Ann made a Spanish omelet with fresh fennel, which we ate beneath the austere eye of our beautiful fish.

As you well know, there are certain necessary tasks that coarsen the quality of everyday life, and while Lois-Ann and I went about ours, we felt calmed by the heft of our solemn, gleaming fish. My health improved from the first day, and before long Lois-Ann and I were on better terms, often sharing workaday anecdotes or pointing out curious items to each other in the newspaper. I rediscovered the girlish angularity of her arms and shoulders as she wriggled in and out of her little nylon nightgowns, smoothing down the skirts with a sly, sweet glance in my direction. For the first time in years she left the lamp burning on the bedside table and, as in our early days, she covered me with kisses, a long nibbling trail up and down the ridge of my vertebrae. In the morning, drinking our coffee at the breakfast table, we looked up, regarded our orange fish, smiled at each other, but were ritualistically careful to say nothing.

We didn't ask ourselves, for instance, what kind of fish this was, whether it was a carp or a flounder or a monstrously out-of-scale gold-fish. Its biological classification, its authenticity, seemed splendidly irrelevant. Details, just details; we swept them aside. What mattered was the prismatic disjection of green light that surrounded it. What mattered was that it existed. That it had no age, no history. It simply *was*. You can understand that to speculate, to analyze overmuch, interferes with that narrow gap between symbol and reality, and it was precisely in the folds of that little gap that Lois-Ann and I found our temporary refuge.

Soon an envelope arrived in the mail, an official notice. We were advised that the ten owners of *The Orange Fish* met on the third Thursday evening of each month. The announcement was photocopied, but on decent paper with an appropriate logo. Eight-thirty was the regular time, and there was a good-natured reminder at the bottom of the page about the importance of getting things going punctually.

Nevertheless we were late. At the last minute Lois-Ann discovered a run in her pantyhose and had to change. I had difficulty getting the car started, and of course traffic was heavy. Furthermore, the meeting was in a part of the city that was unfamiliar to us. Lois-Ann, although a clever lawyer, has a poor sense of spatial orientation and told me to turn left when I should have turned right. And then there was the usual problem with parking, for which she seemed to hold me responsible. We arrived at eight-forty-five, rather agitated and out of breath from climbing the stairs.

Seeing that roomful of faces, I at first experienced a shriek in the region of my upper colon. Lois-Ann had a similar shock of alarm, what she afterwards described to me as a jolt to her imagination, as though an axle in her left brain had suddenly seized.

Someone was speaking as we entered the room. I recognized the mono-tone of the born chairman. "It is always a pleasure," the voice intoned, "to come together to express our concerns and compare experiences."

At that moment the only experience I cared about was the sinuous river of kisses down my shoulders and backbone, but I managed to sit straight on my folding chair and to look alert and responsible. Lois-Ann, in lawyerlike fashion, inspected the agenda, running a little gold pencil down the list of items, her tongue tight between her teeth.

The voice rumbled on. Minutes from the previous meeting were read and approved. There was no old business. Nor any new business. "Well, then," the chairman said, "who would like to speak first?"

Someone at the front of the room rose and gave his name, a name that conveyed the double-pillared boom of money and power. I craned my neck, but could see only a bush of fine white hair. The voice was feeble yet dignified, a persisting quaver from a soft old silvery throat, and I realized after a minute or two that we were listening to a testimonial. A mystical experience was described. Something, too, about the "search for definitions" and about "wandering in the wilderness" and about the historic symbol of the fish in the Western Tradition, a secret sign, an icon expressing providence. "My life has been altered," the voice concluded, "and given direction."

The next speaker was young, not more than twenty I would say. Lois-Ann and I took in the flare of dyed hair, curiously angled and distinctively punk in style. You can imagine our surprise: here of all places to find a spiked bracelet, black nails, cheeks outlined in blue paint, and a forehead tattooed with the world's most familiar expletive. *The Orange Fish* had been a graduation gift from his parents. The framing alone cost two hundred dollars. He had stared at it for weeks, or possibly months, trying to understand what it meant; then revelation rushed in. "Fishness" was a viable alternative. The orange fins and sneering mouth said no to "all that garbage that gets shoveled on your head by society. So keep swimming and don't take any junk," he wound up, then sat down to loud applause.

A woman in a neatly tailored mauve suit spoke for a quarter of an hour about her investment difficulties. She'd tried stocks. She'd tried the bond market. She'd tried treasury bills and mutual funds. In every instance she found herself buying at the peak and selling just as the market bottomed out. Until she found out about investing in art. Until she found *The Orange Fish*. She was sure, now, that she was on an upward curve. That success was just ahead. Recently she had started to be happy, she said.

A man rose to his feet. He was in his mid-fifties, we guessed, with good teeth and an aura of culture lightly worn. "Let me begin at the beginning," he said. He had been through a period of professional burnout, arriving every day at his office exhausted. "Try to find some way to brighten up the place," he told his secretary, handing her a blank check. *The Orange Fish* appeared the next day. Its effect had been instantaneous: on himself, his staff, and also on his clients. It was as though a bright banner had been raised. Orange, after all, was the color of celebration, and it is the act of celebration which has been crowded out of contemporary life.

The next speaker was cheered the moment he stood. He had, we discovered, traveled all the way from Japan, from the city of Kobe— making our little journey across the city seem trivial. As you can imagine, his accent was somewhat harsh and halting, but I believe we understood something of what he said. In the small house where he lives, he has hung *The Orange Fish* in the traditional tokonoma alcove,[1] just above the black lacquered slab of wood on which rests a bowl of white flowers. The contrast between the sharp orange of the fish's scales and the unearthly whiteness of the flowers' petals reminds him daily of the contradictions that abound in the industrialized world. At this no one clapped louder than myself.

A fish is devoid of irony, someone else contributed in a brisk, cozy voice, and is therefore a reminder of our lost innocence, of the era which predated double meanings and trial balloons. But, at the same time, a fish is more and also less than its bodily weight.

A slim, dark-haired woman, hardly more than a girl, spoke for several minutes about the universality of fish. How three-quarters of the earth's surface is covered with water, and in this water leap fish by the millions. There are people in this world, she said, who have never seen a sheep or a cow, but there is no one who is not acquainted with the organic shape of the fish.

"We begin our life in water," came a hoarse and boozey squawk from the back row, "and we yearn all our days to return to our natural element. In water we are free to move without effort, to be most truly ourselves."

"The interior life of the fish is unknowable," said the next speaker, who was Lois-Ann. "She swims continuously, and is as mute, as voiceless as a dahlia. She speaks at the level of gesture, in circling patterns revived and repeated. The purpose of her eye is to decode and rearrange the wordless world."

"The orange fish," said a voice which turned out to be my own, "will never grow old."

---

[1] In a traditional Japanese home, art is displayed only in an alcove reserved for that purpose.

I sat down. Later my hand was most warmly shaken. During the refreshment hour I was greeted with feeling and asked to sign the membership book. Lois-Ann put her arms around me, publicly, her face shining, and I knew that when we got home she would offer me a cup of cocoa. She would leave the bedside lamp burning and bejewel me with a stream of kisses. You can understand my feeling. Enchantment. Ecstasy. But waking up in the morning we would not be the same people.

I believe we all felt it, standing in that brightly lit room with our coffee cups and cookies: the woman in the tailored mauve suit, the fifty-ish man with the good teeth, even the young boy with his crown of purple hair. We were, each of us, speeding along a trajectory, away from each other, and away from that one fixed point in time, the orange fish.

But how helplessly distorted our perspective turned out to be. What none of us could have known that night was that *we* were the ones who were left behind, sheltered and reprieved by a rare congeniality and by the pleasure that each of us feels when our deepest concerns have been given form.

That very evening, in another part of the city, ten thousand posters of the orange fish were rolling off a press. These posters—which would sell first for $10, then $8.49, and later $1.95—would decorate the rumpled bedrooms of teenagers and the public washrooms of filling stations and beer halls. Within a year a postage stamp would be issued, engraved with the image of the orange fish, but a fish whose eye, miniaturized, would hold a look of mild bewilderment. And sooner than any of us would believe possible, the orange fish would be slapped across the front of a Sears flyer, given a set of demeaning eyebrows, and cruelly bisected with an invitation to stock up early on back-to-school supplies.

There can be no turning back at this point, as you surely know. Winking off lapel buttons and earrings, stamped onto sweatshirts and neckties, doodled on notepads and in the margin of love letters, the orange fish, without a backward glance, will begin to die.

—1989

Alistair MacLeod b. 1936

Not a prolific author—in thirty years he has published two collections of short stories and the award-winning novel No Great Mischief *(1999)—Alistair MacLeod creates narratives of immense power. (A single volume,* Island, *which appeared in 2000, brings together all his short fiction to date.) "The Closing Down of Summer" is, like most of his work, located on Cape Breton Island, within the Scots culture still strongly rooted there. Speaking for himself and his fellow miners, the story's narrator describes the emotional costs of a trade that carries them far away from home and family. Longing to "tell the nature of my work and perhaps some of my entombed feelings to those that I would love, if they would care to listen," he finds himself struggling against inarticulate loneliness.*

Like this story's "transparent vodka bottles [that] both show and keep their simple secret," MacLeod reveals much about his subjects yet leaves his readers with a strong sense of things unsaid. He achieves this paradoxical effect while creating miniature epics about heroic individuals, weighing each word in a heightened style that provides enough distance to lift its subject out of the quotidian world and into the realm of "ballads and folktales of the distant lonely past."

The Closing Down of Summer

It is August now, towards the end, and the weather can no longer be trusted. All summer it has been very hot. So hot that the gardens have died and the hay has not grown and the surface wells have dried to dampened mud. The brooks that flow to the sea have dried to trickles and the trout that inhabit them and the inland lakes are soft and sluggish and gasping for life. Sometimes they are seen floating dead in the over-warm water, their bodies covered with fat grey parasites. They are very unlike the leaping, spirited trout of spring, battling and alive in the rushing, clear, cold water; so electrically filled with movement that it seems no parasite could ever lodge within their flesh.

The heat has been bad for fish and wells and the growth of green, but for those who choose to lie on the beaches of the summer sun the weather has been ideal. This is a record year for tourists in Nova Scotia, we are constantly being told. More motorists have crossed the border at Amherst than ever before. More cars have landed at the ferry docks in Yarmouth. Motels and campsites have been filled to capacity. The highways are heavy with touring buses and camper trailers and cars with the inevitable lobster traps fastened to their roofs. Tourism is booming as never before.

Here on this beach, on Cape Breton's west coast, there are no tourists. Only ourselves. We have been here for most of the summer. Surprised at the endurance and consistency of the heat. Waiting for it to break and perhaps to change the spell. At the end of July we said to ourselves and to each other, "The August gale will come and shatter all of this." The August gale is the traditional storm that comes each August, the forerunner of the hurricanes that will sweep up from the Caribbean and beat and lash this coast in the months of autumn. The August gale with its shrieking winds and crashing muddied waves has generally signalled the unofficial end of summer and it may come in August's very early days. But this year, as yet, it has not come and there are only a few days left. Still we know that the weather cannot last much longer and in another week the tourists will be gone and the schools will reopen and the pace of life will change. We will have to gather ourselves together then in some way and make the decisions that we have been postponing in the back of our minds. We are perhaps the best crew of shaft and development miners in the world and we were due in South Africa on the seventh of July.

But as yet we have not gone and the telegrams from Renco Development in Toronto have lain unanswered and the telephone calls have been unreturned. We are waiting for the change in the weather that will make it impossible for us to lie longer on the beach and then we will walk, for the final time, the steep and winding zigzagged trail that climbs the rocky face of Cameron's Point. When we reach the top of the cliff we will all be breathing heavily and then we will follow the little path that winds northward along the cliff's edge to the small field where our cars are parked, their hoods facing out to sea and their front tires scant feet from the cliffside's edge. The climb will take us some twenty minutes but we are all still in good shape after a summer of idleness.

The golden little beach upon which we lie curves in a crescent for approximately three-quarters of a mile and then terminates at either end in looming cliffs. The north cliff is called Cameron's Point after the family that once owned the land, but the south cliff has no name. Both cliffs protect the beach, slowing the winds from both north and south and preserving its tranquillity.

At the south cliff a little brook ends its journey and plummets almost vertically some fifty feet into the sea. Sometimes after our swims or after lying too long in the sand, we stand underneath its fall as we would a shower, feeling the fresh water fall upon our heads and necks and shoulders and run down our bodies' lengths to our feet which stand within the sea.

All of us have stood and turned our naked bodies unknown, unaccountable times beneath the spraying shower nozzles of the world's mining developments. Bodies that when free of mud and grime and the singed-hair smell of blasting powder are white almost to the colour of milk or ivory. Perhaps of leprosy. Too white to be quite healthy; for when we work we are often twelve hours in the shaft's bottom or in the development drifts, and we do not often feel the sun. All summer we have watched our bodies change their colour and seen our hair grow bleached and ever lighter. Only the scars that all of us bear fail to respond to the healing power of the sun's heat. They seem to stand out even more vividly now, long running pink welts that course down our inner forearms or jagged saw-toothed ridges on the taut calves of our legs.

Many of us carry one shoulder permanently lower than the other where we have been hit by rockfalls or the lop of the giant clam that swings down upon us in the narrow closeness of the shaft's bottom. And we have arms that we cannot raise above our heads, and touches of arthritis in our backs and in our shoulders, magnified by the water that chills and falls upon us in our work. Few of us have all our fingers and some have lost either eyes or ears from falling tools or discharged blasting caps or flying stone or splintering timbers. Yet it is damage to our feet that we fear most of all. For loss of toes or damage to the intricate bones of heel or ankle means that we cannot support our bodies for the gruelling twelve-hour stand-up shifts. And injury to one foot means that the other must bear double its weight, which it can do for only a short time before poor circulation sets in to numb the leg and make it, too, inoperative. All of us are big men, over six feet tall and near two hundred pounds, and our feet have at the best of times a great deal of pressure bearing down upon them.

We are always intensely aware of our bodies and the pains that course and twinge through them. Even late at night when we would sleep they jolt us unexpectedly as if from an electric current, bringing tears to our eyes and causing our fists to clench in the whiteness of knuckles and the biting of nails into palms. At such times we desperately shift our positions, or numb ourselves from the tumblers of alcohol we keep close by our sides.

Lying now upon the beach we see the external scars on ourselves and on each other and are stirred to the memories of how they occurred. When we are clothed the price we pay for what we do is not so visible as it is now.

Beside us on the beach lie the white Javex containers filled with alcohol. It is the purest of moonshine made by our relatives back in the hills and is impossible to buy. It comes to us only as a gift or in exchange for long-past favours: bringing home of bodies, small loans of forgotten dollars, kindnesses to now-dead grandmothers. It is as clear as water, and a teaspoonful of it when touched by a match will burn with the low blue flame of a votive candle until it is completely consumed, leaving the teaspoon hot and totally dry. When we are finished here we will pour what remains into forty-ounce vodka bottles and take it with us on the long drive to Toronto. For when we decide to go we will be driving hard and fast and all of our cars are big: Cadillacs with banged-in fenders and Lincolns and Oldsmobiles. We are often stopped for speeding on the stretch outside Mt. Thom, or going through the Wentworth Valley, or on the narrow road to Fredericton, or on the fast straight road that leads from Rivière-du-Loup to Lévis, sometimes even on the 401. When we say that we must leave for Africa within hours we are seldom fined or in odd instances are allowed to pay our speeding fines upon the spot. We do not wish to get into the entanglement of moonshine brought across provincial lines and the tedium that accompanies it. The fine for open commercial liquor is under fifteen dollars in most places and the transparent vodka bottles both show and keep their simple secret.

But we are not yet ready to leave, and in the sun we pour the clear white fluid into styrofoam cups and drink it in long burning swallows, sometimes following such swallows with mouthfuls of Teem or Sprite or Seven-Up. No one bothers us here because we are so inaccessible. We can see any figure that would approach us from more than a mile away, silhouetted on the lonely cliff and the rocky and treacherous little foot-path that is the only route to where we are. None of the RCMP who police this region are in any way local and it is unlikely that they even know this beach exists. And in the legal sense there is no public road that leads to the cliff where our cars now stand. Only vague paths and sheep trails through the burnt-out grass and around the clumps of alders and blueberry bushes and protruding stones and rotted stumps. The resilient young spruce trees scrape against the mufflers and oilpans of our cars and scratch against the doors. Hundreds of miles hence, when we stop by the roadsides in Quebec and Ontario, we will find small sprigs of this same spruce still wedged within the grillework of our cars or stuck beneath the headlight bulbs. We will remove them and take them with us to Africa as mementos or talismans or symbols of identity. Much as our Highland ancestors, for centuries, fashioned crude badges of heather or of whortleberries to accompany them on the battlefields of the world. Perhaps so that in the closeness of their work with death they might find nearness to their homes and an intensified realization of themselves. We are lying now in the ember of summer's heat and in the stillness of its time.

Out on the flatness of the sea we can see the fishermen going about their work. They do not make much money any more and few of them take it seriously. They say that the grounds have been over-fished by the huge factory fleets from Russia, Spain and Portugal. And it is true that on the still warm nights we can see the lights of such floating factories shining brightly off the coast. They appear as strange, moveable, brilliant cities and when they are far out their blazing lights seem to mingle with those of the stars. The fishermen before us are older men or young boys. Grandfathers with their grandsons acting out their ancient rituals. At noon or at one or two, before they start for home, they will run their little boats into our quiet cove until their bows are almost touching the sand. They will toss us the gleaming blue-black mackerel and the silver herring and the brown-and-white striped cod and talk to us for a while, telling us anything that they think we should know. In return we toss them the whitened Javex bottles so that they may drink the pure clear contents. Sometimes the older men miss the toss and the white cylindrical bottles fall into the sea where they bob and toss like marker buoys or a child's duck in the bathtub until they are gaffed by someone in the boat or washed back in to shore. Later we cook the fish over small, crackling driftwood fires. This, we know too, cannot go on much longer.

In the quiet graveyards that lie inland the dead are buried. Behind the small white wooden churches and beneath the monuments of polished black granite they take their silent rest. Before we leave we will visit them to pray and take our last farewell. We will perhaps be afraid then, reading the dates of our brothers and uncles and cousins; recalling their youth and laughter and the place and manner of each death.

Death in the shafts and in the drifts[1] is always violent and very often the body is so crushed or so blown apart that it can not be reassembled properly for exposure in the coffin. Most of us have accompanied the grisly remains of such bodies trussed up in plastic bags on trains and planes and automobiles, and delivered them up to the local undertaker. During the two or three days of the final wake and through the lonely all-night vigils kept in living rooms and old-fashioned parlours only memories and youthful photographs recall the physical reality that lies so dismembered and disturbed within each grey, sealed coffin. The most flattering photograph is placed upon the coffin's lid in an attempt to remind us of what was. I am thinking of this now, of the many youthful deaths I have been part of, and of the long homeward journeys in other seasons of other years. The digging of graves in the bitterness of February's cold, the shovelling of drifts of snow from the barren earth, and then the banging of the pick into the frozen ground, the striking of sparks from steel on stone and the scraping of shovels on earth and rock.

Some twenty years ago, when first I went to the uranium shafts of Ontario's Elliot Lake and short-lived Bancroft, we would have trouble getting our dead the final few miles to their high white houses. Often, in winter, we would have to use horses and sleighs to get them up the final hills, standing in chest-high snow, taking out window casings so that we might pass the coffin in and then out again for the last time. Or sometimes in the early spring we would again have to resort to horses when the leaving of the frost and the melting of the winter snow turned the brooks into red and roiling rivers and caused the dirt roads that led into the hills to become greasy and impassable. Sometimes in such seasons the underground springs beneath such roads erupt into tiny geysers, shooting their water upward and changing the roadbeds around them into quivering bogs that bury vehicles up to their hubs and axles.

And in November the rain is chill and cold at the graveside's edge. It falls upon our necks and splatters the red mud upon our gleaming shoes and on the pantlegs of our expensive suits. The bagpiper plays "Flowers of the Forest," as the violinist earlier played his haunting laments from the high choir loft. The music causes the hair to bristle on the backs of our necks and brings out the wildness of our grief and dredges the depths of our dense dark sorrow. At the graveside people sometimes

---

[1] Horizontal passages dug by miners as they follow veins of minerals.

shout farewells in Gaelic or throw themselves into the mud or upon the coffin as it is being lowered on its straps into the gaping earth.

Fifteen years ago when the timbers gave way in Springdale, Newfoundland, my younger brother died, crushed and broken amidst the constant tinkle of the dripping water, and lying upon a bed of tumbled stone. We could not get him up from the bottom in time, as his eyes bulged from his head and the fluids of his body seeped quietly onto the glistening rock. Yet even as we tried we realized our task was hopeless and that he would not last, even on the surface. Would not last long enough for any kind of medical salvation. And even as the strength of his once-powerful grip began to loosen on my hand and his breath to rattle in his throat, we could see the earthly road that stretched before us as the witnesses and survivors of his death: the report to the local authorities, the statements to the company, to the police, to the coroner and then the difficult phone calls made on badly connected party lines or, failing those, the more efficient and more impersonal yellow telegrams. The darkness of the midnight phone call seems somehow to fade with the passing of time, or to change and be recreated like the ballads and folk-tales of the distant lonely past. Changing with each new telling as the tellers of the tales change, as they become different, older, more bitter or more serene. It is possible to hear descriptions of phone calls that you yourself have made some ten or fifteen years ago and to recognize very little about them except the undeniable kernel of truth that was at the centre of the messages they contained. But the yellow telegram is more blunt and more permanent in the starkness of its message and it is never, ever thrown away. It is kept in vases and in Bibles and in dresser drawers beneath white shirts and it is stumbled upon sometimes unexpectedly, years later, sometimes by other hands, in little sandalwood boxes containing locks of the baby's hair or tucked inside the small shoes in which he learned to walk. A simple obituary of a formal kind.

When my brother died in Springdale, Newfoundland, it was the twenty-first of October and when we brought his body home we were already deep into fall. On the high hardwood hills the mountain ash and the aspen and the scarlet maple were ablaze with colour beneath the weakened rays of the autumn sun. On alternate days the rain fell; sometimes becoming sleet or small hard hailstones. Sometimes the sun would shine in the morning, giving way to the vagaries of precipitation in the afternoon. And sometimes the cloud cover would float over the land even as the sun shone, blocking the sun out temporarily and casting shadows

as if a giant bird were passing overhead. Standing beneath such a glid-
ing cloud and feeling its occasional rain we could see the sun shining
clearly at a distance of only a mile away. Seeing warmth so reachably
near while feeling only the cold of the icy rain. But at the digging of his
grave there was no sun at all. Only the rain falling relentlessly down upon
us. It turned the crumbling clay to the slickest of mud, as slippery and
glistening as that of the potter's wheel but many times more difficult to
control. When we had dug some four feet down, the earthen walls began
to slide and crumble and to give way around us and to fall upon our
rubber boots and to press against the soaking pantlegs that clung so
clammily to our blue-veined legs. The deeper we dug, the more intensely
the rain fell, the drops dripping from our eyebrows and from our noses
and the icy trickles running down the backs of our necks and down our
spines and legs and into our squishing and sucking boots. When we had
almost reached the required depth one of the walls that had been continuously crumbling and falling suddenly collapsed and with a great
whoosh rolled down upon us. We were digging in our traditional family
plot and when the wall gave way it sent the box that contained my
father's coffin sliding down upon us. He had been dead for five years
then, blown apart in Kirkland Lake, and at the time of his burial his
coffin had been sealed. We were wildly and irrationally frightened by the
slide and braced our backs against the splintered and disintegrating box,
fearful lest it should tip and fall upon us and spill and throw whatever
rotting relics remained of that past portion of our lives. Of little flesh but
maybe green decaying bones or strands of silver matted hair.

We had held it there, braced by our backs in the pouring rain, until
timbers were brought to shore up the new grave's side and to keep the
past dead resting quietly. I had been very frightened then, holding the old
dead in the quaking mud so that we might make room for the new in that
same narrow cell of sliding earth and cracking wood. The next day at his
funeral the rain continued to fall and in the grave that received him the
unsteady timbers and the ground they held so temporarily back seemed
but an extension of those that had caused his life to cease.

Lying now in the precarious heat of this still and burning summer I
would wish that such thoughts and scenes of death might rise like the
mists from the new day's ocean and leave me dry and somehow emptied
on this scorching fine-grained sand.

In Africa it will be hot, too, in spite of the coming rainy season, and
on the veldt the heat will shimmer and the strange, fine-limbed animals

will move across it in patterns older than memory. The nomads will follow their flocks of bleating goats in their constant search for grass and moisture, and the women will carry earthen jars of water on their heads or baskets of clothes to slap against the rocks where the water is found.

In my own white house my wife does her declining wash among an increasingly bewildering battery of appliances. Her kitchen and her laundry room and her entire house gleam with porcelain and enamel and an ordered cleanliness that I can no longer comprehend. Little about me or about my work is clean or orderly and I am always mildly amazed to find the earnings of the violence and dirt in which I make my living converted into such meticulous brightness. The lightness of white and yellow curtains rustling crisply in the breeze. For us, most of our working lives are spent in rough, crude bunkhouses thrown up at the shafthead's site. Our bunks are made of two-by-fours sometimes roughly hammered together by ourselves, and we sleep two men to a room or sometimes four or sometimes in the development's early stages in the vast "ram pastures" of twenty or thirty or perhaps even forty men crowded together in one vast, rectangular, unpartitioned room. Such rooms are like hospital wards without the privacy of the dividing curtains and they are filled, constantly, day and night, with the sounds of men snoring and coughing or spitting into cans by their bedsides, the incoherent moans and mumbles of uneasy sleepers and the thuds of half-conscious men making groaning love to their passive pillows. In Africa we will sleep, mostly naked, under incongruous structures of mosquito netting, hearing the occasional rain on the roofs of corrugated iron. In the near twenty-four-hour winter darkness of the Yukon, we have slept in sleeping bags, weighted down with blankets and surrounded by various heaters, still to wake to our breath as vapour in the coldness of the flashlight's gleam.

It is difficult to explain to my wife such things, and we have grown more and more apart with the passage of the years. Meeting infrequently now almost as shy strangers, communicating mostly over vast distances through ineffectual say-nothing letters or cheques that substitute money for what once was conceived as love. Sometimes the cheques do not even come from me, for in the developing African nations the political situation is often uncertain and North American money is sometimes suddenly and almost whimsically "frozen" or "nationalized," making it impossible to withdraw or remove. In times and places of such uneasiness, shaft crews such as ours often receive little or no actual money, only slips of paper to show our earnings, which are deposited in the metropolitan banks of New York or Toronto or London and from which our families are issued monthly cheques.

I would regain what was once real or imagined with my wife. The long nights of passionate lovemaking that seemed so short, the creating and birth of our seven children. Yet I was never home for the birth of any of my children, only for their fathering. I was not home when two of them died so shortly after birth, and I have not been home to participate or to share in many of the youthful accomplishments of the other five. I have attended few parents' nights or eighth-grade graduations or father-and-son hockey banquets, and broken tricycle wheels and dolls with crippled limbs have been mended by other hands than mine.

Now my wife seems to have gone permanently into a world of avocado appliances and household cleanliness and vicarious experiences provided by the interminable soap operas that fill her television afternoons. She has perhaps gone as deeply into that life as I have into the life of the shafts, seeming to tunnel ever downward and outward through unknown depths and distances and to become lost and separated and unavailable for communication. Yet we are not surprised or critical of each other for she, too, is from a mining family and grew up largely on funds sent home by an absentee father. Perhaps we are but becoming our previous generation.

And yet there are times, even now, when I can almost physically feel the summer of our marriage and of our honeymoon and of her singing the words of the current popular songs into my then-attentive ears. I had been working as part of a crew in Uranium City all winter and had been so long without proper radio reception that I knew nothing of the music of that time's hit parade. There was always a feeling of mild panic then, on hearing whole dance floors of people singing aloud songs that had come and flourished since my departure and which I had never heard. As if I had been on a journey to the land of the dead.

It would be of little use now to whisper popular lyrics into my ears for I have become partially deaf from the years of the jackleg drill's relentless pounding into walls of constant stone. I cannot hear much of what my wife and children say to me, and communicate with the men about me through nods and gestures and the reading of familiar lips. Musically, most of us have long abandoned the modern hit parades and have gone, instead, back to the Gaelic songs remembered from our early youth. It is these songs that we hum now on the hotness of this beach and which we will take with us on our journey when we go.

We have perhaps gone back to the Gaelic songs because they are so constant and unchanging and speak to us as the privately familiar. As a youth and as a young man I did not even realize that I could understand or speak Gaelic and entertained a rather casual disdain for those who did. It was not until the isolation of the shafts started that it began to bubble up somehow within me, causing a feeling of unexpected surprise at finding it there at all. As if it had sunk in unconsciously through some strange osmotic process while I had been unwittingly growing up. Growing up without fully realizing the language of the conversations that swirled around me. Now in the shafts and on the beach we speak it almost constantly, though it is no longer spoken in our homes. There is a "Celtic Revival" in the area now, fostered largely by government grants, and the younger children are taught individual Gaelic words in the classrooms for a few brief periods during each month. It is a revival that is very different from our own and it seems, like so much else, to have little relevance for us and to have largely passed us by. Once, it is true, we went up to sing our Gaelic songs at the various Celtic concerts which have become so much a part of the summer culture and we were billed by the bright young schoolteachers who run such things as MacKinnon's Miners' Chorus; but that too seemed as lonely and irrelevant as it was meaningless. It was as if we were parodies of ourselves, standing in rows, wearing our miners' gear, or being asked to shave and wear suits, being plied with rum while waiting for our turn on the program, only then to mouth our songs to batteries of tape recorders and to people who did not understand them. It was as if it were everything that song should not be, contrived and artificial and non-spontaneous and lacking in communication.

I have heard and seen the Zulus dance until they shook the earth. I have seen large splendid men leap and twist and bend their bodies to the hard-baked flatness of the reddened soil. And I have followed their gestures and listened to their shouts and looked into their eyes in the hope that I might understand the meaning of their art. Hoping to find there a message that is recognizable only to primitive men. Yet, though I think I have caught glimpses of their joy, despair or disdain, it seems that in the end they must dance mainly for themselves. Their dancing speaks a language whose true meaning will elude me forever; I will never grasp the full impact of the subtleties and nuances that are spoken by the small head gesture or the flashing fleck of muscle.

I would like to understand more deeply what they have to say in the vague hope that it might be in some way akin to what is expressed in our own singing. That there might be some message that we share. But I can never enter deeply enough into their experience, can never penetrate behind the private mysteries of their eyes. Perhaps, I think sometimes, I am expecting too much. Yet on those occasions when we did sing at the concerts, I would have liked to reach beyond the tape recorders and the faces of the uninvolved to something that might prove to be more substantial and enduring. Yet in the end it seemed we too were only singing to ourselves. Singing songs in an archaic language as we too became more archaic, and recognizing the nods of acknowledgement and shouted responses as coming only from our own friends and relatives. In many cases the same individuals from whom we had first learned our songs. Songs that are for the most part local and private and capable of losing almost all of their substance in translation. Yet in the introduction to the literature text that my eldest daughter brings home from university it states that "the private experience, if articulated with skill, may communicate an appeal that is universal beyond the limitations of time or landscape." I have read that over several times and thought about its meaning in relation to myself.

When I was a boy my father told me that I would never understand the nature of sex until I had participated in it in some worthwhile way, and that there was little point in trying to grasp its meaning through erotic reading or looking at graphic pictures or listening to the real or imagined experiences of older men. As if the written or the spoken word or the mildly pornographic picture were capable of reaching only a small portion of the distance it might hope to journey on the road to understanding. In the early days of such wistful and exploratory reading the sexual act seemed most frequently to be described as "like flying." A boggling comparison at the time to virginal young men who had never been airborne. In the future numbness of our flight to Africa we will find little that is sexual if it is to be like our other flights to such distant destinations.

We will not have much to say about our flight to those we leave behind, and little about our destinations when we land. Sending only the almost obligatory postcards that talk about the weather continents and oceans away. Saying that "things are going as expected," "going well." Postcards that have as their most exciting feature the exotic postage stamps sought after by the younger children for games of show and tell.

I have long since abandoned any hope of describing the sexual act or having it described to me. Perhaps it is enough to know that it is not at all like flying, though I do not know what it is really like. I have never been told, nor can I, in my turn, tell. But I would like somehow to show and tell the nature of my work and perhaps some of my entombed feelings to those that I would love, if they would care to listen.

I would like to tell my wife and children something of the way my years pass by on the route to my inevitable death. I would like to explain somehow what it is like to be a gladiator who fights always the impassiveness of water as it drips on darkened stone. And what it is like to work one's life in the tightness of confined space. I would like somehow to say how I felt when I lost my father in Kirkland Lake or my younger brother in Springdale, Newfoundland. I would like to say how frightened I am sometimes of what I do. And of how I lie awake at night aware of my own decline and of the diminishing of the men around me. For all of us know we will not last much longer and that it is unlikely we will be replaced in the shaft's bottom by members of our own flesh and bone. For such replacement, like our Gaelic, seems to be of the past and now largely over.

Our sons will go to the universities to study dentistry or law and to become fatly affluent before they are thirty. Men who will stand over six feet tall and who will move their fat, pudgy fingers over the limited possibilities to be found in other people's mouths. Or men who sit behind desks shuffling papers relating to divorce or theft or assault or the taking of life. To grow prosperous from pain and sorrow and the desolation of human failure. They will be far removed from the physical life and will seek it out only through jogging or golf or games of handball with friendly colleagues. They will join expensive private clubs for the pleasures of perspiration and they will not die in falling stone or chilling water or thousands of miles from those they love. They will not die in any such manner, partially at least because we have told them not to and have encouraged them to seek out other ways of life which lead, we hope, to gentler deaths. And yet because it seems they will follow our advice instead of our lives, we will experience, in any future that is ours, only an increased sense of anguished isolation and an ironic feeling of confused bereavement. Perhaps it is always so for parents who give the young advice and find that it is followed. And who find that those who follow such advice must inevitably journey far from those who give it, to distant lonely worlds which are forever unknowable to those who wait behind. Yet perhaps those who go find in the regions to which they travel but another kind of inarticulate loneliness. Perhaps the dentist feels mute anguish as he circles his chair, and the lawyer who lives in a world of words finds little relationship between professional talk and what he would hope to be true expression. Perhaps he too in his quiet heart sings something akin to Gaelic songs, sings in an old archaic language private words that reach to no one. And perhaps both lawyer and dentist journey down into an Africa as deep and dark and distant as ours. I can but vaguely imagine what I will never know.

I have always wished that my children could see me at my work. That they might journey down with me in the dripping cage to the shaft's bottom or walk the eerie tunnels of the drifts that end in walls of staring stone. And that they might see how articulate we are in the accomplishment of what we do. That they might appreciate the perfection of our drilling and the calculation of our angles and the measuring of our powder, and that they might understand that what we know through eye and ear and touch is of a finer quality than any information garnered by the most sophisticated of mining engineers with all their elaborate equipment.

I would like to show them how professional we are and how, in spite of the chill and the water and the dark and the danger, there is perhaps a certain eloquent beauty to be found in what we do. Not the beauty of stillness to be found in gleaming crystal or in the polished hardwood floors to which my wife devotes such care but rather the beauty of motion on the edge of violence, which by its very nature can never long endure. It is perhaps akin to the violent motion of the huge professional athletes on the given days or nights of their many games. Men as huge and physical as are we; polished and eloquent in the propelling of their bodies toward their desired goals and in their relationships and dependencies on one another, but often numb and silent before the microphones of sedentary interviewers. Few of us get to show our children what we do on national television; we offer only the numbness and silence by itself. Unable either to show or tell.

I have always wished to be better than the merely mediocre and I have always wanted to use the power of my body in the fulfilling of such a wish. Perhaps that is why I left the university after only one year. A year which was spent mainly as an athlete and as a casual reader of English literature. I could not release myself enough physically and seemed always to be constricted and confined. In sleeping rooms that were too low, by toilet stalls that were too narrow, in lecture halls that were too hot, even by the desks in those lecture halls, which I found always so difficult to get into and out of. Confined, too, by bells and buzzers and curfews and deadlines, which for me had little meaning. I wanted to burst out, to use my strength in some demanding task that would allow me somehow to feel that I was breaking free. And I could not find enough release in the muddy wars on the football field or in the thudding contact of the enclosed and boarded rink. I suppose I was drawn too by the apparent glamour of the men who followed the shafts. Impressed by their returning here in summer with their fast cars and expensive clothes; also by the fact that I was from a mining family that has given itself for generations to the darkened earth.

I was aware even then of the ultimate irony of my choice. Aware of how contradictory it seemed that someone who was bothered by confinement should choose to spend his working days in the most confined of spaces. Yet the difference seems to be that when we work we are never still. Never merely entombed like the prisoner in the passive darkness of his solitary confinement. For we are always expanding the perimeters of our seeming incarceration. We are always moving downward or inward or forward or, in the driving of our raises, even upward. We are big men engaged in perhaps the most violent of occupations and we have chosen as our adversary walls and faces of massive stone. It is as if the stone of the spherical earth has challenged us to move its weight and find its treasure and we have accepted the challenge and responded with drill and steel and powder and strength and all our ingenuity. In the chill and damp we have given ourselves to the breaking down of walls and barriers. We have sentenced ourselves to enclosures so that we might taste the giddy joy of breaking through. Always hopeful of breaking through, though we know we never will break free.

Drilling and hammering our way to the world's resources, we have left them when found and moved on. Left them for others to expand or to exploit and to make room for the often stable communities that come in our wake: the sewer lines and the fire hydrants and the neat rows of company houses; the over-organized athletic leagues and the ever-hopeful schools; the junior Chambers of Commerce. We have moved about the world, liberating resources, largely untouched by political uncertainties and upheavals, seldom harmed by the midnight plots, the surprising coups and the fast assassinations. We were in Haiti with Duvalier in 1960 and in Chile before Allende and in the Congo before it became associated with Zaire. In Bolivia and Guatemala and in Mexico and in a Jamaica that the tourists never see. Each segment of the world aspires to the treasure, real or imagined, that lies encased in its vaults of stone, and those who would find such booty are readily admitted and handsomely paid, be they employed by dictator or budding democracy or capitalists expanding their holdings and their wealth. Renco Development on Bay Street will wait for us. They will endure our summer on the beach and our lack of response to their seemingly urgent messages. They will endure our Toronto drunkenness and pay our bail and advance us personal loans. And when we go they will pay us thousands of dollars for our work, optimistically hoping that they may make millions in their turn. They will wait for us because they know from years of many contracts that we are the best bet to deliver for them in the end.

There are two other crews in Canada as strong, perhaps even stronger than we are. They are in Rouyn-Noranda; and as our crew is known as MacKinnon, theirs are known by the names of Lafrenière and Picard. We have worked beside them at various times, competed with them and brawled with them in the hall-like beer parlours of Malarctic and Temiskaming, and occasionally we have saved one another's lives. They will not go to Africa for Renco Development because they are imprisoned in the depths of their language. And because they speak no English they will not move out of Quebec or out of northern or northeastern Ontario. Once there was also the O'Leary crew, who were Irish Newfoundlanders. But many of them were lost in a cave-in in India, and of those who remained most have gone to work with their relatives on high-steel construction in New York. We see them sometimes, now, in the bars of Brooklyn or sometimes in the summers at the ferry terminal in North Sydney before they cross to Port-aux-Basques. Iron work, they say, also pays highly for the risk to life; and the long fall from the towering, swaying skyscrapers can occur for any man but once. It seems, for them, that they have exchanged the possibility of being fallen upon for that of falling itself. And that after years of dodging and fearing falling objects from above, they have become such potential objects themselves. Their loss diminishes us, too, because we know how good they were at what they did, and know, too, that the mangled remnants of their dead were flown from India in sealed containers to lie on such summer days as these beneath the nodding wild flowers that grow on outport graves.

I must not think too much of death and loss, I tell myself repeatedly. For if I am to survive I must be as careful and calculating with my thoughts as I am with my tools when working so far beneath the earth's surface: I must always be careful of sloppiness and self-indulgence lest they cost me dearly in the end.

Out on the ocean now it is beginning to roughen and the southwest wind is blowing the smallish waves into larger versions of themselves. They are beginning to break upon the beach with curling whitecaps at their crests, and the water that they consist of seems no longer blue but rather a dull and sombre grey. There are no longer boats visible on the once-flat sea, neither near at hand nor on the horizon's distant line. The sun no longer shines with the fierceness of the earlier day and the sky has begun to cloud over. Evening is approaching. The sand is whipped by the wind and blows into our faces and stings our bodies as might a thousand pinpricks or the tiny tips of many scorching needles. We flinch and shake ourselves and reach for our protective shirts. We leave our prone positions and come restlessly to our feet, coughing and spitting and moving uneasily like nervous animals anticipating a storm. In the sand we trace erratic designs and patterns with impatient toes. We look at one another, arching our eyebrows like bushy question marks. Perhaps this is what we have been waiting for? Perhaps this is the end and the beginning?

And now I can feel the eyes of the men upon me. They are waiting for me to give interpretations of the signals, waiting for my sign. I hesitate for a moment, running my eyes along the beach, watching water touching sand. And then I nod my head. There is almost a collective sigh that is more sensed than really heard. Almost like distant wind in far-off trees. Then suddenly they begin to move. Rapidly they gather their clothes and other belongings, shaking out the sand, folding and packing. Moving swiftly and with certainty they are closing down their summer even as it is closing down on them. MacKinnon's miners are finished now and moving out. We are leaving the beach of the summer sun and perhaps some of us will not see it any more. For some of us may not return alive from the Africa for which we leave.

We begin to walk. First along the beach toward the north cliff of Cameron's Point, and then up the steep and winding zigzagged trail that climbs its face. When I am halfway up I stop and look back at the men strung out in single file behind me. We are mountain climbers in our way, though bound together by no physical ropes of any kind. They stop and look back, too; back and down to the beach we have so recently vacated. The waves are higher now and are breaking and cresting and rolling farther in. They have obliterated the outlines of our bodies in the sand and our footprints of brief moments before already have been washed away. There remains no evidence that we have ever been. It is as if we have never lain, nor ever walked nor ever thought what thoughts we had. We leave no art or mark behind. The sea has washed its sand slate clean.

And then the rain begins to fall. Not heavily but almost hesitantly. It is as if it has been hot and dry for so long that the act of raining has almost been forgotten and has now to be slowly and almost painfully relearned.

We reach the summit of the cliff and walk along the little path that leads us to our cars. The cars are dusty and their metal is still hot from the earlier sun. We lean across their hoods to lift the windshield wipers from the glass. The rubber of the wiper blades has almost melted into the windshields because of heat and long disuse, and when we lift them, slender slivers of rubber remain behind. These blades will have to be replaced.

The isolated raindrops fall alike on windshield and on roof, on hood and trunk. They trace individual rivulets through the layers of grime and then trickle down to the parched and waiting earth.

And now it is two days later. The rain has continued to fall and in it we have gone about preparing and completing our rituals of farewell. We have visited the banks and checked out all the dates on our insurance policies. And we have gathered our working clothes, which when worn continents hence will make us loom even larger than we are in actual life. As if we are Greek actors or mastodons of an earlier time. Soon to be replaced or else perhaps to be extinct.

We have stood bareheaded by the graves and knelt in the mud by the black granite stones. And we have visited privately and in tiny self-conscious groups the small white churches which we may not see again. As we have become older it seems we have become strangely more religious in ways that border on superstition. We will take with us worn family rosaries and faded charms, and loop ancestral medals and crosses of delicate worn fragility around our scar-lashed necks and about the thickness of our wrists, seemingly unaware of whatever irony they might project. This, too, seems but a further longing for the past, far removed from the "rational" approaches to religion that we sometimes encounter in our children.

We have said farewells to our children, too, and to our wives, and I have offered kisses and looked into their eyes and wept outwardly and inwardly for all I have not said or done and for my own clumsy failure at communication. I have not been able, as the young say, "to tell it like it is," and perhaps now I never shall.

By four o'clock we are ready to go. Our cars are gathered with their motors running and we will drive them hard and fast and be in Toronto tomorrow afternoon. We will not stop all night except for a few brief moments at the gleaming service stations and we will keep one sober and alert driver at the wheel of each of our speeding cars. Many of the rest of us will numb ourselves with moonshine for our own complex and diverse reasons: perhaps to loosen our thoughts and tongues or perhaps to deaden and hold them down; perhaps to be as the patient who takes an anaesthetic to avoid operational pain. We will hurtle in a dark night convoy across the landscapes and the borders of four waiting provinces.

As we move out, I feel myself a figure in some mediaeval ballad who has completed his formal farewells and goes now to meet his fatalistic future. I do not particularly wish to feel this way and again would shake myself free from thoughts of death and self-indulgence.

As we gather speed the land of the seacoast flashes by. I am in the front seat of the lead car, on the passenger side next to the window. In the side mirror I can see the other cars stretched out behind us. We go by the scarred and abandoned coal workings of our previous generations and drive swiftly westward into the declining day. The men in the back seat begin to pass around their moonshine and attempt to adjust their long legs within the constricted space. After a while they begin to sing in Gaelic, singing almost unconsciously the old words that are so worn and so familiar. They seem to handle them almost as they would familiar tools. I know that in the other cars they are doing the same even as I begin silently to mouth the words myself. There is no word in Gaelic for good-bye, only for farewell.

More than a quarter of a century ago in my single year at university, I stumbled across an anonymous lyric from the fifteenth century. Last night while packing my clothes I encountered it again, this time in the literature text of my eldest daughter. The book was very different from the one that I had so casually used, as different perhaps as is my daughter from me. Yet the lyric was exactly the same. It had not changed at all. It comes to me now in this speeding car as the Gaelic choruses rise around me. I do not particularly welcome it or want it, and indeed I had almost forgotten it. Yet it enters now, regardless of my wants or wishes, much as one might see out of the corner of the eye an old acquaintance one has no wish to see at all. It comes again, unbidden and unexpected and imperfectly remembered. It seems borne up by the mounting, surging Gaelic voices like the flecked white foam on the surge of the towering, breaking wave. Different yet similar, and similar yet different, and in its time unable to deny:

> *I wend to death, knight stith in stour;*[2]
> *Through fight in field I won the flower;*
> *No fights me taught the death to quell—*
> *I wend to death, sooth I you tell.*
>
> *I wend to death, a king iwis;*[3]
> *What helpes honour or worlde's bliss?*
> *Death is to man the final way—*
> *I wende to be clad in clay.*

—1986

Jack Hodgins b. 1938

Geography, particularly that of Vancouver Island, is important to Jack Hodgins' fiction. However, as the critic W.H. New observed, the attention Hodgins pays to milieu has not made him a regionalist: "Setting is important in his stories, but as setting and as metaphor, not as the main subject; his aim in writing is not to record what it looks like to live in a place, but what it feels like" (from the Introduction to On Coasts of Eternity: Jack Hodgins' Fictional Universe*).*

From the stories of his first book, Spit Delaney's Island *(1976) to the recent* Damage Done by the Storm *(2004), Hodgins shows in his narratives that being "islanded" is a psychological condition as much as a physical one. Individuals find limits both reassuring and constraining. And "Over Here" suggests that, in the era immediately after World War II, stereotypes remain the most pervasive boundaries of all.*

Over Here

Will you take a look at this, my dad said. This here's how you and me will make our fortune.

He opened a jack-knife and ran a slit along the bark of a fallen tree.

He'd chopped down three of them. Chips flew. You had to hold up your arm to protect your eyes. The trees creaked and groaned as they

---

[2] Upright in battle.
[3] Certainly.

tilted, then they fell with a swish. You could feel the thump through your feet. This was out in a back corner of the farm. Even the huckleberries were tall.

Now he cut a ring around the trunk. Using his fingers and the blade of the knife, he started to pry off strips of bark. Thin as leather, orange behind the grey. The inside was wet and yellow.

We'll lay these out on the barn roof to dry in the sun, he said. Then we'll sack 'em up and take them in to the depot.

The depot was where we took the beer bottles from Sunday morning ditches, and burlap sacks of sticky fir cones in summer.

What will they do with it? I said.

Here, smell. You like that?

He held the inside of a piece of bark to my face. A sharp sweet smell.

Tastes good too, he said, but I wouldn't go licking it, you'd spend the rest of the day on the run.

What is it?

They make stuff in bottles out of it, for people who'd be glad to run to the toilet for a change. It's cascara. Here—

He rooted around in his pocket and came up with another jack-knife like his own, and gave it to me. Cracked mother-of-pearl on one side, with four different blades folded along the length.

You can do this just as good as I can. Start on that one over there.

I had to press hard with the point to get it started. I used both hands and leaned my weight into it. He gave me a flat wide chisel for where the bark didn't want to come away. The knife blade was wet. I didn't lick.

It was like skinning something alive.

It was like being one of the Indians we'd learned about in school. The Blackfoot, the Iroquois. Burning missionaries at the stake, cutting out hearts, peeling off a living man's skin. Putting on parties where they gave away everything they owned. Miss Percy cooked a pot of fish-head soup. We sat under a tree and listened to her read from a book about a talking raven. You had to have courage to be an Indian. You had to be strong. Miss Percy had known an Indian who died in the recent War.

Any minute now a band of warbling braves would burst into this clearing and capture me. They would scalp my dad and drag me off to be a slave in their village. I'd have to fight with the dogs for food scraps thrown to the ground. Until one day I saved the tribe from extinction. Then they'd reward me by making me their chief.

You think there was ever an Indian village here?

Well now, my dad said. Have you seen pictures of Indian villages in this part of the world?

Wooden longhouses, I said, with totem poles out front.

Always along a beach. Do we live on a beach, can you tell me?

The beach is two miles away.

Well, do we live on a river filled with salmon then?

We don't even have a creek.

What kind of Indians would build a village on this here gravel pit here? They'd rather sit back and laugh at some idiot white man, breaking his neck to grow puny spuds and stunted hay from this goddam rocky soil.

My dad drank from the wide-mouth mason jar of cherry Freshie he'd kept in the shade. Then he leaned back against a standing tree and rolled a cigarette.

Do you think there were any wars? I said.

On our ranch, you mean?

It was never a farm, it was always a ranch, though we had only twelve acres left, most of it bush. One cow. Thirteen chickens. A pig.

Tribes slaughtering one another, I said. Battles.

Only if they wanted to make sure they never found each other, my dad said. Back in them days trees here were as thick as the hair on your head. Didn't that teacher tell you anything? Wars happen on plains— the Plains of Abraham weren't populated with Douglas firs.

We don't have any plains around here.

He set fire to the scraggly tobacco at the end of his cigarette.

That's my point. They'd have their battles out on the water maybe, in their longboats. Or down along the beach.

I guess I'll never find any arrowheads then, I said.

No Indian ever wanted this here place, said my dad. They were smarter'n that. It took a bureaucrat in Ottawa to decide this land should be opened up. Gave it to Great War vets like your fool grandfather, that didn't know nothing better than the rocks of Connemara.[1]

Without their bark, the cascara trunks were as slick and pale as human flesh in the bath. The naked legs of giants.

*

[1] The rocky coast of Western Ireland.

There were no Indians at school. Some Indians lived on a Reserve twenty miles to the north, some lived ten miles to the south. They went to other schools. Miss Percy invited a woman from a Reserve to speak about their way of life. She told us how they smoked salmon. She told us about making oolichan grease. Once, when a raiding party was coming south they sent their women and children to safety up into the mountains, but when they went to get them afterwards they'd disappeared. Nobody ever found them. Nobody even found bones, or footprints. Today, the band was mostly well-to-do fishermen with a chief who didn't look like an Indian at all. She held up a picture for us to see.

Then one Indian came to school, but she didn't know that that was what she was.

And don't you ever tell her, said my dad.

Why not?

The Tremblays would have your hide. So would I. You could ruin that girl's life. They want her to have a chance to make something of herself.

A priest had driven up Wolf Lake Road on Tuesday and handed her over to the Tremblays, who lived across from us. On Wednesday she was sitting across the aisle from me in school.

As if raising five boys of their own isn't enough work for that poor woman, my dad said. The priest don't care how hard she works, they do what he tells them to do.

The Tremblays were the only Catholics in this part of the district and had to drive all the way in to town for church. My dad was scared that Mr. Tremblay might take it into his head to donate a corner of his property for a church out here in the bush. Right across the road from us, he imagined. Right smack in front of our kitchen window. Cars boiling up dust down the gravel road, parking all over the place, ruining our breakfast.

What did they tell her she was? I said.

Who know? A child of God, maybe. She's got five brothers now to tell her she's a Norwegian queen.

Nettie Tremblay. I watched her out of the corner of my eye across the aisle. You weren't supposed to stare. How could you not know something that was known by everyone else? I could change everything, if I wanted. A scrap of paper with the news scribbled on it. No name. Just knowing I could do this made me feel warm and generous towards her. I was protecting her. We all were. One word and her life would be blown apart.

She'd go nuts and pull out her hair. She wouldn't be able to stand it. She'd kill herself.

Except, why wouldn't she want to know?

If we knew something about Nettie Tremblay that she didn't know herself, this could be true of me as well. When I turned twenty-one maybe I would find out that I'd been an Indian brave all along. Grandson of a Huron chief, sent out to learn the ways of the white man before being called home to rule my people. I wouldn't fall apart when I heard. I'd have my own hut, my own animal skin robes. I would have my own slaves who did everything I told them to do. I'd be the richest man in the tribe.

*

On Saturdays my father cut down half a dozen trees and left me to peel cascara bark on my own. He'd thought of another way to get rich. Nettie Tremblay came across to watch. I offered her a share of my allowance if she'd fill the gunny sacks and help me lay out the bark on the roof of the barn.

You like the smell of that? I said.

She nodded. It was a pleasant smell. Sometimes it was almost impossible not to lick the inside of the bark, except that you remembered what would happen.

I guess you've eaten bark before, I said.

No, she said. Why would I?

Do you like smoked fish better than beef? I said.

I don't know.

Her eyes went blank, as though she'd gone away inside. She must have been lying.

Do you like to eat berries? I said.

Sure, she said. She snatched huckleberries off a nearby bush and ate them.

Not like that, I said. You break off a whole branch, like this. Then you carry it around.

There was a war here once, I said. Right where we're standing. An Indian war. Seventy-six braves were slaughtered right here, their blood soaked into the earth. Some of them were skinned alive. Pieces of flesh were cut off and fed to the dogs. Had you heard about that? You could be standing right on top of a Kwakiutl skull.

She wasn't interested in my war. She carried slabs of bark to the gunny sack and stuffed them inside.

I wouldn't mind being an Indian, I said. *Hyas klahowyum nikt.*

I'd memorized some Chinook, since I didn't know which language I would need when the time came.[2]

She made a face. I'm going to be a movie actress.

You can't be a movie actress.

Why not?

Because.

I can if I want. Why can't I?

Because. You don't look like a movie actress.

I will when I'm older.

No you won't. They'll make you go and be a servant to the nuns.

She blew a raspberry. Maybe I'll be a nun myself.

I bet you won't.

I bet I will.

I bet you'll have eighteen kids and some of them will die.

She dropped her armload of bark to the ground and started to leave.

They won't die, I said. I'll be a doctor by then and I'll save them.

Nettie Tremblay's skin was the dark red-brown of the soil around rotted stumps. Her hair was black as crows but it was not parted down the middle with two long braids at the back. Mrs. Tremblay hacked it off short and curled it. She didn't have the beauty of a Mohawk girl in a book. She was chubby. Her face was wide and quite flat, like the drunks outside the beer parlour of the Lorne Hotel.

*

Are there any Indians in our family? I asked my dad at the supper table. He was prying stubborn eggs off the frying pan.

Not so nobody'd notice, he said. Some figured Aunt Elsie's Frank for one but he turned out to be just another Italian.

He put my plate down in front of me. Fried potatoes with an egg broken over them. Boiled peas.

I mean in our veins, I said. Uncle Leo's pretty dark.

Uncle Leo was my mother's brother. Maybe my mother had had Indian blood in her veins. Maybe when she went off for a better life she'd gone to rejoin her tribe.

[2] Chinook jargon was a synthetic language used as a lingua franca by nineteenth-century traders in the Pacific Northwest.

He pulled in his chair and started forking up his food. My dad ate fast, hardly noticing what he was doing. His left hand picked at the flaking paint on the table.

I'd like to be an Iroquois, I said. No, I'd like to be a Blackfoot and live in a teepee. Moving around. It'd be fun to shoot buffalo.

I'd rather be a Haida myself, my dad said. Then I could lie around carving sticks of wood while my slaves did all the work.

He could say things that made you wonder if he read your mind. He winked. The patch of bared table grew larger every day, like a continent expanding and changing shape, eating up the paint.

Maybe you'd rather be one of their whalers, I said. In a boat hollowed out of a log. Throwing spears.

I wouldn't like that at all, my dad said. I'd have to drag the whales back to shore and cut them up. Too much work.

He mopped the broken egg-yolk off his plate with a piece of bread.

Then I'd have to eat the blubber, he said. I guess I'll stay the way I am, ignorant and poor and white. At least I've got spuds on the table, and once in a while a chicken.

Maybe even beautiful Iroquois maidens had flat plain faces when they were young. Maybe Nettie Tremblay would be pretty when she grew up. She'd never be a movie actress but she might be beautiful enough to marry.

Our children would be half-breeds. Half Indian, half mongrel Irish. We'd go in search of her roots, and find out that she was a hereditary princess. The first thing I would do is order a raiding party to go off and capture a dozen slaves—white, brown, it didn't matter. My father would be amongst them. Maybe I'd pretend I'd never seen him before. My throat tightened when I thought of this. My father would give his life for me in a minute but I was an ungrateful son who would take my time about deciding what to do with him. After all, he'd had no business stealing me and bringing me up as his own.

*

The brothers kept an eye on her at school. Five wild Tremblays—Lucien, Paul, Rene, Pierre, Antoine. They'd kill you if you told.

They'd kill you even if you said something to someone else. You could never find out who else had been warned. Everyone, you guessed. Because anybody could see what she was. Anyone could blurt it out.

You couldn't take a chance. Even if you said, "Look at the squaw scratching her bum," it could be to someone who might tell her and you'd be to blame. Nettie Tremblay would go nuts and kill herself. And the brothers would rip off your head.

You'd never get off the school bus alive. And if you did, you'd never run fast enough to get home. And if you did, they'd climb in through your bedroom window and smother you with your pillow. After they'd pulled all your teeth, and cut off your dick. Paul Tremblay was sixteen, still in Grade Five, a hundred and seventy pounds. He could do that all himself, while the others sawed off your toes.

If you whispered for Nettie to lend an eraser, you could see Pierre trying to hear what you said.

If you looked too long at Nettie, you'd find Miss Percy glaring. She wasn't as scary as the Tremblay brothers but she folded her arms like a sentry on guard, her face clenched up like a fist. Paul Tremblay asked her to a movie once, but she laughed. So he rammed his elbow into Warner Hilton's nose. It was a blood bath. Miss Percy mopped it up.

There were no more lessons about life in an Indian village. No more stories about ravens. We learned about Incas and Mayans instead. They threw maidens into wells but never set foot on this island.

You couldn't even be mean, not without risking your life. When Neil Saunders made a face behind Nettie's back, the brothers dragged him into the woods and beat him up. Then they took off his clothes and left him behind a tree. They stuffed his pants and shirt down the toilet but passed his underpants around on a stick.

Nettie Tremblay didn't notice. She might have been the only person in class. She did her work. She ate her lunch. She smiled and nodded if you said a few words but she acted like someone who lived in a world with glass around it.

You'd think being so protected would make her proud. But she didn't stand with her gaze on the horizon, like an Iroquois princess waiting for the warriors to come home. She walked with her head tilted down, her eyes on the ground. She scuffed along with one pigeon-toed foot in front of the other. She wasn't like an Indian at all, not the Indians we'd read about in books. Not the Indians Miss Percy had told us about in her lessons on Our Proud Neighbours.

Nettie Tremblay didn't know how much trouble we went to, to keep her ignorant and safe, or she might have tried a little harder. After a while you wondered if she was worth it.

She was different on Saturdays, though. She talked a blue streak while she helped. She didn't want to be a movie star any more, she wanted to be a nurse. She'd be a nurse for a while and then a doctor, in a giant city hospital.

Her brothers didn't follow when she came across the road. It was because they trusted me, my dad said. The Tremblays knew what sort of people we were, over here.

*

One day she showed up at the bus shelter wearing glasses. Purple frames. Who ever heard of an Indian wearing glasses?

Why are you wearing those things?

So I can see, she said.

You could see before.

Doctor says I'm short-sighted, like Miss Percy.

She pushed them up with her thumb. She didn't have enough nose to keep them from sliding down.

Four eyes, they called her when we got to school, but not where her brothers could hear.

Goggle face.

Everyone wearing glasses was called something. It didn't count.

The next day she showed up at the bus shelter wearing lipstick as well as the glasses. She'd never worn lipstick before. No girl in our class wore lipstick, you had to be thirteen or fourteen for that. It didn't make her look pretty, it made her look dumb.

Does you mother know you painted your face? I said.

My mother's the one put it on.

She opened her lunch bag and showed me a lipstick tube next to her sandwiches. Maybe her mother wanted to make her feel better about wearing glasses.

War paint, I said.

It makes you look cheap, Eleanor Laitinen said. The Tremblay brothers weren't close enough to hear. They'd murder Eleanor if they'd heard her, even if she was a girl.

You better wipe it off before we get to school, I said. You don't want to look like a tramp.

Tramp was my dad's word for women who painted themselves up and smoked and swung their purses. My mother had not been a tramp, but she'd thought she was too good for us and went off to live somewhere else.

It didn't really make her look like a tramp. Tramps were supposed to be pretty, even if they looked cheap. She probably thought the lipstick made her look pretty but it didn't. She needed someone smarter than those brothers to protect her. She'd make a fool of herself.

I sat beside her on the bus. Her brothers sat at the back, but you could be sure they kept an eye open. You had to be careful they didn't hear. Lucien. Paul. Rene. Antoine. Pierre.

It doesn't suit you, I said, It doesn't look nice on you the way it does on some girls.

She looked out the window.

You're not old enough, I said.

She pulled in both her lips as though she might swallow them. This flattened her nose. She had to push her glasses up again.

You don't want people to laugh at you, I said, you're not like Shelley Price.

Shelley Price was fourteen, six grades ahead of us. She was blonde, and pretty. She was the first girl to wear nylon stockings to school.

Drop dead, she said. I'll do what I want. Go sit somewhere else.

I hated her. She didn't even know how lucky she was. I didn't *have* to feel sorry for her. Let them laugh, if she was going to be like that.

West Coast Indians aren't real Indians, I told my dad that night. Charlie Morris said they came from China on a raft.

That must've been some raft, my dad said. I'd like to see it.

I'd rather be an Algonquin, I said.

Good idea, my dad said. You'll be closer to Ottawa. You can dance for the Great White Father when he's in town. Tell him he's welcome to a night on the kitchen cot if he's ever short of funds in this neck of the woods.

*

The whole south slope of the barn roof was covered with bark. Slabs were nearly dry enough. Some had curled up, and cracked when I stomped on them. Their colour was a dark red now—dried blood. I thought of the little bottles, for people who couldn't go to the toilet without some help.

From the peak of the barn I could look out over the small green field. The pig's smelly pen was below. Our house had not been painted since some time before I was born. Flecks of white were stuck here and there on the weather-blackened boards. My dad was going to paint it one day soon.

When Nettie came across the field I said I didn't need her today.

You can go home. My dad didn't cut any trees.

She came up the ladder anyway.

You want me to go so you won't have to pay me, she said.

Maybe that's why she'd kept coming over. She wouldn't talk to me at school any more but she talked to me while we worked. Money.

Not true, I said.

She came up the roof on all fours, and sat on the peak beside me. She didn't wear lipstick on weekends, but she wore her glasses every day.

How rich will I be? she said.

I don't know. My dad never said how much they pay.

How do you know you'll get any of it?

He gives me an allowance.

Most of it's gonna be mine.

Not most.

You said fifty cents for every day I helped.

I didn't say that.

You did so.

You didn't help all day, you only helped for a couple of hours each time. When you got bored you went home.

He won't pay you anyway, she said. You won't get any allowance, he needs the money for groceries. Daddy says you're only a step away from the poorhouse over here.

Whaddaya mean by that?

Just look at this place, she said. Daddy says a man with one arm and a wooden leg could make better use of it than your father does.

You're lying, I said. My Dad's always been nice to Mr. Tremblay.

He says if you were Catholics the priests would take you away from your father and put you in a home.

That's dumb, I said.

They would.

Nobody's going to take me away from my dad.

You don't know everything. Maybe somebody will.

No.

Somebody could be coming to get you right now. You don't know everything.

Yeah? I know something.

What?

I know something you don't know, I said.

What?

Something about yourself.

What?

If I tell you, you have to promise you won't tell anyone else. You have to promise you won't tell anyone that I told you.

It was like standing on the edge of a cliff. She was at my mercy. She had always been at my mercy. One word and over she'd go. Nothing would be the same.

What is it? she said. I won't believe you anyhow. You lie.

I won't tell you then.

Tell me.

Promise?

Okay, I promise. What is it?

What do you think you are?

Whaddaya mean?

What kind of ancestors do you think you have? Do you think you're a Swede?

Don't be stupid, she said. She laughed.

The priest brought you here from somewhere. Didn't you ever ask?

She went away from behind her eyes again. She didn't deserve to know. I wouldn't tell her. She could be a Haida princess. She could be descended from Big Bear. She could be Sitting Bull's niece. But she didn't deserve to know. Let her think she was just an ordinary girl who looked silly in glasses and stupid wearing lipstick.

What do you think you know? she said.

Nothing.

You better tell me, you think you're so smart.

I don't.

She stood up and hit me across the head with a slab of bark.

Stupid! Stupid! Stupid! Stupid!

She hit me again and again. Then she scrambled down the roof and turned to go down the ladder. Stupid stupid stupid. She knows, doesn't she? I said to my dad. I bet she's known all along.

I suppose she must've, he said.

We were filling the burlap bags, for the trip to the depot in town. Nine sacks. First we'd broken the dried bark into smaller pieces.

And you knew she did too, I said.

I suppose I did.

So why'd you tell me not to tell her?

Everybody was told not to tell her. Do you think if they'd just asked everybody not to call her names they wouldn't? Did you hear anyone call her names?

No.

And why is that, do you think?

Because of the brothers.

The brothers aren't always there. The brothers wouldn't be in the girls' washroom, for instance. Do you think anyone ever called her things in the washroom?

I guess not.

I guess not, he said. Do you know why people would've called her names, if they had?

I don't know, I said. To make her cry? To make themselves feel better'n her?

I'll tell you why they didn't, he said. Because they were part of a conspiracy. They didn't have to call her names, they could feel superior just by being part of a plot to keep her from knowing the facts. Them Tremblays are not so dumb.

The gunny sacks leaned against one another with their tops gaping open. My dad began to tie them closed with binder twine.

Was anything said between you? he said.

No.

Then leave it up to her. Maybe she'll go to school in beaded moccasins one day and tell you to call her Laughing Squirrel.

It isn't fair, I said.

Maybe she'd agree with you there, he said.

What would they do if I wore animal skins to school and told them to call me Mighty Warrior?

They'd laugh in your face.

What would they say?

Worse than they'd ever say to Nettie Tremblay, I'll tell you that. Maybe they'd just tell you to your face what they say behind your back.

This was something new. My skin felt funny and cold.

What do they say behind my back?

Maybe there's more than one plot out there, I bet you never thought of that. Maybe there's a plot to keep you from finding out something too.

Do you think there's something they could say about us, if they decided they didn't give a hoot for your feelings?

He winked. We're not so dumb either, is what he meant. We know who we are.

I don't know, I said.

You don't? Then they must have a better grip on their tongues than I thought.

Anyway, I said, it wouldn't be my fault.

He laughed. Poor thing, stuck with your old man. C'mon, let's get these buggers onto the truck.

I could have killed him. I could run off to look for my mother. It wasn't fair. I was the one who should have been related to Big Bear. I was the one who ought to be Sitting Bull's son. You can be sure I'd stand up and give them a fight. I'd chase the white people right off the land, I'd drive them into the sea. I'd make them all go back to Ireland where they'd have nothing to eat but rotted spuds and rain, where you could die just from being poor.

—2004

Margaret Atwood   b. 1939

Margaret Atwood has achieved enormous critical and popular success as an author of short stories, poems, novels, essays, and book-length critical studies. In all of these she presents a vision of a world that is difficult yet intriguing. "Death by Landscape" recalls a central thesis in Survival, *her 1972 reading guide to Canadian literature—which is that the Canadian landscape is one of "ever-present menace." It is not so much a story of the main character, Lois, or of her friend Lucy, a girl who has gone missing from camp, as of their relationship to nature and the haunted northern wilderness. Atwood contrasts the direct experience of the north woods that the Canadian-born Lois and the American-born Lucy shared at camp with that of Lois's later mediated experience of that landscape as it has been envisioned by Canadian painters, particularly in the representations associated with Tom Thomson and the Group of Seven—visual art that has come to seem the pictorial embodiment of the Canadian north. Like "Death by Landscape," which has some of the qualities of a Gothic ghost story, these paintings are neither picturesque nor sublime. They depict disorienting landscapes—"a tangle of bush and . . . interlaced branches"—that seem to hide something from Lois's lost past, something she needs but cannot have.*

Death by Landscape

Now that the boys are grown up and Rob is dead, Lois has moved to a condominium apartment in one of the newer waterfront developments. She is relieved not to have to worry about the lawn, or about the ivy pushing its muscular little suckers into the brickwork, or the squirrels gnawing their way into the attic and eating the insulation off the wiring, or about strange noises. This building has a security system, and the only plant life is in pots in the solarium.

Lois is glad she's been able to find an apartment big enough for her pictures. They are more crowded together than they were in the house, but this arrangement gives the walls a European look: blocks of pictures, above and beside one another, rather than one over the chesterfield, one over the fireplace, one in the front hall, in the old acceptable manner of sprinkling art around so it does not get too intrusive. This way has more of an impact. You know it's not supposed to be furniture.

None of the pictures is very large, which doesn't mean they aren't valuable. They are paintings, or sketches and drawings, by artists who were not nearly as well known when Lois began to buy them as they are now. Their work later turned up on stamps, or as silk-screen reproductions hung in the principals' offices of high schools, or as jigsaw puzzles, or on beautifully printed calendars sent out by corporations as Christmas gifts, to their less important clients. These artists painted mostly in the twenties and thirties and forties; they painted landscapes. Lois has two Tom Thomsons, three A. Y. Jacksons, a Lawren Harris. She has an Arthur Lismer, she has a J. E. H. MacDonald. She has a David Milne. They are pictures of convoluted tree trunks on an island of pink wave-smoothed stone, with more islands behind; of a lake with rough, bright, sparsely wooded cliffs; of a vivid river shore with a tangle of bush and two beached canoes, one red, one grey; of a yellow autumn woods with the ice-blue gleam of a pond half-seen through the interlaced branches.

It was Lois who'd chosen them. Rob had no interest in art, although he could see the necessity of having something on the walls. He left all the decorating decisions to her, while providing the money, of course. Because of this collection of hers, Lois's friends—especially the men— have given her the reputation of having a good nose for art investments.

But this is not why she bought the pictures, way back then. She bought them because she wanted them. She wanted something that was in them, although she could not have said at the time what it was. It was not peace:

she does not find them peaceful in the least. Looking at them fills her with a wordless unease. Despite the fact that there are no people in them or even animals, it's as if there is something, or someone, looking back out.

When she was thirteen, Lois went on a canoe trip. She'd only been on overnights before. This was to be a long one, into the trackless wilderness, as Cappie put it. It was Lois's first canoe trip, and her last.

Cappie was the head of the summer camp to which Lois had been sent ever since she was nine. Camp Manitou, it was called; it was one of the better ones, for girls, though not the best. Girls of her age whose parents could afford it were routinely packed off to such camps, which bore a generic resemblance to one another. They favoured Indian names and had hearty, energetic leaders, who were called Cappie or Skip or Scottie. At these camps you learned to swim well and sail, and paddle a canoe, and perhaps ride a horse or play tennis. When you weren't doing these things you could do Arts and Crafts and turn out dingy, lumpish clay ashtrays for your mother—mothers smoked more, then—or bracelets made of coloured braided string.

Cheerfulness was required at all times, even at breakfast. Loud shouting and the banging of spoons on the tables were allowed, and even encouraged, at ritual intervals. Chocolate bars were rationed, to control tooth decay and pimples. At night, after supper, in the dining hall or outside around a mosquito-infested campfire ring for special treats, there were singsongs. Lois can still remember all the words to "My Darling Clementine," and to "My Bonnie Lies Over the Ocean," with acting-out gestures: a rippling of the hands for "the ocean," two hands together under the cheek for "lies." She will never be able to forget them, which is a sad thought.

Lois thinks she can recognize women who went to these camps, and were good at it. They have a hardness to their handshakes, even now; a way of standing, legs planted firmly and farther apart than usual; a way of sizing you up, to see if you'd be any good in a canoe—the front, not the back. They themselves would be in the back. They would call it the stern.

She knows that such camps still exist, although Camp Manitou does not. They are one of the few things that haven't changed much. They now offer copper enamelling, and functionless pieces of stained glass baked in electric ovens, though judging from the productions of her friends' grandchildren the artistic standards have not improved.

To Lois, encountering it in the first year after the war, Camp Manitou seemed ancient. Its log-sided buildings with the white cement in between the half-logs, its flagpole ringed with whitewashed stones, its weathered grey dock jutting out into Lake Prospect, with its woven rope bumpers and its rusty rings for tying up, its prim round flowerbed of petunias near the office door, must surely have been there always. In truth it dated only from the first decade of the century; it had been founded by Cappie's parents, who'd thought of camping as bracing to the character, like cold showers, and had been passed along to her as an inheritance, and an obligation.

Lois realized, later, that it must have been a struggle for Cappie to keep Camp Manitou going, during the Depression and then the war, when money did not flow freely. If it had been a camp for the very rich, instead of the merely well off, there would have been fewer problems. But there must have been enough Old Girls, ones with daughters, to keep the thing in operation, though not entirely shipshape: furniture was battered, painted trim was peeling, roofs leaked. There were dim photographs of these Old Girls dotted around the dining hall, wearing ample woollen bathing suits and showing their fat, dimpled legs, or standing, arms twined, in odd tennis outfits with baggy skirts.

In the dining hall, over the stone fireplace that was never used, there was a huge moulting stuffed moose head, which looked somehow carnivorous. It was a sort of mascot; its name was Monty Manitou. The older campers spread the story that it was haunted, and came to life in the dark, when the feeble and undependable lights had been turned off or, due to yet another generator failure, had gone out. Lois was afraid of it at first, but not after she got used to it.

Cappie was the same: you had to get used to her. Possibly she was forty, or thirty-five, or fifty. She had fawn-coloured hair that looked as if it was cut with a bowl. Her head jutted forward, jigging like a chicken's as she strode around the camp, clutching notebooks and checking things off in them. She was like their minister in church: both of them smiled a lot and were anxious because they wanted things to go well; they both had the same overwashed skins and stringy necks. But all this disappeared when Cappie was leading a singsong, or otherwise leading. Then she was happy, sure of herself, her plain face almost luminous. She wanted to cause joy. At these times she was loved, at others merely trusted.

There were many things Lois didn't like about Camp Manitou, at first. She hated the noisy chaos and spoon-banging of the dining hall, the rowdy singsongs at which you were expected to yell in order to show that you were enjoying yourself. Hers was not a household that encouraged yelling. She hated the necessity of having to write dutiful letters to her parents claiming she was having fun. She could not complain, because camp cost so much money.

She didn't much like having to undress in a roomful of other girls, even in the dim light, although nobody paid any attention, or sleeping in a cabin with seven other girls, some of whom snored because they had adenoids or colds, some of whom had nightmares, or wet their beds and cried about it. Bottom bunks made her feel closed in, and she was afraid of falling out of top ones; she was afraid of heights. She got homesick, and suspected her parents of having a better time when she wasn't there than when she was, although her mother wrote to her every week saying how much they missed her. All this was when she was nine. By the time she was thirteen she liked it. She was an old hand by then.

Lucy was her best friend at camp. Lois had other friends in winter, when there was school and itchy woollen clothing and darkness in the afternoons, but Lucy was her summer friend.

She turned up the second year, when Lois was ten, and a Bluejay. (Chickadees, Bluejays, Ravens, and Kingfishers—these were the names Camp Manitou assigned to the different age groups, a sort of totemic clan system. In those days, thinks Lois, it was birds for girls, animals for boys: wolves, and so forth. Though some animals and birds were suitable and some were not. Never vultures, for instance; never skunks, or rats.)

Lois helped Lucy to unpack her tin trunk and place the folded clothes on the wooden shelves, and to make up her bed. She put her in the top bunk right above her, where she could keep an eye on her. Already she knew that Lucy was an exception, to a good many rules; already she felt proprietorial.

Lucy was from the United States, where the comic books came from, and the movies. She wasn't from New York or Hollywood or Buffalo, the only American cities Lois knew the names of, but from Chicago. Her house was on the lake shore and had gates to it, and grounds. They had a maid, all of the time. Lois's family only had a cleaning lady twice a week.

The only reason Lucy was being sent to *this* camp (she cast a look of minor scorn around the cabin, diminishing it and also offending Lois, while at the same time daunting her) was that her mother had been a camper here. Her mother had been a Canadian once, but had married her father, who had a patch over one eye, like a pirate. She showed Lois the picture of him in her wallet. He got the patch in the war. "Shrapnel," said Lucy. Lois, who was unsure about shrapnel, was so impressed she could only grunt. Her own two-eyed, unwounded father was tame by comparison.

"My father plays golf," she ventured at last.

"*Everyone* plays golf," said Lucy. "My *mother* plays golf."

Lois's mother did not. Lois took Lucy to see the outhouses and the swimming dock and the dining hall with Monty Manitou's baleful head, knowing in advance they would not measure up.

This was a bad beginning; but Lucy was good-natured, and accepted Camp Manitou with the same casual shrug with which she seemed to accept everything. She would make the best of it, without letting Lois forget that this was what she was doing.

However, there were things Lois knew that Lucy did not. Lucy scratched the tops off all her mosquito bites and had to be taken to the infirmary to be daubed with Ozonol. She took her T-shirt off while sailing, and although the counsellor spotted her after a while and made her put it back on, she burnt spectacularly, bright red, with the X of her bathing-suit straps standing out in alarming white; she let Lois peel the sheets of whispery-thin burned skin off her shoulders. When they sang "Alouette" around the campfire, she did not know any of the French words. The difference was that Lucy did not care about the things she didn't know, whereas Lois did.

During the next winter, and subsequent winters, Lucy and Lois wrote to each other. They were both only children, at a time when this was thought to be a disadvantage, so in their letters they pretended to be sisters, or even twins. Lois had to strain a little over this, because Lucy was so blonde, with translucent skin and large blue eyes like a doll's, and Lois was nothing out of the ordinary—just a tallish, thinnish, brownish person with freckles. They signed their letters LL, with the L's entwined together like the monograms on a towel. (Lois and Lucy, thinks Lois. How our names date us. Lois Lane, Superman's girlfriend, enterprising female reporter; "I Love Lucy." Now we are obsolete, and it's little Jennifers, little Emilys, little Alexandras and Carolines and Tiffanys.)

They were more effusive in their letters than they ever were in person. They bordered their pages with X's and O's, but when they met again in the summers it was always a shock. They had changed so much, or Lucy had. It was like watching someone grow up in jolts. At first it would be hard to think up things to say.

But Lucy always had a surprise or two, something to show, some marvel to reveal. The first year she had a picture of herself in a tutu, her hair in a ballerina's knot on the top of her head; she pirouetted around the swimming dock, to show Lois how it was done, and almost fell off. The next year she had given that up and was taking horseback riding. (Camp Manitou did not have horses.) The next year her mother and father had been divorced, and she had a new stepfather, one with both eyes, and a new house, although the maid was the same. The next year, when they had graduated from Bluejays and entered Ravens, she got her period, right in the first week of camp. The two of them snitched some matches from their counsellor, who smoked illegally, and made a small fire out behind the farthest outhouse, at dusk, using their flashlights. They could set all kinds of fires by now; they had learned how in Campcraft. On this fire they burned one of Lucy's used sanitary napkins. Lois is not sure why they did this, or whose idea it was. But she can remember the feeling of deep satisfaction it gave her as the white fluff singed and the blood sizzled, as if some wordless ritual had been fulfilled.

They did not get caught, but then they rarely got caught at any of their camp transgressions. Lucy had such large eyes, and was such an accomplished liar.

This year Lucy is different again: slower, more languorous. She is no longer interested in sneaking around after dark, purloining cigarettes from the counsellor, dealing in black-market candy bars. She is pensive, and hard to wake in the mornings. She doesn't like her stepfather, but she doesn't want to live with her real father either, who has a new wife. She thinks her mother may be having a love affair with a doctor; she doesn't know for sure, but she's seen them smooching in his car, out on the driveway, when her stepfather wasn't there. It serves him right. She hates her private school. She has a boyfriend, who is sixteen and works as a gardener's assistant. This is how she met him: in the garden. She describes to Lois what it is like when he kisses her—rubbery at first, but then your knees go limp. She has been forbidden to see him, and threatened with boarding school. She wants to run away from home.

Lois has little to offer in return. Her own life is placid and satisfactory, but there is nothing much that can be said about happiness.

"You're so lucky," Lucy tells her, a little smugly. She might as well say *boring* because this is how it makes Lois feel.

Lucy is apathetic about the canoe trip, so Lois has to disguise her own excitement. The evening before they are to leave, she slouches into the campfire ring as if coerced, and sits down with a sigh of endurance, just as Lucy does.

Every canoe trip that went out of camp was given a special send-off by Cappie and the section leader and counsellors, with the whole section in attendance. Cappie painted three streaks of red across each of her cheeks with a lipstick. They looked like three-fingered claw marks. She put a blue circle on her forehead with fountain-pen ink, and tied a twisted bandanna around her head and stuck a row of frazzle-ended feathers around it, and wrapped herself in a red-and-black Hudson's Bay blanket. The counsellors, also in blankets but with only two streaks of red, beat on tom-toms made of round wooden cheese boxes with leather stretched over the top and nailed in place. Cappie was Chief Cappeosota. They all had to say "How!" when she walked into the circle and stood there with one hand raised.

Looking back on this, Lois finds it disquieting. She knows too much about Indians: this is why. She knows, for instance, that they should not even be called Indians, and that they have enough worries without other people taking their names and dressing up as them. It has all been a form of stealing.

But she remembers, too, that she was once ignorant of this. Once she loved the campfire, the flickering of light on the ring of faces, the sound of the fake tom-toms, heavy and fast like a scared heartbeat; she loved Cappie in a red blanket and feathers, solemn, as a chief should be, raising her hand and saying, "Greetings, my Ravens." It was not funny, it was not making fun. She wanted to be an Indian. She wanted to be adventurous and pure, and aboriginal.

"You go on big water," says Cappie. This is her idea—all their ideas— of how Indians talk. "You go where no man has ever trod. You go many moons." This is not true. They are only going for a week, not many moons. The canoe route is clearly marked, they have gone over it on a map, and there are prepared campsites with names which are used year after year. But when Cappie says this—and despite the way Lucy rolls up her eyes—Lois can feel the water stretching out, with the shores twisting away on either side, immense and a little frightening.

"You bring back much wampum," says Cappie. "Do good in war, my braves, and capture many scalps." This is another of her pretences: that they are boys, and bloodthirsty. But such a game cannot be played by substituting the word "squaw." It would not work at all.

Each of them has to stand up and step forward and have a red line drawn across her cheeks by Cappie. She tells them they must follow in the paths of their ancestors (who most certainly, thinks Lois, looking out the window of her apartment and remembering the family stash of daguerreotypes and sepia-coloured portraits on her mother's dressing table, the stiff-shirted, black-coated, grim-faced men and the beflounced women with their severe hair and their corseted respectability, would never have considered heading off onto an open lake, in a canoe, just for fun).

At the end of the ceremony they all stood and held hands around the circle, and sang taps. This did not sound very Indian, thinks Lois. It sounded like a bugle call at a military post, in a movie. But Cappie was never one to be much concerned with consistency, or with archaeology.

After breakfast the next morning they set out from the main dock, in four canoes, three in each. The lipstick stripes have not come off completely, and still show faintly pink, like healing burns. They wear their white denim sailing hats, because of the sun, and thin-striped T-shirts, and pale baggy shorts with the cuffs rolled up. The middle one kneels, propping her rear end against the rolled sleeping bags. The counsellors going with them are Pat and Kip. Kip is no-nonsense; Pat is easier to wheedle, or fool.

There are white puffy clouds and a small breeze. Glints come from the little waves. Lois is in the bow of Kip's canoe. She still can't do a J-stroke very well, and she will have to be in the bow or the middle for the whole trip. Lucy is behind her; her own J-stroke is even worse. She splashes Lois with her paddle, quite a big splash.

"I'll get you back," says Lois.

"There was a stable fly on your shoulder," Lucy says.

Lois turns to look at her, to see if she's grinning. They're in the habit of splashing each other. Back there, the camp has vanished behind the first long point of rock and rough trees. Lois feels as if an invisible rope has broken. They're floating free, on their own, cut loose. Beneath the canoe the lake goes down, deeper and colder than it was a minute before.

"No horsing around in the canoe," says Kip. She's rolled her T-shirt sleeves up to the shoulder; her arms are brown and sinewy, her jaw determined, her stroke perfect. She looks as if she knows exactly what she is doing.

The four canoes keep close together. They sing, raucously and with defiance; they sing "The Quartermaster's Store," and "Clementine," and "Alouette." It is more like bellowing than singing.

After that the wind grows stronger, blowing slantwise against the bows, and they have to put all their energy into shoving themselves through the water.

Was there anything important, anything that would provide some sort of reason or clue to what happened next? Lois can remember everything, every detail; but it does her no good.

They stopped at noon for a swim and lunch, and went on in the afternoon. At last they reached Little Birch, which was the first campsite for overnight. Lois and Lucy made the fire, while the others pitched the heavy canvas tents. The fireplace was already there, flat stones piled into a U. A burned tin can and a beer bottle had been left in it. Their fire went out, and they had to restart it. "Hustle your bustle," said Kip. "We're starving."

The sun went down, and in the pink sunset light they brushed their teeth and spat the toothpaste froth into the lake. Kip and Pat put all the food that wasn't in cans into a packsack and slung it into a tree, in case of bears.

Lois and Lucy weren't sleeping in a tent. They'd begged to be allowed to sleep out; that way they could talk without the others hearing. If it rained, they told Kip, they promised not to crawl dripping into the tent over everyone's legs: they would get under the canoes. So they were out on the point.

Lois tried to get comfortable inside her sleeping bag, which smelled of musty storage and of earlier campers, a stale salty sweetness. She curled herself up, with her sweater rolled up under her head for a pillow and her flashlight inside her sleeping bag so it wouldn't roll away. The muscles of her sore arms were making small pings, like rubber bands breaking.

Beside her Lucy was rustling around. Lois could see the glimmering oval of her white face.

"I've got a rock poking into my back," said Lucy.

"So do I," said Lois. "You want to go into the tent?" She herself didn't, but it was right to ask.

"No," said Lucy. She subsided into her sleeping bag. After a moment she said, "It would be nice not to go back."

"To camp?" said Lois.

"To Chicago," said Lucy. "I hate it there."

"What about your boyfriend?" said Lois. Lucy didn't answer. She was either asleep or pretending to be.

There was a moon, and a movement of the trees. In the sky there were stars, layers of stars that went down and down. Kip said that when the stars were bright like that instead of hazy it meant bad weather later on. Out on the lake there were two loons, calling to each other in their insane, mournful voices. At the time it did not sound like grief. It was just background.

The lake in the morning was flat calm. They skimmed along over the glassy surface, leaving V-shaped trails behind them; it felt like flying. As the sun rose higher it got hot, almost too hot. There were stable flies in the canoes, landing on a bare arm or leg for a quick sting. Lois hoped for wind.

They stopped for lunch at the next of the named campsites, Lookout Point. It was called this because, although the site itself was down near the water on a flat shelf of rock, there was a sheer cliff nearby and a trail that led up to the top. The top was the lookout, although what you were supposed to see from there was not clear. Kip said it was just a view.

Lois and Lucy decided to make the climb anyway. They didn't want to hang around waiting for lunch. It wasn't their turn to cook, though they hadn't avoided much by not doing it, because cooking lunch was no big deal, it was just unwrapping the cheese and getting out the bread and peanut butter, but Pat and Kip always had to do their woodsy act and boil up a billy tin for their own tea.

They told Kip where they were going. You had to tell Kip where you were going, even if it was only a little way into the woods to get dry twigs for kindling. You could never go anywhere without a buddy.

"Sure," said Kip, who was crouching over the fire, feeding driftwood into it. "Fifteen minutes to lunch."

"Where are they off to?" said Pat. She was bringing their billy tin of water from the lake.

"Lookout," said Kip.

"Be careful," said Pat. She said it as an afterthought, because it was what she always said.

"They're old hands," Kip said.

Lois looks at her watch: it's ten to twelve. She is the watchminder; Lucy is careless of time. They walk up the path, which is dry earth and rocks, big rounded pinky-grey boulders or split-open ones with jagged edges. Spindly balsam and spruce trees grow to either side, the lake is blue fragments to the left. The sun is right overhead; there are no shadows anywhere. The heat comes up at them as well as down. The forest is dry and crackly.

It isn't far, but it's a steep climb and they're sweating when they reach the top. They wipe their faces with their bare arms, sit gingerly down on a scorching-hot rock, five feet from the edge but too close for Lois. It's a lookout all right, a sheer drop to the lake and a long view over the water, back the way they've come. It's amazing to Lois that they've travelled so far, over all that water, with nothing to propel them but their own arms. It makes her feel strong. There are all kinds of things she is capable of doing.

"It would be quite a dive off here," says Lucy.

"You'd have to be nuts," says Lois.

"Why?" says Lucy. "It's really deep. It goes straight down." She stands up and takes a step nearer the edge. Lois gets a stab in her midriff, the kind she gets when a car goes too fast over a bump. "Don't," she says.

"Don't what?" says Lucy, glancing around at her mischievously. She knows how Lois feels about heights. But she turns back. "I really have to pee," she says.

"You have toilet paper?" says Lois, who is never without it. She digs in her shorts pocket.

"Thanks," says Lucy.

They are both adept at peeing in the woods: doing it fast so the mosquitoes don't get you, the underwear pulled up between the knees, the squat with the feet apart so you don't wet your legs, facing down-hill. The exposed feeling of your bum, as if someone is looking at you from behind. The etiquette when you're with someone else is not to look. Lois stands up and starts to walk back down the path, to be out of sight.

"Wait for me?" says Lucy.

Lois climbed down, over and around the boulders, until she could not see Lucy; she waited. She could hear the voices of the others, talking and laughing, down near the shore. One voice was yelling, "Ants! Ants!" Someone must have sat on an ant hill. Off to the side, in the woods, a raven was croaking, a hoarse single note.

She looked at her watch: it was noon. This is when she heard the shout.

She has gone over and over it in her mind since, so many times that the first, real shout has been obliterated, like a footprint trampled by other footprints. But she is sure (she is almost positive, she is nearly certain) that it was not a shout of fear. Not a scream. More like a cry of surprise, cut off too soon. Short, like a dog's bark.

"Lucy?" Lois said. Then she called "Lucy!" By now she was clambering back up, over the stones of the path. Lucy was not up there. Or she was not in sight.

"Stop fooling around," Lois said. "It's lunch-time." But Lucy did not rise from behind a rock or step out, smiling, from behind a tree. The sunlight was all around; the rocks looked white. "This isn't funny!" Lois said, and it wasn't, panic was rising in her, the panic of a small child who does not know where the bigger ones are hidden. She could hear her own heart. She looked quickly around; she lay down on the ground and looked over the edge of the cliff. It made her feel cold. There was nothing.

She went back down the path, stumbling; she was breathing too quickly; she was too frightened to cry. She felt terrible—guilty and dismayed, as if she had done something very bad, by mistake. Something that could never be repaired. "Lucy's gone," she told Kip.

Kip looked up from her fire, annoyed. The water in the billy can was boiling. "What do you mean, gone?" she said. "Where did she go?"

"I don't know," said Lois. "She's just gone."

No one had heard the shout, but then no one had heard Lois calling, either. They had been talking among themselves, by the water.

Kip and Pat went up to the lookout and searched and called, and blew their whistles. Nothing answered.

Then they came back down, and Lois had to tell exactly what had happened. The other girls all sat in a circle and listened to her. Nobody said anything. They all looked frightened, especially Pat and Kip. They were the leaders. You did not just lose a camper like this, for no reason at all.

"Why did you leave her alone?" said Kip.

"I was just down the path," said Lois. "I told you. She had to go to the bathroom." She did not say *pee* in front of people older than herself.

Kip looked disgusted.

"Maybe she just walked off into the woods and got turned around," said one of the girls.

"Maybe she's doing it on purpose," said another.

Nobody believed either of these theories.

They took the canoes and searched around the base of the cliff, and peered down into the water. But there had been no sound of falling rock; there had been no splash. There was no clue, nothing at all. Lucy had simply vanished.

That was the end of the canoe trip. It took them the same two days to go back that it had taken coming in, even though they were short a paddler. They did not sing.

After that, the police went in a motorboat, with dogs; they were the Mounties and the dogs were German shepherds, trained to follow trails in the woods. But it had rained since, and they could find nothing.

Lois is sitting in Cappie's office. Her face is bloated with crying, she's seen that in the mirror. By now she feels numbed; she feels as if she has drowned. She can't stay here. It has been too much of a shock. Tomorrow her parents are coming to take her away. Several of the other girls who were on the canoe trip are also being collected. The others will have to stay, because their parents are in Europe, or cannot be reached.

Cappie is grim. They've tried to hush it up, but of course everyone in camp knows. Soon the papers will know too. You can't keep it quiet, but what can be said? What can be said that makes any sense? "Girl vanishes in broad daylight, without a trace." It can't be believed. Other things, worse things, will be suspected. Negligence, at the very least. But they have always taken such care. Bad luck will gather around Camp Manitou like a fog; parents will avoid it, in favour of other, luckier places. Lois can see Cappie thinking all this, even through her numbness. It's what anyone would think.

Lois sits on the hard wooden chair in Cappie's office, beside the old wooden desk, over which hangs the thumb-tacked bulletin board of normal camp routine, and gazes at Cappie through her puffy eyelids. Cappie is now smiling what is supposed to be a reassuring smile. Her manner is too casual: she's after something. Lois has seen this look on Cappie's face when she's been sniffing out contraband chocolate bars, hunting down those rumoured to have snuck out of their cabins at night.

"Tell me again," says Cappie, "from the beginning."

Lois has told her story so many times by now, to Pat and Kip, to Cappie, to the police, that she knows it word for word. She knows it, but she no longer believes it. It has become a story. "I told you," she said. "She wanted to go to the bathroom. I gave her my toilet paper. I went down the path, I waited for her. I heard this kind of shout . . ."

"Yes," says Cappie, smiling confidingly, "but before that. What did you say to one another?"

Lois thinks. Nobody has asked her this before. "She said you could dive off there. She said it went straight down."

"And what did you say?"

"I said you'd have to be nuts."

"Were you mad at Lucy?" says Cappie, in an encouraging voice.

"No," says Lois. "Why would I be mad at Lucy? I wasn't ever mad at Lucy." She feels like crying again. The times when she has in fact been mad at Lucy have been erased already. Lucy was always perfect.

"Sometimes we're angry when we don't know we're angry," says Cappie, as if to herself. "Sometimes we get really mad and we don't even know it. Sometimes we might do a thing without meaning to, or without knowing what will happen. We lose our tempers."

Lois is only thirteen, but it doesn't take her long to figure out that Cappie is not including herself in any of this. By *we* she means Lois. She is accusing Lois of pushing Lucy off the cliff. The unfairness of this hits her like a slap. "I didn't!" she says.

"Didn't what?" says Cappie softly. "Didn't what, Lois?"

Lois does the worst thing, she begins to cry. Cappie gives her a look like a pounce. She's got what she wanted.

Later, when she was grown up, Lois was able to understand what this interview had been about. She could see Cappie's desperation, her need for a story, a real story with a reason in it; anything but the senseless vacancy Lucy had left for her to deal with. Cappie wanted Lois to supply the reason, to be the reason. It wasn't even for the newspapers or the parents, because she could never make such an accusation without proof. It was for herself: something to explain the loss of Camp Manitou and of all she had worked for, the years of entertaining spoiled children and buttering up parents and making a fool of herself with feathers stuck in her hair. Camp Manitou was in fact lost. It did not survive.

Lois worked all this out, twenty years later. But it was far too late. It was too late even ten minutes afterwards, when she'd left Cappie's office and was walking slowly back to her cabin to pack. Lucy's clothes were still there, folded on the shelves, as if waiting. She felt the other girls in the cabin watching her with speculation in their eyes. *Could she have done it? She must have done it.* For the rest of her life, she has caught people watching her in this way.

Maybe they weren't thinking this. Maybe they were merely sorry for her. But she felt she had been tried and sentenced, and this is what has stayed with her: the knowledge that she had been singled out, condemned for something that was not her fault.

Lois sits in the living room of her apartment, drinking a cup of tea. Through the knee-to-ceiling window she has a wide view of Lake Ontario, with its skin of wrinkled blue-grey light, and of the willows of Centre Island shaken by a wind, which is silent at this distance, and on this side of the glass. When there isn't too much pollution she can see the far shore, the foreign shore; though today it is obscured.

Possibly she could go out, go downstairs, do some shopping; there isn't much in the refrigerator. The boys say she doesn't get out enough. But she isn't hungry, and moving, stirring from this space, is increasingly an effort.

She can hardly remember, now, having her two boys in the hospital, nursing them as babies; she can hardly remember getting married, or what Rob looked like. Even at the time she never felt she was paying full attention. She was tired a lot, as if she was living not one life but two: her own, and another, shadowy life that hovered around her and would not let itself be realized—the life of what would have happened if Lucy had not stepped sideways, and disappeared from time.

She would never go up north, to Rob's family cottage or to any place with wild lakes and wild trees and the calls of loons. She would never go anywhere near. Still, it was as if she was always listening for another voice, the voice of a person who should have been there but was not. An echo.

While Rob was alive, while the boys were growing up, she could pretend she didn't hear it, this empty space in sound. But now there is nothing much left to distract her.

She turns away from the window and looks at her pictures. There is the pinkish island, in the lake, with the intertwisted trees. It's the same landscape they paddled through, that distant summer. She's seen travelogues of this country, aerial photographs; it looks different from above, bigger, more hopeless: lake after lake, random blue puddles in dark green bush, the trees like bristles.

How could you ever find anything there, once it was lost? Maybe if they cut it all down, drained it all away, they might find Lucy's bones, some time, wherever they are hidden. A few bones, some buttons, the buckle from her shorts.

But a dead person is a body; a body occupies space, it exists somewhere. You can see it; you put it in a box and bury it in the ground, and then it's in a box in the ground. But Lucy is not in a box, or in the ground. Because she is nowhere definite, she could be anywhere.

And these paintings are not landscape paintings. Because there aren't any landscapes up there, not in the old, tidy European sense, with a gentle hill, a curving river, a cottage, a mountain in the background, a golden evening sky. Instead there's a tangle, a receding maze, in which you can become lost almost as soon as you step off the path. There are no backgrounds in any of these paintings, no vistas; only a great deal of foreground that goes back and back, endlessly, involving you in its twists and turns of tree and branch and rock. No matter how far back in you go, there will be more. And the trees themselves are hardly trees; they are currents of energy, charged with violent colour.

Who knows how many trees there were on the cliff just before Lucy disappeared? Who counted? Maybe there was one more, afterwards.

Lois sits in her chair and does not move. Her hand with the cup is raised halfway to her mouth. She hears something, almost hears it: a shout of recognition, or of joy.

She looks at the paintings, she looks into them. Every one of them is a picture of Lucy. You can't see her exactly, but she's there, in behind the pink stone island or the one behind that. In the picture of the cliff she is hidden by the clutch of fallen rocks towards the bottom, in the one of the river shore she is crouching beneath the overturned canoe. In the yellow autumn woods she's behind the tree that cannot be seen because of the other trees, over beside the blue sliver of pond; but if you walked into the picture and found the tree, it would be the wrong one, because the right one would be further on.

Everyone has to be somewhere, and this is where Lucy is. She is in Lois's apartment, in the holes that open inwards on the wall, not like windows but like doors. She is here. She is entirely alive.

—1991

Sandra Birdsell   b. 1942

Sandra Birdsell is the author of three collections of short stories and three novels. Her fiction is often set in the community of Aggasiz, an imagined version of the town of Morris, Manitoba, where Birdsell was raised by her Metis father and Russian–Mennonite mother. Her first two books (Night Travellers, *from which "The Wednesday Circle" comes, and* Ladies of the House—*reissued in 1987 in one volume as* Agassiz Stories) *explore the lives of the Lafreniere family: Mika, her Metis husband, Maurice, and their seven children. In these stories the open sky and vast landscape of the prairies contrast with a closed human world—one in which fears are silenced and individuals try to protect themselves from human suffering by using codified statements derived from the language of the Bible and Protestant belief. In "The Wednesday Circle," Betty, the most adventurous of the Lafrenieres, seeks a new language, one that will allow her to distinguish between being a victim and taking responsibility for her own fate.*

The Wednesday Circle

Betty crosses the double planks that span the ditch in front of Joys' yard. Most people have only one plank. But Mrs. Joy needs two. Mrs. Joy is a possible candidate for the circus. Like sleeping with an elephant, Betty's father says often. But Mr. and Mrs. Joy, the egg people, don't sleep together. Betty knows this even though she's never gone further than inside their stale smelling kitchen.

The highway is a smeltering strip of gunmetal grey at her back. It leads to another town like the one she lives in. If you kept on going south, you would get to a place called Pembina in the States and a small dark tavern where a woman will serve under-age kids beer. Laurence, Betty's friend, knows about this. But if you turn from the highway and go west, there are dozens of villages and then the Pembina Hills which Betty has seen on one occasion, a school trip to the man-made lake at Morden. Home of the rich and the godly, Betty's father calls these villages. Wish the godly would stay home. Can't get a seat in the parlour on Friday nights.

Beyond her lies a field in summer fallow and a dirt road rising to a slight incline and then falling as it meets the highway. Before her is the Joys' crumbling yellow cottage, flanked on all sides by greying bales of straw which have swollen and broken free from their bindings and are scattered about the yard. Behind the cottage is the machine shed. Behind the machine shed and bumping up against the prairie is the chicken coop.

Because Mika, Betty's mother, sends her for the eggs instead of having them delivered by Mr. Joy, she gets them cheaper.

Betty balances the egg cartons beneath her chin and pushes open the gate. It shrieks on its rusty hinges. The noise doesn't affect her as it usually does. Usually, the noise is like a door opening into a dark room and she is filled with dread. Today, she is prepared for it. Today is the day for the Wednesday Circle. The church ladies are meeting at her home. Even now, they're there in the dining room, sitting in a circle with their Bibles in their laps. It's like women and children in the centre. And arrows flying. Wagons are going up in flames and smoke. The goodness and matronly wisdom of the Wednesday Circle is a newly discovered thing. She belongs with them now. They can reach out to protect her even here, by just being what they are. And although she wants nothing to happen today, she is prepared for the worst.

"Come on in," Mrs. Joy calls from the kitchen.

Betty sets the egg cartons down on the steps and enters the house. Mrs. Joy's kitchen resembles a Woolworth store. There are porcelain dogs and cats in every corner on knick-knack shelves. Once upon a time, she used to love looking at those figurines but now she thinks they're ugly.

The woman sits in her specially made chair which is two chairs wired together. Her legs are stretched out in front resting up on another chair. Out of habit, Betty's heart constricts because she knows the signs. Mrs. Joy is not up to walking back to the chicken coop with her. And that's how it all began.

"Lo, I am with you always even unto the end of the world," her mind recites.

These verses rise unbidden. She has memorized one hundred of them and won a trip to a summer Bible camp at Lake Winnipeg. She has for the first time seen the ocean on the prairie and tried to walk on water. The waves have lifted and pulled her out where her feet couldn't touch the sandy bottom and she has been swept beneath that mighty sea and heard the roaring of the waves in her head and felt the sting of fish water in her nostrils. Like a bubble of froth she is swept beneath the water, back and forth by the motion of the waves. She is drowning. What happens is just as she's heard. Her whole life flashes by. Her head becomes a movie screen playing back every lie and swearing, malicious and unkind deeds, thoughts, words. There is not one thing that makes her look justified for having done or said them. And then her foot touches a rock and she pushes herself forward in desperation, hoping it's the right direction.

Miraculously, it is. She bounces forward from the depths to where she can tiptoe to safety, keeping her nose above the waves. She runs panting with fear to her cabin. She pulls the blankets over her. She tells no one. But that evening in the chapel during devotions, the rustling wind in the poplars against the screen causes her to think of God. When they all sing, "Love Lifted Me," the sunset parts the clouds above the water so there is a crack of gold where angels hover, watching. So she goes forward to the altar with several others and has her name written in the Book of Life. They tell her the angels are clapping and she thinks she can hear them there at that crack of gold which is the door to heaven. She confesses every sin she's been shown in the water except for one. For some reason, it wasn't there in the movie. And they are such gentle, smiling nice people who have never done what she's done. So she can't bring herself to tell them that Mr. Joy puts his hands in her pants.

"Rainin' today, ain't it child?" Mrs. Joy asks.

"No, not yet," Betty says. "It's very muggy."

"Don't I know it," she says.

"Are your legs sore?" Betty asks.

"Oh Lord, yes, how they ache," Mrs. Joy says and rolls her eyes back into her head. Her jersey dress is a tent stretched across her knees. She cradles a cookie tin in her lap.

"That's too bad," Betty says.

A chuckle comes from deep inside her mammoth chest. "You sound just like your mother," she says. "And you're looking more and more like her each time I see you. You're just like an opal, always changing."

God's precious jewels, Mrs. Joy calls them when she visits Mika. She lines them up verbally, Betty and her sisters and brothers, comparing chins, noses. This one here, she says about Betty, she's an opal. You oughta keep a watch over that one. Always changing. But it just goes to show, His mysteries does He perform. Not one of them the same.

"Thank you," Betty says, but she hates being told she looks like her mother. Mika has hazel eyes and brown hair. She is blonde and blue-eyed like her Aunt Elizabeth.

"Well, you know where the egg pail is," Mrs. Joy says, dismissing her with a flutter of her pudgy hand.

"Aren't you coming?" Betty asks.

"Not today, girl. It aches me so to walk. You collect the eggs and then you jest find Mr. Joy and you pay him. He gets it in the end anyhow."

Betty looks around the kitchen. His jacket is missing from its hook on the wall. She goes over to the corner by the window and feigns interest in the porcelain figures. She picks one up, sets it down. His truck is not in the yard.

"Where is he?"

"Went to town for something," Mrs. Joy says. "But I thought he'd be back by now. Doesn't matter though, jest leave the money in the back porch."

The egg pail thumps against her leg as she crosses the yard to the chicken coop. She walks towards the cluttered wire enclosure, past the machine shed. The doors are open wide. The hens scratch and dip their heads in her direction as she approaches. Hope rises like an erratic kite as she passes the shed and there are no sounds coming from it. She stamps her feet and the hens scatter before her, then circle around and approach her from behind, silently. She quickly gathers three dozen of the warm, straw-flecked eggs, and then steps free of the stifling smelly coop out into the fresh moist air. She is almost home-free. She won't have to face anything today. It has begun to rain. Large spatters spot her white blouse, feel cool on her back. She sets the pail down on the ground beside the egg cartons and begins to transfer the eggs.

"Here, you don't have to do that outside." His sudden voice, as she fills the egg cartons, brings blood to her face, threatens to pitch her forward over the pail.

He strides across the yard from the shed. "Haven't got enough sense to come in out of the rain," he says "Don't you know you'll melt? Be nothing left of you but a puddle."

He carries the pail, she carries the cartons. He has told her: Mrs. Joy is fat and lazy, you are my sunshine, my only sunshine. I would like six little ones running around my place too, but Mrs. Joy is fat and lazy. His thin hand has gone from patting her on the head with affection, to playfully slapping her on the behind, graduated then to tickling her armpits and ribs and twice now, his hands have been inside her underpants.

"Be not afraid," a verse leaps into her head, "For I am with you." She will put her plan into action. The Wednesday Circle women are strong and mighty. She knows them all, they're her mother's friends. She'll just go to them and say, Mr. Joy feels me up, and that will be the end of it.

She walks behind him, her heart pounding. He has an oil rag hanging from his back pocket and his boots are caked with clay, adding inches to his height.

"I'm waiting for my parts," he says over his shoulder. "Can't do anything until I get that truck fixed." Sometimes he talks to her as though she were an adult. Sometimes as though she were ten again and just coming for the eggs for the first time. How old are you, he'd asked the last time and was surprised when she said, fourteen. My sunshine has grown up.

They enter the machine shed and he slides the doors closed behind them, first one and then the other, leaving a sliver of daylight beaming through where the doors join. A single light bulb dangles from a wire, shedding a circle of weak yellow light above the truck, not enough to clear the darkness from the corners.

"Okay-dokey," he says and puts the pail of eggs on the workbench. "You can work here. I've got things to do." He goes over to the truck, disappears beneath its raised hood.

Then he's back at the workbench, searching through his tool-box. "Seen you with your boyfriend the other day," he says. "That Anderson boy."

"He's not my boyfriend," she says.

"I saw you," he says. His usual bantering tone is missing. "The two of you were in the coulee." Then his breath is warm on the side of her face as he reaches across her. His arm knocks against her breast, sending pain shooting through her chest. I need a bra, she has told Mika. Whatever for? Wear an undershirt if you think you really need to.

"Do you think it's a good idea to hang around in the coulee with your boyfriend?"

"He's not my boyfriend," she says. "I told you."

He sees her flushed cheeks, senses her discomfort. "Aha," he says. "So he is. You can't fool me."

She moves away from him. Begins to stack the cartons up against her chest, protection against his nudgings. Why is it that everyone but her own mother notices that she has breasts now?

"Don't rush off," he says. "Wait until the rain passes." The sound of it on the tin roof is like small pebbles being dropped one by one.

He takes the cartons from her and sets them back on the workbench. He smiles and she can see that perfect decayed circle between his front teeth. His hair is completely grey even though he's not as old as her father. He starts to walk past her, back towards the truck and then suddenly he grasps her about the waist and begins to tickle her ribs. She is slammed up against him and gasping for breath. His whiskers prickle against her neck. She tastes the bitterness of his flannel shirt.

She pushes away. "Stop."

He holds her tighter. "You're so pretty," he says. "No wonder the boys are chasing you. When I'm working in here, know what I'm thinking all the time?"

"Let me go." She continues to push against his bony arms.

"I'm thinking about all the things I could do to you."

Against her will, she has been curious to know. She feels desire rising when he speaks of what he would like to do. He has drawn vivid word-pictures that she likes to reconstruct until her face burns. Only it isn't Mr. Joy in the pictures, it's Laurence. It's what made her pull aside her underpants so he could fumble inside her moist crevice with his grease-stained fingers.

"Show me your tits," he whispers into her neck. "I'll give you a dollar if you do."

She knows the only way out of this is to tell. When the whole thing is laid out before the Wednesday Circle, she will become whiter than snow. "No," she says.

"What do you mean, no," he says, jabbing her in the ribs once again.

"I'm going to tell," she says. "You can't make me do anything anymore because I'm going to tell on you." She feels as though a rock has been taken from her stomach. He is ugly. He is like a salamander dropping from the sky after a rainstorm into a mincemeat pail. She doesn't know how she could ever have liked him.

"Make you?" he says. "Make you? Listen here, girlie, I've only done what you wanted me to do."

She knows this to be true and not true. She isn't certain how she has come to accept and even expect his fondling. It has happened over a course of four years, gradually, like growing.

She walks to the double doors where the light shines through. "Open them, please," she says.

"Open them yourself," he says. She can feel the presence of the Wednesday Circle. The promise of their womanly strength is like a lamp unto her feet. They will surround her and protect her. Freedom from his word-pictures will make her a new person.

"You say anything," he says. "You say one thing and I'll have some pretty stories to tell about you. You betcha."

"That woman," Mika is saying to the Wednesday Circle as Betty enters the dining room. "That woman. She has absolutely no knowledge of the scriptures. She takes everything out of context." Mika is standing at the buffet with a china teacup in her hand. Betty steps into the circle of chairs and sits down in Mika's empty one. Mika stops talking, throws her a look of surprise and question. The other women greet her with smiles, nods.

"Did you get the eggs?" Mika asks.

Betty feels her mouth stretching, moving of its own accord into a silly smile. She knows the smile irritates Mika but she can't help it. At times like these, her face moves on its own. She can hear her own heartbeat in her ears, like the ocean, roaring.

"What now?" Mika asks, worried.

"What do you mean, she takes everything out of context?" Mrs. Brawn asks, ignoring Betty. It's her circle. She started it off, arranging for the church women to meet in each others' homes twice a month to read scripture and sew things which they send to a place in the city where they are distributed to the poor. The women are like the smell of coffee to Betty and at the same time, they are like the cool opaque squares of Mika's lemon slice which is arranged on bread and butter plates on the table. They are also like the sturdy varnished chairs they sit on. To be with them now is the same as when she was a child and thought that if you could always be near an adult when you were ill, you wouldn't die.

"My, my," Mika mimics someone to demonstrate to Mrs. Brawn what she means. She places her free hand against her chest in a dramatic gesture. "They are different, ain't they? God's precious jewels. Just goes to show. His mysteries does He perform."

Betty realizes with a sudden shock that her mother is imitating Mrs. Joy.

Mrs. Brawn takes in Mika's pose with a stern expression and immediately Mika looks guilty, drops her hand from her breast and begins to fill cups with coffee.

"I suppose that we really can't expect much from Mrs. Joy," Mika says with her back to them. Betty hears the slight mocking tone in her voice that passes them by.

Heads bent over needlework nod their understanding. The women's stitches form thumbs, forest-green fingers; except for the woman who sits beside Betty. With a hook she shapes intricate spidery patterns to lay across varnished surfaces, the backs of chairs. What the poor would want with those, I'll never know, Mika has said privately. But they include the doilies in their parcels anyway because they have an understanding. They whisper that this white-haired woman has known suffering.

She works swiftly. It seems to Betty as though the threads come from the ends of her fingers, white strings with a spot of red every few inches. It looks as though she's cut her finger and secretly bleeds the colour into the lacy scallops. The women all unravel and knit and check closely for evenness of tension.

Mika enters the circle of chairs then, carrying the tray of coffee, and begins to make her way around it. She continues to speak of Mrs. Joy.

"Are you looking forward to school?" the white-haired woman asks Betty. Her voice is almost a whisper, a knife peeling skin from a taut apple. Betty senses that it has been difficult for her to speak, feels privileged that she has.

"Yes, I miss school."

The woman blinks as she examines a knot in her yarn. She scrapes at it with her large square thumbnail which is flecked oddly with white fish-hook-shaped marks. "Your mother tells us you were at camp," she says. "What did you do there?"

Mika approaches them with the tray of coffee. "I just wish she hadn't picked me out, that's all," Mika says. "She insists on coming over here in the morning and it's impossible to work with her here. And Mr. Joy is just as bad. I send Betty for the eggs now because he used to keep me at the door talking."

Mr. Joy is just as bad. Mr. Joy makes me ashamed of myself and I let him do it. The woman shakes loose the doily; it unfolds into the shape of a star as she holds it up.

"You like it?" the white-haired woman asks Betty.

"It's pretty."

"Maybe I give it to you."

"Ah Mika," a woman across the circle says, "she just knows where she can find the best baking in town."

Then they all laugh; even the quiet woman beside Betty has a dry chuckle over the comment, only Mrs. Brawn doesn't smile. She stirs her coffee with more force than necessary and sets the spoon alongside it with a clang.

"Obesity is no laughing matter," she says. "Mrs. Joy is a glutton and that's to be pitied. We don't laugh at sin, the wages of sin is death."

"But the gift of God is eternal life through Jesus Christ our Lord," the woman says so softly, the words are nail filings dropping into her lap. If Betty hadn't seen her lips moving, she wouldn't have heard it. "God forgives," the woman says then, louder. She is an odd combination of young and old. Her voice and breasts are young but her hair is white.

Mika stands before them with the tray of coffee. "Not always," Mika says. "There's the unpardonable sin, don't forget about that." She seems pleased to have remembered this.

"Which is?" the woman asks.

"Well, suicide," Mika says. "It has to be, because when you think of it, it's something you can't repent of once the deed is done." Mika smiles around the circle as if to say to them, see, I'm being patient with this woman who has known suffering.

"Perhaps there is no need to repent," the woman says.

"Pardon?"

"In Russia," the woman begins and then stops to set her thread down into her lap. She folds her hands one on top of the other and closes her eyes. The others, sensing a story, fall silent.

"During the revolution in Russia, there was once a young girl who was caught by nine soldiers and was their prisoner for two weeks. She was only thirteen. These men had their way with her many times, each one taking their turn, every single night. In the end, she shot herself. What about her?"

"I've never heard of such a case," Mika says. She sounds as though she resents hearing of it now.

"There are always such cases," the woman says. "If God knows the falling of a single sparrow, He is also merciful. He knows we're only human."

Mrs. Brawn sets her knitting down on the floor in front of her chair, leans forward slightly. "Oh, He knows," she says. "But He never gives us more than we can bear. When temptation arises, He gives us the strength to resist." She closes her statement with her hands, like a conductor pinching closed the last sound.

Betty watches as the white-haired woman twists and untwists her yarn into a tight ring around her finger. "I don't believe for one moment," she says finally, "that God would condemn such a person to hell. Jesus walked the earth and so He knows."

"No, no," Mika says from the buffet. "He doesn't condemn us, don't you see? That's where you're wrong. We condemn ourselves. We make that choice."

"And what choice did that young girl have?" the woman asks. "It was her means of escape. God provided the gun."

Mika holds the tray of lemon squares up before her as though she were offering them to the sun. She looks stricken. Deep lines cut a sharp V above her nose. "You don't mean that," she says. "Suicide is unpardonable. I'm sure of it. Knowing that keeps me going. Otherwise, I would have done it myself long ago."

There is shocked silence and a rapid exchange of glances around the circle at Betty, to see if she's heard.

"You shouldn't say such things," Mrs. Brawn says quietly. "For shame. You have no reason to say that."

The white-haired woman speaks with a gaunt smile. "Occasionally," she says, "in this room, someone dares to speak the truth."

"What do you mean?" asks Mrs. Brawn.

"Look at us," the woman says. "We're like filthy rags to Him in our self-righteousness. We obey because we fear punishment, not because we love."

Betty sees the grease spot on her blouse where his arm has brushed against her breast. Her whole body is covered in handprints. The stone is back in her stomach. She feels betrayed. For a moment the women are lost inside their own thoughts and they don't notice as she rises from her chair and sidles over to the door. Then, as if on some signal, their conversation resumes its usual level, each one waiting impatiently for the other to be finished so they can speak their words. Their laughter and goodwill have a feeling of urgency, of desperation. Betty stands at the door; a backward glance and she sees the white-haired woman bending over her work once again, eyes blinking rapidly, her fingers moving swiftly and the doily, its flecked pattern spreading like a web across her lap.

—1982

Isabel Huggan   b. 1943

Isabel Huggan's preferred form has been the short story. She followed The Elizabeth Stories *(1984), a moving sequence about a girl growing up in small-town Ontario, with the collection* You Never Know *(1993). More recently, she chose to end her award-winning memoir,* Belonging: Home Away from Home *(2003), about her struggle to understand the meaning of home while living abroad with her husband, with three works of short fiction that emerge from her recollections.*

In "End of Empire" the main character recalls her childhood and the comforts of having had a "private mythology" and chronicles the loss that results when fantasy is disrupted by real events. The story captures not just a personal moment in the life of one character but also suggests much about a transitional era in Canadian history and the cultural changes that took place after World War II and the death of King George VI.

End of the Empire

Long ago, when I was young, I was in love with King George the Sixth. It was, as you might imagine, a rather lopsided relationship, but within its limitations so real that his death, in 1952, diminished for some time my expectations for happiness on this earth. Even now I sometimes suffer from a vague and aching sadness, a sorrow wandering in the halls of memory, as if in some hidden part of myself I am still mourning the day he died.

In King George, I recognized a soul very like my own—someone who had, inadvertently, without having any say about it, landed in the wrong life. In him I recognized such a gentle and bewildered dignity my heart was quite pierced through with arrows of devotion. Neither his daughter's well-meaning and anxious stiffness nor his grandson's self-deprecating wit can duplicate the winsome charm of his stammer, his long-faced sincerity and sweetness. Nothing can bring him back, he is forever gone; and without him, both the world and I have changed.

The day he died I was so stricken with grief I had to be kept home from school that afternoon, my face swollen and purple from crying. We received the news of his death on the CBC at noon, from the small brown radio on top of the refrigerator. My father was on evening shift at the foundry that week so he was home and we were all sitting at the kitchen table eating lunch, our usual Campbell's chicken noodle soup and soda crackers and carrot sticks. As the announcer's deep rolling voice and the tolling British bells brought the truth home to us and the rest of Canada, I fell from my chair in a swoon, and with a terrible gasp of "Oh no, my King!" toppled to the floor at my mother's feet. My father, never one for emotional display, told me to straighten round immediately if I didn't want the belt, and my mother said, "Now, now, there's no need for that," but it was not clear whether it was to me or to my father that she spoke.

I gathered myself up and ran sobbing from the kitchen to the bedroom I shared with my older sister, whose jeering laughter I still heard as I slammed the door—cold, older-sister laughter. I flung myself across the white chenille bedspread, lay there face down and felt the fuzzy ridges of its pattern pressing against my cheek as I wept out my despair. My hope for rescue was gone, gone to the grave.

My love for King George had been, until that moment in the kitchen, a private thing, a passion too rare to be shared with a family such as mine. I'd always known that: it was part of what made my royal life a necessary secret. My mother said she had no notion of what made me tick and whenever she said that, my father would mutter she had better be careful, because bombs tick too and then go off. It was meant as a joke, suggesting I was a tricky bit of business he didn't understand, and although it seemed rather a mean thing to say about his child—a bomb, indeed!—he was essentially correct.

Offsetting them, in fortuitous counterbalance, King George understood me absolutely. He and I were united at a deep and invisible level, as if connected by a silent underground river running beneath our lives. This became apparent the first time he saw me, the lids of his blue eyes fluttering momentarily and then opening with something like astonishment or delight. He saw me for the first time many times, as I refined the pleasurable details of the scene. But always the heart of it remained the same: we belonged together, the King and I. Because of his age, and mine, the way in which we would fit would be father and daughter, but that was merely a matter of convenience and fate. Our destiny was interwoven, of that I was sure.

The events leading up to King George's happy discovery of me, Hannah Louise Clement, were always the same. I would have been found in a large green park by his younger daughter, Princess Margaret Rose, who would take me home to the Palace. Although I knew her to be a dozen years older, on this occasion she always appeared to be nearer my age, looking rather as she did in the photograph of herself and her older sister that hung on the dining room wall at my grandmother's house. She and Elizabeth were seated at a grand piano, wearing matching dresses of pink lace and tulle tied round with satin ribbon; they were smiling, and there were two small brown Corgi dogs at their feet.

Even in the park where it was rainy and chilly, dusk coming on, mist rising from the lawns, Margaret Rose appeared to be perfectly turned out, as if royal radiance kept her dry. The park in my mind's eye bore a fairly strong resemblance to Victoria Park, a few blocks from where I lived in London, Ontario. A small and very ordinary city park criss-crossed with asphalt paths, it extended in my imagination far past its normal boundaries, became larger and greener, full of rose beds and glass-globe lamps shining dimly in the fog. The weather was always English and wet in this sequence: there was never sunshine, never snow, as if I knew instinctively the climatic demands of my private mythology.

Although Princess Margaret Rose seemed above ordinary physical discomfort, it distressed her royal heart to see me, Hannah Louise, huddled on a park bench . . . hungry, outcast, alone. She would scrutinize me by bringing her dimpled face in its nest of curls very close to mine and then she would stand back, and pronounce her sentence very clearly: she would take me home to her father, the King.

Exactly how I knew that King George would want to adopt me as soon as he set eyes on me, I am not to this day sure. I saw *him* only infrequently in black-and-white newsreels at the movie house on Saturdays, and in a few colour photographs in magazines or in the corridors at school. But I knew, with the intuition of the truly blessed, that he and I were cut from the same cloth. That is not to say that I had delusions of grandeur or believed myself to be of royal blood, my lineage lost and muddled over the years because of some Dickensian nursemaid. Rather, it was from the fine and innocent certainty that station in life meant nothing, a kind of childish notion of pure equality. Nobody gets to choose who her parents are, nobody gets to choose the time and place of his birth—we all start out the same, having no say in anything at all. I felt sure that King George was not any different from, and longed to be attached to, the real world of common people. Like me. And I sensed that he was, like me, a little scared. And I knew that he knew that I knew.

I was a thin, unadventurous child who preferred fantasy because less than a decade in this world had convinced me that reality was a punishing and difficult affair. Sometime shortly after kindergarten, perhaps as a result of a determined teacher insisting I use my right hand instead of my left, I developed a slight stutter, which had a way of coming and going so that I never knew exactly when I was going to stumble and fall over a syllable. The very random nature of this thing meant no one could find a way to cure it, and the family doctor simply assured my mother that I would, eventually, grow out of it. Which, of course, I did, except for occasional lapses when I am angry or afraid.

As a child, I found a lot to be afraid of. My mother used to say she thought I looked for trouble and she was probably right. In those years after the war, it was hard for a child to differentiate between the horrors one saw in magazines and newsreels and the horrors one imagined. It was impossible to grasp the levels of hate and fear in the world and translate it all properly so that none of it applied to you.

There were, for example, in our end of the city, several "foreign" families known as the DPs, who'd come out of central Europe after 1945. Tough, hardened survivors ready to make a new life in the new land, these *displaced persons* did not fit into the already established patterns of London, Ontario, and they were discriminated against at every turn, especially in working-class neighborhoods such as mine where their presence was a continuing reminder of the ups and downs of fate.

Their children who went to my school were known as the Dumb DPs, and were mocked and scorned and treated with disdain. In my fearful heart, I knew how these kids felt, in their moth-eaten, hand-me-down cardigans, with their funny accents and garlicky breath and knobby knees. I felt like that when I was teased for my stutter or for being a beanpole or a smartypants. It was all the same, and it wasn't fair. And pity swelled within me for their awful plight.

It did not make me open my heart to them, you understand. I befriended not one solitary DP child. I turned instead for companionship and solace to the King of England.

Margaret Rose, on the other hand, had a heart of gold, and I feel for her still a grateful fondness. She did not hesitate to rescue a wet little waif from the park and to share, with angelic generosity, her father and her life. Elizabeth generally I found a touch surly, a bit sulky in a selfish way—much like my older sister. I could see *she* wanted to remain the apple of her Daddy's eye, unthwarted by any snotty-nosed stranger; and I always had the shaky feeling that if Elizabeth had her way she'd whisk me out of Buckingham Palace quick as a wink, no matter what her silly sister said.

I would be led to the throne room by Margaret Rose, who'd take my hand in a bossy but kindly way. As a rule the Queen was never present but her absence was easily explainable—a Queen was meant to be out and about, hovering by veterans' wheelchairs, offering sticks of candy to poor children, cutting ribbons, pouring tea, the impersonal, dutiful charities of *noblesse oblige*, requiring little of her but large hats and powdery smiles. I was not cynical but I knew the Queen did not matter.

The King, however, preferred sticking closer to home and that was as it should be, a king on his throne, ruling. He didn't wear a crown, but he usually had on a peacock-blue smoking jacket, made of shiny, patterned brocade. It must have been handed down by his brother, I think. It made a nice, if surprising, change from the military gear he so often wore, and the informality of the costume made him appear relaxed, nearly jolly. He would be sitting with his hands folded in his lap, as if he'd been waiting for me to appear, and when I did, he would say to Margaret Rose, "What's this, then?"

I would walk carefully up the long purple carpet to where he sat, and make a deep curtsey, and he would rise from his throne and touch my hair with his hand and say, "There, there, child. Enough." And I would look up at his face—the long, sad cheeks, the remarkable expanse from nose to lip, the thin lip itself—and see in his lovely eyes the perfect understanding of which I spoke earlier, and the flicker of paternal joy.

Bashfully, for neither of us were any good at making conversation, we would talk to each other about our lives. This episode would usually serve as a review of what I was doing in school at the time, and I would tell the King everything I knew. The routes of the explorers, the toughest multiplication tables, all the verses of the poems I had memorized by Walter de la Mare and Christina Rossetti—all these things and more, without hesitation or stutter. And he too spoke clearly and calmly, in a voice rich and warm and even, in the voice a king should have. In the voice I gave him. And he would say, in this wonderful voice, that he was amazed at the depth and breadth of my knowledge.

"Why, I think you know more than either of my girls do," he would say. And then: "What would you think about coming to live here at the Palace? You are just the sort of girl I like to talk to."

It was the kind of swift decision-making one might expect from a king. For although the invitation was phrased as a question, there was no doubt that it was a royal command, and that I would now live there forever, with him.

Conveniently, I was only recently orphaned, my insensitive family having perished in a car accident or a tragic fire or from food poisoning at a picnic, and thus there were no obstacles to surmount. I would shyly nod my assent, and the court stenographer would be called to draw up immediately the adoption papers. I'd sign my name, Hannah Louise, with a flourish, and King George would raise his eyebrows in appreciation of my fine hand, and then apply himself to his own signature. This would be followed by a hot wax seal, red and dripping, as the parchment would be lifted up, and the announcement made: "Hannah Louise Clement is now of the House of Windsor."

Generally speaking, I never progressed beyond this point. The ceremony in itself was the culmination of all my hopes and dreams, and there was no need for dénouement. And it was only the King's death that brought me back to the suburban street and two-storey frame house in which I dwelled with a father and mother who couldn't figure me out, and a sister who thought, if she ever gave me a thought, that I was weird.

Her name was Phyllis Anne, and in the weeks following my downfall in the kitchen she needled and teased me and made me miserable at every turn. Three years older than I, she was exactly the right age to take the approaching Coronation seriously, and she began a scrapbook, starting with newspaper clippings which told how Princess Elizabeth had been given the news she'd be Queen while she was at Treetops in faraway Africa. Then she added to her collection the countless magazine articles and pamphlets flourishing in those days leading up to the event, full of Windsor family photographs, charts of royal succession, historical essays on the meaning of the Coronation, the symbolism of the orb and crown and etcetera, etcetera.

All very cheery and positive, this business of putting that Elizabeth on the throne. Phyllis Anne purposely left stuff out on the bureau, knowing I would see it and read it, knowing it would make me suffer. Well, perhaps she didn't do it on purpose; but the bitterness of my grief must have been apparent to her, she must have seen how I mourned.

I had longed for that name change with my whole being—I had heard in the King's last name the *win* and *wind* and *soar* of Windsor— and it made me feel strong and free, an eagle, a lark, lifted high above the ground where my unimaginative family congealed around me, dull and hard as cement. Clement, cement, stuck in my name forever. I felt so weighted with sadness I could not bear to think of it, and tried to avoid facing the dreadful truth. Spurred by some self-preserving impulse I trudged off to the public library where I took books off shelves and flipped over pages, searching for something, anything to take me away from my life.

And by a chance as serendipitous as being discovered by Margaret Rose, one day I took from the top of a return cart an old novel by Zane Grey,[1] and within a few paragraphs found what I'd been looking for. The words seemed to blaze from the page, so vivid and real I could feel the heat from the small campfire against my face and the dark prairie night cold at my back. I knew, as deeply as anything I had ever experienced, what it was to ride for hours across sand blowing with tumbleweed, through the cactus and the sagebrush and up into the purple hills, riding and riding and riding. And I turned to the Wild West with a passion.

It was only a small step from those novels to the cowboy comic books and movies suddenly surrounding me—how had I never noticed them before? Waiting for me, as if they'd known I'd be coming just at that moment, were Roy Rogers and Dale Evans, King and Queen of the Cowboys. They welcomed me into their movies—I spent every cent of my allowance on the Saturday matinees, often the only girl for rows around—and met me once a week on the little brown radio, which I was allowed to take upstairs for the precious half hour of the Roy Rogers Show. I would lie on the bed looking up at the ceiling where my imagination brought me the unfolding adventures of Roy and Dale. And I always took the radio back down to the kitchen feeling calm and contented, prepared to ride along my own happy trails until, next week, I would meet them again.

The universe expanded, allowing me to accompany Roy's sidekick Pat Brady in his jeep Nellybelle, but in no time I found myself riding my own palomino, Golden Girl, just a little behind Roy and Trigger. Often he would turn toward me rather than to Dale or Pat when things got tough and he needed a hand. Almost overnight I became a rip-snorting cowgirl who never rode sissy sidesaddle, who could blast the eyes out of a rattlesnake with her six-shooter, who was vigilant in her defence of justice out there on the lone prairie. Roy and Dale said they didn't know how they'd ever managed before I came along, and I wondered myself as well.

My mutable soul transformed itself in all that sunshine and fresh air and my allegiance transferred itself—effortlessly, painlessly—from one king to another. The hot dry winds of the desert swept away the park

[1] Prolific and popular writer, best known for *The Last of the Plainsmen* (1908) and *Riders of the Purple Sage* (1912), Grey was one of the chief architects of the American Western.

bench where Margaret Rose had found me; even Buckingham Palace receded into the distant fog. It had been easier to believe that things were all of a piece when King George was on the throne—England, Canada, Canada, England, hardly any difference, really—but now with Elizabeth up there, well, things weren't the same any more.

I didn't care. Once I discovered riding the range I was no longer waiting to be adopted in order to make life happen. I was becoming tough, brave, independent, and prickly as a cactus. Maybe even a little dangerous. I was growing up. The Palace, if it ever did come to mind, seemed an awfully dull and confining place compared to sleeping out under the stars and listening to the coyotes howl.

One day, as I was riding on ahead of Roy and the sheriff's posse to show them the way, the entire Royal Family slipped into the cold grey ocean separating their little island from the land of the free. They vanished from my thoughts as completely as if they had drowned, they dissolved into the mists of time with the ghost of King George. I kept on riding into the wind and left all my old dreams behind—I had to git along, I couldn't look back.

Only now, all these years later, do I wish I'd turned to say good-bye.

—1993

Thomas King   b. 1943

In delivering the Massey lectures for CBC Radio, published as The Truth about Stories: A Native Narrative *(2003), Thomas King said: "The truth about stories is that that's all we are." A writer of short stories, as well as novels, drama, and a comic radio series* (Dead Dog Cafe Comedy Hour), *and also an editor and professor of English, King, who is of Cherokee and German descent, has explored North American Native traditions with comedy and compassion, seeking to bring the power of oral narratives into the contemporary era. His work was particularly affected by his discovery of Harry Robinson's stories, but he draws widely on Native and non-Native culture, whether it is manifested in oral storytelling, visual art, popular culture, literature, history, or myth.*

Employing the Native trickster figure also seen in Robinson's "Coyote Tricks Owl," King creates, in "The One about Coyote Going West," a tale in which old elements are honoured, while handled in a radically new way. Playing freely with

*the traditional Native tale of Coyote and the dancing ducks, this story challenges
European history and myth. Intentionally disorienting, it opens with a frame tale in
which Coyote and an I-narrator begin to tell stories to one another, and in which the
narrator then tries to distract Coyote from her planned trip west by telling a story
about the first Coyote going west.*

The One about Coyote Going West

This one is about Coyote. She was going west. Visiting her relations. That's
what she said. You got to watch that one. Tricky one. Full of bad business.
No, no, no, no, that one says. I'm just visiting. Going to see Raven.

Boy, I says. That's another tricky one.

Coyote comes by my place. She wag her tail. Make them happy
noises. Sit on my porch. Look around. With them teeth. With that smile.
Coyote put her nose in my tea. My good tea.

Get that nose out of my tea, I says.

I'm going to see my friends, she says. Tell those stories. Fix this
world. Straighten it up.

Oh boy, pretty scary that, Coyote fix the world, again.

Sit down, I says. Eat some food. Hard work that, fix up the world.
Maybe you have a song. Maybe you have a good joke.

Sure, says Coyote. That one wink her ears. Lick her whiskers.

I tuck my feet under that chair. Got to hide my toes. Sometimes that
tricky one leave her skin sit in that chair. Coyote skin. No Coyote. Sneak
around. Bite them toes. Make you jump.

I been reading those books, she says.

You must be one smart Coyote, I says.

You bet, she says.

Maybe you got a good story for me, I says.

I been reading about that history, says Coyote. She sticks that nose
back in my tea. All about who found us Indians.

Ho, I says. I like those old ones. Them ones are the best. You tell me
your story, I says. Maybe some biscuits will visit us. Maybe some moose-
meat stew come along, listen to your story.

Okay, she says and she sings her story song.

Snow's on the ground the snakes are asleep.
Snow's on the ground my voice is strong.
Snow's on the ground the snakes are asleep.
Snow's on the ground my voice is strong.

She sings like that. With that tail, wagging. With that smile. Sitting there.

Maybe I tell you the one about Eric The Lucky and the Vikings play hockey for the Oldtimers, find us Indians in Newfoundland, she says. Maybe I tell you the one about Christopher Cartier looking for something good to eat. Find us Indians in a restaurant in Montreal. Maybe I tell you the one about Jacques Columbus come along that river. Indians waiting for him. We all wave and say here we are, here we are.

Everyone knows those stories, I says. Whiteman stories. Baby stories you got in your mouth.

No, no, no, no, says that Coyote. I read these ones in that old book.

Ho, I says. You are trying to bite my toes. Everyone knows who found us Indians. Eric The Lucky and that Christopher Cartier and that Jacques Columbus come along later. Those ones get lost. Float about. Walk around. Get mixed up. Ho, ho, ho, ho, those ones cry, we are lost. So we got to find them. Help them out. Feed them. Show them around. Boy, I says. Bad mistake that one.

You are very wise grandmother, says Coyote, bring her eyes down, like she is sleepy. Maybe you know who discovered Indians.

Sure, I says. Everyone knows that. It was Coyote. She was the one.

Oh, grandfather, that Coyote says. Tell me that story. I love those stories about that sneaky one. I don't think I know that story, she says.

Alright, I says. Pay attention.

Coyote was heading west. That's how I always start this story. There was nothing else in this world. Just Coyote. She could see all the way, too. No mountains then. No rivers then. No forests then. Pretty flat then. So she starts to make things. So she starts to fix this world.

This is exciting, says Coyote, and she takes her nose out of my tea.

Yes, I says. Just the beginning, too. Coyote got a lot of things to make.

Tell me, grandmother, says Coyote. What does the clever one make first?

Well, I says. Maybe she makes that tree grows by the river. Maybe she makes that buffalo. Maybe she makes that mountain. Maybe she makes them clouds.

Maybe she makes that beautiful rainbow, says Coyote.

No, I says. She don't make that thing. Mink makes that.

Maybe she makes that beautiful moon, says Coyote.

No, I says. She don't do that either. Otter finds that moon in a pond later on.

Maybe she make the oceans with that blue water, says Coyote.

No, I says. Oceans are already here. She don't do any of that. The first thing Coyote makes, I tell Coyote, is a mistake.

Boy, Coyote sit up straight. Them eyes pop open. That tail stop wagging. That one swallow that smile.

Big one, too, I says. Coyote is going west thinking of things to make. That one is trying to think of everything to make at once. So she don't see that hole. So she falls in that hole. Then those thoughts bump around. They run into each other. Those ones fall out of Coyote's ears. In that hole.

Ho, that Coyote cries. I have fallen into a hole, I must have made a mistake. And she did.

So there is that hole. And there is that Coyote in that hole. And there is that big mistake in that hole with Coyote. Ho, says that mistake. You must be Coyote.

That mistake is real big and that hole is small. Not much room. I don't want to tell you what that mistake looks like. First mistake in the world. Pretty scary. Boy, I can't look, I got to close my eyes. You better close your eyes, too, I tell Coyote.

Okay, I'll do that, she says, and she puts her hands over her eyes. But she don't fool me. I can see she's peeking.

Don't peek, I says.

Okay, she says. I won't do that.

Well you know, that Coyote thinks about the hole. And she thinks about how she's going to get out of that hole. She thinks how she's going to get that big mistake back in her head.

Say, says that mistake. What is that you're thinking about?

I'm thinking of a song, says Coyote. I'm thinking of a song to make this hole bigger.

That's a good idea, says that mistake. Let me hear your hole song.

But that's not what Coyote sings. She sings a song to make the mistake smaller. But that mistake hears her. And that mistake grabs Coyote's nose. And that one pulls off her mouth so she can't sing. And that one jumps up and down on Coyote until she is flat. Then that one leaps out of that hole, wanders around looking for things to do.

Well, Coyote is feeling pretty bad all flat her nice fur coat full of stomp holes. So she thinks hard, and she thinks about a healing song. And she tries to sing a healing song, but her mouth is in other places. So she thinks harder and tries to sing that song through her nose. But that nose don't make any sound, just drip a lot. She tries to sing that song out her ears, but those ears don't hear anything.

So, that silly one thinks real hard and tries to sing out her butt hole. Pssst! Pssst! That is what that butt hole says, and right away things don't smell so good in that hole. Pssst.

Boy, Coyote thinks. Something smells.

That Coyote lies there flat and practice and practice. Pretty soon, maybe two days, maybe one year, she teach that butt hole to sing. That song. That healing song. So that butt hole sings that song. And Coyote begins to feel better. And Coyote don't feel so flat anymore. Pssst! Pssst! Things smell pretty bad, but Coyote is okay.

That one look around in that hole. Find her mouth. Put that mouth back. So, she says to that butt hole. Okay, you can stop singing now. You can stop making them smells now. But, you know, that butt hole is liking all that singing, and so that butt hole keeps on singing.

Stop, says Coyote. You are going to stink up the whole world. But it don't. So Coyote jumps out of that hole and runs across the prairies real fast. But that butt hole follows her. Pssst. Pssst. Coyote jumps into a lake, but that butt hole don't drown. It just keeps on singing.

Hey, who is doing all that singing, someone says.

Yes, and who is making that bad smell, says another voice.

It must be Coyote, says a third voice.

Yes, says a fourth voice. I believe it is Coyote.

That Coyote sit in my chair, put her nose in my tea, say, I know who that voice is. It is that big mistake playing a trick. Nothing else is made yet.

No, I says. That mistake is doing other things.

Then those voices are spirits, says Coyote.

No, I says. Them voices belong to them ducks.

Coyote stand up on my chair. Hey, she says, where did them ducks come from?

Calm down, I says. This story is going to be okay. This story is doing just fine. This story knows where it is going. Sit down. Keep your skin on. So.

Coyote look around, and she see them four ducks. In that lake. Ho, she says. Where did you ducks come from? I didn't make you yet.

Yes, says them ducks. We were waiting around, but you didn't come. So we got tired of waiting. So we did it ourselves.

I was in a hole, says Coyote.

Pssst. Pssst.

What's that noise, says them ducks. What's that bad smell?

Never mind, says Coyote. Maybe you've seen something go by. Maybe you can help me find something I lost. Maybe you can help me get it back.

Those ducks swim around and talk to themselves. Was it something awful to look at?

Yes, says Coyote, it certainly was.

Was it something with ugly fur?

Yes, says Coyote. I think it had that, too.

Was it something that made a lot of noise, ask them ducks.

Yes, it was pretty noisy, says Coyote.

Did it smell bad, them ducks want to know.

Yes, says Coyote. I guess you ducks have seen my something.

Yes, says them ducks. It is right there behind you.

So that Coyote turn around, and there is nothing there.

It's still behind you, says those ducks.

So Coyote turn around again but she don't see anything.

Pssst! Pssst!

Boy, says those ducks. What a noise! What a smell! They say that, too. What an ugly thing with all that fur!

Never mind, says that Coyote again. That is not what I'm looking for. I'm looking for something else.

Maybe you're looking for Indians, says those ducks.

Well, that Coyote is real surprised because she hasn't created Indians, either. Boy, says that one, mischief is everywhere. This world is getting bent.

Alright.

So Coyote and those ducks are talking, and pretty soon they hear a noise. And pretty soon there is something coming. And those ducks says, oh, oh, oh, oh. They say that like they see trouble, but it is not trouble. What comes along is a river.

Hello, says that river. Nice day. Maybe you want to take a swim. But Coyote don't want to swim, and she looks at that river and she looks at that river again. Something's not right here, she says. Where are those rocks? Where are those rapids? What did you do with them waterfalls? How come you're so straight?

And Coyote is right. That river is nice and straight and smooth without any bumps or twists. It runs both ways, too, not like a modern river.

We got to fix this, says Coyote, and she does. She puts some rocks in that river, and she fixes it so it only runs one way. She puts a couple of waterfalls in and makes a bunch of rapids where things get shallow fast.

Coyote is tired with all this work, and those ducks are tired just watching. So that Coyote sits down. So she closes her eyes. So she puts her nose in her tail. So those ducks shout, wake up, wake up! Something big is heading this way! And they are right.

Mountain come sliding along, whistling. Real happy mountain. Nice and round. This mountain is full of grapes and other good things to eat. Apples, peaches, cherries. Howdy-do, says that polite mountain, nice day for whistling.

Coyote looks at that mountain, and that one shakes her head. Oh no, she says, this mountain is all wrong. How come you're so nice and round. Where are those craggy peaks? Where are all them cliffs? What happened to all that snow? Boy, we got to fix this thing, too. So she does.

Grandfather, grandfather, says that Coyote, sit in my chair put her nose in my tea. Why is that Coyote changing all those good things?

That is a real sly one, ask me that question. I look at those eyes. Grab them ears. Squeeze that nose. Hey, let go my nose, that Coyote says.

Okay, I says. Coyote still in Coyote skin. I bet you know why Coyote change that happy river. Why she change that mountain sliding along whistling.

No, says that Coyote, look around my house, lick her lips, make them baby noises.

Maybe it's because she is mean, I says.

Oh no, says Coyote. That one is sweet and kind.

Maybe it's because that one is not too smart.

Oh no, says Coyote. That Coyote is very wise.

Maybe it's because she made a mistake.

Oh no, says Coyote. She made one of those already.

Alright, I says. Then Coyote must be doing the right thing. She must be fixing up the world so it is perfect.

Yes, says Coyote. That must be it. What does that brilliant one do next?

Everyone knows what Coyote does next, I says. Little babies know what Coyote does next.

Oh no, says Coyote. I have never heard this story. You are a wonderful storyteller. You tell me your good Coyote story.

Boy, you got to watch that one all the time. Hide them toes.

Well, I says. Coyote thinks about that river. And she thinks about that mountain. And she thinks somebody is fooling around. So she goes looking around. She goes looking for that one who is messing up the world.

She goes to the north, and there is nothing. She goes to the south, and there is nothing there either. She goes to the east, and there is still nothing there. She goes to the west, and there is a pile of snow tires.

And there is some televisions. And there is some vacuum cleaners. And there is a bunch of pastel sheets. And there is an air humidifier. And there is a big mistake sitting on a portable gas barbecue reading a book. Big book. Department store catalog.

Hello, says that mistake. Maybe you want a hydraulic jack.

No, says that Coyote. I don't want one of them. But she don't tell that mistake what she wants because she don't want to miss her mouth again. But when she thinks about being flat and full of stomp holes, that butt hole wakes up and begins to sing. Pssst. Pssst.

What's that noise, says that big mistake.

I'm looking for Indians, says that Coyote real quick. Have you seen any? What's that bad smell?

Never mind, says Coyote. Maybe you have some Indians around here.

I got some toaster ovens, says that mistake.

We don't need that stuff, says Coyote. You got to stop making all those things. You're going to fill up this world.

Maybe you want a computer with a color monitor. That mistake keeps looking through that book and those things keep landing in piles all around Coyote.

Stop, stop, cries Coyote. Golf cart lands on her foot. Golf balls bounce off her head. You got to give me that book before the world gets lopsided.

These are good things, says that mistake. We need these things to make up the world. Indians are going to need this stuff.

We don't have any Indians, says that Coyote.

And that mistake can see that that's right. Maybe we better make some Indians, says that mistake. So that one looks in that catalog, but it don't have any Indians. And Coyote don't know how to do that either. She has already made four things.

I've made four things already, she says. I got to have help.

We can help, says some voices and it is those ducks come swimming along. We can help you make Indians, says that white duck. Yes, we can do that, says that green duck. We have been thinking about this, says that blue duck. We have a plan, says that red duck.

Well, that Coyote don't know what to do. So she tells the ducks to go ahead because this story is pretty long and it's getting late and everyone wants to go home.

You still awake, I says to Coyote. You still here?

Oh yes, grandmother, says Coyote. What do those clever ducks do?

So I tell Coyote that those ducks lay some eggs. Ducks do that you know. That white duck lay an egg, and it is blue. That red duck lay an egg, and it is green. That blue duck lay an egg, and it is red. That green duck lay an egg, and it is white.

Come on, says those ducks. We got to sing a song. We got to do a dance. So they do. Coyote and that big mistake and those four ducks dance around the eggs. So they dance and sing for a long time, and pretty soon Coyote gets hungry.

I know this dance, she says, but you got to close your eyes when you do it or nothing will happen. You got to close your eyes tight. Okay, says those ducks. We can do that. And they do. And that big mistake closes its eyes, too.

But Coyote, she don't close her eyes, and all of them start dancing again, and Coyote dances up close to that white duck, and she grabs that white duck by her neck.

When Coyote grabs that duck, that duck flaps her wings, and that big mistake hears the noise and opens them eyes. Say, says that big mistake, that's not the way the dance goes.

By golly, you're right, says Coyote, and she lets that duck go. I am getting it mixed up with another dance.

So they start to dance again. And Coyote is very hungry, and she grabs that blue duck, and she grabs his wings, too. But Coyote's stomach starts to make hungry noises, and that mistake opens them eyes and sees Coyote with the blue duck. Hey, says that mistake, you got yourself mixed up again.

That's right, says Coyote, and she drops that duck and straightens out that neck. It sure is good you're around to help me with this dance.

They all start that dance again, and, this time, Coyote grabs the green duck real quick and tries to stuff it down that greedy throat, and there is nothing hanging out but them yellow duck feet. But those feet are flapping in Coyote's eyes, and she can't see where she is going, and she bumps into the big mistake and the big mistake turns around to see what has happened.

Ho, says that big mistake, you can't see where you're going with them yellow duck feet flapping in your eyes, and that mistake pulls that green duck out of Coyote's throat. You could hurt yourself dancing like that.

You are one good friend, look after me like that, says Coyote.

Those ducks start to dance again, and Coyote dances with them, but that red duck says, we better dance with one eye open, so we can help Coyote with this dance. So they dance some more, and then, those eggs begin to move around, and those eggs crack open. And if you look hard, you can see something inside those eggs.

I know, I know, says that Coyote jump up and down on my chair, shake up my good tea. Indians come out of those eggs. I remember this story, now. Inside those eggs are the Indians Coyote's been looking for.

No, I says. You are one crazy Coyote. What comes out of those duck eggs are baby ducks. You better sit down, I says. You may fall and hurt yourself. You may spill my tea. You may fall on top of this story and make it flat.

Where are the Indians, says that Coyote. This story was about how Coyote found the Indians. Maybe the Indians are in the eggs with the baby ducks.

No, I says, nothing in those eggs but little baby ducks. Indians will be along in a while. Don't lose your skin.

So.

When those ducks see what has come out of the eggs, they says, boy, we didn't get that quite right. We better try that again. So they do. They lay them eggs. They dance that dance. They sing that song. Those eggs crack open and out comes some more baby ducks. They do this seven times and each time, they get more ducks.

By golly, says those four ducks. We got more ducks than we need. I guess we got to be the Indians. And so they do that. Before Coyote or that big mistake can mess things up, those four ducks turn into Indians, two women and two men. Good-looking Indians, too. They don't look at all like ducks anymore.

But those duck-Indians aren't too happy. They look at each other and they begin to cry. This is pretty disgusting, they says. All this ugly skin. All these bumpy bones. All this awful black hair. Where are our nice soft feathers? Where are our beautiful feet? What happened to our wonderful wings? It's probably all that Coyote's fault because she didn't do the dance right, and those four duck-Indians come over and stomp all over Coyote until she is flat like before. Then they leave. That big mistake leave, too. And that Coyote, she starts to think about a healing song.

Pssst. Pssst.

That's it, I says. It is done.

But what happens to Coyote, says Coyote. That wonderful one is still flat.

Some of these stories are flat, I says. That's what happens when you try to fix this world. This world is pretty good all by itself. Best to leave it alone. Stop messing around with it.

I better get going, says Coyote. I will tell Raven your good story. We going to fix this world for sure. We know how to do it, now. We know how to do it right.

So, Coyote drinks my tea and that one leave. And I can't talk anymore because I got to watch the sky. Got to watch out for falling things that land in piles. When that Coyote's wandering around looking to fix things, nobody in this world is safe.

—1993

Bronwen Wallace 1945–1989

The compassion exhibited in Bronwen Wallace's career as a political and social activist (she campaigned for workers' and women's rights and worked for a time in a shelter for battered women) is evident in the deep-felt humanity that pervades her writing. Before completing her single collection of short stories, People You'd Trust Your Life To *(published posthumously in 1990), Wallace had established her reputation, in five books of poetry, as an author of witty and touching anecdotal poems. Both poems and stories leave us feeling as if someone were talking directly to us as readers, someone sitting across a table perhaps, having a cup of tea, and filling us in on recent events. This familiar, almost chatty, quality of Wallace's writing and poetry is the product of her keen ear for speech rhythms and her ability to capture the dialogic nature of human interactions. Wallace took as a credo the American writer Jessamyn West's observation that "fiction reveals truths that reality obscures." One of the truths Wallace offers for her readers' consideration is the suggestion in "For Puzzled in Wisconsin" that we must learn to love the pasts we carry forward into the present.*

For Puzzled in Wisconsin

Dear Allie: My husband has an intricate tattoo on his chest. I am very fond of it, and don't want to see it go with him when he dies.

I'm wondering if there is a way to have it taken off and preserved somehow at the time of his passing. Is this against the law? If not, who would look after this sort of thing, should it be possible: a taxidermist, the funeral director, or someone else?

My husband enjoys the best of health now, but I'd like to know what your answer is so that I can prepare myself.

—Puzzled in Wisconsin

My daughter reads me your letter, laughing.

"Do you believe this?" she says, in the voice she has for the tabloids at the checkout at Loblaws. "Baby Born Repeating Message from Aliens!" "I Saw My Husband Snatched by a Mermaid."

"Do you believe this!" Not a question, of course, since for her the answer is obvious.

After she goes off to do her homework, I pick up the paper and read your letter through again, two or three times, until I can see you there at your kitchen table writing it. Beside you is a coffee mug and a pack of Player's Light. The mug says I ♥ my mutt and there's a picture on it of a dog like the one that's lying by the door watching you.

You're just about due for a perm and a rinse. Your hair's showing grey at the roots, greyer than mine, I think, but fine like mine and straggly. Faded blonde, like your skin, which is dry and washed-out looking under your blush and your blue eye shadow.

When your husband gets off work tonight—he's on afternoons this week—the letter will be in your purse, which is on the sideboard in the dining room. I can see you in the living room with your bathrobe on, watching "Johnny Carson." Your husband usually brings home a pizza or some Chinese and you both have a couple of beers. Then he'll start sucking on your earlobe or tickling your breasts. It's fun, not having to worry anymore about the kids hearing. Your baby, Tommy, moved out on his own three months ago.

At this point, your husband pulls his T-shirt off. You like to run your tongue over his tattoo. Sometimes, that's all you do. Sometimes, that's just for starters.

Dear Puzzled: Ask the funeral director when the time comes. He (or she) will be able to answer your questions. In the meantime, perhaps someone who knows will see this and let me know if anything of the sort has been done before, and, if so, how they handled it.

I, too, am puzzled.

Well, she didn't exactly bust her ass trying to find an answer, did she? *I, too, am puzzled.* When you read that out loud it sounds kind of snotty, as if she thinks this can't be serious. *When the time comes . . .* Oh, brilliant. When the time comes you'll have a million other things on your mind. The boys'll make fun of you, the undertaker will pat you on the arm and say: "There, there, you're just upset." It gets you upset, all right, just thinking about it.

Your husband just thinks you're weird. "But what the hell," he says, "go ahead if you want to. They're already gonna take my eyes and my liver. Might as well have my tattoo, too."

He doesn't know about the letter, of course. He never reads "Dear Allie." "They just make that shit up," he says, "to sell papers."

The summer I was eighteen, I worked as a waitress at the Bangor Lodge in Muskoka. Most of the other waitresses were girls like me, just finished high school, earning money for university in the fall, but the cooking staff were all local, from Bracebridge or Huntsville. They worked there every summer and on into the off-season after the rest of us left. Most of them were women my mother's age, except for the girl who did the salads and the bread baskets and stuff.

Gwen MacIntyre. She was my age, though she looked older. Short and busty with thick black hair and huge violet eyes. Like Liz Taylor, of course, and she emphasized that, piling her hair up in thick curls and wearing lots of dark eyeliner. On her it was okay, too. She really was beautiful, just as Liz herself was beautiful, temporarily, but perfectly, before she got all bloated and silly.

Usually the waitresses didn't hang around much with the kitchen staff, but Gwen and I soon found we had something in common. Our boyfriends both worked in Toronto. Gwen's boyfriend, Chuck, was a welder; my boyfriend, Jeff, was working at a paint factory for the summer.

"I suppose he's comin' up on the weekend, eh?" Gwen asked, though she didn't really put it as a question. It was just sort of assumed. She'd already told me that Chuck came up every Saturday.

"Probably not, actually." I tried to sound casual, but I felt, somehow, apologetic. "He doesn't have a car."

"Well, why didn't you say so? He can drive up with Chuck and we can do something together. It'll be great."

That night, Gwen phoned Chuck to tell him the plan.

"He'll pay half the gas," she said, which is what we'd agreed she'd say, "and he can get over to your place, easy. All you have to do is call him up and introduce yourself. Anna's gonna call him first, right after I hang up. She's really nice, honey. It'll be great. See you Saturday. Bye, hon."

She always called him "honey" or "hon." He called her "babe." I couldn't imagine Jeff calling me anything.

"Jesus, I don't even know the guy," he kept saying. "Why didn't you call me first."

"If you don't want to come," I said after a few minutes of this, "don't bother." And I hung up, hard.

We were using the phone in the little office just off the kitchen where the cook made up the orders and paid the delivery men. You had to reverse the charges. There'd been a minute at the start when I thought Jeff wasn't going to accept and, now that I'd hung up, I realized he couldn't call me back. Even if he bothered to find out, the only number listed for the lodge was the front desk. They didn't take personal calls for staff.

Gwen was in the kitchen putting the last of the dishes in the dishwasher, but she didn't try to hide the fact that she was listening. As soon as I banged the phone down, she came to the door with a coffee and my cigarettes.

"Don't worry," she said, "he'll show up."

As it turned out, she was right. Jeff said he thought Chuck was a bit of an asshole, but he could stand it, so the summer was set. They both had to work Saturdays and, what with holiday traffic and all, they usually didn't get to the lodge before 9:30 or 10:00 p.m. By that time, we'd be pretty well finished. If I had a late table, Gwen'd help me set up for breakfast, though she wasn't supposed to.

Chuck had an old Ford pickup that his father had sold him for a dollar when he started working in Toronto. The passenger door was so rusted he'd had to weld it shut, so everyone piled in from the driver's side. By half past ten, we'd be heading out to a spot he knew about along the lake where there was a bit of a beach and no other cottages. We'd build a fire and sit around drinking beer and listening to Jeff's radio. After an hour or so, Chuck'd grab Gwen and say, "C'mon, babe, come and say hello to your old man," and they'd move off a ways into the little woods while Jeff and I stretched out by the fire.

The air was always hot and close and still. You could hear everything. Especially Chuck.

"Oh, babe!" he'd say. "Oh, babe!" And then louder and louder. "Oh, babe, oh, Gwennie, oh-h, oh-h, babe!" Then silence. Then it would start again.

Later, driving back to the lodge, I'd try to fit Chuck's face—which was broad and fair and sort of *eager*, I guess, but in the way a kid's face is eager, one front tooth chipped, the other missing—to the sounds I heard in the woods, but I never could. It was like it never happened. Jeff never even let on, but one night, just as he came inside me, he started whining in this forced, stupid whisper: "Oh, babe, oh, babe." I pushed him away and tried to stand up.

"Hey"—he held me—"c'mon. I was only fooling."

"Yeah, I know." I wanted to punch him, to hurt him in some way I knew I never could. I don't know why.

Jeff and I always used a safe, of course, but I knew for a fact, because she told me, that Gwen and Chuck never did. I wasn't surprised. There'd been lots of Gwens at my high school. I knew exactly what would happen.

By the end of August, Gwen was pregnant. Chuck was ecstatic. He even brought a bottle of champagne up the next weekend. He'd already found a bigger apartment. They planned to get married on the Labour Day weekend, though Gwen would go on working at the lodge until it closed in October. They could use the extra money.

Jeff and I used to talk about getting married, too, but it was just talk. He was going to Queen's, to med school, in the fall and he kept saying he wanted me to come there instead of going to Western. He talked about how a small apartment would be cheaper than residence.

Knowing what I know now, this would have meant my getting a part-time job to help with expenses, failing courses, getting pregnant and then finding out five years down the road that Jeff was in love with some night nurse and wanted a divorce. At the time, I just didn't like the way he kept kissing the back of my neck when I tried to talk about something I'd read or even about one of my customers.

"Is this what you really want to do?" I asked Gwen once.

She looked as if she thought I must be joking. "Of course. Don't you?"

That was all she said. I thought it was because she was too stupid to want anything else. I guess I saw her as a victim of her own life, forced into it because she hadn't been smart enough to plan ahead. I never even considered then that she might see me in the same light.

Peter, the man I *did* marry, sixteen years ago, is an archivist at the university. When our daughter read him your letter, he laughed with her, but for different reasons. He can believe it all right, some people are probably like that, he just doesn't think it has anything to do with him. When they laugh, both Peter and our daughter, Jennifer, dip their heads slightly to the side at precisely the same angle, mouths wide open, showing the same even teeth.

That night in bed, I ask Peter, "Is there anything like that of mine you'd want to save?"

"Like what?"

"You know, that 'Dear Allie' letter Jennifer read about the tattoo."

"Of course not; I'd never even think of it."

"Well, think about it now. *If* you were going to do something like that, what would you want? Some of my stretch marks? The mole on my left breast?"

"I can't imagine it, Anna. Really, this is silly."

He lies flat on his back, his hands at his sides, his eyes closed, his face set in the pained expression he wears for conversations like this—"What if's" speculations. When Jennifer and I sit in a restaurant making up stories about the people around us, he closes his eyes, just as he's doing now.

"Tightass. You never even try."

"I just can't, Anna. You know that. I don't know what you want me to do."

"I don't, either." I try to make it light, nonchalant. "Night." I kiss him lightly as I reach across him to turn off the lamp, then roll over as if to sleep. I don't want him to think I'm angry, it's just a silly game, after all.

I don't even want to *be* angry, dammit. It's not like he isn't imaginative. He is—about gifts, for example, and vacations. I don't think this other is something he can do anything about, and why should he? Once I asked him if he ever made up stories about the material at the archives, the people whose bits and pieces he sorts and labels.

"Of course not, Anna. I'd never get any work done."

And I can see what he means. His job is to organize the known world, after all. It's up to someone else to explore the rest. Why should I hold it against him?

But I do. Just because I understand doesn't mean it doesn't poke at me, niggling and sore, like the pea under all those mattresses in the fairy story.

After a few minutes, I get up and slip on my bathrobe. Peter, who can sleep through anything, doesn't move, even his breathing stays slow and regular.

Downstairs, the house has that smooth, mirror-like quality that always makes me feel like a figure in someone else's dream. I grab a glass and the bourbon and go out on the deck at the back. It's hot tonight. All the houses are open, relaxed, letting go of their secrets. A toilet flushes, a baby cries, a man's voice coaxes a cat inside. "Susie, c'mon now, Susie, come and see Daddy." It's not very often that I sit here, late like this, with my feet on the railing, drinking bourbon. I wish I had a cigarette. I wish I could stay up all night, drinking and smoking.

The first time I ever drank bourbon was with Gwen and Chuck and Jeff at Chuck's parents' house. The boys had come up one Saturday, as usual, but just as they pulled in, it started to rain, hard. We didn't know what to do.

"Hop in," Chuck said. "We'll go see my folks. They won't mind."

Chuck's parents, Roy and Joan, were sitting at the kitchen table when we came up to the back porch. Roy was an older version of Chuck with the same eager face, even the missing tooth. He was wearing a baggy pair of Bermuda shorts and a green T-shirt with ART'S ESSO in black across the chest. Joan was wearing shorts, too, white, with a white halter top and a man's plaid flannel shirt, open, over the whole thing. Her hair, which was dark brown (obviously, but gloriously dyed), was teased and piled into a high beehive. On her feet she had gold, high-heeled slippers.

They both jumped up as soon as they saw us.

"Hey there, Chuckie boy!" Roy shouted. "C'mon in outta the rain." He pulled chairs up around the table, while Joan brought over glasses and a forty-ouncer of bourbon.

"You're workin' with Gwen at the lodge then," she said, handing me a drink and holding out her pack of cigarettes.

"Yeah, in the dining room, though. I'm a waitress."

"Tips good?"

"Yeah, I guess so. I get about one hundred dollars a week."

"Shit!" Joan exhaled smoke sharply. "You hear that Roy? One hundred lousy bucks a week in tips at Bangor. Cheapskates. What you don't have to put up with, eh?"

She laughed, but even her laugh had an edge to it, angry, as if she were personally involved.

I took another sip of my bourbon. I'd never drunk liquor straight before. I was beginning to like the way it stung my tongue, burned my whole mouth frozen all the way down. One hundred a week in tips had seemed like a lot to me, but now I could see what Joan meant. I thought about how people's voices sounded when they gave their order, how they always stopped talking to each other when I came up to the table.

We sat around drinking and smoking for what seemed like hours. Food kept appearing. Some doughnuts Joan had made fresh that morning, salami and cheese, crackers, homemade pickles.

All of a sudden Roy leaned back in his chair and pulled his T-shirt up almost to his neck.

"What do ya think of this baby here?" he asked.

Across his middle, from his belt line to just below his left nipple was a wide, jagged, white scar. He had a lot of hair, but it hadn't grown back over the scar, which was thicker in some places than others. It glistened and bulged in the yellow kitchen light, stretched taut over his gut as if the skin couldn't take much more.

"Quite a mess, eh?" he said. "I used to be a guard at the Pen in Kingston, there. Had some trouble one night. One of the guys had a shank. Ripped me open in one swipe. Felt like he'd sliced my liver out. Next thing I know, I'm wakin' up in the hospital."

He took another swig of bourbon and lit a cigarette off the one he had going. "Turned out I lost a lot of blood, but that was about it. The guy missed every single vital organ. Can you believe it? Every single goddamn vital organ. The doctors said I was the luckiest sonofabitch they'd ever seen. I wanted to go right back as soon as the stitches were out, but Joan here, she said she couldn't take it, what with the kids and all, especially the nights. So I let 'er go. Ten years seniority, pension, the whole goddamn shot."

He let go of his shirt so that it dropped slightly and wrinkled around his gut. Nobody said anything, but it wasn't from embarrassment or shock or anything like that. It was more as if we weren't expected to.

Whenever I have told this story—and I have, many times—I always tell about Roy and the scar, of course, but it's just part of it, part of the story about that summer and about Gwen and Chuck (neither of whom I ever saw again, after the season ended, though we promised we'd visit), and about drinking bourbon all night. I tell about going out to drive back to the lodge and seeing the sky lightening over the trees and realizing that we'd been up all night, Gwen and me working all day Sunday, no sleep, hung-over and never giving it a thought. That's how the story ends when I've told it lately. How you can do it when you're young.

Not now though. So I haul myself off the deck, rinse the glass and tiptoe back upstairs. Peter doesn't wake up when I crawl into bed, but he says my name, out loud. "Anna." As if he were checking it off a list, some part of him still awake until everything's accounted for. He always does this and I always sort of like it, even though I'm still a little angry.

I'm just drifting off when I see something else. It's almost as if I'm watching a movie of the six of us in that kitchen, sitting around the table and the camera moves in all of a sudden, so that what I can see now is a close-up of Joan's hand, reaching out to Roy's bare gut, caressing it so intimately I can't believe she's doing it in front of us. And then, with the tip of her index finger, gently, very gently, she traces the scar, every turn and bulge, from Roy's nipple to his waist, as if to show us exactly what it's like.

As if his belly were a map, almost, and the scar was this road she was pointing out, wanting us to see where he'd been. And where she'd been, too. After he got out of the hospital, when he spent days just sitting there, staring, and she had to keep the kids quiet, not knowing what he was going to do next, what was going to happen to them. That was part of it. And more, that we could never know.

It's just for a minute that I see this, mind you, Joan's hand on Roy's scar like that. But it's what I would want to tell you, Puzzled in Wisconsin, if I ever had the chance, or knew how.

—1990

Jane Urquhart   b. 1949

Early in her career as a writer, Jane Urquhart published Storm Glass *(1987), a short story collection of delicate imagery. A fascination with visual art, also evident in her poems and novels, shapes both theme and technique in these stories.*

In "Italian Postcards," which comes from this volume, adults carry with them emotionally laden images acquired in childhood. What initially seems a simple infatuation with Italy (especially with Pompeii), begun when Clara was a young girl looking at postcards, becomes more complicated when she visits Assisi as an adult. There she learns about her namesake Saint Clare (Santa Chiara) and—in this story of layers, correspondences, and gradually emerging significances—tries to come to terms, within the real landscape she once so vividly imagined, with the effect St. Francis had on that woman's life.

Italian Postcard

Whenever she is sick, home from school, Clara the child is allowed to examine her mother's Italian postcards, a large pile of them, which are normally bound by a thick leather band and kept in a bureau drawer. Years later when she touches postcards she will be amazed that her hands are so large. Perhaps she feels that the hands of a child are proportionally correct to rest like book-ends on either side of land-scapes. Or maybe it's not that complicated; maybe she just feels that, as an adult, she can't really see these colours, those vistas, and so, in the odd moments when she does, she must necessarily be a child again.

The room she lies in on weekdays, when she has managed to stay home from school, is all hers. She'll probably carry it around with her for the rest of her life. Soft grey wallpaper with sprays of pink apple blossom. Pink dressing-table (under the skirts of which her dolls hide, resting on their little toy beds), cretonne curtains swathed over a window at the foot of the bed she occupies, two or three pink pillows propping her up. Outside the window a small back garden and some winter city or another. It doesn't really matter which.

And then the postcards: turquoise, fuchsia, lime green—improbable colours placed all over the white spread and her little hands picking up one, then another, and her little mind trying to imagine her mother walking through such passionate surroundings.

In time, her mother appears at the side of the bed. Earlier in the morning she has brought the collection of postcards. Now she holds a concoction of mustard and water wrapped in white flannel and starts to undo the little buttons on the little pyjama top.

While the mustard plaster burns into her breastbone Clara continues to look at the postcards. Such flowers, such skies, such suns burning down on such perfect seas. Her mother speaks the names of foreign towns; *Sorrento*, she says, *Capri, Fiesole, Garda, Como*, and then after a thoughtful pause, *You should see Como. But most of all you should see Pompeii.*

Clara always saves Pompeii, however, until the end—until after her mother has removed the agonizing poultice and has left the room—until after she has gone down the stairs and has resumed her orderly activities in the kitchen. Then the child allows the volcano to erupt, to spill molten lava all over the suburban villas, the naughty frescos, the religious mosaics. And all over the inhabitants of the unsuspecting ancient town.

In the postcards Pompeii is represented, horrifyingly, fascinatingly, by the inhabitants themselves, frozen in such attitudes of absolute terror or complete despair that the child learns everything she needs to know from them about heartbreak and disaster: how some will put their arms up in front of their faces to try to ward it off, how others will resign themselves, sadly, to its strength. What she doesn't understand is how such heat can freeze, make permanent, the moment of most intense pain. A scream in stone that once was liquid. What would happen, she wonders, to these figures if the volcano were to erupt again? How permanent are they?

And she wonders about the archaeologists who have removed the stone bodies from the earth and, without disturbing a single gesture, have placed them in glass display cases inside the museum where they seem to float in the air of their own misfortune—clear now, the atmosphere empty of volcanic ash, the glass polished.

These are the only postcards of Pompeii that Clara's mother has. No bright frescos, no recently excavated villas, no mosaics; only these clear cases full of grey statues made from what was once burning flesh.

Twenty-five years later when Clara stands with her husband at the entrance to Hotel Oasie in Assisi she has seen Sorrento, Como, Capri and has avoided Pompeii altogether.

"Why not?" her husband asks.

"Nobody lives there," she replies.

But people live here, in this Tuscan hill town; the sun has burned life into their faces. And the colours in the postcards were real after all—they spill out from red walls into the vegetable displays on the street, they flash by on the backs of over-dressed children. Near the desk of the hotel they shout out from travel posters. But in this space there is no sun; halls of cool remote marble, sparse furnishings, and, it would seem, no guests but themselves.

"Dinner," the man behind the desk informs them, "between seven and nine in the big salon."

Then he leads them, through arched halls, to the room.

Clara watches the thick short back of the Italian as she walks behind him, realizing as she does, that it is impossible to imagine muscle tone when it is covered by smooth black cloth. She looks at the back of his squarish head. Cumbersome words such as *Basilica, portcullis, Etruscan,* and *Vesuvius* rumble disturbingly, and for no apparent reason, through her mind.

Once the door has clicked behind them and the echoing footsteps of the desk clerk have disappeared from the outside hall, her husband examines the two narrow beds with displeasure and shrugs.

"Perhaps we'll find a way," he says, "marble floors are cold." Then looking down, "Don't think these small rugs will help much."

Then, before she can reply, they are both distracted by the view outside the windows. Endless olive groves and vineyards and a small cemetery perched halfway up the hill. Later in the evening, after they have eaten pasta and drunk rough, red wine in the enormous empty dining-room, they will see little twinkling lights shine up from this spot, like a handful of stars on the hillside. Until that moment it will never have occurred to either of them that anyone would want to light a tomb at night.

> *Go and light a tomb at night*
> *Get with child a mandrake root.*[1]

Clara is thinking Blake—in Italy of all places, wandering through the empty halls of Hotel Oasie, secretly inspecting rooms. All the same so far: narrow cots, tiny rugs, views of vineyards and the graveyard, olive

---

[1] This second line is from John Donne's early seventeenth-century poem, "Song: Go and Catch a Falling Star," a light complaint about the unfaithfulness of women. The first line recalls the work of several poets of the Graveyard School (the designation given to a group of eighteenth-century poets who wrote extensively about mortality and tombs). Clara's thoughts may therefore turn to Blake because he illustrated two of the best-known works of that school, Edward Young's *Night Thoughts* and Robert Blair's *The Grave.*

trees. Plain green walls. These rooms, she thinks, as Blake evaporates from her mind, these rooms could use the services of *Mr. Domado's Wallpaper Company*, a company with one employee—the very unhappy *Mr. Domado himself.* He papered her room once when she was a sick child and he was sick with longing for his native land. When Italian postcards coincidentally littered her bedspread like fallen leaves, *Ah yes,* said Mr. Domado, sadly picking up one village and then another. *Ah yes.*

And he could sing—Italian songs. Arias that sounded as mournful as some of the more lonely villages looked. Long, long sobbing notes trembling in the winter sunshine, while she lay propped on pink pillows and her mother crept around in the kitchen below silently preparing mustard plasters. Mr. Domado with tears in his voice, eliminating spray after spray of pink apple blossoms, replacing them with rigid geometric designs, while Clara studied the open mouths of the stone Pompeii figures and wondered whether, at the moment of their death, they were praying out loud. Or whether they were simply screaming.

Screaming, she thinks now as she opens door after door of Hotel Oasie, would be practically a catastrophe in these echoing marble halls. One scream might go on for hours, as her footsteps seem to every time she moves twenty feet or so down to the next door, as the click of the latch seems to every time she has closed whatever door she has been opening. The doors are definitely an addition to the old, old building and appear to be pulled by some new longitudinal force back into the closed position after she releases her fingers from their cold, steel knobs. Until she opens the door labelled *Sala Beatico Angelico* after which no hotel room will ever be the same.

Neither Clara nor her husband speak Italian, so to ask for a complete explanation would be impossible.

"A Baroque church!" she tells him later. "Not a chapel but a complete church. All the doors are the same, *this* door is the same except for the words on it, and you open it and there, instead of a hotel room, is a complete church."

"It appears," he says after several moments of reflection, "that we have somehow checked into a monastery."

Sure enough when she takes herself out to the rose garden later in the afternoon to sit in the sun and read *The Little Flowers of Santa Chiara* in preparation for the next day's trip to the Basilica, the hotel clerk greets her, dressed now in a clerical collar. Clara shows no surprise, as if she had known all along that hers was not to be a secular vacation; as if the idea of a retreat had been in her mind when she planned the trip. She shifts the book a little so that the monastic gardener will notice that she is reading about St. Francis' holy female friend. He, however, is busy with roses; his own little flowers, and though he faces her while he works his glance never once meets hers. She is able, therefore, to observe him quite closely—the dark tan of his face over the white of his collar, his hands that move carefully, but easily, through the roses, avoiding thorns. Clara tries, but utterly fails, to imagine the thoughts of a priest working in a rose garden. Are they concerned, as they should be, with GOD, the thorns, perhaps, signifying a crown, the dark red stain of the flower turning in his mind to the blood of Christ? Or does he think only of roses and their health: methods of removing the insect from the leaf, the worm from the centre of the scarlet bud? His face gives her no clue; neither that nor the curve of his back as he stoops to remove yet another vagrant weed from the soft brown earth surrounding the bushes.

Clara turns again to her book, examining the table of contents: *The Circle of Ashes, The Face in the Well, The Hostage of Heaven, The Bread of Angels, The Meal in the Woods,* and finally, at the bottom of the list, *The Retinue of Virgins.* St. Francis, she discovers, had never wanted to see Chiara. The little stories made this perfectly clear. Sentence after sentence described his aversion. After he had clothed her in sackcloth and cut off all her hair in the dark of the Italian night, after he had set her on the path of poverty and had left her with her sisters at St. Damiens, after she had turned into a *hostage of heaven* and had given up eating altogether, Francis withdrew. *Beware of the poison of familiarity with women,* he had told his fellow friars. In a chapter entitled *The Roses,* the book stated that Francis had wanted to place an entire season between himself and Chiara. *We will meet again when the roses bloom,* he had said, standing with his bare feet in the snow. Then God had decided to make the roses bloom, spontaneously, right there, right then, in the middle of winter.

Clara cannot decide, now, what possible difference that would make. As a matter of fact, it looks to her as if God were merely playing a trick on Chiara and Francis. If Francis said they would meet again when the roses bloom, why not have the roses bloom right now? Perhaps then there would be no subsequent meeting since the roses had already bloomed. This would have certainly been a puzzle for Chiara to work on during the dreary winter days that stretched ahead of her in the unheated convent. She could work it over and over in her mind like a rosary. It might have kept her, in some ways, very busy.

Francis, on the other hand, was always very busy. As the book said: *Francis came and went freely from St. Mary of the Angels but Chiara found herself like a prisoner at St. Damiens.* Francis might have dropped by to see Chiara while he was out rushing around, but he didn't. *On the other hand, Francis stayed well away from St. Damiens,* the book continued, *for he did not wish the common people should take scandal from seeing him going in and out.* So basically, it would appear that poor Chiara, poison that she was, rarely spoke to her mentor, the man whose principles she built her life around. At least not until *The Meal in the Woods.*

After she had asked him repeatedly to share a meal with her, Francis finally relented. Speaking once again to his fellow friars (he seemed never to have spoken to Chiara), he argued, *She has been a long time at St. Damiens. She will be happy to come out for a little while and to see in the daytime that place to which she first came at night, where her hair was cut from her, and where she was received among us. In the name of Jesus Christ we will picnic in the woods.* Somehow, during the course of this unusual picnic, the woods began to glow as if they were on fire. It is not clear to Clara whether God or Francis was responsible for this miracle. It may have been a collaboration. It is perfectly clear, however, that Chiara had nothing to do with it. Her role was that of appreciator—one that she, no doubt, played very well. And, as usual, she wasn't eating. The chapter ends with this statement: *Finally Chiara and Francis rose from the ground, overjoyed and filled with spiritual nourishment, not having touched as much as a crumb of the food.*

Clara is beginning to feel hungry. Delicious smells are coming from what she now knows is the refectory. The gardener is placing his tools, one by one, in the wheelbarrow. Then, without looking in her direction, he pushes the little vehicle away from her, toward the potting-shed.

"Our hotel clerk," she informs her husband at dinner, "is a gardener as well as a priest. I was reading up on my namesake out on the terrace and I saw him in the garden, working away."

"I discovered the other part of the building," her husband replies. "There is a glass door with *Keep Out* written on it in four languages, and then an entire wing where the priests must stay when they open the place to tourists."

"You didn't peek?" asks Clara, fully aware that, had she discovered it, she might have opened the door.

"No—written rules you know," and then, "Have you decided to like your namesake? Do you think you take after her?"

Clara reflects for a while. "I think she was a very unhappy woman. She kept on wanting to see Francis and he kept not wanting to see her."

"Probably just propriety, don't you think? You can't have Saint Francis spending a lot of time hanging around the convent you know, wouldn't look good."

"Possibly . . . but maybe it was just an excuse. Maybe he really *didn't* want to see her. The poor girl—she was in love with him, I expect. He was probably God to her."

"Maybe *he* was in love with her. Did that ever occur to you? Maybe that's why he stayed away." Her husband glances down to the end of the room. "Look who is coming," he says. "Our desk clerk is not only a gardener and a priest, he is also a waiter."

The next afternoon Clara decides she will not visit the Basilica after all. She would rather read in the rose garden than gaze at frescos.

"Later," she tells her husband. "You check it out, tell me about it."

Postcard views and skies are outside the walls of the hotel as usual, and now the closer, more exaggerated colours of the roses. It is hotter than the previous day so the priest has abandoned his collar. Clara notices that he has a perfect mole situated right in the centre of his throat. A sort of natural stigmata, she decides.

The chapter entitled *The Door of the Dead* is fascinating her. She is reading it for the fourth time. It seems that the ancient houses in Assisi often had two doors: a large one through which the family normally came and went, and a smaller one, elevated above the ground, through which the dead were passed, feet first in their coffins. Chiara, on the night she went to meet Francis in the woods, decided to leave the house through the second door. *She wanted to get away secretly*, the book states, *and she was absolutely sure she would meet no one on the threshold of that door.* With the help of a minor miracle on God's part she was able to slide bolts and move hinges that had been rusted in position for fifteen years. Then she jumped lightly to the ground and ran out of the village. *Never again would she be able to return to her family*; the chapter concludes. *Chiara was dead. Chiara was lost. Chiara had passed over into another life.*

Clara wonders if the priest, who is working directly in front of her, has also passed over into another life, and whether, if this is so, the roses look redder to him than they do to her. Whether he lives a sort of *Through the Looking Glass* existence.

She adjusts the angle of her chair. He is working close enough now that their shadows almost touch. A vague sadness stirs near Clara's heart, stops, then moves again. Restless lava shifting somewhere in the centre of a mountain.

Her husband has decided that they will stay at Hotel Oasie for the remainder of their vacation. He likes it there. He likes Assisi. He is moved by all of it, as much, he says, by the electrified confessionals in the Basilica as by the Giottos. He claims that the former are like the washrooms on a jumbo jet in that they have automatic *occupied* and *vacant* signs that are lighted from behind. He is amazed, he continues, at how easily the Italians have adapted their highly super-stitious religion to modern technology—the lighted tombs, the electric candles in front of religious statues, the *occupied* signs. This amuses and pleases him. He will write a sociological paper on it when they return to North America.

She isn't listening to him very carefully because she has fallen in love, just like that, bang, with the gardener, waiter, desk clerk, priest. She has, by now, spent four long afternoons with him in the rose garden and he has never once looked her way. Unless, she speculates, he looks her way when she is absorbed in *The Little Flowers of Santa Chiara*, which is possible. On the third afternoon she made up a little rule for herself that she would not lift her eyes from the book until a chapter was completely finished. In that way she has balanced her activities. Ten minutes of reading followed by ten minutes of studying the priest. This means, of course, that he is never in the same location after she finishes reading, say, *The Door of the Dead* as he was after she finished reading *A Kiss For the Servant*. She is then forced to look around for him, which makes the activity more intriguing. One afternoon, after finishing the chapter called *Infirmity and Suffering*, she looked up and around and discovered that he had disappeared completely, simply slipped away while she was reading. Almost every other time, though, she is able to watch him collect his tools, place them in the wheelbarrow and walk toward the potting-shed. And this makes her grieve a little, as one often does when a lengthy ritual has been appropriately completed.

"Did you know," she asks her husband angrily at dinner, "did you know that he wouldn't even let her come to see him when he was DYING? I mean, isn't that taking it a bit too far? The man was dying and she asked if she could see him and he said no, not until I'm *dead.* "

The priestly waiter serves the pasta. Clara watches his brown left hand approach the table and withdraw. "Scusi" he says as he places the dish in front of her. She cannot accuse him of never speaking to her. He has said "Scusi" in her presence now a total of seventeen times and once, when a meal was over, he had looked directly into her eyes and had asked, "You feeneesh?"

Now she stabs her fork deliberately into the flesh of the ravioli. "Moreover," she continues, "that little book I am reading has next to nothing to do with Chiara; mostly it's about Francis—until he dies, of course—then it's about her dying." Forgetting to chew, Clara swallows the little piece of pasta whole.

"Well," says her husband, "at least Giotto included her in some of the frescos."

"Hmm," she replies, decidedly unimpressed.

Clara gazes at the priest and her heart turns soft. He is staring absently into space. Imagining miracles, she decides, waiting out the tenure of the dinner hour so that he can return to his quiet activities. Evening mass, midnight mass. Lighting candles, saying prayers. Does he make them up or follow rituals? Are there beads involved? Does he kneel before male or female saints? Any of this information is important to her. Still, she would never dare enter the church she has discovered at the end of the hall. In fact, with the exception of the Basilica with its electrified confessionals and famous frescos, she has not dared to open the door of any church in town. They are spaces that are closed to her and she knows it.

"Have you ever felt that a church was closed to you?" she asks her husband.

"Of course not," he answers. "After all, they are not only religious institutions, they are great public monuments, great works of art. They are open to all of us."

Clara sighs and turns her eyes, once again, to the priest. The way he is carrying the crockery back to the kitchen, as if it were a collection of religious artifacts he has recently blessed, almost breaks her heart.

It is her fifth afternoon in the rose garden. He is there too, of course, pinning roses onto stakes. "Crucifying them perhaps," she thinks vaguely, lovingly.

By now she knows that this man will never EVER respond to her, never EVER speak to her; not in his language or hers—except at meal time when it is absolutely necessary. Because of this, the sadness of this, she loves him even harder. It is this continuous rejection that sets him apart. Rejection without object, without malice, a kind of healing rejection; one that causes a cleansing ache.

The ache washes over her now as she watches him stand back to survey his labours. She loves the way he just stands there looking, completely ignoring her. She is of absolutely no consequence in the story of his life, none whatsoever, and she loves him for this. She has no desire for change; no mediaeval fantasies about being the rose that he fumbles with, the Saint that he prays to. She wants him just as he is, oblivious to her, causing her to ache, causing her to understand the true dimensions of hopelessness, how they are infinite.

She turns to the chapter in the book called *The Papal Bull*. This is an oddly political section and her least favourite. It concerns the legitimization of the various Franciscan orders including Santa Chiara's Poor Sisters—the legitimization of lives of chosen self-denial. At this point Clara is finding it difficult to concentrate on what the Pope had to say, finds it difficult to care whether it was legitimate or not.

She is surprised, when she allows herself to look up, to find the priest's gaze aimed in her direction. She prepares to be embarrassed until she realizes that he is, at last, reading the title of her book.

"She wanted words from him," Clara tells her husband later. "Words, you know, spiritual advice. You know what she got instead?"

"What?"

"She got a circle of ashes—a circle of goddamn ashes! The book tries to make this seem profound; the usual, he put a circle of ashes on the convent floor to demonstrate that all humans were merely dust, or some such nonsense. You know what I think it meant? It think it meant that regardless of what Chiara wanted from him, regardless of how badly she might have wanted it, regardless of whether or not she ever swallowed a single morsel of food, or wore hairshirts, or humiliated herself in any number of ways, regardless of what she did, all she was EVER going to get from him was a circle of ashes. I think it meant that she was entirely powerless and he was going to make damn certain that she stayed that way."

"Quite a theory. I doubt the church would approve."

"God, how she must have suffered!"

"Well," he replies, "wasn't that what she was supposed to do?"

In the middle of her seventh afternoon in the rose garden, after she has finished reading a chapter entitled *The Canticle of the Creatures* (which she practically knows now by heart), and while she is studying the gestures of the priest who has moved from roses to vegetables, Clara decides that her heart is permanently broken. How long, she wonders, has it been this way? And why did it take this priest, this silent man who thinks and prays in a foreign language, to point it out to her. This is not a new disease, she knows suddenly. It's been there for a long, long time; a handicap she has managed to live with somehow, by completely ignoring it. How strange. Not to feel that pain that is always there by never identifying it, never naming it. Now she examines the wound and it burns in the centre of her chest the way her mother's mustard plasters used to, the way molten lava must have in the middle of Vesuvius. Her broken heart has burned inside her for so long she assumed it was normal. Now the pain of it moves into her whole body; past the pulse at her wrists, down the fronts of her thighs, up into her throat. Then it moves from there out into the landscape she can see from the garden, covering all of it, every detail; each grey, green olive leaf, each electric candle in front of each small pathetic tomb, every bird, all of the churches she can never enter, poppies shouting in a distant field, this terrible swath of blue sky overhead, the few pebbles that cover the small area of terrace at her feet. And all the air that moves up and down her throat until she is literally gasping in pain.

Pure eruption. Shards of her broken heart are everywhere, moving through her bloodstream, lacerating her internally on their voyage from the inside out into the landscape, until every sense is raw. She can actually see the sound waves that are moving in front of her. She wonders if she has begun to shout but then gradually, gradually, isolated sound dissolves into meaning as her brain begins its voyage back into the inside of her skull.

"Meesus," the priest is saying, pointing to her book. "She is still here, Santa Chiara. You go see her—you go to Chiesa Santa Chiara—you go there and you see her."

Then he collects his gardening tools, places them in his wheelbarrow and walks purposefully away.

She goes alone, of course, two days later when she feels better and when she knows for sure they will be leaving Assisi the following morning. She is no longer in love with the priest; he has become what he always was, a small brown Italian busy with kitchen, clerical and gardening tools. The heartbreak, however, which preceded him and will continue, is still with her, recognized now and accepted as she stands across the road from the Church of Santa Chiara watching a small cat walk on top of its shadow in the noonday sun.

Inside the door total darkness for a while, followed by a gradual adjustment of the eyes to dark inscrutable paintings and draped altars and the slow movements of two nuns who are walking toward the front of the church. She follows them, unsure now how to make her request and then, suddenly, the request is unnecessary. There, boom, illuminated by the ever present electricity, is the Saint, laid out for all to see in her glass coffin. "She is, you see," one of the nuns explains, "incorruptible. She is here 700 years and she does not decay because she is holy."

Clara moves closer to see the dead woman's face, now glowing under the harsh twentieth-century light, and there, as she expects, is the pain. Frozen on Chiara's face the terrifying, wonderful pain; permanent, incorruptible, unable to decay. The dead mouth is open, shouting pain silently up to the electricity, past the glass, into the empty cave of the church, out into the landscape, up the street to the Basilica where images of the live Chiara appear, deceitfully serene, in the frescos. It is the heartbreak that is durable, Clara thinks to herself, experiencing the shock of total recognition. Everything else will fade away. No wonder the Saint didn't decay. A flutter of something sharp and cutting in Clara's own bloodstream and then she turns away.

Before she steps out into the street again she buys a postcard from one of the nuns. Santa Chiara in her glass coffin, as permanent as a figure from Pompeii in her unending, incorruptible anguish.

Clara places the card in an inside pocket of her handbag. There it will stay through the long plane ride home while her husband makes jokes about the washrooms resembling Italian confessionals. It will stay there and she will clutch the leather close to her broken heart, clutch the image of the dead woman's mouth. The permanent pain that moves past the postcard booth into the colours of the Italian landscape.

—1987

Guy Vanderhaeghe b. 1951

Like many of his generation who later became successful novelists, Guy Vanderhaeghe first established himself as a short story writer—with Man Descending *(1982), for which he received a Governor General's Award for fiction. Vanderhaeghe has since published two more collections of stories,* The Trouble with Heroes *(1986) and* Things as They Are *(1992), as well as four novels and two plays. Having lived most of his life in Saskatchewan, he sets his narratives chiefly in the prairies. In stories such as "How the Story Ends," he explores generational relationships and conflicting western codes. When Carl Tollefson, an aging and sick man, moves in with his niece's family, his botched attempt to teach the boy about the Bible not only calls attention to how stories end but to how they get understood, interpreted, and applied to our daily lives.*

How the Story Ends

Carl Tollefson was what people, only a short time ago, commonly used to refer to as a *nice, clean old bachelor.* In any event, that was the manner in which Little Paul's mother, Tollefson's niece, chose to characterize him to Big Paul while their guest unpacked in his room upstairs.

"I was so pleased to see he was a *nice, clean old bachelor,*" she said, buttering toast for her husband, who refused to go to bed on an empty stomach. "Most old men get awful seedy if they don't marry. And I really had no idea what to expect. I hadn't seen him since I was a little girl— I couldn't have been more than ten. Eleven maybe."

"Christ, Lydia," said Big Paul, "don't you think they keep them clean in that T.B. sanatorium? They don't have no choice about bathing in a place like that. They make them. Sure he looks clean. *Now.*"

"Did you notice he wears elastic sleeve garters to keep his cuffs even? When was the last time you saw somebody wear sleeve garters, Paul?" She slid the plate deftly in front of him. "I think it's real cute."

"You make sure he has his own plate and cup," said Big Paul, who was mortally afraid of illness. "And make sure it's a different colour from the dish set. I don't want his stuff getting mixed with ours. I'm not eating off no goddamn T.B. plate."

"You know better than to talk such ignorance," his wife answered him. "He'd die of embarrassment. Anyway, he isn't contagious. Do you think he'd get a foot in the door if he was?" She tilted her head and lifted an eyebrow ever so slightly in the direction of their son, as if to say: Do you really think I'd put him in jeopardy?

Little Paul stood with his thin shoulders jammed against the wall, and a harried look on his face as he scratched the red scale of eczema which covered his hands. His hair, which had been cropped short because of the skin disorder, appeared to have been gnawed down to his skull by a ravenous rodent, rather than cut, and made the scalp which showed through the fine hair seem contused and raw.

He was six years old and slow to read, or count, or do most things people seemed to expect of him. In school he gave the impression of a small, pale spider hung in the centre of a web of stillness, expecting at any moment to feel one of the fragile threads vibrate with a warning.

"Give him a chipped plate then," said Big Paul around a mouthful of toast. "You can keep track of that easy enough. He'll never notice."

"You might buy three or four weanling pigs," his wife replied, ignoring him, "and he could look after them. I'm sure he wouldn't mind doing light chores for his room and board. We could feed them garden trash. It would keep him busy pottering around until he found a place."

"Where's he going to find a place?" asked Big Paul with that easy contemptuousness which had first attracted his wife to him. "Nobody is going to hire an old fart like him."

"He's not so *old*. Sixty-six isn't *so* old. And it's not as if farm work is all bull labour any more. He could get on with a dairy farm and run the milking machines, say. Or maybe work a cattle auction. He knows cattle; he said so himself."

"Anybody can say anything. Saying something doesn't make it so."

"Tollefsons were never blowhards nor braggers."

"One lung," said Big Paul moodily, "he won't last long. You saw him. The old bugger looks like death warmed over."

"Paul," his wife returned sharply, "not in front of the boy."

"Why did he come here?" whined Little Paul, who felt something vaguely like jealousy, and decided he could exercise it now that his presence had been formally recognized.

"To die in my upstairs bed," his father said unhappily, apparently speaking to himself, "that's why. To die on a goddamn spanking-new box-spring mattress."

"Don't listen to your father," said his mother. "He's only joking."

"What do you want?" Tollefson said, startled to see the silent, solemn boy standing in the doorway dressed in pyjamas. He tried hard to remember the child's name. He couldn't.

"That's my dad's bed," Little Paul said pointing to where Tollefson sat. "He owns it."

"Yes." The old man took exception to what he read as a note of belligerence in the boy's voice. "And this is my room. Nobody is welcome here who doesn't knock." Little Paul's settled gaze made him uncomfortable. He supposed it was being shirtless and exposing the scar of his operation—an L of ridged, plum-coloured tissue, the vertical of which ran alongside his spine, the horizontal directly beneath and parallel to the last bone of his rib cage. Whenever Tollefson thought of his missing lung he felt empty, hollow, unbalanced. He felt that way now.

"Why can't I come in here without knocking?" the boy demanded listlessly his eyes shifting about the room, looking into things, prying. "This is my dad's house."

"Because I have certain rights. After all, I'm sixty-six and you're only . . ." He didn't know. "How old are you anyway?"

"Almost seven."

"Almost seven," Tollefson said. He extended one blunt-fingered hand scrolled with swollen blue veins, grasped a corner of the dresser and dragged himself upright. Then he unzipped a cracked leather case and removed two old-fashioned gentleman's hairbrushes, which he slipped on his hands.

"What are you doing?" said the boy, advancing cautiously into the room. He thrust his tattered head from side to side like some wary buzzard fledgling.

What an ugly child, Tollefson thought, and was immediately ashamed. He glanced at the hairbrushes on his hands and remembered he had originally intended to have them initialled. *Vanity of vanities, saith the preacher, vanity of vanities, all is vanity* rang in his mind.[1]

What exactly had his married sister, Elizabeth, said to him forty-five years ago on the occasion of his twenty-first birthday party?

"Carlie," she had sung in the lilting voice he had been pleased to hear her daughter Lydia had inherited, "you're a handsome young devil. You do know that, don't you?"

No. He hadn't. Never dreamed it. The notion had surprised and confounded him. He would have liked to ask someone else's opinion on the matter, but that was hardly the thing a person did.

[1] Ecclesiastes 1:2.

This startling information, however, did lead him to begin to take great pains with his appearance. He refused any longer to let his father cut his hair. Instead, he went to the barber in town for a "trim" and his first baptism with bay rum.[2] His sideburns crept past his ear-lobes; his hair appeared to be trying to mount a plausible pompadour. He bought elastic-sided boots, took to looking at himself in store windows when he sauntered past, and lounged on street corners with his thumbs hooked in his belt loops. Carl Tollefson began to suspect more than one girl of being in love with him.

Nobody told him any different until, in a moment of fanciful speculation, insane even for him, he remarked to his brother-in-law Roland that he thought the butcher's wife had her "eye on me."

Elizabeth spoke to him a second time. "Carlie, you remember what I said to you about being a handsome devil? I'm sorry, but I only meant to give you a little confidence—you're so shy around girls. The thing is, Carlie, there never was a Tollefson born who was anything but plain. I swear to God Roland married me out of charity. Still, I learned some time ago that nothing much helps; you can't make a silk purse out of a sow's ear. So let me give you a little advice—the girls around here don't much run to hair oil and elastic-sided boots. What they want is steady, and God knows you're steady. Just remember, Carlie, we're all in the same boat—there never was a Tollefson who turned a head with his profile."

"You think I don't know that," he had replied with a tight, pinched laugh. "What kind of fool do you think I am?"

Studying his face in the mirror he was puzzled by the mystery of how he had been able to believe in his supposed good looks, even for a second. Evidence to the contrary stared out at him from the mirror as it had every one of those mornings forty-five years ago as he had so carefully shaved.

Of course, age hadn't improved him. But, by and large, it was the same old face, only a little more used up. An indifferent kind of face: mild blue eyes which in a certain light appeared unfocussed; a limp mouth which he often caught himself breathing through; a decent, ordinary, serviceable nose for a decent, ordinary face; and a set of small, neat ears which lay close to his skull and gave him the surprised look of a man caught in a fierce wind.

Perhaps it was from the moment he realized what he *was* in comparison with what he hoped to be that he turned in upon himself. And

---

[2] Once the chief cologne used in barbershops.

although he bore no resentment against his sister for planting the seed that flowered in his humiliation, he always sensed that the story of his life might have been very different if she had never said what she had. Not better, only different.

After all, he did not renounce all of what he had come to be; that would have been an admission that everything stemmed from self-delusion, and he was too proud to do that. The sideburns disappeared and the never-to-be-completed edifice of his pompadour crumbled from neglect, but the elastic-sided boots and the trips to the barber endured.

Nor did he dare court the local girls, imagining that they scorned the memory of his debonair days and thought him a poor thing, likely simple. Yet when the chrome-backed hairbrushes he had ordered from the catalogue finally arrived, he hadn't returned them and requested a refund. He was not quite the same young man he had been before his twenty-first birthday.

"What are you doing?" said Little Paul again, with greater emphasis.

"I'm going to brush my hair," Tollefson told him, cocking his head and looking at himself in the glass from a different angle.

"And then what?"

"I'll get myself ready for breakfast. Like you should. I'll wash my face and hands."

"Why?"

"Cleanliness is next to godliness."

"Why can't I come to your room without knocking?" the boy asked again.

"Because I might be doing something I don't want anybody to see."

"Like what?"

"Praying. Having my private talks with God that nobody has any business butting into," said Tollefson sternly. "For Jesus told us: 'When thou prayest, enter into thy closet, and when thou hast shut thy door, pray to thy Father which is in secret; and thy Father which seeth in secret shall reward thee openly.'"

"Here? In this room? God would come here in this room?" the boy said excitedly, his fingers digging and twisting at the crotch of his pyjamas. "Come here and talk to you?"

"Yes, in a way He would."

Little Paul thought for a moment, sucking his bottom lip. "I don't believe you," he said. "God wouldn't fit in such a little room. Jesus might fit, but not God."

"Same thing, son," said Tollefson, slipping into his shirt.

Little Paul appeared to be sceptical of Tollefson's contention, but he let the subject drop. "My dad's buying you pigs," he informed the old man.

"That a fact?"

"Can I help you look after them pigs?"

"You can if you promise not to come here in my room without knocking any more."

"All right." He climbed on to the bed and crossed and locked his legs.

"Why don't you go to the bathroom, son?"

"Don't need to."

"Suit yourself. But no accidents on my bed, eh?"

Little Paul giggled at the idea. Somehow Tollefson heard this as a plaintive sound. The boy didn't seem to have acquired the knack of laughter. Tollefson began to do up his shirt.

"Why did you come here?" the boy asked abruptly.

Tollefson paused at his collar-button. He always did up his collars. He was that kind of man. "I never thought about it," he said. "I suppose because there was no place else to go." He considered further. "No, God brought me here," he decided at last.

"To die in this upstairs bed," added Little Paul conversationally, patting the bedclothes with a hand crusted with eczemic lesions.

That terrible spring Big Paul often inquired of Tollefson, "Did you bring this goddamn miserable weather with you, or what?" He made a point of the goddamn, always careful to stress it after he learned from Lydia that her uncle had turned "churchy" some time during the past twenty years.

"I don't remember hearing anything about his being religious from Mom," she said. "He didn't catch it from home; I know that for sure. Grandpa Tollefson's acquaintance with church was of the marrying and burying variety."

"Why do they have to creep?" said Big Paul. "He minces around like he was walking on eggs. They all walk the same and they all talk the same. They're so jeezly *nice*. I never thought there'd come a day when I'd have to sidle past some creeping christer slipping and sliding around *my* house."

"There's nothing the matter with religion," declared his wife. "You could do with a little yourself."

"What really frosts my ass about guys like him," said Big Paul, who found anything out of the ordinary offensive, "is they got no idea of what's *normal*. Take him. He wouldn't say shit if his mouth was full of it. Yesterday he fell down in that slop in the corral. Know what he says?"

"Can't imagine."

"'Oh Lord, how long?' he says. 'How long what?' I asks. 'Oh Lord, how long will it rain?' he says, and then laughs like he was in his right mind. That's his idea of a joke!"

"If God happens to answer his question, let me in on the secret," said Lydia. "I want to hang washing some time this week."

But April was not a month to hang washing. April was a month of cruel rains. The eaves on the house choked on ice water; the poplars behind the cow sheds glistened in an agony of chilling sweats; and sparrows shrank to black clots of damp feathers which rode telephone wires that vibrated dolefully in the wind.

Big Paul's farmyard swam in water. The early calves were dropped from the warm bath of the womb into numbing puddles—where four drowned before they found the strength to gain their feet. Others shook in the steady drizzles until they contracted hemorrhagic septicemia, shat blood, and died between their mother's legs.

Under the pressure of circumstances, Tollefson tried to do more than he was capable of. The muck in the corrals sucked the strength out of his legs and left him trembling from head to foot, his single lung straining, the blood surging in his temples. When the old man stumbled in pursuit of new-born calves, his mouth gaped in a mute appeal for oxygen; his breath was barely visible in the cold as a thin, exhausted vapour. The wound on his back became a fiery letter, and one grey day in the mindlessness of utter fatigue, trying to wrestle a struggling calf to shelter in a pelting rain, he found himself muttering over and over, "L . . . , L . . . , L . . . ," in cadence with the thrumming of the blood in his ears and scar.

In mid-month, on April 18, the temperature dropped and the rain resolved itself into a stinging sleet which came driving out of a flat impassive sky and froze to whatever it struck. Fence posts were sheathed in ice; barbed wire turned to glass, its spikes to frosty thorns. The cattle humped their backs to the bitter onslaught and received it dumbly, until their coats crackled when they stirred uneasily during lulls in the wind.

Big Paul and Tollefson began to search the bushes behind the cowsheds for calves when it became clear, after an hour, that the storm was not going to abate. They panted over deadfalls, forced their way through blinds of saskatoon and chokecherry bushes, slogged through the low spots where the puddles lay thick and sluggish, a porridge of ice crystals.

Within half an hour Tollefson's flannel shirt stuck to his back, heavy and damp with a sickly sweat. Thirty minutes later he had the feeling that his legs were attempting to walk out from underneath him. They felt as light and airy as balsa wood; it was only by an exertion of great will that he made them carry him. At some point, however, the cold gnawed through the gristle of his resolve and concentration, his mind wandered, his legs did what they wished—and folded under him. Tollefson was surprised to find himself kneeling in mud and slush, the wet seeping through his pant-legs and draining slowly into his boots, while he listened to his heart ticking over, and felt the scar blaze on his back.

"I found him," Big Paul would tell the beer parlour crowd later, "else he'd have froze stiff as a tinker's dink. It was just behind my barley bin, about a quarter-mile from where he says his legs gave out. I guess the old bugger got pooped out and sat down for a minute, and then his legs cramped with the cold and he couldn't get up. When I seen him he was just a lump of snow by the granary skids. He must have had horseshoes up his ass, because I could have easy missed him. I looked twice, mind you.

"But as I was saying, I saw this bump and first thing I says to myself is, 'That's another christly calf down and sure as Carter's got liver pills he's dead, son of a bitch.' I nearly crapped my drawers when I got close up and saw it wasn't no calf but the wife's uncle. I hadn't seen him for an hour, but I'd figured he'd got cold and went back to the house.

"He didn't have a thing left in him. He was on his side with an arm over his face to keep the sleet off. He could have been sleeping. Didn't hear me until I was practically standing on him.

"'Hey!' I hollered. 'Hey!' I figured he was tits up. I wasn't too crazy about touching a dead man. But he wasn't dead. 'You found me,' he says, real quiet. Then he takes his arm off his face. No teeth. He lost his teeth somewhere.

"'You broke a leg, or what?' I says. 'Can you get up?'

"'No, I can't get up,' he mumbles. 'I'm beat.' He didn't talk so good without his teeth and he was so tired I could barely make out what he was saying. I yelled at him: 'You broke a leg or had a heart attack or what?'

"'I'm tired,' he says. 'My legs give up on me.'

"Now he's old but he ain't light, and I was thinking how the hell was I going to get him out of there? He seen I was wondering how I was going to pack his arse out of there. I couldn't get a truck in there; she'd go down to the axles.

"'Go hook the stoneboat to the Ford tractor,' he says, 'and pull me out of here.' He had it all figured out. Of course, he had plenty of time, didn't he?

"'I got a pile of manure on it!' I hollers. 'I'll have to throw it off first!'

"'I can't wait,' he says. 'I can't feel my toes.' Then he says, 'You bring her in here and load me on. That Ford can pull a double load of b.s., can't it?' And he laughs. I tell you, I figure he was pretty far gone for him to say that. That's pretty strong stuff for that old man. He's a regular Bible-banger. I never heard him say so much as damn before that.

"So that's how I dragged him out of there. Rolled him onto a pile of cow shit and pulled him up to the house. He just lay there with his arms flung out on either side, the sleet coming down in his face. He didn't even try to cover up. I don't think he cared for nothing at that point."

Eric, who was seated across the table from Paul, said: "You say he crawled a half-mile? You ought to race him against Charlie's kid," he laughed, poking Charlie. "I was over to his place yesterday, and his rug rat can really rip. I'd put a dollar on him."

"I paced it off next day," Big Paul said, and his voice hinted at wonder. "That was what it was, just under a quarter-mile. And he gets the pension. I didn't think he had it in him."

"How's he now?" asked Charlie.

"Seems he's okay. We brought him home from the hospital a week ago. He spends most of the day laying in bed, then he reads to the kid when he comes home from school. Reads him mostly Bible stories. The old bird ain't nothing if he ain't odd. Lydia thinks it helps the kid. He don't do much at school."

"Sounds just like his old man," said Eric, "a regular little shit-disturber."

"No," said Big Paul, honesty itself, "he just don't learn."

"He won't grow up to be a shit-disturber with a preacher in the house," said Charlie, draining his glass.

"You ought to seen the kid," Big Paul said, suddenly struck by the recollection. "The things he comes up with. The things he thinks of. The other day I come in from feeding the stock and Little Paul's traipsing around the kitchen with a towel tied on his head and a piece of butcher's tape stuck on his chin for a beard.

"'Who the hell are you?' I says.

"'Moses leading the Jews out of Egypt,' he says. Do you believe that? Moses leading the Jews out of Egypt.

"'Well, lead the bastards over the nearest cliff,' I says." Big Paul winked at his companions and rubbed his palms on his knees. "'Over the nearest cliff,' I says," he repeated, laughing.

"A preacher in the house," said Eric, shaking his head. "That's trouble. You know what they say about preachers. Hornier than a two-peckered owl is what my old man used to say. Watch that old bugger; he might preach the pants off the wife."

"Keep him away from the goats," snorted Charlie. "He'll turn the cheese."

Big Paul hated it when they teased him. Every time they started in on him he began to feel confused and helpless. "Ah, not him," he said nervously, "for chrissakes show some respect. He's her uncle, for crying out loud."

"Any port in a storm," said Eric, poking Charlie.

"He don't like women much," said Big Paul, "he never got married." He paused, and, suddenly inspired, saw a solution. "You know," he said, "if anything, he's a little fruity. He's got fruity ways. Irons his own shirts. Cleans his fingernails every day before dinner. Queer, eh?"

"That reminds me," said Charlie. "Did you ever hear the one about the priest and the altar boy?"

"What?" said Big Paul sharply.

Tollefson's four volumes of *Bible Tales for Children* were twenty years old. He had bought them for his own edification weeks after his conversion at a Pentecostal meeting he had been taken to by a widow who had thoughts of marriage. She never landed that fish, but Jesus did.

Tollefson bought the books for two reasons. He admired the bright illustrations, particularly the angels who were sweetness itself; and he thought that in those children's books the great mysteries of the Trinity, the Incarnation, and the Resurrection would be so simply and obviously stated that his perplexities on those matters would evaporate. He found they helped.

Now the first volume lay open on the scarlet counterpane that covered Tollefson's bed and Little Paul was huddled beside him, his head drawn into his bony shoulders, his face intent.

"But why did God ask Abraham to do that?" the boy demanded, his voice much too loud for the narrow bedroom.

"Can't you wait for nothing?" said Tollefson. "The book'll say. It'll all come out in the end." The old man resumed reading, his words muffled and moist because his lost teeth had not been found.

"*So Abraham took his only son Isaac, whom he loved more than life itself, two trusty servants, a donkey, and bundles of sticks to make a fire, and began his journey to the land of Moriah where God had told him he would point out the mountain on which he was to sacrifice his son Isaac to God.*"

Tolleffson paused and wiped at his slack lips with the back of his hand. Little Paul wound his fingers together and grimaced suddenly, like a small ape displaying his teeth.

"Why is God doing this?" he said nervously. "Little Isaac is scared, I bet."

"He doesn't know," Tollefson reminded him.

"Why is God doing this?" the boy said. "Why?"

"Wait and see, it's like a mystery. Wait until the end of the story. Listen now," he said, beginning to read in a flat, uninspired monotone. "*Can you imagine what pain was in Abraham's heart when he watched Isaac skipping light-heartedly beside him? How he longed to disobey God?*"

"He won't do it," Little Paul said under his breath. "Isaac's daddy won't do it. Not when he sees how scared he is."

"*And all through the trip,*" Tollefson read, "*Isaac kept repeating one question over and over again. 'Father,' he said, 'we are carrying these big bundles of sticks to make a fire, but what will we offer to the Lord our God, since we have forgotten a lamb to sacrifice?'*"

"*But Abraham ignored the question, because he could not tell his son that he was the sacrifice.*"

Little Paul stared down at the stark print; for the first time in his life his mind wrestled with the hard words. He wanted to spell out the conclusion to this fearsome puzzle. He hated the story. He hated the book. He hated all books. They said he could read if he wanted to. That he could count. *Your tests prove it,* they said. *You could read if you'd try.* But he wouldn't. Little Paul was not going down that long tunnel. Count maybe. His head could count. One, two, three, four . . . on and on you could go. Numbers never stopped. But they would never find out he counted in his head. He just would never say the numbers out loud.

"*After many weary days and thirsty miles Isaac and Abraham arrived at the mountain in Moriah. Abraham climbed it with oh so sad a heart, his son beside him. When they arrived at the top they gathered stones and built an altar.*"

Little Paul had begun to rock himself on the bed, his arms clasping his knees tightly. He slowly waggled his prison-camp head with its shorn hair and scent of powerful medication from side to side. "No," he said softly, his lips carefully forming before he sounded the word, "no-o-o, he won't."

Tollefson, his ears numbed by the singsong cadences of his own voice, did not hear Little Paul. He had a picture of his own forming behind his eyes. A great golden angel crouched behind a rock on a barren, sandy mountain top. Rescue. Unconsciously, his voice began to rise with his own excitement. *"Suddenly, after the last stone was lifted, Abraham seized his son, bound him, placed him on the altar amongst the sticks, and lifted his sharp dagger high, high above his head!"*

A sob, a darting hand, and the page was torn. The old man, stunned, caught Little Paul; but the boy's body wriggled violently upward, his eyes staring, his mouth a pocket of blackness—a diver with bursting lungs breaking the surface. For a moment the boy's body throbbed with inchoate fury as he strained silently in Tollefson's grasp, speechless, and full of wonder at what had passed through his mind. Then he screamed: "It's stupid! It's stupid! *You're* stupid!"

"Paul! Stop it!"

"He killed him!" shouted Little Paul. "The little boy is dead! There's nothing left of him! He's all gone! All of him!"

"No," said Tollefson, and he said it with such assurance and sincerity that the boy went quiet in his hands. "No, he isn't. The little boy's alive. There's an angel, and the angel tells Abraham not to kill Isaac, and there's a ram in the thicket," he went on quickly, "and they sacrifice that instead. The little boy . . . Isaac, he isn't dead."

"Yes?"

"Yes," said Tollefson. Once more on familiar ground, he was recovering his stride and filling with annoyance. "What kind of performance was that?" he asked, handling the book. "You can't get away with stunts like that. You know, people won't stand for it. Look at the book."

Little Paul was not interested in the book. "Why did God tell him to kill the little boy? Was he bad?"

"No, he wasn't bad. God told Abraham to kill Isaac to see if Abraham loved God enough to obey. And Abraham did love God enough. He loved God so much that he was willing to sacrifice his only son, just as God was willing to sacrifice his only son, Jesus, because He so loved the world and wished to wash it clean of sin, as white as snow, by the saving mercy of His blood."

Little Paul could see blood. Pails and pails of blood were needed to wash away the sins of the world. He had seen his father catch blood in a pail to make sausage. Blood pumping hot out of a slashed throat in bright jets. Later, when it cooled, it turned black and thick like pudding.

"And because Abraham loved God," said Tollefson, "he would do anything God asked. No matter how hard."

"Would you?"

"I'd try very hard. We must always try our hardest to please God. You must too, Paul, because He loves you."

"Did he love Isaac?"

"Of course. He loves all his children."

"I don't like the story."

"Oh, you didn't *at first*," said Tollefson, "because you didn't wait for the end. But everything came out all right in the end, didn't it? That's the point."

It didn't seem the point to Little Paul. It seemed to him that God, being who he was, could have as easily ended the story the other way. *That*, to Little Paul, seemed the point.

"What do you mean," said Big Paul, "he wet the bed?"

"He wet the bed, that's what I mean. And keep your voice down."

"Jesus, he's seven years old."

"It's the nightmares," Lydia said. "They all have them at his age. Myrna's youngest had them for months and then, just like that, they stopped."

Big Paul felt uneasy. "He never plays with other kids. He's always with that sick old man. It's as if he's afraid to take his eyes off him. No wonder the goddamn kid has nightmares."

"Maybe if you didn't talk about Uncle dying in front of Paul, he wouldn't have bad dreams."

"Shit."

"And he spends time with Uncle because of the pigs. He likes to help him."

"That's another thing. I told you to tell that kid those pigs weren't supposed to become pets. That they were going to be butchered.

Yesterday I go down to the pens and he shows me how they'll roll over to have their bellies scratched. Jesus H. Murphy, doesn't anybody listen to me around here any more?"

"He knows they've got to be butchered. I've told him and told him."

"And something else," Big Paul said, his voice rising with outrage, "the old boy is butchering those pigs. I'm not looking like a shit-head in my kid's eyes killing those pigs. I didn't teach them cute tricks!"

"My God, Paul, are you jealous?" Lydia asked, surprised and a little pleased at the notion.

"And last of all," he yelled, "tell that old son of a bitch to leave the bedroom door open when he's in there with Little Pauly! Better still, keep the kid out of there!"

"You *pig*," she said.

"What are you telling Uncle?" Little Paul whispered, his head twisting at the keyhole in a futile attempt to see more of Tollefson's bedroom.

"Don't you listen, Uncle Carl," he muttered fiercely. "Don't you listen to him."

Through the keyhole the boy could see only part of the room, and that part contained Tollefson's bed, by which the old man knelt praying, his bare back turned to the door, and the scar, faded by time, a faint letter formed by a timid hand.

What was out of view, in that portion of the bedroom that contained the unseen wardrobe, toward which Tollefson's head was beseechingly turned, Little Paul could only imagine.

The old man and the boy picked their way between the dusty rows of garden vegetables under a stunning August sun, collecting refuse for the pigs. Little Paul trudged along listlessly behind Tollefson, pulling a wagon heaped with old pea vines; tiny, sun-scalded potatoes; beet and carrot tops. Their two shadows, black as pitch, crept over the dry, crumbling soil; shattered on the plant tops shaking in the breeze; squatted, stooped, and stretched.

Tollefson was admitting to himself he was a sinful man, a deceitful man. For months, ever since the April storm in which he had collapsed, he had known he was incapable of any longer earning his way in the world. His working days were over. He really was an old man, and in his talks with God he had come to realize that he was close to death. Yet he had pretended it was only a matter of time before he regained his strength and left to find work. But this deception was no longer enough. His niece and her husband were becoming impatient with him. Perhaps they would soon invite him to leave.

Tollefson didn't want to leave. He was an old man with nowhere to go. A man with no place of his own; no people of his own. All his life he had lived in other men's houses; played with other men's children; even, on occasion, slept with other men's wives before he had come to know Jesus. He was lonely and frightened.

That was why he had hit on the idea of making Little Paul the beneficiary of his will. He had worked very hard all his life and saved more money than anybody would suspect. Thirty-nine thousand dollars. When he told Lydia what he was going to do, they wouldn't dare ask him to leave for fear he would take the boy out of his will. What had Jesus said? *"Or what man is there of you, whom if his son ask bread, will he give him a stone? Or if he ask a fish, will he give him a serpent?"*

Big Paul might hate his guts, but he wouldn't deny his son a stake in thirty-nine thousand dollars. He was sure of that.

Tollefson looked down at Paul grubbing under a tomato plant for wormy fruit. Lydia had told him the child was suffering from bad dreams and nervous diarrhea.

The boy glanced up at him with his flat, guarded eyes. "Tomorrow will be too hot to kill pigs," he said out of the blue. Although Little Paul hadn't phrased his sentence as a question, Tollefson knew it was. For a week the boy had heard his father and Tollefson discuss whether they would soon have "killing weather"—cooler temperatures and a wind to prevent flies swarming on the pigs as they were scalded and gutted.

"Can't wait any longer," said Tollefson matter-of-factly, shading his eyes and studying the glowing blue glaze of the sky. "Your dad made a booking to have the meat cut and wrapped at the locker plant tomorrow afternoon. I'll have to do the pigs in the morning." The old man paused, adjusted his shirt sleeves, and then inquired, "Are you going to give me a hand?"

"It's too hot to kill pigs," the boy said sullenly.

"You got to learn some time," Tollefson said, "if you want to be a farmer. I told you all along them pigs would be butchered and your mother told you. You knew it. That's a farmer's job to grow things for people to eat. Now, you like bacon, don't you? Where do you think bacon comes from?"

"God," said Little Paul automatically. He thought he'd learned how to please Tollefson.

His answer took the old man momentarily aback. "Well yes . . . that's right. But pigs is what I meant. It comes from pigs. It's pork. But you're right. Everything God made, he made for a reason. He made pigs for men to eat."

"I'd puke," said Little Paul vehemently. "I'd puke it all up."

Tollefson took off his long-billed cap and peered into it as if he expected to find there an answer to his predicament. "Listen," he said at last, taking the boy by the shoulders and looking directly into his face, "you got to learn to see things through. Believe me when I tell you it's the most important thing in life. You can't feed a pig and keep a pig and grow a pig and then leave the end, the dirty part, for another man to do. You had the fun of it all, and now you don't want the rest. It isn't right, Little Paul," he said. "You got to learn that. Remember when I read you the story of Abraham and Isaac? You didn't want to hear the end of the story because you thought it didn't suit. Just the way now you think butchering those pigs doesn't suit. But it does. There's nothing finer in God's eyes than a farmer, because the work he does, it does good for all people. A farmer feeds people and that's good. Don't you see?" he pleaded to the pale, intractable face.

"No." The boy's shoulders twisted under his hand. "No."

"God wants them pigs butchered," said Tollefson, trying to make sense of it for the boy. "They won't feel nothing. I'm a top-notch pig shot. I shot hundreds."

"You talk to him," said the boy, speaking very quickly, his face a strained mask. "You two got secrets from me. I talk and talk but he doesn't answer me what you got planned for me. I asked and asked and asked. But it's a secret. Why don't he tell me!"

"Who?" said Tollefson, reaching for the boy, alarmed by the fear which had lain in the shallows of the child's eyes all those months, but which he recognized only then for the first time.

"Is he hungry?" implored Little Paul. "Is he hungry? Please, is that how the story ends?"

—1982

Rohinton Mistry   b. 1952

Since launching his career with the accomplished book of short stories Tales from Firozsha Baag *in 1987, Rohinton Mistry has published three novels—all of them short-listed for the prestigious Booker Prize. While these novels have been set entirely in the India in which Mistry grew up, his short story collection draws both on his early years in Bombay and on his experience of immigrating to Toronto as a young man.*

Firozsha Baag is the name of an apartment complex that serves to unify his sequence of eleven stories about a Parsi community in Bombay. "Squatter," the eighth story in the book, provides a comical and satirical look at the idea of immigrant assimilation and can be read both as a serious parable and as an ironic parody of the familiar story of failed immigration. Making use of the self-reflexive form that became popular in narratives at the end of the twentieth century, it is a humorous story about a storyteller and about the act of telling stories that reworks some of the oldest motifs in the storyteller's repertoire: the journey into a strange land, the test, and the rash promise.

Squatter

Whenever Nariman Hansotia returned in the evening from the Cawasji Framji Memorial Library in a good mood the signs were plainly evident.

First, he parked his 1932 Mercedes-Benz (he called it the apple of his eye) outside A Block, directly in front of his ground-floor veranda window, and beeped the horn three long times. It annoyed Rustomji who also had a ground-floor flat in A Block. Ever since he had defied Nariman in the matter of painting the exterior of the building, Rustomji was convinced that nothing the old coot did was untainted by the thought of vengeance and harassment, his retirement pastime.

But the beeping was merely Nariman's signal to let Hirabai inside know that though he was back he would not step indoors for a while. Then he raised the hood, whistling "Rose Marie," and leaned his tall frame over the engine. He checked the oil, wiped here and there with a rag, tightened the radiator cap, and lowered the hood. Finally, he polished the Mercedes star and let the whistling modulate into the march from *The Bridge on the River Kwai*. The boys playing in the compound knew that Nariman was ready now to tell a story. They started to gather round.

"*Sahibji,* Nariman Uncle," someone said tentatively and Nariman nodded, careful not to lose his whistle, his bulbous nose flaring slightly. The pursed lips had temporarily raised and reshaped his Clark Gable moustache. More boys walked up. One called out, "How about a story, Nariman Uncle?" at which point Nariman's eyes began to twinkle, and he imparted increased energy to the polishing. The cry was taken up by others, "Yes, yes, Nariman Uncle, a story!" He swung into a final verse of the march. Then the lips relinquished the whistle, the Clark Gable moustache descended. The rag was put away, and he began.

"You boys know the great cricketers: Contractor, Polly Umrigar, and recently, the young chap, Farokh Engineer. Cricket *aficionados,* that's what you all are." Nariman liked to use new words, especially big ones, in the stories he told, believing it was his duty to expose young minds to as shimmering and varied a vocabulary as possible; if they could not spend their days at the Cawasji Framji Memorial Library then he, at least, could carry bits of the library out to them.

The boys nodded; the names of the cricketers were familiar.

"But does any one know about Savukshaw, the greatest of them all?" They shook their heads in unison.

"This, then, is the story about Savukshaw, how he saved the Indian team from a humiliating defeat when they were touring in England." Nariman sat on the steps of A Block. The few diehards who had continued with their games could not resist any longer when they saw the gathering circle, and ran up to listen. They asked their neighbours in whispers what the story was about, and were told: Savukshaw the greatest cricketer. The whispering died down and Nariman began.

"The Indian team was to play the indomitable MCC as part of its tour of England. Contractor was our captain. Now the MCC being the strongest team they had to face, Contractor was almost certain of defeat. To add to Contractor's troubles, one of his star batsmen, Nadkarni, had caught influenza early in the tour, and would definitely not be well enough to play against the MCC. By the way, does anyone know what those letters stand for? You, Kersi, you wanted to be a cricketer once."

Kersi shook his head. None of the boys knew, even though they had heard the MCC mentioned in radio commentaries, because the full name was hardly ever used.

Then Jehangir Bulsara spoke up, or Bulsara Bookworm, as the boys called him. The name given by Pesi *paadmaroo*[1] had stuck even though it was now more than four years since Pesi had been sent away to boarding-school, and over two years since the death of Dr. Mody. Jehangir was still unliked by the boys in the Baag, though they had come to accept his aloof-ness and respect his knowledge and intellect. They were not surprised that he knew the answer to Nariman's question: "Marylebone Cricket Club."

"Absolutely correct," said Nariman, and continued with the story. "The MCC won the toss and elected to bat. They scored four hundred and ninety-seven runs in the first inning before our spinners could get them out. Early in the second day's play our team was dismissed for one hundred and nine runs, and the extra who had taken Nadkarni's place was injured by a vicious bumper that opened a gash on his fore-head." Nariman indicated the spot and the length of the gash on his furrowed brow. "Contractor's worst fears were coming true. The MCC waived their own second inning and gave the Indian team a follow-on, wanting to inflict an inning's defeat. And this time he had to use the second extra. The second extra was a certain Savukshaw."

The younger boys listened attentively; some of them, like the two sons of the chartered accountant in B Block, had only recently been deemed old enough by their parents to come out and play in the compound, and had not received any exposure to Nariman's stories. But the others like Jehangir, Kersi, and Viraf were familiar with Nariman's technique.

Once, Jehangir had overheard them discussing Nariman's stories, and he could not help expressing his opinion: that unpredictability was the brush he used to paint his tales with, and ambiguity the palette he mixed his colours in. The others looked at him with admiration. Then Viraf asked what exactly he meant by that. Jehangir said that Nariman sometimes told a funny incident in a very serious way, or expressed a significant matter in a light and playful manner. And these were only two rough divisions, in between were lots of subtle gradations of tone and texture. Which, then, was the funny story and which the serious? Their opinions were divided, but ultimately, said Jehangir, it was up to the listener to decide.

"So," continued Nariman, "Contractor first sent out his two regular openers, convinced that it was all hopeless. But after five wickets were

---

[1] In "The Ghost of Firozsha Baag," the third story in *Tales from Firozsha Baag*, the narrator explains that they called the late Dr. Mody's son "Pesi Paadmaroo because he makes dirty wind all the time." The fifth story, "The Collectors," tells more about Pesi and gives the full story of Dr. Mody.

lost for just another thirty-eight runs, out came Savukshaw the extra. Nothing mattered any more."

The street lights outside the compound came on, illuminating the iron gate where the watchman stood. It was a load off the watchman's mind when Nariman told a story. It meant an early end to the hectic vigil during which he had to ensure that none of the children ran out on the main road, or tried to jump over the wall. For although keeping out riff-raff was his duty, keeping in the boys was as important if he wanted to retain the job.

"The first ball Savukshaw faced was wide outside the off stump. He just lifted his bat and ignored it. But with what style! What panache! As if to say, come on, you blighters, play some polished cricket. The next ball was also wide, but not as much as the first. It missed the off stump narrowly. Again Savukshaw lifted his bat, boredom written all over him. Everyone was now watching closely. The bowler was annoyed by Savukshaw's arrogance, and the third delivery was a vicious fast pitch, right down on the middle stump.

"Savukshaw was ready, quick as lightning. No one even saw the stroke of his bat, but the ball went like a bullet towards square leg.

"Fielding at square leg was a giant of a fellow, about six feet seven, weighing two hundred and fifty pounds, a veritable Brobdingnagian,[2] with arms like branches and hands like a pair of huge *sapaat*, the kind that Dr. Mody used to wear; you remember what big feet Dr. Mody had." Jehangir was the only one who did; he nodded. "Just to see him standing there was scary. Not one ball had got past him, and he had taken some great catches. Savukshaw purposely aimed his shot right at him. But he was as quick as Savukshaw, and stuck out his huge *sapaat* of a hand to stop the ball. What do you think happened then, boys?"

The older boys knew what Nariman wanted to hear at this point. They asked, "What happened, Nariman Uncle, what happened?" Satisfied, Nariman continued.

"A howl is what happened. A howl from the giant fielder, a howl that rang through the entire stadium, that soared like the cry of a banshee right up to the cheapest seats in the furthest, highest corners, a howl that echoed from the scoreboard and into the pavilion, into the kitchen, startling the chap inside who was preparing tea and scones for after the match, who spilled boiling water all over himself and was severely hurt. But not nearly as bad as the giant fielder at square leg. Never at any

[2] In Jonathan Swift's *Gulliver's Travels*, Brobdingnag is a land inhabited by giants. *Sapaat* are shoes.

English stadium was a howl heard like that one, not in the whole history of cricket. And why do you think he was howling, boys?"

The chorus asked, "Why, Nariman Uncle, why?"

"Because of Savukshaw's bullet-like shot, of course. The hand he had reached out to stop it, he now held up for all to see, and *dhur-dhur, dhur-dhur* the blood was gushing like a fountain in an Italian piazza, like a burst water-main from the Vihar-Powai reservoir, dripping onto his shirt and his white pants, and sprinkling the green grass, and only because he was such a giant of a fellow could he suffer so much blood loss and not faint. But even he could not last forever; eventually, he felt dizzy, and was helped off the field. And where did you think the ball was, boys, that Savukshaw had smacked so hard?"

And the chorus rang out again on the now dark steps of A Block: "Where, Nariman Uncle, where?"

"Past the boundary line, of course. Lying near the fence. Rent asunder. Into two perfect leather hemispheres. All the stitches had ripped, and some of the insides had spilled out. So the umpires sent for a new one, and the game resumed. Now none of the fielders dared to touch any ball that Savukshaw hit. Every shot went to the boundary, all the way for four runs. Single-handedly, Savukshaw wiped out the deficit, and had it not been for loss of time due to rain, he would have taken the Indian team to a thumping victory against the MCC. As it was, the match ended in a draw."

Nariman was pleased with the awed faces of the youngest ones around him. Kersi and Viraf were grinning away and whispering something. From one of the flats the smell of frying fish swam out to explore the night air, and tickled Nariman's nostrils. He sniffed appreciatively, aware that it was in his good wife Hirabai's pan that the frying was taking place. This morning he had seen the pomfret she had purchased at the door, waiting to be cleaned, its mouth open and eyes wide, like the eyes of some of these youngsters. It was time to wind up the story.

"The MCC will not forget the number of new balls they had to produce that day because of Savukshaw's deadly strokes. Their annual ball budget was thrown badly out of balance. Any other bat would have cracked under the strain, but Savukshaw's was seasoned with a special combination of oils, a secret formula given to him by a *sadhu*[3] who had seen him one day playing cricket when he was a small boy. But

---

[3] Holy man.

Savukshaw used to say his real secret was practice, lots of practice, that was the advice he gave to any young lad who wanted to play cricket."

The story was now clearly finished, but none of the boys showed any sign of dispersing. "Tell us about more matches that Savukshaw played in," they said.

"More nothing. This was his greatest match. Anyway, he did not play cricket for long because soon after the match against the MCC he became a champion bicyclist, the fastest human on two wheels. And later, a pole-vaulter—when he glided over on his pole, so graceful, it was like watching a bird in flight. But he gave that up, too, and became a hunter, the mightiest hunter ever known, absolutely fearless, and so skilful, with a gun he could have, from the third floor of A Block, shaved the whisker of a cat in the backyard of C Block."

"Tell us about that," they said, "about Savukshaw the hunter!"

The fat ayah, Jaakaylee, arrived to take the chartered accountant's two children home. But they refused to go without hearing about Savukshaw the hunter. When she scolded them and things became a little hysterical, some other boys tried to resurrect the ghost she had once seen: "Ayah *bhoot!* Ayah *bhoot!*"[4] Nariman raised a finger in warning—that subject was still taboo in Firozsha Baag; none of the adults was in a hurry to relive the wild and rampageous days that Pesi *paadmaroo* had ushered in, once upon a time, with the *bhoot* games.

Jaakaylee sat down, unwilling to return without the children, and whispered to Nariman to make it short. The smell of frying fish which had tickled Nariman's nostrils ventured into and awakened his stomach. But the story of Savukshaw the hunter was one he had wanted to tell for a long time.

"Savukshaw always went hunting alone, he preferred it that way. There are many incidents in the life of Savukshaw the hunter, but the one I am telling you about involves a terrifying situation. Terrifying for us, of course; Savukshaw was never terrified of anything. What happened was, one night he set up camp, started a fire and warmed up his bowl of chicken-*dhansaak.*"

The frying fish had precipitated famishment upon Nariman, and the subject of chicken-*dhansaak* suited him well. His own mouth watering, he elaborated: "Mrs. Savukshaw was as famous for her

[4] In "The Ghost of Firozsha Baag," the aging ayah (domestic servant) Jaakaylee believes she has seen a *bhoot* (ghost).

dhansaak as Mr. was for hunting. She used to put in tamarind and brinjal, coriander and cumin, cloves and cinnamon, and dozens of other spices no one knows about. Women used to come from miles around to stand outside her window while she cooked it, to enjoy the fragrance and try to penetrate her secret, hoping to identify the ingredients as the aroma floated out, layer by layer, growing more complex and delicious. But always, the delectable fragrance enveloped the women and they just surrendered to the ecstasy, forgetting what they had come for. Mrs. Savukshaw's secret was safe."

Jaakaylee motioned to Nariman to hurry up, it was past the children's dinner-time. He continued: "The aroma of savoury spices soon filled the night air in the jungle, and when the *dhansaak* was piping hot he started to eat, his rifle beside him. But as soon as he lifted the first morsel to his lips, a tiger's eyes flashed in the bushes! Not twelve feet from him! He emerged licking his chops! What do you think happened then, boys?"

"What, what, Nariman Uncle?"

Before he could tell them, the door of his flat opened. Hirabai put her head out and said, "*Chaalo ni*, Nariman, it's time. Then if it gets cold you won't like it."

That decided the matter. To let Hirabai's fried fish, crisp on the outside, yet tender and juicy inside, marinated in turmeric and cayenne—to let that get cold would be something that *Khoedaiji* above would not easily forgive. "Sorry boys, have to go. Next time about Savukshaw and the tiger."

There were some groans of disappointment. They hoped Nariman's good spirits would extend into the morrow when he returned from the Memorial Library or the story would get cold.

But a whole week elapsed before Nariman again parked the apple of his eye outside his ground-floor flat and beeped the horn three times. When he had raised the hood, checked the oil, polished the star and swung into the "Colonel Boogie March," the boys began drifting towards A Block.

Some of them recalled the incomplete story of Savukshaw and the tiger, but they knew better than to remind him. It was never wise to prompt Nariman until he had dropped the first hint himself, or things would turn out badly.

Nariman inspected the faces: the two who stood at the back, always looking superior and wise, were missing. So was the quiet Bulsara boy, the intelligent one. "Call Kersi, Viraf, and Jehangir," he said, "I want them to listen to today's story."

Jehangir was sitting alone on the stone steps of C Block. The others were chatting by the compound gate with the watchman. Someone went to fetch them.

"Sorry to disturb your conference, boys, and your meditation, Jehangir," Nariman said facetiously, "but I thought you would like to hear this story. Especially since some of you are planning to go abroad."

This was not strictly accurate, but Kersi and Viraf did talk a lot about America and Canada. Kersi had started writing to universities there since his final high-school year, and had also sent letters of inquiry to the Canadian High Commission in New Delhi and to the U.S. Consulate at Breach Candy. But so far he had not made any progress. He and Viraf replied with as much sarcasm as their unripe years allowed, "Oh yes, next week, just have to pack our bags."

"Riiiight," drawled Nariman. Although he spoke perfect English, this was the one word with which he allowed himself sometimes to take liberties, indulging in a broadness of vowel more American than anything else. "But before we go on with today's story, what did you learn about Savukshaw, from last week's story?"

"That he was a very talented man," said someone.

"What else?"

"He was also a very lucky man, to have so many talents," said Viraf.

"Yes, but what else?"

There was silence for a few moments. Then Jehangir said, timidly: "He was a man searching for happiness, by trying all kinds of different things."

"Exactly! And he never found it. He kept looking for new experiences, and though he was very successful at everything he attempted, it did not bring him happiness. Remember this, success alone does not bring happiness. Nor does failure have to bring unhappiness. Keep it in mind when you listen to today's story."

A chant started somewhere in the back: "We-want-a-story! We-want-a-story!"

"Riiiight," said Nariman. "Now, everyone remembers Vera and Dolly, daughters of Najamai from C Block." There were whistles and hoots; Viraf nudged Kersi with his elbow, who was smiling wistfully. Nariman held up his hand: "Now now, boys, behave yourselves. Those two girls went abroad for studies many years ago, and never came back. They settled there happily.

"And like them, a fellow called Sarosh also went abroad, to Toronto, but did not find happiness there. This story is about him. You probably don't know him, he does not live in Firozsha Baag, though he is related to someone who does."

"Who? Who?"

"Curiosity killed the cat," said Nariman, running a finger over each branch of his moustache, "and what's important is the tale. So let us continue. This Sarosh began calling himself Sid after living in Toronto for a few months, but in our story he will be Sarosh and nothing but Sarosh, for that is his proper Parsi name. Besides, that was his own stipulation when he entrusted me with the sad but instructive chronicle of his recent life." Nariman polished his glasses with his handkerchief, put them on again, and began.

"At the point where our story commences, Sarosh had been living in Toronto for ten years. We find him depressed and miserable, perched on top of the toilet, crouching on his haunches, feet planted firmly for balance upon the white plastic oval of the toilet seat.

"Daily for a decade had Sarosh suffered this position. Morning after morning, he had no choice but to climb up and simulate the squat of our Indian latrines. If he sat down, no amount of exertion could produce success.

"At first, this inability was no more than mildly incommodious. As time went by, however, the frustrated attempts caused him grave anxiety. And when the failure stretched unbroken over ten years, it began to torment and haunt all his waking hours."

Some of the boys struggled hard to keep straight faces. They suspected that Nariman was not telling just a funny story, because if he intended them to laugh there was always some unmistakable way to let them know. Only the thought of displeasing Nariman and prematurely terminating the story kept their paroxysms of mirth from bursting forth unchecked.

Nariman continued: "You see, ten years was the time Sarosh had set himself to achieve complete adaptation to the new country. But how could he claim adaptation with any honesty if the acceptable catharsis continually failed to favour him? Obtaining his new citizenship had not helped either. He remained dependent on the old way, and this unalterable fact, strengthened afresh every morning of his life in the new country, suffocated him.

"The ten-year time limit was more an accident than anything else. But it hung over him with the awesome presence and sharpness of a guillotine. Careless words, boys, careless words in a moment of lightheartedness, as is so often the case with us all, had led to it.

"Ten years before, Sarosh had returned triumphantly to Bombay after fulfilling the immigration requirements of the Canadian High Commission in New Delhi. News of his imminent departure spread amongst relatives and friends. A farewell party was organized. In fact, it was given by his relatives in Firozsha Baag. Most of you will be too young to remember it, but it was a very loud party, went on till late in the night. Very lengthy and heated arguments took place, which is not the thing to do at a party. It started like this: Sarosh was told by some what a smart decision he had made, that his whole life would change for the better; others said he was making a mistake, emigration was all wrong, but if he wanted to be unhappy that was his business, they wished him well.

"By and by, after substantial amounts of Scotch and soda and rum and Coke had disappeared, a fierce debate started between the two groups. To this day Sarosh does not know what made him raise his glass and announce: 'My dear family, my dear friends, if I do not become completely Canadian in exactly ten years from the time I land there, then I will come back. I promise. So please, no more arguments. Enjoy the party.' His words were greeted with cheers and shouts of hear! hear! They told him never to fear embarrassment; there was no shame if he decided to return to the country of his birth.

"But shortly, his poor worried mother pulled him aside. She led him to the back room and withdrew her worn and aged prayer book from her purse, saying, 'I want you to place your hand upon the *Avesta* and swear that you will keep that promise.'

"He told her not to be silly, that it was just a joke. But she insisted: '*Kassum khà*—on the *Avesta*.[5] One last thing for your mother. Who knows when you will see me again?' and her voice grew tremulous as it always did when she turned deeply emotional. Sarosh complied, and the prayer book was returned to her purse.

"His mother continued: 'It is better to live in want among your family and your friends, who love you and care for you, than to be unhappy

---

[5] Swear on the Zoroastrian scriptures.

surrounded by vacuum cleaners and dishwashers and big shiny motor cars.' She hugged him. Then they joined the celebration in progress.

"And Sarosh's careless words spoken at the party gradually forged themselves into a commitment as much to himself as to his mother and the others. It stayed with him all his years in the new land, reminding him every morning of what must happen at the end of the tenth, as it reminded him now while he descended from his perch."

Jehangir wished the titters and chortles around him would settle down, he found them annoying. When Nariman structured his sentences so carefully and chose his words with extreme care as he was doing now, Jehangir found it most pleasurable to listen. Sometimes, he remembered certain words Nariman had used, or combinations of words, and repeated them to himself, enjoying again the beauty of their sounds when he went for his walks to the Hanging Gardens or was sitting alone on the stone steps of C Block. Mumbling to himself did nothing to mitigate the isolation which the other boys in the Baag had dropped around him like a heavy cloak, but he had grown used to all that by now.

Nariman continued: "In his own apartment Sarosh squatted barefoot. Elsewhere, if he had to go with his shoes on, he would carefully cover the seat with toilet paper before climbing up. He learnt to do this after the first time, when his shoes had left telltale footprints on the seat. He had had to clean it with a wet paper towel. Luckily, no one had seen him.

"But there was not much he could keep secret about his ways. The world of washrooms is private and at the same time very public. The absence of feet below the stall door, the smell of faeces, the rustle of paper, glimpses caught through the narrow crack between stall door and jamb—all these added up to only one thing: a foreign presence in the stall, not doing things in the conventional way. And if the one outside could receive the fetor of Sarosh's business wafting through the door, poor unhappy Sarosh too could detect something malodorous in the air: the presence of xenophobia and hostility."

What a feast, thought Jehangir, what a feast of words! This would be the finest story Nariman had ever told, he just knew it.

"But Sarosh did not give up trying. Each morning he seated himself to push and grunt, grunt and push, squirming and writhing unavailingly on the white plastic oval. Exhausted, he then hopped up, expert at balancing now, and completed the movement quite effortlessly.

"The long morning hours in the washroom created new difficulties. He was late going to work on several occasions, and one such day, the supervisor called him in: 'Here's your time-sheet for this month. You've been late eleven times. What's the problem?'"

Here, Nariman stopped because his neighbour Rustomji's door creaked open. Rustomji peered out, scowling, and muttered: "*Saala* loafers, sitting all evening outside people's houses, making a nuisance, and being encouraged by grownups at that."

He stood there a moment longer, fingering the greying chest hair that was easily accessible through his *sudra*, then went inside. The boys immediately took up a soft and low chant: "Rustomji-the-curmudgeon! Rustomji-the-curmudgeon!"

Nariman held up his hand disapprovingly. But secretly, he was pleased that the name was still popular, the name he had given Rustomji when the latter had refused to pay his share for painting the building. "Quiet, quiet!" said he. "Do you want me to continue or not?"

"Yes, yes!" The chanting died away, and Nariman resumed the story.

"So Sarosh was told by his supervisor that he was coming late to work too often. What could poor Sarosh say?"

"What, Nariman Uncle?" rose the refrain.

"Nothing, of course. The supervisor, noting his silence, continued: 'If it keeps up, the consequences could be serious as far as your career is concerned.'

"Sarosh decided to speak. He said embarrassedly, 'It's a different kind of problem. I . . . I don't know how to explain . . . it's an immigration-related problem.'

"Now this supervisor must have had experience with other immigrants, because right away he told Sarosh, 'No problem. Just contact your Immigrant Aid Society. They should be able to help you. Every ethnic group has one: Vietnamese, Chinese—I'm certain that one exists for Indians. If you need time off to go there, no problem. That can be arranged, no problem. As long as you do something about your lateness, there's no problem.' That's the way they talk over there, nothing is ever a problem.

"So Sarosh thanked him and went to his desk. For the umpteenth time he bitterly rued his oversight. Could fate have plotted it, concealing the western toilet behind that shroud of anxieties which had appeared out of nowhere to beset him just before he left India? After all, he had readied himself meticulously for the new life. Even for the great, merciless Canadian cold he had heard so much about. How could he have overlooked preparation for the western toilet with its matutinal demands unless fate had conspired? In Bombay, you know that offices of foreign businesses offer both options in their bathrooms. So do all hotels with three stars or more. By practising in familiar surroundings, Sarosh was convinced he could have mastered a seated evacuation before departure.

"But perhaps there was something in what the supervisor said. Sarosh found a telephone number for the Indian Immigrant Aid Society and made an appointment. That afternoon, he met Mrs. Maha-Lepate at the Society's office."

Kersi and Viraf looked at each other and smiled. Nariman Uncle had a nerve, there was more *lepate*[6] in his own stories than anywhere else.

"Mrs. Maha-Lepate was very understanding, and made Sarosh feel at ease despite the very personal nature of his problem. She said, 'Yes, we get many referrals. There was a man here last month who couldn't eat Wonder Bread—it made him throw up.'

"By the way, boys, Wonder Bread is a Canadian bread which all happy families eat to be happy in the same way; the unhappy families are unhappy in their own fashion by eating other brands." Jehangir was the only one who understood, and murmured: "Tolstoy," at Nariman's little joke.[7] Nariman noticed it, pleased. He continued.

"Mrs. Maha-Lepate told Sarosh about that case: 'Our immigrant specialist, Dr. No-Ilaaz, recommended that the patient eat cake instead. He explained that Wonder Bread caused vomiting because the digestive system was used to Indian bread only, made with Indian flour in the village he came from. However, since his system was unfamiliar with cake, Canadian or otherwise, it did not react but was digested as a newfound food. In this way he got used to Canadian flour first in cake form. Just yesterday we received a report from Dr. No-Ilaaz. The patient successfully ate his first slice of whole-wheat Wonder Bread with no ill effects. The ultimate goal is pure white Wonder Bread.'

"Like a polite Parsi boy, Sarosh said, 'That's very interesting.' The garrulous Mrs. Maha-Lepate was about to continue, and he tried to interject: 'But I—' but Mrs. Maha-Lepate was too quick for him: 'Oh, there are so many interesting cases I could tell you about. Like the woman from Sri Lanka—referred to us because they don't have their own Society—who could not drink the water here. Dr. No-Ilaaz said it was due to the different mineral content. So he started her on Coca-Cola and

[6] Endless tale-spinning.
[7] Nariman is playfully paraphrasing the famous opening line of Leo Tolstoy's novel *Anna Karenina*: "All happy families are alike; every unhappy family is unhappy in its own way."

then began diluting it with water, bit by bit. Six weeks later she took her first sip of unadulterated Canadian water and managed to keep it down.'

"Sarosh could not halt Mrs. Maha-Lepate as she launched from one case history into another: 'Right now, Dr. No-Ilaaz is working on a very unusual case. Involves a whole Pakistani family. Ever since immigrating to Canada, none of them can swallow. They choke on their own saliva, and have to spit constantly. But we are confident that Dr. No-Ilaaz will find a remedy. He has never been stumped by any immigrant problem. Besides, we have an information network with other third-world Immigrant Aid Societies. We all seem to share a history of similar maladies, and regularly compare notes. Some of us thought these problems were linked to retention of original citizenship. But this was a false lead.'

"Sarosh, out of his own experience, vigorously nodded agreement. By now he was truly fascinated by Mrs. Maha-Lepate's wealth of information. Reluctantly, he interrupted: 'But will Dr. No-Ilaaz be able to solve my problem?'

"'I have every confidence that he will,' replied Mrs. Maha-Lepate in great earnest. 'And if he has no remedy for you right away, he will be delighted to start working on one. He loves to take up new projects.'"

Nariman halted to blow his nose, and a clear shrill voice travelled the night air of the Firozsha Baag compound from C Block to where the boys had collected around Nariman in A Block: "Jehangoo! O Jehangoo! Eight o'clock! Upstairs now!"

Jehangir stared at his feet in embarrassment. Nariman looked at his watch and said, "Yes, it's eight." But Jehangir did not move, so he continued.

"Mrs. Maha-Lepate was able to arrange an appointment while Sarosh waited, and he went directly to the doctor's office. What he had heard so far sounded quite promising. Then he cautioned himself not to get overly optimistic, that was the worst mistake he could make. But along the way to the doctor's, he could not help thinking what a lovely city Toronto was. It was the same way he had felt when he first saw it ten years ago, before all the joy had dissolved in the acid of his anxieties."

Once again that shrill voice travelled through the clear night: "*Arré* Jehangoo! *Muà*, do I have to come down and drag you upstairs!"

Jehangir's mortification was now complete. Nariman made it easy for him, though: "The first part of the story is over. Second part continues tomorrow. Same time, same place." The boys were surprised,

Nariman did not make such commitments. But never before had he told such a long story. They began drifting back to their homes.

As Jehangir strode hurriedly to C Block, falsettos and piercing shrieks followed him in the darkness: "*Arré* Jehangoo! *Muà* Jehangoo! Bulsara Bookworm! Eight o'clock Jehangoo!" Shaking his head, Nariman went indoors to Hirabai.

Next evening, the story punctually resumed when Nariman took his place on the topmost step of A Block: "You remember that we left Sarosh on his way to see the Immigrant Aid Society's doctor. Well, Dr. No-Ilaaz listened patiently to Sarosh's concerns, then said, 'As a matter of fact, there is a remedy which is so new even the IAS does not know about it. Not even that Mrs. Maha-Lepate who knows it all,' he added drolly, twirling his stethoscope like a stunted lasso. He slipped it on around his neck before continuing: 'It involves a minor operation which was developed with financial assistance from the Multicultural Department. A small device, *Crappus Non Interruptus*, or CNI as we call it, is implanted in the bowel. The device is controlled by an external handheld transmitter similar to the ones used for automatic garage door-openers—you may have seen them in hardware stores.'"

Nariman noticed that most of the boys wore puzzled looks and realized he had to make some things clearer. "The Multicultural Department is a Canadian invention. It is supposed to ensure that ethnic cultures are able to flourish, so that Canadian society will consist of a mosaic of cultures—that's their favourite word, mosaic—instead of one uniform mix, like the American melting pot. If you ask me, mosaic and melting pot are both nonsense, and ethnic is a polite way of saying bloody foreigner. But anyway, you understand Multicultural Department? Good. So Sarosh nodded, and Dr. No-Ilaaz went on: 'You can encode the handheld transmitter with a personal ten-digit code. Then all you do is position yourself on the toilet seat and activate your transmitter. Just like a garage door, your bowel will open without pushing or grunting.'"

There was some snickering in the audience, and Nariman raised his eyebrows, whereupon they covered up their mouths with their hands. "The doctor asked Sarosh if he had any questions. Sarosh thought for a moment, then asked if it required any maintenance.

"Dr. No-Ilaaz replied: 'CNI is semi-permanent and operates on solar energy. Which means you would have to make it a point to get some sun periodically, or it would cease and lead to constipation. However, you don't have to strip for a tan. Exposing ten percent of your skin surface once a week during summer will let the device store sufficient energy for year-round operation.'

"Sarosh's next question was: 'Is there any hope that someday the bowels can work on their own, without operating the device?' at which Dr. No-Ilaaz grimly shook his head: 'I'm afraid not. You must think very, very carefully before making a decision. Once CNI is implanted, you can never pass a motion in the natural way—neither sitting nor squatting.'

"He stopped to allow Sarosh time to think it over, then continued: 'And you must understand what that means. You will never be able to live a normal life again. You will be permanently different from your family and friends because of this basic internal modification. In fact, in this country or that, it will set you apart from your fellow countrymen. So you must consider the whole thing most carefully.'

"Dr. No-Ilaaz paused, toyed with his stethoscope, shuffled some papers on his desk, then resumed: 'There are other dangers you should know about. Just as a garage door can be accidentally opened by a neighbour's transmitter on the same frequency, CNI can also be activated by someone with similar apparatus.' To ease the tension he attempted a quick laugh and said, 'Very embarrassing, eh, if it happened at the wrong place and time. Mind you, the risk is not so great at present, because the chances of finding yourself within a fifty-foot radius of another transmitter on the same frequency are infinitesimal. But what about the future? What if CNI becomes very popular? Sufficient permutations may not be available for transmitter frequencies and you could be sharing the code with others. Then the risk of accidents becomes greater.'

Something landed with a loud thud in the yard behind A Block, making Nariman startle. Immediately, a yowling and screeching and caterwauling went up from the stray cats there, and the *kuchrawalli's*[8] dog started barking. Some of the boys went around the side of A Block to peer over the fence into the backyard. But the commotion soon died down of its own accord. The boys returned and, once again, Nariman's voice was the only sound to be heard.

"By now, Sarosh was on the verge of deciding against the operation. Dr. No-Ilaaz observed this and was pleased. He took pride in being able to dissuade his patients from following the very remedies which he first so painstakingly described. True to his name, Dr. No-Ilaaz believed no

[8] A *kuchrawalli* is a sweeper.

remedy is the best remedy, rather than prescribing this-mycin and that-mycin for every little ailment. So he continued: 'And what about our sons and daughters? And the quality of their lives? We still don't know the long-term effects of CNI. Some researchers speculate that it could generate a genetic deficiency, that the offspring of a CNI parent would also require CNI. On the other hand, they could be perfectly healthy toilet seat-users, without any congenital defects. We just don't know at this stage.'

"Sarosh rose from his chair: 'Thank you very much for your time, Dr. No-Ilaaz. But I don't think I want to take such a drastic step. As you suggest, I will think it over very carefully.'

"'Good, good,' said Dr. No-Ilaaz, 'I was hoping you would say that. There is one more thing. The operation is extremely expensive, and is not covered by the province's Health Insurance Plan. Many immigrant groups are lobbying to obtain coverage for special immigration-related health problems, if they succeed, then good for you.'

"Sarosh left Dr. No-Ilaaz's office with his mind made up. Time was running out. There had been a time when it was perfectly natural to squat. Now it seemed a grotesquely aberrant thing to do. Wherever he went he was reminded of the ignominy of his way. If he could not be westernized in all respects, he was nothing but a failure in this land—a failure not just in the washrooms of the nation but everywhere. He knew what he must do if he was to be true to himself and to the decade-old commitment. So what do you think Sarosh did next?"

"What, Nariman Uncle?"

"He went to the travel agent specializing in tickets to India. He bought a fully refundable ticket to Bombay for the day when he would complete exactly ten immigrant years—if he succeeded even once before that day dawned, he would cancel the booking.

"The travel agent asked sympathetically, 'Trouble at home?' His name was Mr. Rawaana, and he was from Bombay too.

"'No,' said Sarosh, 'trouble in Toronto.'

"'That's a shame,' said Mr. Rawaana. 'I don't want to poke my nose into your business, but in my line of work I meet so many people who are going back to their homeland because of problems here. Sometimes I forget I'm a travel agent, that my interest is to convince them to travel. Instead, I tell them: don't give up, God is great, stay and try again. It's bad for my profits but gives me a different, a spiritual kind of satisfaction when I succeed. And I succeed about half the time. Which means,' he added with a wry laugh, 'I could double my profits if I minded my own business.'

"After the lengthy sessions with Mrs. Maha-Lepate and Dr. No-Ilaaz, Sarosh felt he had listened to enough advice and kind words. Much as he disliked doing it, he had to hurt Mr. Rawaana's feelings and leave his predicament undiscussed: 'I'm sorry, but I'm in a hurry. Will you be able to look after the booking?'

"'Well, okay,' said Mr. Rawaana, a trifle crestfallen; he did not relish the travel business as much as he did counselling immigrants. 'Hope you solve your problem. I will be happy to refund your fare, believe me.'

"Sarosh hurried home. With only four weeks to departure, every spare minute, every possible method had to be concentrated on a final attempt at adaptation.

"He tried laxatives, crunching down the tablets with a prayer that these would assist the sitting position. Changing brands did not help, and neither did various types of suppositories. He spent long stretches on the toilet seat each morning. The supervisor continued to reprimand him for tardiness. To make matters worse, Sarosh left his desk every time he felt the slightest urge, hoping: maybe this time.

"The working hours expended in the washroom were noted with unflagging vigilance by the supervisor. More counselling sessions followed. Sarosh refused to extinguish his last hope, and the supervisor punctiliously recorded 'No Improvement' in his daily log. Finally, Sarosh was fired. It would soon have been time to resign in any case, and he could not care less.

"Now whole days went by seated on the toilet, and he stubbornly refused to relieve himself the other way. The doorbell would ring only to be ignored. The telephone went unanswered. Sometimes, he would awake suddenly in the dark hours before dawn and rush to the washroom like a madman."

Without warning, Rustomji flung open his door and stormed: "Ridiculous nonsense this is becoming! Two days in a row, whole Firozsha Baag gathers here! This is not Chaupatty beach, this is not a squatters' colony, this is a building, people want to live here in peace and quiet!" Then just as suddenly, he stamped inside and slammed the door. Right on cue, Nariman continued, before the boys could say anything.

"Time for meals was the only time Sarosh allowed himself off the seat. Even in his desperation he remembered that if he did not eat well, he was doomed—the downward pressure on his gut was essential if there was to be any chance of success.

"But the ineluctable day of departure dawned, with grey skies and the scent of rain, while success remained out of sight. At the airport Sarosh checked in and went to the dreary lounge. Out of sheer habit he started towards the washroom. Then he realized the hopelessness of it and returned to the cold, clammy plastic of the lounge seats. Airport seats are the same almost anywhere in the world.

"The boarding announcement was made, and Sarosh was the first to step onto the plane. The skies were darker now. Out of the window he saw a flash of lightning fork through the clouds. For some reason, everything he'd learned years ago in St. Xavier's about sheet lightning and forked lightning went through his mind. He wished it would change to sheet, there was something sinister and unpropitious about forked lightning."

Kersi, absorbedly listening, began cracking his knuckles quite unconsciously. His childhood habit still persisted. Jehangir frowned at the disturbance, and Viraf nudged Kersi to stop it.

"Sarosh fastened his seat-belt and attempted to turn his thoughts towards the long journey home: to the questions he would be expected to answer, the sympathy and criticism that would be thrust upon him. But what remained uppermost in his mind was the present moment—him in the plane, dark skies lowering, lightning on the horizon—irrevocably spelling out: defeat.

"But wait. Something else was happening now. A tiny rumble Inside him. Or was it his imagination? Was it really thunder outside which, in his present disoriented state, he was internalizing? No, there it was again. He had to go.

"He reached the washroom, and almost immediately the sign flashed to 'Please return to seat and fasten seat-belts.' Sarosh debated whether to squat and finish the business quickly, abandoning the perfunctory seated attempt. But the plane started to move and that decided him; it would be difficult now to balance while squatting.

"He pushed. The plane continued to move. He pushed again, trembling with the effort. The seat-belt sign flashed quicker and brighter now. The plane moved faster and faster. And Sarosh pushed hard, harder than he had ever pushed before, harder than in all his ten years of trying in the new land. And the memories of Bombay, the immigration interview in New Delhi, the farewell party, his mother's tattered prayer hook, all these, of their own accord, emerged from beyond the region of the ten years to push with him and give him newfound strength."

Nariman paused and cleared his throat. Dusk was falling, and the frequency of B.E.S.T. buses plying the main road outside Firozsha Baag had dropped. Bats began to fly madly from one end of the compound to the other, silent shadows engaged in endless laps over the buildings.

"With a thunderous clap the rain started to fall. Sarosh felt a splash under him. Could it really be? He glanced down to make certain. Yes, it was, he had succeeded!

"But was it already too late? The plane waited at its assigned position on the runway, jet engines at full thrust. Rain was falling in torrents and takeoff could be delayed. Perhaps even now they would allow him to cancel his flight, to disembark. He lurched out of the constricting cubicle.

"A stewardess hurried towards him: 'Excuse me, sir, but you must return to your seat immediately and fasten your belt.'

"'You don't understand!' Sarosh shouted excitedly. 'I must get off the plane! Everything is all right, I don't have to go anymore . . .'

"'That's impossible, sir!' said the stewardess, aghast. 'No one can leave now. Takeoff procedures are in progress!' The wild look in his sleepless eyes, and the dark rings around them scared her. She beckoned for help.

"Sarosh continued to argue, and a steward and the chief stewardess hurried over: 'What seems to be the problem, sir? You must resume your seat. We are authorized, if necessary, to forcibly restrain you, sir.'

"The plane began to move again, and suddenly Sarosh felt all the urgency leaving him. His feverish mind, the product of nightmarish days and torturous nights, was filled again with the calm which had fled a decade ago, and he spoke softly now: 'That . . . that will not be necessary . . . it's okay, I understand.' He readily returned to his seat.

"As the aircraft sped down the runway, Sarosh's first reaction was one of joy. The process of adaptation was complete. But later, he could not help wondering if success came before or after the ten-year limit had expired. And since he had already passed through the customs and security check, was he really an immigrant in every sense of the word at the moment of achievement?

"But such questions were merely academic. Or were they? He could not decide. If he returned, what would it be like? Ten years ago, the immigration officer who had stamped his passport had said, 'Welcome to Canada.' It was one of Sarosh's dearest memories, and thinking of it, he fell asleep.

"The plane was flying above the rainclouds. Sunshine streamed into the cabin. A few raindrops were still clinging miraculously to the windows, reminders of what was happening below. They sparkled as the sunlight caught them."

Some of the boys made as if to leave, thinking the story was finally over. Clearly, they had not found this one as interesting as the others Nariman had told. What dolts, thought Jehangir, they cannot recognize a masterpiece when they hear one. Nariman motioned with his hand for silence.

"But our story does not end there. There was a welcome-home party for Sarosh a few days after he arrived in Bombay. It was not in Firozsha Baag this time because his relatives in the Baag had a serious sickness in the house. But I was invited to it anyway. Sarosh's family and friends were considerate enough to wait till the jet lag had worked its way out of his system. They wanted him to really enjoy this one.

"Drinks began to flow freely again in his honour: Scotch and soda, rum and Coke, brandy. Sarosh noticed that during his absence all the brand names had changed—the labels were different and unfamiliar. Even for the mixes. Instead of Coke there was Thums-Up, and he remembered reading in the papers about Coca-Cola being kicked out by the Indian Government for refusing to reveal their secret formula.

"People slapped him on the back and shook his hand vigorously, over and over, right through the evening. They said: 'Telling the truth, you made the right decision, look how happy your mother is to live to see this day,' or they asked: 'Well, bossy, what changed your mind?' Sarosh smiled and nodded his way through it all, passing around Canadian currency at the insistence of some of the curious ones who, egged on by his mother, also pestered him to display his Canadian passport and citizenship card. She had been badgering him since his arrival to tell her the real reason: '*Saachoo kahé*,[9] what brought you back?' and was hoping that tonight, among his friends, he might raise his glass and reveal something. But she remained disappointed.

"Weeks went by and Sarosh found himself desperately searching for his old place in the pattern of life he had vacated ten years ago. Friends who had organized the welcome-home party gradually disappeared. He went walking in the evenings along Marine Drive, by the sea-wall, where the old crowd used to congregate. But the people who sat on the parapet while waves crashed behind their backs were strangers. The tetrapods were still there, staunchly protecting the reclaimed land from

[9] Truthfully.

the fury of the sea.[10] He had watched as a kid when cranes had lowered these cement and concrete hulks of respectable grey into the water. They were grimy black now, and from their angularities rose the distinct stench of human excrement. The old pattern was never found by Sarosh; he searched in vain. Patterns of life are selfish and unforgiving.

"Then one day, as I was driving past Marine Drive, I saw someone sitting alone. He looked familiar, so I stopped. For a moment I did not recognize Sarosh, so forlorn and woebegone was his countenance. I parked the apple of my eye and went to him, saying, 'Hullo, Sid, what are you doing here on your lonesome?' And he said, 'No no! No more Sid, please, that name reminds me of all my troubles.' Then, on the parapet at Marine Drive, he told me his unhappy and wretched tale, with the waves battering away at the tetrapods, and around us the hawkers screaming about coconut-water and sugar-cane juice and *paan*.

"When he finished, he said that he had related to me the whole sad saga because he knew how I told stories to boys in the Baag, and he wanted me to tell this one, especially to those who were planning to go abroad. 'Tell them,' said Sarosh, 'that the world can be a bewildering place, and dreams and ambitions are often paths to the most pernicious of traps.' As he spoke, I could see that Sarosh was somewhere far away, perhaps in New Delhi at his immigration interview, seeing himself as he was then, with what he thought was a life of hope and promise stretching endlessly before him. Poor Sarosh. Then he was back beside me on the parapet.

"'I pray you, in your stories,' said Sarosh, his old sense of humour returning as he deepened his voice for his favourite *Othello* lines"— and here, Nariman produced a basso profundo of his own—"'When you shall these unlucky deeds relate, speak of me as I am; nothing extenuate, nor set down aught in malice: tell them that in Toronto once there lived a Parsi boy as best as he could. Set you down this; and say, besides, that for some it was good and for some it was bad, but for me life in the land of milk and honey was just a pain in the posterior.'"

And now, Nariman allowed his low-pitched rumbles to turn into chuckles. The boys broke into cheers and loud applause and cries of "Encore!" and "More!" Finally, Nariman had to silence them by pointing warningly at Rustomji-the-curmudgeon's door.

---

[10] Tetrapods, concrete structures on four stubby legs used on breakwaters to dissipate the energy of waves, protect the seawall on Chaupatty Beach, stabilizing Marine Drive by slowing erosion at the point sewage is released into the mouth of the sea.

While Kersi and Viraf were joking and wondering what to make of it all, Jehangir edged forward and told Nariman this was the best story he had ever told. Nariman patted his shoulder and smiled. Jehangir left, wondering if Nariman would have been as popular if Dr. Mody was still alive. Probably, since the two were liked for different reasons: Dr. Mody used to be constantly jovial, whereas Nariman had his periodic story-telling urges.

Now the group of boys who had really enjoyed the Savukshaw story during the previous week spoke up. Capitalizing on Nariman's extraordinarily good mood, they began clamouring for more Savukshaw: "Nariman Uncle, tell the one about Savukshaw the hunter, the one you had started that day."

"What hunter? I don't know which one you mean." He refused to be reminded of it, and got up to leave. But there was loud protest, and the boys started chanting, "We-want-Savukshaw! We-want-Savukshaw!"

Nariman looked fearfully towards Rustomji's door and held up his hands placatingly: "All right, all right! Next time it will be Savukshaw again. Savukshaw the artist. The story of the Parsi Picasso."

—1987

Dionne Brand b. 1953

Born in the village of Guayguayare in Trinidad, Dionne Brand moved to Toronto when she was seventeen and completed her education there, earning a Ph.D. in Women's Studies. A political activist, she has worked on documentary film, served as an editor, and published books of poetry, fiction, and essays grounded in her experience as an immigrant, as a member of a racial minority, and as a lesbian.

Her writing engages oppositionally with established dominant discourses. In a section of "At the Lisbon Plate," for example, she writes back to Albert Camus' L'Étranger, a novel that helped define the Existentialist movement (it is translated into English as The Stranger *or* The Outsider*), decentring its western European point of view and replacing it with that of an Arab. "At the Lisbon Plate" is more generally a meditation on how history is filled with injustices —especially those of slavery and empire. Taking the form of a monologue, its narrative begins in the real world but becomes increasingly fantastic, even allegorical.*

At the Lisbon Plate

The sky in the autumn is full of telephone and telegraph wires; it is not like sitting in the Portuguese bar on Kensington in the summer, outside—the beer smell, the forgetful waiter. I wonder what happened to Rosa. She was about forty and wore a tight black dress, her face appliquéed with something I could barely identify as life. Her false mole, the one she wore beside her mouth, shifted everyday and faded by evening. She had a look that was familiar to me. Possibly she had lived in Angola or Mozambique and was accustomed to Black women, so she looked at me kindly, colonially.

"Do you have fish, Rosa?" I would ask.

"Oh yes, good Portuguese fish."

"From the take or from the sea."

"Ah the sea, of course."

This would be our conversation every time I would come to the bar, her "of course" informing me of her status in our relationship.

My life was on the upswing, and whenever that happened I went to the bar on Kensington. That was usually in the summertime. After twenty years and half my life in this city I still have to wait for the summertime to get into a good mood. My body refuses to appreciate dull, grey days. Truthfully, let me not fool you, my life was neither up nor down, which for me is an upswing and I don't take chances, I celebrate what little there is. Which is why I come to this bar. This is my refuge, as it is. I believe in contradictions.

So Rosa ran from Angola and Mozambique.[1] Well, well! By the looks of it she'd come down a peg or two. At the Lisbon Plate, Rosa seems quite ordinary, quite different from the woman who entertained in the European drawing rooms in Luanda and Lorenços Marques. Then, she gave orders to Black women, whom she called "as pretinhas."[2] Then, she minced over to the little consul from Lisbon and the general, whose family was from Oporto and whom she made promise to give her a little gun for her protection when the trouble started.

I figured anyone who left Angola was on the other side, on the run. Rosa did have a kind enough look, personally. The wholesale merchant

[1] Both Angola and Mozambique were colonized by Portugal in the fifteenth century and became centres of a flourishing slave trade. During the 1960s, independence movements arose and intense fighting forced the Portuguese to withdraw in 1975; a destructive civil war subsequently broke out in Angola.
[2] Little black ones. Luanda is the capital of Angola; Lorenços Marques was once the capital of Mozambique.

she was married to or his general manager, whom she slept with from time to time, had to leave. So, Rosa left too. This does not absolve Rosa, however. I'm sure that she acquired her plumpness like a bed bug, sucking a little blood here, a little there.

As I've said, my life was on the upswing. Most other times it was a bitch. But I had spent two successive days with no major setbacks. Nobody called me about money, nobody hurt my feelings, and I didn't wake up feeling shaky in the stomach about how this world was going. And, I had twenty clear bucks to come to the bar. This is my refuge. It is where I can be invisible or, if not invisible, at least drunk. Drinking makes me introspective, if not suicidal. In these moments I have often looked at myself from the third floor window of the furniture store across from the bar. Rheumy-eyed, I have seen a woman sitting there, whom I recognize as myself. A Black woman, legs apart, chin resting in the palm of her hand, amusement and revulsion travelling across her face in uneasy companionship; the years have taken a bit of the tightness out of my skin but the expression has not changed, searching and uneasy, haunted like a plantation house. Surrounded by the likes of Rosa and her compadres. A woman in enemy territory.

It has struck me more than once that a little more than a century ago I may have been Rosa's slave and not more than twenty-five years ago, her maid, whom she maimed, playing with the little gun that she got from the general from Oporto. My present existence is mere chance, luck, syzygy.

Rosa's brother, Joao the priest, was now living in New Jersey. He used to live in Toronto, but before that he lived in Angola. One day, in a village there, during the liberation war, two whites were kidnapped and the others, including Rosa's brother, the priest, went into the village and gunned down a lot of people—women, children—to death, everything. He told this story to Maria de Conseçao, my friend, and she told me. Women and children, everything. People think that saying women and children were killed makes the crime more disgusting. I was sorry that Maria de Conseçao told me, because whenever I think about it I see Joao the priest confiding this crime as if he relished it, rather than repented it. I think Maria de Conseçao told me the story just to get rid of it. It's the kind of story which occurs to you when you're doing something pleasant and it's the kind of story you can't get rid of. I've kept it.

I am not a cynical woman under ordinary circumstances, but if you sit here long enough anyone can see how what appears to be ordinary, isn't.

For, on the other hand, I look like a woman I met many years ago. As old as dirt, she sat at a roadside waiting her time, an ivory pipe stuck in her withered lips and naked as she was born. That woman had stories, more lucid than mine and more frightening for that.

The day I met her, her bones were black powder and her fingers crept along my arm causing me to shiver. She was a dangerous woman. I knew it the moment I saw her and I should have left her sitting there, the old grave-digger. But no. Me, I had to go and look. I had to follow that sack of dust into places I had no right being. Me, I had to look where she pointed. She wanted to show me her condiments and her books. I thought nothing of it. Why not humour an old woman, I said in my mind. They were old as ashes. All tied up and knotted in a piece of cloth and, when she opened it up, you would not believe the rattling and the odour, all musty and sweet. A bone here and a fingernail there. They looked like they'd been sitting in mud for centuries, like her. When it came to the books, it was before they had pages and the writing was with stones, which the old thing threw on the ground and read to me. I never laughed so much as I laughed at her jokes, not to mention her stories, which made me cry so much I swore I'd turn to salt water myself. It was one of her stories which led me here, in search of something I will recognize, once I see it.

But back to things that we can understand, because I want to forget that harridan in the road and her unpleasantness.

Today I am waiting for Elaine, as usual. She likes to make entrances of the type that white girls make in movies. The truth is she's always getting away from something or someone. She is always promising too much and escaping. Which is why we get along. I never believe a promise and I, myself, am in constant flight.

Elaine is a mysterious one. Two days ago she told me to meet her here at one o'clock. I've been sitting here ever since. I know that she'll turn up a new woman. She'll say that she's moving to Tanzania to find her roots. She'll have her head tied in a wrap and she'll have gold bracelets running up her arms. She'll be learning Swahili, she'll show me new words like "jambo" and she'll be annoyed if I don't agree to go with her. Elaine wants to be a queen in ancient Mali or Songhai.[3] A rich woman with gold and land.

The bar has a limited view of Kensington market. Across the street from it there's a parkette, in the centre of which there is a statue of

---

[3] Mali and Songhai were wealthy medieval West African kingdoms that have been largely ignored in western accounts of world history. "Jambo" is "Hello" in Swahili.

Cristobal Colon.[4] Columbus, the carpet-bagger. It's most appropriate that they should put his stoney arse right where I can see it. I know bitterness doesn't become me, but that son of a bitch will get his soon enough too. The smell from the market doesn't bother me. I've been here before, me and the old lady. We know the price of things. Which is why I feel safe in telling stories here. They will be sure to find me. For fish you must have bait; for some people you must have blood. Spread the truth around enough, and you must dig up a few liars.

In the summertime, I come to the bar practically every day. After my first beer I'm willing to talk to anyone. I'm willing to reveal myself entirely. Which is a dirty habit, since it has made me quite a few enemies. Try not to acquire it. The knots in my head loosen up and I may start telling stories about my family.

I keep getting mixed up with old ladies; for instance. I have an old aunt, she used to be beautiful. Not in the real sense, but in that sense that you had to be, some years ago. Hair slicked back to bring out the Spanish and hide the African. You could not resemble your mother or your father. This would only prove your guilt. This aunt went mad in later years. I think that it must have been from so much self-denial or, given the way that it turned out. . . .

Anyway, when I was a child we used to go to their house. It was made of stone and there was a garden around it. A thick green black garden. A forest. My aunt worked in the garden every day, pruning and digging. There was deep red hibiscus to the far right wall. The soil was black and loose and damp and piled around the roots of roses and xoras and anthuriums and orchids. In the daylight, the garden was black and bright; in the night, it was shadowy and dark. Only my aunt was allowed to step into the garden. At the edges, shading the forest-garden were great calabash mango trees. Their massive trunks and roots gave refuge from my aunt when she climbed into a rage after merely looking at us all day. She would run after us screaming, "beasts! worthless beasts!" Her rage having not subsided, she would grab us and scrub us, as if to take the black out of our skins. Her results would never please her. Out we would come five still bright-black little girls, blackness intent on our skins. She would punish us by having us stand utterly still, dressed in stiffly starched dresses.

Elaine never reveals herself and she is the most frustrating storyteller. She handles a story as if stories were scarce. "Well," she says, as

[4] The Spanish name for Christopher Columbus.

she sits down at the table. Then she pauses, far too long a pause, through which I say, in my mind, "I'm going to last out this pause." Then quickly getting upset, I say, "For god's sake, tell me." Then I have to drag it out of her, in the middle of which I say, "Forget it, I don't want to hear," then she drops what she thinks is the sinker and I nonchalantly say, "Is that it?" to which she swears that never again would she tell me a story. The truth is that Elaine picks up on great stories, but the way she tells them makes people suffer. I, on the other hand, am quite plain. Particularly when I'm in my waters. Drink, I mean. I've noticed that I'm prepared to risk anything. But truthfully, what makes a good story if not for the indiscretions we reveal, the admissions of being human. In this way, I will tell you some of my life; though I must admit that some of it is fiction, not much mind you, but what is lie, I do not live through with any less tragedy. Anyway, these are not state secrets, people live the way that they have to and handle what they can. But don't expect any of the old woman's tales. There are things that you know and things that you tell. Well, soon and very soon, as they say.

Listen, I can drink half a bottle of whisky and refuse to fall down. It's from looking at Rosa that I get drunk and it's from looking at Rosa that I refuse to fall down. I was a woman with a face like a baby before I met Rosa, a face waiting to hold impressions.

I saw the little minx toddle over to the statue of Columbus, the piss-face in the parkette, and kiss his feet. Everyone has their rituals, I see. And then, before her mirror, deciding which side to put the mole on. Her face as dry as a powder. Perfuming herself in her bedroom in Lorenços Marques, licking the oil off that greasy merchant of hers. Even though the weather must have been bad for her, she stuck it out until they were driven away. It's that face that Rosa used cursing those "sons of bitches in the bush," when the trouble started. "When the trouble started," indeed. These European sons of bitches always say "when the trouble started" when *their* life in the colonies begins to get miserable.

I never think of murder. I find it too intimate and there's a smell in the autumn that I do not like. I can always tell. The first breath of the fall. It distracts me from everyone. I will turn down the most lucrative dinner invitation to go around like a bloodhound smelling the fall. Making sure and making excuses, suggesting and insinuating that the summer is not over. But of course, as soon as I get a whiff of that smell I know. It's the autumn. Then the winter comes in, as green and fresh as spring and I know that I have to wait another ten months for the old woman's prophecy to come true. That hag by the road doesn't know what she gave me and what an effort I must make to see it through. On top of that, I have to carry around her juju belt full of perfidious mixtures and insolent smells and her secrets. Her secrets. My god, you don't know what a soft pain in the chest they give me. I grow as withered as the old hag with their moaning. She's ground them up like seasoning and she's told me to wear them close to my skin, like a poultice. I thought nothing of it at first. A little perfume, I said, a little luxury. I now notice that I cannot take the juju off. I lift up my camisole and have a look. It's hardly me there anymore. There's a hole like a cave with an echo.

The old hag hates the winter too; says it dries her skin out. God knows she's no more than dust, but vain as hell. She migrates like a soucouyant[5] in the winter, goes back to the tropics, says she must mine the Sargasso[6] for bones and suicides. I must say, I envy the old bagsnatcher. Though she's promised me her memories, her maps and her flight plans, when it's over. Until then, I wait and keep watch here, frozen like a lizard in Blue Mountain,[7] while she suns her quaily self in some old slave port.

At this bar, as I have my first beer and wait for the African princess, Elaine, I discover substantive philosophical arguments concerning murder. The beauty is, I have a lot of time. I have watched myself here, waiting. A woman so old her skin turned to water, her eyes blazing like a dead candle. I'm starting to resemble that bag of dust, the longer I live.

Now they have a man waiting on tables at the bar. I suppose the pay must be better. Elaine says he resembles Rosa except for her beauty mole and her breasts. It doesn't matter how Rosa looks in her disguises, I am doomed to follow her like a bloodhound after a thief. He is quite forgetful. Twenty minutes ago I asked him for another beer and up to now he hasn't brought it. Elaine's the one who got me into beer drinking anyway. In the old days—before the great mother old soul in the road and before I sussed out Rosa and her paramour, Elaine and I used to roam the streets together, looking. The old bone digger must have spotted my vacant look then. Elaine, on the other hand, had very definite ideas. Even then Elaine

---

[5] In Trinidadian mythology, a soucoyant is an evil being who inhabits the body of an old woman and, shedding her skin at night, becomes a ball of fire that flies through the air and sucks blood from its sleeping victims.

[6] The Sargasso Sea is a sluggish part of the Atlantic Ocean between the Azores and the West Indies known for its sargasso seaweed floating on the surface: in old sailors' legends the Sargasso Sea was said to entrap ships in this mass of vegetation.

[7] The area around the highest point in Jamaica, near the eastern tip of the island.

was looking for a rich African to help her make her triumphal return to the motherland.

Still, a rumour went around that Elaine and I were lovers. It wouldn't have bothered either of us if it were true at the time or if it wasn't said in such a malicious way. But it was because of how we acted. Simply, we didn't defer to the men around and we didn't sleep with them, or else when we did we weren't their slaves for ever or even for a while. So both factions, those we slept with and those we didn't, started the rumour that we were lovers. Actually, Elaine and I laughed at the rumours. We liked to think of ourselves as free spirits and realists. We never attempted to dispel the rumours; it would have taken far too much of a commitment to do that. It would be a full time job of subjecting yourself to any prick on two legs. And anyway if the nastiest thing that they could say about you is that you loved another woman, well. . . .

Elaine and I would take the last bus home, bags full of unopened beer, or pay a taxi, after I had persuaded her that the man she was looking at was too disgusting to sleep with, just for a ride home. Elaine takes the practical to the absurd sometimes.

We've been to other bars. Elaine looked for the bars, she scouted all the hangouts. She determined the ambience, the crowd, and then she asked me to meet her there. There's no accounting for her taste. I'd get to the appointed bar and it would be the grungiest, with the most oily food, the most vulgar horrible men and a juke box with music selected especially to insult women. This was during Elaine's nationalist phase. Everything was culture, rootsy. The truth is, I only followed Elaine to see if I could shake the old woman's stories or, alternatively, if I could find the something for her and get her off my back. It's not that I don't like the old schemer. At first I didn't mind her, but then she started to invade me like a spirit. So I started to drink. You get drunk enough and you think you can forget, but you get even greater visions. At the beginning of any evening the old woman's stories are a blip on the horizon; thirteen ounces into a bottle of scotch or four pints of beer later the stories are as lurid as a butcher's block.

I had the fever for two days and dreamt that the stove had caught afire. My big sister was just standing there as I tried furiously to douse the fire which kept getting bigger and bigger. Finally, my sister dragged the stove from the wall and with a knowledgeable air, put the fire out. When I woke up, I heard that the stock exchange in Santiago had been blown up by a bomb in a suitcase and that some group called the communist fighting cell had declared war on NATO by destroying troop supply lines in Belgium. Just as I was thinking of Patrice Lumumba.[8] For you Patrice! From this I surmised that my dreams have effects. Though, they seem somewhat unruly. They escape me. They have fires in them and they destine at an unknown and precipitous pace.

I followed Elaine through her phases, though there were some that she hid from me. Now we come to this bar, where we cannot understand the language most of the time. Here Elaine plans the possibilities of living grandly and, if not, famously. As for me, I tolerate her dreams because when Elaine found this bar I knew it was my greatest opportunity. All of the signs were there. The expatriates from the colonial wars, the money changers and the skin dealers, the whip handlers, the coffle[9] makers and the boatswains. Their faces leathery from the African sun and the tropical winter. They were swilling beer like day had no end. Rosa was in her glory, being pawed and pinched. Of course, they didn't notice me in my new shape. Heavens, I didn't notice me. It scared the hell out of me when the juju surged to my head and I was a thin smoke over the Lisbon Plate. What a night! They said things that shocked even me, things worse than Joao, the priest. The old-timers boasted about how many piezas de indias[10] they could pack into a ship for a bauble or a gun. The young soldiers talked about the joys of filling a black with bullets and stuffing a black cunt with dynamite. Then they gathered around Columbus, the whoremaster, and sang a few old songs. The old woman and I watched the night's revelry with sadness, the caves in our chest rattling the echo of unkindness, but I noticed the old woman smiling as she counted them, pointing and circling with her hand, over and over again, mumbling "jingay, jingay where you dey, where you dey, where you dey, spirit nah go away." Before you know it, I was mumbling along with her too, "jingay, jingay, where you dey. . . ." We stayed with them all night, counting and mumbling. Now, all I have to do is choose the day and the spot and it's done. The old woman loves fanfare and flourish, so it will have to be spectacular. If Elaine knew what a find this bar was, she'd charge me money.

[8] Santiago, the capital of Chile, was the site of a 1973 CIA-supported coup overthrowing the elected president Salvador Allende (who had promised nationalization of banks, industries, and communications) and installing Augusto Pinochet, a bloody dictator subsequently responsible for the disappearance of thousands of Chileans. Patrice Lumumba: In 1960, the anti-colonialist Lumumba was elected premier of the Congo while it was still a colony of Belgium; he was deposed later that same year and murdered in 1961. (The Congo subsequently became a republic; it was known as Zaire from 1971 to 1996.)

[9] A coffle is a gang of slaves chained together for travel to market.

[10] Slaves were once referred to as pieces. This Spanish phrase (literally "pieces of female Indians") is therefore offensive.

Elaine never cared for Rosa one way or the other, which is where Elaine and I are different. Some people would have no effect on her whatsoever. This way she remained friends with everyone. Me, I hate you or I love you. Always getting into fights, always adding enemies to my lists. Which is why I'll never get any place, as they say. But Elaine will. Elaine, sadly, is a drunk without vision. I, unfortunately, am a drunk with ideas. Which is probably why the old woman chose me to be her steed.

I pride myself with keeping my ear to the ground. I read the news and listen to the radio every day, even if it is the same news. I look for nuances, changes in the patter. It came to me the other night, when listening to the news. One Polish priest had been killed and the press was going wild. At the same time, I don't know how many African labourers got killed and, besides that, fell to their deaths from third floor police detention rooms in Johannesburg; and all that the scribes talked about was how moderate the Broderbond is.[11] We should be grateful I suppose.

It occurred to me that death, its frequency, causes, sequence and application to written history, favours, even anticipates, certain latitudes. The number of mourners, their enthusiasms, their entertainments, their widows' weeds, all mapped by a cartographer well schooled in pre-Galileo geography. I'm waxing. Don't stop me. I couldn't tell you the things I know.

Meanwhile back at the bar, still waiting for Elaine to surface, there have been several interesting developments. Speaking of politics. First, I hear that the entire bourgeoisie of Bolivia is dead. It was on the radio not more than half an hour ago. The deaths are not significant in and of themselves. What is interesting is that only a few days ago, when I heard that president Suazo was kidnapped in La Paz and that there was possibly a coup, I said in my mind, that the entire bourgeoisie should perish. It was the Bolivian army who killed Ernesto Che Guevara, you see.[12] They put his body in the newspapers with their smiles. Now, I hear the news that the entire bourgeoisie of Bolivia is dead. Of course, from this I learned that as I become more and more of a spirit, I have more and more possibilities. First Santiago and Belgium and now Bolivia.

---

[11] The Afrikaner Broderbond (or *Broederbond*: Association of Brothers). This secret racist society functioned as a para-government in South Africa to ensure that those who supported the murderous policies of apartheid and white supremacy were in positions of power.
[12] Ernesto "Che" Guevara, a leader of the Cuban revolution with Fidel Castro, spearheaded Castro's efforts to "export revolution" to other South American countries. He was killed by the U.S.-supported Bolivian army in 1967. Siles Suazo, part of a middle-class left-activist movement that emerged in Bolivia in the 1930s, was elected president in 1978 but vanished during a bloody military coup before he could take office. (He later emerged from hiding and, in 1982, assumed the presidency.)

Second, and most, most important, the big white boy has arrived here. He's ordered a beer from Rosa's brother. I would know those eyes anywhere. The last time I saw them, I was lying in the hold of a great ship leaving Conakry[13] for the new world. It was just a glimpse, but I remember as if it were yesterday. I am a woman with a lot of time and I have waited, like shrimp wait for tide. I have waited, like dirt waits for worms. That hell-hole stank of my own flesh before I left it, its walls mottled with my spittle and waste. For days I lived with my body rotting and the glare of those eyes keeping me alive, as I begged to die and follow my carcass. This is the story the old road woman told me. Days and days and night and nights, dreaming death like a loved one; but those hellish eyes kept me alive and dreadfully human until reaching a port in the new world. His pitiless hands placed me on a block of wood like a yoke, when my carcass could not stand any more for the worms had eaten my soul. Running, running a long journey over hot bush, I found a cliff one day at the top of an island and jumped—jumped into the jagged blue water of an ocean, swimming, swimming to Conakry.

Elaine has also arrived and disappeared again, she's always disappearing into the bar to make phone calls. I never get an explanation of these phone calls mainly because I simply continue with my story. But I have the feeling, as the afternoon progresses into evening, and as different moods cross Elaine's face after every phone call, that some crisis is being made, fought and resolved. I have a feeling that Elaine needs my stories as a curtain for her equally spyish dramas.

The big white boy was sitting with his dog. I did not see his face at first, but I recognized him as you would recognize your hands. His hair was cut with one patch down the middle. He was wearing black and moaning as he sat there smoking weed. Like Rosa, he had fallen on his luck. I heard him say this.

"I don't have nobody, no friends, I ain't got no love, no nothing, just my dog."

He was blond. At least, that was the colour of his hair presently. I felt for him the compassion of a warship, the maudlin sentiment of a boot stepping on a face. He said this to Rosa, who gave him an unsympathetic look as she picked her teeth. I'm not fooled by their lack of affection for each other. They are like an alligator and a parasite. I felt like rushing to his throat, but something held me back. The old woman's

---

[13] Seaport capital of Guinea, West Africa; historically an important slave port.

burning hand. I've seen him and Rosa whispering behind my back. What would a punk ku klux klansman and a washed-up ex-colonial siren have in common. Except me and the old lady. I suppose they're wondering who I am. Wonder away you carrion! I wonder if they recognize me as quickly as I, them. I saw them do their ablutions on the foot of the statue in the parkette. How lovingly they fondled his bloody hands. They have their rituals, but I've lived longer than they.

Listen, I neglected to say that my old aunt of the forest has gone mad. She told my sister, and indeed the whole town of Monas Bay, that on Easter Sunday of 1979, this year, jesus christ had descended from the heavens and entered her bedroom and had been there ever since. She had had a vision. After days of fasting and kneeling on the mourning ground, she had entered a desert where nothing grew. No water and inedible shrubs. The sun's heat gave the air a glassiness upon looking into the distance. Then she saw christ. He was withered and young as a boy of twenty. Christ and my aunt conversed for many days and planned to marry three years from the time of their meeting. They would have a son who would grow to be the new christ. My aunt related this incident to any one who would listen and cursed into hell and damnation anyone who did not believe. Few, needless to say, didn't. Anyone with a vision was helpful in bad times and people said that at least she had the guts to have a vision, which was not like the politicians in those parts.

Even my aunt's garden had descended into sand and tough shrub. It had become like the desert of her vision. She no longer made any attempt to grow plants, she said that armageddon was at hand anyway. Her bedroom, she turned into a shrine on the very day of her meeting with christ. On the wall hung bits of cardboard with glossy photographs of her fiancé cut out of the *Plain Truth*,[14] and candles burnt endlessly in the four corners of the shrine. Sundry chaplets of jumbie beads, plastic and ivory manoeuvred themselves on the windows and bedposts. My aunt knows that some people think that she is mad; so, in the style of her affianced, she prays for their salvation. If she is mad. . . . Which is a debate that I will never personally enter, having seen far too much in my short life and knowing that if you live in places with temporary electricity and plenty of hard work, jesus christ (if not god) is extant. Not to mention that, the last time that I saw her, she stood at what was once the gate to the forest garden and was now dead wire, wearing a washed-out flowered dress and

---

[14] A magazine published by the once-powerful Christian evangelical organization known as the World Wide Church of God.

her last remaining tooth, even though she was only a woman of fifty, and told me that the land tax for the forest and the stone house was paid up or would be as soon as she went to town. This, to me, attested to her sanity. Come hell or high water, as they say, though these might be the obvious causes of her madness, if she were mad, they were certainly legal. Anyway, if she is mad, her vision is clearly not the cause of it. Rather it has made her quite sane. At any rate she no longer uses face powder.

This trick that I learned in Bolivia and the dream in Santiago has set me to thinking. She, the old poui stick,[15] is not the only one who can have plans. The dear old lady only gave me seven red hot peppers and told me to write their names seven times on seven scraps of paper. Then put the seven pieces of paper into the seven red hot peppers and throw them into seven latrines. This, she said, would do for them. This and sprinkling guinea pepper in front of their door every morning. Then, she said, I should wait for the rest. The old hag is smart, but she never anticipated the times or perhaps that's what she means.

Elaine thinks I'm taking things too far, of course. But, I cannot stand this endless waiting. I've practically turned into a spirit with all this dreadfulness around the Lisbon Plate. I want to get back to my life and forget this old woman and her glamorous ideas. So, what must be done, must be done. Elaine's on her way to Zaire, at any moment anyway. I think she's landed Mobutu Sese Seku.[16]

For now I've taken to hiding things from her. She doesn't care about anything. Each time I mention it she says, "Oh, for god's sake, forget them." As if it's that easy. You tell me! When there's a quaily skinned battle-axe riding on your shoulder and whispering in your ear. Well fine, if Elaine can have her secret telephone calls, and I don't think that I mentioned her disappearances, I can have my secret fires too. She can't say that I didn't try to warn her.

Wait! Well, I'll be damned! They're coming in like flies, old one. I eavesdrop on conversations here. I listen for plots, hints. You never know what these people are up for. This way, I amuse myself and scout for my opportunity. Listen,

"Camus' *Outsider* can be interpreted as the ultimate alienation!"

Ha! Did you hear that? Now, literature! Jesus. That's the one who looks like a professor, all scruffy and sensitive. If the truth be known

[15] The wood of the poui tree (which is indigenous to the tropics in the Americas) is used to make batons and has associations with *juju* (Caribbean beliefs in magic).
[16] Dictator of Zaire after he was installed by the army in 1965.

several hundred years ago he made up the phrase "Dark Ages," then he attached himself to an expedition around the Bight of Benin[17] from which, as the cruder of his sea company packed human cargo into the hold of their ship, he rifled the gold statues and masks and he then created a "museum of primitive art" to store them. Since his true love was phrase-making he made up "museum of primitive art," elaborating his former success "Dark Ages." Never trust white men who look sensitive. They're the worst kind of phonies. They want the best of both worlds. Compared to him, the big white boy looks like a saint.

Anyway, alienation, my ass! Camus! Camus wrote a novel about a European, un pied noir,[18] killing an Arab on a beach outside Algiers. He works it so that the sun gets into the European's eyes (they have their rituals) and the heat and his emotionlessness to his mother's dying and all this. But killing an Arab, pumping successive bullets into an Arab is not and never has been an alienating experience for a European. It was not unusual. It need not symbolize any alienation from one's being or anything like that. It was customary in Algeria, so how come all this high shit about Camus. Didn't it ever strike you that Meursault was a European and the Arab on the beach was an Arab? And the Arab was an Arab, but this European was Meursault.

You want to hear a story? Let me tell you a real story. I have no art for phraseology, I'll warn you.

Ahmed. Ahmed. Ahmed. Ahmed came to the beach with Ousmane to get away. The town, stiffly hot, drove him from the bicycle factory, making an excuse to his boss. Headache, my little brother has a headache three days now. He needs the salt air. The grimy hands of the boss closed around a dry cigar in the tin can ashtray. "Ahmed, if you leave I don't pay for the week. That's it. That's it you hear." Ahmed retreating, feeling free already, sweat trickling and drying under his chin. He would go to the beach, Ousmane was waiting for him, the sand would be damp. Ousmane was at the corner, he held his flute anxiously looking up and down the narrow street. His face lit up as he saw Ahmed. "You got away, good Ahmed," running beside Ahmed's bicycle. Ousmane climbed onto the handle bars. Ahmed pedalled in the hot silence toward the beach. Nearing the sea, their legs and arms eased from the tension of the town. Ousmane's bare feet leapt from the makeshift seat at the same time that Ahmed braked. They headed for

---

[17] A broad bay on the coast of western Africa.
[18] A term for the French colonists in North Africa, especially Algerians.

their favourite rock wheeling and lifting the bicycle through the sand, hot and stinging. Already he felt tranquil as the thin wind shaking the flowers. He dropped the bicycle, raced Ousmane to the water, crushing softly underfoot the vine and silky mangrove. Ahmed and Ousmane fell into the sea fully clothed, he washing away the sticky oil of the bicycle shop, Ousmane drowning his headache. Then they lay beside the rock, talking and falling asleep.

Ousmane awakening, felt hungry; his dungarees, still damp, felt steamy on his legs. Shading his eyes from the sun which had narrowed the shadow of the rock, his headache came back. He stood up, lifted his flute and played a tune he'd made over and over again as if to tame the ache in his head. After a while he wandered down the beach, looking for a foodseller.

Ahmed. Ahmed. Ahmed awoke, feeling Ousmane's absence at the same moment that he heard an explosion close to his ear. Ahmed felt his eyes taking an eternity to open into the glassy haze of the afternoon. A blurred white form wobbling in the heat's haze. Sound exploded on the other side of Ahmed. He barely raised his body, shielding his eyes as he made out the white form of a European. Far out in the ocean a steamer was passing. The sand around Ahmed pulsated with the heat and the loud ringing in his ears. Ousmane! Run!

Ahmed's vision pinpointed the white's face, the toothpick between the white's teeth and lip moving. The gun transfixed his arms. Beneath a veil of brine and tears, his eyes were blinded; they watched the steamer's latitude longingly. "Born slackers!" Ahmed's chest sprang back, tendrilled. "Born liars!" A pump of blood exploded in his left side. "Born criminals!" Sheets of flame poured down his ribs. "Born. . . .!" Ahmed![19]

That is what happened! And as for Camus. Murderer.

This is it baby. The old woman has given the go-ahead. Now that they're all gathered—Rosa, the big white boy, the professor, the money-changers and the skin dealers, the whip handlers, the coffle makers and the boatswains, the old timers and the young soldiers. I'm going to kill them. I'll tell them I have something to sell. That'll get them going; it always has. Then we'll strangle them. It'll be a night for the old woman to remember. That'll make up for it. Then that'll be the end of it.

---

[19] In a note to this passage Brand explains: "'Ahmed's death' is intended to echo and counterpoint the corresponding scene in *L'Étranger* and therefore echoes the language of the Penguin edition, English language translation."

We chained them around the statue of Cristobal Colon, the prick head. The old woman and I slashed his face to ribbons then we chewed on the stones and spit them into the eyes of the gathering. When that was over and they were all jumping and screaming, the old woman drew out her most potent juju and sprayed them all with oceans of blood which, she said, she had carried for centuries.

"En't is blood all you like?!" she whispered in their ears maliciously.

Then we sang "jingay . . ." and made them call out everything that they had done over and over again, as they choked on the oceans of blood from the old hag's juju. Then we marinated them in hot peppers, like the old woman wanted. What an everlasting sweet night we had. The old woman was so happy, she laughed until her belly burst.

When Elaine returned from her continuous phone call, I convinced her to stuff the bodies in her trunk to Zaire. It wasn't easy, as she almost could not see me and kept saying how much my face had changed. I promised her the Queendom and riches of Songhai. She bought it. The old lady has promised me her big big juju, so this is where the African princess and I must part. I'm off to see my new love and companion, the old hag of a banyan tree.

—1988

Antanas Sileika   b. 1953

Antanas Sileika has worn many hats: literary magazine editor, literary journalist on TV and radio, creative writing instructor, Director of the Humber School for Writers, raconteur, essayist, short story writer, novelist. His Buying on Time *(1997) is a series of linked stories that deals humorously with the serious problems of an immigrant family seeking a New World life in a Toronto suburb in the 1950s. Like "anthropologists trying to fathom the local customs," they disturb the orderly conformist community they have sought when their father moves them into a dugout on the land he purchases and then builds a house around them. As "The Man Who Read Voltaire" (the third story in the book) makes evident, the conflict is not simply one of European versus North American values. The young I-narrator of the sequence learns of an opposition within Old World attitudes after the arrival of his uncle. The man, who is fond of Voltaire — the great freethinker of the Enlightenment — represents a commitment to reason that stands in opposition to his father's narrow Catholicism.*

The Man Who Read Voltaire

Gerry and I were marooned on the concrete front porch in long sleeves and ties. We weren't allowed to roll up our sleeves because we might lose the cufflinks, and besides, the sleeves of our starched shirts would look wrinkled when we rolled them back down again. My mother bought the neck sizes big enough to last two years, so the collars drooped low and showed the white crew-neck T-shirts below. We had clip-on bow ties, but no jackets. We looked like a tap dance team at the church basement amateur night.

"They're only boys," my father had said. "What do they need jackets for?"

"I want them to look nice."

"Just clean their fingernails and make sure they don't talk too much when the guests get here. I don't want them yapping the whole day."

"I can get two jackets for twenty-seven dollars at Bi-Rite."

"Money again. That's all you ever talk about."

My father had stuffed his pipe, and that was the end of the conversation.

That morning, my mother fell purposefully to her knees with a painful thud. Painful to my ears, anyway. She was wearing an old flowered cotton dress that I still remembered on her at church only two years before. Now it looked like a nightgown she had been wearing too long. She hunched over the floor with the rag in one hand and the paste wax in the other, and started to rub the floor in tight, angry circles.

"Go sit on the porch and wait. If they show up early, God forbid, you run right in here and let me know. Otherwise, stay out of the house. And don't step on the yard either. I don't want your shoes to get dirty."

It was hot on the porch.

"What if he's just like the Old Man?" Gerry asked. He had started to call our father the Old Man, but I couldn't bring myself to do the same. Gerry was like that. Starting things that worried me a bit, and then looking to see if I'd follow, ready to sneer if I didn't.

"There can't be two like him," I said.

"But they're brothers, so how different could they be? A younger brother is just kind of an imitation of the older one, so the odds are that he's going to be like the Old Man, only more."

My father was puttering around the shed in the back because he too had been banished from the house. My mother had caught him sneaking shots of whisky right after breakfast.

"Eight years you haven't seen your brother, so you want to be dead drunk when he arrives. What a genius you are."

"I only had one drink."

"Liar."

"Two."

"Liar."

His face became a mask of hurt forbearance. She nicked the label on the bottle of Five Star whisky with her thumbnail, and then she checked the seal on the other bottle to make sure it wasn't broken.

But she expelled him from the house for his second misdemeanour, the salting of cabbage.

"You don't even know how to cook," she said, wagging a wooden spoon like a long finger.

"What's to know? Turn on the oven and put in the food. Add salt."

In some arenas, very, very few, my father could not win against my mother. He tucked his suit pants into the tops of his black boots and went out to the back yard.

We stayed in the front yard, where off-cuts of lumber still lay around, and the thin wild grass and weeds had been beaten down to dust by me and Gerry. The only other house on the street belonged to the Taylors, and theirs was an oasis of lawn and garden. The rest of the street was being dug up by contractors as they built houses in our new sub-division. Small contractors appeared at the dusty lots with pickup trucks of Italians, and Ukrainians, and Poles. Sometimes the men would show up at our door to ask for a glass of water. The clipped green lawn of the Taylors' yard was as good as a No Trespassing sign to them.

Our town of Weston lay in the shadow of Toronto, and our new suburb fattened itself on the old farms and orchards as Toronto loomed, waiting for us to gain enough weight to be taken to the slaughter.

My father had finally finished the shell of the house, and then he rushed to make sure the hardwood floors were in and the walls painted. He ran out of money for the interior doors. We all moved up from the basement where we had been living for almost a year, and Gerry and I shared a small bedroom beside my parents' room on the ground floor. The second floor was going to be rented, and we were not allowed up there in case we put smudgy fingerprints on the walls. He managed to buy one door for the bathroom when he found out our uncle was coming to visit, but he had lost the pins to the hinges and slipped in straight nails instead. There was no need to lock the door because half the time it wouldn't open properly anyway.

Gerry and I sat on the concrete front porch for two hours, as the sun swung around and put our east-facing porch into the shade. My mother brought out sandwiches once. She almost caught Gerry urinating off the porch into the dust of the yard.

"I wish they'd get here," I said.

"Yeah, but Detroit is a long way away."

"Six and a half hours."

We still did not have our citizenship papers, and could not hope to go to Detroit to visit my uncle for years. In the grit of our new suburb, Gerry and I longed for America. That was where real life happened. All of our favourite radio shows came from there. Kids in the radio serials ate candy bars we never even saw in the stores—Fifth Avenue and Three Musketeers. It was the kind of place where a man in a cape could fly over the city. In Weston, a man in a cape would be arrested.

Gerry's teacher let him borrow the class atlas for one night, and together with my mother we had found Detroit.

"It's so close on the map," I said.

"Everything's close on the map, stupid," said Gerry. "Look, I can walk my fingers down to New York and see the Yankees. Down the coast to Florida and get some oranges, big juicy ones that I pick off the tree. Across to Texas where I wrestle a couple of longhorns."

"To California," my mother continued, "where I stand on the beach and look across the Pacific to Hawaii and the mysterious Orient."

"You could swim all the way to Japan," my father said from his armchair. He didn't bother to look at the map with us, "right to some other DP camp outside Hiroshima."

We'd been sitting on the front porch a long time when our mother came out and joined us after she locked the back door to make sure my father could not sneak in for another drink. She had changed into a new dress and imitation pearl earrings and a hat she usually wore to church. It was a straw hat with a white veil folded up above the brim.

"You going out?" Gerry asked.

"No."

"What's the hat for?"

"I want to look nice."

"You going to wear the hat indoors?"

"Just until your uncle gets here. I'll take it off when we go in."

"That's stupid."

"If you were a girl, you'd understand."

"If I was a girl, I'd cut my throat."

"You know something? A pipe would suit you."

Gerry didn't get it, but I laughed. She looked down the street where a perpetual haze of dust hung in the air from the construction that went on during the week. It got so that the taste of it in my mouth made me think of home on my way back from school. It was a strange kind of dust that was so light it never settled, but it was scratchy too, and I could always feel it between my collar and my neck, especially now that I was wearing a tie.

"When your uncle gets here, I don't want you to badger him," said my mother. "I want you to entertain your cousins."

"Yeah, yeah," Gerry said. "Just our luck that the only cousins we have are girls."

"Tease those girls once, and I'll spank you right in front of your uncle."

Gerry sneered.

"Besides, the girls are both a couple of years older than you. They could probably beat you up if they wanted."

Gerry ground his teeth.

"Just be thankful you've got anyone at all. Your uncle and aunt are the only relatives you have on this continent, and if anything happened to your father and me, they're the ones who would take care of you."

"So what could happen?"

"Anything. One night during the war, your father answered the door and someone stuck the barrel of a rifle inside."

"What did he do?"

"Your father had a revolver in his other hand, so he fired through the door."

"Did he kill the guy?" Gerry asked.

"No. The man ran away."

"Too bad."

"Your father and his brother made a deal during the war," my mother went on. "If something happened to them, we'd raise their girls, and if anything happened to us, they'd raise you boys. It almost happened, too."

"What?"

"They got caught in Dresden."[1]

Neither of us knew if Dresden was a city or a country, but I didn't care and Gerry hated to ask questions. We'd heard the war stories a hundred times.

But I wondered what it would be like to have sisters. Older sisters probably did not beat you up. If they were old enough, they might even buy you things. I had a vision of blond sympathy that would take all my share of the housework.

The heat was rising up off the street in wavy lines. Between the dust and the heat, I felt like I was in a dream when the brown car with the running boards glided up beside the ditch at the end of our yard, and stopped as silently as a ship slipping into anchorage. The woman in the passenger seat wore a hat with a veil lowered over her face. She turned to look at us from under her veil, and she raised a gloved hand against the window in a gesture so small it could hardly be called a wave.

"Go around the back and get your father," my mother said to Gerry.

"Why can't Dave go?"

"Just do it."

Gerry spat into the dust at the side of the porch, dropped his head between hunched shoulders, and went around the back, kicking up as much dust as he could onto his new leather shoes.

There was no crunch of gravel under his shoes as my uncle stepped out of the car and waved at us over its roof. Thin as the Prince of Wales,[2] he wore a white shirt and tie, but a long one, not a bow tie. He walked around to the passenger side of the car and opened the door. A slim woman in a suit came out of the car. Both of them had cigarettes in their hands.

My father came round the corner of the house with Gerry at his heels. He had not bothered to take off his rubber boots, and his pants were bunched up at the knees.

---

[1] A large number of civilians, many of them refugees fleeing the Red Army, were killed in the German city of Dresden as a result of Allied firebombing in February 1945, the last year of World War II. (Estimates of casualties vary from 35 000 to over 135 000 of Dresden's 650 000 inhabitants.)

[2] Edward George (1894–1972), the Prince of Wales from 1894 to 1936, was a boyishly handsome man and regarded as a highly desirable eligible bachelor before his marriage to Wallis Simpson. (He became King Edward VIII of England in January 1936 and abdicated at the end of that year, accepting the title of the Duke of Windsor.)

"What, so old?" my father shouted across the yard as he approached them. "Can this be my brother, this old man who's losing his hair? And what happened to the girl he married? Who's this stocky matron he brought along? You must have to tie two belts together to make it around that waist."

Beneath the veil, a masked frown played over my aunt's face.

"Look who hasn't changed at all," my aunt said. "Eight years and one war later, and he's still talking like a smart-mouthed peasant boy."

She was not fat at all, but my father never cared what he said. My mother told us that God was going to be in for an earful when my father died.

"Where are the girls?" my mother asked.

"Measles. We had to leave them at home with their grandmother."

"Poor girls."

I could feel their weightlessness. Their feet were only lightly fixed to the ground, and I was afraid that if I breathed too hard they would blow away like angels.

"So these are the boys," my uncle said. He walked up to us and kissed us both on the lips. His smell of tobacco was different from my father's. The American cigarettes left an exotic aroma, as if he'd just come back from Egypt.

"Do you smoke?" he asked.

I hesitated, but Gerry nodded immediately.

My uncle walked back to the car, and took two packages of Lucky Strikes off the seat.

"Here you are, boys."

I looked anxiously at my mother and father, but they were both smiling, so I ripped off the cellophane and opened up the package. Chocolate cigarettes. Gerry and I put them into our mouths, and we all walked into the house.

Visitors to the house had always been a mixed blessing. It was the only time there was ginger ale in the house, reserved for the highballs of rye and ginger that the women sipped while the men took their shots neat. But the women were generous, and they let us pour glasses of ginger ale for ourselves, although some of them clung to the notion that ice cubes were bad for the throat, and one of my mother's friends had dug the cubes out of my glass with her red-painted fingernails. The "mix," as they called all pop, was a double blessing, because we could sneak some of the bottles to the store when the adults were all hung over the next day, and get the refund.

The men were less predictable than the women. They might come bearing gifts of Schneider's salami or boxes of chocolate-coated cherries that ran a sticky liquid onto our hands when we bit them in half. The fools among them, as far as Gerry and I were concerned, brought flowers. The happy drinkers might give us money for ice cream after the meal, or send us out to buy cigarettes and let us keep the change. But most of the men ignored us altogether, indifferent to our merit, indifferent to our longing for gifts. They told long and boring stories about adventures with the Red Army, or clashes with the Nazi labour battalions that combed the refugee columns for able-bodied men and women to dig earthworks against the Russians. Deep in their cups, the men banged on tables to show anguish over the families they had left behind, or else they described in infinite detail the hunger of everyday life in the refugee camps before the British or Americans arrived. These stories were boring enough in themselves, but sometimes a man might begin to cry at the memories enlivened by alcohol, and then Gerry and I despised them with all our hearts. What did we care for the sorrows and longings of grown men who could not recognize the longing of children who sat at the same table?

But my uncle and his wife were not ordinary guests.

My aunt walked beside me as my father showed them the rooms he had built, and as she walked, she rested her hand gently on my shoulder, and I did not dare to look at it for fear that she might take it away. Women all smelled of powders and hair spray and perfume, but the scent of my aunt was different from all the others. It was powerful but elusive, and I did not want to take myself away from it. It smelled faintly of citrus, as if she had driven through an orange grove in an open car, yet smoky too, as if she had spent the night in a jazz cafe where black men blew strange sounds through horns that said nothing about our lives in Canada, or the lives of our parents in Europe.

My aunt refused to laugh at my father's lame jokes, and she walked into each room as if she could own it if she chose. Her hips swung more than the hips of Canadian women. She had raised the veil of her hat to kiss us all, but then let the veil drop again as we walked through the house. I did not dare to look at her full in the face, but I stole glances at her nevertheless, and she seemed far younger than any mother I had ever known. This was a woman who must have been lucky enough to work in an office. She neither cooked nor cleaned, nor made things with her hands, but went to a place that was clean and sat at a desk all day and answered the phone and got paid for it.

Back downstairs, after the tour, my aunt pinned up the veil of her hat, and then I took my father's matches to light the first of many Parliaments that she smoked in the house. Even Tom fell under her spell, and he crawled across the floor and pawed at my aunt's legs until she lifted him onto her lap. Tom reached up for the gauze veil on her hat and pulled it back down over her face. Like a child before God, he had no fear, and he stared at her face through the veil with his lips turned into a tiny "o."

Gerry talked all the time until my father told him to shut up. As usual, he grew sullen, but he did not leave, because he had fallen under their spell as well. The adults talked without stopping, and sometimes I heard the words, spoken in our language but mixed with English incantations like "Singer," "Ford," or "Westinghouse." Sometimes I just watched my uncle and aunt as they gestured with movements far smaller than the European ones we knew, yet firmer and more knowing than the flapping from the elbows that was the Canadian norm. My uncle had brought a bottle of cognac from America, and he showed my father how to make a Nikolashka by putting a few grains of sugar and coffee on a lemon wedge, and then biting down on it after taking the cognac straight up.

When my aunt went up to the bathroom, I waited for her at the bottom of the stairs so I could have a moment alone as she came back down. When she was done, I heard her try the door, but it was stuck.

I was at the top of the stairs in a moment.

"The door sticks sometimes," I said. "You have to lift it up a bit as you pull."

I could hear her trying, but it did no good.

"Stand back," I said, and I twisted the knob with my hand, lifted as much as I could, and threw my weight against the door. It resisted for a moment, and then gave way suddenly with a splintering of the veneer where it met the jamb. The door came open and I flew into the arms of my aunt. She caught me with both arms and held me to her breast, and I could feel the movement in her as she began to laugh.

"My hero," she said through her laughter, and she held me back at arm's length. "My hero," she said again, and she led me into her bedroom and let go of my hand. From her purse she took an American dollar and placed it in my palm.

"Father's going to be furious about the door."

"That's nothing," she said, shrugging. "I'll tell him I did it."

I was ready to march into hell for her.

After dinner, my uncle took Gerry and me out in his car, and the two of us sat up as straight as we could so any kids on the street could see how fine we were.

"How many horsepower?" asked Gerry.

"I'm not sure."

"It's got to be close to two hundred. Just listen to that purr. Eight cylinders or six?"

"Six."

"That's okay for now. You can get eight in your next car."

"Six is enough," I said.

"Shut up," said Gerry. "Can't you see I'm talking to my uncle?"

My uncle spoke in English as soon as we stepped out of the car, and Gerry winked at me, appreciative of his linguistic wisdom. In public, we spoke English. We walked in together to the Kresge store, and he stood for a moment on the dull wooden floorboards, getting his bearings.

"Come on, boys." He led us straight to the glass candy bins, but there was no one there. My uncle took out a Parliament and lighted it, and then rapped on the glass bin with his wedding ring. An old woman with tight white curls walked purposefully to her place behind the counter. She wore a blue smock and an expression unsweetened by the candies she sold.

"Thank you, madam," said my uncle. "How are you this afternoon?"

The stern face softened a little.

"My feet are killing me, if you want to know the truth."

"It's almost the end of the day. Please give the boys a pound of candy each. You boys choose what you like."

He stood back and finished his cigarette as Gerry and I agonized over our selection, and after he paid for us, he saluted the woman with a finger brought loosely to his forehead.

She smiled.

"Where did you learn your English?" Gerry asked in the car, where we held on to our pound bags of candy, afraid to open them because we had never had so much wealth before. We were now speaking in our own language again.

"I studied in Germany and France when I was a student," my uncle said, "and once you have those two languages, English is not so hard.

You just put German and French into a bag, add some absurdity and ridiculous spelling, and English comes spilling right out."

Back home, they ate, and they smoked, and they drank right into the evening and on into the night. As it grew dark around nine o'clock, my father's voice became louder and louder and his face more flushed. They talked of prewar politics, and the coming war between Russia and America, and at nine-thirty my father stood up from the table and walked away. My mother and uncle and aunt talked on, and an hour later my father returned to the table, but he did not sit down. He was dressed in his boxer shorts and an undershirt that looped low under his arms. He looked dazed.

"What, still up?" he asked.

"Go back to bed, or put on some clothes," my mother said.

"Like drunks, all of you, sitting up into the small hours. Everybody go to bed!"

It was the voice that Gerry and I knew all too well. He was taking control of the situation again, like a madman who takes over a sinking ship.

"Nice underwear," my aunt said.

"I told you all to go to bed. I won't have this house turning into a den of drunkards."

I was afraid for my aunt. If she provoked him, he would rage even more.

"You go back to bed right now," my uncle said sharply. "You heard me. To bed. And not another word out of your ridiculous mouth."

My father swayed as if he had been punched.

"To bed!" my uncle repeated, and my father turned on his heel, and walked through the dark kitchen to his bedroom.

Gerry and I stared at one another in awe.

In our new small bedroom, Gerry and I had separate beds, and when we talked, we had to do it very quietly, because if our father heard us, he would come storming in. He had once caught Gerry with a flashlight and a book under the covers, and he had thrown the flashlight across the room in a rage, and broken the glass and the bulb. Gerry said he was an idiot because it was cheaper to replace the bulb than the batteries, and who needed the glass on the front anyway?

"He told off the Old Man," I said, rolling the words around in my mouth because they gave me so much pleasure.

"Yeah. When push comes to shove, the older brother is the one with the authority."

"You said he was going to be just like the Old Man."

"Naw. The Old Man must have been adopted or something. Maybe he was raised by wolves, and they found him in the fields when he was a little kid."

"I wish I could go back with them."

"He's got two daughters. You want to live with girls?"

"I'd put up with it."

"You'd like it. You could try on their nylons."

I threw my pillow across the room in the darkness.

"Great! Two pillows," said Gerry.

As we lay in the darkness, we could hear the talk that still came from the dining room. My father's snoring from the next bedroom was loud and irregular, and sometimes he muttered in his sleep, as if he knew they were saying evil things about him.

Gerry was up first, and I came into the kitchen to find him washing the crumbs of a napoleon cake off his lips.

"Are you nuts? We have to go to communion."[3]

"Shut up."

He washed the crumbs from his face just as my father came into the kitchen. His hair was standing up in tufts, and his eyes were bleary, and he was still in his boxer shorts and undershirt. He nodded at us, washed his face and smoothed his hair with his hand, and then started towards the stairs.

"Dad," said Gerry, "you better put on some clothes if you're going up there."

"They're family," my father said. "What do they care?"

He went heavily up the steps, like Frankenstein's monster. We could hear him stop and stand at the open doorway.

"So what, are you living or dead?"

Gerry and I heard everything from the bottom of the steps. There was hardly any furniture upstairs, and the sounds bounced off the empty walls. We could hear the springs creak as my father sat down on the edge of their bed.

"What time is it?" my uncle asked.

"Seven-thirty," my aunt said.

"I thought maybe he'd grown out of this by now."

"He never changes, no matter what continent he lives on."

[3] Catholics were once expected to fast after midnight (even abstaining from water) to prepare themselves for communion the next day.

"Enough philosophy," my father roared. "Get up and dress. We have to be at church by nine."

"Why the early mass?" my aunt asked.

"Because we have to take communion, and I get too hungry if we go any later."

"I'll go to mass for your sake," my uncle said, "but I'm not taking communion."

"You have to," my father said. "Think of the two boys down there. They like you. They admire you, and if you don't go to communion, you're going to make them fry in hell."

"I wish you'd stop with all that superstition. You sound like someone out of the last century."

"I won't argue with you," my father said. "I don't argue on Sundays. Just do as I say for the good of the boys."

Gerry and I raced away from the bottom of the steps as our father came down. He whistled tunelessly in his dry mouth.

Oh, the agony of Catholic hangover on a Sunday morning before communion. Not even water passed the lips of my father, although I suspected that my aunt and uncle drank freely from the tap after they had closed the bathroom door behind them.

Gerry and I were used to hungover adults. Our lives were filled with them, for all of my father's friends drank the same way he did—to oblivion—to the bottom of any bottle on the table. We grew wise in avoiding them on mornings after, especially on Sunday mornings. My mother claimed that aspirin and water were not food, but my father did not believe it.

In the alcove between the door and the bottom of the steps, my uncle whispered to us, conspiratorially.

"When you get older, promise me you will do one thing."

"Anything," Gerry whispered back.

"Promise me you will read Voltaire."

He paused, and looked worried, as if he had said too much.

"But promise me another thing. Wait until you are twenty-one before you do it."

My father was uncommonly gay that Sunday morning. He looked as if he had snatched two savages for the faith, and he held his hand lightly on his brother's back as the two of them lined up for communion. I watched carefully to see if the wafer would fly from my atheistic uncle's mouth, but it went inside his lips just as it did for all the others.

My mother had managed to hide half a bottle the night before, so when they sat down to eat after mass, the reinjection of alcohol brightened them again, and I willed them to sit there until I could summon my courage. When it came time for them to leave, Gerry and I volunteered to put their bags in the trunk, and my uncle gave us the keys to do it.

I told Gerry my plans.

He went red in the face as soon as I explained.

"I'm going too," he said.

"You can't. Who's going to close the trunk?"

"Then I'll go instead. I'm the one who's older."

"I thought of it first."

"I don't care. The Old Man is going to be pissed off, and he's going to take it out on whoever gets left behind."

I left the trunk open, and walked back towards the house. Gerry came running after me.

"You can't do this. I'm the one who thinks of things like this. You're supposed to be the good one."

"Either you close that trunk after me, or I'll find a piece of string and do it myself."

"So what do you think will happen even if you make it? They'll just send you back."

"At least I'll get a look at America. Maybe they'll let me stay."

"What happens if you die in there?"

"Why should I die?"

"There could be a hole in the floor. Exhaust could seep in from a hole in the tail pipe."

"It's not an old car. There won't be any exhaust in the trunk."

"But it's hot today. You could cook in there—you could die of thirst before you got to Detroit. The car might break down and they would have to leave it in a garage overnight."

"Will you close the trunk after me or not?"

Gerry chewed on his lower lip. It looked like he was going to cry. I knew I'd won when the sullen look returned to his face.

My uncle and aunt were already standing in the living room. I had to move fast. I hugged them and kissed them, but all the adults I knew took forever to say goodbye, so there was still time. Gerry and I returned the keys, and then we shot back outside. There was plenty of room for me in the trunk. Gerry slammed it down. He waited a few seconds, and then gave two raps. I gave two raps back as an all clear.

My aunt's dresses were on hangers, and I lay down on the mat deep in the trunk, and pulled the dresses over me in case someone opened the trunk before they left. It took a long time for the car to start. They had to be wondering why I wasn't standing next to the car to say good-bye. I imagined my father's rage at this impoliteness, but then I would never have to worry about his rage any more. I did not want to think about my mother.

The engine finally started, and the car jerked away from the side of the road. I pulled off the dresses, and looked carefully in the darkness for pinpoints of light in the floor of the trunk, just to make sure that there was no way the exhaust from a leaky tail-pipe could get inside. There were no lights, but I kept sniffing for the tell-tale gas, and wondered if my aunt and uncle would hear me if I rapped on the inside of the trunk. I sniffed, and I could smell many things; it was difficult to tell what might be poisonous. There were gasoline and oil in the back-ground, the smell of the clothes under me, and my aunt's perfume in them. Sometimes I thought I could smell something burning, and hoped it was only the Parliaments that my aunt and uncle smoked.

I had prepared myself for the thirst and the heat that I soon came to feel, but I had forgotten to go to the bathroom before we left. Not that I had to go yet, but the knowledge of it was worrisome to me. The car started and stopped often, in those days before highways, and the rock-ing motion and the heat that began to fill the trunk made me dozy. I half slept and then dreamed, and awoke to wonder if I had died from poison-ous gas, and then I slept again. I finally came fully awake when the pres-sure in my bladder grew unbearable, and then I rocked myself back and forth to ease the need to urinate. I thought that if I let out just a little, not enough to be noticeable, the pressure would go away, but when I began to urinate in my pants, I could no longer stop, and for a moment the relief was too delicious for words. Then I thought of my girl cousins greeting me, and there I would be with my pants all wet, like an infant. They would hate me then, and my uncle would turn away in his shame.

I had no watch, and I could not have seen it in any case, but it seemed we would go on forever. Twice, the car stopped, and each time I thought the trunk would open and we would be in front of my uncle's house in Detroit. When finally the trunk did open, all I could see in the brightness of the late afternoon sun was the outline of a military hat.

"It's Dave," I heard my aunt say.

"So you do know the boy," the man in the hat said.

"Of course I know him. He's my nephew."

"Most of the time, people claim it's some kid they've never seen before in their lives. You'd better come along with me."

It had never occurred to me that trunks were sometimes opened when people re-entered their country, especially the trunks of men with accents. The American customs officers took us into a low row of offices.

My father met me at the bus station in downtown Toronto late that night. I got off the bus with the wet pants in a paper bag, and a new pair of pants that someone in the customs office had found. They were adult pants, and looked ridiculous with the cuffs rolled up to fit my legs.

In silence, we rode back to Weston on the last bus. My mother did not look up at me as I walked through the door. She was knitting something, and she stared resolutely at the knitting needles just above her lap. Gerry was already in bed. My father directed me straight down to the basement. I could hear him working to get his belt undone as we went down the steps.

I stood in the customary corner, and he talked as he lashed the belt across my buttocks.

"We had the police here all evening. They had dogs to sniff around the bushes in the fields in case someone had killed you and stuffed your body in there. Your mother was crying the whole afternoon. Let me tell you something. That uncle of yours works on the assembly line at Ford. He works a blowtorch, and every day he welds the same joint. Hundreds of times a day—day in and day out. Your aunt is a saleslady at Kroger's, and all day long she sells socks. Now if you think their life is so much better than ours, you can go and live there if you want. But you'll have to wait until you're twenty-one, and then as soon as you cross the border, they'll draft you into the army and they'll send you to be killed in Korea, or some other place where they kill American boys. Until that time, you'll live here and you'll like it, and you'll listen to every word I say or we'll come down here again and again until you learn."

Gerry whispered to me after we heard my mother and father go to bed.

"Does it hurt?"

"Kind of."

"He gave it to me too."

"You told?"

"After the police came around again and told him where they found you. He didn't believe you closed the trunk yourself."

"Yeah."

He was quiet for a couple of minutes.

"They said you actually made it to the American side of the bridge."

"I guess so."

"So you're the only one in this family who's ever been to the States."

"Yeah."

"Was it beautiful there?"

"I couldn't see much. But when he drove me back over the bridge to the Canadian side, I looked out the window. It's this huge bridge—so high it feels like you're going to shoot right into the sky. There's a wide river, and Detroit is on the other side."

"What does it look like?"

"All these factories along the river, and barges and ships, and behind that these skyscrapers."

"How many?"

"A lot. All packed together, and tall as the bridge—maybe taller."

"How many storeys?"

I thought for a while.

"Hundreds, I guess."

He whistled low.

"But the Canadian side was different. I didn't see any factories at all. Just green, you know? Like a lot of lawns that come down to the water."

"Nothing ever happens on this side of the border."

"Nothing ever will."

We talked for a little while longer, but it was late. Gerry fell silent. He must have fallen asleep, because he did not say anything when the door to our room opened and my mother walked in. It was dark, but my eyes were used to it and I could make out the white nightgown.

She sat down on the edge of the bed and stroked my hair for a while.

"I know you're awake," she said. She didn't sound angry at all. Maybe just a little sad, and that was worse. She was quiet for a time.

"There's just one thing I want to know," she said. "Was it beautiful?"

—1997

André Alexis   b. 1957

Born in Trinidad of African–Caribbean descent, André Alexis was left with his grandmother as an infant when his parents immigrated to Petrolia, Ontario; he did not join them there until he was four, a dislocation reflected in his dream-like and Kafkaesque writing. This surrealism is evident in his play Lambton Kent *(1999), his novel* Childhood *(1998), and his collection of short stories,* Despair and Other Stories of Ottawa *(1994). In "Kuala Lumpur," the story of a father's wake in Ottawa, the family home is filled with people, both familiar and strange, who bring with them rituals and traditions that fail to comfort a mourning son.*

Although "Kuala Lumpur" does not take place in Kuala Lumpur, the Malaysian capital's contradictory qualities may be relevant to the story: the city is known for the way its bustling independence overlays a still visible colonial inheritance and for its heterogeneous architecture, which juxtaposes modern buildings with traditional Moorish ones, and the golden arches of fast food chains with mosques and Hindu temples.

Kuala Lumpur

The house was filled with mourners.

One of them stood up and called for quiet:

—I would just like to say a few words about Doctor Williams. In my opinion, he was the very best of men. One would have to search far and wide to find his equal, to find someone as kind, generous and honest as the Doctor. I would not presume to judge this man, this paragon of virtue, but I, like so many of you here today, must despair of finding one so good. I say, with the great poets, we will not soon see his like again. I myself remember when I first met the Doctor. It was not a happy occasion for me. I had a boil on my bottom, because my pants had chafed and it was torture for me to sit down . . . It was not the most auspicious of introductions, as I was sensitive about my injury, but the Doctor put me at ease, and before I knew what happened, he lanced the offending thing, put a bandage on for me, and sent me on my way with the smile we have all come to know and love. After that, I did not hesitate to visit him for my problems, and not once, no matter how private the matter, did the Doctor turn me away . . . I would like all of you to join me now in a toast to his memory: To the Doctor, and may God look after him as he looked after us!

And they all stood up and drank to his father's memory.

For Michael, this wake was more upsetting than his father's death had been. His father's death had come after a painful struggle, peacefully. There had been no time to say this or that, and very little contact between them. (The day before he died, he tried to squeeze Michael's hand, but Michael had pulled his hand away immediately.)

Now, three days later, he was in a living-room he barely recognized, with people he had met once or twice, if at all, and a handful of relatives.

A young woman in a black dress put her hand on his shoulder. Her hair was thick and black as a stage wig, and on her head she had what looked like a white lace doily.

—Poor boy, she said. You'll have to be strong now. For your dear mother . . .

She couldn't have been much older than he was, but she spoke maternally.

—He's so strong for his age, she said.

And that's how it had been all day. The mourners evidently felt they owed him the benefit of their wisdom, but when it came right down to it, they had none to offer.

Mr. Taylor, the man who'd given the toast to his father's memory, approached and said:

—How're you, young fellow?

—Fine, Michael answered.

—He was a damned good man, the Doctor . . .

Mr. Taylor smelled of alcohol and, beneath that, moth balls.

—Your father brought my own two into the world, he said. Wouldn't have anyone else do it. My wife, that's her, she felt the same way about it. Wouldn't have anyone else do it. The way these doctors are today, you don't find a good one too soon, that's for sure . . . Did you like my speech?

—Yes, Michael politely said.

—Two days to write it, said Mr. Taylor. Just to show how much we loved the Doctor.

He put his hand on Michael's shoulder, and then he moved on.

Michael's mother was in the kitchen with his aunt Edna. It was they who had made the peas and rice, the stewed chicken and the fishcakes. They had also made the ginger ale, and all the little sweets left on white plates, on tables and counters around the house. The two of them had been in the kitchen for days, for weeks it seemed. And before that, they had moved the furniture around, turned the paintings to face the wall and hung crêpe over all the mirrors.

His mother was in a dowdy, black dress, her face made up; cheeks rouged, eyelashes blackened, and she smelled of the *Chanel* they had given her for Christmas years ago.

One of the guests said:

—I've never had a better peas and rice . . .

—Thank you, Russell, his mother said.

She sounded tired.

His uncle Horace, who sat with two men Michael had never met, called him over. He put his arm around Michael's waist.

—Michael, this is Fred Hosein, and this is Melvin Fernandez. They were your father's friends back home.

—He looks just like Sonny, said Mr. Fernandez.

—You find?

Horace held him loosely. The men went on talking about Trinidad.

As soon as it was polite, Michael moved away from them. He made for the kitchen, but before he could get there a woman pulled him to her breast and held him. She smelled of rose-water and baby powder. She held on to him until he thought he would suffocate, but no, she let him go, held him again, then let him go for good: all without a word.

—Michael! Come give your mother a hand, his aunt Edna called.

But there was nothing for him to do, really. The latest course was ready, but as with the drink, people preferred to help themselves. (The mourners had finished the ginger beer, the coffee, the innocuous things. They were now on to stronger smack.)

—What do you want me to do? Michael asked.

But nobody was listening. His mother and his aunt were bickering about the salt in the stewed chicken.

—Don't put too much, you'll ruin it, his mother said.

As Michael retreated from the kitchen, a certain Mr. Andrew took hold of his arm. He introduced Michael to Mrs. Andrew. Mrs. Andrew was short, thin and grey-haired. She was dressed in black and, despite the heat, she still wore her black, pill-box hat.

—This is the Doctor's son, said Mr. Andrew.

—He looks so much like the Doctor, said Mrs. Andrew.

The sound of people chatting, of glasses clinking, of subdued laughter: it was annoying.

—Lovely funeral, said Mrs. Andrew.

Mr. Andrew said:

—The Doctor would have liked it.

Michael smiled politely, but it was impossible for him to imagine his father pleased with *any* funeral, much less his own. (Still, he doesn't have to make conversation, Michael thought, and the thought consoled him.)

—You know, said Mr. Andrew, not to change the conversation, but do you watch television?

—Yes.

—Of course . . . so I wonder if you saw . . . what was the name? . . . The one about funerals?

He turned to Mrs. Andrew.

—"The Hour of Our Death," she said.

—That's it: "The Hour of Our Death." Did you see it?

—No, said Michael.

Mr. Andrew said:

—It was remarkable. Where was it? Kuala Lumpur? It said the people in Kuala Lumpur, they put the son to death when the father dies . . . Isn't that something? If the son looks too much like the father, they put him to death . . .

The Andrews stared at Michael as if there were a correct response to this.

—I look like my mother, Michael said. Mr. Andrew said:

—No, no . . . I didn't mean . . .

Mrs. Andrew put her hand on Michael's arm.

—He didn't mean . . .

—It's alright, said Michael.

But he moved away from them.

There were people everywhere. Downstairs, a young couple had discovered his bedroom. They were sitting on his bed.

—I hope we're not in the way, said the woman.

—Your father was a good man, said the man. They went on talking to each other.

It really was a peculiar wake, but he wasn't sure his own feelings weren't behind its quirks. It was lacking solemnity, but he himself didn't feel solemn. (There were too many people. It was difficult to feel anything at all.) There should have been more sorrow or more distress. Instead, everyone spoke of The Doctor, and they held on to him. (It was like being wrapped in wet cotton.) And then, periodically, like a wave of nausea, his own grief rose and it was all he could do to keep from crying.

He went from room to room looking for quiet. There were people in all of them: in the kitchen, in all three bathrooms, in the living-room, in all five bedrooms, in the dining-room, in the bar, in the family room . . . no sanctuary.

Worse, as time went on their voices were less hushed; their laughter not quite restrained.

—Come hear this . . .

—Remember Admiral Nelson?

—Is there a little more sorrel?

—I'm so sorry, Mrs. Williams. He was a good man . . .

And then Mr. Taylor, who'd been drinking since his first eulogy, called for quiet. He didn't get it, though his wife managed to shush a few of the people around him.

—I want to say a few words about Dr. Williams, said Mr. Taylor. The Doctor was a good man. He was . . . generous, and good, and kind, and he never looked down on people who didn't have money . . . I remember the first time I saw the Doctor. It was a happy occasion . . . No, it wasn't happy. I had a boil, and the Doctor had to lance it, but the Doctor didn't hesitate. After that, I didn't hesitate to bring up private matters, because I knew the Doctor wouldn't mind. That was the kind of man he was . . .

Though very few people were listening to him, Mr. Taylor struggled manfully to remember the rest of his speech. His wife encouraged him. Nothing more would come though.

—The Doctor! he said at last.

And the people nearest him drank politely from their glasses.

There *were* a few who seemed genuinely upset by his father's death. Even now, hours after the burial, they wiped the tears from their eyes. Were they upset by his father's death, by death itself, or was there something else?

Having listened to Mr. Taylor's second, sad eulogy, Michael again made his way through the crowd. (It had grown.) He was on his way downstairs when Father Albert pulled him aside.

—Michael? How're you holding up?

—I'm fine.

—Don't be afraid to let it out, Michael. I know sometimes we men tend to keep things in, but it's good to let things out . . .

—Thank you, Father.

—Women are better with their emotions. No doubt about it . . . Just last month I was at a funeral in Wakefield. Not a dry eye in the house, *except* for the son. You'd think he didn't care peanuts. And then, next thing you know, schizophrenia. He's looking, speaking and acting like his father. You couldn't have told them apart. Lost himself entirely. Isn't that something?

—Yes, said Michael.

—So you just let it out.

—Thank you, Father.

In his bedroom, the couple were intimate: he now had his hand politely placed on her knee; she had hers on his shoulder. They sat facing each other, each with one foot on the floor, their bodies slightly reclined on his bed.

—I hope we're not in the way, the woman said.

Neither of them moved.

—No, said Michael.

It was he who was in the way, though all he wanted was to lie in his own bed with the lights out.

—Your father was a good man, the man said.

What was he supposed to say to that? His feelings for his father would not fit under the word "good." "Good" was no help at all. His father had been loving, kind, cruel, mean, headstrong, unloving, play-ful, gentle, and on until all the adjectives were exhausted. He had loved his father, he supposed, though here, as ever, the word "love" was puny. It wasn't love he felt for his father, but it was love also.

By the time he had made his way back upstairs, the mourners had become even more animated. (There were more of them.) There was some confusion. Someone was arguing about Jamaican cooking. Someone else excitedly spoke of a television program on the life of molluscs. And every time Michael passed a clump of people, someone would reach out for him.

—Your father . . . , they'd say.

Or:

—He loved you . . .

Or:

—You look so much like him . . .

And someone said:

—There was a something on "Nature" last week about Kuala Lumpur . . .

And it reminded Michael of eucalyptus trees.

Who were these people, anyway? He was beginning to wonder if it was such a good thing that so many people's lives had been salved by his father's art.

An older woman pulled his arm as he passed.

—You know, she said, your father loved you. He told me so himself, but . . . I don't know how to say this . . . maybe he was a little worried about you, too. And he wasn't exactly sure what you were doing with your life. I mean, here you are eighteen . . . Are you eighteen? Seventeen? Anyway, you need direction in life, and he wasn't really sure what direction you were taking . . . He wanted to see direction, that's all . . . I'd call that a good father, wouldn't you? To love you like that when you were breaking his heart a little, even though you didn't mean to . . . but you were a little bit of a disappointment, you know . . . not a disappointment, exactly, just a sliver of a disappointment . . . but that goes to show how much he loved you, doesn't it? Even though you were a disappointment . . .

Then she let go of him and turned away as if she hadn't spoken to him at all.

There were more people crying, now. Two or three of them were in real distress. One stood sobbing in a corner of the living-room. There was a respectful distance between him and those nearby.

And then it was as if his family disappeared. He couldn't find them in the crush of strangers. But no, there they were, when he actually looked for them: his mother and his aunt in the kitchen, his sister and her husband in the dining-room, the rest of them dispersed throughout, drinking.

Again, he ventured downstairs. The man and woman were still in his bedroom. Their relationship had progressed. His hand was frankly near her breast. It was there in a friendly way, but it had an intent of some sort. Her hand was casually open on his lap. Their faces were inches apart.

He was about to say something when the woman looked up.

—Oh, she said. I hope we're not in the way . . .

Michael stood before them, watching their hands. He knew their hands.

—Your father was a good man, the man said.

His room was no longer his to use. (He didn't want to face those two again.) That left only four rooms to which he could retire for privacy. There was the bathroom downstairs: newly wainscotted, it smelled of pine. There was the bathroom upstairs: tiled not two months ago, it smelled of caulking. There was the bathroom adjoining his parents' bedroom: it was too small. Finally, there was the furnace room. From each bathroom he would have to chase mourners or, worse, mourners engaged in the legitimate use of the accommodations. In any case, he didn't want to spend the day chasing people from bathrooms.

That left the furnace room. It was a clean chamber at the other end of the basement. It was well lit and smelled only a little of oil, and it was unlikely anyone would choose to do their mourning there. It was, suddenly, a haven.

He made his way through the dark suits and dresses as if he were penetrating a thick curtain, feeling for the part.

—Excuse me, young fellow, said Mr. So-and-So.

—Michael? said Father Albert. How're you holding up?

—I'm so sorry, said an older woman with white hair.

She held on to him.

—Are you Michael? said an older man.

He held on to him.

The place was now unbearably loud. It smelled of powders, colognes, sweat and alcohol. It was a relief to reach the furnace room, and then, as he should have guessed, the furnace room was occupied. There were three people inside: his uncle Roger; a stranger in a blue suit; and a woman in a blue dress wearing a floppy, blue hat with a wide, white band.

—Just close the door there for me will you, Michael?

—Is this Michael? the woman asked. She hugged him.

—We knew your father, said the man.

He touched Michael's shoulder.

—He was a good man.

They stared at him, as though admiring his clothes, and tried to engage him in conversation.

Bitterly disappointed, Michael made his way back through the crowd. As he did, he happened to see the clock behind the bar. Six o'clock! Four hours had passed since his father had been put in the ground. Time was an accordion. Certain things felt as if they'd gone on forever (a speech, a discussion) while others had breezed by (a speech, an encounter). The wake was like a fever, like lying in bed, the smell of a blanket like a horse's mane, the hours short, the minutes eternal.

Upstairs, the noise of conversation fought with the noise of grief. The man in the corner was even more distraught. He beat his chest and cried out. It was grotesque, but his grief was contagious. Hundreds of mourners were in tears. Now, when they held Michael they inadvertently dug their nails into his biceps or shook him or forced his head on to their breasts and held it there, his nose crushed on their sterna.

Once again, Mr. Taylor called for silence. He tried to stand up on a chair, failed, tried again, one hand on his wife's head for support. Mrs. Taylor was stoic under pressure. Mr. Taylor held up his hands.

—Shhh . . . , he said. Shhhh . . .

It would have been difficult to hear him, even if one were paying close attention. No one was.

—The Doctor, he said. The Doctor . . . boils and all . . . stand still dammit! . . . a paragon of injury . . . you stand there naked while he's sticking your boils . . . nothing personal . . . you better believe it . . . he was a good man . . . stand still!

And then he was helped down from the chair, or pulled down, by several men who thought he might hurt himself if he fell. Mr. Taylor was insulted by the idea. He attacked his wife.

—You bitch! he said.

But his insults were as slurred as his eulogy had been. They were lost in the din. And when he saw that most of the people around him were openly weeping, Mr. Taylor began to weep as well.

A woman in a navy-blue dress pulled back the wire-mesh curtain on the fireplace. She sprinkled ashes on her forehead. And then, the rest of them began to do the same. They took handfuls of ashes. They opened their shirts and dresses to find expanses of skin to cover. They ripped their clothes. A cloud of ashes rose over the living-room.

Someone dug their nails into Michael's elbow. (It was as if he'd cut himself on a broken bottle.)

—Spitting image, she said.

Father Albert held him by the collar.

—Let it out, he said.

But he couldn't. The ground shook from the mourners who stamped their feet as they covered themselves with ashes and called out his father's name. Michael could barely make his way through the crowd. The basement was no longer accessible, but the confusion and grief had certainly found their way downstairs. The noise that came from below was just as frightening as that from the main floor.

—In Malé . . .
—In Kuala Lumpur . . .
—In Kuala Lumpur?

Just what was the point of a wake, anyway? To revel in the memory of the dead? To share a common sorrow? Canadians didn't do that kind of thing, did they? He himself couldn't revel and he felt no sorrow. He felt nothing definite: sadness, longing, fear, resentment . . . there was even a small place where he was relieved by his father's death. He couldn't cry, while these people, many of whom knew his father only as The Doctor, these were the people who wept and covered themselves with ashes. Their tears were real; their cries were convincing, while all he could manage was to wander about, pushing his way through the mourners like an usher. He deserved whatever they had planned for him.

Briefly, he caught sight of his mother. Her face was pale, her hair dishevelled, her clothes rumpled. Her eye-shadow had run and her make-up had noticeably pebbled. She was no more than two yards away, but there were too many people between them. She was eclipsed by a tall man with ashes on his forehead.

An old man pinched Michael's cheek. A woman held him from behind.
—It's been so long, she said. Don't you recognize me?
—No, Michael said.

He couldn't even see her. She held on, squeezing the wind out of him.
—Where's Michael? someone shouted.

And from somewhere else came the sound of breaking glass.

The mourners still took great handfuls of ash from the fireplace. (I should have cleaned the fireplace when he asked me, Michael thought.) A woman tore the front of her own dress and then ripped the arm from the jacket of the man beside her. He in turn pulled his white shirt open with such force the buttons hit the wall like hail on shutters. (I should have cleaned the ashes in February or March, thought Michael.) Three women stood by the stairs to the basement. They had torn their dresses down to their petticoats. They were covered in ashes, and they sang:
—Save me, O God; for the waters are come in unto my soul . . .[1]

As if there weren't enough noise in the house.

---

[1] Psalm 61:1.

And the noise had become something like a long groan of anguish. Michael finally broke free of the woman holding him.

—The boy doesn't remember his mother's best friend! What kind of son is that?

More than anything else in the world, Michael needed to get outside. The wake had degenerated into something ecstatic and unhealthy. There were people shouting, crying, pulling their clothes from their bodies, breaking dishes against the wall, calling out his father's name. They moved aside at his approach, thousands of them, pushing him towards the living-room, towards the fireplace. (It was like drowning, with someone there to push you down or pull you under.)

And Michael began to struggle. He saw himself in the third person, fighting their will. He noticed peculiar details as he resisted: the rouge on a man's face, a false eyelash that hung down like a spider, a yellow shirt, a small turquoise ring, gold cuff-links, a handprint in ashes on the forehead of a young woman. He struggled, but on towards the fireplace he went. They wanted him. They wanted to touch him, to say: "Cry, it's alright. We care for you. He was a good man. You look just like him." And then they were going to burn him. It was all clear to him, in the fever of grief. He sank to his hands and knees and crawled through the wilderness of legs and feet, towards the nearest wall.

—Where's Michael? someone shouted.

—Excuse me, Michael said, as he snuck through their legs. I've lost my contact lenses.

He didn't wear contact lenses, but the mourners moved aside just the same. It took him five minutes to reach a wall, and when he did he held to it.

—Michael! his mother called.

And then her voice was lost in the noise. What did she want? It didn't matter. He kept moving.

They looked down at him, but all they could see clearly was the back of his suit, his neck bent forward, his knuckles and fingers in the deep carpet. He was anonymous, but his progress through the crowd was slow.

And then he could see the door, but the foyer was empty. Should he remain where he was, hidden by the legs of a few mourners, or should he make a break for the door? If he stayed where he was, the mourners would find him or trample him underfoot. If he made for the door, they would see him in the foyer. It was ten yards to the door, plenty of room to tackle him if he were seen.

—Michael? someone said softly.

And touched his shoulder. So the decision was made for him. He ran for the door. He made it across the foyer and, pulling frantically, twisted the large, brass doorknob this way and that.

—Michael?

Was the last thing he heard.

Outside, the sun was on its way down. It was still light, but the earth smelled of weeds and the close of day. The river ran softly by. The houses on the other shore were small and bright.

It was strange to go from such commotion to such peace. Standing there beside the water, looking across at the other shore, he felt the weight of silence. There was no one else in the world. There was Michael, and there was earth, sky, trees and water.

Gradually, the stillness of the world settled on him.

And then, for a moment, he distinctly felt his father's hand in his. He looked up at his father's face as they crossed a street in Petrolia, Ontario . . .

He remembered the warmth of his father's hand.

Everything else was hidden in a confusion of emotions . . .

A confusion, a welter, a tangle, a tumult . . .

—1994

Timothy Taylor   b. 1963

Born in Venezuela of peripatetic parents, Timothy Taylor grew up in Vancouver. He studied economics at the University of Alberta and, after completing an M.B.A. at Queen's University in Kingston, Ontario, worked for four years in banking before deciding to move back to Vancouver and write full time. Taylor's hat trick of having three stories chosen for a single volume of The Journey Prize Stories *in 2000 marked the emergence of an important new talent. His novel* Stanley Park, *published the following year, and the novella and eight stories brought together in* Silent Cruise *in 2002, show his abilities to create highly polished surfaces, to record the way life is lived today, and to capture the nuances and rhythms of contemporary speech, with all its disjunctions, unexpected connections, and hidden conflicts.*

"The Resurrection Plant" is an account of prejudice and the need to find a place within the difficult peer culture of boys. Its narrator, who has moved from a coastal community to Edmonton (as Taylor himself did), feels lost on "a buff-coloured planet full of hostile, sun-toughened Prairie kids."

The Resurrection Plant

Dad struck oil in 1976 when I was fifteen. "Struck" maybe isn't the right word. More like, was struck by. He read an enthusiastic article about it and became, himself, enthusiastic. That was his way. And so we moved from Halifax to an acreage outside Edmonton, Alberta.

I sat on the front steps of our new house and looked at the dead grass stretching away to the fence by the dirt road, the shrubs lining the drive ready to burst into flames. I was stunned by the heat, by the lack of moisture and colour. I felt like an exile. Marooned on a buff-coloured planet full of hostile, sun-toughened Prairie kids.

Mom dealt with it her own way. She was inside unpacking. Not pots or clothes. First, her South American hat collection. Panamas and bowlers. Next, the record player. Dad phoned from his new office in downtown Edmonton.

"Helping your mom, Colin?"

I didn't tell him mom was lying flat on her back in the empty living room listening to the Tijuana Brass. Wearing a Mayan bowler. What I did tell him was that I was going to go look for the river.

"Attaboy," Dad said optimistically. "The Atlantic, see . . . it just goes in and out. The river is always coming from someplace, and then going on to some other place."

There were black-and-white birds that shrieked challenges and followed me from branch to branch partway down the ravine. I climbed through papery grass and some thin silver trees, up over a weed-covered berm, and discovered the mighty North Saskatchewan.

It was brown. I threw dirt clods into it.

My locker partner was Ted Shuchuk. He had a virgin upper lip, never shaved, which aspired to a moustache and achieved only a faint black smudge that disappeared entirely if you looked at it from a certain angle. His closest friend was a failed eleventh-grader everyone called Snowblower. He stored his broken binders, a dumb-bell and stray sandwiches on a rickety homemade set of plywood shelves. Almost every morning I had to brush piles of mouse shit off my books.

Ted spruced up the locker with an Olivia Newton John poster and a Nazi flag.

The gym teacher, Mr. Cartwright, was the first to see the flag, and he cuffed Ted in the side of the head and told him to take it down. Ms.

Davison, the drama coach, said hanging up that particular flag was hateful, insulting and immature, but Ted's legal right.

I waited a week before mentioning it to my mom. She wrote a carefully worded letter to *The Edmonton Journal* and the next day there was a long, if somewhat oblique, editorial about the Holocaust. The swastika came down.

"That was my grandfather's flag," Ted said, breathing menthol tobacco breath on me.

"You must be very proud," I said to him.

"Get out of the way, turkey, I'm going to work out." And he began pumping his dumb-bell right in front of the locker. I had to lean over him to put my liverwurst sandwiches up on that tiny top shelf.

My mom said to me, "He can't hurt you. Don't forget that." It was late September. We were walking through a warm wind on a hard blue night.

After Hitler was gone, my mom emerged from her hiding place in the Black Forest and took a boat to Argentina. (This is how she told it.) She was drinking hot chocolate on the lower deck, an indescribable luxury, and someone said, "Eichmann is on this very boat!"[1] An old woman, her voice shaking with rage at the diabolical irony of it. And my mom had heard this and been sick: all at once, over the rail, a deep hot-chocolate-coloured, evacuating sickness. Then she fainted, toppling like a spent gyro and hitting her head on a deck bollard. She woke up wrapped in a horse blanket, her head pounding, and delivered her signature line, in broken English with her eyes still pinched shut: "Damn to Eichmann." My grandmother and the old lady cried. My mom never did. She said simply, "Then we went to Rio de Janeiro, and I prayed for a husband. Canadian or maybe from California."

I have a photograph from the New Year's Eve party at the Canadian consulate in Rosario where they met. My dad is flushed and brush-cut. My mother looks wide-eyed, frozen in the headlights of her own prayers. He took her to Nova Scotia the next year.

Phil Levine wore a black kangaroo jacket and carried an asthma inhaler. We used to eat lunch out at the hockey rink, on the visitors' bench. Phil always had a Vonnegut on him, an old dog-eared Dell paperback edition

---

[1] Adolf Eichmann, who was in charge of the Nazi genocide of European Jews during World War II, supervised the mass killing of over six million men, women, and children. After the war he hid from the Allies, first in Germany for five years and later, under an assumed name, in Argentina (where a number of Nazis had already fled) until he was captured by Israeli agents in 1960. Tried for crimes against humanity, and executed in 1962, he is infamous for having defended himself by saying, "I was only following orders." Hermann Goering (mentioned later) was Hitler's second in command, responsible for military operations.

Player Piano, Cat's Cradle, Jailbird. Phil's brother once spent an entire year indoors, reading and underlining bits in his Vonnegut collection, then moved to the Yucatan Peninsula. It was enough to make anyone read the underlined bits. So we sat out there at the rink and talked about fascism and nuclear winter and setting things on fire, until a tanker truck pulled up and flooded the rink. Then suddenly there were hockey players everywhere.

"Goofs with dentures," said Phil, who had a fine eye for details.

We went inside.

"Phil's a Zionist," I announced at dinner.

Scott Miller was not a Zionist, but he knew aircraft statistics and had read half of *Slaughterhouse-Five*. Phil, Scott and I ended up in the same science group. Our fourth was Ted. He came over and surveyed his team-mates: "Fatso, Nerdball and Psycho Asthmahead."

"You can be Goering," said Phil.

"But I was Fatso last year," Scott said, and Ted hit him without even looking in his direction.

"Anyone know what this is?" Mr. Duke, our science teacher, stood at the front of the class behind the lab bench, holding a brown crust above his head between his fingers. Holding it like it might break. It looked dead, whatever it was. The rad hummed.

"It's a dried dog turd," Ted said, laughing.

"It's a resurrection plant," Duke said. The brown crust didn't deny this. It was curled in on itself tight as a pine cone.

"And if I said it was alive would you believe me?" he asked, and somebody near the window answered aloud, "No-o-o."

"Well," he said, "how could you prove me wrong?"

One of the girls got it right. "Absolutely," Duke said. "Living things need oxygen."

So, we tried to suffocate it. Duke and Snowblower put it under the vacuum beaker set up on the corner of the lab bench.

"If it still looks the same in a week, what'll we know then?" Duke asked. "Anyone?"

"That it's definitely a dog turd," said Ted.

"What'll we know?" he asked again after Ted had disappeared to the principal's office.

"That it's dead," I said aloud. My first unsolicited class answer and, in fact, the right answer.

After school, Ted and Snowblower hung out and smoked in the east stairwell. We didn't talk to them. They hung out with girls, knit-vested princesses with platforms, pooka shells and three-dimensional breasts.

Phil got moods. He'd walk all the way home and not say a thing.

Scott walked between us, always talking, sticking a hand out on either side of him so we all had to stop and listen to him.

"Someone ask me what the fuel capacity of an L-1011 is."

Or, "Got your jockstraps for wrestling next week? No, really, what size did you get?"

After we dropped Scott off at his house, I'd try to draw Phil out.

"Shuchuk's into knives, hey?" I said once.

"And flags," Phil said tightly.

"You know he hung it up again," I asked.

"I know he hung it up again," he nodded.

"I could be a Zionist, you know," I tried.

"With a name like McCluskey?" he said and peeled off for home. I waved at his back.

At night we played ping-pong and Yahtzee round robins, and my mom and I listened to talk radio. Every Albertan held a personal opinion on whether the northern lights made a noise. I saw them a couple times and didn't hear anything. They just waved back and forth and then faded away.

At breakfast, Dad read the "Exposed-flesh-freezes-in-how-many-seconds" statistics out of the newspaper: "Ten seconds. Coldest November day since nine-teen-oh-too. Says here scientists have proven it's actually colder than a witch's tit. Sorry."

Duke let everyone come up with a way to kill the resurrection plant. Carbon monoxide, X-rays, two weeks of darkness, chlorine and ammonia gas. By December, I was rooting for the plant.

"Just burn the fucking thing," Ted said, right in one of those unexpected canyons of silence that a classroom will pass through.

Everyone turned to look at him. Duke closed his eyes and clenched his jaw. We decided to put it in a deep freeze until after the holidays.

The bell rang. "All right. The jockstrap hour," Scott said.

The sponge mat was rolled out in the gym. Phil tripped Scott and fell elbow first onto his back. "Body slam," he shouted. They bounced up, tapped into the finely strung mania webbing throughout the room.

"Get off the mat!" Cartwright emerged from the equipment room. Whistle, stopwatch, green sweatsuit cut like real pants with a wide yellow stripe down the outside of each leg. Red eyebrows the same width as his moustache. Black eyes flicking left and right.

He called me Mr. Vocabulary.

"Ring the mat!" We scattered like ants under a magnifying glass.

"Sutcliffe and Nesbitt," Cartwright read off his clipboard from the centre of the gym, glaring around him for silence.

"Sutcliffe, referee's position." Sutcliffe hit the mat on all fours. Nesbitt kneeled beside him, hands on Sutcliffe's back, fingers spread. There was silence. I looked up at the ceiling. Green rings around the gym lights were a bad omen. Silence hovered. And then the sound of the whistle was swamped by pandemonium.

"Nesbitt!" Scott yelled beside me. Sutcliffe had done a sit-out, sliding out from under Nesbitt's hands and scrambling to his feet. They grappled and fell. All knees and ribs.

"Nesbitt!" Phil and I joined in.

Nesbitt was chest down. Sutcliffe was on his back reefing on a half nelson. Snowblower was chanting, "Sutty, Sutty, Sutty."

Nesbitt's underwear climbed out the top of his shorts.

"Gonch pull," shouted Ted.

And that appeared to break his spirit. Nesbitt resigned with his eyes and rolled. One. Two. Three.

"Who backed the loser?" Cartwright paced the edge of the mat looking at each of us.

Our betrayal of Nesbitt was unanimous.

"I heard some of you yelling," Cartwright said, smiling, enjoying the moment. "Some of you, I know, backed the loser."

After gym, Phil and Scott and I sat in the hallway with our backs against the lockers and ate lunch.

"Meat loaf," Scott said, looking depressed. "What do ya got?"

"Gefilte fish and a Ding Dong," Phil said.

"Very Yiddish, Levine, congratulations. What do ya got, Colin?"

"I'm not trading."

"What though?"

"A granola bar," I said.

"All right. Meat loaf for the granola bar." Scott opened a corner of his sandwich. "It's got ketchup and mayo. What kind of granola bar is it?"

"My mom makes them," I said.

"Oh, forget it," Scott said. "What else you got?"

"A herring sandwich," I admitted.

"Herring sandwich?" Scott said. "What's with the Yid food, guys, how'm I supposed to trade here?"

"Well, I'm kind of Jewish, you know?" I said.

We ate and watched the janitor string up red letters that spelled Merry Christmas along the main hallway.

"You spelled it wrong," Scott called over to him.

"What?" he said.

"Your sign is spelled wrong."

He climbed down off his stepladder, wiped his forehead with a rag he took from the pocket of his railway overalls and looked at the sign.

"So how'd you spell it?" he said after several minutes.

"H-A-N-U-K-K-A-H," Scott said. So Phil and I punched him until he coughed up a piece of sandwich. Then we went over to Poon's to buy Sno-Jos.

"What's this about you being kind of Jewish," Phil said later. We were standing outside the store squinting in the clear bright sun.

"My Oma and Opa[2] were, so my mom kind of is," I said. "I mean they're not really, because they're Lutheran, but they could be if they wanted to switch back."

Phil took some Wink Sno-Jo into his straw, covered the end with his thumb and dribbled the green slush onto the sidewalk. "Moms pass the Jewish bloodline," he said. And Phil scraped the frozen green pattern he'd made on the sidewalk with the side of his boot.

We went skating in Mayfair Park after Christmas. Dad bought us all new Bauer Supremes. I asked my mom while we were skating, "When does it warm up here?" I had two pairs of gloves on.

"Don't you like this?"

She skated with her bare hands behind her back.

"It's crisp, it's fresh," she said.

The air felt sharp on my cheek for the first while, then I didn't feel anything on my cheek.

"I'm going numb," I said.

---

[2] Grandmother and grandfather (German).

"You shouldn't complain so much," she said. And we skated on a bit in silence. It was true that she never complained, not about physical pain.

"Ted hung that flag back in our locker," I said.

She kept skating. The ice was covered with a whisper of snow.

"Phil's a Zionist," I said. Still she just skated. Bare hands behind her back. Ear muffs, no toque.

"I want to be Jewish," I said finally.

Then she stopped, so I stopped. She looked at me.

"What do you want to be?" she asked.

"Jewish," I said.

"No, what do you want most of all. Right this minute."

"I'd like to be warm," I said, without thinking.

She smiled a sort of halfway smile I couldn't interpret.

Then she said, "Well, that's not so complicated then. In the spring you will get what you want."

Phil and I planned a camping trip out to Elk Island Park to see buffaloes in the spring. I was talking about this on the way to school and he cut me off.

"I want you to put this in your locker," he said, just outside the schoolyard gate. It was a taped-up Birks box. I held it in my glove. It seemed weightless.

"What is it?" I asked.

"It's the resurrection plant," he said.

"No, really," I said.

Phil stopped walking. "Do you have to know? I'm asking you a favour. A favour I couldn't ask just anyone. Hide this box in the back of your locker. Forget about it. As my brother, do me this favour." And he took my hand and shook it slowly and firmly, something he'd never done before.

"Well, I don't have to exactly know about it," I said. "Except maybe if it's explosive or flammable. I'd like to know whether to put it on the upper or lower shelf." Phil didn't smile. At school I dropped the box behind Ted's shelves and blew into my cold hands.

"All right," Phil said, grinning, happy. I felt guilty-good.

Plus we were late.

"Glad you could join us, gentlemen," Duke said.

We sidled in like desperadoes. The room stayed silent after we sat down. No one was looking around.

"One of us is a thief," Duke said. And I noticed that Ted's chair was empty.

By the time I got out the door after class, and sprinted to the locker, Ted was hunched over, digging into the papers that filled the bottom shelf.

"Where'd you put it?" Ted said to me.

My legs actually felt weak. I was hyperventilating. "Behind the shelves," I said.

Ted leaned into the locker. "Oh, here it is." And he pulled out his dumb bell, turned around and started pumping it up and down solemnly.

"You been using this?" he asked me.

"No, I haven't at all. I promise."

"Just be cool," Phil said from behind me. He sounded cool.

There was a muscle on the right side of Ted's neck pressing out and relaxing rhythmically as he pumped. I stretched around him to put my science binder away.

"Hey, turkey," he said. "I need your notes from today."

"Sure. Where were you?" I asked.

Ted looked disgusted. "Principal. It was nothing."

"What was nothing, Shuchuk?" Phil leaned into our conversation, a big fake smile pasted on.

"Mind your own fucking business, Levine."

"No, seriously, I want to know. I mean, we never talk, you know. How was Christmas, get any cool stuff at all? Guns? Grenades? Gas maybe? Hey, nice flag."

"Hey, happy Hanukkah, Levine, all right?" Ted turned to his locker.

"And back to you, Shuchuk. Happy, happy, happy Hanukkah."

Ted was walking away.

"What a pin-dick," Phil said. He was wheezing. He took a drag on his inhaler.

"What's your problem?" I said to him.

"No problem," he said.

"What did you do? What did I do?" I asked.

He smiled, took another drag.

"Take it easy, McCluskey," he said. And we walked after Ted down the hall towards the gym.

Cartwright was pacing the circle at the centre of the mat, spinning his whistle. "And now," he said to the assembled class. "A special match."

Every light in the ceiling cast a green ring.

Cartwright was grinning broadly. "Will you welcome please, the Snowblower."

Whoops. Ted was on his feet. "Me. Me. Me. Let Snowblower and me go."

Not likely. Never friends. Cartwright's eyes were flicking around the ring. My arms goose-pimpled.

"In the blue trunks . . . Mr.Voca-aaa-bulary."

Snowblower's face went flat with surprise, then hardened into something like sadistic amusement. I stood slowly, trying and failing to hold Cartwright's stare.

"Oh man, that's unfair," Scott said.

"Thanks," I said. "Any advice?"

"The balls," Scott said, "definitely the balls."

"His that is," Phil added. "Kick them, or pull on them."

"Oh, and if you hit him like this, you can drive his nose bone into his brain," Scott said, demonstrating on himself.

"Snowblower, referee," Cartwright barked, smiling at me from behind his whistle as I entered the centre ring.

I spread my hands on Snowblower's sweating back. The whistle sounded far above us and I did exactly as taught. I lunged for his far arm, reaching under his chest, got it, and drove with my shoulder against his ribs. Snowblower rocked a bit and settled. Then he stood up and shook me off. I was hanging from his neck. He grabbed my head. I jerked downward and escaped.

We circled. I could hear Ted screaming, "Snowblower. Snowblower." And Scott foghorning away on my behalf.

Then Snowblower grappled, lifted me and dropped me on the mat. Damn. My face was going to burst. He was working on my right shoulder. I twisted over onto my chest, crossed my legs, tucked in my hands and elbows. My last defence, the Armadillo.

Snowblower was scrambling around my back. I felt one hand on my neck, one on my ankles. I felt his head butt into my side, just above the waist. Phil was looking at me. He shrugged and shook his head. Snowblower was bending me like a bow and arrow, pulling on my head and feet, pushing with his head. I flipped onto my back, a husk, airless. Pinned.

Everyone was shouting. Cartwright helped me up and put a towel in my face. "It's just a nosebleed," he said. I pulled the towel away from my face. The white terry cloth was sticky red in the middle, still connected to me by a slick string of pink mucus.

I got what I wanted most. It did warm up.

Above the dirt-brown snow drifts, the skinny poplars next to the fire station were muscling out buds. There was a mouse population explosion at school. I began losing ground to the shit at the bottom of our locker. There were mice in the halls, streaking for cover in the corners behind doors. Disappearing into the wall under the water fountain.

On a Monday I slushed up the street, the air light and breathable, past sand-crusted front lawns.

Duke came out of the storeroom and stepped up behind the lab bench. He took his time, cleared his throat. Ted not being there didn't even register with me until I saw the blue Birks box.

Conversations slowly stopped, heads turned, seats were readjusted. Phil and Scott were the last to stop talking. I had forgotten the thing existed, and recognized it now like a toy lost in grade four and rediscovered. Like the Bluenose II model in the box in the basement that I had found before Christmas and repacked. That I had recognized every detail of, and immediately wanted forgotten.

He stood with the blue Birks box in his right palm. Then he reached over and pulled the lid off and rolled a blackened briquette-sized lump onto the desk. There was no question what it was. Burnt to a nub of its former size. We might have doubted. We had all doubted, I suppose, but the resurrection plant was now most definitely dead.

"At least we found it," Duke said. "The mouse exterminators were looking for nests in the lockers and . . . and the person responsible . . ." His face was a quilt of red and white splotches. "The person responsible has been expelled."

Phil showed nothing. He stared straight ahead, and so I did as well. Scott's jaw was slack. Around us, people seemed to breathe relief and delight, in unison.

The next part happened fast. I went to the locker after the three o'clock bell without talking to Phil. I was thinking of going home. Of confessing to someone or going to the Yucatan or both. And then I opened the locker and saw the flag gone. And something did flush through me. Like I had won something. Pride. Anger.

Scott came up behind me. "You going over to the fire station? Phil's already there."

And when we got into the poplars, it seemed like everyone was waiting for us. Ted was shadow-boxing Snowblower, dumb-bell biceps evident under his Edmonton Eskimos T-shirt. Phil stood a few yards away in the long grass, shaking his wire-thin arms by his sides.

"This is nuts," I said to him. "This is very stupid."

"And your better idea is?" he said to me.

"We'll get killed," I said.

Ted approached through the thick grass to where we stood. "I didn't burn that fucking thing. He told Duke I did. He's a weasel. You're both weasels. You're both dead weasels."

"I never said anything to anyone," Phil said.

"Fuck you, Levine."

"Fuck yourself, Shuchuk."

"Right now, man, right now."

"Don't you think—" I started a sentence I didn't have an ending for anyway.

"Hey, you're next, all right?" Ted said right into my face. He was at one of the angles from which I could see the moustache. It was filling out.

Snowblower was smacking Ted in the arm, bop, bop, get him, man, you're gonna kill him. A crowd fanned hungrily around us.

I looked at Phil, who gave a shrug.

"Let me have the first go," he said.

So I got out of the way and they did that mandatory circling manoeuvre. I can't say they were really sizing each other up. Ted was doing it for effect, swinging his fist near his waist, his stance open and confident. He was appraising a certain kill, thinking about maximizing crowd value maybe, but at his own speed.

Phil was just waiting. He could have been waiting for the bus. Except his elbows were tucked in at his sides, his white-knuckled fists trembled at eye level and he was leading left. A useless formality before going out with good form.

The crowd's calls for blood became persuasive, even from those who didn't want blood, those who probably wanted to go home but couldn't or wouldn't, because leaving at that moment was inconceivable. Girls hopped up and down on the spot. The few junior high school kids there, boys, were pushing each other back and forth, infected by what lay ahead.

"Ted. Ted. Ted." No one was yelling for Phil.

"Kill him, Phil," I screamed. And Phil stepped off his back foot, closed quickly and threw what everyone in the lot must have known was a one-in-a-million haymaker. A sweeping arc. A hate-filled cartoon of a punch, with enough power to remove an opponent's head as long as he'd been immobilized first.

Ted didn't even look at it. But he brought a fist up from his waist hard and fast into Phil's throat. A short, blunt movement. Phil's right arm feathered off Ted's shoulder and followed him to the grass. His face was white, his eyes pinched shut, his hands around his own neck, breathing like a stick in bike spokes. Then Ted kicked him in the stomach, a considered, methodical kick. Phil moved his hands, rolled tighter. Ted kicked again. The side of the head. It sounded like *clack*.

Phil rolled away, bloody face in the grass.

"Enough. Fuck," I said and ran toward them. The air was alive with movement. The crowd was draining out of the lot around me.

Scott was crying and yelling, "If you killed him, my dad'll sue." He was on his bike already.

I rolled Phil over. He was bleeding, but breathing.

Snowblower came over. "Oh, leave him, he's fine."

"You better not've fucking killed him," Scott yelled again, his face red and wet, and then he pedalled away. Standing up for speed, not looking back.

"You later, Vocabulary," Ted said, standing over Levine and me.

"Me now, cheese dick," I heard myself say as I stood up. Clearly I had lost my mind. Maybe I wouldn't feel anything. I felt strong. Maybe I was coursing full of some kind of Judaic adrenaline, making me impervious to pain, to fear.

"Come on, Brownshirt," I found myself saying. "You want to hit me. Hit me. Fucking hit me. What? Knock me down, pussy. Burnt a fucking plant so now you're a tough guy?"

Ted took a step back toward me but Snowblower stopped him.

"Don't," Snowblower said. Ted shook his arm away. "Listen to this little shit."

"Come on, gas me, you Ukrainian fuck. Try to kill me, Eichmann."

"Oh, I'm going to enjoy this," said Ted.

"You want Duke to come out?" Snowblower had Ted by the arm again. "Let's get out of here, man."

"Bastards took my flag. Let me kill him," Ted said.

"Come on, Eichmann, I'm not fucking afraid of you," I said.

"Leave the girls here," Snowblower said, almost softly.

They walked out of the lot, Snowblower pulling Ted through the grass. I wanted them dead.

"Anytime," I yelled after them. I was delirious.

But they didn't come back.

"Nice work," Phil said. He was sitting up behind me holding his throat and laughing. It looked painful. He had to go into his Adidas bag and get out his inhaler before he could speak again.

"Eichmann?" he said, wheezing, bleeding, laughing. "Fucking Eichmann."

Then Phil reached into his bag again, took out the resurrection plant and handed it to me. I had never felt it before. It was crumbled, a little worse for the wear. Tender to the touch, like dried cedar. But all there. A tough little plant. Completely unburned. As alive as ever.

"Just do something with it. Anything," he said to me.

"I thought this was burnt. What's that in the school?" I said, confused.

Phil winced and strained some blood through his teeth into the grass. "A pine cone. A burnt pine cone," he said finally, coughed, spat some more. Laughed another painful laugh.

"Jesus," I said. I felt light, and I sat down suddenly, then lay back in the grass. The sky full of horsetails.

I kept the resurrection plant for three days before I talked to my mom. Even then I didn't tell her anything, only that I had something that wasn't mine. She said, "Is it from a store?" And then when I shook my head she said, "Does it have a proper owner?"

I said that its real owner thought it was dead. And that made her think for a minute. "Then put it where it belonged before its real owner even knew it was alive."

Of course it only needed water. I carried the resurrection plant down into the river valley. I found a spot near the sludgy bank. Buried it halfway in the moist brown soil, full of bugs and worms. The bowl-blue sky held out space above me. And in less than a week there was a fist-sized bush that sprang roots and pushed itself deep into the prairie.

The magpies still follow and fall away, their insults tapering. Their cackles trail behind them as they turn back toward the highway, toward roadkill and other concerns. The papery grass still catches in my cuffs and laces. The muddy bank gums my leather soles.

I kneel. It has grown as high as my chest.

I hold the branches, which I think smell of musty pine and pepper. The branches aren't dry. Aren't lifeless. They're full of the earth's moisture. Full of the water that the earth holds from the air. Moisture churned by beetles and fertilized by generations seeking to be reborn.

—2002

Lisa Moore   b. 1964

Lisa Moore, a member of the Burning Rock Collective, a St. John's writers' group, and part of the recent literary renaissance in Newfoundland, is the author of two volumes of short stories: Degrees of Nakedness *(1995) and* Open *(2002). One of the most striking features of Moore's fiction is its frankness: her characters speak directly about desire as they try to sort out the new rules that govern relationships.*

Moore's stories are more than just reports on mating patterns. As "The Lonely Goatherd" shows, her characters exist with uneasy intensity in a world that is still defined by their local milieu yet flooded by denaturing media: there are snapshots, television programs, videos, paintings, sculpture, book illustrations, film, songs, and buzzers; a home stereo system unexpectedly picks up a message from a taxi dispatcher; a woman paints images of golf courses based on photographs of videotaped TV broadcasts. Contexts increasingly come from elsewhere—from literature (the name of the St. John's cab company recalls Gulliver's Travels*), from popular culture (the story's title comes from* The Sound of Music*), and from myth, fable, and fairy tales.*

The Lonely Goatherd

The houses dig their heels into the hill to stop from tumbling into the harbour. The clapboard faces are stained with last night's rain. Everything is squeezed together and sad. Carl loves Anita but lately he's been sleeping with other women. It's not idiosyncrasies he's been sleeping with, it's bones. Cheek bones, hip bones, knees. He sees inside apartments of St. John's he will never see again.

Two nights ago he was in an apartment over Gulliver's Taxi Stand. The girl's stereo speaker picked up radio messages of the Dispatcher. At about four in the morning Carl heard the taxi driver say, Sure that's only your imagination, almost as if he were tangled in the bed sheets with them. Carl felt like a kid.

The sad thing is Anita's art. She is painting golf courses from the TV set. The old man she nurses watches golf, tapes it with his VCR. She takes polaroid snapshots of the screen. She wants to capture in her paintings the glossy finish of the polaroid, the snowy texture of the video, the play of light on the manicured lawns, and the slow motion time of the ball flying through the air. She says it's an analytical reduction she's after, always keeping herself distanced from the subject. They don't talk about their problem, but when he looks at her paintings he feels she is stripping him like an onion, layer by layer, her eyes watering.

Carl works at the Arts and Culture Centre, building sets. He makes an adequate living working chiefly with styrofoam. This week he is building sets for a fairy tale amusement park. He shows his own sculpture once a year.

A sea of white styrofoam beads covers the floor, clings to his pants, his bald head, and sticks to his hands like warts. Thumb-tacked on the wall are several eighteenth century fairy tale illustrations, before illustration got cute. Red Riding Hood in the gnarled forest, eyes wide, the wolf, saliva drooling from his fangs. Where Red Riding Hood's cape parts you glimpse a white vulnerable breast. Carl flicks his pocket knife into the illustration like a dart. Carl has been provided with an assistant from the Student Employment Office. The assistant studies day care management. Her name is Sarah. She is about ten years younger than Carl, and is now sweating in her paper suit over the giant chunk of styrofoam from which the wolf will be carved.

Anita found out she was pregnant the same time she took the job nursing Mr. Crawhall. He sleeps most of the time she's there. This gives her an opportunity to paint. The house is on Circular Road, surrounded by trees which block the sound of traffic. Toward the end of the first week with Mr. Crawhall she entered the house and was assaulted by a loud consistent buzzing. She thought it was the buzzer by his bed, that Mr. Crawhall had died and his hand had fallen on the buzzer, but it was the egg timer on the stove. She has to serve him a three-and-a-half minute egg every day. Her fingers shake a little on the silver teaspoon when she brings it near his mouth. It's different from feeding a baby, there's the question of Mr. Crawhall's dignity. Because of her condition the egg makes her nauseous. Once a hairline crack ran down the side of the egg and yolk seeped through it over the gold rimmed egg cup down to the saucer, threatening Mr. Crawhall's thin white bread. He said quite slowly, with his hands squeezed in the effort to speak, Oh, how have we managed to waste all that lovely yellow yolk?

Anita thinks of painting the egg as seen from under Mr. Crawhall's magnifying glass, but the jelly of it and the overt symbolism make her sick. She's planning an abortion. The baby isn't Carl's.

Sarah, the assistant, is more of a hindrance than a help. Her professional opinion after six weeks in day care training is that Carl is making fairy tale props too realistic. The Momma Bear and Poppa Bear look like real bears. Strands of melted clear plastic hang from their teeth. She says they'll have a damaging psychological effect. She feels fairy tales are violent and sexist. She thinks we should ship loads of grain to India, she talks about McDonald's hamburger containers polluting the environment, American aggression in Nicaragua, and acid rain. Carl is building a cage for her out of two-by-four and plastic sheeting so she can work with contact cement and the fumes will be contained within the cage. He gives her a gas mask, tightening the rubber strap around her fine hair. He puts her in the cage with one of the wolves. It's impossible to talk with a gas mask on. The rest of the afternoon the studio is quiet, except for the chain saw.

Anita watches *The Sound of Music* with Mr. Crawhall. He tells her to fast forward over the scene with Lisel and her boyfriend in the gazebo where she sings *I am sixteen going on seventeen, innocent as a lamb.* This scene bores Mr. Crawhall, so they watch it in fast forward. The dance number changes Lisel into a maddened butterfly batting the wings of her white skirt against the boy's head. She circles round and round him, flinging her arms this way and that, trapped in the amorphous white cloud. Her face in the close up is contorted and pulled like plastic across the jiggling screen. When Anita presses "play," Julie Andrews sings, *These are a few of my favourite things.*

When Carl gets round to asking Sarah to sleep with him he tells her he is bored sleeping with his wife. Sarah asks, Is she intelligent?

Carl says, Yes, of course, she's a very articulate woman.

Does her conversation bore you? asks Sarah.

No, I love her.

Then I don't see why she should bore you in bed.

Well, her conversation might bore me if she were the only woman I had a conversation with in seven years.

He says after a moment, Don't worry about Anita; she gets it whenever she wants it. She has no idea how I feel.

Although Sarah feigns moral indignation, Carl feels her going soft like butter. She blushes when he compliments her and enjoys the special attention she gets around the workshop.

Mr. Crawhall's house is designed to allow as much sunlight as possible. When he's asleep Anita watches a white chair with faint apricot flowers. The shadows of the leaves on the chair are in constant motion. At about seven in the evening it's almost as though the chair catches fire, a silent fire. It's the only moving thing in the stiff-backed room besides the two goldfish. They are kept in a clear glass bowl with no plants or coloured stones. A soft spoken friend speaks to Anita over the phone, You really have no choice, Anita. This will hurt Carl so much. It was a one night stand.

The goldfish are identical. Anita calls one fish the option of keeping the baby and the other the abortion. She watches them swim around and makes a game of seeing how long she can tell which is which.

That night Anita says to Carl, about her new painting, If you spend enough time alone the pain of emptiness passes and you realize your own voice is the only company you need.

The image is entirely nonrepresentational, red and yellow dots only, but the canvas shimmers with anxiety.

Carl tries to remember what it is he loves about Anita. The smell of turpentine on her flannel painting smock, burnt match sticks and beer bottle caps between the bed sheets. The squeezed paint tubes in her leather box, curled in on themselves, the limbs of their shirts and jeans twisted together on the floor. The photographs in his sock drawer, in the beaten Tooton's envelope, of the night they walked to Signal Hill. It was summer and the sky was a skin of ticklish rain. Anita was drinking pop that turned the down of her upper lip and tongue orange. She tasted like summer, childhood. In the photographs the lights of the city at night burned coloured sizzles on the film. They made love on the grass, watching out for broken beer bottles, an aureole of amber glitter around their bodies.

Anita slept with a tourist named Hans. He was a German gymnast who had trained for the Olympics for eleven years and gave it up. Now he was driving a VW van across Canada. St. John's was his starting point. He was golden, muscular, but small. He walked with his hands loosely by his sides. He seemed to place his steps, walking on the balls of his feet as if he were stepping onto a mat in front of a large audience. He had been sitting alone at the Ship Inn drinking milk. It was as though the blondness of his hair alarmed almost anyone who might have joined him. Hans and Anita discussed what was scenic, the hospitable Newfoundlander, and Jiggs dinner, briefly. He had come from California, that was his first stop in North America. He had learned to speak English in a place called Pure Springs, a self-awareness camp with hot springs where they practised Gestalt and taught hyperventilation to relax. Hans talked about group therapy.

You are one of twenty-five for a month. You come to know each other very well and one day you step outside the room and the others decide on one word or a simple phrase that describes your essence. Sometimes it's very painful, but for the first time you see your true self. Everyone hugs and is supportive.

Anita asks, What was your word?

Cold fish.

Outside the Ship Inn a rusted sign pole stuck out from the brick wall. The sign itself had been removed. Hans climbed on the windowsill easily and, jumping, gripped the bar. He swung back and forth, then with his legs straight, toes pointed, lifted himself into a handstand. It was the moment while he was upside down that Anita realized she would sleep with him because he was passing through and because her faithfulness to Carl was a burden. When he swung down, Anita felt the pocket of warm night air he cut with his body.

Hans swept the seats of the VW van with a small hand brush before she got in. The van was spotless. There was a string bag full of fruit, none of it bruised. On the wall was a calendar from Pure Springs. The photograph for June was four pairs of naked feet, toes twisted, all caught in the same hammock net. Nestled between the hand-brake and the driver's seat was a glossy purple diary. Anita picked it up and opened it.

What's this?

Inside were poems written in German, diary entries, dried flowers, and coloured pencil drawings of mountain peaks.

My ex-fiancee made that for me.

Hans took out his shiny Swiss Army knife from the glove compartment and effortlessly cut the rind from a pineapple while he spoke. She was a gypsy. Long dark hair, black eyes, small like me, we wore each other's clothes. We hiked together in the mountains of Switzerland for two and three months at a time. We were together for ten years and were to be married. The invitations were sent. One hundred invitations. A week later she said she wanted to go to Africa. She met another fellow there, a German. The wedding was called off.

Hans held a quivering slice of pineapple out to Anita on the blade of the knife.

You must be very hurt, said Anita.

No, at Pure Springs they taught me to see myself as I really am. When I have finished my trip I will return there as a counsellor.

They sat in silence looking at the stars over Long Pond.

The fruit is very sour, remarked Hans. In the morning Anita could see the Arts and Culture Centre from where they had parked. She saw Carl get out of his car.

Hans dropped her off later at Mr. Crawhall's. When he left she could only imagine him in a hat with a little red feather, shorts with straps, and a walking stick; Julie Andrews' voice echoing off the Alps. *Such is the cry of the lonely goatherd la-he-o, la-he-o, dee-lo.*

It shocked her later to think her baby might be blond with eyes like an iceberg, if she had it.

Carl's troll is hunched under the bridge, naked, its long green fingers hanging between its knees. Carl is placing glass eyeballs in the carved eye sockets. Sarah is standing on a wooden chair, perfectly still, her pressed lips full of pins. She's modelling the Red Riding Hood costume for the seamstress. She's identical in size to the five styrofoam Red Riding Hoods standing in various positions around the warehouse. The roar of the chain saw subsides. Carl holds the glass eyeballs over his own eyes and tilts his head mechanically from one side to the other. He laughs and snorts, feigning a limp.

My dear, what firm milky breasts you have, all the better to . . .

He pops the glass eyeball into his mouth, rolling it between his lips, which close over it like eyelids. Slowly he reaches for Sarah's throat and pulls the bow of her cloak so it falls off her shoulders onto the floor. Sarah squeals through tightly pressed lips.

For Christ's sake, Carl, she'll catch her death of cold, says the seamstress.

Carl and Sarah have been using a glue that foams into a cement. It has been taken off the market because the fumes are highly toxic, but over the years Carl has grown accustomed to using it and he knows a guy who imports it from Italy. It's a two-part solution and becomes active when the two separate solutions are mixed. Sarah and Carl are the only ones in the workshop. She's pouring the solution and he's holding the bucket for her. She spills the solution over his hands and frantically tries to wipe it. The foam has an acid base, and in her effort their hands have become stuck together. Carl shouts obscenities between his teeth and drags her to the sink. It's difficult for him to get at the cold water tap. Sarah is crying hysterically and his other hand is stuck to the bucket. It takes him fifteen minutes to separate their hands. The seamstress hears the commotion from the kitchen down the hall and gets the first aid kit. She wraps their hands with burn ointment and gauze. Carl apologizes for cursing at Sarah and sends her home. He stays a long time in the empty warehouse, his burnt hands cradled between his knees.

—1995

Michael Crummey b. 1965

How short can a short story be? Very brief stories like Michael Crummey's "Bread" invite such questions. One of the new generation of writers from Newfoundland, Crummey has published a novel, The River Thieves *(2001), and a book of short stories of conventional lengths* (Flesh & Blood, *1998). He is the author of several books of poetry, one of which,* Hard Light *(1998), contains a section of prose pieces called "Little Stories." It is here that "Bread" may be found. Just over 300 words, "Bread" provides a complete narrative and offers a rich glimpse into a fully realized world.*

Bread

I was twenty years younger than my husband, his first wife dead in childbirth. I agreed to marry him because he was a good fisherman, because he had his own house and he was willing to take in my mother and father when the time came. It was a practical decision and he wasn't expecting more than that. Two people should never say the word love before they've eaten a sack of flour together, he told me.

The night we married I hiked my night dress around my thighs and shut my eyes so tight I saw stars. Afterwards I went outside and I was sick, throwing up over the fence. He came out the door behind me and put his hand to the small of my back. It happens your first time, he said. It'll get better.

I got pregnant right away and then he left for the Labrador. I dug the garden, watched my belly swell like a seed in water. Baked bread, bottled bakeapples for the winter store, cut the meadow grass for hay. After a month alone I even started to miss him a little.

The baby came early, a few weeks after my husband arrived home in September. We had the minister up to the house for the baptism the next day, Angus Maclean we named him, and we buried him in the graveyard in the Burnt Woods a week later. I remember he started crying at the table the morning of the funeral and I held his face against my belly until he stopped, his head in my hands about the size of the child before it was born. I don't know why sharing a grief will make you love someone.

I was pregnant again by November. I baked a loaf of bread and brought it to the table, still steaming from the oven. Set it on his plate whole and stood there looking at him. That's the last of that bag of flour, I told him. And he smiled at me and didn't say anything for a minute. I'll pick up another today, he said finally.

And that's how we left it for a while.

—1998

Michael Redhill b. 1966

Michael Redhill is the author of the novel, Martin Sloane *(2001), of several plays and books of poetry, and of one collection of stories,* Fidelity *(2003). Also an editor with Coach House Press, he became the publisher of the prominent literary journal* Brick *in 2003.*

As the title suggests, the stories in Fidelity *all deal in some way with faithfulness—which proves a difficult virtue. In "Human Elements," the I-narrator, Russell, flees a broken relationship and retreats into nature. The story—which asks us to consider whether eroding conditions are indications of entropy brought on by pollution and imbalance, or if our present moment is part of a large cyclical pattern that we can never fully comprehend—can be read as a meditation on the problematics of love at the beginning of the twenty-first century, or as an ecological fable, or as an anti-pastoral romance.*

Human Elements

As sometimes happens, I had a depression. It ought to be reassuring to know that half of humankind has had one, and there they all are, up and walking around again. It ought to be.

The best way to describe depression is that it can take seven hours to do a load of laundry. If you drink while you're doing the laundry it will take eight, but it will seem to go faster, and you won't mind so much the red stains on your whites, or at least it will not seem to you to be confirmation of the hopelessness of everything.

Before I was depressed, I had mostly been lonesome. I was lonesome with people and without them. This condition led to my moving out of a house I'd been sharing with a woman named J—. I took a bachelor apartment in a university neighbourhood, and my loneliness metastasized. As winter came on, I realized that I was planning on dying there. I started to smoke, a disgusting habit, and I drank more. On the weekends, I went to loud parties thrown by the fraternities on my street. It was easy enough to walk into one and claim I was from another frat or another school, and someone would point out the keg and that was that. I brought home what my mother would once have called co-eds, and did the kinds of things that one was supposed to do with co-eds. It was a pleasant routine, but I'd already become immune to beauty, and once that happens, you're almost there. I'd been cured of the mating sickness that had always animated my life and I imagined my death would be like a plant drying out on a radiator, seemingly gradual, but ending with an ashy spasm. In all, it was an excellent plan, but then the spring came and the park beside the building filled up with children in strollers and the sun rose earlier and set later, and worse, spring training started and on every channel ballplayers were talking in the idiom of stupid but irrefutable hope. The black flame flared down and I came back to the dessicated kernel of my self. And, like a sign of life, simple loneliness came back. I decided to get out of the city.

In those days, I was still a poet. When I was with J— I wrote a great deal of poetry, but I never published it. I poured it into one black hard-covered notebook after another. J— thought I was keeping a diary and it freaked her out. She'd never met a man who kept a diary. I told her it was poetry, and no, she couldn't see it. So she came to believe I was writing things about her anyway, and in a sense I was. So I stopped, and poetry left me like a chronic condition suddenly clearing up. Although in the case of poetry, I would have been happy to go on suffering.

I left my little apartment in the university district and rented a cabin on a lake outside of tourist country, three hours north of the city. My thought was that I could start writing poetry again, and if that didn't work, at least I could smoke and read. There was no phone. Trying to live without a phone can make you realize how weird it is to be "modern." In a place where a phone never rings it starts to feel like someone's dropped you into a hole, although all it means is that you're in nature.

I found, for a few days, that talking to myself was reassuring. A human voice is a human voice. I didn't indulge in real dialogue; I wasn't crazy anymore, so there was no *Well, Russell, how are we this morning?* Or *Ha ha, good one Russell.* I just narrated my day to myself. *It's a beautiful morning,* I'd say. *Time for coffee.* I'd talk to my books. *Mr. Sorel,* I said to Stendhal's misanthropist,[1] *make up your fucking mind.* And at night, down at the lakeshore, in the web of animal calls and the unseen water lapping against the rocks, I'd look up and name the alarming sky. Orion, Cassiopeia, Gemini. Constellations of the north. Even most of the sky was hidden from my sight.

I tried to write poems, but mainly I sat on the porch looking down the unkempt lawn to the ridge. Below the ridge, the land fell away in scrub and blackberry canes to the water. Pine trees and oaks were scattered all

---

[1] Julian Sorel, a character in Stendhal's novel *The Red and the Black* (1831), who—torn between his desires for social status (in the army or in the church) and his sexual appetites—is indifferent to the needs of others.

over the property, and a variety of birds visited the branches and performed their various tasks. I'd spent my summer childhood in places like this, under curving skies and jumping into lakes with the shadows of black branches laid on their surfaces. Outside of the city, my natural existential skittishness faded somewhat, even though the country can make you feel awesomely tiny, with its skies and wilderness. It was true I felt alone, I did crave another human voice. But at least I was supposed to feel alone there. After another couple of weeks passed, I stopped speaking to myself and slipped into a peaceable silence.

One morning around this time, I went outside to the porch with a cup of coffee, a plate of fried eggs, and the poems of Francis Ponge.[2] When I looked up after an hour or so, I saw that there was something sticking up beyond the ridge. It looked as if someone had leaned a large piece of wet cardboard against it. I put down my book and walked to the edge of the porch, and in the changing perspective I saw I was looking at the top of a tent.

I stood there for a while, reassured to be in a space that was clearly defined as my own, but then I told myself I had nothing to fear and I went inside to grab a couple of friendly-gesture beers and walked down to the ridge. A pot of coffee sat on a portable gas stove to one side of the tent, and a duffel bag poked out of the front flap. On the other side was a large plastic tub with a lid on it; the faint sound of water moving around came from inside it. I continued down onto the thin line of grey sand that passed for the beach there, and off to the left, standing on the shore and peering down into the weeds, were a man and a woman. They each wore a headset with a microphone that arced over their mouths. They looked like a pair of badly lost telemarketers. I held up the beers and they exchanged glances, then the man looked at his watch and shrugged and they both came over.

"Thanks," said the woman. She was dressed in a well-rounded yellow bikini, and he was wearing a Speedo and a worn-out T-shirt that said *Be Kind to Your Mother* and had a big picture of the planet on it. He was over six feet, and terminated in a patch of thorny black hair. He was also comprehensively pierced. Neither of them made any move to explain what they were doing on my rented property. Finally, I said, "What are you doing here?"

---

[2] French modernist writer (1899–1988) who rejected symbolism and formal poetic styles for a way of writing based on the close observation of things expressed in rational yet lyric terms.

"Oh, I'm Kate," said the woman, "and this is Sylvain. We're on a ministry capture." I stared at her blankly, so she added, "Frogs. We're catching and counting frogs for the Ministry of the Environment."

"I see," I said. "Well, nice to meet you. I'm Russell."

"Thanks for the beers, Russell. Are you a cottager?"

Given that she was in a bikini catching frogs for the government, I felt free to say, "I'm writing poetry in a rented cabin to get over a breakup."

Sylvain lifted his head a little. "Is it working?"

"I don't think so."

"Too bad," he said.

"But you're not in *that* place, are you?" Kate gestured with the beer bottle to the roof of the cabin. It was all we could see.

"I am. Why."

"See?" she said angrily to Sylvain. She really was quite lovely. Her long brown hair swayed up and covered her face for a moment when she swung her head over to him. She was a good foot shorter than he was. "So you're wondering what we're doing here?"

"It's okay," I said. "It's not really my place."

"We were told there wasn't anyone here. Otherwise, we would have introduced ourselves."

"As a courtesy," said Sylvain.

"I won't report you," I said. That seemed to make us equals again, and Sylvain raised his bottle to me before draining it. Kate put her bottle down in the cool muck at the shore.

"I'll bring them both up later, okay?" she said. Sylvain was already walking back along the bushes, his head down, his eyes sweeping back and forth like a metal detector. Kate whispered, "We just took a break."

"Well then, back to the mines."

She waved to me with her fingers, then went to join Sylvain. One of them had smelled like coconut and I was pretty sure it was her.

In my time in the north, I'd been trying to force diligence on myself in a vain effort to get some creative results. I'd been starting my days with whiskey-splashed coffee and reversing the ratio as the day went on, and this might have been playing a role in my output. It certainly had a deleterious effect on my ability to read. I'd come armed with enough books to last me my stay, but, especially after lunchtime, I had trouble understanding what exactly was happening on the page. I would see the words, and I'd *hear* them in my head, and for the first time in my life, that seemed like a very odd thing. If I saw the word H-U-M-A-N-I-T-Y, I would hear *hyoo-MAN-itty*, and I realized those two things were not the same. There was some filter that caused what was out in the world to make a sound in my head. And so I became frightened of reading and had no other agenda after that except to write, and that was not going well, either. It was a relief, then, that some hint of human activity was taking place down by the water. It relaxed me.

The morning after the frog-catchers' appearance, I once again took my coffee and my notebook out to the porch. They had already left for their work, creeping through the reeds at the lake perimeter, armed with a couple of clipboards. I got out a cigarette and opened the notebook. I'd written two lines of what I presumed was poetry since I'd got there, about three weeks earlier. There were also some drawings of tree limbs and my own hand. The two lines of poetry were:

> *quadrabalance of the elements*
> *human limbs, months, and hours*

I wasn't sure what they were leading to, what they meant, or even if they were mathematically accurate. At least they didn't sound like conversation, so I wasn't going to give up quite yet. I'd always felt that if I didn't know exactly what I was doing, there was still a chance I'd write something worth the time it took to write anything.

Below, I heard someone splashing along the water's edge and then, I presumed, come up on the beach. A moment later, Kate appeared, walking up the wood-stump steps. "Do you have a minute?"

"I have one or two," I said. "Beer?" It was probably 10 A.M.

"Maybe later." She was still in that yellow bikini, but there was a towel around her waist. I turned a chair to her and she sat down. Her shins were covered in thin patches of mud from the lake-bottom.

"Looks like you've been giving chase."

She looked down and slapped lightly at her legs. Little brown flakes fell off. "I look like this all summer. You writing?"

"Yep!" I waved the notebook in the air manically. "Writing writing!" I stole a glance at her shoulders—brown and spotted—then her hands. They were just girl hands, thin fingers and nails like almond slivers. Hard to imagine them full of frog. "So what is it you two do all day?"

"We catch frogs, sex them, and mark them. Then we let them go."

"Do they like it?" I asked.

"No."

"But it's for their own good." She squinted her eyes at me because I was trying to be funny, but the sentiment was true. Nature hadn't made animals like frogs with the ability to distinguish between when they were about to be eaten and when they were just going to be sexed and marked. "What are the secret-agent headsets for?"

"Have you ever seen a frog?"

"I'm pretty sure I have."

"They have huge tympana—those are the eardrums, the big circles on the sides of their heads. Their ears are even larger than elephants', relatively speaking."

"Okay," I said.

"Anyway, they're attuned to certain frequencies, like the beating of a dragonfly's wings or the buzzing of a fly. We try not to make much noise in the field, since some of the frequencies of the human voice are like those of insects or predators. We just whisper to each other over a radio channel."

"Coming in under the radar."

"Kinda," she said. "Look, uh, we wanted to ask you something, me and Sylvain. We're going to be here for like another eight days, and all we've got down there is a gas stove and two pots. But we have lots of food. So we were wondering if we could interest you in a swap." She tucked some hair over her ear.

"You want to use my kitchen."

"We cook, you eat our food, and we all have a bit of company."

I'd been eating cereal for supper and the idea of a hot meal was appealing. "Sylvain's *French*, isn't he?"

"Yeah," she said, catching my drift. "But he doesn't cook. I cook."

"Are you two . . ."

"We used to be." She picked some invisible lint off her towel. When she looked up, she pointed her eyes away. "To be honest with you," she said, "having another person around would be kind of good for us. You know, make things seem normal."

"They're not normal?"

"They are for me," she said.

That first night, they came in around seven o'clock, lugging their huge cooler into the cabin. That they would unpack their groceries into my fridge had not been discussed, but I was pleased by what I saw. Vacuum-packed bags of frozen meat and fish, frozen tetrapacks of corn, spinach, and strawberries, fresh mushrooms, milk and cream, bacon, eggs, and butter. A rucksack on Sylvain's back disgorged whole wheat bread, pasta, coffee, and corn chips. It was half their provisions; the other half would be delivered after the fifth day. We weren't that remote, but the ministry apparently wanted them to focus on their work. Someone else could do the shopping.

Kate was putting things in the fridge and freezer. "What have you been eating?"

"Just light things," I said. "I eat light."

"I think you've been living on Rice Krispies."

"I have potatoes, too. And apples."

"You need meat," she said.

"Potatoes have protein," said Sylvain, and we both looked at him. He was setting the table. "They do."

"Whatever," said Kate.

I was relegated to a chair as the two of them commandeered the kitchen. I hadn't seen either of them wash their hands, but I wasn't going to make an issue out of it. When I had been alive enough to cook, I wasn't bad. There had even been a time in my life when I made pizza dough from scratch. But when I'd been with J— she'd been the cook. I had the traditional male role: chopping, tasting, complimenting. Complimenting was very important. Sylvain was a little more useful than I was. He was cutting the mushrooms and holding one of the frozen meat packs under his arm to thaw it. It was still in its bag.

I filled three glasses with ice and poured us all scotch. I knew instinctively that Kate drank scotch, but when she took it and rolled the liquor around the ice and then let a bit of it fall into her mouth, that was the first thing. That was the thing you always look back on and you think, yes, that was it.

Kate took the meat from Sylvain and opened it, then cut it into slices. "Venison Stroganoff," she said. There was no cognac, so she poured the rest of her scotch into the skillet. She put on a pot of water to boil the noodles and in about half an hour it was all ready. I'd never eaten venison before. It seemed somehow disrespectful to take a creature like that out of the forest, antlers and all, and poach it in cheap liquor. But it was delicious all the same.

"Why do you keep looking at your watch?" I asked Sylvain when we were done. All through the meal he kept glancing outside and then looking at his watch. It was one of those heavy watches you could swim with underwater as well as calibrate stuff. We'd had scotch with dinner, too.

"I have to finish every day with a count," he said, "and the count has to start at the same sun-time every day. That's whatever time I did it yesterday minus eight minutes."

"The sun sets a little earlier every day," Kate said. "So they start calling a bit earlier, too. Go on out with him, you two can do it together. I'll clean up."

Sylvain stood—the wild was about to start calling—and waited for me. I made a murmuring sound that suggested maybe I wasn't entitled to such a wonderful experience as standing out in the water at dusk with a heavily pierced Frenchman, but Kate started shooing us away from the table. So I went outside with Sylvain, when all I really wanted was the sensual pleasure of being passed wet dishes and drying them while talking about this and that. I looked back and saw Kate through the window above the sink, not aware she was being watched, and I imagined that after I saw Sylvain off to wherever he lived I would be going back up to the cabin and we'd sit down on the couch and Kate would put her feet in my lap while she read a novel. Afterwards, we'd talk about the novel and she'd be really smart about it, although not intellectual, and then she'd say, "Let's go to bed, babe, long day tomorrow."

"Hold this," said Sylvain. It was a clipboard with a pencil tucked in at the top. There was a list of frogs on it: *Bullfrog, Green, Mink, Northern Leopard, Pickerel, Spring Peeper, Western Chorus.* We were down on the little grey beach. "I say a name and you make a tick-mark. That's all."

"Okay."

He stood completely still. I realized that the fact of the frogs' calling wasn't to help lead him to where they were in the failing light: he was just going to count them by *sound.* This was impressive. To me, the sounds along the lake-edge were without distinction. It was a general commotion, high and low sounds mixing together, repeating sounds flowering up over singular sounds. It was a hubbub and a buzz and nothing stood out of it for me.

"Pickerel," said Sylvain.

"Just one?"

"We can't talk right now. Green. Mink. Take my watch and tell me when exactly ten minutes is up. Another green. Bull."

I started dashing the marks onto the page. At first the pickerels were winning, but then they went pretty much head-to-head with the northern leopards. The spring peepers and western choruses were no-shows. Sylvain stood there as tensed as a pointer and spat out the names. I wondered when Kate had fallen in love with him. It wasn't when he was leaning into the frog-filled dusk, his ear turned slightly toward the water, croaking the names of his prey.

"Northern," he said.

"You sure that wasn't a pickerel?" I said. "Just joking."

When we were done, he took the list away from me and tilted it into the light from the cottage as it gave up its secrets to him. He nodded a couple of times. "Are you interested in this?"

"Sure," I said.

"Last year, we did this lake and two others nearby, and the pickerel and northern leopard populations were lower by twenty-five per cent. Can you guess what that means?"

"They were quieter then?"

He smiled. He surprised himself by doing it; he wasn't expecting that I'd be anything but a drag. "That could be," he said. "But it probably means that the predator population has dropped off in this area. Snakes and herons, some kinds of fish. Maybe they overfed and went elsewhere, or maybe there was a die-off. More pollution in the water."

"Why wouldn't that affect the frogs?"

"It would, but then so would the reduction in the predator groups. We don't really know what causes these fluctuations. That's why we're studying them."

What I didn't like about Sylvain at this particular moment was that I was starting to think he was a pretty decent guy. To care like this. I'd learned by experience plenty of times that there's no vig in judging people too early. Doing that had landed me with J—. Mere attraction can get the better of you and it usually does. "So, will the increase in these kinds of frogs bring back the snakes and fish?" I said, trying to stay on his wavelength.

"If that's the reason why their numbers are increasing, then maybe. That'll be a question we come out here with next year."

"You and Kate?"

He shrugged; that wasn't the point. "Whoever the ministry sends."

Kate's voice came over the ridge just then. It was saying *coffee* and something else, so we started walking back up. "It probably won't be me and Kate," Sylvain said. "But you never can tell."

I pinched my lips together and nodded knowingly. I think this gesture started in the movies and then men all around the world started doing it. It means *you don't have to say another word.*

"Anyway," said Sylvain, and that was the end of it. We came up past the tent, and the tub I'd seen earlier started making sounds again.

"What's in there?"

"Bullfrogs. The big ones go to the lab for blood tests. You know, a three-quarter-pound bullfrog can tell you the ratios of all the various minerals and chemicals in a lake. They're mirror images of the bodies of water they live in. It's actually quite amazing."

I was nodding enthusiastically. Maybe he was a loon. "Then what happens after?"

"Don't worry—they come home. We show the elders the respect they deserve." He smiled at me again.

Kate had made Rice Krispie squares. "I didn't want to deprive you of your evening's ration of cereal," she said. She had piled them onto a plate into a pyramid and they looked exactly like the photo in the Kraft Foods recipe book my mother had when I was a kid.

Maybe I'd suffered depression as a child, but I don't remember. How many kids would pass for sane anyway?

Many nights during the worst of it in the city, I'd lain awake in bed and tried to recall if there had been anything really wrong with me as a kid. I supposed that the big difference between then and now was that now I knew what things were called, and I knew what was generally accepted to be normal. As a child, I'd succumbed on a couple of occasions to strange behaviour, and perhaps it had been in line with what children of my generation and demographic were supposed to do. All of childhood is training the animal out of the human—who's to say that the animal doesn't need to manifest these last wild desires? One night I'd run out of the house after some small thwarting—a television show denied, or some insignificant punishment levied—out onto the street, crying and waving my hands around. Neighbours called to me from their front stoops (had I done such a thing more than once?) and I ran past them. I stopped to catch my breath outside of my school and saw my mother turn the corner in her car and come toward me. I ran again, even diving over hedges to keep her from seeing me, and when she drove past she seemed to float by over the street in a bubble of pale light, her face yellowed by the dashboard into a grave frieze of worry.

Another time, a whole summer in fact, I tried to kill animals. I didn't go for the easy ones, like fish, which you could catch on a line and smack with a stick, or even birds, which you could catch with a net if they were feeding on the ground. My prey that summer was squirrels. I figured the match-up was fair: they could run and go right up the sides of trees, and I could throw rocks. They seemed to have a second sight when it came to rocks—they knew to go where the rocks wouldn't. And even when, in rare instances, I made contact, they just shrugged it off. Then I got one. It was eating an apple core on a rock and my own rock caught it there. It tumbled unnaturally off the back and fell into the grass. I went to the rock and looked down, and there it was on its side, some of its ribs sticking out of its fur. And it was breathing, just as it had been when it was eating the apple core. It looked up calmly into the sky for a while, its eye moving back and forth quickly, and then it shook one of its limbs and the eye stopped moving.

I brought it into the house weeping. I told my father it had fallen out of a tree. We buried it and marked the grave and nothing else was said about it.

Maybe I was mad that summer. Or maybe there was more animal left in me than there should have been.

Kate and Sylvain argued that night. Their voices rose to a pitch and then they realized they could be heard and they became quiet again. For a while, there was a lamp on in the tent, and I could see from their shadows that they were sitting as far apart as they could in the pinched space. Then the lamp went out, and Kate appeared, coming up toward the lawn. I returned inside quickly and switched the lights off. She came up below the cabin and spread her sleeping bag on the grass, then slipped herself into it and arranged a pile of clothes under her head. It was a warm night, so she wasn't going to freeze out there. I sat down, worrying that I was seeing their problems as an opportunity. That, I thought, didn't make me a very good person, never mind a good host. But I knew I wouldn't sleep if I didn't go out there.

When she heard my approach, she turned over and shielded her eyes against the porchlight I'd turned on as a sort of signal that I was coming down.

"Are you okay?"

"I'm fine," she said. Her face was a little swollen. "I spent the second half of last summer sleeping outside."

"I can get you another blanket if you want."

She hesitated for a second. Accepting something for herself alone would mean that she was having a separate relationship with me. This I understood: to that point, it had been a relationship with both of them. "That would be great," she said. "And maybe a pillow."

I went in and gathered what she needed, then came down with the whiskey. She sat up and drank a little and we passed the bottle back and forth.

"Are you *okay* okay?"

"Don't worry about us," she said. "We'll be fine. He just has to accept it, is all."

"You've known each other for a long time."

"We were in the same program. He doesn't look the part, but he's amazingly dedicated. He'd do this all year if the lakes didn't freeze." She looked over her shoulder down to the top of the tent and her face changed. "I don't *want* to hurt him."

"I understand."

"But I can't force myself. I mean, to feel something I don't."

I drank. I had the unpleasant sensation that my simple listening was a form of falsehood. Most men have this instinct. Watching her talk, I was filled with tenderness for her, for the trouble she was willing to invite into her life. "Well," I said, "if he can accept what you're offering, it sounds like he'll have a good friend."

"He will," she said resolutely. She put the cap back on the bottle. "You're kind to let us invade your privacy here. I'm sure this is no good for your writing."

"Anything can help," I said. "It's impossible to know in advance what might unlock you."

"Is this unlocking you?" She lay down and put her arms up under her head. In certain books and movies, that would have been my cue. But excruciating experience had taught me that women's come-on lines were never what men thought they would be.

I said, "A little."

"I guess you can't really force that, either."

"You really can't." I collected the bottle off the grass and stood up. "Goodnight then," I said.

I lay in bed after that, and felt her presence out there on the grass. I couldn't have drunk myself unconscious if I'd wanted to. I got up around three in the morning and went back out into the front room to look at her, but she was gone and the light in the tent was back on. The two of them were unable to leave it alone, this relationship that wanted to devour them.

In the morning, I felt uneven. I took my spiked coffee and went out to my spot. Kate and Sylvain were nowhere to be seen, already on the survey's schedule. I took out my two lines of poetry, lonesome lines with no source and no destination, and I experimented with them, removing various words to see if anything about the lines was absolute, inevitable.

of the elements:
human limbs, months, and hours

quadrabalance of human limbs,
and months

quadrabalance of the elements
human months and hours

human elements

This turned out to be a distressing exercise, since it seemed to me that all the lines that were left by these mechanical amputations were all better than the ones I'd sweated so hard to create from will. It started to seem as if poetry followed natural laws that perhaps I had once known, but that now were an alien algebra to me. Probably Sylvain, with his training in the systems of nature, had an innate connection to the very things that had abandoned me. It certainly seemed to me that what he was doing, his head tilted into the night air, was a better lightning rod for the phenomenological world than was the feeble apparatus of my language. In disgust, I wrote *jugorum* in my book, then slammed it shut and went inside.

Since it would still be hours until dinner (how quickly the shape of my days was changing), I gave in to the pull of television, which to that point I'd treated as a piece of furniture. When I switched it on, the signal came through like light cast through a tunnel. There was a cooking show on one channel, an American game show on another. The sound on that channel was as clear as a person standing behind you, even though the picture swayed like a silk curtain. A woman told something of herself to the host. Where she was from and how many children. That was her, that little list of things. Had she always been this happy? Did she do with her life as she had intended? What threads of circumstance saw her born in that town, give birth to those children, end up guessing the names of songs for money? Her image, almost insubstantial, drifted across; she was as fragile as the signals that came down through space carrying her in them.

"Can you even *see* anything?" asked Kate. She was standing in the kitchen.

"Whoops," I said. "I'm taking a break. You want a coffee?"

"Actually, I was coming up to tell you that if you want, in a couple of hours you can come out with me and I'll show you how to catch a frog. Sylvain's offered to make dinner."

"I thought you said he didn't cook."

"He doesn't. But he thinks he owes me something for last night." She tried to make it sound like an amusing side effect of an experience that had left her with pale grey sacs under each eye.

"You went back to the tent," I said.

"I did." She looked out at the lake. There had been a couple of moments like this, when it seemed that she was on the verge of crossing a line with me. But then she said, "If you thought you were the reason someone was unhappy, you'd probably find it hard to walk away. I do."

"Didn't your mom ever tell you it takes two to tango?"

"Dancing's supposed to be fun." Her eyes drifted to the television for a moment, where the ghostly woman was frantically clapping and weeping. I shut it off.

"If you want to talk . . ."

She turned her eyes on me. "If I want to talk, you're a good listener?"

"Yeah. I am."

"Yeah. I'm sure you are, Russell. Maybe later." She turned on one heel and started out. "Come down around four."

She went out. I had an extra minute or two, so I watched her walk all the way down. Being around Kate for even those two days made me wonder if there could be a world where sex and love weren't so gloomy a business. It seemed that somewhere, people were enjoying carnal lives, unencumbered by ineptness or shyness. But I'd never met these people, or been to where they were. I looked at Kate and felt as if she were pulling the scent of that world into this one, where the great unloved might learn to be more at ease with themselves.

I went down at five minutes past four, after washing my face and changing into some shorts. I had no swim trunks; I hadn't intended on swimming while I was up there, and I generally stayed away from water. I met Sylvain on the way up and he scanned my attire with a jaundiced eye. "You'll get those filthy," he said, stopping me on the path.

"It's just dirt. It'll come out."

"She'll laugh at you and call you a city boy."

"I *am* a city boy," I said.

He looked up to the cabin and then back to me. "How long have you been here? Writing your poems."

"Almost a month." Kate had come across to the beach and was looking up at us. I waved to her. Sylvain didn't turn around. "Why?"

"Maybe I'll rent it after you go. See if I have better luck than you."

"At what."

"Getting over something."

"Sylvain!" Kate called, and now he turned around and shielded his eyes. I noticed for the first time that his irises were so dark they could have been black. They were what gave him his permanently wounded look. "Let him come down. You start on dinner."

"You're next," he said and patted me on the shoulder.

Kate stood on the tiny beach and when I got closer she slid her arm in mine and brought me into the water. "Nice get-up," she said. "All you're missing is the metal detector."

"Sylvain warned me you'd laugh at my *ensemble*."

"He was right." We were standing in five-inch-deep water now. "What else did he say?"

"Sylvain? He wanted to know if he could rent the cabin after me. To get over you."

She stopped and took back her arm. She had a look on her face that was somewhere between amused and disgusted. "Maybe the two of you could live here after I go and drink whiskey and keen at the moon together. Maybe turn the place into a retreat for broken-hearted men."

"That's an idea."

"You could offer some kind of package deal: a long weekend up here with mementoes of the old girlfriend, all the chocolate you can eat, and then at the end, someone rows you out to the middle of the lake and puts a bullet in your brain. Charge, like, $399."

I narrowed my eyes at her and smiled carefully. "Men don't do the chocolate thing, Kate. That's girls."

"Whatever."

"How come you sound guilty one minute and pissed off the next?"

She started to talk, but it came out as a huff, and then she gestured helplessly toward the cabin. Her hand went up and then flopped down on her thigh with a wet slap. "He thinks I never loved him. I've been with three guys whose last words were that I never loved them. Must be something about me, huh?"

"Maybe you're attracted to the same kind of man."

"Sylvain's line is that I was with him because I felt *sorry* for him."

"He's only saying that."

"When I met him, he was sick, you know that? He was in and out of hospital—and I'll let you in on something, it wasn't for any physical problems, okay? And that was fucking hard! I didn't do it out of pity, I loved him."

"You shouldn't take someone who's in this state too seriously."

"He's always in this state. That's why I'm finished. So he's giving me one last helping for good measure." She waved her hand dismissively. "Anyway, good listener, you came down here to catch a frog."

"We don't have to. I like talking to you."

She walked around me to a clearing on the shore a few feet away where she or Sylvain had pushed back the lakegrass for a spot to sit, and she sat down and draped her arms over her knees. The insides of her elbows gleamed. "He says to me, the Indians have this saying that if you save someone's life, you're responsible for it. How's that for a fucking guilt trip?"

"Of course you're not responsible for it." To this point, I'd tried to ignore that Kate and Sylvain had a past. My attraction to her allowed me to discount that the two of them were probably as inextricably joined to each other as I had once been to J—, the woman I claimed I was getting over. That I'd told a white lie about that in service of not having to tell two strangers that I was trying to win a footrace with depression made me feel pathetic now. It made me feel that I'd lost a chance to say anything of substance to Kate. Now I was in the position of trying to be sensitive so I'd seem appealing to this woman who probably wouldn't otherwise have invited a person like me into her life. But, I told myself, I'm over it now. I'm ready for someone like Kate. Maybe Sylvain just got to her too soon. Maybe the timing's perfect for me, for her. These kinds of thoughts go in circles, and as long as you stop them before they reach their inevitable end (where once again the likely decline of everything you care about features as the main outcome) you can convince yourself there are things worth living for. Such conviction, report those who have it, is as good as its being true. I went and sat down beside her. "What are you going to do?"

"I don't know. I think I'm going to wait and see." She pushed her hair back behind her neck and leaned away a little so she could see me. "He thinks we're attracted to each other, you and me."

"He would, I guess. Part of his condition."

"Right."

"What did you tell him?"

"I told him I didn't know what *you* were thinking, but *I* thought you were ugly and you smelled bad."

"Did he fall for it?"

"It was hard to convince him you smelled bad." She stood up. "I'm bored talking about relationships now. I'm finished with men. I want to show you how to catch a frog."

"So that's it?"

"For now."

We stood and walked to where there was another concentration of lilypads and reeds. I just wanted to keep on walking until we came around the other side of the lake and could walk back to some road somewhere that would lead away. But I was aware now that I was stepping into a sequence of some kind. Kate unhooked one of the headsets from her bikini strap and put it on me, then slipped her own on. "Can you hear me?" she said.

"I can hear the real you as well as the microphoned you."

"Walk away now, and don't make too much noise. Go on." I reluctantly started off toward the reeds. I didn't want to catch anything that lived in water. "There's a bullfrog in there, about two o'clock from where you are right now. I've already caught her a couple of times, so she's tired. As long as you don't act all clumsy, she'll probably give up without a fight."

"They fight?" I whispered into the headpiece.

"They struggle. Wouldn't you? Keep going."

I walked toward the edge of the lilypads and scanned the water's edge. The feeling I was being visited with was one I hadn't had in some time—that there was something taking shape, ever-so-vaguely, in my future. Maybe that's what my illness had been about: not knowing where I was going, or what to want when I got there. Or maybe, as I suspected at the time and still do, it was about nothing I could possibly understand, except the work of being alive and not being good at it.

"Do you see her?" Kate said quietly into my ear.

"Not yet."

"Maybe she's gone." I continued closer to the edge of the water. I could hear Kate's breathing in my ears. It was like she was a ghost in my mind. "The trick," she said, "is to know they can't see in front of themselves that well. Frogs have great peripheral vision, but if you come at them front on, they don't really notice. That's how snakes get them."

"Maybe that just makes them stupid."

"Good scientific insight, poet-boy." She gave a quiet, scornful laugh. After another moment, though, she said, "What?" and after a moment, I realized she wasn't talking to me. I looked up to where she was and saw Sylvain standing at the edge of the lake. He had a windbreaker on and a duffel bag was on the beach. She went back toward him. "Where are you going?" she said.

She dropped the headset down around her neck as she approached him, and he retreated onto the grass. Her voice was fainter now, his even more so. I made out that he was leaving to go back to the city. His voice became agitated.

". . . that isn't true," she said, tired with pleading her version to him. "You believe what you want then."

He said something else and I heard her say, "Jesus Christ, Sylvain. We're not going to get paid if we don't finish."

I started to walk back toward where they were, not sure what kind of person he might really be, or if she was in any danger. I got a few steps closer and then stopped and turned. There was the frog. It sat, shaded in the cover of the low scrub, looking out serenely into the lake as if daydreaming.

I spoke quietly into the headset. "Kate?"

"Just a second," I heard her say, and then she put her earphones back on. "What is it, Russell?"

"I see something here."

"I'm going to be a while, okay?"

"Do you need any help?"

"No," she said, and she took the headset off again. I imagined her turning her face back to Sylvain, trying, as perhaps she'd been trying all along, to convince him that whatever love she had for him, it still meant *something*. I waited, wondering if she would come back on and instruct me somehow, but I could hear nothing. After a moment, they moved into view closer to the cabin, and I watched them, the discussion their bodies were having, and I saw her take him into her arms. She held him against her, and he let himself be held. That was the kind of embrace it was. Then they vanished from view behind the cabin.

I didn't know then what was required of me, so I kept moving slowly to where Kate's frog was and extended my hand. The animal didn't register me at all, or at least not in a way I understood. I moved forward as slowly as I was able. I knew I'd been taken away from my purpose here, I'd been more than waylaid, but this was as good a reason to be here as any. Letting life come in from the side was a wise thing, I thought. It worked for frogs. Although perhaps they'd settle for a little more of knowing what was right in front of them, in the long, forward view. I was only a couple of feet away now, and the frog turned itself a little to the side, like a mechanical toy. I shifted position as well. I heard a car door shut—it must have been my car—and at that moment, I shot my hand out and tried to grab the thing, but it vaulted into the air, its limbs flailing wildly, and plunged into the water near my foot in a flash of white and green. I felt it brush against me, a glancing of flesh, and then it was gone. I waited a moment to see if it would come up, but it must have known to go somewhere I couldn't see into.

When I got back to the beach, the tent and the rest of their gear was gone. I went into the cabin and looked around, but there was only silence there, and my keys were gone from the bowl on the front table. I took off the headset and lay it in the bowl, where it gave off a faint crackling, still bringing her in, still connecting us. I had a proper appetite now and started cooking. I had some sense of faith as well, but why and in what, I wasn't sure. I was settled in myself for once, and had the feeling that I had done something with my day even though it hadn't been remotely like poetry, and probably it wouldn't be like poetry again.

—2003

Eden Robinson   b. 1968

Traplines *(1996), the first of Eden Robinson's two books (the second was her novel* Monkey Beach, *published in 2000), comprises four thematically related stories told in a stark and understated style. Although Robinson grew up on the Haisla Nation Kitamaat Reserve in British Columbia,* Traplines *does not emphasize Native identity. The tensions that permeate these stories come from differences in class and status, from competition between peers, and from conflicts within dysfunctional families. In the title story, danger comes not only from the threat of brutality from a family member but from family patterns that seem impossible to escape. It is hard to say where the trap really lies and who the trapper is.*

Traplines

Dad takes the white marten from the trap.

"Look at that, Will," he says.

It is limp in his hands. It hasn't been dead that long.

We tramp through the snow to the end of our trapline. Dad whistles. The goner marten is over his shoulder. From here, it looks like Dad is wearing it. There is nothing else in the other traps. We head back to the truck. The snow crunches. This is the best time for trapping, Dad told me a while ago. This is when the animals are hungry.

Our truck rests by the roadside at an angle. Dad rolls the white marten in a gray canvas cover separate from the others. The marten is flawless, which is rare in these parts. I put my animals beside his and cover them. We get in the truck. Dad turns the radio on and country twang fills the cab. We smell like sweat and oil and pine. Dad hums. I stare out the window. Mrs. Smythe would say the trees here are like the ones on Christmas postcards, tall and heavy with snow. They crowd close to the road. When the wind blows strong enough, the older trees snap and fall on the power lines.

"Well, there's our Christmas money," Dad says, snatching a peek at the rearview mirror.

I look back. The wind ruffles the canvases that cover the martens. Dad is smiling. He sits back, steering with one hand. He doesn't even mind when we are passed by three cars. The lines in his face are loose now. He sings along with a woman who left her husband—even that doesn't make him mad. We have our Christmas money. At least for now, there'll be no shouting in the house. It will take Mom and Dad a few days to find something else to fight about.

The drive home is a long one. Dad changes the radio station twice. I search my brain for something to say but my headache is spreading and I don't feel like talking. He watches the road, though he keeps stealing looks at the back of the truck. I watch the trees and the cars passing us.

One of the cars has two women in it. The woman that isn't driving waves her hands around as she talks. She reminds me of Mrs. Smythe. They are beside us, then ahead of us, then gone.

Tucca is still as we drive into it. The snow drugs it, makes it lazy. Houses puff cedar smoke and the sweet, sharp smell gets in everyone's clothes. At school in town, I can close my eyes and tell who's from the village and who isn't just by smelling them.

When we get home, we go straight to the basement. Dad gives me the ratty martens and keeps the good ones. He made me start on squirrels when I was in grade five. He put the knife in my hand, saying, "For Christ's sake, it's just a squirrel. It's dead, you stupid knucklehead. It can't feel anything."

He made the first cut for me. I swallowed, closed my eyes, and lifted the knife.

"Jesus," Dad muttered. "Are you a sissy? I got a sissy for a son. Look. It's just like cutting up a chicken. See? Pretend you're skinning a chicken."

Dad showed me, then put another squirrel in front of me, and we didn't leave the basement until I got it right.

Now Dad is skinning the flawless white marten, using his best knife. His tongue is sticking out the corner of his mouth. He straightens up and shakes his skinning hand. I quickly start on the next marten. It's perfect except for a scar across its back. It was probably in a fight. We won't get much for the skin. Dad goes back to work. I stop, clench, unclench my hands. They are stiff.

"Goddamn," Dad says quietly. I look up, tensing, but Dad starts to smile. He's finished the marten. It's ready to be dried and sold. I've finished mine too. I look at my hands. They know what to do now without my having to tell them. Dad sings as we go up the creaking stairs. When we get into the hallway I breathe in, smelling fresh baked bread.

Mom is sprawled in front of the TV. Her apron is smudged with flour and she is licking her fingers. When she sees us, she stops and puts her hands in her apron pockets.

"Well?" she says.

Dad grabs her at the waist and whirls her around the living room.

"Greg! Stop it!" she says, laughing.

Flour gets on Dad and cedar chips get on Mom. They talk and I leave, sneaking into the kitchen. I swallow three aspirins for my headache, snatch two buns, and go to my room. I stop in the doorway. Eric is there, plugged into his electric guitar. He looks at the buns and pulls out an earphone.

"Give me one," he says.

I throw him the smaller bun, and he finishes it in three bites.

"The other one," he says.

I give him the finger and sit on my bed. I see him thinking about tackling me, but he shrugs and plugs himself back in. I chew on the bun, roll bits of it around in my mouth. It's still warm, and I wish I had some honey for it or some blueberry jam.

Eric leaves and comes back with six buns. He wolfs them down, cramming them into his mouth. I stick my fingers in my ears and glare at him. He can't hear himself eat. He notices me and grins. Opens his mouth so I can see. I pull out a mag and turn the pages.

Dad comes in. Eric's jaw clenches. I go into the kitchen, grabbing another bun. Mom smacks my hand. We hear Eric and Dad starting to yell. Mom rolls her eyes and puts three more loaves in the oven.

"Back later," I say.

She nods, frowning at her hands.

I walk. Think about going to Billy's house. He is seeing Elaine, though, and is getting weird. He wrote her a poem yesterday. He couldn't find anything nice to rhyme with "Elaine" so he didn't finish it.

"Pain," Craig said. "Elaine, you pain."

"Plain Elaine," Tony said.

Billy smacked Tony and they went at it in the snow. Billy gave him a face wash. That ended it, and we let Billy sit on the steps and write in peace.

"Elaine in the rain," I say. "Elaine, a flame. Cranes. Danes. Trains. My main Elaine." I kick at the slush on the ground. Billy is on his own.

I let my feet take me down the street. It starts to snow, tiny ladybug flakes. It is only four but already getting dark. Streetlights flicker on. No one but me is out walking. Snot in my nose freezes. The air is starting to burn my throat. I turn and head home. Eric and Dad should be tired by now.

Another postcard picture. The houses lining the street look snug. I hunch into my jacket. In a few weeks, Christmas lights will go up all over the village. Dad will put ours up two weeks before Christmas. We use the same set every year. We'll get a tree a week later. Mom'll decorate it. On Christmas Eve, she'll put our presents under it. Some of the presents will be wrapped in aluminum because she never buys enough wrapping paper. We'll eat turkey. Mom and Dad will go to a lot of parties and get really drunk. Eric will go to a lot of parties and get really stoned. Maybe this year I will too. Anything would be better than sitting around with Tony and Craig, listening to them gripe.

I stamp the snow off my sneakers and jeans. I open the door quietly. The TV is on loud. I can tell that it's a hockey game by the announcer's voice. I take off my shoes and jacket. The house feels really hot to me after being outside. My face starts to tingle as the skin thaws. I go into the kitchen and take another aspirin.

The kitchen could use some plants. It gets good light in the winter. Mrs. Smythe has filled her kitchen with plants, hanging the ferns by the window where the cats can't eat them. The Smythes have pictures all over their walls of places they have been—Europe, Africa, Australia. They've been everywhere. They can afford it, she says, because they don't have kids. They had one, a while ago. On the TV there's a wallet-sized picture of a dark-haired boy with his front teeth missing. He was their kid but he disappeared. Mrs. Smythe fiddles with the picture a lot.

Eric tries to sneak up behind me. His socks make a slithering sound on the floor. I duck just in time and hit him in the stomach.

He doubles over. He has a towel stretched between his hands. His choking game. He punches at me, but I hop out of the way. His fist hits the hot stove. Yelling, he jerks his hand back. I race out of the kitchen and down to the basement. Eric follows me, screaming my name. "Come out, you chicken," he says. "Come on out and fight."

I keep still behind a stack of plywood. Eric has the towel ready. After a while, he goes back upstairs and locks the door behind him.

I stand. I can't hear Mom and Dad. They must have gone out to celebrate the big catch. They'll probably find a party and go on a bender until Monday, when Dad has to go back to work. I'm alone with Eric, but he'll leave the house around ten. I can stay out of his way until then.

The basement door bursts open. I scramble under Dad's tool table. Eric must be stoned. He's probably been toking up since Mom and Dad left. Pot always makes him mean.

He laughs. "You baby. You fucking baby." He doesn't look for me that hard. He thumps loudly up the stairs, slams the door shut, then tiptoes back down and waits. He must think I'm really stupid.

We stay like this for a long time. Eric lights up. In a few minutes, the whole basement smells like pot. Dad will be pissed off if the smoke ruins the white marten. I smile, hoping it does. Eric will really get it then.

"Fuck," he says and disappears upstairs, not locking the door. I crawl out. My legs are stiff. The pot is making me dizzy.

The woodstove is cooling. I don't open it because the hinges squeal. It'll be freezing down here soon. Breathing fast, I climb the stairs. I crack the door open. There are no lights on except in our bedroom. I pull on my jacket and sneakers. I grab some bread and stuff it in my jacket, then run for the door but Eric is blocking it, leering.

"Thought you were sneaky, hey," he says.

I back into the kitchen. He follows. I wait until he is near before I bend over and ram him. He's slow because of the pot and slips to the floor. He grabs my ankle, but I kick him in the head and am out the door before he can catch me. I take the steps two at a time. Eric stands on the porch and laughs. I can't wait until I'm bigger. I'd like to smear him against a wall. Let him see what it feels like. I'd like to smear him so bad.

I munch on some bread as I head for the exit to the highway. Now the snow is coming down in thick, large flakes that melt when they touch my skin. I stand at the exit and wait.

I hear One Eye's beat-up Ford long before I see it. It clunks down the road and stalls when One Eye stops for me.

"You again. What you doing out here?" he yells at me.

"Waiting for Princess fucking Di," I say.

"Smart mouth. You keep it up and you can stay out there."

The back door opens anyway. Snooker and Jim are there. One Eye and Don Wilson are in the front. They all have silver lunch buckets at their feet.

We get into town and I say, "Could you drop me off here?"

One Eye looks back, surprised. He has forgotten about me. He frowns. "Where you going this time of night?"

"Disneyland," I say.

"Smart mouth," he says. "Don't be like your brother. You stay out of trouble."

I laugh. One Eye slows the car and pulls over. It chokes and sputters. I get out and thank him for the ride. One Eye grunts. He pulls away and I walk to Mrs. Smythe's.

The first time I saw her house was last spring, when she invited the English class there for a barbecue. The lawn was neat and green and I only saw one dandelion. There were rose bushes in the front and raspberry bushes in the back. I went with Tony and Craig, who got high on the way there. Mrs. Smythe noticed right away. She took them aside and talked to them. They stayed in the poolroom downstairs until the high wore off.

There weren't any other kids from the village there. Only townies. Kids that Dad says will never dirty their pink hands. They were split into little groups. They talked and ate and laughed and I wandered around alone, feeling like a dork. I was going to go downstairs to Tony and Craig when Mrs. Smythe came up to me, carrying a hot dog. I never noticed her smile until then. Her blue sundress swayed as she walked.

"You weren't in class yesterday," she said.

"Stomachache."

"I was going to tell you how much I liked your essay. You must have done a lot of work on it."

"Yeah." I tried to remember what I had written.

"Which part was the hardest?" she said.

I cleared my throat. "Starting it."

"I walked right into that one," she said, laughing. I smiled.

A tall man came up and hugged her. She kissed him. "Sam," she said. "This is the student I was telling you about."

"Well, hello," Mr. Smythe said. "Great paper."

"Thanks," I said.

"Is it William or Will?" Mr. Smythe said.

"Will," I said. He held out his hand and shook mine.

"That big, huh?" he said.

Oh no, I thought, remembering what I'd written. Dad, Eric, Grandpa, and I had gone out halibut fishing once and caught a huge one. It took forever to get it in the boat and we all took turns clubbing it. But it wouldn't die, so Dad shot it. In the essay I said it was seven hundred pounds, but Mrs. Smythe had pointed out to the whole class that halibut didn't get much bigger than five hundred. Tony and Craig bugged me about that.

"Karen tells me you've written a lot about fishing," Mr. Smythe said, sounding really cheerful.

"Excuse me," Mrs. Smythe said. "That's my cue to leave. If you're smart, you'll do the same. Once you get Sam going with his stupid fish stories you can't get a word—"

Mr. Smythe goosed her. She poked him with her hot dog and left quickly. Mr. Smythe put his arm around my shoulder, shaking his head. We sat out on the patio and he told me about the time he caught a marlin and about scuba diving on the Great Barrier Reef. He went down in a shark cage once to try to film a great white eating. I told him about Uncle Bernie's gillnetter. He wanted to know if Uncle Bernie would take him out, and what gear he was going to need. We ended up in the kitchen, me using a flounder to show him how to clean a halibut.

I finally looked at the clock around eleven. Dad had said he would pick me and Tony and Craig up around eight. I didn't even know where Tony and Craig were anymore. I couldn't believe it had gotten so late without my noticing. Mrs. Smythe had gone to bed. Mr. Smythe said he would drive me home. I said that was okay, I'd hitch.

He snorted. "Karen would kill me. No, I'll drive you. Let's phone your parents and tell them you're coming home."

No one answered the phone. I said they were probably asleep. He dialed again. Still no answer.

"Looks like you've got the spare bedroom tonight," he said.

"Let me try," I said, picking up the phone. There was no answer, but after six rings I pretended Dad was on the other end. I didn't want to spend the night at my English teacher's house. Tony and Craig would never shut up about it.

"Hi, Dad," I said. "How come? I see. Car trouble. No problem. Mr. Smythe is going to drive me home. What? Sure, I—"

"Let me talk to him," Mr. Smythe said, snatching the phone. "Hello! Mr. Tate! How are you? My, my, my. Your son is a lousy liar, isn't he?" He hung up. "It's amazing how much your father sounds like a dial tone."

I picked up the phone again. "They're sleeping, that's all." Mr. Smythe watched me as I dialed. There wasn't any answer.

"Why'd you lie?" he said quietly.

We were alone in the kitchen. I swallowed. He was a lot bigger than me. When he reached over, I put my hands up and covered my face. He stopped, then took the phone out of my hands.

"It's okay," he said. "I won't hurt you. It's okay."

I put my hands down. He looked sad. That annoyed me. I shrugged, backing away. "I'll hitch," I said.

Mr. Smythe shook his head. "No, really, Karen would kill me, then she'd go after you. Come on. We'll be safer if you sleep in the spare room."

In the morning Mr. Smythe was up before I could sneak out. He was making bacon and pancakes. He asked if I'd ever done any freshwater fishing. I said no. He started talking about fishing in the Black Sea and I listened to him. He's a good cook.

Mrs. Smythe came into the kitchen dressed in some sweats and a T-shirt. She ate without saying anything and didn't look awake until she finished her coffee. Mr. Smythe phoned my house but no one answered. He asked if I wanted to go up to Old Timer's Lake with them. He had a new Sona reel he wanted to try out. I didn't have anything better to do.

The Smythes have a twenty-foot speedboat. They let me drive it around the lake a few times while Mrs. Smythe baked in the sun and Mr. Smythe put the rod together. We lazed around the beach in the afternoon, watching the people go by. Sipping their beers, the Smythes argued about who was going to drive back. We rode around the lake some more and roasted hot dogs for dinner.

Their porch light is on. I go up the walk and ring the bell. Mrs. Smythe said just come in, don't bother knocking, but I can't do that. It doesn't feel right. She opens the door, smiling when she sees me. She is wearing a fluffy pink sweater. "Hi, Will. Sam was hoping you'd drop by. He says he's looking forward to beating you."

"Dream on," I say.

She laughs. "Go right in." She heads down the hall to the washroom.

I go into the living room. Mr. Smythe isn't there. The TV is on, some documentary about whales.

He's in the kitchen, scrunched over a game of solitaire. His new glasses are sliding off his nose and he looks more like a teacher than Mrs. Smythe. He scratches the beard he's trying to grow.

"Come on in," he says, patting the chair beside him.

I take a seat and watch him finish the game. He pushes his glasses up. "What's your pleasure?" he says.

"Pool," I say.

"Feeling lucky, huh?" We go down to the poolroom. "How about a little extra this week?" he says, not looking at me.

I shrug. "Sure. Dishes?"

He shakes his head. "Bigger."

"I'm not shoveling the walk," I say.

He shakes his head again. "Bigger."

"Money?"

"Bigger."

"What?"

He racks up the balls. Sets the cue ball. Wipes his hands on his jeans.

"What?" I say again.

Mr. Smythe takes out a quarter. "Heads or tails?" he says, tossing it.

"Heads," I say.

He slaps the quarter on the back of his hand. "I break."

"Where? Let me see that," I say, laughing. He holds it up. The quarter is tails.

He breaks. "How'd you like to stay with us?" he says, very quietly.

"Sure," I say. "But I got to go back on Tuesday. We got to check the traplines again."

He is quiet. The balls make thunking sounds as they bounce around the table. "Do you like it here?"

"Sure," I say.

"Enough to live here?"

I'm not sure I heard him right. Maybe he's asking a different question from the one I think he's asking. I open my mouth. I don't know what to say. I say nothing.

"Those are the stakes, then," he says. "I win, you stay. You win, you stay."

He's joking. I laugh. He doesn't laugh. "You serious?" I ask.

He stands up straight. "I don't think I've ever been more serious."

The room is suddenly very small.

"Your turn," he says. "Stripes."

I scratch, missing the ball by a mile. He takes his turn.

"We don't want to push you," he says. He leans over the table, squints at a ball. "We just think that you'd be safer here. Hell, you practically live with us already." I watch my sneakers. He keeps playing. "We aren't rich. We aren't perfect. We . . ." He looks at me. "We thought maybe you'd like to try it for a couple of weeks first."

"I can't."

"You don't have to decide right now," he says. "Think about it. Take a few days."

It's my turn again but I don't feel like playing anymore. Mr. Smythe is waiting, though. I pick a ball. Aim, shoot, miss.

The game goes on in silence. Mr. Smythe wins easily. He smiles. "Well, I win. You stay."

If I wanted to get out of the room, there is only one door and Mr. Smythe is blocking it. He watches me. "Let's go upstairs," he says.

Mrs. Smythe has shut off the TV. She stands up when we come into the living room. "Will—"

"I asked him already," Mr. Smythe says.

Her head snaps around. "You what?"

"I asked him."

Her hands clench at her sides. "We were supposed to do it together, Sam." Her voice is flat. She turns to me. "You said no."

I can't look at her. I look at the walls, at the floor, at her slippers. I shouldn't have come tonight. I should have waited for Eric to leave. She stands in front of me, trying to smile. Her hands are warm on my face. "Look at me," she says. "Will? Look at me." She is trying to smile. "Hungry?" she says.

I nod. She makes a motion with her head for Mr. Smythe to follow her into the kitchen. When they're gone I sit down. It should be easy. It should be easy. I watch TV without seeing it. I wonder what they're saying about me in the kitchen.

It's now almost seven and my ribs hurt. Mostly, I can ignore it, but Eric hit me pretty hard and they're bruised. Eric got hit pretty hard by Dad, so we're even, I guess. I'm counting the days until Eric moves out. The rate he's going, he'll be busted soon anyway. Tony says the police are starting to ask questions.

It's a strange night. We all pretend that nothing has happened and Mrs. Smythe fixes some nachos. Mr. Smythe gets out a pack of Uno cards and we play a few rounds and watch the Discovery Channel. We go to bed.

I lie awake. My room. This could be my room. I already have most of my books here. It's hard to study with Eric around. I still have a headache. I couldn't get away from them long enough to sneak into the kitchen for an aspirin. I pull my T-shirt up and take a look. There's a long bruise under my ribs and five smaller ones above it. I think Eric was trying to hit my stomach but he was so wasted he kept missing. It isn't too bad. Tony's dad broke three of his ribs once. Billy got a concussion a couple of weeks ago. My dad is pretty easy. It's only Eric who really bothers me.

The Smythes keep the aspirin by the spices. I grab six, three for now and three for the morning. I'm swallowing the last one when Mr. Smythe grabs my hand. I didn't even hear him come in. I must be sleepy.

"Where'd they hit you this time?" he says.

"I got a headache," I say. "A bad one."

He pries open the hand with the aspirins in it. "How many do you plan on taking?"

"These are for later."

He sighs. I get ready for a lecture. "Go back to bed" is all he says. "It'll be okay." He sounds very tired.

"Sure," I say.

I get up around five. I leave a note saying I have things to do at home. I catch a ride with some guys coming off the graveyard shift.

No one is home. Eric had a party last night. I'm glad I wasn't around. They've wrecked the coffee table and the rug smells like stale beer and cigarettes. Our bedroom is even worse. Someone puked all over Eric's bed and there are two used condoms on mine. At least none of the windows were broken this time. I start to clean my side of the room, then stop. I sit on my bed.

Mr. Smythe will be getting up soon. It's Sunday, so there'll be waffles or french toast. He'll fix a plate of bacon and eat it before Mrs. Smythe comes downstairs. He thinks she doesn't know that he does this. She'll get up around ten or eleven and won't talk to anyone until she's had about three coffees. She starts to wake up around one or two. They'll argue about something. Whose turn to take out the garbage or do the laundry. They'll read the paper.

I crawl into bed. The aspirin isn't working. I try to sleep but it really reeks in here. I have a biology test tomorrow. I forgot to bring the book back from their place. I lie there awake until our truck pulls into the driveway. Mom and Dad are fighting. They sound plastered. Mom is bitching about something. Dad is not saying anything. Doors slam.

Mom comes in first and goes straight to bed. She doesn't seem to notice the house is a mess. Dad comes in a lot slower.

"What the—Eric!" he yells. "Eric!"

I pretend to sleep. The door bangs open.

"Eric, you little bastard," Dad says, looking around. He shakes me. "Where the fuck is Eric?"

His breath is lethal. You can tell he likes his rye straight.

"How should I know?"

He rips Eric's amplifiers off the walls. He throws them down and gives them a good kick. He tips Eric's bed over. Eric is smart. He won't come home for a while. Dad will have cooled off by then and Eric can give him some money without Dad's getting pissed off. I don't move. I wait until he's out of the room before I put on a sweater. I can hear him down in the basement chopping wood. It should be around eight by now. The RinkyDink will be open in an hour.

When I go into the kitchen, Mom is there. She sees me and makes a shushing motion with her hands. She pulls out a bottle from behind the stove and sits down at the kitchen table.

"You're a good boy," she says, giggling. "You're a good boy. Help your old mother back to bed, hey."

"Sure," I say, putting an arm around her. She stands, holding onto the bottle with one hand and me with the other. "This way, my lady."

"You making fun of me?" she says, her eyes going small. "You laughing at me?" Then she laughs and we go to their room. She flops onto the bed. She takes a long drink. "You're fucking laughing at me, aren't you?"

"Mom, you're paranoid. I was making a joke."

"Yeah, you're really funny. A laugh a minute," she says, giggling again. "Real comedian."

"Yeah, that's me."

She throws the bottle at me. I duck. She rolls over and starts to cry. I cover her with the blanket and leave. The floor is sticky. Dad's still chopping wood. They wouldn't notice if I wasn't here. Maybe people would talk for a week or two, but after a while they wouldn't notice. The only people who would miss me are Tony and Craig and Billy and maybe Eric, when he got toked up and didn't have anything for target practice.

Billy is playing Mortal Kombat at the RinkyDink. He's chain-smoking. As I walk up to him, he turns around quickly.

"Oh, it's you," he says, going back to the game.

"Hi to you too," I say.

"You seen Elaine?" he says.

"Nope."

He crushes out his cigarette in the ashtray beside him. He plays for a while, loses a life, then shakes another cigarette out one-handed. He sticks it in his mouth, loses another man, then lights up. He sucks deep. "Relax," I say. "Her majesty's limo is probably stuck in traffic. She'll come."

He glares at me. "Shut up."

I go play pool with Craig, who's decided that he's James Dean. He's wearing a white T-shirt, jeans, and a black leather jacket that looks like his brother's. His hair is blow-dried and a cigarette dangles from the corner of his mouth.

"What a loser," he says.

"Who you calling a loser?"

"Billy. What a loser." He struts to the other side of the pool table.

"He's okay."

"That babe," he says. "What's-her-face. Ellen? Irma?"

"Elaine."

"Yeah, her. She's going out with him 'cause she's got a bet."

"What?"

"She's got to go out with him a month, and her friend will give her some coke."

"Billy's already giving her coke."

"Yeah. He's a loser."

I look over at Billy. He's lighting another cigarette.

"Can you imagine a townie wanting anything to do with him?" Craig says. "She's just doing it as a joke. She's going to dump him in a week. She's going to put all his stupid poems in the paper."

I see it now. There's a space around Billy. No one is going near him. He doesn't notice. Same with me. I catch some guys I used to hang out with grinning at me. When they see me looking at them, they look away.

Craig wins the game. I'm losing a lot this week.

Elaine gets to the RinkyDink after lunch. She's got some townie girl-friends with her who are tiptoeing around like they're going to get jumped. Elaine leads them right up to Billy. Everyone's watching. Billy gives her his latest poem. I wonder what he found to rhyme with "Elaine."

The girls leave. Billy holds the door open for Elaine. Her friends start to giggle. The guys standing around start to howl. They're laughing so hard they're crying. I feel sick. I think about telling Billy but I know he won't listen.

I leave the RinkyDink and go for a walk. I walk and walk and end up back in front of the RinkyDink. There's nowhere else to go. I hang out with Craig, who hasn't left the pool table.

I spend the night on his floor. Craig's parents are Jehovah's Witnesses and preach at me before I go to bed. I sit and listen because I need a place to sleep. I'm not going home until tomorrow, when Mom and Dad are sober. Craig's mom gets us up two hours before the bus that takes the village kids to school comes. They pray before we eat. Craig looks at me and rolls his eyes. People are always making fun of Craig because his parents stand on the corner downtown every Friday and hold up the *Watchtower* mags. When his parents start to bug him, he says he'll take up devil worship or astrology if they don't lay off. I think I'll ask him if he wants to hang out with me on Christmas. His parents don't believe in it.

Between classes I pass Mrs. Smythe in the hall. Craig nudges me. "Go on," he says, making sucking noises. "Go get your A."

"Fuck off," I say, pushing him.

She's talking to some girl and doesn't see me. I think about skipping English but know that she'll call home and ask where I am.

At lunch no one talks to me. I can't find Craig or Tony or Billy. The village guys who hang out by the science wing snicker as I go past. I don't stop until I get to the gym doors, where the headbangers have taken over. I don't have any money and I didn't bring a lunch, so I bum a cigarette off this girl with really tight jeans. To get my mind off my stomach I try to get her to go out with me. She looks at me like I'm crazy. When she walks away, the fringe on her leather jacket swings.

I flunk my biology test. It's multiple choice. I stare at the paper and kick myself. I know I could have passed if I'd read the chapter. Mr. Kellerman reads out the scores from lowest to highest. My name is called out third.

"Mr. Tate," he says. "Three out of thirty."

"All riiight," Craig says, slapping my back.

"Mr. Davis," Mr. Kellerman says to Craig, "three and a half."

Craig stands up and bows. The guys in the back clap. The kids in the front laugh. Mr. Kellerman reads out the rest of the scores. Craig turns to me. "Looks like I beat the Brain," he says.

"Yeah," I say. "Pretty soon you're going to be getting the Nobel Prize."

The bell rings for English. I go to my locker and take out my jacket. If she calls home no one's going to answer anyway.

I walk downtown. The snow is starting to slack off and it's even sunning a bit. My stomach growls. I haven't eaten anything since break-fast. I wish I'd gone to English. Mrs. Smythe would have given me something to eat. She always has something left over from lunch. I hunch down into my jacket.

Downtown, I go to the Paradise Arcade. All the heads hang out there. Maybe Eric'll give me some money. More like a belt, but it's worth a try. I don't see him anywhere, though. In fact, no one much is there. Just some burnouts by the pinball machines. I see Mitch and go over to him, but he's soaring, laughing at the ball going around the machine. I walk away, head for the highway, and hitch home. Mom will have passed out by now, and Dad'll be at work.

Sure enough, Mom is on the living room floor. I get her a blanket. The stove has gone out and it's freezing in here. I go into the kitchen and look through the fridge. There's one jar of pickles, some really pathetic-looking celery, and some milk that's so old it smells like cheese. There's no bread left over from Saturday. I find some Rice-A-Roni and cook it. Mom comes to and asks for some water. I bring her a glass and give her a little Rice-A-Roni. She makes a face but slowly eats it.

At six Dad comes home with Eric. They've made up. Eric has bought Dad a six-pack and they watch the hockey game together. I stay in my room. Eric has cleaned his bed by dumping his mattress outside and stealing mine. I haul my mattress back onto my bed frame. I pull out my English book. We have a grammar test this Friday. I know Mrs. Smythe will be unhappy if she has to fail me. I read the chapter on nouns and get through most of the one on verbs before Eric comes in and kicks me off the bed.

He tries to take the mattress but I punch him in the side. Eric turns and grabs my hair. "This is my bed," he says. "Understand?"

"Fuck you," I say. "You had the party. Your fucked-up friends trashed the room. You sleep on the floor."

Dad comes in and sees Eric push me against the wall and smack my face. He yells at Eric, who turns around, his fist frozen in the air. Dad rolls his sleeves up.

"You always take his side!" Eric yells. "You never take mine!"

"Pick on someone your own size," Dad says. "Unless you want to deal with me."

Eric gives me a look that says he'll settle with me later. I pick up my English book and get out. I walk around the village, staying away from the RinkyDink. It's the first place Eric will look.

I'm at the village exit. The sky is clear and the stars are popping out. Mr. Smythe will be at his telescope trying to map the Pleiades. Mrs. Smythe will be marking papers while she watches TV.

"Need a ride?" this guy says. There's a blue pickup stopped in front of me. The driver is wearing a hunting cap.

I take my hand out of my mouth. I've been chewing my knuckle like a baby. I shake my head. "I'm waiting for someone," I say.

He shrugs and takes off. I stand there and watch his headlights disappear.

They didn't really mean it. They'd get bored of me quick when they found out what I'm like. I should have just said yes. I could have stayed until they got fed up and then come home when Eric had cooled off.

Two cars pass me as I walk back to the village. I can hide at Tony's until Eric goes out with his friends and forgets this afternoon. My feet are frozen by the time I get to the RinkyDink. Tony is there.

"So. I heard Craig beat you in biology," he says.

I laugh. "Didn't it just impress you?"

"A whole half a point. Way to go," he says. "For a while there we thought you were getting townie."

"Yeah, right," I say. "Listen, I pissed Eric off—"

"Surprise, surprise."

"—and I need a place to crash. Can I sleep over?"

"Sure," he says. Mitch wanders into the RinkyDink, and a crowd of kids slowly drifts over to him. He looks around, eyeing everybody. Then he starts giving something out. Me and Tony go over.

"Wow," Tony says, after Mitch gives him something too.

We leave and go behind the RinkyDink, where other kids are gathered. "Fucking all right," I hear Craig say, even though I can't see him.

"What?" I say. Tony opens his hand. He's holding a little vial with white crystals in it.

"Crack," he says. "Man, is he stupid. He could have made a fortune and he's just giving it away."

We don't have a pipe, and Tony wants to do this right the first time. He decides to save it for tomorrow, after he buys the right equipment. I'm hungry again. I'm about to tell him that I'm going to Billy's when I see Eric.

"Shit," I say and hide behind him.

Tony looks up. "Someone's in trou-ble," he sings.

Eric's looking for me. I hunch down behind Tony, who tries to look innocent. Eric spots him and starts to come over. "Better run," Tony whispers.

I sneak behind some other people but Eric sees me and I have to run for it anyway. Tony starts to cheer and the kids behind the RinkyDink join in. Some of the guys follow us so they'll see what happens when Eric catches up with me. I don't want to find out so I pump as hard as I can.

Eric used to be fast. I'm glad he's a dopehead now because he can't really run anymore. I'm panting and my legs are cramping but the house is in sight. I run up the stairs. The door is locked.

I stand there, hand on the knob. Eric rounds the corner to our block. There's no one behind him. I bang on the door but now I see that our truck is gone. I run around to the back but the basement door is locked too. Even the windows are locked.

Eric pops his head around the corner of the house. He grins when he sees me, then disappears. I grit my teeth and start running across our backyard. Head for Billy's. "You shithead," Eric yells. He has a friend with him, maybe Brent. I duck behind our neighbor's house. There's snow in my sneakers and all the way up my leg, but I'm sweating. I stop. I can't hear Eric. I hope I've lost him, but Eric is really pissed off and when he's pissed off he doesn't let go. I look down. My footprints are clear in the snow. I start to run again, but I hit a thick spot and have to wade through thigh-high snow. I look back. Eric is nowhere. I keep slogging. I make it to the road again and run down to the exit.

I've lost him. I'm shaking because it's cold. I can feel the sweat cooling on my skin. My breath goes back to normal. I wait for a car to come by. I've missed the night shift and the graveyard crew won't be by until midnight. It's too cold to wait that long.

A car, a red car. A little Toyota. Brent's car. I run off the road and head for a clump of trees. The Toyota pulls over and Eric gets out, yelling. I reach the trees and rest. They're waiting by the roadside. Eric is peering into the trees, trying to see me. Brent is smoking in the car. Eric crosses his arms over his chest and blows into his hands. My legs are frozen.

After a long time, a cop car cruises to a stop beside the Toyota. I wade out and wave at the two policemen. They look startled. One of them turns to Eric and Brent and asks them something. I see Eric shrug. It takes me a while to get over to where they're standing because my legs are slow.

The cop is watching me. I swear I'll never call them pigs again. I swear it. He leans over to Brent, who digs around in the glove compartment. The cop says something to his partner. I scramble down the embankment.

Eric has no marks on his face. Dad probably hit him on the back and stomach. Dad has been careful since the social worker came to our house. Eric suddenly smiles at me and holds out his hand. I move behind the police car.

"Is there a problem here?" the policeman says.

"No," Eric says. "No probulum. Li'l misunnerstanin'."

Oh, shit. He's as high as a kite. The policeman looks hard at Eric. I look at the car. Brent is staring at me, glassy-eyed. He's high too.

Eric tries again to reach out to me. I put the police car between us. The policeman grabs Eric by the arm and his partner goes and gets Brent. The policeman says something about driving under the influence but none of us are listening. Eric's eyes are on me. I'm going to pay for this. Brent is swearing. He wants a lawyer. He stumbles out of the Toyota and slips on the road. Brent and Eric are put in the backseat of the police car. The policeman comes up to me and says, "Can you make it home?"

I nod.

"Good. Go," he says.

They drive away. When I get home, I walk around the house, trying to figure out a way to break in. I find a stick and jimmy the basement door open. Just in case Eric gets out tonight, I make a bed under the tool table and go to sleep.

No one is home when I wake up. I scramble an egg and get ready for school. I sit beside Tony on the bus.

"I was expecting to see you with black eyes," he says.

My legs are still raw from last night. I have something due today but I can't remember what. If Eric is in the drunk tank, they'll let him out later.

The village guys are talking to me again. I skip gym. I skip history. I hang out with Craig and Tony in the Paradise Arcade. I'm not sure if I want to be friends with them after they joined in the chase last night, but it's better to have them on my side than not. They get a two-for-one pizza special for lunch and I'm glad I stuck with them because I'm starved. They also got some five-finger specials from Safeway. Tony is proud because he swiped a couple of bags of chips and two Pepsis and no one even noticed.

Mitch comes over to me in the bathroom.

"That was a really cheap thing to do," he says.

"What?" I haven't done anything to him.

"What? What? Getting your brother thrown in jail. Pretty crummy."

"He got himself thrown in jail. He got caught when he was high."

"That's not what he says." Mitch frowns. "He says you set him up."

"Fuck." I try to sound calm. "When'd he tell you that?"

"This morning," he says. "He's waiting for you at school."

"I didn't set him up. How could I?"

Mitch nods. He hands me some crack and says, "Hey, I'm sorry," and leaves. I look at it. I'll give it to Tony and maybe he'll let me stay with him tonight.

Billy comes into the Paradise with Elaine and her friends. He's getting some glances but he doesn't notice. He holds the chair out for Elaine, who sits down without looking at him. I don't want to be around for this. I go over to Tony.

"I'm leaving," I say.

Tony shushes me. "Watch," he says.

Elaine orders a beer. Frankie shakes his head and points to the sign that says WE DO NOT SERVE MINORS. Elaine frowns. She says something to Billy. He shrugs. She orders a Coke. Billy pays. When their Cokes come, Elaine dumps hers over Billy's head. Billy stares at her, more puzzled than anything else. Her friends start to laugh, and I get up and walk out.

I lean against the wall of the Paradise. Billy comes out a few minutes later. His face is still and pale. Elaine and her friends follow him, reciting lines from the poems he wrote her. Tony and the rest spill out too, laughing. I go back inside and trade the crack for some quarters for the video games. I keep losing. Tony wants to go now and we hitch back to the village. We raid his fridge and have chocolate ice cream coconut sundaes. Angela comes in with Di and says that Eric is looking for me. I look at Tony and he looks at me.

"Boy, are you in for it," Tony says. "You'd better stay here tonight."

When everyone is asleep, Tony pulls out a weird-looking pipe and does the crack. His face goes very dreamy and far away. A few minutes later he says, "Christ, that's great. I wonder how much Mitch has?"

I turn over and go to sleep.

The next morning Billy is alone on the bus. No one wants to sit with him so there are empty seats all around him. He looks like he hasn't slept. Tony goes up to him and punches him in the arm.

"So how's Shakespeare this morning?" Tony says.

I hope Eric isn't at the school. I don't know where else I can hide.

Mrs. Smythe is waiting at the school bus stop. I sneak out the back door of the bus, with Tony and the guys pretending to fight to cover me.

We head back to the Paradise. I'm starting to smell bad. I haven't had a shower in days. I wish I had some clean clothes. I wish I had some money to buy a toothbrush. I hate the scummy feeling on my teeth. I wish I had enough for a taco or a hamburger.

Dad is at the Paradise, looking for me.

"Let's go to the Dairy Queen," he says.

He orders a coffee, a chocolate milk shake, and a cheeseburger. We take the coffee and milk shake to a back table, and I pocket the order slip. We sit there. Dad folds and unfolds a napkin.

"One of your teachers called," he says.

"Mrs. Smythe?"

"Yeah." He looks up. "Says she'd like you to stay there."

I try to read his face. His eyes are bloodshot and red-rimmed. He must have a big hangover.

The cashier calls out our number. I go up and get the cheeseburger and we split it. Dad always eats slow to make it last longer.

"Did you tell her you wanted to?"

"No," I say. "They asked me, but I said I couldn't."

Dad nods. "Did you tell them anything?"

"Like what?"

"Don't get smart," he says, sounding beat.

"I didn't say anything."

He stops chewing. "Then why'd they ask you?"

"Don't know."

"You must have told them something."

"Nope. They just asked."

"Did Eric tell them?"

I snort. "Eric? No way. They would . . . He wouldn't go anywhere near them. They're okay, Dad. They won't tell anybody."

"So you did tell them."

"I didn't. I swear I didn't. Look, Eric got me on the face a couple of times and they just figured it out."

"You're lying."

I finished my half of the cheeseburger. "I'm not lying. I didn't say anything and they won't either."

"I never touched you."

"Yeah, Eric took care of that," I say. "You seen him?"

"I kicked him out."

"You what?"

"Party. Ruined the basement," Dad says grimly. "He's old enough. Had to leave sooner or later."

He chews his last mouthful of cheeseburger. Eric will really be out of his mind now.

We drive out to check the trapline. The first trap has been tripped with a stick. Dad curses, blaming the other trappers who have lines near ours. "I'll skunk them," he says. But the last three traps have got some more martens. We even get a little lynx. Dad is happy. We go home. The basement is totally ripped apart.

Next day at school, I spend most of the time ducking from Eric and Mrs. Smythe before I finally get sick of the whole lot and go down to the Paradise. Tony is there with Billy, who asks me if I want to go to Vancouver with him until Eric cools off.

"Now?"

"No better time," he says.

I think about it. "When you leaving?"

"Tonight."

"I don't know. I don't have any money."

"Me neither," he says.

"Shit," I say. "How we going to get there? It's a zillion miles from here."

"Hitch to town, hitch to Smithers, then down to Prince George."

"Yeah, yeah, but what are we going to eat?"

He wiggles his hand. Five-finger special. I laugh.

"You change your mind," he says, "I'll be behind the RinkyDink around seven. Get some thick boots."

We're about to hitch home when I see Mrs. Smythe peer into the Paradise. It's too late to hide because she sees me. Her face stiffens. She walks over to us and the guys start to laugh. Mrs. Smythe looks at them, then at me.

"Will?" she says. "Can I talk to you outside?"

She glances around like the guys are going to jump her. I try to see what she's nervous about. Tony is grabbing his crotch. Billy is cleaning his nails. The other guys are snickering. I suddenly see them the way she does. They all have long, greasy hair, combed straight back. We're all wearing jeans, T-shirts, and sneakers. We don't look nice.

She's got on her school uniform, as she calls it. Dark skirt, white shirt, low black heels, glasses. She's watching me like she hasn't seen me before. I hope she never sees my house.

"Later?" I say. "I'm kind of busy."

She blushes, the guys laugh hard. I wish I could take the words back. "Are you sure?" she says.

Tony nudges my arm. "Why don't you introduce us to your girl-friend," he says. "Maybe she'd like—"

"Shut up," I say. Mrs. Smythe has no expression now.

"I'll talk to you later, then," she says, and turns around and walks out without looking back. If I could, I'd follow her.

Billy claps me on the shoulder. "Stay away from them," he says. "It's not worth it."

It doesn't matter. She practically said she didn't want to see me again. I don't blame her. I wouldn't want to see me again either.

She'll get into her car now and go home. She'll honk when she pulls into the driveway so Mr. Smythe will come out and help her with the groceries. She always gets groceries today. The basics and sardines. Peanut butter. I lick my lips. Diamante frozen pizzas. Oodles of Noodles. Waffles. Blueberry Mueslix.

Mr. Smythe will come out of the house, wave, come down the drive-way. They'll take the groceries into the house after they kiss. They'll kick the snow off their shoes and throw something in the microwave. Watch *Cheers* reruns on Channel 8. Mr. Smythe will tell her what happened in his day. Maybe she will say happened in hers.

We catch a ride home. Billy yabbers about Christmas in Vancouver, and how great it's going to be, the two of us, no one to boss us around, no one to bother us, going anywhere we want. I turn away from him. Watch the trees blur past. I guess anything'll be better than sitting around, listening to Tony and Craig gripe.

—1996

David Bezmozgis   b. 1973

David Bezmozgis's book, the short story sequence Natasha and Other Stories
*(2004), was a success before it was published because so many of its stories had
already appeared in prominent journals—including* The New Yorker, Harper's,
The Walrus, *Francis Ford Coppola's* Zoetrope, *and* Prairie Fire. *In contrast to
the deliberate calling attention to style and textuality that characterizes postmodern
metafictional works like P.K. Page's "Ex Libris," the transparency of Bezmozgis's
fiction looks back to the ideals of modernist writers such as Hemingway and
Callaghan. In his presentation of an immigrant family trying to make sense of the
new culture in which they find themselves and to make themselves comprehensible to
their new countrymen, Bezmozgis handles his characters with both humour and
respect, avoiding didactic anger and self-deprecation. "The Second Strongest Man"
shows the poignancy and loss that results from necessary emigration but also
suggests that the passage of time is itself an inevitable dislocation, one that removes
us from the past whether we remain at home or go abroad.*

The Second Strongest Man

In the winter of 1984, as my mother was recovering from a nervous
breakdown and my father's business hovered precipitously between failure and near failure, the international weightlifting championships were
held at the Toronto Convention Centre. One evening the phone rang and
a man invited my father to serve on the panel of judges. The job paid
next to nothing but my father took it for the sake of his dignity. If only
for a few days, he would wear his old IWF blazer and be something
other than a struggling massage therapist and schlepper of chocolate
bars.[1] In the bedroom my father retrieved a passport with his
International Weightlifting Federation credentials. The passport
contained a photo of him taken years before the trials of immigration.
In the picture his face carried the detached confidence of the highly
placed Soviet functionary. I had seen the picture many times, and occasionally, when my father wasn't home, I took it out and studied it. It was
comforting to think that the man in the picture and my father were once
the same person.

Several days after the phone call we received an official package from
the IWF. I joined my parents at the kitchen table and scanned through

---

[1] *Schlepper* is a deprecating Yiddish expression that literally means someone who carries or drags
heavy objects around. Here, a door-to-door salesman.

the list of competitors. There, as part of the Soviet delegation, were the names Sergei Federenko and Gregory Ziskin. My mother asked my father what this meant. Did it mean we would get to see them? Did it mean they would see our apartment? It had been little more than a week since the last time the paramedics had come, wrapped my mother in an orange blanket, strapped her to a gurney and taken her to Branson Hospital. For months she had been stricken with paralyzing anxiety and a lethargy that made it impossible for her to undertake even the most basic household tasks. These had been months of boiled eggs, Lipton chicken noodle soup, an accumulation of sticky patches on the kitchen floor, and dust in the corners. My God, Sergei can't see the apartment like this, she said.

I sprang up from the table, unable to restrain my enthusiasm. I pranced around the apartment singing, Seryozha, Seryozha, Seryozha. Seryozha is coming!

My father told me to be quiet already.

—Seryozha, Seryozha, Seryozha.

My mother got up and handed me the broom.

—If you can't sit still, start sweeping.

—Seryozha is coming, I sang to the broom.

Five years before we left Latvia my father operated a very successful side venture out of the gym at Riga Dynamo. At that time he was one of the head administrators at Dynamo and was responsible for paper shuffling and budget manipulation. Before that he had been a very good varsity athlete and an accomplished coach of the VEF radio factory's soccer team. For a Jew, he was well liked by his superiors, and so they turned a blind eye when he and Gregory Ziskin—a fellow administrator and Jew—started their bodybuilding program in the evenings. At best, the directors hoped that the class would lead to the discovery of a new lifter; at worst, it meant they would get a piece of the action.

Every Monday, Wednesday, and Friday from six to nine my father and Gregory unlocked the back door of the Dynamo gym and admitted their eager bodybuilders. Most of these were Jewish university students and young professionals who wanted to look good on the beaches of Jurmala. They were hardly inspired athletes but they came regularly and were pleased with their results. My father and Gregory assigned routines and oversaw their exercises. For my father the class was a welcome break from the obligations of Soviet bureaucracy—the endless documents, detailed reports, and formal presentations to the Dynamo directors and visiting dignitaries. Also, the money was good. After kick-backs to the Dynamo directors and a few rubles to the janitor, my father and Gregory each pocketed thirty extra rubles a month—more than double the rent on our three-room apartment.

My father and Gregory ran the class for several years without incident. The directors received their cut and kept quiet. As long as the Dynamo teams were placing well, nobody was willing to mess with a good thing, and at the time, Riga Dynamo was clicking along: Victor Tikhonov worked magic with the hockey team before being promoted to Moscow and Red Army; Ivanchenko became the first middleweight to lift a combined 500 kilos; and the basketball and volleyball teams were feared across Europe. So nobody paid much attention to my father's class.

It was only in the mid-1970s that things started to turn. As Jews began to emigrate many of my father's bodybuilders requested visas to Israel. Dynamo represented the KGB and someone at the ministry started making connections. It was pointed out to one of my father's directors that there was a disturbing correlation between my father's bodybuilders and Jews asking for exit visas. My father and Gregory were invited into the director's office and informed of the suspicions. These were the sorts of suspicions that could get them all into trouble. It wouldn't look good at all if the Riga Dynamo gym was sponsoring anti-Soviet activities. The director, an old friend, asked my father whether the bodybuilding class was a front for Zionist agitation. It was an unpleasant conversation, but everyone understood that this could only be the beginning of the unpleasantness. The class was now being closely monitored. The only way to keep from shutting it down would be to justify its existence in an official capacity. In other words, they had better discover some talent.

After the meeting with the director, my father suggested to Gregory that the smart thing to do would be to end the class. They'd made their money, and since my parents had already resolved to leave the Soviet Union, this was exactly the sort of incident that could create serious problems. Gregory, who had no plans to emigrate, but who also had no interest in a trip to Siberia, agreed. They decided not to continue the class beyond the end of the month.

The following day my father discovered Sergei Federenko.

On the night my father discovered Sergei Federenko the class ended later than usual. Gregory left early and my father remained with five students.

It was almost ten when my father opened the back door of the gym and stepped out into the alley where three young soldiers were singing drunken songs. The smallest of the three was pissing against the wall. My father turned in the opposite direction, but one of his students decided to flex his new muscles. He accused the little soldier of uncivilized behavior, called him a dog, and said unflattering things about his mother.

The little soldier continued pissing as if nothing had happened, but the two bigger soldiers got ready to crack skulls.

—Would you listen to Chaim? A real tough Jew bastard.

—You apologize, Chaim, before it's too late.

My father envisioned a catastrophe. Even if by some miracle he and his students weren't killed, the police would get involved. The consequences of police involvement would be worse than any beating.

Before his student could respond, my father played the conciliator. He apologized for the student. He explained that he was part of a body-building class. His head was still full of adrenaline. He didn't know what he was saying. Doctors had proven that as muscles grow the brain shrinks. He didn't want any trouble. They should accept his apology and forget the whole thing.

As my father spoke the little soldier finished pissing on the wall and buttoned up his trousers. Unlike his two friends, he was completely unperturbed. He reached into his pants pocket and retrieved a small bottle of vodka. One of the other soldiers pointed to a black Moskvich sedan parked in the alley.

—Listen, faggot, if one of your boys can lift the Moskvich we'll forget the whole thing.

They made a deal. The Moskvich had to be lifted from the back and held at least a meter off the ground. Even though the engine was at the front, the back of the car was sufficiently heavy. Taking into account the frame, wheels, tires, and whatever might be kept in the trunk, the total would be in the hundreds of pounds. Maybe three hundred? Maybe four? It was an impossible bet. None of his students would be able to do it. It would be an exercise in futility. They would certainly be humiliated, but from my father's perspective, humiliation was better than a beating and a police inquiry. So, out of respect for my father, his students shut up and endured the ridicule. One by one they squatted under the car's bumper.

—Careful, Chaim, don't shit your pants.

—Lift it for Mother Russia.

—Lift it for Israel.

As expected, none of them could so much as get it off the ground. When they were done, one of the soldiers turned to the student who had started the trouble.

—Not so tough now, Chaim?

—It's impossible.

—Impossible for Chaim.

—Impossible even for a stupid cocksucker like you.

Amazingly, instead of killing the student, the big soldier turned to the little soldier.

—Sergei, show Chaim what's impossible.

The little soldier put his bottle back into his pocket and walked over to the Moskvich.

—Chaim, you watch the stupid cocksucker.

Sergei squatted under the bumper, took a deep breath, and lifted the car a meter off the ground.

From the time I was four until we left Riga two years later, Sergei was a regular visitor to our apartment on Kasmonaftikas. As a rule, he would come and see us whenever he returned from an international competition. Two years after my father discovered him, Sergei was a member of the national team, had attained the prestigious tide of "International Master of Sport," and possessed all three world records in his weight class. My father called him the greatest natural lifter he had ever seen. He was blessed with an economy of movement and an intuition for the mechanics of lifting. He loved to lift the way other people love drugs or chocolate. Growing up on a kolkhoz,[2] he had been doing a man's work since the age of twelve. Life had consisted of hauling manure, bailing hay, harvesting turnips, and lugging bulky farm equipment. When the army took him at eighteen he had never been more than thirty kilometers from the kolkhoz. Once he left he never intended to return. His father was an alcoholic and his mother had died in an accident when he was three. His gratitude to my father for rescuing him from the army and the kolkhoz was absolute. As he rose through the ranks, his loyalty remained filial and undiminished. And in 1979, when we left Riga, Sergei was as devoted to my father as ever. By then he could no longer walk down the street without being approached by strangers. In Latvia, he was as recognizable as any movie star. Newspapers in many countries called him, pound for pound, the strongest man in the world.

---

[2] A collective farm.

Sergei left a deep impression on my four-, five-, and six-year-old mind. There wasn't much I remembered from Riga—isolated episodes, little more than vignettes, mental artifacts—but many of these recollections involved Sergei. My memories, largely indistinct from my parents' stories, constituted my idea of Sergei. A spectrum inverted through a prism, stories and memories refracted to create the whole: Sergei as he appeared when he visited our apartment on Kasmonafrikas. Dressed in the newest imported fashions, he brought exotic gifts: pineapples, French perfume, Swiss chocolate, Italian sunglasses. He told us about strange lands where everything was different—different trains, different houses, different toilets, different cars. Sometimes he arrived alone, other times he was accompanied by one of the many pretty girls he was dating. When Sergei visited I was spastic with a compulsion to please him. I shadowed him around the apartment, I swung from his biceps like a monkey, I did somersaults on the carpet. The only way I could be convinced to go to sleep was if Sergei followed my mother into my bedroom. We developed a routine. Once I was under the covers Sergei said good night by lifting me and my little bed off the floor. He lifted the bed as though it weighed no more than a newspaper or a sandwich. He raised me to his chest and wouldn't put me back down until I named the world's strongest man.

—Seryozha, Seryozha Federenko!

My father took me with him to the Sutton Place Hotel where the Soviet delegation had their rooms. A KGB agent always traveled with the team, but it turned out that my father knew him. My father had met him on the two or three occasions when he had toured with Dynamo through Eastern Europe. The agent was surprised to see my father.

—Roman Abramovich, you're here? I didn't see you on the plane.

My father explained that he hadn't taken the plane. He lived here now. A sweep of my father's arm defined "here" broadly. The sweep included me. My jacket, sneakers, and Levi's were evidence. Roman Abramovich and his kid lived here. The KGB agent took an appreciative glance at me. He nodded his head.

—You're living well?

—I can't complain.

—It's a beautiful country. Clean cities. Big forests. Nice cars. I also hear you have good dentists.

In the hotel lobby, the KGB agent opened his mouth and showed my father the horrific swelling around a molar. He had been in agony for weeks. In Moscow, a dentist had extracted a neighboring tooth and the wound had become infected. On the plane, with the cabin pressure, he had thought he would go insane. Eating was out of the question and sleep was impossible without 1,000 grams of vodka, minimum. But he couldn't very well do his job if he was drunk all the time. Also, he'd been told that vodka was very expensive here. What he needed was a dentist. If my father could arrange for a Toronto dentist to help him he would owe him his life. The pain was already making him think dark thoughts. In his room on the twenty-eighth floor he had stood at the window and considered jumping.

Using the hotel phone, my father called Dusa, our dentist. A top professional in Moscow, she had not yet passed her Canadian exams. In the interim, she worked nights as a maid for a Canadian dentist with whom she had an informal arrangement which allowed her to use his office to see her own patients, for cash, under the table. The Canadian dentist got fifty percent with the understanding that in the event of trouble, he would deny everything and it would be Dusa's ass on the line. Fortunately, after months and months of work, there had been no trouble. And several times a week, after she finished cleaning the office, Dusa saw her motley assortment of patients. All of them Russian immigrants without dental insurance. My father explained this to the KGB officer and told him that if he wasn't averse to seeing a dentist at one in the morning, he had himself an appointment.

As a token of his gratitude, the KGB agent personally escorted us up to Sergei's room. So long as Sergei appeared at the competition and was on the flight to Moscow with the rest of the team, everything else was of no consequence. We could see him as much as we liked. The KGB agent swore on his children's eyes that there would be no problems.

At Sergei's door, the agent knocked sharply.

—Comrade Federenko, you have important visitors!

Dressed in official gray slacks and buttoning his shirt, Sergei opened the door. He hesitated to speak until the KGB agent slapped my father's back and confessed that he was always deeply moved to witness a reunion of old friends. Then, Dusa's address in his pocket, he turned and departed down the carpeted hall.

In the hallway, Sergei embraced my father and kissed him in the Soviet style. Next to Sergei, my father—five feet six and 170 pounds—looked big. I hadn't expected the physical Sergei to be so small—even though I had memorized his records the way American kids memorized box scores and knew that he was in the lowest weight class at 52 kilos.

—That bastard, he scared the hell out of me.

—The KGB, they know how to knock on a door.

—Especially that one. A true Soviet patriot.

Sergei looked down the hall in the direction of the KGB agent's departure. My father looked. So did I. The man had gone.

Sergei turned back, looked at my father, and grinned.

—I was in the washroom, I almost pissed myself. I thought, if I'm lucky, it's only another drug test.

—Since when are you afraid of drug tests?

—Since never.

—Do I need to remind you of our regard for drug tests?

In his capacity as Dynamo administrator it had been my father's responsibility to ensure that all the weightlifters were taking their steroids. At the beginning of each week he handed out the pills along with the special food coupons. Everyone knew the drill: no pills, no food.

—Absolutely not. Keeps the sport clean.

—And, of course, you're clean.

—I'm clean. The team is clean. Everyone is clean.

—Good to hear nothing has changed.

—Nothing.

Sergei clapped my father on the shoulder.

—What a wonderful surprise.

On our way to the hotel, I had been rabid with excitement to see Sergei, but seeing him in person, I couldn't speak. I stood behind my father and waited to be acknowledged. It seemed like a very long time before Sergei turned his attention to me. When he finally did, he looked down and appeared not to know me.

—And who is this?

—You don't recognize him?

—He looks familiar.

—Think.

—It's hard to say.

—Take a guess.

—Well, if I had to guess, I would say he looks a little like Mark. But he's too small.

—Too small?

—Mark was much bigger. He could do fifteen, maybe even twenty push-ups. This one looks like he couldn't even do ten.

—I can do twenty-five! I do them every morning.

—I don't believe it.

I dropped down onto the red and gold Sutton Place carpet and Sergei counted them from one to twenty-five. Panting, I got back up and waited for Sergei's reaction. He smiled and spread his arms.

—Come on, boy, jump.

I leapt. Sergei carried me into the hotel room and I hung from his arm as my father called Gregory's room. Sergei's competition was two days away and it was decided that he would spend a little time with us the next day and then he and Gregory would come for dinner after his competition.

When my father and I returned from the hotel with the good news, my mother was scrubbing every available surface. Floors, oven, furniture, windows. She presented us with several bags of garbage which we dropped down the smelly chute in the hallway. My father told her that Sergei looked good. As though he hadn't changed at all in the last five years.

—What did he say about the way you look?

—He said I looked good. Canadian. Younger than the last time he saw me.

—If you look young, then I must be a schoolgirl.

—You are a schoolgirl.

—The ambulance comes once a week. Some schoolgirl.

The next morning my father stopped at the hotel on his way to judge events in the middleweight class. Sergei wasn't competing that day and I took the subway with my father so that I could guide Sergei back to our apartment, where my mother was waiting to take him shopping. As we crossed the lobby toward the elevator I noticed the KGB agent making his way over to intercept us. I noticed before my father noticed. From a distance I had the vague impression that there was something not quite the same about the agent. As he drew closer I saw that his face was badly swollen. With every step he took the swelling became more prominent. It was as though the swelling preceded his face. From a distance he had been arms, legs, torso, haircut, but up close he was a swollen jaw. My father, distracted by his obligations to the competition and nervous about being late, didn't appear to recognize the man until he was standing directly in front of him. But then, on seeing the agent's face, my father stiffened and seized me by the shoulder. My God, he said, and simultaneously drew me back, putting himself between me and the KGB agent.

The KGB agent clapped his hands and broke into what appeared to be a lopsided grin. His distended lips barely parted but parted enough to reveal white cotton gauze clamped between his teeth. When he spoke, it was through this gruesome leer, like a man with his jaw wired shut. My father tightened his grip on the back of my neck.

—Roman Abramovich, looks like you really did me a favor.

—She's the dentist for my family. I go to her. My wife. My son. I swear she always does good work.

The agent's jaw muscles twitched as he clamped tighter into his grin.

—Good work. Look at me. I couldn't ask for better. She put in three crowns and a bridge.

—She's a very generous woman.

—She knows how to treat a man. Anesthetic and a bottle of vodka. I left at four in the morning. A very generous woman. And beautiful. It was a wonderful night, you understand.

—I'm glad to hear you're happy

—Roman Abramovich, remember, you always have a friend in Moscow. Visit anytime.

Laughing at his joke, the agent turned, and we proceeded to the elevator and rode up to Sergei's floor. In the elevator my father leaned against the wall and finally loosened his grip on my neck.

—Don't ever forget. This is why we left. So you never have to know people like him.

We knocked on Sergei's door, and after some shuffling, Sergei answered. He was in the middle of his push-ups when he let us into his room. He was wearing an undershirt and his arms were a bold relief of muscles, tendons, and veins. In Italy during our six-month purgatory between Russia and Canada, I had seen statues with such arms. I understood that the statues were meant to reflect the real arms of real men, but except for Sergei I had never met anyone with arms like that.

As my father was in a hurry, he left me with Sergei as he rushed back out to the convention center. I waited while Sergei dressed.

—So where are you taking me today?

—Mama says we'll go to the supermarket. She thinks you'll like it.

—The supermarket.

—The good supermarket. They have every kind of food.

—And you know how to get there?

—Yes. First we take the subway and then the bus. By the subway and the bus I know how to go almost anywhere.

—How about California?

—The subway doesn't go to California.

—Then maybe we should take a plane.

The way he said it I didn't know if he was joking or serious until he laughed. I wanted to laugh too but I hadn't understood the joke. I sensed that I wasn't intended to understand it in the first place. I was hurt because I wanted very much to be Sergei's equal, his friend, and I suspected that Sergei wasn't laughing at his joke but rather at me.

Seeing that he had upset me, Sergei tried to make up for it by asking about the supermarket.

—We sometimes go to another one that isn't as good. In the other one they don't have the things they show on the television. But at the good supermarket you can find everything.

On the bus ride home I pointed out the landmarks that delineated our new life. To compensate for the drabness of the landscape I animated my hands and voice. I felt the tour guide's responsibility to show Sergei something interesting. At the northern edge of the city, home to Russian immigrants, brown apartment buildings, and aging strip malls, there wasn't much to show. I stressed our personal connection to each mundane thing, hoping in that way to justify its inclusion. There was the Canadian Tire store where I got my bicycle, the Russian Riviera banquet hall where my father celebrated his birthday, one delicatessen called Volga and another called Odessa, a convenience store where I played video games, my school, my hockey arena, my soccer fields. Sergei looked and nodded. I kept talking and talking even though I could tell that what I was showing and what he was seeing were not the same things.

When the bus pulled up near our apartment building I was relieved to stop talking. Sergei followed me into the lobby. I used my key and let us inside. Upstairs, my mother was waiting. For the first time in months she was wearing makeup and what appeared to be a new dress. In the dining room there was a vase with flowers. There was a bowl on the coffee table with yellow grapes. There was another bowl beside it containing assorted Russian bonbons: Karakum, Brown Squirrel, Clumsy Bear. When my mother saw Sergei, her face lit up with true happiness. Involuntarily, I looked away. After so many miserable months I was surprised by my reaction. I had been praying for her to get better, but there was something about the pitch of her happiness that made me feel strangely indecent. I had felt this way once before when I accidentally glimpsed her undressing through a doctor's office door. Here as there, instinct proscribed against looking at my mother's nakedness.

From our apartment my mother drove our green Pontiac to the good supermarket and then the mall where Sergei bought blue jeans for himself and for the woman he was dating. Also, on my recommendation, he bought some shirts with the Polo logo on them which were very popular at the time. Against my mother's protestations he also insisted on buying a shirt for me and one for my father.

—Bellachka, don't forget, you wake up in the morning, you get into your car, you go to a store, you can buy anything you want. In Riga people now line up just for permission to line up.

I was grateful when my mother didn't say anything to contradict him, since both she and I knew that the only way we could afford fifty-dollar shirts was if Sergei paid for them.

When my father returned from the convention center that night he was exhilarated. He had witnessed two world records. One by a Soviet lifter he had known. He was energized by the proximity to his former life. He had seen old friends. People recognized him. He had also spent a few hours with Gregory Ziskin and they had been able to have a drink in Gregory's hotel room. Gregory had filled him in on the Dynamo gossip. Colleagues who had received promotions, others who had retired. The politics with directors. New athletes on the rise. Gregory was proud that, including Sergei, the national team had three weightlifters from Riga Dynamo. There was a new young lifter named Krutov in Sergei's weight class who showed considerable promise. He had been taking silver behind Sergei for the past year. Having the gold and silver medalists was doing wonders for Gregory's profile with the ministry. He'd heard rumors of a transfer to Moscow and a permanent position with Red Army.

As a souvenir, my father surprised me with a poster signed by the Soviet national team. We, in turn, surprised him with his Polo shirt. In the living room, my father and I tried on our new shirts. My father said he couldn't think of when he would wear it. He had plenty of shirts. I had plenty of shirts too, but I felt as though I had only one.

Along with the poster my father also secured tickets for me and my mother for the next day's competition. My mother, anxious about preparing dinner, felt she couldn't go. Even though she wanted very much to see Sergei compete. I had no obligations. The competition was on a Saturday. I had no school, no homework. Nothing that could keep me from watching Sergei perform.

At the convention center dozens of wooden risers had been joined together to create a stage. At one edge of the stage was a long table for the officials. My father had his place there along with the two other judges. A small black electrical box sat squarely in front of each judge. The box was connected by wires to a display board. On the box were two buttons, one button for a good lift, the second button for failure. Before the competition started my father allowed me to sit in his seat and press the buttons. As I sat there Gregory Ziskin approached. I had only faint memories of Gregory who, unlike Sergei, hadn't often come to the apartment. He was my father's friend and business partner, but there was a quality to his demeanor that stressed the professional over the personal. He looked perpetually impatient.

At my father's suggestion Gregory agreed to take me behind the stage so I could watch the lifters warming up. In Riga it was something my father had enjoyed doing. He always liked the energy of the warm-up room. But now, as a judge, it was unacceptable for him to give even the impression of bias or impropriety. Leaving my father to review papers, I followed Gregory through a heavy curtain toward the sounds of grunting and clanging iron.

Standing in the wings, I watched a scene I recognized as familiar only once I saw it. The warm-up room was very big, the size of a high school gymnasium. There was activity everywhere. In small groups, coaches and trainers attended to their athletes. Teams could be distinguished from one another by the colors of their Adidas training suits. Some of the lifters wore the suits, others had stripped down to their tights. In one corner I watched as trainers wrapped and taped knees, in another corner other trainers had set up massage tables. In the center of the room a large section of the floor had been covered with plywood. Several bars had been set up for the lifters. There were also chalk caddies. I looked on with fascination as the men went through their rituals of applying the chalk to their hands, arms, and shoulders. To handle the perfect white cakes of chalk seemed reason enough to become a weightlifter.

Gregory, who had important matters to attend to, left me with a plastic press pass and instructions not to get into any trouble. I could stick around as long as I liked, or at least until someone told me to leave.

I watched him head over to the Soviet delegation, where Sergei was stretching beside a young blond weightlifter. From every corner came the sounds of exertion, of metal striking metal and metal striking wood. Nobody paid me any attention as I wandered around. I finally took up a position near the center of the room and watched men lift heavy things in preparation for lifting very heavy things.

The competition took hours. My father reserved me a seat in the front so that my view wouldn't be obscured by the heads of adults. Sergei's weight class was one of the last on the schedule. Until Sergei performed I spent most of my time watching my father. Up onstage with the other judges, he looked very much like his old picture in the IWF passport.

Sergei's weight class competed in the afternoon. Very quickly it became clear that it was a competition between two men: Sergei and Krutov, the blond weightlifter. Their first lifts exceeded those of the rest of the competitors by several kilos. After that, from attempt to attempt, they performed only against each other. I watched first as Sergei eclipsed his world record in the snatch and then as Krutov matched it. Each one lifting fluidly, in one motion, almost twice his own weight.

When it came time for the clean and jerk Sergei declined the opening weight and watched as Krutov successfully approached and then matched Sergei's world record. To catch Krutov, Sergei had three attempts. During Sergei's lifts, Krutov waited silently in the wings. I sat on my hands and watched as Sergei failed on his first attempt, and then, minutes later, on his second. Both times, straining under the bar, he managed to get the weight up to his chest and no farther. Until Sergei's final lift, it hadn't occurred to me that he could lose. But as he chalked his hands in preparation for the lift, it not only occurred to me that he might lose, but, all at once, I knew he would. I looked at the people around me and sensed that they also knew it. Sergei seemed to know it too. He paced the stage almost until his time expired. I watched the seconds on the huge dock behind him tick away. Just to stay in the competition, he had to match his own world record. And when he failed to do it, when he was unable to steady the bar above his head, when all three judges' lights—including my father's—glowed red, I felt sick. As I watched Sergei embrace Krutov and then Krutov embrace Gregory, I tasted and then swallowed the eggs I had eaten for breakfast.

After the awards ceremony I followed my father over to Sergei. He was standing slightly apart from Gregory, Krutov, and the rest of the Soviet team. When he saw us he forced a smile. My father congratulated him and Sergei held up his silver medal. He took it off his neck and let me hold it. He kept the smile on his face.

—A silver medal. It's not gold, but I guess you don't find them lying in the street.

Sergei looked over to where Gregory was standing with his arm around Krutov.

—Don't forget to congratulate Comrade Ziskin on another great day for Dynamo. Another one-two finish. What difference does it make to him if all of a sudden one is two and two is one?

At home, my mother had prepared a large and elaborate dinner. There were salads, a cold borscht, smoked pike, smoked whitefish, a veal roast, and tea, cake, and ice cream for dessert. She had set the table for five and used crystal glasses and her good china. I wore my clean new Polo shirt. My father told amusing stories about our immigration in Italy. He made an effort to reminisce with Gregory about their old bodybuilding students. The ones who remained in Riga, those who were now in Toronto, others who sometimes wrote letters from New York and Israel. My mother inquired after some of her girlfriends. People in the Jewish community whom Gregory would have known even though he and my mother were almost a generation apart. Even I talked about what my school was like, what sorts of cars my Hebrew school friends had. The only person who didn't talk was Sergei. He listened to all the conversations and drank. My father had placed a bottle of vodka on the table, and after the requisite toasts, only Sergei continued to address the bottle. With the bottle almost gone, he suddenly turned on Gregory and accused him of plotting against him. He knew that Gregory planned to recommend that he be removed from the team.

—He wants to put me out to pasture. Soviet pasture. The rest of my life grazing in the dust. The only way he'll get me back there is with a bullet through my head.

Sergei kept drinking, even though it looked like he was having a hard time keeping his eyes open.

—Roman, you did the right thing. You got the hell out of that cemetery. Now you can look forward to a real life. And what do we look forward to? What kind of life, Gregory Davidovich, you KGB cocksucker!

After another drink Sergei's head began to drift toward his plate and he accepted my father's help and rose from the table. His arm draped over my father's shoulder, Sergei stumbled into my bedroom and onto my single bed. My father closed the door and returned to the table. He lowered himself wearily into his chair. Submitting to gravity, he looked again like my old father.

As my mother served the tea Gregory confessed that Sergei was more right than wrong. But this was something my father knew as well as he did. A weightlifter's career was five, maybe seven years. After that there was a nice arrangement. A position with Dynamo. A lucrative job with customs. Maybe a coaching placement, or moving papers from one corner of the desk to the other. Sergei would get what everyone else got. He'd keep his three-room apartment, he'd have his garage for his car, he'd never have to worry about a salary. That Russia was becoming a colossal piece of shit was a different story. That my father had proven himself a genius by leaving was undeniable. Dunking biscuits into his tea, Gregory admitted he should have left when he had the chance. Now it was too late.

My father looked at my mother before speaking.

—Don't be fooled, Grisha. I often think of going back.

—Are you insane? Look at what you have. Take a walk outside. I saw beggars on the street wearing Levi's jeans and Adidas running shoes.

—Three days out of five I'm afraid I'll join them.

—Roman, come on, I've known you for thirty years. You don't have to lie on my account.

—I'm not lying. Every day is a struggle.

—Look, I'm not blind. I see your car. I see your apartment. I see how you struggle. Believe me, your worst day is better than my best.

Leaving my parents and Gregory at the table, I went down the hall and into my bedroom. Even though I knew every step blind, I waited for my eyes to become accustomed to the dark. Sergei was stretched out on my single bed, his feet barely hanging over the edge. I went over and stood beside him. I listened to his breathing and considered his body through his suit jacket. Again, I was amazed at how small he was. I bent closer to examine his face. I didn't mind that he was in my bed, although I wondered where I would sleep if he stayed. When he suddenly opened his eyes, I was startled.

—Well, boy, what do you see?

He raised himself to a sitting position and looked me over. He put his hands on my shoulders and my arms and gripped for a proper appraisal.

—How many push-ups can you do?

—Twenty-five.

—Only twenty-five?

—I think so.

—For a boy like you, anything less than fifty is a disgrace.

He climbed off the bed and kneeled on the floor. He patted a spot beside him.

—Come on, come on.

When I hesitated his hand shot up and seized me by my new Polo shirt. I felt the fabric tear and heard two buttons strike the floor.

—Let's go. You and me. Fifty push-ups.

At first I managed to keep up with him, but after a while he began to race ahead. I strained not to fall behind, afraid of what he might do to me. But he continued to do the exercise, counting to himself, not minding me at all. When he finished I finished as well.

—See, it feels good.

I nodded my head in agreement.

Sergei looked over at my alarm clock. It read past ten.

—Look at how late it is. Shouldn't you be asleep?

—It's okay. Sometimes I stay up until eleven.

—When you were in Riga it was nine o'clock sharp. You remember how you liked it when I used to put you to sleep?

—I remember.

—It wasn't so long ago.

—No.

—Come on, into bed.

—It's okay. I don't really have to.

—Into bed. Into bed.

His tone left no room for negotiation. I kicked off my shoes and lifted the covers.

—Good.

Sergei knelt down beside my bed and gripped the wooden frame.

—Comfortable?

—Yes.

His face straining, he used his legs and rose from the floor; my bed resisting, scratching the wall, but leaving the ground. At first the bed tottered and I gripped the sides, but then he steadied it. Smiling triumphantly, he looked at me. I heard the door opening behind him. I recognized my father's footsteps. Then other footsteps. My mother's. Gregory's.

—Nu, boy, tell me. Who is the world's strongest man?

Looking past Sergei at my father, I waited to see if he was going to do something. My mother started to take a step forward but my father restrained her.

—Nu, boy? Who is the world's strongest man?

—Seryozha. Seryozha Federenko.

—Wrong, boy. That was yesterday's answer.

He laughed and turned to face Gregory.

—Isn't that right Gregory Davidovich?

—Put him down, you idiot.

Seryozha emitted something that was a cross between a cough and a laugh. He carefully eased my bed to the ground and proceeded to slump down on the floor. Gregory and my father both moved to help him up, but as Gregory reached for his arm Sergei violently slapped it aside.

—You bastard, don't you dare put a hand on me.

Gregory stepped back. My father carefully took hold of Sergei's armpits and helped him up. Without protesting, Sergei put his arms across my father's shoulders.

—Roman, you were the only one who gave a shit about me, and we will never see each other again.

With faltering steps, my father supported Sergei into the hall. I got out of my bed and stood in my doorway. Gregory followed my father and Sergei into the hall and toward the front door. My mother came over and stood with me.

My father offered to drive or call them a cab.

Gregory shook his head and smiled the familiar Soviet smile.

—What for? Have you forgotten? There is always a car waiting downstairs.

Still holding on to my father, Sergei permitted himself to be led down the hall and into the elevator. Gregory said goodbye to my mother as she closed the door behind him. I went to my bedroom window and waited. Below, in the parking lot, I saw a man smoking beside a dark sedan. In slightly more than the amount of time it took for the elevator to descend to the lobby, my father appeared in the parking lot with Sergei clinging to his shoulders. Gregory followed. The man opened the rear door and my father eased Sergei into the car. I watched as my father shook hands with Gregory and with the man. As my father turned back in the direction of our building the man opened the driver's-side door. For an instant, the light from the car's interior was sufficient to illuminate his swollen face.

—2004

Madeleine Thien   b. 1974

Born in Canada to Chinese-Malaysian immigrants, Madeleine Thien published Simple Recipes *(2001) while still in her twenties. Alice Munro, who has only rarely given her imprimatur to young writers, wrote of Thien's collection of short stories: "I am astonished by the clarity and ease of the writing, and a kind of emotional purity." The disturbing title story, which uses food preparation and consumption as a source of narrative unity, balances the simplicity of cooking against the complex cultural negotiations within immigrant family life.*

Simple Recipes

There is a simple recipe for making rice. My father taught it to me when I was a child. Back then, I used to sit up on the kitchen counter watching him, how he sifted the grains in his hands, sure and quick, removing pieces of dirt or sand, tiny imperfections. He swirled his hands through the water and it turned cloudy. When he scrubbed the grains clean, the sound was as big as a field of insects. Over and over, my father rinsed the rice, drained the water, then filled the pot again.

The instructions are simple. Once the washing is done, you measure the water this way—by resting the tip of your index finger on the surface of the rice. The water should reach the bend of your first knuckle.

My father did not need instructions or measuring cups. He closed his eyes and felt for the waterline.

Sometimes I still dream my father, his bare feet flat against the floor, standing in the middle of the kitchen. He wears old buttoned shirts and faded sweatpants drawn at the waist. Surrounded by the gloss of the kitchen counters, the sharp angles of the stove, the fridge, the shiny sink, he looks out of place. This memory of him is so strong, sometimes it stuns me, the detail with which I can see it.

Every night before dinner, my father would perform this ritual—rinsing and draining, then setting the pot in the cooker. When I was older, he passed this task on to me but I never did it with the same care. I went through the motions, splashing the water around, jabbing my finger down to measure the water level. Some nights the rice was a mushy gruel. I worried that I could not do so simple a task right. "Sorry," I would say to the table, my voice soft and embarrassed. In answer, my father would keep eating, pushing the rice into his mouth as if he never expected anything different, as if he noticed no difference between what he did so well and I so poorly. He would eat every last mouthful, his chopsticks walking quickly across the plate. Then he would rise, whistling, and clear the table, every motion so clean and sure, I would be convinced by him that all was well in the world.

*

My father is standing in the middle of the kitchen. In his right hand he holds a plastic bag filled with water. Caught inside the bag is a live fish.

The fish is barely breathing, though its mouth opens and closes. I reach up and touch it through the plastic bag, trailing my fingers along the gills, the soft, muscled body, pushing my finger overtop the eyeball. The fish looks straight at me, flopping sluggishly from side to side.

My father fills the kitchen sink. In one swift motion he overturns the bag and the fish comes sailing out with the water. It curls and jumps. We watch it closely, me on my tiptoes, chin propped up on the counter. The fish is the length of my arm from wrist to elbow. It floats in place, brushing up against the sides of the sink.

I keep watch over the fish while my father begins the preparations for dinner. The fish folds its body, trying to turn or swim, the water nudging overtop. Though I ripple tiny circles around it with my fingers, the fish stays still, bobbing side-to-side in the cold water.

For many hours at a time, it was just the two of us. While my mother worked and my older brother played outside, my father and I sat on the couch, flipping channels. He loved cooking shows. We watched *Wok with Yan*, my father passing judgement on Yan's methods. I was enthralled when Yan transformed orange peels into swans. My father sniffed. "I can do that," he said. "You don't have to be a genius to do that." He placed a sprig of green onion in water and showed me how it bloomed like a flower. "I know many tricks like this," he said. "Much more than Yan."

Still, my father made careful notes when Yan demonstrated Peking Duck. He chuckled heartily at Yan's punning. "Take a wok on the wild side!" Yan said, pointing his spatula at the camera.

"Ha ha!" my father laughed, his shoulders shaking. "*Wok* on the wild side!"

In the mornings, my father took me to school. At three o'clock, when we came home again, I would rattle off everything I learned that day. "The brachiosaurus," I informed him, "eats only soft vegetables."

My father nodded. "That is like me. Let me see your forehead." We stopped and faced each other in the road. "You have a high forehead," he said, leaning down to take a closer look. "All smart people do."

I walked proudly, stretching my legs to match his steps. I was overjoyed when my feet kept time with his, right, then left, then right, and we walked like a single unit. My father was the man of tricks, who sat for an hour mining a watermelon with a circular spoon, who carved the rind into a castle.

My father was born in Malaysia and he and my mother immigrated to Canada several years before I was born, first settling in Montreal, then finally in Vancouver. While I was born into the persistence of the Vancouver rain, my father was born in the wash of a monsoon country. When I was young, my parents tried to teach me their language but it never came easily to me. My father ran his thumb gently over my mouth, his face kind, as if trying to see what it was that made me different.

My brother was born in Malaysia but when he immigrated with my parents to Canada the language left him. Or he forgot it, or he refused it, which is also common, and this made my father angry. "How can a child forget a language?" he would ask my mother. "It is because the child is lazy. Because the child chooses not to remember." When he was twelve years old, my brother stayed away in the afternoons. He drummed the soccer ball up and down the back alley, returning home only at dinner time. During the day, my mother worked as a sales clerk at the Woodward's store downtown, in the building with the red revolving W on top.

In our house, the ceilings were yellowed with grease. Even the air was heavy with it. I remember that I loved the weight of it, the air that was dense with the smell of countless meals cooked in a tiny kitchen, all those good smells jostling for space.

The fish in the sink is dying slowly. It has a glossy sheen to it, as if its skin is made of shining minerals. I want to prod it with both hands, its body tense against the pressure of my fingers. If I hold it tightly, I imagine I will be able to feel its fluttering heart. Instead, I lock eyes with the fish. *You're feeling verrrry sleepy,* I tell it. *You're getting verrrry tired.*

Beside me, my father chops green onions quickly. He uses a cleaver that he says is older than I am by many years. The blade of the knife rolls forward and backward, loops of green onion gathering in a pyramid beside my father's wrist. When he is done, he rolls his sleeve back from his right hand, reaches in through the water and pulls the plug.

The fish in the sink floats and we watch it in silence. The water level falls beneath its gills, beneath its belly. It drains and leaves the sink dry. The fish is lying on its side, mouth open and its body heaving. It leaps sideways and hits the sink. Then up again. It curls and snaps, lunging for its own tail. The fish sails into the air, dropping hard. It twitches violently.

My father reaches in with his bare hands. He lifts the fish out by the tail and lays it gently on the counter. While holding it steady with one hand, he hits the head with the flat of the cleaver. The fish falls still, and he begins to clean it.

*

In my apartment, I keep the walls scrubbed clean. I open the windows and turn the fan on whenever I prepare a meal. My father bought me a rice cooker when I first moved into my own apartment, but I use it so rarely it stays in the back of the cupboard, the cord wrapped neatly around its belly. I have no longing for the meals themselves, but I miss the way we sat down together, our bodies leaning hungrily forward while my father, the magician, unveiled plate after plate. We laughed and ate, white steam fogging my mother's glasses until she had to take them off and lay them on the table. Eyes closed, she would eat, crunchy vegetables gripped in her chopsticks, the most vivid green.

*

My brother comes into the kitchen and his body is covered with dirt. He leaves a thin trail of it behind as he walks. The soccer ball, muddy from outside, is encircled in one arm. Brushing past my father, his face is tense.

Beside me, my mother sprinkles garlic onto the fish. She lets me slide one hand underneath the fish's head, cradling it, then bending it backwards so that she can fill the fish's insides with ginger. Very carefully, I turn the fish over. It is firm and slippery, and beaded with tiny, sharp scales.

At the stove, my father picks up an old teapot. It is full of oil and he pours the oil into the wok. It falls in a thin ribbon. After a moment, when the oil begins crackling, he lifts the fish up and drops it down into the wok. He adds water and the smoke billows up. The sound of the fish frying is like tires on gravel, a sound so loud it drowns out all other noises. Then my father steps out from the smoke. "Spoon out the rice," he says as he lifts me down from the counter.

My brother comes back into the room, his hands muddy and his knees the colour of dusty brick. His soccer shorts flutter against the backs of his legs. Sitting down, he makes an angry face. My father ignores him.

Inside the cooker, the rice is flat like a pie. I push the spoon in, turning the rice over, and the steam shoots up in a hot mist and condenses on my skin. While my father moves his arms delicately over the stove, I begin dishing the rice out: first for my father, then my mother, then my brother, then myself. Behind me the fish is cooking quickly. In a crockery pot, my father steams cauliflower, stirring it round and round.

My brother kicks at a table leg.

"What's the matter?" my father asks.

He is quiet for a moment, then he says, "Why do we have to eat fish?"

"You don't like it?"

My brother crosses his arms against his chest. I see the dirt lining his arms, dark and hardened. I imagine chipping it off his body with a small spoon.

"I don't like the eyeball there. It looks sick."

My mother tuts. Her nametag is still clipped to her blouse. It says *Woodward's*, and then, *Sales Clerk*. "Enough," she says, hanging her purse on the back of the chair. "Go wash your hands and get ready for supper."

My brother glares, just for a moment. Then he begins picking at the dirt on his arms. I bring plates of rice to the table. The dirt flies off his skin, speckling the tablecloth. "Stop it," I say crossly.

"*Stop it*," he says, mimicking me.

"Hey!" My father hits his spoon against the counter. It *pings*, high-pitched. He points at my brother. "No fighting in this house."

My brother looks at the floor, mumbles something, and then shuffles away from the table. As he moves farther away, he begins to stamp his feet.

Shaking her head, my mother takes her jacket off. It slides from her shoulders. She says something to my father in the language I can't understand. He merely shrugs his shoulders. And then he replies, and I think his words are so familiar, as if they are words I should know, as if maybe I did know them once but then I forgot them. The language that they speak is full of soft vowels, words running together so that I can't make out the gaps where they pause for breath.

My mother told me once about guilt. Her own guilt she held in the palm of her hands, like an offering. But your guilt is different, she said. You do not need to hold on to it. Imagine this, she said, her hands running along my forehead, then up into my hair. Imagine, she said. Picture it, and what do you see?

A bruise on the skin, wide and black.

A bruise, she said. Concentrate on it. Right now, it's a bruise. But if you concentrate, you can shrink it, compress it to the size of a pinpoint. And then, if you want to, if you see it, you can blow it off your body like a speck of dirt.

She moved her hands along my forehead.

I tried to picture what she said. I pictured blowing it away like so much nothing, just these little pieces that didn't mean anything, this complicity that I could magically walk away from. She made me believe in the strength of my own thoughts, as if I could make appear what had never existed. Or turn it around. Flip it over so many times you just lose sight of it, you lose the tail end and the whole thing disappears into smoke.

My father pushes at the fish with the edge of his spoon. Underneath, the meat is white and the juice runs down along the side. He lifts a piece and lowers it carefully onto my plate.

Once more, his spoon breaks skin. Gingerly, my father lifts another piece and moves it towards my brother.

"I don't want it," my brother says.

My father's hand wavers. "Try it," he says, smiling. "Take a wok on the wild side."

"No."

My father sighs and places the piece on my mother's plate. We eat in silence, scraping our spoons across the dishes. My parents use chopsticks, lifting their bowls and motioning the food into their mouths. The smell of food fills the room.

Savouring each mouthful, my father eats slowly, head tuned to the flavours in his mouth. My mother takes her glasses off, the lenses fogged, and lays them on the table. She eats with her head bowed down, as if in prayer.

Lifting a stem of cauliflower to his lips, my brother sighs deeply. He chews, and then his face changes. I have a sudden picture of him drowning, his hair waving like grass. He coughs, spitting the mouthful back onto his plate. Another cough. He reaches for his throat, choking.

My father slams his chopsticks down on the table. In a single movement, he reaches across, grabbing my brother by the shoulder. "I have tried," he is saying. "I don't know what kind of son you are. To be so ungrateful." His other hand sweeps by me and bruises into my brother's face.

My mother flinches. My brother's face is red and his mouth is open. His eyes are wet.

Still coughing, he grabs a fork, tines aimed at my father, and then in an unthinking moment, he heaves it at him. It strikes my father in the chest and drops.

"I hate you! You're just an asshole, you're just a fucking asshole chink!" My brother holds his plate in his hands. He smashes it down and his food scatters across the table. He is coughing and spitting. "I wish you weren't my father! I wish you were dead."

My father's hand falls again. This time pounding downwards. I close my eyes. All I can hear is someone screaming. There is a loud voice. I stand awkwardly, my hands covering my eyes.

"Go to your room," my father says, his voice shaking.

And I think he is talking to me so I remove my hands.

But he is looking at my brother. And my brother is looking at him, his small chest heaving.

A few minutes later, my mother begins clearing the table, face weary as she scrapes the dishes one by one over the garbage.

I move away from my chair, past my mother, onto the carpet and up the stairs.

Outside my brother's bedroom, I crouch against the wall. When I step forward and look, I see my father holding the bamboo pole between his hands. The pole is smooth. The long grains, fine as hair, are pulled together, at intervals, jointed. My brother is lying on the floor, as if thrown down and dragged there. My father raises the pole into the air.

I want to cry out. I want to move into the room between them, but I can't.

It is like a tree falling, beginning to move, a slow arc through the air.

The bamboo drops silently. It rips the skin on my brother's back. I cannot hear any sound. A line of blood edges quickly across his body.

The pole rises and again comes down. I am afraid of bones breaking. My father lifts his arms once more.

On the floor, my brother cries into the carpet, pawing at the ground. His knees folded into his chest, the crown of his head burrowing down. His back is hunched over and I can see his spine, little bumps on his skin.

The bamboo smashes into bone and the scene in my mind bursts into a million white pieces.

My mother picks me up off the floor, pulling me across the hall, into my bedroom, into bed. Everything is wet, the sheets, my hands, her body, my face, and she soothes me with words I cannot understand because all I can hear is screaming. She rubs her cool hands against my forehead. "Stop," she says. "Please stop," but I feel loose, deranged, as if everything in the known world is ending right here.

In the morning, I wake up to the sound of oil in the pan and the smell of French toast. I can hear my mother bustling around, putting dishes in the cupboards.

No one says anything when my brother doesn't come down for breakfast. My father piles French toast and syrup onto a plate and my mother pours a glass of milk. She takes everything upstairs to my brother's bedroom.

As always, I follow my father around the kitchen. I track his footprints, follow behind him and hide in the shadow of his body. Every so often, he reaches down and ruffles my hair with his hands. We cast a spell, I think. The way we move in circles, how he cooks without thinking because this is the task that comes to him effortlessly. He smiles down at me, but when he does this, it somehow breaks the spell. My father stands in place, hands dropping to his sides as if he has forgotten what he was doing mid-motion. On the walls, the paint is peeling and the floor, unswept in days, leaves little pieces of dirt stuck to our feet.

My persistence, I think, my unadulterated love, confuse him. With each passing day, he knows I will find it harder to ignore what I can't comprehend, that I will be unable to separate one part of him from another. The unconditional quality of my love for him will not last forever, just as my brother's did not. My father stands in the middle of the kitchen, unsure. Eventually, my mother comes downstairs again and puts her arms around him and holds him, whispering something to him, words that to me are meaningless and incomprehensible. But she offers them to him, sound after sound, in a language that was stolen from some other place, until he drops his head and remembers where he is.

Later on, I lean against the door frame upstairs and listen to the sound of a metal fork scraping against a dish. My mother is already there, her voice rising and falling. She is moving the fork across the plate, offering my brother pieces of French toast.

I move towards the bed, the carpet scratchy, until I can touch the wooden bed-frame with my hands. My mother is seated there, and I go to her, reaching my fingers out to the buttons on her cuff and twisting them over to catch the light.

"Are you eating?" I ask my brother.

He starts to cry. I look at him, his face half hidden in the blankets.

"Try and eat," my mother says softly.

He only cries harder but there isn't any sound. The pattern of sunlight on his blanket moves with his body. His hair is pasted down with sweat and his head moves forward and backward like an old man's.

At some point I know my father is standing at the entrance of the room but I cannot turn to look at him. I want to stay where I am, facing the wall. I'm afraid that if I turn around and go to him, I will be complicit, accepting a portion of guilt, no matter how small that piece. I do not know how to prevent this from happening again, though now I know, in the end, it will break us apart. This violence will turn all my love to shame and grief. So I stand there, not looking at him or my brother. Even my father, the magician, who can make something beautiful out of nothing, he just stands and watches.

A face changes over time, it becomes clearer. In my father's face, I have seen everything pass. Anger that has stripped it of anything recognizable, so that it is only a face of bones and skin. And then, at other times, so much pain that it is unbearable, his face so full of grief it might dissolve. How to reconcile all that I know of him and still love him? For a long time, I thought it was not possible. When I was a child, I did not love my father because he was complicated, because he was human, because he needed me to. A child does not know yet how to love a person that way.

How simple it should be. Warm water running over, the feel of the grains between my hands, the sound of it like stones running along the pavement. My father would rinse the rice over and over, sifting it between his fingertips, searching for the impurities, pulling them out. A speck, barely visible, resting on the tip of his finger.

If there were some recourse, I would take it. A cupful of grains in my open hand, a smoothing out, finding the impurities, then removing them piece by piece. And then, to be satisfied with what remains.

Somewhere in my memory, a fish in the sink is dying slowly. My father and I watch as the water runs down.

—2001

Credits

André Alexis, "Kuala Lumpur." Taken from *Despair* by André Alexis. Used by permission, McClelland & Stewart Ltd. *The Canadian Publishers.*

Margaret Atwood, "Death by Landscape." Taken from *Wilderness Tips* by Margaret Atwood. Used by permission, McClelland & Stewart Ltd. *The Canadian Publishers.*

David Bezmozgis, "The Second Strongest Man" by David Bezmozgis from *Natasha and Other Stories.* Published by HarperCollins Publishers Ltd. Copyright © 2004 by David Bezmozgis. All rights reserved.

Sandra Birdsell, "The Wednesday Circle." Taken from *Agassiz Story* by Sandra Birdsell. Used by permission, McClelland & Stewart Ltd. *The Canadian Publishers.*

Dionne Brand, "At theLisbon Plate" from *Sans Souci and Other Stories.* Toronto: Women's Press, 1994. Reprinted by permission of Canadian Scholars' Press Inc. and/or Women's Press and the author.

Morley Callaghan, "Rigmarole." © Exile Editions & Estate of Morley Callaghan, 2003. Reprinted with permission from Morley Callaghan, *The Complete Stories,* Volume One.

Michael Crummey, "Bread" from *Hard Light,* p. 27. © 1998 by Michael Crummey. Reprinted by permission of Brick Books Inc.

Timothy Findley, "Stones" from *Stones* by Timothy Findley. Copyright © Pebble Productions Inc., 1988. Reprinted by permission of Penguin Group (Canada), a Division of Pearson Education Canada Inc.

Mavis Gallant, "My Heart Is Broken" from *My Heart Is Broken* by Mavis Gallant. Copyright © 1964 by Mavis Gallant. Reprinted by permission of Georges Borchardt, Inc.

Frederick Philip Grove, "Lazybones" from *Tales from the Margin,* pp. 20–29. Copyright © 1971 Frederick Philip Grove. Reprinted with permission of McGraw-Hill Ryerson Ltd.

Thomas Chandler Haliburton, "A Cure for Smuggling" from *The Clockmaker* (second series). Reprinted in *The Clockmaker, Series One, Two, and Three* (Ottawa: Carleton University Press, 1995). pp. 368–376. Reprinted with permission of McGill-Queen's University Press.

Jack Hodgins, "Over Here" from the 2004 collection *Damage Done by the Storm: Stories by Jack Hodgins* (McClelland & Stewart) is used with permission of the author.